WILLIAM M. THACKERAY

VANITY FAIR

A NOVEL WITHOUT A HERO

Premier
CLASSICS

VANITY FAIR

CHRONOLOGY

DATE	AUTHOR'S LIFE	LITERARY CONTEXT
1811	Born, Calcutta, India, 18 July.	Jane Austen: *Sense and Sensibility.*
1812		Birth of Dickens.
		Byron: Cantos I and II of *Childe Harold.*
1813		Jane Austen: *Pride and Prejudice.*
1814		Walter Scott: *Waverley.*
		Jane Austen: *Mansfield Park.*
1815	Death of his father, Richmond Thackeray.	Walter Scott: *Guy Mannering.*
1816		Jane Austen: *Emma.*
1817	Sent home to England to the care of his great-grandmother and great-aunt. Mother marries Captain Henry Carmichael Smyth.	Walter Scott: *Rob Roy.*
1818		Jane Austen: *Northanger Abbey* and *Persuasion.*
		Mary Shelley: *Frankenstein.*
1819	At school in Chiswick. Mother and step-father return to England.	Walter Scott: *Ivanhoe.*
		Birth of George Eliot.
1820		
1821		Walter Scott: *Kenilworth.*
		Baudelaire, Dostoevsky, Flaubert born.
		Death of Keats.
1822–8	At Charterhouse School, London.	
1822		Death of Shelley.
1824		Walter Scott: *Redgauntlet.*
		Death of Byron.
1825		Manzoni: *I Promessi Sposi.*
1828		Birth of Tolstoy.
		Bulwer-Lytton: *Pelham.*
1829	Enters (January) Trinity College, Cambridge.	
1830	Leaves Cambridge (June) without a degree. Spends the	Tennyson: *Poems, Chiefly Lyrical.*

HISTORICAL EVENTS

Prince of Wales appointed Prince Regent.

Napoleon invades Russia, but is forced to retreat.

Napoleon abdicates and is banished to Elba.

Napoleon returns: the 'Hundred Days' end in his defeat at Waterloo.
Napoleon banished to St Helena.

Birth of Queen Victoria. 'Peterloo' massacre.

Accession of George IV.
Death of Napoleon.

Stockton–Darlington railway opened.
Wellington becomes Prime Minister.

Accession of William IV.
July Revolution in France; accession of Louis Philippe.

DATE	AUTHOR'S LIFE	LITERARY CONTEXT
	next nine months in Germany, mostly at Weimar, where he meets Goethe.	Balzac begins to group his novels into *La Comédie Humaine*.
1831	Admitted to Middle Temple.	
1832–6	Living mostly in Paris, studying art and contributing to various journals.	
1832		Deaths of Goethe, Scott. Bulwer-Lytton: *Eugene Aram*.
1833		Carlyle: *Sartor Resartus*. Dickens: *Sketches by Boz*.
1834		Balzac: *Le Père Goriot*.
1836	Marries Isabella Shawe. Paris correspondent of *The Constitutional* newspaper.	Dickens: *Pickwick Papers*.
1837	Settles in London. Birth (June) of eldest daughter, Anne Isabella. *The Constitutional* ceases publication. (July) *The Yellowplush Correspondence*, his first literary success, begins to appear in *Fraser's Magazine* (November).	Carlyle: *The French Revolution*.
1838	Birth of second daughter, Jane (July).	Dickens: *Oliver Twist* and *Nicholas Nickleby*.
1839	Death of Jane Thackeray (March). *Catherine*, Thackeray's first novel, serialized in *Fraser's Magazine* (May to February 1840).	Stendhal: *La Chartreuse de Parme*.
1840	Birth (May) of third daughter, Harriet Marian. *A Shabby Genteel Story* serialized in *Fraser's*. *The Paris Sketch Book*. Thackeray's wife becomes mentally ill. He entrusts his children to the care of his mother in Paris.	
1841	*The Second Funeral of Napoleon*. *The Great Hoggarty Diamond*.	Dickens: *Barnaby Rudge* and *The Old Curiosity Shop*. Carlyle: *On Heroes, Hero-worship and the Heroic in Literature*. *Punch* founded. The London Library founded.

CHRONOLOGY

DATE	AUTHOR'S LIFE	LITERARY CONTEXT
1842	First contribution to *Punch*.	
1843	*The Irish Sketch Book*.	Dickens: *A Christmas Carol*.
1844	*Barry Lyndon* serialized in *Fraser's*. Makes a tour of the Mediterranean.	Dickens: *Martin Chuzzlewit*.
1845	Writing early draft of *Vanity Fair*. Moves his wife, judged incurably insane, from Paris to London.	Disraeli: *Sybil, or the Two Nations*.
1846	*Notes of a Journey from Cornhill to Grand Cairo*. *The Snobs of England* published in *Punch*. Moves to Young Street, Kensington, and brings his children to live with him. *Mrs. Perkins's Ball*.	Balzac: *La Cousine Bette*.
1847-8	*Vanity Fair* published in monthly numbers.	
1847		Charlotte Brontë: *Jane Eyre*. Emily Brontë: *Wuthering Heights*.
1848-50	*Pendennis* published in monthly numbers; interrupted, September–November 1849, by a serious illness.	
1848		Dickens: *Dombey and Son*. Elizabeth Gaskell: *Mary Barton*. Macaulay: *History of England* (first two volumes). Dumas *fils*: *La Dame aux Camélias*.
1849		Charlotte Brontë: *Shirley*.
1850		Deaths of Wordsworth, Balzac. Dickens: *David Copperfield*. *Household Words* founded.
1851	Lectures on *The English Humourists*. Resigns from *Punch*.	Melville: *Moby-Dick*.
1852	*The History of Henry Esmond*.	Harriet Beecher Stowe: *Uncle Tom's Cabin*.
1852-3	Lectures in the USA.	
1853-5	*The Newcomes* published in monthly numbers.	

CHRONOLOGY

DATE	AUTHOR'S LIFE	LITERARY CONTEXT
1853		Dickens: *Bleak House*. Charlotte Brontë: *Villette*.
1854–6		
1854	*The Rose and the Ring*.	Dickens: *Hard Times*.
1855–6	Lectures in the USA on *The Four Georges*.	
1855		Trollope: *The Warden*. Death of Charlotte Brontë.
1856–7	Lectures in England.	
1857	Stands for Parliament in Oxford; defeated.	Dickens: *Little Dorrit*. Trollope: *Barchester Towers*.
1857–8		Flaubert: *Madame Bovary*.
1857–9	*The Virginians* published in monthly numbers.	Baudelaire: *Les Fleurs du mal*.
1858	Quarrel with Dickens, who sides with Edmund Yates against Thackeray in the 'Garrick Club affair'.	George Eliot: *Scenes of Clerical Life*. Carlyle: *Frederick the Great*.
1859	Becomes first editor of *The Cornhill Magazine*.	Dickens: *A Tale of Two Cities*. George Eliot: *Adam Bede*. Tennyson: *Idylls of the King*.
1860	*Lovel the Widower* published in *Cornhill*. *The Four Georges* published in *Cornhill*. *The Roundabout Papers* published in *Cornhill* (to 1863).	Wilkie Collins: *The Woman in White*. George Eliot: *The Mill on the Floss*.
1861–2	*Philip* published in *Cornhill*.	
1861		Dickens: *Great Expectations*. George Eliot: *Silas Marner*. Trollope: *Framley Parsonage*. Turgenev: *Fathers and Sons*. Dostoevsky: *The House of the Dead*.
1861–5		
1862	Resigns editorship of *Cornhill*. Moves to 2 Palace Green, Kensington.	George Eliot: *Romola*. Trollope: *Orley Farm*. Hugo: *Les Misérables*.
1863	Begins writing *Denis Duval*. Dies; buried, Kensal Green cemetery.	Elizabeth Gaskell: *Sylvia's Lovers*.
1864	*Denis Duval* (uncompleted) published in *Cornhill*.	

HISTORICAL EVENTS

Crimean War.

Indian Mutiny.

Franco–Austrian War.

Death of Prince Consort.

American Civil War.

A NOTE ON THE TEXT

———

The text of this edition of *Vanity Fair* is taken from the first single-volume edition of 1848.

CONTENTS

CONTENTS

To

B. W. PROCTER

this story is affectionately dedicated.

BEFORE THE CURTAIN

As the Manager of the Performance sits before the curtain on the boards, and looks into the Fair, a feeling of profound melancholy comes over him in his survey of the bustling place. There is a great quantity of eating and drinking, making love and jilting, laughing and the contrary, smoking, cheating, fighting, dancing, and fiddling: there are bullies pushing about, bucks ogling the women, knaves picking pockets, policemen on the look-out, quacks (*other* quacks, plague take them!) bawling in front of their booths, and yokels looking up at the tinselled dancers and poor old rouged tumblers, while the light-fingered folk are operating upon their pockets behind. Yes, this is VANITY FAIR; not a moral place certainly; nor a merry one, though very noisy. Look at the faces of the actors and buffoons when they come off from their business; and Tom Fool washing the paint off his cheeks before he sits down to dinner with his wife and the little Jack Puddings behind the canvas. The curtain will be up presently, and he will be turning over head and heels, and crying 'How are you?'

A man with a reflective turn of mind, walking through an exhibition of this sort, will not be oppressed, I take it, by his own or other people's hilarity. An episode of humour or kindness touches and amuses him here and there; – a pretty child looking at a gingerbread stall; a pretty girl blushing whilst her lover talks to her and chooses her fairing; – poor Tom Fool, yonder behind the wagon, mumbling his bone with the honest family which lives by his tumbling; – but the general impression is one more melancholy than mirthful. When you come home, you sit down, in a sober, contemplative, not uncharitable frame of mind, and apply yourself to your books or your business.

I have no other moral than this to tag to the present story of *Vanity Fair*. Some people consider Fairs immoral altogether, and eschew such, with their servants and families: very likely they are right. But persons who think otherwise, and are of a lazy, or a benevolent, or a sarcastic mood, may perhaps like to step in for half an hour, and look at the performances. There are scenes of all sorts; some dreadful combats, some grand and lofty horse-riding, some scenes of high life, and some of very middling indeed; some love-making for the sentimental, and some light comic business; the whole accompanied by appropriate scenery, and brilliantly illuminated with the Author's own candles.

What more has the Manager of the Performance to say? – To acknowledge the kindness with which it has been received in all the principal towns of England through which the Show has passed, and where it has been most favourably noticed by the respected conductors of the Public Press, and by the Nobility and Gentry. He is proud to think that his Puppets have given satisfaction to the very best company in this empire. The famous little Becky Puppet has been pronounced to be uncommonly flexible in the joints, and lively on the wire: the Amelia Doll, though it has had a smaller circle of admirers, has yet been carved and dressed with the greatest care by the artist: the Dobbin Figure, though apparently clumsy, yet dances in a very amusing and natural manner: the Little Boys' Dance has been liked by some; and please to remark the richly-dressed figure of the Wicked Nobleman, on which no expense has been spared, and which Old Nick will fetch away at the end of this singular performance.

And with this, and a profound bow to his patrons, the Manager retires, and the curtain rises.

LONDON, June 28, 1848.

VANITY FAIR

A Novel without a Hero

CHAPTER I

CHISWICK MALL

W HILE the present century was in its teens, and on one
sunshiny morning in June, there drove up to the great
iron gate of Miss Pinkerton's academy for young ladies, on
Chiswick Mall, a large family coach, with two fat horses in
blazing harness, driven by a fat coachman in a three-cornered
hat and wig, at the rate of four miles an hour. A black servant,
who reposed on the box beside the fat coachman, uncurled his
bandy legs as soon as the equipage drew up opposite Miss
Pinkerton's shining brass plate, and as he pulled the bell, at
least a score of young heads were seen peering out of the
narrow windows of the stately old brick house. Nay, the acute
observer might have recognized the little red nose of good-
natured Miss Jemima Pinkerton herself, rising over some gera-
nium-pots in the window of that lady's own drawing-room.

'It is Mrs. Sedley's coach, sister,' said Miss Jemima.
'Sambo, the black servant, has just rung the bell; and the
coachman has a new red waistcoat.'

'Have you completed all the necessary preparations incident to Miss Sedley's departure, Miss Jemima?' asked Miss
Pinkerton herself, that majestic lady; the Semiramis of Hammersmith, the friend of Doctor Johnson, the correspondent
of Mrs. Chapone herself.

'The girls were up at four this morning, packing her trunks,
sister,' replied Miss Jemima; 'we have made her a bow-pot.'

'Say a bouquet, sister Jemima, 'tis more genteel.'

'Well, a booky as big almost as a haystack; I have put up
two bottles of the gillyflower-water for Mrs. Sedley, and the
receipt for making it, in Amelia's box.'

'And I trust, Miss Jemima, you have made a copy of Miss Sedley's account. This is it, is it? Very good – ninety-three pounds, four shillings. Be kind enough to address it to John Sedley, Esquire, and to seal this billet which I have written to his lady.'

In Miss Jemima's eyes an autograph letter of her sister, Miss Pinkerton, was an object of as deep veneration, as would have been a letter from a sovereign. Only when her pupils quitted the establishment, or when they were about to be married, and once, when poor Miss Birch died of the scarlet fever, was Miss Pinkerton known to write personally to the parents of her pupils; and it was Jemima's opinion that if anything *could* console Mrs. Birch for her daughter's loss, it would be that pious and eloquent composition in which Miss Pinkerton announced the event.

In the present instance, Miss Pinkerton's 'billet' was to the following effect:–

THE MALL, CHISWICK, June 15, 18–.

MADAM, – After her six years' residence at the Mall, I have the honour and happiness of presenting Miss Amelia Sedley to her parents, as a young lady not unworthy to occupy a fitting position in their polished and refined circle. Those virtues which characterize the young English gentlewoman, those accomplishments which become her birth and station, will not be found wanting in the amiable Miss Sedley, whose *industry* and *obedience* have endeared her to her instructors, and whose delightful sweetness of temper has charmed her *aged* and her *youthful* companions.

In music, in dancing, in orthography, in every variety of embroidery and needlework, she will be found to have realized her friends' *fondest wishes*. In geography there is still much to be desired; and a careful and undeviating use of the backboard, for four hours daily during the next three years, is recommended as necessary to the acquirement of that dignified *deportment and carriage*, so requisite for every young lady of *fashion*.

In the principles of religion and morality, Miss Sedley will be found worthy of an establishment which has been honoured by the presence of *The Great Lexicographer*, and the patronage of the admirable Mrs. Chapone. In leaving the Mall, Miss Amelia carries with her the hearts of her companions, and the affectionate regards of her mistress, who has the honour to subscribe herself,

Madam,
Your most obliged humble servant,
BARBARA PINKERTON.

PS. – Miss Sharp accompanies Miss Sedley. It is particularly requested that Miss Sharp's stay in Russell Square may not exceed ten days. The family of distinction with whom she is engaged desire to avail themselves of her services as soon as possible.'

This letter completed, Miss Pinkerton proceeded to write her own name, and Miss Sedley's, in the fly-leaf of a Johnson's Dictionary – the interesting work which she invariably presented to her scholars, on their departure from the Mall. On the cover was inserted a copy of 'Lines addressed to a young lady on quitting Miss Pinkerton's school, at the Mall; by the late revered Doctor Samuel Johnson.' In fact, the lexicographer's name was always on the lips of this majestic woman, and a visit he had paid to her was the cause of her reputation and her fortune.

Being commanded by her elder sister to get 'the Dictionary' from the cupboard, Miss Jemima had extracted two copies of the book from the receptacle in question. When Miss Pinkerton had finished the inscription in the first, Jemima, with rather a dubious and timid air, handed her the second.

'For whom is this, Miss Jemima?' said Miss Pinkerton, with awful coldness.

'For Becky Sharp,' answered Jemima, trembling very much, and blushing over her withered face and neck, as she turned her back on her sister. 'For Becky Sharp: she's going too.'

'MISS JEMIMA!' exclaimed Miss Pinkerton, in the largest capitals. 'Are you in your senses? Replace the Dixonary in the closet, and never venture to take such a liberty in future.'

'Well, sister, it's only two-and-ninepence, and poor Becky will be miserable if she don't get one.'

'Send Miss Sedley instantly to me,' said Miss Pinkerton. And so venturing not to say another word, poor Jemima trotted off, exceedingly flurried and nervous.

Miss Sedley's papa was a merchant in London, and a man of some wealth; whereas Miss Sharp was an articled pupil, for whom Miss Pinkerton had done, as she thought, quite enough, without conferring upon her at parting the high honour of the Dixonary.

Although schoolmistresses' letters are to be trusted no

more nor less than churchyard epitaphs; yet, as it sometimes happens that a person departs this life, who is really
deserving of all the praises the stone-cutter carves over
his bones; who *is* a good Christian, a good parent, child,
wife or husband; who actually *does* leave a disconsolate family
to mourn his loss; so in academies of the male and female
sex it occurs every now and then, that the pupil is fully
worthy of the praises bestowed by the disinterested instruc-
tor. Now, Miss Amelia Sedley was a young lady of this
singular species, and deserved not only all that Miss Pinkerton said in her praise, but had many charming qualities
which that pompous old Minerva of a woman could not see,
from the differences of rank and age between her pupil and
herself.

For she could not only sing like a lark, or a Mrs.
Billington, and dance like Hillisberg or Parisot; and embroider
beautifully; and spell as well as the Dixonary itself; but she
had such a kindly, smiling, tender, gentle, generous heart of
her own, as won the love of everybody who came near her,
from Minerva herself down to the poor girl in the scullery,
and the one-eyed tartwoman's daughter, who was permitted
to vend her wares once a week to the young ladies in the
Mall. She had twelve intimate and bosom friends out of the
twenty-four young ladies. Even envious Miss Briggs never
spoke ill of her: high and mighty Miss Saltire (Lord Dexter's
granddaughter) allowed that her figure was genteel: and as
for Miss Swartz, the rich woolly-haired mulatto from St.
Kitts, on the day Amelia went away, she was in such a
passion of tears, that they were obliged to send for Dr. Floss,
and half tipsify her with sal volatile. Miss Pinkerton's
attachment was, as may be supposed, from the high position
and eminent virtues of that lady, calm and dignified; but
Miss Jemima had already whimpered several times at the
idea of Amelia's departure; and, but for fear of her sister,
would have gone off in downright hysterics, like the heiress
(who paid double) of St. Kitts. Such luxury of grief, however, is only allowed to parlour-boarders. Honest Jemima
had all the bills, and the washing, and the mending, and the
puddings, and the plate and crockery, and the servants to
superintend. But why speak about her? It is probable that
we shall not hear of her again from this moment to the end
of time, and that when the great filigree iron gates are once

closed on her, she and her awful sister will never issue therefrom into this little world of history.

But as we are to see a great deal of Amelia, there is no harm in saying, at the outset of our acquaintance, that she was a dear little creature; and a great mercy it is, both in life and in novels, which (and the latter especially) abound in villains of the most sombre sort, that we are to have for a constant companion, so guileless and good-natured a person. As she is not a heroine, there is no need to describe her person; indeed I am afraid that her nose was rather short than otherwise, and her cheeks a great deal too round and red for a heroine; but her face blushed with rosy health, and her lips with the freshest of smiles, and she had a pair of eyes, which sparkled with the brightest and honestest good-humour, except indeed when they filled with tears, and that was a great deal too often; for the silly thing would cry over a dead canary bird; or over a mouse, that the cat haply had seized upon; or over the end of a novel, were it ever so stupid; and as for saying an unkind word to her, were any persons hardhearted enough to do so – why, so much the worse for them. Even Miss Pinkerton, that austere and god-like woman, ceased scolding her after the first time, and though she no more comprehended sensibility than she did algebra, gave all masters and teachers particular orders to treat Miss Sedley with the utmost gentleness, as harsh treatment was injurious to her.

So that when the day of departure came, between her two customs of laughing and crying, Miss Sedley was greatly puzzled how to act. She was glad to go home, and yet most wofully sad at leaving school. For three days before, little Laura Martin, the orphan, followed her about, like a little dog. She had to make and receive at least fourteen presents, – to make fourteen solemn promises of writing every week: 'Send my letters under cover to my grandpapa, the Earl of Dexter,' said Miss Saltire (who, by the way, was rather shabby): 'Never mind the postage, but write every day, you dear darling,' said the impetuous and woolly-headed, but generous and affectionate Miss Swartz; and the orphan, little Laura Martin (who was just in round-hand), took her friend's hand and said, looking up in her face wistfully, 'Amelia, when I write to you I shall call you mamma.' All which details, I have no doubt, Jones, who reads this book at his Club, will pronounce to be excessively foolish, trivial, twaddling, and ultra-sentimental. Yes; I can see Jones at this minute (rather flushed with his joint of mutton and half-pint of wine), taking out his pencil and scoring under the words 'foolish, twaddling,' &c., and adding to them his own remark of '*quite true*'. Well, he is a lofty man of genius, and admires the great and heroic in life and novels; and so had better take warning and go elsewhere.

Well, then. The flowers, and the presents, and the trunks, and bonnet-boxes of Miss Sedley having been arranged by Mr. Sambo in the carriage, together with a very small and weather-beaten old cow's-skin trunk with Miss Sharp's card neatly nailed upon it, which was delivered by Sambo with a grin, and packed by the coachman with a corresponding sneer – the hour for parting came; and the grief of that moment was considerably lessened by the admirable discourse which Miss Pinkerton addressed to her pupil. Not that the parting speech caused Amelia to philosophize, or that it armed her in any way with a calmness, the result of argument; but it was intolerably dull, pompous, and tedious; and having the fear of her schoolmistress greatly before her eyes, Miss Sedley did not venture, in her presence, to give way to any ebullitions of private grief. A seed-cake and a bottle of wine were produced in the drawing-room, as on the solemn occasions of the visit of parents, and these refreshments being partaken of, Miss Sedley was at liberty to depart.

You'll go in and say good-bye to Miss Pinkerton, Becky!' said Miss Jemima to a young lady of whom nobody took any notice, and who was coming downstairs with her own bandbox.

'I suppose I must,' said Miss Sharp calmly, and much to the wonder of Miss Jemima; and the latter having knocked at the door and receiving permission to come in, Miss Sharp advanced in a very unconcerned manner, and said in French, and with a perfect accent, '*Mademoiselle, je viens vous faire mes adieux.*'

Miss Pinkerton did not understand French; she only directed those who did: but biting her lips and throwing up her venerable and Roman-nosed head (on the top of which figured a large and solemn turban), she said, 'Miss Sharp, I wish you a good morning.' As the Hammersmith

Semiramis spoke, she waved one hand, both by way of adieu, and to give Miss Sharp an opportunity of shaking one of the fingers of the hand which was left out for that purpose.

Miss Sharp only folded her own hands with a very frigid smile and bow, and quite declined to accept the proffered honour; on which Semiramis tossed up her turban more indignantly than ever. In fact, it was a little battle between the young lady and the old one, and the latter was worsted. 'Heaven bless you, my child,' said she, embracing Amelia, and scowling the while over the girl's shoulder at Miss Sharp. 'Come away, Becky,' said Miss Jemima, pulling the young woman away in great alarm, and the drawing-room door closed upon them for ever.

Then came the struggle and parting below. Words refuse to tell it. All the servants were there in the hall – all the dear friends – all the young ladies – the dancing-master who had just arrived; and there was such a scuffling, and hugging, and kissing, and crying, with the hysterical *yoops* of Miss Swartz, the parlour-boarder, from her room, as no pen can depict, and as the tender heart would fain pass over. The embracing was over; they parted – that is, Miss Sedley parted from her friends. Miss Sharp had demurely entered the carriage some minutes before. Nobody cried for leaving *her*.

Sambo of the bandy-legs slammed the carriage-door on his young weeping mistress. He sprang up behind the carriage. 'Stop!' cried Miss Jemima, rushing to the gate with a parcel.

'It's some sandwiches, my dear,' said she to Amelia. 'You may be hungry, you know; and Becky, Becky Sharp, here's a book for you that my sister – that is, I – Johnson's Dixonary, you know; you mustn't leave us without that. Good-bye. Drive on, coachman. God bless you!'

And the kind creature retreated into the garden, overcome with emotions.

But, lo! and just as the coach drove off, Miss Sharp put her pale face out of the window, and actually flung the book back into the garden.

This almost caused Jemima to faint with terror. 'Well, I never,' – said she – 'what an audacious —' Emotion prevented her from completing either sentence. The carriage rolled

away; the great gates were closed; the bell rang for the
dancing lesson. The world is before the two young ladies;
and so, farewell to Chiswick Mall.

CHAPTER II

IN WHICH MISS SHARP AND MISS SEDLEY PREPARE
TO OPEN THE CAMPAIGN

WHEN Miss Sharp had performed the heroical act mentioned in the last chapter, and had seen the Dixonary
flying over the pavement of the little garden, fall at length
at the feet of the astonished Miss Jemima, the young lady's
countenance, which had before worn an almost livid look
of hatred, assumed a smile that perhaps was scarcely more
agreeable, and she sank back in the carriage in an easy frame
of mind, saying, 'So much for the Dixonary; and, thank
God, I'm out of Chiswick.'

Miss Sedley was almost as flurried at the act of defiance
as Miss Jemima had been; for, consider, it was but one
minute that she had left school, and the impressions of six
years are not got over in that space of time. Nay, with some
persons those awes and terrors of youth last for ever and
ever. I know, for instance, an old gentleman of sixty-eight,
who said to me one morning at breakfast, with a very agitated
countenance, 'I dreamed last night that I was flogged by Dr.
Raine.' Fancy had carried him back five-and-fifty years in
the course of that evening. Dr. Raine and his rod were just
as awful to him in his heart, then, at sixty-eight, as they
had been at thirteen. If the Doctor, with a large birch, had
appeared bodily to him, even at the age of three score and
eight, and had said in awful voice, 'Boy, take down your
pant —'? Well, well, Miss Sedley was exceedingly alarmed
at this act of insubordination.

'How could you do so, Rebecca?' at last she said, after a
pause.

'Why, do you think Miss Pinkerton will come out and
order me back to the black-hole?' said Rebecca, laughing.

'No: but —'

'I hate the whole house,' continued Miss Sharp, in a fury.
'I hope I may never set eyes on it again. I wish it were in
the bottom of the Thames, I do; and if Miss Pinkerton were

there, I wouldn't pick her out, that I wouldn't. Oh, how I should like to see her floating in the water yonder, turban and all, with her train streaming after her, and her nose like the beak of a wherry.'

'Hush!' cried Miss Sedley.

'Why, will the black footman tell tales?' cried Miss Rebecca, laughing. 'He may go back and tell Miss Pinkerton that I hate her with all my soul; and I wish he would; and I wish I had a means of proving it, too. For two years I have only had insults and outrage from her. I have been treated worse than any servant in the kitchen. I have never had a friend or a kind word, except from you. I have been made to tend the little girls in the lower schoolroom, and to talk French to the misses until I grew sick of my mother-tongue. But that talking French to Miss Pinkerton was capital fun, wasn't it? She doesn't know a word of French, and was too proud to confess it. I believe it was that which made her part with me; and so thank Heaven for French. *Vive la France! Vive l'Empereur! Vive Bonaparte!*'

'O Rebecca, Rebecca, for shame!' cried Miss Sedley; for this was the greatest blasphemy Rebecca had as yet uttered; and in those days, in England, to say 'Long live Bonaparte!' was as much as to say 'Long live Lucifer!' 'How can you – how dare you have such wicked, revengeful thoughts?'

'Revenge may be wicked, but it's natural,' answered Miss Rebecca. 'I'm no angel.' And, to say the truth, she certainly was not.

For it may be remarked in the course of this little conversation (which took place as the coach rolled along lazily by the riverside) that though Miss Rebecca Sharp has twice had occasion to thank Heaven, it has been, in the first place, for ridding her of some person whom she hated, and secondly, for enabling her to bring her enemies to some sort of perplexity or confusion; neither of which are very amiable motives for religious gratitude, or such as would be put forward by persons of a kind and placable disposition. Miss Rebecca was not, then, in the least kind or placable. All the world used her ill, said this young misanthropist, and we may be pretty certain that persons whom all the world treats ill, deserve entirely the treatment they get. The world is a looking-glass, and gives back to every man the reflection of his own face. Frown at it, and it will in turn look sourly upon you; laugh at it and with it, and it is a jolly kind companion; and so let all young persons take their choice. This is certain, that if the world neglected Miss Sharp, she never was known to have done a good action in behalf of anybody; nor can it be expected that twenty-four young ladies should all be as amiable as the heroine of this work, Miss Sedley (whom we have selected for the very reason that she was the best-natured of all, otherwise what on earth was to have prevented us from putting up Miss Swartz, or Miss Crump, or Miss Hopkins, as heroine in her place?) – it could not be expected that every one should be of the humble and gentle temper of Miss Amelia Sedley; should take every opportunity to vanquish Rebecca's hard-heartedness and ill-humour; and, by a thousand kind words and offices, overcome, for once at least, her hostility to her kind.

Miss Sharp's father was an artist, and in that quality had given lessons of drawing at Miss Pinkerton's school. He was a clever man; a pleasant companion; a careless student; with a great propensity for running into debt, and a partiality for the tavern. When he was drunk, he used to beat his wife and daughter; and the next morning, with a headache, he would rail at the world for its neglect of his genius, and abuse, with a good deal of cleverness, and sometimes with perfect reason, the fools, his brother painters. As it was with the utmost difficulty that he could keep himself, and as he owed money for a mile round Soho, where he lived, he thought to better his circumstances by marrying a young woman of the French nation, who was by profession an opera-girl. The humble calling of her female parent, Miss Sharp never alluded to, but used to state subsequently that the Entrechats were a noble family of Gascony, and took great pride in her descent from them. And curious it is, that as she advanced in life this young lady's ancestors increased in rank and splendour.

Rebecca's mother had had some education somewhere, and her daughter spoke French with purity and a Parisian accent. It was in those days rather a rare accomplishment, and led to her engagement with the orthodox Miss Pinkerton. For her mother being dead, her father, finding himself not likely to recover, after his third attack of *delirium tremens*, wrote a manly and pathetic letter to Miss Pinkerton, recommending the orphan child to her protection, and so descended to the grave, after two bailiffs had quarrelled over his corpse. Rebecca was seventeen when she came to Chiswick, and was bound over as an articled pupil; her duties being to talk French, as we have seen; and her privileges to live cost free, and, with a few guineas a year, to gather scraps of knowledge from the professors who attended the school.

She was small and slight in person; pale, sandy-haired, and with eyes habitually cast down: when they looked up they were very large, odd, and attractive; so attractive, that the Reverend Mr. Crisp, fresh from Oxford, and curate to the Vicar of Chiswick, the Reverend Mr. Flowerdew, fell in love with Miss Sharp; being shot dead by a glance of her eyes, which was fired all the way across Chiswick Church from the school-pew to the reading-desk. This infatuated young man used sometimes to take tea with Miss Pinkerton, to whom he had been presented by his mamma, and actually proposed something like marriage in an intercepted note, which the one-eyed applewoman was charged to deliver. Mrs. Crisp was summoned from Buxton, and abruptly carried off her darling boy; but the idea, even, of such an eagle in the Chiswick dovecot caused a great flutter in the breast of Miss Pinkerton, who would have sent away Miss Sharp, but that she was bound to her under a forfeit, and who never could thoroughly believe the young lady's protestations that she had never exchanged a single word with Mr. Crisp, except under her own eyes on the two occasions when she had met him at tea.

By the side of many tall and bouncing young ladies in the establishment, Rebecca Sharp looked like a child. But she had the dismal precocity of poverty. Many a dun had she talked to, and turned away from her father's door; many a tradesman had she coaxed and wheedled into good humour, and into the granting of one meal more. She sat commonly with her father, who was very proud of her wit, and heard the talk of many of his wild companions – often but ill-suited for a girl to hear. But she never had been a girl, she said; she had been a woman since she was eight years old. Oh, why did Miss Pinkerton let such a dangerous bird into her cage?

The fact is, the old lady believed Rebecca to be the meekest creature in the world, so admirably, on the occasions when her father brought her to Chiswick, used Rebecca to perform the part of the *ingénue*; and only a year before the arrangement by which Rebecca had been admitted into her house, and when Rebecca was sixteen years old, Miss Pinkerton majestically, and with a little speech, made her a present of a doll — which was, by the way, the confiscated property of Miss Swindle, discovered surreptitiously nursing it in school hours. How the father and daughter laughed as they trudged home together after the evening party (it was on the occasion of the speeches, when all the professors were invited), and how Miss Pinkerton would have raged had she seen the caricature of herself which the little mimic, Rebecca, managed to make out of her doll. Becky used to go through dialogues with it; it formed the delight of Newman Street, Gerrard Street, and the artists' quarter: and the young painters, when they came to take their gin-and-water with their lazy, dissolute, clever, jovial senior, used regularly to ask Rebecca if Miss Pinkerton was at home: she was well known to them, poor soul! as Mr. Lawrence or President West. Once she had the honour to pass a few days at Chiswick; after which she brought back Jemima, and erected another doll as Miss Jemmy; for though that honest creature had made and given her jelly and cake enough for three children, and a seven-shilling piece at parting, the girl's sense of ridicule was far stronger than her gratitude, and she sacrificed Miss Jemmy quite as pitilessly as her sister.

The catastrophe came, and she was brought to the Mall as to her home. The rigid formality of the place suffocated her: the prayers and the meals, the lessons and the walks, which were arranged with a conventual regularity, oppressed her almost beyond endurance; and she looked back to the freedom and the beggary of the old studio in Soho with so much regret, that everybody, herself included, fancied she was consumed with grief for her father. She had a little room in the garret, where the maids heard her walking and sobbing at night; but it was with rage, and not with grief. She had not been much of a dissembler, until now her loneliness taught her to feign. She had never mingled in the society of women: her father, reprobate as he was, was a man of talent; his conversation was a thousand times more agreeable to her than the talk of such of her own sex as she now encountered. The pompous vanity of the old school-mistress, the foolish good humour of her sister, the silly chat and scandal of the elder girls, and the frigid correctness of the governesses equally annoyed her; and she had no soft maternal heart, this unlucky girl, otherwise the prattle and talk of the younger children, with whose care she was chiefly entrusted, might have soothed and interested her; but she lived among them two years, and not one was sorry that she went away. The gentle tender-hearted Amelia Sedley was the only person to whom she could attach herself in the least; and who could help attaching herself to Amelia?

The happiness – the superior advantages of the young women round about her, gave Rebecca inexpressible pangs of envy. 'What airs that girl gives herself, because she is an earl's granddaughter,' she said of one. 'How they cringe and bow to that Creole, because of her hundred thousand pounds! I am a thousand times cleverer and more charming than that creature, for all her wealth. I am as well-bred as the earl's granddaughter, for all her fine pedigree; and yet every one passes me by here. And yet, when I was at my father's, did not the men give up their gayest balls and parties in order to pass the evening with me?' She deter-mined at any rate to get free from the prison in which she found herself, and now began to act for herself, and for the first time to make connected plans for the future.

She took advantage, therefore, of the means of study the place offered her; and as she was already a musician and a good linguist, she speedily went through the little course of study which was considered necessary for ladies in those days. Her music she practised incessantly, and one day, when the girls were out, and she had remained at home, she was overheard to play a piece so well, that Minerva thought wisely, she could spare herself the expense of a master for the juniors, and intimated to Miss Sharp that she was to instruct them in music for the future.

The girl refused; and for the first time, and to the astonishment of the majestic mistress of the school. 'I am here to speak French with the children,' Rebecca said abruptly, 'not to teach them music, and save money for you. Give me money, and I will teach them.'

Minerva was obliged to yield, and, of course, disliked her

from that day. 'For five-and-thirty years,' she said, and with great justice, 'I never have seen the individual who has dared in my own house to question my authority. I have nourished a viper in my bosom.'

'A viper – a fiddlestick,' said Miss Sharp to the old lady, almost fainting with astonishment. 'You took me because I was useful. There is no question of gratitude between us. I hate this place, and want to leave it. I will do nothing here but what I am obliged to do.'

It was in vain that the old lady asked her if she was aware she was speaking to Miss Pinkerton? Rebecca laughed in her face, with a horrid sarcastic demoniacal laughter, that almost sent the schoolmistress into fits. 'Give me a sum of money,' said the girl, 'and get rid of me – or, if you like better, get me a good place as governess in a nobleman's family – you can do so if you please.' And in their further disputes she always returned to this point, 'Get me a situation – we hate each other, and I am ready to go.'

Worthy Miss Pinkerton, although she had a Roman nose and a turban, and was as tall as a grenadier, and had been up to this time an irresistible princess, had no will or strength like that of her little apprentice, and in vain did battle against her, and tried to overawe her. Attempting once to scold her in public, Rebecca hit upon the before-mentioned plan of answering her in French, which quite routed the old woman. In order to maintain authority in her school, it became necessary to remove this rebel, this monster, this serpent, this firebrand; and hearing about this time that Sir Pitt Crawley's family was in want of a governess, she actually recommended Miss Sharp for the situation, firebrand and serpent as she was. 'I cannot, certainly,' she said, 'find fault with Miss Sharp's conduct, except to myself; and must allow that her talents and accomplishments are of a high order. As far as the head goes, at least, she does credit to the educational system pursued at my establishment.'

And so the schoolmistress reconciled the recommendation to her conscience, and the indentures were cancelled, and the apprentice was free. The battle here described in a few lines, of course lasted for some months. And as Miss Sedley, being now in her seventeenth year, was about to leave school, and had a friendship for Miss Sharp (' 'tis the only point in Amelia's behaviour,' said Minerva, 'which has not been satisfactory to her mistress'), Miss Sharp was invited by her friend to pass a week with her at home, before she entered upon her duties as governess in a private family.

Thus the world began for these two young ladies. For Amelia it was quite a new, fresh, brilliant world, with all the bloom upon it. It was not quite a new one for Rebecca (indeed, if the truth must be told with respect to the Crisp affair, the tart-woman hinted to somebody, who took an affidavit of the fact to somebody else, that there was a great deal more than was made public regarding Mr. Crisp and Miss Sharp, and that his letter was *in answer* to another letter). But who can tell you the real truth of the matter? At all events, if Rebecca was not beginning the world, she was beginning it over again.

By the time the young ladies reached Kensington turn-pike, Amelia had not forgotten her companions, but had dried her tears, and had blushed very much and been delighted at a young officer of the Life Guards, who spied her as he was riding by, and said, 'A dem fine gal, egad!' and before the carriage arrived in Russell Square, a great deal of conversation had taken place about the Drawing-room, and whether or not young ladies wore powder as well as hoops when presented, and whether she was to have that honour: to the Lord Mayor's ball she knew she was to go. And when at length home was reached, Miss Amelia Sedley skipped out on Sambo's arm, as happy and as handsome a girl as any in the whole big city of London. Both he and coachman agreed on this point, and so did her father and mother, and so did every one of the servants in the house, as they stood bobbing, and curtsying, and smiling, in the hall, to welcome their young mistress.

You may be sure that she showed Rebecca over every room of the house, and everything in every one of her drawers; and her books, and her piano, and her dresses, and all her necklaces, brooches, laces, and gimcracks. She insisted upon Rebecca accepting the white cornelian and the turquoise rings, and a sweet sprigged muslin, which was too small for her now, though it would fit her friend to a nicety; and she determined in her heart to ask her mother's permission to present her white Cashmere shawl to her friend. Could she not spare it? and had not her brother Joseph just brought her two from India?

When Rebecca saw the two magnificent Cashmere shawls which Joseph Sedley had brought home to his sister, she said, with perfect truth, 'that it must be delightful to have a brother,' and easily got the pity of the tender-hearted Amelia, for being alone in the world, an orphan without friends or kindred.

'Not alone,' said Amelia; 'you know; Rebecca, I shall always be your friend, and love you as a sister – indeed I will.'

'Ah, but to have parents, as you have – kind, rich, affectionate parents, who give you everything you ask for; and their love, which is more precious than all! My poor papa could give me nothing, and I had but two frocks in all the world! And then, to have a brother, a dear brother! Oh, how you must love him!'

Amelia laughed.

'What! *don't* you love him? you, who say you love everybody?'

'Yes, of course, I do – only —'

'Only what?'

'Only Joseph doesn't seem to care much whether I love him or not. He gave me two fingers to shake when he arrived after ten years' absence! He is very kind and good, but he scarcely ever speaks to me; I think he loves his pipe a great deal better than his —' but here Amelia checked herself, for why should she speak ill of her brother?

'He was very kind to me as a child,' she added; 'I was but five years old when he went away.'

'Isn't he very rich?' said Rebecca. 'They say all Indian nabobs are enormously rich.'

'I believe he has a very large income.'

'And is your sister-in-law a nice pretty woman?'

'La! Joseph is not married,' said Amelia, laughing again.

Perhaps she had mentioned the fact already to Rebecca, but that young lady did not appear to have remembered it; indeed, vowed and protested that she expected to see a number of Amelia's nephews and nieces. She was quite disappointed that Mr. Sedley was not married; she was sure Amelia had said he was, and she doted so on little children.

'I think you must have had enough of them at Chiswick,' said Amelia, rather wondering at the sudden tenderness on her friend's part; and indeed in later days Miss Sharp would never have committed herself so far as to advance opinions, the untruth of which would have been so easily detected. But we must remember that she is but nineteen as yet, unused to the art of deceiving, poor innocent creature! and making her own experience in her own person. The meaning of the above series of queries, as translated in the heart of this ingenious young woman, was simply this: – 'If Mr. Joseph Sedley is rich and unmarried, why should I not marry him? I have only a fortnight, to be sure, but there is no harm in trying.' And she determined within herself to make this laudable attempt. She redoubled her caresses to Amelia; she kissed the white cornelian necklace as she put it on; and vowed she would never, never part with it. When the dinner-bell rang she went downstairs with her arm round her friend's waist, as is the habit of young ladies. She was so agitated at the drawing-room door, that she could hardly find courage to enter. 'Feel my heart, how it beats, dear!' said she to her friend.

'No, it doesn't,' said Amelia. 'Come in, don't be frightened. Papa won't do you any harm.'

CHAPTER III

REBECCA IS IN PRESENCE OF THE ENEMY

A VERY stout, puffy man, in buckskins and hessian boots, with several immense neckcloths, that rose almost to his nose, with a red striped waistcoat and an apple-green coat with steel buttons almost as large as crown pieces (it was the morning costume of a dandy or blood of those days), was reading the paper by the fire when the two girls entered, and bounced off his arm-chair, and blushed excessively, and hid his entire face almost in his neckcloths at this apparition.

'It's only your sister, Joseph,' said Amelia, laughing and shaking the two fingers which he held out. 'I've come home *for good*, you know; and this is my friend, Miss Sharp, whom you have heard me mention.'

'No, never, upon my word,' said the head under the neckcloth, shaking very much, – 'that is, yes, – what abominably cold weather, miss;' – and herewith he fell to poking the fire with all his might, although it was in the middle of June.

'He's very handsome,' whispered Rebecca to Amelia, rather loud.

'Do you think so?' said the latter. 'I'll tell him.'

'Darling! not for worlds,' said Miss Sharp, starting back as timid as a fawn. She had previously made a respectful virgin-like curtsy to the gentleman, and her modest eyes gazed so perseveringly on the carpet that it was a wonder how she should have found an opportunity to see him.

'Thank you for the beautiful shawls, brother,' said Amelia to the fire-poker. 'Are they not beautiful, Rebecca?'

'Oh, heavenly!' said Miss Sharp, and her eyes went from the carpet straight to the chandelier.

Joseph still continued a huge clattering at the poker and tongs, puffing and blowing the while, and turning as red as his yellow face would allow him. 'I can't make you such handsome presents, Joseph,' continued his sister, 'but while I was at school, I have embroidered for you a very beautiful pair of braces.'

'Good Gad! Amelia,' cried the brother, in serious alarm, 'what do you mean?' and plunging with all his might at the bell-rope, that article of furniture came away in his hand, and increased the honest fellow's confusion. 'For heaven's sake see if my buggy's at the door. I *can't* wait. I must go. D— that groom of mine. I must go.'

At this minute the father of the family walked in, rattling his seals like a true British merchant. 'What's the matter, Emmy?' says he.

'Joseph wants me to see if his – his *buggy* is at the door. What is a buggy, papa?'

'It is a one-horse palanquin,' said the old gentleman, who was a wag in his way.

Joseph at this burst out into a wild fit of laughter; in which, encountering the eye of Miss Sharp, he stopped all of a sudden, as if he had been shot.

'This young lady is your friend? Miss Sharp, I am very happy to see you. Have you and Emmy been quarrelling already with Joseph, that he wants to be off?'

'I promised Bonamy of our service, sir,' said Joseph, 'to dine with him.'

'Oh, fie! didn't you tell your mother you would dine here?'

'But in this dress it's impossible.'

'Look at him, isn't he handsome enough to dine any-where, Miss Sharp?'

On which, of course, Miss Sharp looked at her friend, and they both set off in a fit of laughter, highly agreeable to the old gentleman.

'Did you ever see a pair of buckskins like those at Miss Pinkerton's?' continued he, following up his advantage.

'Gracious heavens! father,' cried Joseph.

'There now, I have hurt his feelings. Mrs. Sedley, my dear, I have hurt your son's feelings. I have alluded to his buckskins. Ask Miss Sharp if I haven't? Come, Joseph, be friends with Miss Sharp, and let us all go to dinner.'

'There's a pillau, Joseph, just as you like it, and papa has brought home the best turbot in Billingsgate.'

'Come, come, sir, walk downstairs with Miss Sharp, and I will follow with these two young women,' said the father, and he took an arm of wife and daughter and walked merrily off.

If Miss Rebecca Sharp had determined in her heart upon making the conquest of this big beau, I don't think, ladies, we have any right to blame her; for though the task of husband-hunting is generally, and with becoming modesty, entrusted by young persons to their mammas, recollect that Miss Sharp had no kind parent to arrange these delicate matters for her, and that if she did not get a husband for herself, there was no one else in the wide world who would take the trouble off her hands. What causes young people to 'come *out*', but the noble ambition of matrimony? What sends them trooping to watering-places? What keeps them dancing till five o'clock in the morning through a whole mortal season? What causes them to labour at pianoforte sonatas, and to learn four songs from a fashionable master at a guinea a lesson, and to play the harp if they have handsome arms and neat elbows, and to wear Lincoln green toxopholite hats and feathers, but that they may bring down some 'desirable' young man with those killing bows and arrows of theirs? What causes respectable parents to take up their carpets, set their houses topsy-turvy, and spend a fifth of their year's income in ball suppers and iced champagne? Is it sheer love of their species, and an unadulterated wish to see young people happy and dancing? Psha! they want to marry their daughters; and, as honest Mrs. Sedley has, in the depths of her kind heart, already arranged a score of little schemes for the settlement of her Amelia, so also had our beloved but unprotected Rebecca determined to do her very best to secure the husband, who was even more necessary for her than for her friend. She had a vivid imagination; she had, besides, read the *Arabian Nights* and *Guthrie's Geography*; and it is a fact, that while she was dressing for dinner, and after she had asked Amelia whether her brother was very rich, she had built for herself a most magnificent castle in the air, of which she was mistress, with a husband somewhere in the background (she had not seen him as yet, and his figure would not therefore be very distinct); she had arrayed herself in an infinity of shawls, turbans, and diamond necklaces, and had mounted upon an elephant to the sound of the march in Bluebeard, in order to pay a visit of ceremony to the Grand Mogul. Charming Alnaschar visions! it is the happy privilege of youth to construct you, and many a fanciful young creature besides Rebecca Sharp has indulged in these delightful day-dreams ere now!

Joseph Sedley was twelve years older than his sister Amelia. He was in the East India Company's Civil Service, and his name appeared, at the period of which we write, in the Bengal division of the East India Register, as collector of Boggley Wollah, an honourable and lucrative post, as everybody knows: in order to know to what higher posts Joseph rose in the service, the reader is referred to the same periodical.

Boggley Wollah is situated in a fine, lonely, marshy, jungly district, famous for snipe-shooting, and where not unfrequently you may flush a tiger. Ramgunge, where there is a magistrate, is only forty miles off, and there is a cavalry station about thirty miles farther; so Joseph wrote home to his parents, when he took possession of his collectorship. He had lived for about eight years of his life, quite alone, at this charming place, scarcely seeing a Christian face except twice a year, when the detachment arrived to carry off the revenues which he had collected, to Calcutta.

Luckily, at this time he caught a liver complaint, for the cure of which he returned to Europe, and which was the source of great comfort and amusement to him in his native country. He did not live with his family while in London, but had lodgings of his own, like a gay young bachelor.

Before he went to India he was too young to partake of the delightful pleasures of a man about town, and plunged into them, on his return, with considerable assiduity. He drove his horses in the Park; he dined at the fashionable taverns (for the Oriental Club was not as yet invented); he frequented the theatres, as the mode was in those days, or made his appearance at the opera, laboriously attired in tights and a cocked hat.

On returning to India, and ever after, he used to talk of the pleasure of this period of his existence with great enthusiasm, and give you to understand that he and Brummell were the leading bucks of the day. But he was as lonely here as in his jungle at Boggley Wollah. He scarcely knew a single soul in the metropolis: and were it not for his doctor, and the society of his blue-pill, and his liver complaint, he must have died of loneliness. He was lazy, peevish, and a *bon-vivant*; the appearance of a lady frightened him beyond measure; hence it was but seldom that he joined the paternal circle in Russell Square, where there was plenty of gaiety, and where the jokes of his good-natured old father frightened his *amour-propre*. His bulk caused Joseph much anxious thought and alarm; now and then he would make a desperate attempt to get rid of his superabundant fat; but his indolence and love of good living speedily got the better of these endeavours at reform, and he found himself again at his three meals a day. He never was well dressed; but he took the hugest pains to adorn his big person, and passed many hours daily in that occupation. His valet made a fortune out of his wardrobe: his toilet-table was covered with as many pomatums and essences as ever were employed by an old beauty: he had tried, in order to give himself a waist, every girth, stay, and waistband then invented. Like most fat men, he *would* have his clothes made too tight, and took care they should be of the most brilliant colours and youthful cut. When dressed at length, in the afternoon, he would issue forth to take a drive with nobody in the Park; and then would come back in order to dress again and go and dine with nobody at the piazza Coffee-house. He was as vain as a girl; and perhaps his extreme shyness was one of the results of his extreme vanity. If Miss Rebecca can get the better of *him*, and at her first entrance into life, she is a young person of no ordinary cleverness.

The first move showed considerable skill. When she called Sedley a very handsome man, she knew that Amelia would tell her mother, who would probably tell Joseph, or who, at any rate, would be pleased by the compliment paid to her son. All mothers are. If you had told Sycorax that her son Caliban was as handsome as Apollo, she would have been pleased, witch as she was. Perhaps, too, Joseph Sedley would overhear the compliment – Rebecca spoke loud enough – and he *did* hear, and (thinking in his heart that he was a very fine man) the praise thrilled through every fibre of his big body, and made it tingle with pleasure. Then, however, came a recoil. 'Is the girl making fun of me?' he thought, and straightway he bounced towards the bell, and was for retreating, as we have seen, when his father's jokes and his mother's entreaties caused him to pause and stay where he was. He conducted the young lady down to dinner in a dubious and agitated frame of mind. 'Does she really think I am handsome?' thought he, 'or is she only making game of me?' We have talked of Joseph Sedley being as vain as a girl. Heaven help us! the girls have only to turn the tables, and say of one of their own sex, 'She is as vain as a man,' and they will have perfect reason. The bearded creatures are quite as eager for praise, quite as finikin over their toilets, quite as proud of their personal advantages, quite as conscious of their powers of fascination, as any coquette in the world.

Downstairs, then, they went, Joseph very red and blushing, Rebecca very modest, and holding her green eyes downwards. She was dressed in white, with bare shoulders as white as snow – the picture of youth, unprotected innocence, and humble virgin simplicity. 'I must be very quiet,' thought Rebecca, 'and very much interested about India.'

Now we have heard how Mrs. Sedley had prepared a fine curry for her son, just as he liked it, and in the course of dinner a portion of this dish was offered to Rebecca. 'What is it?' said she, turning an appealing look to Mr. Joseph.

'Capital,' said he. His mouth was full of it: his face quite red with the delightful exercise of gobbling. 'Mother, it's as good as my own curries in India.'

'Oh, I must try some, if it is an Indian dish,' said Miss Rebecca. 'I am sure everything must be good that comes from there.'

'Give Miss Sharp some curry, my dear,' said Mr. Sedley, laughing.

Rebecca had never tasted the dish before.

'Do you find it as good as everything else from India?' said Mr. Sedley.

'Oh, excellent!' said Rebecca, who was suffering tortures with the cayenne pepper.

'Try a chili with it, Miss Sharp,' said Joseph, really interested.

'A chili,' said Rebecca, gasping. 'Oh, yes!' She thought a chili was something cool, as its name imported, and was served with some. 'How fresh and green they look,' she said, and put one into her mouth. It was hotter than the curry; flesh and blood could bear it no longer. She laid down her fork. 'Water, for Heaven's sake, water!' she cried. Mr. Sedley burst out laughing (he was a coarse man, from the Stock Exchange, where they love all sorts of practical jokes). 'They are real Indian, I assure you,' said he. 'Sambo, give Miss Sharp some water.'

The paternal laugh was echoed by Joseph, who thought the joke capital. The ladies only smiled a little. They thought poor Rebecca suffered too much. She would have liked to choke old Sedley, but she swallowed her mortification as well as she had the abominable curry before it, and as soon as she could speak, said, with a comical good-humoured air, 'I ought to have remembered the pepper which the Princess of Persia puts in the cream-tarts in the *Arabian Nights*. Do you put cayenne into your cream-tarts in India, sir?'

Old Sedley began to laugh, and thought Rebecca was a good-humoured girl. Joseph simply said, 'Cream-tarts, miss? Our cream is very bad in Bengal. We generally use goats' milk; and, 'gad, do you know, I've got to prefer it?'

'You won't like *everything* from India now, Miss Sharp,' said the old gentleman; but when the ladies had retired after dinner, the wily old fellow said to his son, 'Have a care, Joe; that girl is setting her cap at you.'

'Pooh! nonsense!' said Joe, highly flattered. 'I recollect, sir, there was a girl at Dumdum, a daughter of Cutler of the Artillery, and afterwards married to Lance, the surgeon, who made a dead set at me in the year '4 – at me and Mulligatawney, whom I mentioned to you before dinner – a devilish good fellow Mulligatawney – he's a magistrate at

Budgebudge, and sure to be in council in five years. Well, sir, the Artillery gave a ball, and Quintin, of the King's 14th, said to me, "Sedley," said he, "I bet you thirteen to ten that Sophy Cutler hooks either you or Mulligatawney before the rains." "Done," says I; and egad, sir – this claret's very good. Adamson's or Carbonell's? —'

A slight snore was the only reply: the honest stockbroker was asleep, and so the rest of Joseph's story was lost for that day. But he was always exceedingly communicative in a man's party, and has told this delightful tale many scores of times to his apothecary, Dr. Gollop, when he came to inquire about the liver and the blue-pill.

Being an invalid, Joseph Sedley contented himself with a bottle of claret, besides his madeira at dinner, and he managed a couple of plates full of strawberries and cream, and twenty-four little rout cakes, that were lying neglected in a plate near him, and certainly (for novelists have the privilege of knowing everything), he thought a great deal about the girl upstairs. 'A nice, gay, merry young creature,' thought he to himself. 'How she looked at me when I picked up her handkerchief at dinner! She dropped it twice. Who's that singing in the drawing-room? 'Gad! shall I go up and see?'

But his modesty came rushing upon him with uncontrollable force. His father was asleep: his hat was in the hall: there was a hackney-coach stand hard by in Southampton Row. 'I'll go and see the *Forty Thieves*,' said he, 'and Miss Decamp's dance;' and he slipped away gently on the pointed toes of his boots, and disappeared, without waking his worthy parent.

'There goes Joseph,' said Amelia, who was looking from the open windows of the drawing-room, while Rebecca was singing at the piano.

'Miss Sharp has frightened him away,' said Mrs. Sedley. 'Poor Joe, why *will* he be so shy?'

CHAPTER IV

THE GREEN SILK PURSE

POOR Joe's panic lasted for two or three days; during which he did not visit the house, nor during that period did Miss Rebecca ever mention his name. She was all respectful gratitude to Mrs. Sedley; delighted beyond measure at the bazaars; and in a whirl of wonder at the theatre, whither the good-natured lady took her. One day, Amelia had a headache, and could not go upon some party of pleasure to which the two young people were invited: nothing could induce her friend to go without her. 'What! you who have shown the poor orphan what happiness and love are for the first time in her life – quit *you?* never!' and the green eyes looked up to Heaven and filled with tears; and Mrs. Sedley could not but own that her daughter's friend had a charming kind heart of her own.

As for Mr. Sedley's jokes, Rebecca laughed at them with a cordiality and perseverance which not a little pleased and softened that good-natured gentleman. Nor was it with the chiefs of the family alone that Miss Sharp found favour. She interested Mrs. Blenkinsop by evincing the deepest sympathy in the raspberry-jam preserving, which operation was then going on in the housekeeper's room; she persisted in calling Sambo 'Sir', and 'Mr. Sambo', to the delight of that attendant; and she apologized to the lady's maid for giving her trouble in venturing to ring the bell, with such sweetness and humility that the Servants' Hall was almost as charmed with her as the Drawing-room.

Once, in looking over some drawings which Amelia had sent from school, Rebecca suddenly came upon one which caused her to burst into tears and leave the room. It was on the day when Joe Sedley made his second appearance.

Amelia hastened after her friend to know the cause of this display of feeling, and the good-natured girl came back without her companion, rather affected too. 'You know, her father was our drawing-master, mamma, at Chiswick, and used to do all the best parts of our drawings.'

'My love! I'm sure I always heard Miss Pinkerton say that he did not touch them – he only *mounted* them.'

'It was called mounting, mamma. Rebecca remembers the drawing, and her father working at it, and the thought of it came upon her rather suddenly – and so, you know, she —'

'The poor child is all heart,' said Mrs. Sedley.

'I wish she could stay with us another week,' said Amelia.

'She's devilish like Miss Cutler that I used to meet at Dumdum, only fairer. She's married now to Lance, the

Artillery surgeon. Do you know, ma'am, that once Quintin, of the 14th, bet me —'

'Oh, Joseph, we know that story,' said Amelia, laughing. 'Never mind about telling that; but persuade mamma to write to Sir Something Crawley, for leave of absence for poor dear Rebecca: – here she comes, her eyes red with weeping.'

'I'm better now,' said the girl, with the sweetest smile possible, taking good-natured Mrs. Sedley's extended hand and kissing it respectfully. 'How kind you all are to me! All,' she added with a laugh, 'except you, Mr. Joseph.'

'Me!' said Joseph, meditating an instant departure. 'Gracious Heavens! Good Gad! Miss Sharp!'

'Yes; how could you be so cruel as to make me eat that horrid pepper dish at dinner, the first day I ever saw you? You are not so good to me as dear Amelia.'

'He doesn't know you so well,' cried Amelia.

'I defy anybody not to be good to you, my dear,' said her mother.

'The curry was capital; indeed it was,' said Joe, quite gravely. 'Perhaps there was *not* enough citron juice in it; – no, there was *not*.'

'And the chilis?'

'By Jove, how they made you cry out!' said Joe, caught by the ridicule of the circumstance, and exploding in a fit of laughter which ended quite suddenly, as usual.

'I shall take care how I let *you* choose for me another time,' said Rebecca, as they went down again to dinner. 'I didn't think men were fond of putting poor harmless girls to pain.'

'By Gad, Miss Rebecca, I wouldn't hurt you for the world.'

'No,' said she, 'I *know* you wouldn't;' and then she gave him ever so gentle a pressure with her little hand, and drew it back quite frightened, and looked first for one instant in his face, and then down at the carpet-rods; and I am not prepared to say that Joe's heart did not thump at this little involuntary, timid, gentle motion of regard on the part of the simple girl.

It was an advance, and as such, perhaps, some ladies of indisputable correctness and gentility will condemn the action as immodest; but, you see, poor dear Rebecca had all this work to do for herself. If a person is too poor to keep a servant, though ever so elegant, he must sweep his own rooms: if a dear girl has no dear mamma to settle matters with the young man, she must do it for herself. And oh, what a mercy it is that these women do not exercise their powers oftener! We can't resist them, if they do. Let them show ever so little inclination, and men go down on their knees at once: old or ugly, it is all the same. And this I set down as a positive truth. A woman with fair opportunities, and without an absolute hump, may marry WHOM SHE LIKES. Only let us be thankful that the darlings are like the beasts of the field, and don't know their own power. They would overcome us entirely if they did.

'Egad!' thought Joseph, entering the dining-room, 'I exactly begin to feel as I did at Dumdum with Miss Cutler.' Many sweet little appeals, half tender, half jocular, did Miss Sharp make to him about the dishes at dinner; for by this time she was on a footing of considerable familiarity with the family, and as for the girls, they loved each other like sisters. Young unmarried girls always do, if they are in a house together for ten days.

As if bent upon advancing Rebecca's plans in every way – what must Amelia do, but remind her brother of a promise made last Easter holidays. 'When I was a girl at school,' said she, laughing – a promise that he, Joseph, would take her to Vauxhall. 'Now,' she said, 'that Rebecca is with us, will be the very time.'

'Oh, delightful!' said Rebecca, going to clap her hands; but she recollected herself, and paused, like a modest creature as she was.

'To-night is not the night,' said Joe.

'Well, to-morrow.'

'To-morrow your papa and I dine out,' said Mrs. Sedley.

'You don't suppose that *I*'m going, Mrs. Sed.?' said her husband, 'and that a woman of your years and size is to catch cold, in such an abominable damp place?'

'The children must have some one with them,' cried Mrs. Sedley.

'Let Joe go,' said his father, laughing. 'He's *big* enough.' At which speech even Mr. Sambo at the sideboard burst out laughing, and poor fat Joe felt inclined to become a parricide almost.

'Undo his stays!' continued the pitiless old gentleman. 'Fling some water in his face, Miss Sharp, or carry him upstairs: the dear creature's fainting. Poor victim! carry him up; he's as light as a feather!'

'If he stand this, sir, I'm d——!' roared Joseph.

'Order Mr. Jos's elephant, Sambo!' cried the father. 'Send to Exeter 'Change, Sambo;' but seeing Jos ready almost to cry with vexation, the old joker stopped his laughter, and said, holding out his hand to his son, 'It's all fair on the Stock Exchange, Jos, – and, Sambo, never mind the elephant, but give me and Mr. Jos a glass of champagne. Boney himself hasn't got such in his cellar, my boy!'

A goblet of champagne restored Joseph's equanimity, and before the bottle was emptied, of which as an invalid he took two-thirds, he had agreed to take the young ladies to Vauxhall.

'The girls must have a gentleman apiece,' said the old gentleman. 'Jos will be sure to leave Emmy in the crowd, he will be so taken up with Miss Sharp here. Send to 96, and ask George Osborne if he'll come.'

At this, I don't know in the least for what reason, Mrs. Sedley looked at her husband and laughed. Mr. Sedley's eyes twinkled in a manner indescribably roguish, and he looked at Amelia; and Amelia, hanging down her head, blushed as only young ladies of seventeen know how to blush, and as Miss Rebecca Sharp never blushed in her life – at least not since she was eight years old, and when she was caught stealing jam out of a cupboard by her godmother. 'Amelia had better write a note,' said her father; 'and let George Osborne see what a beautiful handwriting we have brought back from Miss Pinkerton's. Do you remember when you wrote to him to come on Twelfth Night, Emmy, and spelt twelfth without the f?'

'That was years ago,' said Amelia.

'It seems like yesterday, don't it, John?' said Mrs. Sedley to her husband; and that night in a conversation which took place in a front room in the second floor, in a sort of tent, hung round with chintz of a rich and fantastic India pattern, and *doublé* with calico of a tender rose-colour; in the interior of which species of marquee was a featherbed, on which were two pillows, on which were two round red faces, one in a laced nightcap, and one in a simple cotton one, ending

in a tassel: − in *a curtain lecture*, I say, Mrs. Sedley took
her husband to task for his cruel conduct to poor Joe.

'It was quite wicked of you, Mr. Sedley,' said she, 'to
torment the poor boy so.'

'My dear,' said the cotton-tassel in defence of his conduct,
'Jos is a great deal vainer than you ever were in your life,
and that's saying a good deal. Though, some thirty years
ago, in the year seventeen hundred and eighty − what was
it? − perhaps you had a right to be vain. − I don't say no.
But I've no patience with Jos and his dandified modesty. It
is out-Josephing Joseph, my dear, and all the while the boy
is only thinking of himself, and what a fine fellow he is. I
doubt, ma'am, we shall have some trouble with him yet.
Here is Emmy's little friend making love to him as hard as
she can; that's quite clear; and if she does not catch him
some other will. That man is destined to be a prey to woman,
as I am to go on 'Change every day. It's a mercy he did
not bring us over a black daughter-in-law, my dear. But,
mark my words, the first woman who fishes for him, hooks
him.'

'She shall go off to-morrow, the little artful creature,'
said Mrs. Sedley, with great energy.

'Why not she as well as another, Mrs. Sedley? The girl's
a white face at any rate. *I* don't care who marries him. Let
Joe please himself.'

And presently the voices of the two speakers were hushed,
or were replaced by the gentle but unromantic music of the
nose; and save when the church bells tolled the hour and
the watchman called it, all was silent at the house of John
Sedley, Esquire, of Russell Square, and the Stock Exchange.

When morning came, the good-natured Mrs. Sedley no
longer thought of executing her threats with regard to Miss
Sharp; for though nothing is more keen, nor more common,
nor more justifiable, than maternal jealousy, yet she could
not bring herself to suppose that the little, humble, grateful,
gentle governess, would dare to look up to such a magnificent personage as the collector of Boggley Wollah. The
petition, too, for an extension of the young lady's leave of
absence had already been dispatched, and it would be difficult to find a pretext for abruptly dismissing her.

And as if all things conspired in favour of the gentle
Rebecca, the very elements (although she was not inclined

at first to acknowledge their action in her behalf) interposed to aid her. For on the evening appointed for the Vauxhall party, George Osborne having come to dinner, and the elders of the house having departed, according to invitation, to dine with Alderman Balls, at Highbury Barn, there came on such a thunder-storm as only happens on Vauxhall nights, and as obliged the young people, perforce, to remain at home. Mr. Osborne did not seem in the least disappointed at this occurrence. He and Joseph Sedley drank a fitting quantity of port wine, *tête à tête*, in the dining-room, – during the drinking of which Sedley told a number of his best Indian stories; for he was extremely talkative in man's society; – and afterwards Miss Amelia Sedley did the honours of the drawing-room; and these four young persons passed such a comfortable evening together, that they declared they were rather glad of the thunder-storm than otherwise, which had caused them to put off their visit to Vauxhall.

Osborne was Sedley's godson, and had been one of the family any time these three-and-twenty years. At six weeks old, he had received from John Sedley a present of a silver cup; at six months old, a coral with gold whistle and bells; from his youth, upwards, he was 'tipped' regularly by the old gentleman at Christmas: and on going back to school, he remembered perfectly well being thrashed by Joseph Sedley, when the latter was a big, swaggering hobbledehoy, and George an impudent urchin of ten years old. In a word, George was as familiar with the family as such daily acts of kindness and intercourse could make him.

'Do you remember, Sedley, what a fury you were in, when I cut off the tassels of your Hessian boots, and how Miss – hem! – how Amelia rescued me from a beating, by falling down on her knees and crying out to her brother Jos, not to beat little George?'

Jos remembered this remarkable circumstance perfectly well, but vowed that he had totally forgotten it.

'Well, do you remember coming down in a gig to Dr. Swishtail's to see me, before you went to India, and giving me half a guinea and a pat on the head? I always had an idea that you were at least seven feet high, and was quite astonished at your return from India to find you no taller than myself.'

'How good of Mr. Sedley to go to your school and give

you the money!' exclaimed Rebecca, in accents of extreme delight.

'Yes, and after I had cut the tassels of his boots too. Boys never forget those tips at school, nor the givers.'

'I delight in Hessian boots,' said Rebecca. Jos Sedley who admired his own legs prodigiously, and always wore his ornamental *chaussure*, was extremely pleased at this remark, though he drew his legs under his chair as it was made.

'Miss Sharp,' said George Osborne, 'you who are so clever an artist, you must make a grand historical picture of the scene of the boots. Sedley shall be represented in buckskins, and holding one of the injured boots in one hand; by the other he shall have hold of my shirt-frill. Amelia shall be kneeling near him, with her little hands up; and the picture shall have a grand allegorical title, as the frontispieces have in the Medulla and the spelling-book.'

'I shan't have time to do it here,' said Rebecca. 'I'll do it when – when I'm gone.' And she dropped her voice, and looked so sad and piteous, that everybody felt how cruel her lot was, and how sorry they would be to part with her.

'Oh, that you could stay longer, dear Rebecca,' said Amelia.

'Why?' answered the other, still more sadly. 'That I may be only the more unhap – unwilling to lose you?' And she turned away her head. Amelia began to give way to that natural infirmity of tears which, we have said, was one of the defects of this silly little thing. George Osborne looked at the two young women with a touched curiosity; and Joseph Sedley heaved something very like a sigh out of his big chest, as he cast his eyes down towards his favourite Hessian boots.

'Let us have some music, Miss Sedley – Amelia,' said George, who felt at that moment an extraordinary, almost irresistible impulse to seize the above-mentioned young woman in his arms, and to kiss her in the face of the company; and she looked at him for a moment, and if I should say that they fell in love with each other at that single instant of time, I should perhaps be telling an untruth, for the fact is, that these two young people had been bred up by their parents for this very purpose, and their banns had, as it were, been read in their respective families any time these ten years. They went off to the piano, which was situated, as pianos usually are, in the back drawing-room; and as it was rather dark, Miss Amelia, in the most unaffected way in the world, put her hand into Mr. Osborne's, who, of course, could see the way among the chairs and ottomans a great deal better than she could. But this arrangement left Mr. Joseph Sedley *tête à tête* with Rebecca, at the drawing-room table, where the latter was occupied in netting a green silk purse.

'There is no need to ask family secrets,' said Miss Sharp. 'Those two have told theirs.'

'As soon as he gets his company,' said Joseph, 'I believe the affair is settled. George Osborne is a capital fellow.'

'And your sister the dearest creature in the world,' said Rebecca. 'Happy the man who wins her!' With this, Miss Sharp gave a great sigh.

When two unmarried persons get together, and talk upon such delicate subjects as the present, a great deal of confidence and intimacy is presently established between them. There is no need of giving a special report of the conversation which now took place between Mr. Sedley and the young lady; for the conversation, as may be judged from the foregoing specimen, was not especially witty or eloquent; it seldom is in private societies, or anywhere except in very high-flown and ingenious novels. As there was music in the next room, the talk was carried on, of course, in a low and becoming tone, though, for the matter of that, the couple in the next apartment would not have been disturbed had the talking been ever so loud, so occupied were they with their own pursuits.

Almost for the first time in his life, Mr. Sedley found himself talking, without the least timidity or hesitation, to a person of the other sex. Miss Rebecca asked him a great number of questions about India, which gave him an opportunity of narrating many interesting anecdotes about that country and himself. He described the balls at Government House, and the manner in which they kept themselves cool in the hot weather, with punkahs, tatties, and other contrivances; and he was very witty regarding the number of Scotchmen whom Lord Minto, the Governor-General, patronized; and then he described a tiger-hunt; and the manner in which the mahout of his elephant had been pulled off his seat by one of the infuriated animals. How delighted Miss Rebecca was at the Government balls, and how she laughed at the stories of the Scotch aides de camp, and called Mr. Sedley a sad wicked satirical creature; and how frightened she was at the story of the elephant! 'For your mother's sake, dear Mr. Sedley,' she said, 'for the sake of all your friends, promise *never* to go on one of those horrid expeditions.'

'Pooh, pooh, Miss Sharp,' said he, pulling up his shirt-collars; 'the danger makes the sport only the pleasanter.' He had never been but once at a tiger-hunt, when the accident in question occurred, and when he was half killed – not by the tiger, but by the fright. And as he talked on, he grew quite bold, and actually had the audacity to ask Miss Rebecca for whom she was knitting the green silk purse? He was quite surprised and delighted at his own graceful familiar manner.

'For any one who wants a purse,' replied Miss Rebecca, looking at him in the most gentle winning way. Sedley was going to make one of the most eloquent speeches possible, and had begun, 'Oh, Miss Sharp, how —' when some song which was performed in the other room came to an end, and caused him to hear his own voice so distinctly that he stopped, blushed, and blew his nose in great agitation.

'Did you ever hear anything like your brother's eloquence?' whispered Mr. Osborne to Amelia. 'Why, your friend has worked miracles.'

'The more the better,' said Miss Amelia; who, like almost all women who are worth a pin, was a matchmaker in her heart, and would have been delighted that Joseph should carry back a wife to India. She had, too, in the course of this few days' constant intercourse, warmed into a most tender friendship for Rebecca, and discovered a million of virtues and amiable qualities in her which she had not perceived when they were at Chiswick together. For the affection of young ladies is of as rapid growth as Jack's beanstalk, and reaches up to the sky in a night. It is no blame to them that after marriage this *Sehnsucht nach der Liebe* subsides. It is what sentimentalists, who deal in *very* big words, call a yearning after the Ideal, and simply means that women are commonly not satisfied until they have husbands and children on whom they may centre affections, which are spent elsewhere, as it were, in small change.

Having expended her little store of songs, or having stayed long enough in the back drawing-room, it now appeared proper to Miss Amelia to ask her friend to sing. 'You would not have listened to me,' she said to Mr. Osborne (though she knew she was telling a fib), 'had you heard Rebecca first.'

'I give Miss Sharp warning, though,' said Osborne, 'that, right or wrong, I consider Miss Amelia Sedley the first singer in the world.'

'You shall hear,' said Amelia; and Joseph Sedley was actually polite enough to carry the candles to the piano. Osborne hinted that he should like quite as well to sit in the dark; but Miss Sedley, laughing, declined to bear him company any farther, and the two accordingly followed Mr. Joseph. Rebecca sang far better than her friend (though of course Osborne was free to keep his opinion), and exerted herself to the utmost, and, indeed, to the wonder of Amelia, who had never known her perform so well. She sang a French song, which Joseph did not understand in the least, and which George confessed he did not understand, and then a number of those simple ballads which were the fashion forty years ago, and in which British tars, our King, poor Susan, blue-eyed Mary, and the like, were the principal themes. They are not, it is said, very brilliant, in a musical point of view, but contain numberless good-natured, simple appeals to the affections, which people understood better than the milk-and-water *lagrime, sospiri*, and *felicità* of the eternal Donizettian music with which we are favoured nowadays.

Among these ditties was one, the last of the concert, and to the following effect: –

> Ah, bleak and barren was the moor!
> Ah, loud and piercing was the storm!
> The cottage roof was shelter'd sure,
>   The cottage hearth was bright and warm –
> An orphan boy the lattice pass'd,
>   And, as he mark'd its cheerful glow,
> Felt doubly keen the midnight blast, .
>   And doubly cold the fallen snow.

They mark'd him as he onward pressed,
    With fainting heart and weary limb;
Kind voices bade him turn and rest,
    And gentle faces welcomed him.
The dawn is up – the guest is gone,
    The cottage hearth is blazing still;
Heaven pity all poor wanderers lone!
    Hark to the wind upon the hill!

It was the sentiment of the before-mentioned words, 'When I'm gone,' over again. As she came to the last words, Miss Sharp's 'deep-toned voice faltered'. Everybody felt the allusion to her departure, and to her hapless orphan state. Joseph Sedley, who was fond of music, and soft-hearted, was in a state of ravishment during the performance of the song, and profoundly touched at its conclusion. If he had had the courage; if George and Miss Sedley had remained, according to the former's proposal, in the farther room; Joseph Sedley's bachelorhood would have been at an end, and this work would never have been written. But at the close of the ditty, Rebecca quitted the piano, and giving her hand to Amelia, walked away into the front drawing-room twilight; and, at this moment, Mr. Sambo made his appearance with a tray, containing sandwiches, jellies, and some glittering glasses and decanters, on which Joseph Sedley's attention was immediately fixed. When the parents of the house of Sedley returned from their dinner-party, they found the young people so busy in talking, that they had not heard the arrival of the carriage, and Mr. Joseph was in the act of saying, 'My dear Miss Sharp, one little teaspoonful of jelly to recruit you after your immense – your – your *delightful* exertions.'

'Bravo, Jos!' said Mr. Sedley; on hearing the bantering of which well-known voice, Jos instantly relapsed into an alarmed silence, and quickly took his departure. He did not lie awake all night thinking whether or not he was in love with Miss Sharp; the passion of love never interfered with the appetite or the slumber of Mr. Joseph Sedley; but he thought to himself how delightful it would be to hear such songs as those after Cutcherry – what a *distinguée* girl she was – how she could speak French better than the Governor-General's lady herself – and what a sensation she would make at the Calcutta balls. 'It's evident the poor devil's in love with me,' thought he. 'She is just as rich as most of the girls who come out to India. I might go farther and fare worse, egad!' And in these meditations he fell asleep.

How Miss Sharp lay awake, thinking, will he come or not to-morrow? need not be told here. To-morrow came, and, as sure as fate, Mr. Joseph Sedley made his appearance before luncheon. He had never been known before to confer such an honour on Russell Square. George Osborne was somehow there already (sadly 'putting out' Amelia, who was writing to her twelve dearest friends at Chiswick Mall), and Rebecca was employed upon her yesterday's work. As Joe's buggy drove up, and while, after his usual thundering knock and pompous bustle at the door, the ex-collector of Boggley Wollah laboured upstairs to the drawing-room, knowing glances were telegraphed between Osborne and Miss Sedley, and the pair, smiling archly, looked at Rebecca, who actually blushed as she bent her fair ringlets over her netting. How her heart beat as Joseph appeared, – Joseph, puffing from the staircase in shining creaking boots, – Joseph, in a new waistcoat, red with heat and nervousness, and blushing behind his wadded neckcloth. It was a nervous moment for all; and as for Amelia, I think she was more frightened than even the people most concerned.

Sambo, who flung open the door and announced Mr. Joseph, followed grinning, in the collector's rear, and bearing two handsome nosegays of flowers, which the monster had actually had the gallantry to purchase in Covent Garden market that morning – they were not as big as the haystacks which ladies carry about with them nowadays, in cones of filigree paper; but the young women were delighted with the gift, as Joseph presented one to each, with an exceedingly solemn bow.

'Bravo, Jos,' cried Osborne.

'Thank you, dear Joseph,' said Amelia, quite ready to kiss her brother, if he were so minded. (And I think for a kiss from such a dear creature as Amelia, I would purchase all Mr. Lee's conservatories out of hand.)

'O heavenly, heavenly flowers!' exclaimed Miss Sharp, and smelt them delicately, and held them to her bosom, and cast up her eyes to the ceiling, in an ecstasy of admiration. Perhaps she just looked first into the bouquet, to see whether there was a *billet-doux* hidden among the flowers; but there was no letter.

'Do they talk the language of flowers at Boggley Wollah, Sedley?' asked Osborne, laughing.

'Pooh, nonsense!' replied the sentimental youth. 'Bought 'em at Nathan's; very glad you like 'em; and eh, Amelia, my dear, I bought a pineapple at the same time, which I gave to Sambo. Let's have it for tiffin; very cool and nice this hot weather.' Rebecca said she had never tasted a pine, and longed beyond everything to taste one.

So the conversation went on. I don't know on what pretext Osborne left the room, or why, presently, Amelia went away, perhaps to superintend the slicing of the pine-apple; but Jos was left alone with Rebecca, who had resumed her work, and the green silk and the shining needles were quivering rapidly under her white slender fingers.

'What a beautiful, *byoo-ootiful* song that was you sang last night, dear Miss Sharp,' said the collector. 'It made me cry almost; 'pon my honour it did.'

'Because you have a kind heart, Mr. Joseph; all the Sedleys have, I think.'

'It kept me awake last night, and I was trying to hum it this morning in bed; I was, upon my honour. Gollop, my doctor, came in at eleven (for I'm a sad invalid, you know, and see Gollop every day), and, 'gad! there I was, singing away like – a robin.'

'Oh, you droll creature! Do let me hear you sing it.'

'Me? No, you, Miss Sharp; my dear Miss Sharp, do sing it.'

'Not now, Mr. Sedley,' said Rebecca, with a sigh. 'My spirits are not equal to it: besides I must finish the purse. Will you help me, Mr. Sedley?' And before he had time to ask how, Mr. Joseph Sedley, of the East India Company's service, was actually seated *tête à tête* with a young lady, looking at her with a most killing expression; his arms stretched out before her in an imploring attitude, and his hands bound in a web of green silk, which she was unwinding.

*

In this romantic position Osborne and Amelia found the interesting pair, when they entered to announce that tiffin was ready. The skein of silk was just wound round the card; but Mr. Jos had never spoken.

'I am sure he will to-night, dear,' Amelia said, as she pressed Rebecca's hand; and Sedley, too, had communed with his soul, and said to himself, ' 'Gad, I'll pop the question at Vauxhall.'

CHAPTER V

DOBBIN OF OURS

CUFF'S fight with Dobbin, and the unexpected issue of that contest, will long be remembered by every man who was educated at Dr. Swishtail's famous school. The latter youth (who used to be called Heigh-ho Dobbin, Gee-ho Dobbin, and by many other names indicative of puerile contempt) was the quietest, the clumsiest, and, as it seemed, the dullest of all Dr. Swishtail's young gentlemen. His parent was a grocer in the city: and it was bruited abroad that he was admitted into Dr. Swishtail's academy upon what are called 'mutual principles' − that is to say, the expenses of his board and schooling were defrayed by his father in goods, not money; and he stood there − almost at the bottom of the school − in his scraggy corduroys and jacket, through the seams of which his great big bones were bursting − as the representative of so many pounds of tea, candles, sugar, mottled-soap, plums (of which a very mild proportion was supplied for the puddings of the establishment), and other commodities. A dreadful day it was for young Dobbin when one of the youngsters of the school, having run into the town upon a poaching excursion for hardbake and polonies, espied the cart of Dobbin & Rudge, Grocers and Oilmen, Thames Street, London, at the doctor's door, discharging a cargo of the wares in which the firm dealt.

Young Dobbin had no peace after that. The jokes were frightful, and merciless against him. 'Hullo, Dobbin,' one wag would say, 'here's good news in the paper. Sugars is ris', my boy.' Another would set a sum − 'If a pound of mutton-candles cost sevenpence-halfpenny, how much must Dobbin cost?' and a roar would follow from all the circle of young knaves, usher and all, who rightly considered that the selling of goods by retail is a shameful and infamous practice, meriting the contempt and scorn of all real gentlemen.

'Your father's only a merchant, Osborne,' Dobbin said in

private to the little boy who had brought down the storm upon him. At which the latter replied haughtily, 'My father's a gentleman, and keeps his carriage;' and Mr. William Dobbin retreated to a remote out-house in the playground, where he passed a half-holiday in the bitterest sadness and woe. Who amongst us is there that does not recollect similar hours of bitter, bitter childish grief? Who feels injustice; who shrinks before a slight; who has a sense of wrong so acute, and so glowing a gratitude for kindness, as a generous boy? and how many of those gentle souls do you degrade, estrange, torture, for the sake of a little loose arithmetic, and miserable dog-Latin?

Now, William Dobbin, from an incapacity to acquire the rudiments of the above language, as they are propounded in that wonderful book the Eton Latin Grammar, was compelled to remain among the very last of Dr. Swishtail's scholars, and was 'taken down' continually by little fellows with pink faces and pinafores when he marched up with the lower form, a giant amongst them, with his downcast stupefied look, his dog's-eared primer, and his tight corduroys. High and low, all made fun of him. They sewed up those corduroys, tight as they were. They cut his bed-strings. They upset buckets and benches, so that he might break his shins over them, which he never failed to do. They sent him parcels, which, when opened, were found to contain the paternal soap and candles. There was no little fellow but had his jeer and joke at Dobbin; and he bore everything quite patiently, and was entirely dumb and miserable.

Cuff, on the contrary, was the great chief and dandy of the Swishtail Seminary. He smuggled wine in. He fought the town-boys. Ponies used to come for him to ride home on Saturdays. He had his top-boots in his room, in which he used to hunt in the holidays. He had a gold repeater: and took snuff like the Doctor. He had been to the Opera, and knew the merits of the principal actors, preferring Mr. Kean to Mr. Kemble. He could knock you off forty Latin verses in an hour. He could make French poetry. What else didn't he know, or couldn't he do? They said even the Doctor himself was afraid of him.

Cuff, the unquestioned king of the school, ruled over his subjects and bullied them, with splendid superiority. This one blacked his shoes: that toasted his bread, others would fag out, and give him balls at cricket during whole summer afternoons. 'Figs' was the fellow whom he despised most, and with whom, though always abusing him, and sneering at him, he scarcely ever condescended to hold personal communication.

One day in private, the two young gentlemen had had a difference. Figs, alone in the schoolroom, was blundering over a home letter; when Cuff, entering, bade him go upon some message, of which tarts were probably the subject.

'I can't,' says Dobbin; 'I want to finish my letter.'

'You *can't?*' says Mr. Cuff, laying hold of that document (in which many words were scratched out, many were misspelt, on which had been spent I don't know how much thought, and labour, and tears; for the poor fellow was writing to his mother, who was fond of him, although she was a grocer's wife, and lived in a back-parlour in Thames Street). 'You *can't?*' says Mr. Cuff: 'I should like to know why, pray? Can't you write to old Mother Figs to-morrow?'

'Don't call names,' Dobbin said, getting off the bench, very nervous.

'Well, sir, will you go?' crowed the cock of the school.

'Put down the letter,' Dobbin replied; 'no gentleman readth letterth.'

'Well, *now* will you go?' says the other.

'No, I won't. Don't strike, or I'll *thmash* you,' roars out Dobbin, springing to a leaden inkstand, and looking so wicked, that Mr. Cuff paused, turned down his coat-sleeves again, put his hands into his pockets, and walked away with a sneer. But he never meddled personally with the grocer's boy after that; though we must do him the justice to say he always spoke of Mr. Dobbin with contempt behind his back.

Some time after this interview, it happened that Mr. Cuff, on a sunshiny afternoon, was in the neighbourhood of poor William Dobbin, who was lying under a tree in the play-ground, spelling over a favourite copy of the *Arabian Nights* which he had – apart from the rest of the school, who were pursuing their various sports – quite lonely, and almost happy. If people would but leave children to themselves; if teachers would cease to bully them; if parents would not insist upon directing their thoughts, and dominating their feelings – those feelings and thoughts which are a mystery to all (for how much do you and I know of each other, of our children, of our fathers, of our neighbour, and how far more beautiful and sacred are the thoughts of the poor lad or girl whom you govern likely to be, than those of the dull and world-corrupted person who rules him?) – if, I say, parents and masters would leave their children alone a little more, – small harm would accrue, although a less quantity of *as in praesenti* might be acquired.

Well, William Dobbin had for once forgotten the world, and was away with Sindbad the Sailor in the Valley of Diamonds, or with Prince Ahmed and the Fairy Peribanou in that delightful cavern where the prince found her, and whither we should all like to make a tour; when shrill cries, as of a little fellow weeping, woke up his pleasant reverie; and, looking up, he saw Cuff before him, belabouring a little boy.

It was the lad who had peached upon him about the grocer's cart; but he bore little malice, not at least towards the young and small. 'How dare you, sir, break the bottle?' says Cuff to the little urchin, swinging a yellow cricket-stump over him.

The boy had been instructed to get over the playground wall (at a selected spot where the broken-glass had been removed from the top, and niches made convenient in the brick); to run a quarter of a mile; to purchase a pint of rum-shrub on credit; to brave all the Doctor's outlying spies, and to clamber back into the playground again; during the performance of which feat his foot had slipped, and the bottle was broken, and the shrub had been spilt, and his pantaloons had been damaged, and he appeared before his employer a perfectly guilty and trembling, though harm-less, wretch.

'How dare you, sir, break it?' says Cuff; 'you blundering little thief. You drank the shrub, and now you pretend to have broken the bottle. Hold out your hand, sir.'

Down came the stump with a great heavy thump on the child's hand. A moan followed. Dobbin looked up. The Prince Peribanou had fled into the inmost cavern with Prince Ahmed: the Roc had whisked away Sindbad the Sailor out of the Valley of Diamonds out of sight, far into the clouds: and there was everyday life before honest William; and a big boy beating a little one without cause.

'Hold out your other hand, sir,' roars Cuff to his little schoolfellow, whose face was distorted with pain. Dobbin quivered, and gathered himself up in his narrow old clothes.

'Take that, you little devil!' cried Mr. Cuff, and down came the wicket again on the child's hand. – Don't be horrified, ladies, every boy at a public school has done it. Your children will so do and be done by, in all probability. Down came the wicket again; and Dobbin started up.

I can't tell what his motive was. Torture in a public school is as much licensed as the knout in Russia. It would be ungentlemanlike (in a manner) to resist it. Perhaps Dobbin's foolish soul revolted against that exercise of tyranny; or perhaps he had a hankering feeling of revenge in his mind, and longed to measure himself against that splendid bully and tyrant, who had all the glory, pride, pomp, circumstance, banners flying, drums beating, guards saluting, in the place. Whatever may have been his incentive, however, up he sprang, and screamed out, 'Hold off, Cuff; don't bully that child any more; or I'll —'

'Or you'll what?' Cuff asked in amazement at this interruption. 'Hold out your hand, you little beast.'

'I'll give you the worst thrashing you ever had in your life,' Dobbin said, in reply to the first part of Cuff's sentence; and little Osborne, gasping and in tears, looked up with wonder and incredulity at seeing this amazing champion put up suddenly to defend him: while Cuff's astonishment was scarcely less. Fancy our late monarch George III when he heard of the revolt of the North American colonies: fancy brazen Goliath when little David stepped forward and claimed a meeting; and you have the feelings of Mr. Reginald Cuff when this rencontre was proposed to him.

'After school,' says he, of course; after a pause and a look, as much as to say, 'Make your will, and communicate your best wishes to your friends between this time and that.'

'As you please,' Dobbin said. 'You must be my bottle-holder, Osborne.'

'Well, if you like,' little Osborne replied; for you see his papa kept a carriage, and he was rather ashamed of his champion.

Yes, when the hour of battle came, he was almost ashamed to say 'Go it, Figs'; and not a single other boy in the place uttered that cry for the first two or three rounds of this famous combat; at the commencement of which the scientific Cuff, with a contemptuous smile on his face, and as light and as gay as if he was at a ball, planted his blows upon his adversary, and floored that unlucky champion three times running. At each fall there was a cheer; and everybody was anxious to have the honour of offering the conqueror a knee.

'What a licking I shall get when it's over,' young Osborne thought, picking up his man. 'You'd best give in,' he said to Dobbin; 'it's only a thrashing, Figs, and you know I'm used to it.' But Figs, all whose limbs were in a quiver, and whose nostrils were breathing rage, put his little bottle-holder aside, and went in for a fourth time.

As he did not in the least know how to parry the blows that were aimed at himself, and Cuff had begun the attack on the three preceding occasions, without ever allowing his enemy to strike, Figs now determined that he would commence the engagement by a charge on his own part; and accordingly, being a left-handed man, brought that arm into action, and hit out a couple of times with all his might – once at Mr. Cuff's left eye, and once on his beautiful Roman nose.

Cuff went down this time, to the astonishment of the assembly. 'Well hit, by Jove,' says little Osborne, with the air of a connoisseur, clapping his man on the back. 'Give it him with the left, Figs, my boy.'

Figs's left made terrific play during all the rest of the combat. Cuff went down every time. At the sixth round there were almost as many fellows shouting out, 'Go it, Figs,' as there were youths exclaiming, 'Go it, Cuff.' At the twelfth round the latter champion was all abroad, as the saying is, and had lost all presence of mind and power of attack or defence. Figs, on the contrary, was as calm as a quaker. His face being quite pale, his eyes shining open, and a great cut on his under-lip bleeding profusely, gave this young fellow a fierce and ghastly air, which perhaps struck terror into many spectators. Nevertheless, his intrepid adversary prepared to close for the thirteenth time.

If I had the pen of a Napier, or a *Bell's Life*, I should like to describe this combat properly. It was the last charge of the Guard (that is, *it would* have been, only Waterloo had

not yet taken place) – it was Ney's column breasting the hill
of La Haye Sainte, bristling with ten thousand bayonets, and
crowned with twenty eagles – it was the shout of the beef-
eating British, as leaping down the hill they rushed to hug
the enemy in the savage arms of battle – in other words,
Cuff coming up full of pluck, but quite reeling and groggy,
the Fig-merchant put in his left as usual on his adversary's
nose, and sent him down for the last time.

'I think *that* will do for him,' Figs said, as his opponent
dropped as neatly on the green as I have seen Jack Spot's
ball plump into the pocket at billiards; and the fact is, when
time was called, Mr. Reginald Cuff was not able, or did not
choose, to stand up again.

And now all the boys set up such a shout for Figs as
would make you think he had been their darling champion
through the whole battle; and as absolutely brought Dr.
Swishtail out of his study, curious to know the cause of the
uproar. He threatened to flog Figs violently, of course; but
Cuff, who had come to himself by this time, and was washing
his wounds, stood up and said, 'It's my fault, sir – not Figs's
– not Dobbin's. I was bullying a little boy; and he served
me right.' By which magnanimous speech he not only saved
his conqueror a whipping, but got back all his ascendancy
over the boys which his defeat had nearly cost him.

Young Osborne wrote home to his parents an account of
the transaction.

SUGARCANE HOUSE, RICHMOND, March, 18 –.

DEAR MAMA, – I hope you are quite well. I should be much
obliged to you to send me a cake and five shillings. There has been
a fight here between Cuff & Dobbin. Cuff, you know, was the Cock
of the School. They fought thirteen rounds, and Dobbin Licked. So
Cuff is now Only Second Cock. The fight was about me. Cuff was
licking me for breaking a bottle of milk, and Figs wouldn't stand it.
We call him Figs because his father is a Grocer. Figs & Rudge,
Thames St., City – I think as he fought for me you ought to buy
your Tea & Sugar at his father's. Cuff goes home every Saturday, but
can't this, because he has 2 Black Eyes. He has a white Pony to come
and fetch him, and a groom in livery on a bay mare. I wish my Papa
would let me have a Pony, and I am,

Your dutiful Son,
GEORGE SEDLEY OSBORNE.

PS. – Give my love to little Emmy. I am cutting her out a Coach in cardboard. Please not a seed-cake, but a plum-cake.'

In consequence of Dobbin's victory, his character rose prodigiously in the estimation of all his schoolfellows, and the name of Figs, which had been a byword of reproach, became as respectable and popular a nickname as any other in use in the school. 'After all, it's not his fault that his father's a grocer,' George Osborne said, who, though a little chap, had a very high popularity among the Swishtail youth; and his opinion was received with great applause. It was voted low to sneer at Dobbin about this accident of birth. 'Old Figs' grew to be a name of kindness and endearment; and the sneak of an usher jeered at him no longer.

And Dobbin's spirit rose with his altered circumstances. He made wonderful advances in scholastic learning. The superb Cuff himself, at whose condescension Dobbin could only blush and wonder, helped him on with his Latin verses; 'coached' him in play-hours; carried him triumphantly out of the little-boy class into the middle-sized form; and even there got a fair place for him. It was discovered, that although dull at classical learning, at mathematics he was uncommonly quick. To the contentment of all, he passed third in algebra, and got a French prize-book at the public midsummer examination. You should have seen his mother's face when *Télémaque* (that delicious romance) was presented to him by the Doctor in the face of the whole school and the parents and company, with an inscription to Gulielmo Dobbin. All the boys clapped hands in token of applause and sympathy. His blushes, his stumbles, his awkwardness, and the number of feet which he crushed as he went back to his place, who shall describe or calculate? Old Dobbin, his father, who now respected him for the first time, gave him two guineas publicly; most of which he spent in a general tuck-out for the school: and he came back in a tail-coat after the holidays.

Dobbin was much too modest a young fellow to suppose that this happy change in all his circumstances arose from his own generous and manly disposition: he chose, from some perverseness, to attribute his good fortune to the sole agency and benevolence of little George Osborne, to whom henceforth he vowed such a love and affection as is only felt

by children – such an affection as we read in the charming
fairy-book uncouth Orson had for splendid young Valentine
his conqueror. He flung himself down at little Osborne's
feet, and loved him. Even before they were acquainted, he
had admired Osborne in secret. Now he was his valet, his
dog, his man Friday. He believed Osborne to be the possessor of every perfection, to be the handsomest, the bravest,
the most active, the cleverest, the most generous of created
boys. He shared his money with him: bought him uncount-
able presents of knives, pencil-cases, gold seals, toffee, Little
Warblers, and romantic books, with large coloured pictures
of knights and robbers, in many of which latter you might
read inscriptions to George Sedley Osborne, Esquire, from
his attached friend William Dobbin – the which tokens of
homage George received very graciously, as became his
superior merit.

So that when Lieutenant Osborne, coming to Russell
Square on the day of the Vauxhall party, said to the ladies,
'Mrs. Sedley, ma'am, I hope you have room; I've asked
Dobbin of ours to come and dine here, and go with us to
Vauxhall. He's almost as modest as Jos.'

'Modesty! pooh,' said the stout gentleman, casting a
vainqueur look at Miss Sharp.

'He is – but you are incomparably more graceful, Sedley,'
Osborne added, laughing. 'I met him at the Bedford, when
I went to look for you; and I told him that Miss Amelia
was come home, and that we were all bent on going out for
a night's pleasuring; and that Mrs. Sedley had forgiven his
breaking the punch-bowl at the child's party. Don't you
remember the catastrophe, ma'am, seven years ago?'

'Over Mrs. Flamingo's crimson silk gown,' said good-
natured Mrs. Sedley. 'What a gawky it was! And his sisters
are not much more graceful. Lady Dobbin was at Highbury
last night with three of them. Such figures, my dears.'

'The Alderman's very rich, isn't he?' Osborne said archly.
'Don't you think one of the daughters would be a good spec
for me, ma'am?'

'You foolish creature! Who would take *you*, I should like
to know, with your yellow face?'

'Mine a yellow face? Stop till you see Dobbin. Why, he
had the yellow fever three times; twice at Nassau, and once
at St. Kitts.'

'Well, well; yours is quite yellow enough for us. Isn't it, Emmy?' Mrs. Sedley said: at which speech Miss Amelia only made a smile and a blush; and looking at Mr. George Osborne's pale interesting countenance, and those beautiful black, curling, shining whiskers, which the young gentleman himself regarded with no ordinary complacency, she thought, in her little heart, that in His Majesty's army, or in the wide world, there never was such a face or such a hero. 'I don't care about Captain Dobbin's complexion,' she said, 'or about his awkwardness. *I* shall always like him, I know;' her little reason being that he was the friend and champion of George.

'There's not a finer fellow in the service,' Osborne said, 'nor a better officer, though he is not an Adonis, certainly.' And he looked towards the glass himself with much *naïveté;* and in so doing, caught Miss Sharp's eye fixed keenly upon him, at which he blushed a little, and, Rebecca thought in her heart, '*Ah, mon beau monsieur!* I think I have *your* gauge' – the little artful minx!

That evening, when Amelia came tripping into the drawing-room in a white muslin frock, prepared for conquest at Vauxhall, singing like a lark, and as fresh as a rose – a very tall ungainly gentleman, with large hands and feet, and large ears, set off by a closely cropped head of black hair, and in the hideous military frogged coat and cocked hat of those times, advanced to meet her, and made her one of the clumsiest bows that was ever performed by a mortal.

This was no other than Captain William Dobbin, of His Majesty's — Regiment of Foot, returned from yellow fever in the West Indies, to which the fortune of the service had ordered his regiment, whilst so many of his gallant comrades were reaping glory in the Peninsula.

He had arrived with a knock so very timid and quiet, that it was inaudible to the ladies upstairs: otherwise, you may be sure Miss Amelia would never have been so bold as to come singing into the room. As it was, the sweet fresh little voice went right into the captain's heart, and nestled there. When she held out her hand for him to shake, before he enveloped it in his own, he paused and thought – 'Well, is it possible – are you the little maid I remember in the pink frock, such a short time ago – the night I upset the punch-bowl, just after I was gazetted? Are you the little girl

that George Osborne said should marry him? What a blooming young creature you seem, and what a prize the rogue
has got!' All this he thought before he took Amelia's hand
into his own, and as he let his cocked-hat fall.

His history since he left school, until the very moment
when we have the pleasure of meeting him again, although
not fully narrated, has yet, I think, been indicated sufficiently for an ingenious reader by the conversation in the last
page. Dobbin, the despised grocer, was Alderman Dobbin –
Alderman Dobbin was Colonel of the City Light Horse, then
burning with military ardour to resist the French Invasion.
Colonel Dobbin's corps, in which old Mr. Osborne himself
was but an indifferent corporal, had been reviewed by the
Sovereign and the Duke of York; and the colonel and
alderman had been knighted. His son had entered the army:
and young Osborne followed presently in the same regiment.
They had served in the West Indies and in Canada. Their
regiment had just come home, and the attachment of Dobbin
to George Osborne was as warm and generous now, as it
had been when the two were schoolboys.

So these worthy people sat down to dinner presently.
They talked about war and glory, and Boney and Lord
Wellington, and the last *Gazette*. In those famous days every
gazette had a victory in it, and the two gallant young
men longed to see their own names in the glorious list,
and cursed their unlucky fate to belong to a regiment
which had been away from the chances of honour. Miss
Sharp kindled with this exciting talk, but Miss Sedley
trembled and grew quite faint as she heard it. Mr. Jos told
several of his tiger-hunting stories: finished the one about
Miss Cutler and Lance the surgeon; helped Rebecca to
everything on the table, and himself gobbled and drank a
great deal.

He sprang to open the door for the ladies, when they
retired, with the most killing grace – and coming back to
the table, filled himself bumper after bumper of claret, which
he swallowed with nervous rapidity.

'He's priming himself,' Osborne whispered to Dobbin,
and at length the hour and the carriage arrived for Vauxhall.

CHAPTER VI

VAUXHALL

I KNOW that the tune I am piping is a very mild one (although there are some terrific chapters coming presently), and must beg the good-natured reader to remember, that we are only discoursing at present about a stockbroker's family in Russell Square, who are taking walks, or luncheon, or dinner, or talking, and making love as people do in common life, and without a single passionate and wonderful incident to mark the progress of their loves. The argument stands thus – Osborne, in love with Amelia, has asked an old friend to dinner and to Vauxhall – Jos Sedley is in love with Rebecca. Will he marry her? That is the great subject now in hand.

We might have treated this subject in the genteel, or in the romantic, or in the facetious manner. Suppose we had laid the scene in Grosvenor Square, with the very same adventures – would not some people have listened? Suppose we had shown how Lord Joseph Sedley fell in love, and the Marquis of Osborne became attached to Lady Amelia, with the full consent of the duke, her noble father: or instead of the supremely genteel, suppose we had resorted to the entirely low, and described what was going on in Mr. Sedley's kitchen; – how black Sambo was in love with the cook (as indeed he was), and how he fought a battle with the coachman in her behalf; how the knife-boy was caught stealing a cold shoulder of mutton, and Miss Sedley's new *femme de chambre* refused to go to bed without a wax candle; such incidents might be made to provoke much delightful laughter, and be supposed to represent scenes of 'life'. Or if, on the contrary, we had taken a fancy for the terrible, and made the lover of the new *femme de chambre* a professional burglar, who bursts into the house with his band, slaughters black Sambo at the feet of his master, and carries off Amelia in her night-dress, not to be let loose again till the third volume, we should easily have constructed a tale of thrilling interest, through the fiery chapters of which the readers should hurry, panting. But my readers must hope for no such romance, only a homely story, and must be content with a chapter about Vauxhall, which is so short that it scarce deserves to be called a chapter at all. And yet it is a chapter, and a very important one too. Are not there little chapters in everybody's life, that seem to be nothing, and yet affect all the rest of the history?

Let us then step into the coach with the Russell Square party, and be off to the Gardens. There is barely room between Jos and Miss Sharp, who are on the front seat. Mr. Osborne sitting bodkin opposite, between Captain Dobbin and Amelia.

Every soul in the coach agreed, that on that night Jos would propose to make Rebecca Sharp Mrs. Sedley. The parents at home had acquiesced in the arrangement, though, between ourselves, old Mr. Sedley had a feeling very much akin to contempt for his son. He said he was vain, selfish, lazy, and effeminate. He could not endure his airs as a man of fashion, and laughed heartily at his pompous braggadocio stories. 'I shall leave the fellow half my property,' he said; 'and he will have, besides, plenty of his own; but as I am perfectly sure that if you, and I, and his sister were to die to-morrow he would say 'Good Gad!' and eat his dinner just as well as usual, I am not going to make myself anxious about him. Let him marry whom he likes. It's no affair of mine.'

Amelia, on the other hand, as became a young woman of her prudence and temperament, was quite enthusiastic for the match. Once or twice Jos had been on the point of saying something very important to her, to which she was most willing to lend an ear, but the fat fellow could not be brought to unbosom himself of his great secret, and very much to his sister's disappointment he only rid himself of a large sigh and turned away.

This mystery served to keep Amelia's gentle bosom in a perpetual flutter of excitement. If she did not speak with Rebecca on the tender subject, she compensated herself with long and intimate conversations with Mrs. Blenkinsop, the housekeeper, who dropped some hints to the lady's-maid, who may have cursorily mentioned the matter to the cook, who carried the news, I have no doubt, to all the tradesmen, so that Mr. Jos's marriage was now talked of by a very considerable number of persons in the Russell Square world.

It was, of course, Mrs. Sedley's opinion that her son

would demean himself by a marriage with an artist's daughter. 'But, lor', ma'am,' ejaculated Mrs. Blenkinsop, 'we was only grocers when we married Mr. S., who was a stockbroker's clerk, and we hadn't five hundred pounds among us, and we're rich enough now.' And Amelia was entirely of this opinion, to which, gradually, the good-natured Mrs. Sedley was brought.

Mr. Sedley was neutral. 'Let Jos marry whom he likes,' he said; 'it's no affair of mine. This girl has no fortune; no more had Mrs. Sedley. She seems good-humoured and clever, and will keep him in order, perhaps. Better she, my dear, than a black Mrs. Sedley, and a dozen of mahogany grandchildren.'

So that everything seemed to smile upon Rebecca's fortunes. She took Jos's arm, as a matter of course, on going to dinner; she had sat by him on the box of his open carriage (a most tremendous 'buck' he was, as he sat there, serene, in state, driving his greys), and though nobody said a word on the subject of the marriage, everybody seemed to understand it. All she wanted was the proposal, and ah! how Rebecca now felt the want of a mother! – a dear, tender mother, who would have managed the business in ten minutes, and, in the course of a little delicate confidential conversation, would have extracted the interesting avowal from the bashful lips of the young man!

Such was the state of affairs as the carriage crossed Westminster Bridge.

The party was landed at the Royal Gardens in due time. As the majestic Jos stepped out of the creaking vehicle the crowd gave a cheer for the fat gentleman, who blushed and looked very big and mighty, as he walked away with Rebecca under his arm. George, of course, took charge of Amelia. She looked as happy as a rose-tree in sunshine.

'I say, Dobbin,' says George, 'just look to the shawls and things, there's a good fellow.' And so while he paired off with Miss Sedley, and Jos squeezed through the gate into the Gardens with Rebecca at his side, honest Dobbin contented himself by giving an arm to the shawls, and by paying at the door for the whole party.

He walked very modestly behind them. He was not willing to spoil sport. About Rebecca and Jos he did not care a fig. But he thought Amelia worthy even of the brilliant George

Osborne, and as he saw that good-looking couple, threading the walks to the girl's delight and wonder, he watched her artless happiness with a sort of fatherly pleasure. Perhaps he felt that he would have liked to have something on his own arm besides a shawl (the people laughed at seeing the gawky young officer carrying this female burden); but William Dobbin was very little addicted to selfish calculation at all; and so long as his friend was enjoying himself, how should he be discontented? And the truth is, that of all the delights of the Gardens; of the hundred thousand *extra* lamps, which were always lighted; the fiddlers, in cocked-hats, who played ravishing melodies under the gilded cockle-shell in the midst of the Gardens; the singers, both of comic and sentimental ballads, who charmed the ears there; the country dances, formed by bouncing cockneys and cockneyesses, and executed amidst jumping, thumping, and laughter; the signal which announced that Madame Saqui was about to mount skyward on a slack-rope ascending to the stars; the hermit that always sat in the illuminated hermitage; the dark walks, so favourable to the interviews of young lovers; the pots of stout handed about by the people in the shabby old liveries; and the twinkling boxes, in which the happy feasters made believe to eat slices of almost invisible ham; – of all these things, and of the gentle Simpson, that kind smiling idiot, who, I dare say, presided even then over the place – Captain William Dobbin did not take the slightest notice.

He carried about Amelia's white Cashmere shawl, and having attended under the gilt cockle-shell, while Mrs. Salmon performed the Battle of Borodino (a savage Cantata against the Corsican upstart, who had lately met with his Russian reverses) – Mr. Dobbin tried to hum it as he walked away, and found he was humming – the tune which Amelia Sedley sang on the stairs, as she came down to dinner.

He burst out laughing at himself; for the truth is, he could sing no better than an owl.

It is to be understood, as a matter of course, that our young people being in parties of two and two, made the most solemn promises to keep together during the evening, and separated in ten minutes afterwards. Parties at Vauxhall always did separate, but 'twas only to meet again at supper-time, when they could talk of their mutual adventures in the interval.

What were the adventures of Mr. Osborne and Miss Amelia? That is a secret. But be sure of this – they were perfectly happy, and correct in their behaviour; and as they had been in the habit of being together any time these fifteen years, their *tête-à-tête* offered no particular novelty.

But when Miss Rebecca Sharp and her stout companion lost themselves in a solitary walk, in which there were not above five score more of couples similarly straying, they both felt that the situation was extremely tender and critical, and now or never was the moment, Miss Sharp thought, to provoke that declaration which was trembling on the timid lips of Mr. Sedley. They had previously been to the panorama of Moscow, where a rude fellow, treading on Miss Sharp's foot, caused her to fall back with a little shriek into the arms of Mr. Sedley, and this little incident increased the tenderness and confidence of that gentleman to such a degree, that he told her several of his favourite Indian stories over again for, at least, the sixth time.

'How I should like to see India!' said Rebecca.

'*Should* you?' said Joseph, with a most killing tenderness; and was no doubt about to follow up this artful interrogatory by a question still more tender (for he puffed and panted a great deal, and Rebecca's hand, which was placed near his heart, could count the feverish pulsations of that organ), when, oh, provoking! the bell rang for the fireworks, and, a great scuffling and running taking place, these interesting lovers were obliged to follow in the stream of people.

Captain Dobbin had some thoughts of joining the party at supper: as, in truth, he found the Vauxhall amusement not particularly lively – but he paraded twice before the box where the now united couples were met, and nobody took any notice of him. Covers were laid for four. The mated pairs were prattling away quite happily, and Dobbin knew he was as clean forgotten as if he had never existed in this world.

'I should only be *de trop*,' said the captain, looking at them rather wistfully. 'I'd best go and talk to the hermit,' – and so he strolled off out of the hum of men, and noise, and clatter of the banquet, into the dark walk, at the end of which lived that well-known pasteboard Solitary. It wasn't very good fun for Dobbin – and, indeed, to be alone at Vauxhall, I have found, from my own experience, to be one of the most dismal sports ever entered into by a bachelor.

The two couples were perfectly happy then in their box: where the most delightful and intimate conversation took place. Jos was in his glory, ordering about the waiters with great majesty. He made the salad; and uncorked the champagne; and carved the chickens; and ate and drank the greater part of the refreshments on the tables. Finally, he insisted upon having a bowl of rack punch; everybody had rack punch at Vauxhall. 'Waiter, rack punch.'

That bowl of rack punch was the cause of all this history. And why not a bowl of rack punch as well as any other cause? Was not a bowl of prussic acid the cause of Fair Rosamond's retiring from the world? Was not a bowl of wine the cause of the demise of Alexander the Great, or at least, does not Dr. Lemprière say so? – so did this bowl of rack punch influence the fates of all the principal characters in this 'Novel without a Hero', which we are now relating. It influenced their life, although most of them did not taste a drop of it.

The young ladies did not drink it; Osborne did not like it; and the consequence was that Jos, that fat *gourmand*, drank up the whole contents of the bowl; and the consequence of his drinking up the whole contents of the bowl was, a liveliness which at first was astonishing, and then became almost painful; for he talked and laughed so loud as to bring scores of listeners round the box, much to the confusion of the innocent party within it; and, volunteering to sing a song (which he did in that maudlin high key peculiar to gentlemen in an inebriated state), he almost drew away the audience who were gathered round the musicians in the gilt scallop-shell, and received from his hearers a great deal of applause.

'Brayvo, Fat un!' said one; 'Angcore, Daniel Lambert!' said another; 'What a figure for the tight-rope!' exclaimed another wag, to the inexpressible alarm of the ladies, and the great anger of Mr. Osborne.

'For Heaven's sake, Jos, let us get up and go,' cried that gentleman, and the young women rose.

'Stop, my dearest diddle-diddle-darling,' shouted Jos, now as bold as a lion, and clasping Miss Rebecca round the waist. Rebecca started, but she could not get away her hand. The laughter outside redoubled. Jos continued to drink, to make love, and to sing; and, winking and waving his glass gracefully to his audience, challenged all or any to come in and take a share of his punch.

Mr. Osborne was just on the point of knocking down a gentleman in top-boots, who proposed to take advantage of this invitation, and a commotion seemed to be inevitable, when by the greatest good luck a gentleman of the name of Dobbin, who had been walking about the Gardens, stepped up to the box. 'Be off, you fools!' said this gentleman – shouldering off a great number of the crowd, who vanished presently before his cocked-hat and fierce appearance – and he entered the box in a most agitated state.

'Good Heavens! Dobbin, where *have* you been?' Osborne said, seizing the white Cashmere shawl from his friend's arm, and huddling up Amelia in it. – 'Make yourself useful, and take charge of Jos here, whilst I take the ladies to the carriage.'

Jos was for rising to interfere – but a single push from Osborne's finger sent him puffing back into his seat again, and the lieutenant was enabled to remove the ladies in safety. Jos kissed his hand to them as they retreated, and hiccupped out, 'Bless you! Bless you!' Then seizing Captain Dobbin's hand, and weeping in the most pitiful way, he confided to that gentleman the secret of his loves. He adored that girl who had just gone out; he had broken her heart, he knew he had, by his conduct; he would marry her next morning at St. George's, Hanover Square; he'd knock up the Archbishop of Canterbury at Lambeth: he would, by Jove! and have him in readiness; and, acting on this hint, Captain Dobbin shrewdly induced him to leave the Gardens and hasten to Lambeth Palace, and, when once out of the gates, easily conveyed Mr. Jos Sedley into a hackney-coach, which deposited him safely at his lodgings.

George Osborne conducted the girls home in safety, and when the door was closed upon them, and as he walked across Russell Square, laughed so as to astonish the watchman. Amelia looked very ruefully at her friend, as they went upstairs, and kissed her, and went to bed without any more talking.

'He must propose to-morrow,' thought Rebecca. 'He called me his soul's darling four times; he squeezed my hand in

Amelia's presence. He must propose to-morrow.' And so thought Amelia, too. And I dare say she thought of the dress she was to wear as bride's-maid, and of the presents which she should make to her nice little sister-in-law, and of a subsequent ceremony in which she herself might play a principal part, &c., and &c., and &c., and &c.

O, ignorant young creatures! How little do you know the effect of rack punch! What is the rack in the punch, at night, to the rack in the head of a morning! To this truth I can vouch as a man; there is no headache in the world like that caused by Vauxhall punch. Through the lapse of twenty years, I can remember the consequence of two glasses! – two wine-glasses! – but two, upon the honour of a gentleman; and Joseph Sedley, who had a liver complaint, had swallowed at least a quart of the abominable mixture.

That next morning, which Rebecca thought was to dawn upon her fortune, found Sedley groaning in agonies which the pen refuses to describe. Soda-water was not invented yet. Small beer – will it be believed! – was the only drink with which unhappy gentlemen soothed the fever of their previous night's potation. With this mild beverage before him, George Osborne found the ex-collector of Boggley Wollah groaning on the sofa at his lodgings. Dobbin was already in the room, good-naturedly tending his patient of the night before. The two officers, looking at the prostrate Bacchanalian, and askance at each other, exchanged the most frightful sympathetic grins. Even Sedley's valet, the most solemn and correct of gentlemen, with the muteness and gravity of an undertaker, could hardly keep his countenance in order, as he looked at his unfortunate master.

'Mr. Sedley was uncommon wild last night, sir,' he whispered in confidence to Osborne, as the latter mounted the stair. 'He wanted to fight the 'ackney-coachman, sir. The capting was obliged to bring him upstairs in his harms like a babby.' A momentary smile flickered over Mr. Brush's features as he spoke; instantly, however, they relapsed into their usual unfathomable calm, as he flung open the drawing-room door, and announced 'Mr. Hosbin'.

'How are you, Sedley?' that young wag began, after surveying his victim. 'No bones broke? There's a hackney-coachman downstairs with a black eye, and a tied up head, vowing he'll have the law of you.'

'What do you mean, – law?' Sedley faintly asked.

'For thrashing him last night – didn't he, Dobbin? You hit out, sir, like Molyneux. The watchman says he never saw a fellow go down so straight. Ask Dobbin.'

'You *did* have a round with the coachman,' Captain Dobbin said, 'and showed plenty of fight too.'

'And that fellow with the white coat at Vauxhall! How Jos drove at him! How the women screamed! By Jove, sir, it did my heart good to see you. I thought you civilians had no pluck; but *I'll* never get in your way when you are in your cups, Jos.'

'I believe I'm very terrible, when I'm roused,' ejaculated Jos from the sofa, and made a grimace so dreary and ludicrous, that the captain's politeness could restrain him no longer, and he and Osborne fired off a ringing volley of laughter.

Osborne pursued his advantage pitilessly. He thought Jos a milksop. He had been revolving in his mind the marriage-question pending between Jos and Rebecca, and was not over-well pleased that a member of a family into which he, George Osborne, of the –th, was going to marry, should make a *mésalliance* with a little nobody – a little upstart governess. 'You hit, you poor old fellow?' said Osborne. 'You terrible? Why, man, you couldn't stand – you made everybody laugh in the Gardens, though you were crying yourself. You were maudlin, Jos. Don't you remember singing a song?'

'A what?' Jos asked.

'A sentimental song, and calling Rosa, Rebecca, what's her name, Amelia's little friend – your dearest diddle-diddle-darling?' And this ruthless young fellow, seizing hold of Dobbin's hand, acted over the scene, to the horror of the original performer, and in spite of Dobbin's good-natured entreaties to him to have mercy.

'Why should I spare him?' Osborne said to his friend's remonstrances, when they quitted the invalid, leaving him under the hands of Dr. Gollop. 'What the deuce right has he to give himself his patronizing airs, and make fools of us at Vauxhall? Who's this little schoolgirl that is ogling and making love to him? Hang it, the family's low enough already, without *her*. A governess is all very well, but I'd rather have a lady for my sister-in-law. I'm a liberal man; but I've proper pride, and know my own station: let her know hers. And I'll take down that great hectoring nabob, and prevent him from being made a greater fool than he is. That's why I told him to look out, lest she brought an action against him.'

'I suppose you know best,' Dobbin said, though rather dubiously. 'You always were a Tory, and your family's one of the oldest in England. But, —'

'Come and see the girls, and make love to Miss Sharp yourself,' the lieutenant here interrupted his friend; but Captain Dobbin declined to join Osborne in his daily visit to the young ladies in Russell Square.

As George walked down Southampton Row, from Holborn, he laughed as he saw, at the Sedley mansion, in two different stories, two heads on the look-out.

The fact is, Miss Amelia, in the drawing-room balcony, was looking very eagerly towards the opposite side of the Square, where Mr. Osborne dwelt, on the watch for the lieutenant himself; and Miss Sharp, from her little bedroom on the second floor, was in observation until Mr. Joseph's great form should heave in sight.

'Sister Anne is on the watch-tower,' said he to Amelia, 'but there's nobody coming;' and laughing and enjoying the joke hugely, he described in the most ludicrous terms to Miss Sedley the dismal condition of her brother.

'I think it's very cruel of you to laugh, George,' she said, looking particularly unhappy; but George only laughed the more at her piteous and discomfited mien, persisted in thinking the joke a most diverting one, and when Miss Sharp came downstairs, bantered her with a great deal of liveliness upon the effect of her charms on the fat civilian.

'Oh Miss Sharp! if you could but see him this morning,' he said, — 'moaning in his flowered dressing-gown – writhing on his sofa; if you could but have seen him lolling out his tongue to Gollop the apothecary.'

'See whom?' said Miss Sharp.

'Whom? Oh whom? Captain Dobbin, of course, to whom we were all so attentive, by the way, last night.'

'We were very unkind to him,' Emmy said, blushing very much. 'I – I quite forgot him.'

'Of course you did,' cried Osborne, still on the laugh. 'One can't be *always* thinking about Dobbin, you know, Amelia. Can one, Miss Sharp?'

'Except when he overset the glass of wine at dinner.' Miss Sharp said, with a haughty air and a toss of the head, 'I never gave the existence of Captain Dobbin one single moment's consideration.'

'Very good, Miss Sharp, I'll tell him,' Osborne said; and as he spoke Miss Sharp began to have a feeling of distrust and hatred towards this young officer, which he was quite unconscious of having inspired. '*He* is to make fun of me, is he?' thought Rebecca. 'Has he been laughing about me to Joseph? Has he frightened him? Perhaps he won't come.' – A film passed over her eyes, and her heart beat quite quick.

'You're always joking,' said she, smiling as innocently as she could. 'Joke away, Mr. George; there's nobody to defend *me*.' And George Osborne, as she walked away – and Amelia looked reprovingly at him – felt some little manly compunction for having inflicted any unnecessary unkindness upon this helpless creature. 'My dearest Amelia,' said he, 'you are too good – too kind. You don't know the world. I do. And your little friend, Miss Sharp, must learn her station.'

'Don't you think Jos will —'

'Upon my word; my dear, I don't know. He may, or may not. I'm not his master. I only know he's a very foolish vain fellow, and put my dear little girl into a very painful and awkward position last night. My dearest diddle-diddle-darling!' He was off laughing again; and he did it so drolly, that Emmy laughed too.

All that day Jos never came. But Amelia had no fear about this; for the little schemer had actually sent away the page, Mr. Sambo's aide de camp, to Mr. Joseph's lodgings, to ask for some book he had promised, and how he was; and the reply through Jos's man, Mr. Brush, was, that his master was ill in bed, and had just had the doctor with him. He must come to-morrow, she thought, but she never had the courage to speak a word on the subject to Rebecca; nor did that young woman herself allude to it in any way during the whole evening after the night at Vauxhall.

The next day, however, as the two young ladies sat on the sofa, pretending to work, or to write letters, or to read novels, Sambo came into the room with his usual engaging grin, with a packet under his arm, and a note on a tray. 'Note from Mr. Jos, miss,' says Sambo.

How Amelia trembled as she opened it!

So it ran –

DEAR AMELIA, – I send you the *Orphan of the Forest*. I was too ill to come yesterday. I leave town to-day for Cheltenham. Pray excuse me, if you can, to the amiable Miss Sharp, for my conduct at Vauxhall, and entreat her to pardon and forget every word I may have uttered when excited by that fatal supper. As soon as I have recovered, for my health is very much shaken, I shall go to Scotland for some months, and am

Truly yours,
JOS SEDLEY.

It was the death-warrant. All was over. Amelia did not dare to look at Rebecca's pale face and burning eyes, but she dropped the letter into her friend's lap; and got up, and went upstairs to her room, and cried her little heart out.

Blenkinsop, the housekeeper, there sought her presently with consolation; on whose shoulder Amelia wept confidentially, and relieved herself a good deal. 'Don't take on, miss. I didn't like to tell you. But none of us in the house have liked her except at fust. I sor her with my own eyes reading your ma's letters. Pinner says she's always about your trinket-box and drawers, and everybody's drawers, and she's sure she's put your white ribbing into her box.'

'I gave it her, I gave it her,' Amelia said.

But this did not alter Mrs. Blenkinsop's opinion of Miss Sharp. 'I don't trust them governesses, Pinner,' she remarked to the maid. 'They give themselves the hairs and hupstarts of ladies, and their wages is no better than you nor me.'

It now became clear to every soul in the house, except poor Amelia, that Rebecca should take her departure, and high and low (always with the one exception) agreed that that event should take place as speedily as possible. Our good child ransacked all her drawers, cupboards, reticules, and gimcrack boxes – passed in review all her gowns, fichus, tags, bobbins, laces, silk stockings, and fallals – selecting this thing and that and the other, to make a little heap for Rebecca. And going to her papa, that generous British merchant, who had promised to give her as many guineas as she was years old – she begged the old gentleman to give the money to dear Rebecca, who must want it, while she lacked for nothing.

She even made George Osborne contribute, and nothing loath (for he was as free-handed a young fellow as any in the army), he went to Bond Street, and bought the best hat and spencer that money could buy.

'That's George's present to you, Rebecca dear,' said Amelia, quite proud of the bandbox conveying these gifts. 'What a taste he has! There's nobody like him.'

'Nobody,' Rebecca answered. 'How thankful I am to him!' She was thinking in her heart, 'It was George Osborne who prevented my marriage.' – And she loved George Osborne accordingly.

She made her preparations for departure with great equanimity; and accepted all the kind little Amelia's presents, after just the proper degree of hesitation and reluctance. She vowed eternal gratitude to Mrs. Sedley, of course; but did not intrude herself upon that good lady too much, who was embarrassed, and evidently wishing to avoid her. She kissed Mr. Sedley's hand, when he presented her with the purse; and asked permission to consider him for the future as her kind, kind friend and protector. Her behaviour was so affecting that he was going to write her a cheque for twenty pounds more; but he restrained his feelings: the carriage was in waiting to take him to dinner: so he tripped away with a 'God bless you, my dear. Always come here when you come to town, you know. – Drive to the Mansion House, James.'

Finally came the parting with Miss Amelia, over which picture I intend to throw a veil. But after a scene in which one person was in earnest and the other a perfect performer – after the tenderest caresses, the most pathetic tears, the smelling-bottle, and some of the very best feelings of the heart, had been called into requisition – Rebecca and Amelia parted, the former vowing to love her friend for ever and ever and ever.

CHAPTER VII

CRAWLEY OF QUEEN'S CRAWLEY

A MONG the most respected of the names beginning in C, which the Court-Guide contained, in the year 18–, was that of Crawley, Sir Pitt, Baronet, Great Gaunt Street, and

Queen's Crawley, Hants. This honourable name had figured constantly also in the Parliamentary list for many years, in conjunction with that of a number of other worthy gentlemen who sat in turns for the borough.

It is related, with regard to the borough of Queen's Crawley, that Queen Elizabeth, in one of her progresses stopping at Crawley to breakfast, was so delighted with some remarkably fine Hampshire beer which was then presented to her by the Crawley of the day (a handsome gentleman with a trim beard and a good leg), that she forthwith erected Crawley into a borough to send two members to Parliament; and the place, from the day of that illustrious visit, took the name of Queen's Crawley, which it holds up to the present moment. And though by the lapse of time, and those mutations which ages produce in empires, cities, and boroughs, Queen's Crawley was no longer so populous a place as it had been in Queen Bess's time – nay, was come down to that condition of borough which used to be denominated rotten – yet, as Sir Pitt Crawley would say with perfect justice in his elegant way, 'Rotten! be hanged – it produces me a good fifteen hundred a year.'

Sir Pitt Crawley (named after the great Commoner), was the son of Walpole Crawley, first baronet, of the Tape and Sealing-Wax Office in the reign of George II, when he was impeached for peculation, as were a great number of other honest gentlemen of those days; and Walpole Crawley was, as need scarcely be said, son of John Churchill Crawley, named after the celebrated military commander of the reign of Queen Anne. The family tree (which hangs up at Queen's Crawley) furthermore mentions Charles Stuart, afterwards called Barebones Crawley, son of the Crawley of James the First's time; and finally, Queen Elizabeth's Crawley, who is represented as the foreground of the picture in his forked beard and armour. Out of his waistcoat, as usual, grows a tree, on the main branches of which the above illustrious names are inscribed. Close by the name of Sir Pitt Crawley, Baronet (the subject of the present memoir), are written that of his brother, the Reverend Bute Crawley (the great Com-moner was in disgrace when the reverend gentleman was born), rector of Crawley-cum-Snailby, and of various other male and female members of the Crawley family.

Sir Pitt was first married to Grizzel, sixth daughter of

Mungo Binkie, Lord Binkie, and cousin, in consequence, of Mr. Dundas. She brought him two sons: Pitt, named not so much after his father as after the heaven-born minister; and Rawdon Crawley, from the Prince of Wales's friend, whom His Majesty George IV forgot so completely. Many years after her ladyship's demise, Sir Pitt led to the altar Rosa, daughter of Mr. G. Dawson, of Mudbury, by whom he had two daughters, for whose benefit Miss Rebecca Sharp was now engaged as governess. It will be seen that the young lady was come into a family of very genteel connexions, and was about to move in a much more distinguished circle than that humble one which she had just quitted in Russell Square.

She had received her orders to join her pupils, in a note which was written upon an old envelope, and which contained the following words: —

Sir Pitt Crawley begs Miss Sharp and baggidge may be hear on Tuesday, as I leaf for Queen's Crawley to-morrow morning *erly*.
Great Gaunt Street.

Rebecca had never seen a baronet, as far as she knew, and as soon as she had taken leave of Amelia, and counted the guineas which good-natured Mr. Sedley had put into a purse for her, and as soon as she had done wiping her eyes with her handkerchief (which operation she concluded the very moment the carriage had turned the corner of the street), she began to depict in her own mind what a baronet must be. 'I wonder, does he wear a star?' thought she, 'or is it only lords that wear stars? But he will be very handsomely dressed in a court suit, with ruffles and his hair a little powdered, like Mr. Wroughton at Covent Garden. I suppose he will be awfully proud, and that I shall be treated most contemptuously. Still I must bear my hard lot as well as I can — at least, I shall be amongst *gentlefolks*, and not with vulgar city people:' and she fell to thinking of her Russell Square friends with that very same philosophical bitterness with which, in a certain apologue, the fox is represented as speaking of the grapes.

Having passed through Gaunt Square into Great Gaunt Street, the carriage at length stopped at a tall gloomy house between two other tall gloomy houses, each with a hatchment over the middle drawing-room window; as is the custom of houses in Great Gaunt Street, in which gloomy locality death seems to reign perpetual. The shutters of the first-floor windows of Sir Pitt's mansion were closed – those of the dining-room were partially open, and the blinds neatly covered up in old newspapers.

John, the groom, who had driven the carriage alone, did not care to descend to ring the bell; and so prayed a passing milk-boy to perform that office for him. When the bell was rung, a head appeared between the interstices of the dining-room shutters, and the door was opened by a man in drab breeches and gaiters, with a dirty old coat, a foul old neckcloth lashed round his bristly neck, a shining bald head, a leering red face, a pair of twinkling grey eyes, and a mouth perpetually on the grin.

'This Sir Pitt Crawley's?' says John, from the box.

'Ees,' says the man at the door with a nod.

'Hand down these 'ere trunks then,' said John.

'Hand 'n down yourself,' said the porter.

'Don't you see I can't leave my hosses? Come, bear a hand, my fine feller, and miss will give you some beer,' said John, with a horse-laugh, for he was no longer respectful to Miss Sharp, as her connexion with the family was broken off, and as she had given nothing to the servants on coming away.

The bald-headed man, taking his hands out of his breeches-pockets, advanced on this summons, and throwing Miss Sharp's trunk over his shoulder, carried it into the house.

'Take this basket and shawl, if you please, and open the door,' said Miss Sharp, and descended from the carriage in much indignation. 'I shall write to Mr. Sedley, and inform him of your conduct,' said she to the groom.

'Don't,' replied that functionary. 'I hope you've forgot nothink? Miss 'Melia's gownds – have you got them – as the lady's maid was to have 'ad? I hope they'll fit you. Shut the door, Jim, you'll get no good out of 'er,' continued John, pointing with his thumb towards Miss Sharp: 'a bad lot, I tell you, a bad lot,' and so saying, Mr. Sedley's groom drove away. The truth is, he was attached to the lady's maid in question, and indignant that she should have been robbed of her perquisites.

On entering the dining-room, by the orders of the individual in gaiters, Rebecca found that apartment not more cheerful than such rooms usually are, when genteel families are out of town. The faithful chambers seem, as it were, to mourn the absence of their masters. The Turkey carpet has rolled itself up, and retired sulkily under the side-board: the pictures have hidden their faces behind old sheets of brown paper: the ceiling-lamp is muffled up in a dismal sack of brown holland: the window-curtains have disappeared under all sorts of shabby envelopes: the marble bust of Sir Walpole Crawley is looking from its black corner at the bare boards and the oiled fire-irons, and the empty card-racks over the mantelpiece: the cellaret has lurked away behind the carpet: the chairs are turned up heads and tails along the walls; and in the dark corner opposite the statue, is an old-fashioned crabbed knife-box, locked and sitting on a dumb-waiter.

Two kitchen-chairs, and a round table, and an attenuated old poker and tongs were, however, gathered round the fire-place, as was a saucepan over a feeble sputtering fire. There was a bit of cheese and bread, and a tin candlestick on the table, and a little black porter in a pint-pot.

'Had your dinner, I suppose? It is not too warm for you? Like a drop of beer?'

'Where is Sir Pitt Crawley?' said Miss Sharp, majestically.

'He, he! *I*'m Sir Pitt Crawley. Reklect you owe me a pint for bringing down your luggage. He, he! Ask Tinker if I aynt. Mrs. Tinker, Miss Sharp! Miss Governess, Mrs. Char-woman. Ho, ho!'

The lady addressed as Mrs. Tinker at this moment made her appearance with a pipe and a paper of tobacco, for which she had been dispatched a minute before Miss Sharp's arrival; and she handed the articles over to Sir Pitt, who had taken his seat by the fire.

'Where's the farden?' said he. 'I gave you three halfpence. Where's the change, old Tinker?'

'There!' replied Mrs. Tinker, flinging down the coin; 'it's only baronets as cares about farthings.'

'A farthing a day is seven shillings a year,' answered the M.P.; 'seven shillings a year is the interest of seven guineas. Take care of your farthings, old Tinker and your guineas will come quite nat'ral.'

'You may be sure it's Sir Pitt Crawley, young woman,' said Mrs. Tinker, surlily; 'because he looks to his farthings. You'll know him better afore long.'

'And like me none the worse, Miss Sharp,' said the old gentleman, with an air almost of politeness. 'I must be just before I'm generous.'

'He never gave away a farthing in his life,' growled Tinker.

'Never, and never will: it's against my principle. Go and get another chair from the kitchen, Tinker, if you want to sit down; and then we'll have a bit of supper.'

Presently the baronet plunged a fork into the saucepan on the fire, and withdrew from the pot a piece of tripe and an onion, which he divided into pretty equal portions, and of which he partook with Mrs. Tinker. 'You see, Miss Sharp, when I'm not here Tinker's on board wages: when I'm in town she dines with the family. Haw! haw! I'm glad Miss Sharp's not hungry, ain't you, Tink?' And they fell to upon their frugal supper.

After supper Sir Pitt Crawley began to smoke his pipe; and when it became quite dark, he lighted the rushlight in the tin candlestick, and producing from an interminable pocket a huge mass of papers, began reading them, and putting them in order.

'I'm here on law business, my dear, and that's how it happens that I shall have the pleasure of such a pretty travelling companion to-morrow.'

'He's always at law business,' said Mrs. Tinker, taking up the pot of porter.

'Drink and drink about,' said the baronet. 'Yes, my dear, Tinker is quite right: I've lost and won more lawsuits than any man in England. Look here at Crawley, Bart. v. Snaffle. I'll throw him over, or my name's not Pitt Crawley. Podder and another versus Crawley, Bart. Overseers of Snaily parish against Crawley, Bart. They can't prove it's common: I'll defy 'em; the land's mine. It no more belongs to the parish than it does to you or Tinker here. I'll beat 'em, if it cost me a thousand guineas. Look over the papers; you may if you like, my dear. Do you write a good hand? I'll make you useful when we're at Queen's Crawley, depend on it, Miss Sharp. Now the dowager's dead I want some one.'

'She was as bad as he,' said Tinker. 'She took the law of every one of her tradesmen; and turned away forty-eight footmen in four year.'

'She was close – very close,' said the baronet, simply;
'but she was a valyble woman to me, and saved me a
steward.' – And in this confidential strain, and much to the
amusement of the new-comer, the conversation continued
for a considerable time. Whatever Sir Pitt Crawley's qualities
might be, good or bad, he did not make the least disguise
of them. He talked of himself incessantly, sometimes in the
coarsest and vulgarest Hampshire accent; sometimes adopting the tone of a man of the world. And so, with injunctions
to Miss Sharp to be ready at five in the morning, he bade
her good night. 'You'll sleep with Tinker to-night,' he said.
'It's a big bed, and there's room for two. Lady Crawley died
in it. Good night.'

Sir Pitt went off after this benediction, and the solemn
Tinker, rushlight in hand, led the way up the great bleak
stone stairs, past the great dreary drawing-room doors, with
the handles muffled up in paper, into the great front bedroom, where Lady Crawley had slept her last. The bed and
chamber were so funereal and gloomy, you might have
fancied, not only that Lady Crawley died in the room, but
that her ghost inhabited it. Rebecca sprang about the apartment, however, with the greatest liveliness, and had peeped
into the huge wardrobes, and the closets, and the cupboards, and tried the drawers which were locked, and examined the dreary pictures and toilette appointments, while
the old charwoman was saying her prayers. 'I shouldn't like
to sleep in this yeer bed without a good conscience, miss,'
said the old woman. 'There's room for us and a half-dozen
of ghosts in it,' says Rebecca. 'Tell me all about Lady
Crawley and Sir Pitt Crawley, and everybody, my *dear* Mrs.
Tinker.'

But old Tinker was not to be pumped by this little cross-
questioner; and signifying to her that bed was a place for
sleeping, not conversation, set up in her corner of the bed
such a snore as only the nose of innocence can produce.
Rebecca lay awake for a long, long time, thinking of the
morrow, and of the new world into which she was going,
and of her chances of success there. The rushlight flickered
in the basin. The mantelpiece cast up a great black shadow
over half of a mouldy old sampler, which her defunct
ladyship had worked, no doubt, and over two little family
pictures of young lads, one in a college gown, and the other

in a red jacket like a soldier. When she went to sleep, Rebecca chose that one to dream about.

At four o'clock, on such a roseate summer's morning as even made Great Gaunt Street look cheerful, the faithful Tinker, having wakened her bedfellow, and bid her prepare for departure, unbarred and unbolted the great hall-door (the clanging and clapping whereof startled the sleeping echoes in the street), and taking her way into Oxford Street, summoned a coach from a stand there. It is needless to particularize the number of the vehicle, or to state that the driver was stationed thus early in the neighbourhood of Swallow Street, in hopes that some young buck, reeling homeward from the tavern, might need the aid of his vehicle, and pay him with the generosity of intoxication.

It is likewise needless to say that the driver, if he had any such hopes as those above stated, was grossly disappointed; and that the worthy baronet whom he drove to the City did not give him one single penny more than his fare. It was in vain that Jehu appealed and stormed; that he flung down Miss Sharp's bandboxes in the gutter at the 'Necks, and swore he would take the law of his fare.

'You'd better not,' said one of the ostlers; 'it's Sir Pitt Crawley.'

'So it is, Joe,' cried the baronet, approvingly; 'and I'd like to see the man can do me.'

'So should oi,' said Joe, grinning sulkily, and mounting the baronet's baggage on the roof of the coach.

'Keep the box for me, Leader,' exclaims the Member of Parliament to the coachman; who replied, 'Yes, Sir Pitt,' with a touch of his hat, and rage in his soul (for he had promised the box to a young gentleman from Cambridge, who would have given a crown to a certainty), and Miss Sharp was accommodated with a back seat inside the carriage, which may be said to be carrying her into the wide world.

How the young man from Cambridge sulkily put his five great coats in front; but was reconciled when little Miss Sharp was made to quit the carriage, and mount up beside him – when he covered her up in one of his Benjamins, and became perfectly good-humoured – how the asthmatic gentleman, the prim lady, who declared upon her sacred honour she had never travelled in a public carriage before (there is always such a lady in a coach – Alas! was; for the coaches, where are they?), and the fat widow with the brandy-bottle, took their places inside – how the porter asked them all for money, and got sixpence from the gentleman and five greasy halfpence from the fat widow – and how the carriage at length drove away – now threading the dark lanes of Aldersgate, anon clattering by the Blue Cupola of Paul's, jingling rapidly by the strangers' entry of Fleet Market, which, with Exeter 'Change, has now departed to the world of shadows – how they passed the 'White Bear' in Piccadilly, and saw the dew rising up from the market-gardens of Knightsbridge – how Turnham Green, Brentford, Bagshot, were passed – need not be told here. But the writer of these pages, who has pursued in former days, and in the same bright weather, the same remarkable journey, cannot but think of it with a sweet and tender regret. Where is the road now, and its merry incidents of life? Is there no Chelsea or Greenwich for the old honest pimple-nosed coachmen? I wonder where are they, those good fellows? Is old Weller alive or dead? and the waiters, yea and the inns at which they waited, and the cold rounds of beef inside, and the stunted ostler with his blue nose and clinking pail, where is he, and where is his generation? To those great geniuses now in petticoats, who shall write novels for the beloved reader's children, these men and things will be as much legend and history as Nineveh, or Cœur de Lion, or Jack Sheppard. For them stage-coaches will have become romances – a team of four bays as fabulous as Bucephalus or Black Bess. Ah, how their coats shone, as the stablemen pulled their clothes off, and away they went – ah, how their tails shook, as with smoking sides at the stage's end they demurely walked away into the inn-yard. Alas! we shall never hear the horn sing at midnight, or see the pike-gates fly open any more. Whither, however, is the light four-inside 'Trafalgar' coach carrying us? Let us be set down at Queen's Crawley without further divagation, and see how Miss Rebecca Sharp speeds there.

CHAPTER VIII

PRIVATE AND CONFIDENTIAL

Miss Rebecca Sharp to Miss Amelia Sedley, Russell Square, London.

(Free. – Pitt Crawley.)

MY DEAREST, SWEETEST AMELIA – With what mingled joy and sorrow do I take up the pen to write to my dearest friend! Oh, what a change between to-day and yesterday! *Now* I am friendless and alone; yesterday I was at home, in the sweet company of a sister, whom I shall ever, *ever* cherish!

I will not tell you in what tears and sadness I passed the fatal night in which I separated from you. *You* went on Tuesday to joy and happiness, with your mother and *your devoted young soldier* by your side; and I thought of you all night, dancing at the Perkins's, the prettiest, I am sure, of all the young ladies at the Ball. I was brought by the groom in the old carriage to Sir Pitt Crawley's town house, where, after John the groom had behaved most rudely and insolently to me (alas! 'twas safe to insult poverty and misfortune!), I was given over to Sir P.'s care, and made to pass the night in an old gloomy bed, and by the side of a horrid gloomy old charwoman, who keeps the house. I did not sleep one single wink the whole night.

Sir Pitt is not what we silly girls, when we used to read *Cecilia* at Chiswick, imagined a baronet must have been. Anything, indeed, less like Lord Orville cannot be imagined. Fancy an old, stumpy, short, vulgar, and very dirty man, in old clothes and shabby old gaiters, who smokes a horrid pipe, and cooks his own horrid supper in a saucepan. He speaks with a country accent, and swore a great deal at the old charwoman, at the hackney-coachman who drove us to the inn where the coach went from, and on which I made the journey *outside for the greater part of the way*.

I was wakened at daybreak by the charwoman, and having arrived at the inn, was at first placed inside the coach. But, when we got to a place called Leakington, where the rain began to fall very heavily – will you believe it? – I was forced to come outside; for Sir Pitt is a proprietor of the coach, and as a passenger came at Mudbury, who wanted an inside place, I was obliged to go outside in the rain, where, however, a young gentleman from Cambridge College sheltered me very kindly in one of his *several* great-coats.

This gentleman and the guard seemed to know Sir Pitt very well, and laughed at him a great deal. They both agreed in calling him an *old screw;* which means a very stingy, avaricious person. He never gives any money to anybody, they said (and this meanness I hate); and the young gentleman made me remark that we drove very slow for the last two stages on the road, because Sir Pitt was on the box, and because he is proprietor of the horses for this part of the journey. 'But won't I flog 'em on to Squashmore, when I take the ribbons?' said the young *Cantab*. 'And sarve 'em right, Master Jack,' said the guard. When I comprehended the meaning of this phrase, and that Master Jack intended to drive the rest of the way, and revenge himself on Sir Pitt's horses, of course I laughed too.

A carriage and four splendid horses, covered with armorial bearings, however, awaited us at Mudbury, four miles from Queen's Crawley, and we made our entrance to the baronet's park in state. There is a fine avenue of a mile long leading to the house, and the woman at the lodge-gate (over the pillars of which are a serpent and a dove, the supporters of the Crawley arms) made us a number of curtsies as she flung open the old iron carved doors, which are something like those at odious Chiswick.

'There's an avenue,' said Sir Pitt, 'a mile long. There's six thousand pound of timber in them there trees. Do you call that nothing?' He pronounced avenue — *evenue*, and nothing — *nothink*, so droll; and he had a Mr. Hodson, his hind from Mudbury, into the carriage with him, and they talked about distraining and selling up, and draining and subsoiling, and a great deal about tenants and farming — much more than I could understand. Sam Miles had been caught poaching, and Peter Bailey had gone to the work-house at last. 'Serve him right,' said Sir Pitt; 'him and his fam'ly has been cheating me on that farm these hundred and fifty years.' Some old tenant, I suppose, who could not pay his rent. Sir Pitt might have said '*he* and his family', to be sure; but rich baronets do not need to be careful about grammar, as poor governesses must be.

As we passed, I remarked a beautiful church-spire rising above some old elms in the park; and before them, in the midst of a lawn, and some outhouses, an old red house with tall chimneys covered with ivy, and the windows shining in the sun. 'Is that your church, sir?' I said.

'Yes, hang it' (said Sir Pitt, only he used, dear, *a much wickeder word*); 'how's Buty, Hodson? Buty's my brother Bute, my dear — my brother the parson. Buty and the Beast I call him, ha, ha!'

Hodson laughed too, and then looking more grave and nodding his head, said, 'I'm afraid he's better, Sir Pitt. He was out on his pony yesterday, looking at our corn.'

'Looking after his tithes, hang 'un' (only he used the same wicked word). 'Will brandy-and-water never kill him? He's as tough as old whatdyecallum — old Methusalem.'

Mr. Hodson laughed again. 'The young men is home from college. They've whopped John Scroggins till he's wellnigh dead.'

'Whop my second keeper!' roared out Sir Pitt.

'He was on the parson's ground, sir,' replied Mr. Hodson; and Sir Pitt in a fury swore that if ever he caught 'em poaching on his ground, he'd transport 'em, by the lord he would. However, he said, 'I've sold the presentation of the living, Hodson; none of that breed shall get it

I war'nt;' and Mr. Hodson said he was quite right: and I have no doubt from this that the two brothers are at variance – as brothers often are, and sisters too. Don't you remember the two Miss Scratchleys at Chiswick, how they used always to fight and quarrel – and Mary Box, how she was always thumping Louisa?

Presently, seeing two little boys gathering sticks in the wood. Mr. Hodson jumped out of the carriage, at Sir Pitt's order, and rushed upon them with his whip. 'Pitch into 'em, Hodson,' roared the baronet; 'flog their little souls out, and bring 'em up to the house, the vagabonds; I'll commit 'em as sure as my name's Pitt.' And presently we heard Mr. Hodson's whip clacking on the shoulders of the poor little blubbering wretches, and Sir Pitt, seeing that the malefactors were in custody, drove on to the hall.

All the servants were ready to meet us, and

*

Here, my dear, I was interrupted last night by a dreadful thumping at my door; and who do you think it was? Sir Pitt Crawley in his nightcap and dressing-gown, such a figure! As I shrank away from such a visitor, he came forward and seized my candle; 'no candles after eleven o'clock, Miss Becky,' said he. 'Go to bed in the dark, you pretty little hussy' (that is what he called me), 'and unless you wish me to come for the candle every night, mind and be in bed at eleven.' And with this, he and Mr. Horrocks the butler went off laughing. You may be sure I shall not encourage any more of their visits. They let loose two immense bloodhounds at night, which all last night were yelling and howling at the moon. 'I call the dog Gorer,' said Sir Pitt; 'he's killed a man, that dog has, and is master of a bull, and the mother I used to call Flora; but now I calls her Aroarer, for she's too old to bite. Haw, haw!'

Before the house of Queen's Crawley, which is an odious old-fashioned red-brick mansion, with tall chimneys and gables of the style of Queen Bess, there is a terrace flanked by the family dove and serpent, and on which the great hall-door opens. And oh, my dear, the great hall, I am sure, is as big and as glum as the great hall in the dear castle of Udolpho. It has a large fire-place, in which we might put half Miss Pinkerton's school, and the grate is big enough to roast an ox at the very least. Round the room hang I don't know how many generations of Crawleys, some with beards and ruffs, some with huge wigs and toes turned out; some dressed in long straight stays and gowns that look as stiff as towers, and some with long ringlets, and, oh my dear! scarcely any stays at all. At one end of the hall is the great staircase all in black oak, as dismal as may be, and on either side are tall doors with stags' heads over them, leading to the billiard-room and the library, and the great yellow saloon and the morning-rooms. I think there are at least twenty bedrooms on the first floor; one of them has the bed in which Queen Elizabeth slept; and I have been taken by my new pupils through all these fine apartments this morning. They are not rendered less gloomy, I promise you, by having the shutters always shut; and there is scarce one of the apartments, but when the light was let into it, I expected to see a ghost in the room. We have a schoolroom on the second floor, with my bedroom leading into it on one side, and that of the young ladies on the other. Then there are Mr. Pitt's apartments – Mr. Crawley, he is called – the eldest son, and Mr. Rawdon Crawley's rooms – he is an officer like *somebody*, and away with his regiment. There is no want of room, I assure you. You might lodge all the people in Russell Square in the house, I think, and have space to spare.

Half an hour after our arrival, the great dinner-bell was rung, and I came down with my two pupils (they are very thin insignificant little chits of ten and eight years old). I came down in your *dear* muslin gown (about which that odious Mrs. Pinner was so rude, because you gave it me); for I am to be treated as one of the family, except on company days, when the young ladies and I are to dine upstairs.

Well, the great dinner-bell rang, and we all assembled in the little drawing-room where my Lady Crawley sits. She is the second Lady Crawley, and mother of the young ladies. She was an ironmonger's daughter, and her marriage was thought a great match. She looks as if she had been handsome once, and her eyes are always weeping for the loss of her beauty. She is pale and meagre, and high-shouldered; and has not a word to say for herself, evidently. Her step-son, Mr. Crawley, was likewise in the room. He was in full dress, as pompous as an undertaker. He is pale, thin, ugly, silent; he has thin legs, no chest, hay-coloured whiskers, and straw-coloured hair. He is the very picture of his sainted mother over the mantelpiece – Griselda of the noble house of Binkie.

'This is the new governess, Mr. Crawley,' said Lady Crawley, coming forward and taking my hand; 'Miss Sharp.'

'Oh!' said Mr. Crawley, and pushed his head once forward and began again to read a great pamphlet with which he was busy.

'I hope you will be kind to my girls,' said Lady Crawley; with her pink eyes always full of tears.

'Law, ma, of course she will,' said the eldest: and I saw at a glance that I need not be afraid of *that* woman.

'My lady is served,' says the butler in black, in an immense white shirt-frill, that looked as if it had been one of the Queen Elizabeth's ruffs depicted in the hall; and so taking Mr. Crawley's arm, she led the way to the dining-room, whither I followed with my little pupils in each hand.

Sir Pitt was already in the room with a silver jug. He had just been to the cellar, and was in full dress too; that is, he had taken his gaiters off and showed his little dumpy legs in black worsted stockings. The sideboard was covered with glistening old plate – old cups, both gold and silver; old salvers and cruet-stands, like Rundell and Bridge's shop. Everything on the table was in silver too, and two footmen, with red hair and canary-coloured liveries, stood on either side of the sideboard.

Mr. Crawley said a long grace, and Sir Pitt said amen, and the great silver dish-covers were removed.

'What have we for dinner, Betsy?' said the baronet.

'Mutton broth, I believe, Sir Pitt,' answered Lady Crawley.

'*Mouton aux navets*,' added the butler gravely (pronounce, if you please, moutongonavvy); and the soup is *potage de mouton à l'Écossaise*. The side dishes contain *pommes de terre au naturel* and *choufleur à l'eau*.'

'Mutton's mutton,' said the baronet, 'and a devilish good thing. What *ship* was it, Horrocks, and when did you kill?'

'One of the black-faced Scotch, Sir Pitt: we killed on Thursday.'

'Who took any?'

'Steel, of Mudbury, took the saddle and two legs, Sir Pitt; but he says the last was too young and confounded woolly, Sir Pitt.'

'Will you take some *potage*? Miss ah – Miss Blunt,' said Mr. Crawley.

'Capital Scotch broth, my dear,' said Sir Pitt, 'though they call it by a French name.'

'I believe it is the custom, sir, in decent society,' said Mr. Crawley, haughtily, 'to call the dish as I have called it;' and it was served to us on silver soup-plates by the footmen in the canary coats, with the *mouton aux navets*. Then 'ale and water' were brought and served to us young ladies in wine-glasses. I am not a judge of ale, but I can say with a clear conscience I prefer water.

While we were enjoying our repast, Sir Pitt took occasion to ask what had become of the shoulders of the mutton.

'I believe they were eaten in the servants' hall,' said my lady, humbly.

'They was, my lady,' said Horrocks, 'and precious little else we get there neither.'

Sir Pitt burst into a horse-laugh, and continued his conversation with Mr. Horrocks. 'That there little black pig of the Kent sow's breed must be uncommon fat now.'

'It's not quite busting, Sir Pitt,' said the butler with the gravest air, at which Sir Pitt, and with him the young ladies, this time, began to laugh violently.

'Miss Crawley, Miss Rose Crawley,' said Mr. Crawley, 'your laughter strikes me as being exceedingly out of place.'

'Never mind my lord,' said the baronet, 'we'll try the porker on Saturday. Kill 'un on Saturday morning, John Horrocks. Miss Sharp adores pork, don't you, Miss Sharp?'

And I think this is all the conversation that I remember at dinner. When the repast was concluded a jug of hot water was placed before Sir Pitt, with a case-bottle containing, I believe, rum. Mr. Horrocks served myself and my pupils with three little glasses of wine, and a bumper was poured out for my lady. When we retired, she took from her work-drawer an enormous interminable piece of knitting; the young ladies began to play at cribbage with a dirty pack of cards. We had but one candle lighted, but it was in a magnificent old silver candlestick, and after a very few questions from my lady, I had my choice of amusement between a volume of sermons, and a pamphlet on the corn-laws, which Mr. Crawley had been reading before dinner.

So we sat for an hour until steps were heard.

'Put away the cards, girls,' cried my lady, in a great tremor; 'put down Mr. Crawley's books, Miss Sharp:' and these orders had been scarcely obeyed, when Mr. Crawley entered the room.

'We will resume yesterday's discourse, young ladies,' said he, 'and you shall each read a page by turns; so that Miss a – Miss Short may have an opportunity of hearing you;' and the poor girls began to spell a long dismal sermon delivered at Bethesda Chapel, Liverpool, on behalf of the mission for the Chickasaw Indians. Was it not a charming evening?

At ten the servants were told to call Sir Pitt and the household to prayers. Sir Pitt came in first, very much flushed, and rather unsteady in his gait; and after him the butler, the canaries, Mr. Crawley's man, three other men, smelling very much of the stable, and four women, one of whom, I remarked, was very much over-dressed, and who flung me a look of great scorn as she plumped down on her knees.

After Mr. Crawley had done haranguing and expounding, we received our candles, and then we went to bed; and then I was disturbed in my writing, as I have described to my dearest, sweetest Amelia.

Good night. A thousand thousand thousand kisses!

Saturday. – This morning, at five, I heard the shrieking of the little black pig. Rose and Violet introduced me to it yesterday; and to the stables, and to the kennel, and to the gardener, who was picking fruit to send to market, and from whom they begged hard a bunch of hot-house grapes; but he said that Sir Pitt had numbered every 'Man Jack' of them, and it would be as much as his place was worth to give any away. The darling girls caught a colt in a paddock, and asked me if I would ride, and began to ride themselves, when the groom, coming with horrid oaths, drove them away.

Lady Crawley is always knitting the worsted. Sir Pitt is always tipsy, every night; and, I believe, sits with Horrocks, the butler. Mr. Crawley always reads sermons in the evening; and in the morning is locked up in his study, or else rides to Mudbury, on county business, or to Squashmore, where he preaches, on Wednesdays and Fridays, to the tenants there.

A hundred thousand grateful loves to your dear papa and mamma. Is your poor brother recovered of his rack-punch? Oh, dear! Oh, dear! How men should beware of wicked punch!

> Ever and ever thine own,
> REBECCA.

Everything considered, I think it is quite as well for our dear Amelia Sedley, in Russell Square, that Miss Sharp and she are parted. Rebecca is a droll funny creature, to be sure; and those descriptions of the poor lady weeping for the loss of her beauty, and the gentleman 'with hay-coloured whiskers and straw-coloured hair', are very smart, doubtless, and show a great knowledge of the world. That she might, when on her knees, have been thinking of something better than Miss Horrocks's ribbons, has possibly struck both of us. But my kind reader will please to remember that this history has 'Vanity Fair' for a title, and that Vanity Fair is a very vain, wicked, foolish place, full of all sorts of humbugs and falsenesses and pretensions. And while the moralist, who is holding forth on the cover (an accurate portrait of your humble servant), professes to wear neither gown nor bands, but only the very same long-eared livery in which his congregation is arrayed: yet, look you, one is bound to speak the truth as far as one knows it, whether one mounts a cap and bells or a shovel-hat; and a deal of disagreeable matter must come out in the course of such an undertaking.

I have heard a brother of the story-telling trade, at Naples, preaching to a pack of good-for-nothing honest lazy fellows by the sea-shore, work himself up into such a rage and passion with some of the villains whose wicked deeds he was describing and inventing, that the audience could not resist it, and they and the poet together would burst out into a roar of oaths and execrations against the fictitious monster of the tale, so that the hat went round, and the bajocchi tumbled into it, in the midst of a perfect storm of sympathy.

At the little Paris theatres, on the other hand, you will not only hear the people yelling out 'Ah gredin! Ah monstre!' and cursing the tyrant of the play from the boxes; but the actors themselves positively refuse to play the wicked parts, such as those of infâmes Anglais, brutal Cossacks, and what not, and prefer to appear at a smaller salary, in their real characters as loyal Frenchmen. I set the two stories one against the other, so that you may see that it is not from mere mercenary motives that the present performer is desirous to show up and trounce his villains; but because he has a sincere hatred of them, which he cannot keep down, and which must find a vent in suitable abuse and bad language.

I warn my 'kyind friends', then, that I am going to tell a story of harrowing villany and complicated – but, as I trust, intensely interesting – crime. My rascals are no milk-and-water rascals, I promise you. When we come to the proper places we won't spare fine language – No, no! But when we are going over the quiet country we must perforce be calm. A tempest in a slop-basin is absurd. We will reserve that sort of thing for the mighty ocean and the lonely midnight. The present Number will be very mild. Others – but we will not anticipate *those*.

And, as we bring our characters forward, I will ask leave, as a man and a brother, not only to introduce them, but occasionally to step down from the platform, and talk about them: if they are good and kindly, to love them and shake them by the hand; if they are silly, to laugh at them confidentially in the reader's sleeve: if they are wicked and heartless, to abuse them in the strongest terms which politeness admits of.

Otherwise you might fancy it was I who was sneering at the practice of devotion, which Miss Sharp finds so ridiculous; that it was I who laughed good-humouredly at the reeling old Silenus of a baronet – whereas the laughter comes from one who has no reverence except for prosperity, and no eye for anything beyond success. Such people there are living and flourishing in the world – Faithless, Hopeless, Charityless: let us have at them, dear friends, with might and main. Some there are, and very successful too, mere quacks and fools: and it was to combat and expose such as those, no doubt, that Laughter was made.

CHAPTER IX

FAMILY PORTRAITS

S IR PITT CRAWLEY was a philosopher with a taste for what is called low life. His first marriage with the daughter of the noble Binkie had been made under the auspices of his parents; and as he often told Lady Crawley in her lifetime she was such a confounded quarrelsome high-bred jade that when she died he was hanged if he would ever take another of her sort, at her ladyship's demise he kept his promise, and selected for a second wife Miss Rose

Dawson, daughter of Mr. John Thomas Dawson, ironmonger, of Mudbury. What a happy woman was Rose to be my Lady Crawley!

Let us set down the items of her happiness. In the first place, she gave up Peter Butt, a young man who kept company with her, and in consequence of his disappointment in love took to smuggling, poaching, and a thousand other bad courses. Then she quarrelled, as in duty bound, with all the friends and intimates of her youth, who, of course, could not be received by my lady at Queen's Crawley – nor did she find in her new rank and abode any persons who were willing to welcome her. Who ever did? Sir Huddleston Fuddleston had three daughters who all hoped to be Lady Crawley. Sir Giles Wapshot's family were insulted that one of the Wapshot girls had not the preference in the marriage, and the remaining baronets of the county were indignant at their comrade's *mésalliance*. Never mind the commoners, whom we will leave to grumble anonymously.

Sir Pitt did not care, as he said, a brass farden for any one of them. He had his pretty Rose, and what more need a man require than to please himself? So he used to get drunk every night: to beat his pretty Rose sometimes: to leave her in Hampshire when he went to London for the parliamentary session, without a single friend in the wide world. Even Mrs. Bute Crawley, the rector's wife, refused to visit her, as she said she would never give the *pas* to a tradesman's daughter.

As the only endowments with which Nature had gifted Lady Crawley were those of pink cheeks and a white skin, and as she had no sort of character, nor talents, nor opinions, nor occupations, nor amusements, nor that vigour of soul and ferocity of temper which often falls to the lot of entirely foolish women, her hold upon Sir Pitt's affections was not very great. Her roses faded out of her cheeks, and the pretty freshness left her figure after the birth of a couple of children, and she became a mere machine in her husband's house, of no more use than the late Lady Crawley's grand piano. Being a light-complexioned woman, she wore light clothes, as most blondes will, and appeared, in preference, in draggled sea-green, or slatternly sky-blue. She worked that worsted day and night, or other pieces like it. She had counterpanes in the course of a few years to all the beds in

Crawley. She had a small flower-garden, for which she had rather an affection; but beyond this no other like or disliking. When her husband was rude to her she was apathetic: whenever he struck her she cried. She had not character enough to take to drinking, and moaned about, slip-shod and in curl-papers, all day. Oh, Vanity Fair – Vanity Fair! This might have been, but for you, a cheery lass; Peter Butt and Rose a happy man and wife, in a snug farm, with a hearty family, and an honest portion of pleasures, cares, hopes, and struggles: – but a title and a coach and four are toys more precious than happiness in Vanity Fair: and if Harry the Eighth or Bluebeard were alive now, and wanted a tenth wife, do you suppose he could not get the prettiest girl that shall be presented this season?

The languid dullness of their mamma did not, as it may be supposed, awaken much affection in her little daughters, but they were very happy in the servants' hall and in the stables; and the Scotch gardener having luckily a good wife and some good children, they got a little wholesome society and instruction in his lodge, which was the only education bestowed upon them until Miss Sharp came.

Her engagement was owing to the remonstrances of Mr. Pitt Crawley, the only friend or protector Lady Crawley ever had, and the only person, besides her children, for whom she entertained a little feeble attachment. Mr. Pitt took after the noble Binkies, from whom he was descended, and was a very polite and proper gentleman. When he grew to man's estate, and came back from Christchurch, he began to reform the slackened discipline of the hall, in spite of his father, who stood in awe of him. He was a man of such rigid refinement, that he would have starved rather than have dined without a white neckcloth. Once, when just from college, and when Horrocks the butler brought him a letter without placing it previously on a tray, he gave that domestic a look, and administered to him a speech so cutting, that Horrocks ever after trembled before him; the whole household bowed to him: Lady Crawley's curl-papers came off earlier when he was at home: Sir Pitt's muddy gaiters disappeared; and if that incorrigible old man still adhered to other old habits, he never fuddled himself with rum-and-water in his son's presence, and only talked to his servants in a very reserved and polite manner; and those persons remarked that Sir Pitt never swore at Lady Crawley while his son was in the room.

It was he who taught the butler to say 'My lady is served,' and who insisted on handing her ladyship into dinner. He seldom spoke to her, but when he did it was with the most powerful respect; and he never let her quit the apartment, without rising in the most stately manner to open the door, and making an elegant bow at her egress.

At Eton he was called Miss Crawley; and there, I am sorry to say, his younger brother Rawdon used to lick him violently. But though his parts were not brilliant, he made up for his lack of talent by meritorious industry, and was never known, during eight years at school, to be subject to that punishment which it is generally thought none but a cherub can escape.

At college his career was of course highly creditable. And here he prepared himself for public life, into which he was to be introduced by the patronage of his grandfather, Lord Binkie, by studying the ancient and modern orators with great assiduity, and by speaking unceasingly at the debating societies. But though he had a fine flux of words, and delivered his little voice with great pomposity and pleasure to himself, and never advanced any sentiment or opinion which was not perfectly trite and stale, and supported by a Latin quotation; yet he failed somehow, in spite of a mediocrity which ought to have insured any man a success. He did not even get the prize poem, which all his friends said he was sure of.

After leaving college he became Private Secretary to Lord Binkie, and was then appointed Attaché to the Legation at Pumpernickel, which post he filled with perfect honour, and brought home dispatches, consisting of Strasburg pie, to the Foreign Minister of the day. After remaining ten years Attaché (several years after the lamented Lord Binkie's demise), and finding the advancement slow, he at length gave up the diplomatic service in some disgust, and began to turn country gentleman.

He wrote a pamphlet on Malt on returning to England (for he was an ambitious man, and always liked to be before the public), and took a strong part in the Negro Emancipation question. Then he became a friend of Mr. Wilberforce's, whose politics he admired, and had that famous correspondence with the Reverend Silas Hornblower, on the Ashantee Mission. He was in London, if not for the Parliament session, at least in May, for the religious meetings. In the country he was a magistrate, and an active visitor and speaker among those destitute of religious instruction. He was said to be paying his addresses to Lady Jane Sheepshanks, Lord Southdown's third daughter, and whose sister, Lady Emily, wrote those sweet tracts, *The Sailor's True Binnacle*, and *The Applewoman of Finchley Common*.

Miss Sharp's accounts of his employment at Queen's Crawley were not caricatures. He subjected the servants there to the devotional exercises before mentioned, in which (and so much the better) he brought his father to join. He patronized an Independent meeting-house in Crawley parish, much to the indignation of his uncle the rector, and to the consequent delight of Sir Pitt, who was induced to go himself once or twice, which occasioned some violent sermons at Crawley parish church, directed point-blank at the baronet's old gothic pew there. Honest Sir Pitt, however, did not feel the force of these discourses, as he always took his nap during sermon-time.

Mr. Crawley was very earnest, for the good of the nation and of the Christian world, that the old gentleman should yield him up his place in Parliament; but this the elder constantly refused to do. Both were of course too prudent to give up the fifteen hundred a year which was brought in by the second seat (at this period filled by Mr. Quadroon, with carte-blanche on the Slave question); indeed the family estate was much embarrassed, and the income drawn from the borough was of great use to the house of Queen's Crawley.

It had never recovered the heavy fine imposed upon Walpole Crawley, first baronet, for peculation in the Tape and Sealing-Wax Office. Sir Walpole was a jolly fellow, eager to seize and to spend money ('*alieni appetens, sui profusus*,' as Mr. Crawley would remark with a sigh), and in his day beloved by all the county for the constant drunkenness and hospitality which was maintained at Queen's Crawley. The cellars were filled with burgundy then, the kennels with hounds, and the stables with gallant hunters; now, such horses as Queen's Crawley possessed went to plough, or ran in the 'Trafalgar' coach; and it was with a team of these very horses, on an off-day, that Miss Sharp was brought to the Hall; for, boor as he was, Sir Pitt was a stickler for his dignity while at home, and seldom drove out but with four horses, and, though he dined off boiled mutton, had always three footmen to serve it.

If mere parsimony would have made a man rich, Sir Pitt Crawley might have become very wealthy – if he had been an attorney in a country town, with no capital but his brains, it is very possible that he would have turned them to good account, and might have achieved for himself a very considerable influence and competency. But he was unluckily endowed with a good name and a large though encumbered estate, both of which went rather to injure than to advance him. He had a taste for law, which cost him many thousands yearly; and being a great deal too clever to be robbed, as he said, by any single agent, allowed his affairs to be mismanaged by a dozen, whom he all equally mistrusted. He was such a sharp landlord, that he could hardly find any but bankrupt tenants; and such a close farmer, as to grudge almost the seed to the ground, whereupon revengeful Nature grudged him the crops which she granted to more liberal husbandmen. He speculated in every possible way; he worked mines; bought canal-shares; horsed coaches; took government contracts, and was the busiest man and magistrate of his county. As he would not pay honest agents at his granite-quarry, he had the satisfaction of finding that four overseers ran away, and took fortunes with them to America. For want of proper precautions, his coal-mines filled with water: the government flung his contract of damaged beef upon his hands: and for his coach-horses, every mail proprietor in the kingdom knew that he lost more horses than any man in the country, from under-feeding and buying cheap. In disposition he was sociable, and far from being proud; nay, he rather preferred the society of a farmer or a horse-dealer to that of a gentleman, like my lord, his son: he was fond of drink, of swearing, of joking with the farmers' daughters: he was never known to give away a shilling or to do a good action, but was of a pleasant, sly, laughing mood, and would cut his joke, and drink his glass with a tenant and sell him up the next day; or have his laugh with the poacher he was transporting with equal good humour. His politeness for the fair sex has already been hinted at by Miss Rebecca Sharp

– in a word, the whole baronetage, peerage, commonage of England did not contain a more cunning, mean, selfish, foolish, disreputable old man. That blood-red hand of Sir Pitt Crawley's would be in anybody's pocket except his own; and it is with grief and pain that, as admirers of the British aristocracy, we find ourselves obliged to admit the existence of so many ill qualities in a person whose name is in *Debrett*.

One great cause why Mr. Crawley had such a hold over the affections of his father, resulted from money arrangements. The baronet owed his son a sum of money out of the jointure of his mother, which he did not find it convenient to pay; indeed he had an almost invincible repugnance to paying anybody, and could only be brought by force to discharge his debts. Miss Sharp calculated (for she became, as we shall hear speedily, inducted into most of the secrets of the family), that the mere payment of his creditors cost the honourable baronet several hundreds yearly; but this was a delight he could not forgo; he had a savage pleasure in making the poor wretches wait, and in shifting from court to court and from term to term the period of satisfaction. What's the good of being in Parliament, he said, if you must pay your debts? Hence, indeed, his position as a senator was not a little useful to him.

Vanity Fair – Vanity Fair! Here was a man, who could not spell, and did not care to read – who had the habits and the cunning of a boor: whose aim in life was pettifogging: who never had a taste, or emotion, or enjoyment, but what was sordid and foul; and yet he had rank, and honours, and power, somehow: and was a dignitary of the land, and a pillar of the state. He was high sheriff, and rode in a golden coach. Great ministers and statesmen courted him; and in Vanity Fair he had a higher place than the most brilliant genius or spotless virtue.

Sir Pitt had an unmarried half-sister who inherited her mother's large fortune, and though the baronet proposed to borrow this money of her on mortgage, Miss Crawley declined the offer, and preferred the security of the funds. She had signified, however, her intention of leaving her inheritance between Sir Pitt's second son and the family at the rectory, and had once or twice paid the debts of Rawdon

Crawley in his career at college and in the army. Miss Crawley was, in consequence, an object of great respect when she came to Queen's Crawley, for she had a balance at her banker's which would have made her beloved anywhere.

What a dignity it gives an old lady, that balance at the banker's! How tenderly we look at her faults, if she is a relative (and may every reader have a score of such), what a kind, good-natured old creature we find her! How the junior partner of Hobbs and Dobbs leads her smiling to the carriage with the lozenge upon it, and the fat wheezy coachman! How, when she comes to pay us a visit, we generally find an opportunity to let our friends know her station in the world! We say (and with perfect truth) I wish I had Miss MacWhirter's signature to a cheque for five thousand pounds. She wouldn't miss it, says your wife. She is my aunt, say you, in an easy careless way, when your friend asks if Miss MacWhirter is any relative? Your wife is perpetually sending her little testimonies of affection, your little girls work endless worsted baskets, cushions, and footstools for her. What a good fire there is in her room when she comes to pay you a visit, although your wife laces her stays without one! The house during her stay assumes a festive, neat, warm, jovial, snug appearance not visible at other seasons. You yourself, dear sir, forget to go to sleep after dinner, and find yourself all of a sudden (though you invariably lose) very fond of a rubber. What good dinners you have – game every day, Malmsey-Madeira, and no end of fish from London. Even the servants in the kitchen share in the general prosperity; and, somehow, during the stay of Miss MacWhirter's fat coachman, the beer is grown much stronger, and the consumption of tea and sugar in the nursery (where her maid takes her meals) is not regarded in the least. Is it so, or is it not so? I appeal to the middle classes. Ah, gracious powers! I wish you would send me an old aunt – a maiden aunt – an aunt with a lozenge on her carriage, and a front of light coffee-coloured hair – how my children should work work-bags for her, and my Julia and I would make her comfortable! Sweet, sweet vision! Foolish, foolish dream!

CHAPTER X

MISS SHARP BEGINS TO MAKE FRIENDS

A ND now, being received as a member of the amiable
family whose portraits we have sketched in the foregoing
pages, it became naturally Rebecca's duty to make herself,
as she said, agreeable to her benefactors, and to gain their
confidence to the utmost of her power. Who could not
admire this quality of gratitude in an unprotected orphan;
and if there entered some degree of selfishness into her
calculations, who can say but that her prudence was perfectly
justifiable? 'I am alone in the world,' said the friendless girl.
'I have nothing to look for but what my own labour can
bring me; and while that little pinkfaced chit Amelia, with
not half my sense, has ten thousand pounds and an establishment secure, poor Rebecca (and my figure is far better
than hers) has only herself and her own wits to trust to.
Well, let us see if my wits cannot provide me with an
honourable maintenance, and if some day or the other I
cannot show Miss Amelia my real superiority over her. Not
that I dislike poor Amelia: who can dislike such a harmless,
good-natured creature? – only it will be a fine day when I
can take my place above her in the world, as why, indeed,
should I not?' Thus it was that our little romantic friend
formed visions of the future for herself – nor must we be
scandalized that, in all her castles in the air, a husband was
the principal inhabitant. Of what else have young ladies to
think, but husbands? Of what else do their dear mammas
think? 'I must be my own mamma,' said Rebecca; not
without a tingling consciousness of defeat, as she thought
over her little misadventure with Jos Sedley.

So she wisely determined to render her position with the
Queen's Crawley family comfortable and secure, and to this
end resolved to make friends of every one around her who
could at all interfere with her comfort.

As my Lady Crawley was not one of these personages,
and a woman, moreover, so indolent and void of character
as not to be of the least consequence in her own house,
Rebecca soon found that it was not at all necessary to
cultivate her good will – indeed, impossible to gain it. She

used to talk to her pupils about their 'poor mamma'; and, though she treated that lady with every demonstration of cool respect, it was to the rest of the family that she wisely directed the chief part of her attentions.

With the young people, whose applause she thoroughly gained, her method was pretty simple. She did not pester their young brains with too much learning, but, on the contrary, let them have their own way in regard to educating themselves; for what instruction is more effectual than self-instruction? The eldest was rather fond of books, and as there was in the old library at Queen's Crawley a considerable provision of works of light literature of the last century, both in the French and English languages (they had been purchased by the Secretary of the Tape and Sealing-Wax Office at the period of his disgrace), and as nobody ever troubled the bookshelves but herself, Rebecca was enabled agreeably, and, as it were, in playing, to impart a great deal of instruction to Miss Rose Crawley.

She and Miss Rose thus read together many delightful French and English works, among which may be mentioned those of the learned Dr. Smollett, of the ingenious Mr. Henry Fielding, of the graceful and fantastic Monsieur Crébillon the younger, whom our immortal poet Gray so much admired, and of the universal Monsieur de Voltaire. Once, when Mr. Crawley asked what the young people were reading, the governess replied 'Smollett'. 'Oh, Smollett,' said Mr. Crawley, quite satisfied. 'His history is more dull, but by no means so dangerous as that of Mr. Hume. It is history you are reading?' 'Yes,' said Miss Rose; without, however, adding that it was the history of Mr. Humphry Clinker. On another occasion he was rather scandalized at finding his sister with a book of French plays; but as the governess remarked that it was for the purpose of acquiring the French idiom in conversation, he was fain to be content. Mr. Crawley, as a diplomatist, was exceedingly proud of his own skill in speaking the French language (for he was of the world still), and not a little pleased with the compliments which the governess continually paid him upon his proficiency.

Miss Violet's tastes were, on the contrary, more rude and boisterous than those of her sister. She knew the sequestered spots where the hens laid their eggs. She could climb a tree to rob the nests of the feathered songsters of their speckled spoils. And her pleasure was to ride the young colts, and to scour the plains like Camilla. She was the favourite of her father and of the stablemen. She was the darling, and withal the terror, of the cook; for she discovered the haunts of the jampots, and would attack them when they were within her reach. She and her sister were engaged in constant battles. Any of which peccadilloes if Miss Sharp discovered, she did not tell them to Lady Crawley, who would have told them to the father, or, worse, to Mr. Crawley; but promised not to tell if Miss Violet would be a good girl and love her governess.

With Mr. Crawley Miss Sharp was respectful and obedient. She used to consult him on passages of French which she could not understand, though her mother was a Frenchwoman, and which he would construe to her satisfaction: and, besides giving her his aid in profane literature, he was kind enough to select for her books of a more serious tendency, and address to her much of his conversation. She admired, beyond measure, his speech at the Quashimaboo-Aid Society; took an interest in his pamphlet on malt; was often affected, even to tears, by his discourses of an evening, and would say – 'Oh, thank you, sir,' with a sigh, and a look up to heaven, that made him occasionally condescend to shake hands with her. 'Blood is everything, after all,' would that aristocratic religionist say. 'How Miss Sharp is awakened by my words, when not one of the people here is touched. I am too fine for them – too delicate. I must familiarize my style – but she understands it. Her mother was a Montmorency.'

Indeed it was from this famous family, as it appears, that Miss Sharp, by the mother's side, was descended. Of course she did not say that her mother had been on the stage; it would have shocked Mr. Crawley's religious scruples. How many noble *emigrées* had this horrid revolution plunged in poverty! She had several stories about her ancestors ere she had been many months in the house; some of which Mr. Crawley happened to find in D'Hozier's dictionary, which was in the library, and which strengthened his belief in their truth, and in the high-breeding of Rebecca. Are we to suppose from this curiosity and prying into dictionaries, could our heroine suppose, that Mr. Crawley was interested in her? – no, only in a friendly way. Have we not stated that he was attached to Lady Jane Sheepshanks?

He took Rebecca to task once or twice about the propriety of playing at backgammon with Sir Pitt, saying that it was a godless amusement, and that she would be much better engaged in reading *Thrump's Legacy*, or *The Blind Washer-woman of Moorfields*, or any work of a more serious nature; but Miss Sharp said her dear mother used often to play the same game with the old Count de Trictrac and the venerable Abbé du Cornet, and so found an excuse for this and other worldly amusement.

But it was not only by playing at backgammon with the baronet that the little governess rendered herself agreeable to her employer. She found many different ways of being useful to him. She read over, with indefatigable patience, all those law papers, with which, before she came to Queen's Crawley, he had promised to entertain her. She volunteered to copy many of his letters, and adroitly altered the spelling of them so as to suit the usages of the present day. She became interested in everything appertaining to the estate, to the farm, the park, the garden, and the stables; and so delightful a companion was she, that the baronet would seldom take his after-breakfast walk without her (and the children of course), when she would give her advice as to the trees which were to be lopped in the shrubberies, the garden-beds to be dug, the crops which were to be cut, the horses which were to go to cart or plough. Before she had been a year at Queen's Crawley she had quite won the baronet's confidence; and the conversation at the dinner-table, which before used to be held between him and Mr. Horrocks the butler, was now almost exclusively between Sir Pitt and Miss Sharp. She was almost mistress of the house when Mr. Crawley was absent, but conducted herself in her new and exalted situation with such circumspection and modesty as not to offend the authorities of the kitchen and stable, among whom her behaviour was always exceedingly modest and affable. She was quite a different person from the haughty, shy, dissatisfied little girl whom we have known previously, and this change of temper proved great prudence, a sincere desire of amendment, or at any rate great moral courage on her part. Whether it was the heart which dictated this new system of complaisance and humility adopted by our Rebecca, is to be proved by her after-history. A system of hypocrisy, which lasts through whole years, is one seldom satisfactorily practised by a person of one-and-twenty; however, our readers will recollect, that, though young in years, our heroine was old in life and experience, and we have written to no purpose if they have not discovered that she was a very clever woman.

The elder and younger son of the house of Crawley were, like the gentleman and lady in the weather-box, never at home together – they hated each other cordially: indeed, Rawdon Crawley, the dragoon, had a great contempt for the establishment altogether, and seldom came thither except when his aunt paid her annual visit.

The great good quality of this old lady has been mentioned. She possessed seventy thousand pounds, and had almost adopted Rawdon. She disliked her elder nephew exceedingly, and despised him as a milksop. In return he did not hesitate to state that her soul was irretrievably lost, and was of opinion that his brother's chance in the next world was not a whit better. 'She is a godless woman of the world,' would Mr. Crawley say; 'she lives with atheists and Frenchmen. My mind shudders when I think of her awful, awful situation, and that, near as she is to the grave, she should be so given up to vanity, licentiousness, profaneness, and folly.' In fact, the old lady declined altogether to hear his hour's lecture of an evening; and when she came to Queen's Crawley alone, he was obliged to pretermit his usual devotional exercises.

'Shut up your sarmons, Pitt, when Miss Crawley comes down,' said his father; 'she has written to say that she won't stand the preachifying.'

'Oh, sir! consider the servants.'

'The servants be hanged,' said Sir Pitt; and his son thought even worse would happen were they deprived of the benefit of his instruction.

'Why, hang it, Pitt!' said the father to his remonstrance. 'You wouldn't be such a flat as to let three thousand a year go out of the family?'

'What is money compared to our souls, sir?' continued Crawley.

'You mean that the old lady won't leave the money to you?' – and who knows but it *was* Mr. Crawley's meaning?

Old Miss Crawley was certainly one of the reprobate. She had a snug little house in Park Lane, and, as she ate and drank a great deal too much during the season in London, she went to Harrogate or Cheltenham for the summer. She was the most hospitable and jovial of old vestals, and had been a beauty in her day, she said. (All old women were beauties once, we very well know.) She was a *bel esprit*, and a dreadful Radical for those days. She had been in France (where St. Just, they say, inspired her with an unfortunate passion), and loved, ever after, French novels, French cookery, and French wines. She read Voltaire, and had Rousseau by heart; talked very lightly about divorce, and most energetically of the rights of women. She had pictures of Mr. Fox in every room in the house: when that statesman was in opposition, I am not sure that she had not flung a main with him; and when he came into office, she took great credit for bringing over to him Sir Pitt and his colleague for Queen's Crawley, although Sir Pitt would have come over himself, without any trouble on the honest lady's part. It is needless to say that Sir Pitt was brought to change his views after the death of the great Whig statesman.

This worthy old lady took a fancy to Rawdon Crawley when a boy, sent him to Cambridge (in opposition to his brother at Oxford), and, when the young man was requested by the authorities of the first-named University to quit after a residence of two years, she bought him his commission in the Life Guards Green.

A perfect and celebrated 'blood', or dandy about town, was this young officer. Boxing, rat-hunting, the fives-court, and four-in-hand driving were then the fashion of our British aristocracy; and he was an adept in all these noble sciences. And though he belonged to the household troops, who, as it was their duty to rally round the Prince Regent, had not shown their valour in foreign service yet, Rawdon Crawley had already (à propos of play, of which he was immoderately fond) fought three bloody duels in which he gave ample proofs of his contempt for death.

'And for what follows after death,' would Mr. Crawley observe, throwing his gooseberry-coloured eyes up to the ceiling. He was always thinking of his brother's soul, or of the souls of those who differed with him in opinion: it is a sort of comfort which many of the serious give themselves.

Silly, romantic Miss Crawley, far from being horrified at the courage of her favourite, always used to pay his debts after his duels; and would not listen to a word that was whispered against his morality. 'He will sow his wild oats,' she would say, 'and is worth far more than that puling hypocrite of a brother of his.'

CHAPTER XI

ARCADIAN SIMPLICITY

B ESIDES these honest folks at the Hall (whose simplicity and sweet rural purity surely show the advantage of a country life over a town one), we must introduce the reader to their relatives and neighbours at the Rectory, Bute Crawley and his wife.

The Reverend Bute Crawley was a tall, stately, jolly, shovel-hatted man, far more popular in his county than the baronet his brother. At college he pulled stroke-oar in the Christchurch boat, and had thrashed all the best bruisers of the 'town'. He carried his taste for boxing and athletic exercises into private life; there was not a fight within twenty miles at which he was not present, nor a race, nor a coursing match, nor a regatta, nor a ball, nor an election, nor a visitation dinner, nor indeed a good dinner in the whole county, but he found means to attend it. You might see his bay mare and gig-lamps a score of miles away from his rectory house, whenever there was any dinner-party at Fuddleston, or at Roxby, or at Wapshot Hall, or at the great lords of the county, with all of whom he was intimate. He had a fine voice; sang 'A southerly wind and a cloudy sky'; and gave the 'whoop' in chorus with general applause. He rode to hounds in a pepper-and-salt frock, and was one of the best fishermen in the county.

Mrs. Crawley, the rector's wife, was a smart little body, who wrote this worthy divine's sermons. Being of a domestic turn, and keeping the house a great deal with her daughters, she ruled absolutely within the Rectory, wisely giving her husband full liberty without. He was welcome to come and go, and dine abroad as many days as his fancy dictated, for Mrs. Crawley was a saving woman and knew the price of port wine. Ever since Mrs. Bute carried off the young rector

of Queen's Crawley (she was of a good family, daughter of
the late Lieut.-Colonel Hector MacTavish, and she and her
mother played for Bute and won him at Harrogate), she had
been a prudent and thrifty wife to him. In spite of her care,
however, he was always in debt. It took him at least ten
years to pay off his college bills contracted during his father's
lifetime. In the year 179–, when he was just clear of these
incumbrances, he gave the odds of 100 to 1 (in twenties)
against Kangaroo, who won the Derby. The rector was
obliged to take up the money at a ruinous interest, and had
been struggling ever since. His sister helped him with a
hundred now and then, but of course his great hope was in
her death – when 'hang it' (as he would say), 'Matilda *must*
leave me half her money.'

So that the baronet and his brother had every reason
which two brothers possibly can have for being by the ears.
Sir Pitt had had the better of Bute in innumerable family
transactions. Young Pitt not only did not hunt, but set up
a meeting-house under his uncle's very nose. Rawdon, it was
known, was to come in for the bulk of Miss Crawley's
property. These money transactions – these speculations in
life and death – these silent battles for reversionary spoil –
make brothers very loving towards each other in Vanity Fair.
I, for my part, have known a five-pound note to interpose
and knock up a half-century's attachment between two
brethren; and can't but admire, as I think what a fine and
durable thing Love is among worldly people.

It cannot be supposed that the arrival of such a personage
as Rebecca at Queen's Crawley, and her gradual establishment in the good graces of all people there, could be
unremarked by Mrs. Bute Crawley. Mrs. Bute, who knew
how many days the sirloin of beef lasted at the Hall; how
much linen was got ready at the great wash; how many
peaches were on the south wall; how many doses her ladyship
took when she was ill – for such points are matters of intense
interest to certain persons in the country – Mrs. Bute, I say,
could not pass over the Hall governess without making every
inquiry respecting her history and character. There was
always the best understanding between the servants at the
Rectory and the Hall. There was always a good glass of ale
in the kitchen of the former place for the Hall people, whose
ordinary drink was very small – and, indeed, the rector's

lady knew exactly how much malt went to every barrel of Hall beer – ties of relationship existed between the Hall and Rectory domestics, as between their masters; and through these channels each family was perfectly well acquainted with the doings of the other. That, by the way, may be set down as a general remark. When you and your brother are friends, his doings are indifferent to you. When you have quarrelled, all his outgoings and incomings you know, as if you were his spy.

Very soon then after her arrival, Rebecca began to take a regular place in Mrs. Crawley's bulletin from the Hall. It was to this effect: – 'The black porker's killed – weighed x stone – salted the sides – pig's pudding and leg of pork for dinner. Mr. Cramp from Mudbury, over with Sir Pitt about putting John Blackmore in gaol – Mr. Pitt at meeting (with all the names of the people who attended) – my lady as usual – the young ladies with the governess.'

Then the report would come – the new governess be a rare manager – Sir Pitt be very sweet on her – Mr. Crawley too – He be reading tracts to her – 'What an abandoned wretch!' said little, eager, active, black-faced Mrs. Bute Crawley.

Finally, the reports were that the governess had 'come round' everybody, wrote Sir Pitt's letters, did his business, managed his accounts – had the upper hand of the whole house, my lady, Mr. Crawley, the girls and all – at which Mrs. Crawley declared she was an artful hussy, and had some dreadful designs in view. Thus the doings at the Hall were the great food for conversation at the Rectory, and Mrs. Bute's bright eyes spied out everything that took place in the enemy's camp – everything and a great deal besides.

Mrs. Bute Crawley to Miss Pinkerton, The Mall, Chiswick.

RECTORY, QUEEN'S CRAWLEY, December –.

MY DEAR MADAM, – Although it is so *many* years since I profited by your *delightful* and *invaluable* instructions, yet I have *ever* retained the *fondest* and *most reverential* regard for Miss Pinkerton, and *dear* Chiswick. I hope your health is *good*. The world and *the cause of education* cannot afford to lose Miss Pinkerton for *many many years*. When my friend, Lady Fuddleston, mentioned that her dear girls required an instructress (I am *too poor* to engage a governess for mine, but was I not educated at Chiswick?) – 'Who,' I exclaimed, 'can we consult but the excellent, the incomparable Miss Pinkerton?' In a word, have you, dear madam, any ladies on your list, whose services might be made available to my kind friend and neighbour? I assure you she will take no governess *but of your choosing.*

My dear husband is pleased to say that he likes *everything which comes from Miss Pinkerton's school.* How I wish I could present him and my beloved girls to the friend of my youth, and the *admired* of the great lexicographer of our country! If you ever travel into Hampshire, Mr. Crawley begs me to say, he hopes you will adorn our *rural rectory* with your presence. 'Tis the humble but happy home of

Your affectionate
M ARTHA   C RAWLEY.

PS. – Mr. Crawley's brother, the baronet, with whom we are not, alas! upon those terms of *unity* in which it *becomes brethren to dwell,* has a governess for his little girls, who, I am told, had the good fortune to be educated at Chiswick. I hear various reports of her; and as I have the tenderest interest in my dearest little nieces, whom I wish, in spite of family differences, to see among my own children – and as I long to be attentive to *any pupil of yours* – do, my dear Miss Pinkerton, tell me *the history* of this young lady, whom, for *your sake,* I am most anxious to befriend. – M. C.

Miss Pinkerton to Mrs. Bute Crawley.

J OHNSON   H OUSE , C HISWICK , December, 18 –.

D EAR   M ADAM . – I have the honour to acknowledge your polite communication, to which I promptly reply. 'Tis most gratifying to one in my most arduous position to find that my maternal cares have elicited a responsive affection; and to recognize in the amiable Mrs. Bute Crawley my excellent pupil of former years, *the sprightly and accomplished* Miss Martha MacTavish. I am happy to have under my charge now the daughters of many of those who were your contemporaries at my establishment – what pleasure it would give me if your own beloved young ladies had need of my instructive superintendence!

Presenting my respectful compliments to Lady Fuddleston, I have the honour (epistolarily) to introduce to her ladyship my two friends, Miss Tuffin and Miss Hawky.

Either of these young ladies is *perfectly qualified* to instruct in Greek, Latin, and the rudiments of Hebrew; in mathematics and history; in Spanish, French, Italian, and geography; in music, vocal and instrumental; in dancing, without the aid of a master; and in the elements of natural sciences. In the use of the globes both are proficients. In addition to these, Miss Tuffin, who is daughter of the late Reverend Thomas Tuffin (Fellow of Corpus College, Cambridge), can instruct in the Syriac language, and the elements of Constitutional law. But as she is only eighteen years of age, and of exceedingly pleasing personal appearance, perhaps this young lady may be objectionable in Sir Huddleston Fuddleston's family.

Miss Letitia Hawky, on the other hand, is not personally well-favoured. She is twenty-nine; her face is much pitted with the small-pox. She has a halt in her gait, red hair, and a trifling obliquity of vision. Both ladies are endowed with *every moral and religious virtue*. Their terms, of course, are such as their accomplishments merit. With my most grateful respects to the Reverend Bute Crawley, I have the honour to be, Dear Madam,

> Your most faithful and obedient servant,
> BARBARA PINKERTON.

PS. – The Miss Sharp, whom you mention as governess to Sir Pitt Crawley, Bart., M.P., was a pupil of mine, and I have nothing to say in her disfavour. Though her appearance is disagreeable, we cannot control the operations of nature: and though her parents were disreputable (her father being a painter, several times bankrupt; and her mother, as I have since learned, with horror, a dancer at the Opera); yet her talents are considerable, and I cannot regret that I received her *out of charity*. My dread is, lest the principles of the mother – who was represented to me as a French countess, forced to emigrate in the late revolutionary horrors; but who, as I have since found, was a person of the *very lowest order and morals* – should at any time prove to be *hereditary* in the unhappy young woman whom I took as *an outcast*. But her principles have *hitherto* been correct (I believe), and I am sure nothing will occur to injure them in the elegant and refined circle of the eminent Sir Pitt Crawley.

Miss Rebecca Sharp to Miss Amelia Sedley.

I have not written to my beloved Amelia for these many weeks past, for what news was there to tell of the sayings and doings at Humdrum Hall, as I have christened it; and what do you care whether the turnip crop is good or bad; whether the fat pig weighed thirteen stone or fourteen; and whether the beasts thrive well upon mangel-wurzel? Every day since I last wrote has been like its neighbour. Before breakfast, a walk with Sir Pitt and his spud; after breakfast, studies (such as they are) in the schoolroom; reading and writing about lawyers, leases, coal-mines, canals, with Sir Pitt (whose secretary I am become); after dinner, Mr. Crawley's discourses or the baronet's backgammon; during both of which amusements my lady looks on with equal placidity. She has become rather more interesting by being ailing of late, which has brought a new visitor to the Hall, in the person of a young doctor. Well, my dear, young women need never despair. The young doctor gave a certain friend of yours to understand that, if she chose to be Mrs. Glauber, she was welcome to ornament the surgery! I told his impudence that the gilt pestle and mortar was quite ornament enough; as if I was born, indeed, to be a country surgeon's wife! Mr. Glauber went home seriously indisposed at his rebuff, took a cooling draught, and is now quite cured. Sir Pitt applauded my resolution highly; he would be sorry to lose his little secretary, I think; and I believe the old wretch likes me as much as it is in his nature to like any one. Marry, indeed! and with a country apothecary, after – No, no, one cannot so soon forget old associations, about which I will talk no more. Let us return to Humdrum Hall.

For some time past it is Humdrum Hall no longer. My dear, Miss Crawley has arrived with her fat horses, fat servants, fat spaniel – the great rich Miss Crawley, with seventy thousand pounds in the five per cents., whom, or I had better say *which*, her two brothers adore. She looks very apoplectic, the dear soul; no wonder her brothers are anxious about her. You should see them struggling to settle her cushions, or to hand her coffee! 'When I come into the country,' she says (for she has a great deal of humour), 'I leave my toady, Miss Briggs, at home. My brothers are my toadies here, my dear, and a pretty pair they are!'

When she comes into the country our Hall is thrown open, and for a month, at least, you would fancy old Sir Walpole was come to life again. We have dinner-parties, and drive out in the coach-and-four – the footmen put on their newest canary-coloured liveries; we drink claret and champagne as if we were accustomed to it every day. We have wax-candles in the schoolroom, and fires to warm ourselves with. Lady Crawley is made to put on the brightest pea-green in her wardrobe, and my pupils leave off their thick shoes and tight old tartan pelisses, and wear silk stockings and muslin frocks, as fashionable baronets' daughters should. Rose came in yesterday in a sad plight – the Wiltshire sow (an enormous pet of hers) ran her down, and destroyed a most lovely flowered lilac silk dress by dancing over it – had this happened a week ago, Sir Pitt would have sworn frightfully, have boxed the poor wretch's ears, and put her upon bread and water for a month. All he said was, 'I'll serve you out, miss, when your aunt's gone,' and laughed off the accident as quite trivial. Let us hope his wrath will have passed away before Miss Crawley's departure. I hope so, for Miss Rose's sake, I am sure. What a charming reconciler and peacemaker money is!

Another admirable effect of Miss Crawley and her seventy thousand pounds is to be seen in the conduct of the two brothers Crawley. I mean the baronet and the rector, not *our* brothers – but the former, who hate each other all the year round become quite loving at Christmas. I wrote to you last year how the abominable horse-racing rector was in the habit of preaching clumsy sermons at us at church, and how Sir Pitt snored in answer. When Miss Crawley arrives there is no such thing as quarrelling heard of – the Hall visits the Rectory, and vice versa – the parson and the baronet talk about the pigs and the poachers, and the county business, in the most affable manner, and without quarrelling in their cups, I believe – indeed Miss Crawley won't hear of their quarrelling, and vows that she will leave her money to the Shropshire Crawleys if they offend her. If they were clever people, those Shropshire Crawleys, they might have it all, I think; but the Shropshire Crawley is a clergyman like his Hampshire cousin, and mortally offended Miss Crawley (who had fled thither in a fit of rage against her impracticable brethren) by some strait-laced notions of morality. He would have prayers in the house, I believe.

Our sermon-books are shut up when Miss Crawley arrives, and Mr. Pitt, whom she abominates, finds it convenient to go to town. On the other hand, the young dandy – 'blood,' I believe, is the term – Captain Crawley makes his appearance, and I suppose you would like to know what sort of a person he is.

Well, he is a very large young dandy. He is six feet high, and speaks with a great voice; and swears a great deal; and orders about the servants, who all adore him nevertheless; for he is very generous of his money, and the domestics will do anything for him. Last week the keepers almost killed a bailiff and his man who came down from London to arrest the captain, and who were found lurking about the park wall – they beat them, ducked them, and were going to shoot them for poachers, but the baronet interfered.

The captain has a hearty contempt for his father, I can see, and calls him an old *put*, an old *snob*, an old *chaw-bacon*, and numberless other pretty names. He has a *dreadful reputation* among the ladies. He brings his hunters home with him, lives with the squires of the county, asks whom he pleases to dinner, and Sir Pitt dares not say no, for fear of offending Miss Crawley, and missing his legacy when she dies of her apoplexy. Shall I tell you a compliment the captain paid me? I must, it is so pretty. One evening we actually had a dance; there was Sir Huddleston Fuddleston and his family, Sir Giles Wapshot and his young ladies, and I don't know how many more. Well, I heard him say – 'By Jove, she's a neat little filly!' meaning your humble servant; and he did me the honour to dance two country-dances with me. He gets on pretty gaily with the young squires, with whom he drinks, bets, rides, and talks about hunting and shooting; but he says the country girls are *bores:* indeed, I don't think he is far wrong. You should see the contempt with which they look down on poor me! When they dance I sit and play the piano very demurely; but the other night coming in rather flushed from the dining-room, and seeing me employed in this way, he swore out loud that I was the best dancer in the room, and took a great oath that he would have the fiddlers from Mudbury.

'I'll go and play a country-dance,' said Mrs. Bute Crawley, very readily (she is a little, black-faced old woman in a turban, rather crooked, and with very twinkling eyes); and after the captain and your poor little Rebecca had performed a dance together, do you know she actually did me the honour to compliment me upon my steps! Such a thing was never heard of before; the proud Mrs. Bute Crawley, first

cousin to the Earl of Tiptoff, who won't condescend to visit Lady
Crawley, except when her sister is in the country. Poor Lady Crawley!
during most part of these gaieties, she is upstairs taking pills.

Mrs. Bute has all of a sudden taken a great fancy to me. 'My dear
Miss Sharp,' she says, 'why not bring over your girls to the Rectory?
– their cousins will be so happy to see them.' I know what she means.
Signor Clementi did not teach us the piano for nothing; at which price
Mrs. Bute hopes to get a professor for her children. I can see through
her schemes, as though she told them to me; but I shall go, as I am
determined to make myself agreeable – is it not a poor governess's
duty, who has not a friend or protector in the world? The rector's
wife paid me a score of compliments about the progress my pupils
made, and thought, no doubt, to touch my heart – poor, simple,
country soul! – as if I cared a fig about my pupils!

Your India muslin and your pink silk, dearest Amelia, are said to
become me very well. They are a good deal worn now; but, you know,
we poor girls can't afford *des fraiches toilettes*. Happy, happy you! who
have but to drive to St. James's Street, and a dear mother who will
give you anything you ask. Farewell, dearest girl.

> Your affectionate
> REBECCA.

PS. – I wish you could have seen the faces of the Miss Blackbrooks
(Admiral Blackbrook's daughters, my dear): fine young ladies, with
dresses from London, when Captain Rawdon selected poor me for a
partner! Here they are. 'Tis the very image of them. Adieu, adieu!

When Mrs. Bute Crawley (whose artifices our ingenious
Rebecca had so soon discovered) had procured from Miss
Sharp the promise of a visit, she induced the all-powerful
Miss Crawley to make the necessary application to Sir Pitt,
and the good-natured old lady, who loved to be gay herself,
and to see every one gay and happy round about her, was
quite charmed, and ready to establish a reconciliation and
intimacy between her two brothers. It was therefore agreed
that the young people of both families should visit each other
frequently for the future, and the friendship of course lasted
as long as the jovial old mediatrix was there to keep the
peace.

'Why did you ask that scoundrel, Rawdon Crawley, to
dine?' said the rector to his lady, as they were walking home
through the park. '*I* don't want the fellow. He looks down
upon us country people as so many blackamoors. He's never
content unless he gets my yellow-sealed wine, which costs

me ten shillings a bottle, hang him! Besides, he's such an infernal character – he's a gambler – he's a drunkard – he's a profligate in every way. He's shot a man in a duel – he's over head and ears in debt, and he's robbed me and mine of the best part of Miss Crawley's fortune. Waxy says she has him' – here the rector shook his fist at the moon, with something very like an oath, and added, in a melancholious tone – '—, down in her will for fifty thousand; and there won't be above thirty to divide.'

'I think she's going,' said the rector's wife. 'She was very red in the face when we left dinner. I was obliged to unlace her.'

'She drank seven glasses of champagne,' said the reverend gentleman, in a low voice; 'and filthy champagne it is, too, that my brother poisons us with – but you women never know what's what.'

'We know nothing,' said Mrs. Bute Crawley.

'She drank cherry-brandy after dinner,' continued his reverence, 'and took curaçao with her coffee. *I* wouldn't take a glass for a five-pound note: it kills me with heartburn. She can't stand it, Mrs. Crawley – she must go – flesh and blood won't bear it! and I lay five to two, Matilda drops in a year.'

Indulging in these solemn speculations, and thinking about his debts, and his son Jim at college, and Frank at Woolwich, and the four girls, who were no beauties, poor things, and would not have a penny but what they got from the aunt's expected legacy, the rector and his lady walked on for a while.

'Pitt can't be such an infernal villain as to sell the reversion of the living. And that Methodist milksop of an eldest son looks to Parliament,' continued Mr. Crawley, after a pause.

'Sir Pitt Crawley will do anything,' said the rector's wife. 'We must get Miss Crawley to make him promise it to James.'

'Pitt will promise anything,' replied the brother. 'He promised he'd pay my college bills, when my father died; he promised he'd build the new wing to the Rectory; he promised he'd let me have Jibb's field and the Six-acre Meadow – and much he executed his promises! And it's to this man's son – this scoundrel, gambler, swindler, murderer of a Rawdon Crawley, that Matilda leaves the bulk of her money. I say it's unchristian. By Jove, it is. The infamous dog has got every vice except hypocrisy, and that belongs to his brother.'

'Hush, my dearest love! we're in Sir Pitt's grounds,' interposed his wife.

'I say he *has* got every vice, Mrs. Crawley. Don't, ma'am, bully *me*. Didn't he shoot Captain Marker? Didn't he rob young Lord Dovedale at the "Cocoa-Tree"? Didn't he cross the fight between Bill Soames and the Cheshire Trump, by which I lost forty pound? You know he did; and as for the women, why, you heard that before me, in my own magistrate's room —'

'For Heaven's sake, Mr. Crawley,' said the lady, 'spare me the details.'

'And you ask this villain into your house!' continued the exasperated rector. 'You, the mother of a young family – the wife of a clergyman of the Church of England. By Jove!'

'Bute Crawley, you are a fool,' said the rector's wife, scornfully.

'Well, ma'am, fool or not – and I don't say, Martha, I'm so clever as *you* are. I never did. But I won't meet Rawdon Crawley, that's flat. I'll go over to Huddleston, that I will, and see his black greyhound, Mrs. Crawley; and I'll run Lancelot against him for fifty. By Jove, I will; or against any dog in England. But I won't meet that beast Rawdon Crawley.'

'Mr. Crawley, you are intoxicated, as usual,' replied his wife. And the next morning, when the rector woke, and called for small beer, she put him in mind of his promise to visit Sir Huddleston Fuddleston, on Saturday, and as he knew he should have a *wet night*, it was agreed that he might gallop back again in time for church on Sunday morning. Thus it will be seen that the parishioners of Crawley were equally happy in their squire and in their rector.

Miss Crawley had not long been established at the Hall before Rebecca's fascinations had won the heart of that good-natured London rake, as they had of the country innocents whom we have been describing. Taking her accustomed drive, one day, she thought fit to order that 'that little governess' should accompany her to Mudbury. Before they had returned Rebecca had made a conquest of her; having made her laugh four times, and amused her during the whole of the little journey.

'Not let Miss Sharp dine at table!' said she to Sir Pitt, who had arranged a dinner of ceremony, and asked all the neighbouring baronets. 'My dear creature, do you suppose I can talk about the nursery with Lady Fuddleston, or discuss justices' business with that goose, old Sir Giles Wapshot? I insist upon Miss Sharp appearing. Let Lady Crawley remain upstairs, if there is no room. But little Miss Sharp! Why, she's the only person fit to talk to in the county!'

Of course, after such a peremptory order as this, Miss Sharp, the governess, received commands to dine with the illustrious company below stairs. And when Sir Huddleston had, with great pomp and ceremony, handed Miss Crawley into dinner, and was preparing to take his place by her side, the old lady cried out, in a shrill voice, 'Becky Sharp! Miss Sharp! Come you and sit by me and amuse me; and let Sir Huddleston sit by Lady Wapshot.'

When the parties were over, and the carriages had rolled away, the insatiable Miss Crawley would say, 'Come to my dressing-room, Becky, and let us abuse the company,' – which, between them, this pair of friends did perfectly. Old Sir Huddleston wheezed a great deal at dinner; Sir Giles Wapshot had a particularly noisy manner of imbibing his soup, and her ladyship a wink of the left eye; all of which Becky caricatured to admiration; as well as the particulars of the night's conversation; the politics; the war; the quarter-sessions; the famous run with the H. H., and those heavy and dreary themes, about which country gentlemen converse. As for the Misses Wapshot's toilettes and Lady Fuddleston's famous yellow hat, Miss Sharp tore them to tatters, to the infinite amusement of her audience.

'My dear, you are a perfect *trouvaille*,' Miss Crawley would say. 'I wish you could come to me in London, but I couldn't make a butt of you as I do of poor Briggs – no, no, you little sly creature; you are too clever – Isn't she, Firkin?'

Mrs. Firkin (who was dressing the very small remnant of hair which remained on Miss Crawley's pate) flung up her head and said, 'I think miss *is* very clever,' with the most killing sarcastic air. In fact, Mrs. Firkin had that natural jealousy which is one of the main principles of every honest woman.

After rebuffing Sir Huddleston Fuddleston, Miss Crawley ordered that Rawdon Crawley should lead her in to dinner every day, and that Becky should follow with her cushion – or else she would have Becky's arm and Rawdon with the pillow. 'We must sit together,' she said. 'We're the only three Christians in the country, my love' – in which case, it must be confessed, that religion was at a very low ebb in the country of Hants.

Besides being such a fine religionist, Miss Crawley was, as we have said, an ultra-liberal in opinions and always took occasion to express these in the most candid manner.

'What is birth, my dear?' she would say to Rebecca – 'Look at my brother Pitt; look at the Huddlestons, who have been here since Henry II; look at poor Bute at the parsonage; – are any one of them equal to you in intelligence or breeding? Equal to *you* – they are not even equal to poor dear Briggs, my companion, or Bowls, my butler. You, my love, are a little paragon – positively a little jewel – You have more brains than half the shire – if merit had its reward, you ought to be a duchess – no, there ought to be no duchesses at all – but you ought to have no superior, and I consider you, my love, as my equal in every respect; and – will you put some coals on the fire, my dear; and will you pick this dress of mine, and alter it, you who can do it so well?' So this old philanthropist used to make her equal run of her errands, execute her millinery, and read her to sleep with French novels, every night.

At this time, as some old readers may recollect, the genteel world had been thrown into a considerable state of excitement, by two events, which, as the papers say, might give employment to the gentlemen of the long robe. Ensign Shafton had run away with Lady Barbara Fitzurse, the Earl of Bruin's daughter and heiress; and poor Vere Vane, a gentleman who, up to forty, had maintained a most respectable character and reared a numerous family, suddenly and outrageously left his home, for the sake of Mrs. Rougemont, the actress, who was sixty-five years of age.

'That was the most beautiful part of dear Lord Nelson's character,' Miss Crawley said. 'He went to the deuce for a woman. There *must* be good in a man who will do that. I adore all imprudent matches. – What I like best, is for a nobleman to marry a miller's daughter as Lord Flowerdale did – it makes all the women so angry – I wish some great man would run away with *you*, my dear; I'm sure you're pretty enough.'

'Two postboys! – Oh, it would be delightful!' Rebecca owned.

'And what I like next best, is, for a poor fellow to run away with a rich girl. I have set my heart on Rawdon running away with some one.'

'A rich someone, or a poor someone?'

'Why, you goose! Rawdon has not a shilling but what I give him. He is *criblé de dettes* – he must repair his fortunes, and succeed in the world.'

'Is he very clever?' Rebecca asked.

'Clever, my love? – not an idea in the world beyond his horses, and his regiment, and his hunting, and his play; but he must succeed – he's so delightfully wicked. Don't you know he has hit a man, and shot an injured father through the hat only? He's adored in his regiment; and all the young men at Wattier's and the "Cocoa-Tree" swear by him.'

When Miss Rebecca Sharp wrote to her beloved friend the account of the little ball at Queen's Crawley, and the manner in which, for the first time, Captain Crawley had distinguished her, she did not, strange to relate, give an altogether accurate account of the transaction. The captain had distinguished her a great number of times before. The captain had met her in a half-score of walks. The captain had lighted upon her in a half-hundred of corridors and passages. The captain had hung over her piano twenty times of an evening (my lady was now upstairs, being ill, and nobody heeded her), as Miss Sharp sang. The captain had written her notes (the best that the great blundering dragoon could devise and spell; but dullness gets on as well as any other quality with women). But when he put the first of the notes into the leaves of the song she was singing, the little governess, rising and looking him steadily in the face, took up the triangular missive daintily, and waved it about as if it were a cocked hat, and she, advancing to the enemy, popped the note into the fire, and made him a very low curtsy, and went back to her place, and began to sing away again more merrily than ever.

'What's that?' said Miss Crawley, interrupted in her after-dinner doze by the stoppage of the music.

'It's a false note,' Miss Sharp said, with a laugh; and Rawdon Crawley fumed with rage and mortification.

Seeing the evident partiality of Miss Crawley for the new governess, how good it was of Mrs. Bute Crawley not to be jealous, and to welcome the young lady to the Rectory, and not only her, but Rawdon Crawley, her husband's rival in the Old Maid's five per cents! They became very fond of each other's society, Mrs. Crawley and her nephew. He gave up hunting: he declined entertainments at Fuddleston: he would not dine with the mess of the dépôt at Mudbury: his great pleasure was to stroll over to Crawley parsonage – whither Miss Crawley came too; and as their mamma was ill, why not the children with Miss Sharp? So the children (little dears!) came with Miss Sharp; and of an evening some of the party would walk back together. Not Miss Crawley – she preferred her carriage – but the walk over the Rectory fields, and in at the little park wicket, and through the dark plantation, and up the chequered avenue to Queen's Crawley, was charming in the moonlight to two such lovers of the picturesque as the captain and Miss Rebecca.

'Oh, those stars, those stars!' Miss Rebecca would say, turning her twinkling green eyes up towards them. 'I feel myself almost a spirit when I gaze upon them.'

'Oh – ah – Gad – yes, so do I exactly, Miss Sharp,' the other enthusiast replied. 'You don't mind my cigar, do you, Miss Sharp?' Miss Sharp loved the smell of a cigar out of doors beyond everything in the world – and she just tasted one too, in the prettiest way possible, and gave a little puff, and a little scream, and a little giggle, and restored the delicacy to the captain; who twirled his moustache, and straightway puffed it into a blaze that glowed quite red in the dark plantation, and swore – 'Jove – aw – Gad – aw – it's the finest segaw I ever smoked in the world – aw,' – for his intellect and conversation were alike brilliant and becoming to a heavy young dragoon.

Old Sir Pitt, who was taking his pipe and beer, and talking to John Horrocks about a 'ship' that was to be killed, espied the pair so occupied from his study-window, and with dreadful oaths swore that if it wasn't for Miss Crawley, he'd take Rawdon and bundle un out of doors, like a rogue as he was.

'He *be* a bad 'n, sure enough,' Mr. Horrocks remarked; 'and his man Flethers is wuss, and have made such a row in the housekeeper's room about the dinners and hale, as no lord would make – but I think Miss Sharp's a match for 'n, Sir Pitt,' he added, after a pause.

And so, in truth, she was – for father and son too.

CHAPTER XII

QUITE A SENTIMENTAL CHAPTER

WE must now take leave of Arcadia, and those amiable people practising the rural virtues there, and travel back to London, to inquire what has become of Miss Amelia.

'We don't care a fig for her,' writes some unknown correspondent with a pretty little handwriting and a pink seal to her note. 'She is *fade* and insipid,' and adds some more kind remarks in this strain, which I should never have repeated at all, but that they are in truth prodigiously complimentary to the young lady whom they concern.

Has the beloved reader, in his experience of society, never heard similar remarks by good-natured female friends; who always wonder what you *can* see in Miss Smith that is so fascinating; or what *could* induce Major Jones to propose for that silly insignificant simpering Miss Thompson, who has nothing but her wax-doll face to recommend her? What is there in a pair of pink cheeks and blue eyes, forsooth? these dear moralists ask, and hint wisely that the gifts of genius, the accomplishments of the mind, the mastery of *Mangnall's Questions*, and a ladylike knowledge of botany and geology, the knack of making poetry, the power of rattling sonatas in the Herz-manner, and so forth, are far more valuable endowments for a female, than those fugitive charms which a few years will inevitably tarnish. It is quite edifying to hear women speculate upon the worthlessness and the duration of beauty.

But though virtue is a much finer thing, and those hapless creatures who suffer under the misfortune of good looks ought to be continually put in mind of the fate which awaits them; and though, very likely, the heroic female character which ladies admire is a more glorious and beautiful object than the kind, fresh, smiling, artless, tender little domestic goddess, whom men are inclined to worship – yet the latter and inferior sort of women must have this consolation – that the men *do* admire them after all; and that, in spite of all our kind friends' warnings and protests, we go on in our desperate error and folly, and shall to the end of the chapter. Indeed, for my own part, though I have been repeatedly told by persons for whom I have the greatest respect, that Miss Brown is an insignificant chit, and Mrs. White has nothing but her *petit minois chiffonné*, and Mrs. Black has not a word to say for herself; yet I know that I have had the most delightful conversations with Mrs. Black (of course, my dear madam, they are inviolable): I see all the men in a cluster round Mrs. White's chair: all the young fellows battling to dance with Miss Brown; and so I am tempted to think that to be despised by her sex is a very great compliment to a woman.

The young ladies in Amelia's society did this for her very satisfactorily. For instance, there was scarcely any point upon which the Miss Osbornes, George's sisters, and the Mesdemoiselles Dobbin agreed so well as in their estimate of her very trifling merits: and their wonder that their brothers could find any charms in her. 'We are kind to her,' the Misses Osborne said, a pair of fine black-browed young ladies who had had the best of governesses, masters, and milliners; and they treated her with such extreme kindness and condescension, and patronized her so insufferably, that the poor little thing *was* in fact perfectly dumb in their presence, and to all outward appearance as stupid as they thought her. She made efforts to like them, as in duty bound, and as sisters of her future husband. She passed 'long mornings' with them – the most dreary and serious of forenoons. She drove out solemnly in their great family coach with them, and Miss Wirt their governess, that rawboned Vestal. They took her to the ancient concerts by way of a treat, and to the oratorio, and to St. Paul's to see the charity children, where in such terror was she of her friends, she almost did not dare be affected by the hymn the children sang. Their house was comfortable; their papa's table rich and handsome; their society solemn and genteel; their self-respect prodigious; they had the best pew at the Foundling; all their habits were pompous and orderly, and all their amusements intolerably dull and decorous. After every one of her visits (and oh how glad she was when they were over!)

Miss Osborne and Miss Maria Osborne, and Miss Wirt, the vestal governess, asked each other with increased wonder, 'What *could* George find in that creature?'

How is this? some carping reader exclaims. How is it that Amelia, who had such a number of friends at school, and was so beloved there, comes out into the world and is spurned by her discriminating sex? My dear sir, there were no men at Miss Pinkerton's establishment except the old dancing-master; and you would not have had the girls fall out about *him*? When George, their handsome brother, ran off directly after breakfast, and dined from home half a dozen times a week; no wonder the neglected sisters felt a little vexation. When young Bullock (of the firm of Hulker, Bullock & Co., Bankers, Lombard Street) who had been making up to Miss Maria the last two seasons, actually asked Amelia to dance the cotillon, could you expect that the former young lady should be pleased? And yet she said she was, like an artless forgiving creature. 'I'm so delighted you like dear Amelia,' she said quite eagerly to Mr. Bullock after the dance. 'She's engaged to my brother George; there's not much in her, but she's the best-natured and most unaffected young creature: at home we're all *so* fond of her.' Dear girl! who can calculate the depth of affection expressed in that enthusiastic *so*?

Miss Wirt and these two affectionate young women so earnestly and frequently impressed upon George Osborne's mind the enormity of the sacrifice he was making, and his romantic generosity in throwing himself away upon Amelia, that I'm not sure but that he really thought he was one of the most deserving characters in the British army, and gave himself up to be loved with a good deal of easy resignation.

Somehow, although he left home every morning, as was stated, and dined abroad six days in the week, when his sister believed the infatuated youth to be at Miss Sedley's apron-strings: he was *not* always with Amelia, whilst the world supposed him at her feet. Certain it is that on more occasions than one, when Captain Dobbin called to look for his friend, Miss Osborne (who was very attentive to the captain, and anxious to hear his military stories, and to know about the health of his dear mamma), Miss Osborne would laughingly point to the opposite side of the square, and say, 'Oh, you must go to the Sedleys' to ask for George; *we* never see him from morning till night.' At which kind of speech the captain would laugh in rather an absurd constrained manner, and turn off the conversation, like a consummate man of the world, to some topic of general interest, such as the opera, the prince's last ball at Carlton House, or the weather – that blessing to society.

'What an innocent it is, that pet of yours,' Miss Maria would then say to Miss Jane, upon the captain's departure. 'Did you see how he blushed at the mention of poor George on duty?'

'It's a pity Frederick Bullock hadn't some of his modesty, Maria,' replies the elder sister, with a toss of her head.

'Modesty! Awkwardness you mean, Jane. I don't want Frederick to trample a hole in my muslin frock, as Captain Dobbin did in yours at Mrs. Perkins's.'

'In *your* frock, he, he! How could he? Wasn't he dancing with Amelia?'

The fact is, when Captain Dobbin blushed so, and looked so awkward, he remembered a circumstance of which he did not think it was necessary to inform the young ladies, viz., that he had been calling at Mr. Sedley's house already, on the pretence of seeing George, of course, and George wasn't there, only poor little Amelia, with rather a sad wistful face, seated near the drawing-room window, who, after some very trifling stupid talk, ventured to ask, was there any truth in the report that the regiment was soon to be ordered abroad; and had Captain Dobbin seen Mr. Osborne that day?

The regiment was not ordered abroad as yet; and Captain Dobbin had not seen George. 'He was with his sister, most likely,' the captain said. 'Should he go and fetch the truant?' So she gave him her hand kindly and gratefully: and he crossed the square; and she waited and waited, but George never came.

Poor little tender heart! and so it goes on hoping and beating, and longing and trusting. You see it is not much of a life to describe. There is not much of what you call incident in it. Only one feeling all day – when will he come? only one thought to sleep and wake upon. I believe George was playing billiards with Captain Cannon in Swallow Street at the time when Amelia was asking Captain Dobbin about him; for George was a jolly sociable fellow, and excellent in all games of skill.

Once, after three days of absence, Miss Amelia put on her bonnet, and actually invaded the Osborne house. 'What! leave our brother to come to us?' said the young ladies. 'Have you had a quarrel, Amelia? Do tell us!' No, indeed, there had been no quarrel. 'Who could quarrel with him?' says she, with her eyes filled with tears. She only came over to – to see her dear friends; they had not met for so long. And this day she was so perfectly stupid and awkward, that the Miss Osbornes and their governess, who stared after her as she went sadly away, wondered more than ever what George could see in poor little Amelia.

Of course they did. How was she to bare that timid little heart for the inspection of those young ladies with their bold black eyes? It was best that it should shrink and hide itself. I know the Miss Osbornes were excellent critics of a Cashmere shawl, or a pink satin slip; and when Miss Turner had hers dyed purple, and made into a spencer; and when Miss Pickford had her ermine tippet twisted into a muff and trimmings, I warrant you the changes did not escape the two intelligent young women before mentioned. But there are things, look you, of a finer texture than fur or satin, and all Solomon's glories, and all the wardrobe of the Queen of Sheba; – things whereof the beauty escapes the eyes of many connoisseurs. And there are sweet modest little souls on which you light, fragrant and blooming tenderly in quiet shady places; and there are gardenornaments, as big as brass warming-pans, that are fit to stare the sun itself out of countenance. Miss Sedley was not of the sunflower sort; and I say it is out of the rules of all proportion to draw a violet of the size of a double dahlia.

No, indeed; the life of a good young girl who is in the paternal nest as yet, can't have many of those thrilling incidents to which the heroine of romance commonly lays claim. Snares or shot may take off the old birds foraging without – hawks may be abroad, from which they escape or by whom they suffer; but the young ones in the nest have a pretty comfortable unromantic sort of existence in the down and the straw, till it comes to their turn, too, to get on the wing. While Becky Sharp was on her own wing in the country, hopping on all sorts of twigs, and amid a multiplicity of traps, and pecking up her food quite harmless and successful, Amelia lay snug in her home of Russell Square; if she went into the world, it was under the guidance of the elders; nor did it seem that any evil could befall her or that opulent cheery comfortable home in which she was affectionately sheltered. Mamma had her morning duties, and her daily drive, and that delightful round of visits and shopping which forms the amusement, or the profession as you may call it, of the rich London lady. Papa conducted his mysterious operations in the city – a stirring place in those days, when war was raging all over Europe, and empires were being staked; when the *Courier* newspaper had tens of thousands of subscribers; when one day brought you a battle of Vittoria, another a burning of Moscow, or a newsman's horn blowing down Russell Square about dinner-time, announced such a fact as – 'Battle of Leipsic – six hundred thousand men engaged – total defeat of the French – two hundred thousand killed.' Old Sedley once or twice came home with a very grave face; and no wonder, when such news as this was agitating all the hearts and all the Stocks of Europe.

Meanwhile matters went on in Russell Square, Bloomsbury, just as if matters in Europe were not in the least disorganized. The retreat from Leipsic made no difference in the number of meals Mr. Sambo took in the servants' hall; the allies poured into France, and the dinner-bell rang at five o'clock just as usual. I don't think poor Amelia cared anything about Brienne and Montmirail, or was fairly interested in the war until the abdication of the Emperor; when she clapped her hands and said prayers, – oh, how grateful! and flung herself into George Osborne's arms with all her soul, to the astonishment of everybody who witnessed that ebullition of sentiment. The fact is, peace was declared, Europe was going to be at rest; the Corsican was overthrown, and Lieutenant Osborne's regiment would not be ordered on service. That was the way in which Miss Amelia reasoned. The fate of Europe was Lieutenant George Osborne to her. His dangers being over, she sang *Te Deum*. He was her Europe: her emperor: her allied monarchs and august prince regent. He was her sun and moon; and I believe she thought the grand illumination and ball at the Mansion House, given to the sovereigns, were especially in honour of George Osborne.

We have talked of shift, self, and poverty, as those dismal instructors under whom poor Miss Becky Sharp got her education. Now, love was Miss Amelia Sedley's last tutoress, and it was amazing what progress our young lady made under that popular teacher. In the course of fifteen or eighteen months' daily and constant attention to this eminent finishing governess, what a deal of secrets Amelia learned, which Miss Wirt and the black-eyed young ladies over the way, which old Miss Pinkerton of Chiswick herself, had no cognizance of! As, indeed, how should any of those prim and reputable virgins? With Misses P. and W. the tender passion is out of the question: I would not dare to breathe such an idea regarding them. Miss Maria Osborne, it is true, was 'attached' to Mr. Frederick Augustus Bullock, of the firm of Hulker, Bullock & Bullock; but hers was a most respectable attachment, and she would have taken Bullock Senior, just the same, her mind being fixed as that of a well-bred young woman should be, – upon a house in Park Lane, a country house at Wimbledon, a handsome chariot, and two prodigious tall horses and footmen, and a fourth of the annual profits of the eminent firm of Hulker & Bullock, all of which advantages were represented in the person of Frederick Augustus. Had orange blossoms been invented then (those touching emblems of female purity imported by us from France, where people's daughters are universally sold in marriage), Miss Maria, I say, would have assumed the spotless wreath, and stepped into the travelling carriage by the side of gouty, old, bald-headed, bottle-nosed Bullock Senior; and devoted her beautiful existence to his happiness with perfect modesty, – only the old gentleman was married already; so she bestowed her young affections on the junior partner. Sweet, blooming orange flowers! The other day I saw Miss Trotter (that was), arrayed in them, trip into the travelling carriage at St. George's, Hanover Square, and Lord Methuselah hobbled in after. With what an engaging modesty she pulled down the blinds of the chariot – the dear innocent! There were half the carriages of Vanity Fair at the wedding.

This was not the sort of love that finished Amelia's education; and in the course of a year turned a good young girl into a good young woman – to be a good wife presently, when the happy time should come. This young person (perhaps it was very imprudent in her parents to encourage her, and abet her in such idolatry and silly romantic ideas) loved, with all her heart, the young officer in His Majesty's service with whom we have made a brief acquaintance. She thought about him the very first moment on waking; and his was the very last name mentioned in her prayers. She never had seen a man so beautiful or so clever: such a figure on horseback: such a dancer: such a hero in general. Talk of the prince's bow! what was it to George's? She had seen Mr. Brummell, whom everybody praised so. Compare such a person as that to her George! Not amongst all the beaux at the Opera (and there were beaux in those days with actual opera hats) was there any one to equal him. He was only good enough to be a fairy prince; and oh, what magnanimity to stoop to such a humble Cinderella! Miss Pinkerton would have tried to check this blind devotion very likely, had she been Amelia's confidante; but not with much success, depend upon it. It is in the nature and instinct of some women. Some are made to scheme, and some to love; and I wish any respected bachelor that reads this may take the sort that best likes him.

While under this overpowering impression, Miss Amelia neglected her twelve dear friends at Chiswick most cruelly, as such selfish people commonly will do. She had but this subject, of course, to think about; and Miss Saltire was too cold for a confidante, and she couldn't bring her. mind to tell Miss Swartz, the woolly-haired young heiress from St. Kitts. She had little Laura Martin home for the holidays; and my belief is, she made a confidante of her, and promised that Laura should come and live with her when she was married, and gave Laura a great deal of information regarding the passion of love, which must have been singularly useful and novel to that little person. Alas, alas! I fear poor Emmy had not a well-regulated mind.

What were her parents doing, not to keep this little heart from beating so fast? Old Sedley did not seem much to notice matters. He was graver of late, and his City affairs absorbed him. Mrs. Sedley was of so easy and uninquisitive a nature, that she wasn't even jealous. Mr. Jos was away, being besieged by an Irish widow at Cheltenham. Amelia had the house to herself – ah! too much to herself sometimes – not that she ever doubted; for, to be sure, George must be at the Horse Guards; and he can't always get leave from Chatham; and he must see his friends and sisters, and mingle in society when in town (he, such an ornament to every society!); and when he is with the regiment, he is too tired to write long letters. I know where she kept that packet she had — and can steal in and out of her chamber like Iachimo — like Iachimo? No — that is a bad part. I will only act Moonshine, and peep harmless into the bed where faith and beauty and innocence lie dreaming.

But if Osborne's were short and soldierlike letters, it must be confessed, that were Miss Sedley's letters to Mr. Osborne to be published, we should have to extend this novel to such a multiplicity of volumes as not the most sentimental reader could support; that she not only filled sheets of large paper, but crossed them with the most astonishing perverseness; that she wrote whole pages out of poetry-books without the least pity; that she underlined words and passages with quite a frantic emphasis; and, in fine, gave the usual tokens of her condition. She wasn't a heroine. Her letters *were* full of repetition. She wrote rather doubtful grammar sometimes, and in her verses took all sorts of liberties with the metre. But oh, mesdames, if you are not allowed to touch the heart sometimes in spite of syntax, and are not to be loved until you all know the difference between trimeter and tetrameter, may all Poetry go to the deuce, and every schoolmaster perish miserably!

CHAPTER XIII

SENTIMENTAL AND OTHERWISE

I FEAR the gentleman to whom Miss Amelia's letters were addressed was rather an obdurate critic. Such a number of notes followed Lieutenant Osborne about the country, that he became almost ashamed of the jokes of his mess-room companions regarding them, and ordered his servant never to deliver them, except at his private apartment. He was seen lighting his cigar with one, to the horror of Captain Dobbin, who, it is my belief, would have given a bank-note for the document.

For some time George strove to keep the liaison a secret. There *was* a woman in the case, that he admitted. 'And not the first either,' said Ensign Spooney to Ensign Stubbles. 'That Osborne's a devil of a fellow. There was a judge's daughter at Demerara went almost mad about him; then there was that beautiful quadroon girl, Miss Pye, at St. Vincent's, you know; and since he's been home, they say he's regular Don Giovanni, by Jove.'

Stubbles and Spooney thought that to be a 'regular Don Giovanni, by Jove', was one of the finest qualities a man could possess; and Osborne's reputation was prodigious amongst the young men of the regiment. He was famous in field-sports, famous at a song, famous on parade; free with his money, which was bountifully supplied by his father. His coats were better made than any man's in the regiment, and he had more of them. He was adored by the men. He could drink more than any officer of the whole mess, including old Heavytop, the colonel. He could spar better than Knuckles, the private (who would have been a corporal but for his drunkenness, and who had been in the prize-ring); and was the best batter and bowler, out and out, of the regimental club. He rode his own horse, Greased Lightning, and won the Garrison cup at Quebec races. There were other people besides Amelia who worshipped him. Stubbles and Spooney thought him a sort of Apollo; Dobbin took him to be an Admirable Crichton; and Mrs. Major O'Dowd acknowledged he was an elegant young fellow, and put her in mind of Fitzjurld Fogarty, Lord Castlefogarty's second son.

Well, Stubbles and Spooney and the rest indulged in most romantic conjectures regarding this female correspondent of Osborne's, – opining that it was a duchess in London, who was in love with him, – or that it was a general's daughter, who was engaged to somebody else, and madly attached to him, – or that it was a Member of Parliament's lady, who proposed four horses and an elopement, – or that it was some other victim of a passion delightfully exciting, romantic, and disgraceful to all parties, on none of which conjectures would Osborne throw the least light, leaving his young admirers and friends to invent and arrange their whole history.

And the real state of the case would never have been known at all in the regiment but for Captain Dobbin's indiscretion. The captain was eating his breakfast one day in the mess-room, while Cackle, the assistant-surgeon, and the two above-named worthies were speculating upon Osborne's intrigue – Stubbles holding out that the lady was a duchess about Queen Charlotte's court, and Cackle vowing she was an opera-singer of the worst reputation. At this idea Dobbin became so moved, that though his mouth was full of egg and bread-and-butter at the time, and though he ought not to have spoken at all, yet he couldn't help blurting out, 'Cackle, you're a stupid fool. You're always talking nonsense and scandal. Osborne is not going to run off with a duchess or ruin a milliner. Miss Sedley is one of the most charming young women that ever lived. He's been engaged to her ever so long; and the man who calls her names had better not do so in my hearing.' With which, turning exceedingly red, Dobbin ceased speaking, and almost choked himself with a cup of tea. The story was over the regiment in half an hour; and that very evening Mrs. Major O'Dowd wrote off to her sister Glorvina at O'Dowdstown not to hurry from Dublin, – young Osborne being prematurely engaged already.

She complimented the lieutenant in an appropriate speech over a glass of whisky-toddy that evening, and he went home perfectly furious to quarrel with Dobbin (who had declined Mrs. Major O'Dowd's party, and sat in his own room playing the flute, and, I believe, writing poetry in a very melancholy manner) – to quarrel with Dobbin for betraying his secret.

'Who the deuce asked you to talk about my affairs?' Osborne shouted indignantly. 'Why the devil is all the regiment to know that I am going to be married? Why is that tattling old harridan, Peggy O'Dowd, to make free with my name at her d–d supper-table, and advertise my engagement over the three kingdoms? After all, what right have you to say I *am* engaged, or to meddle in my business at all, Dobbin?'

'It seems to me –' Captain Dobbin began.

'Seems be hanged, Dobbin,' his junior interrupted him. 'I am under obligations to you, I know it, a d–d deal too well too; but I won't be always sermonized by you because you're five years my senior. I'm hanged if I'll stand your airs of superiority and infernal pity and patronage. Pity and patronage! I should like to know in what I'm your inferior?'

'Are you engaged?' Captain Dobbin interposed.

'What the devil's that to you or any one here if I am?'

'Are you ashamed of it?' Dobbin resumed.

'What right have you to ask me that question, sir? I should like to know,' George said.

'Good God, you don't mean to say you want to break off?' asked Dobbin, starting up.

'In other words, you ask me if I'm a man of honour,' said Osborne, fiercely; 'is that what you mean? You've adopted such a tone regarding me lately that I'm – if I'll bear it any more.'

'What have I done? I've told you you were neglecting a sweet girl, George. I've told you that when you go to town you ought to go to her, and not to the gambling-houses about St. James's.'

'You want your money back, I suppose,' said George, with a sneer.

'Of course I do – I always did, didn't I?' says Dobbin. 'You speak like a generous fellow.'

'No, hang it, William, I beg your pardon' – here George interposed in a fit of remorse; 'you *have* been my friend in a hundred ways, Heaven knows. You've got me out of a score of scrapes. When Crawley of the Guards won that sum of money of me I should have been done but for you: I know I should. But you shouldn't deal so hardly with me; you shouldn't be always catechizing me. I *am* very fond of Amelia; I adore her, and that sort of thing. Don't look angry. She's faultless; I know she is. But you see there's no fun in winning a thing unless you play for it. Hang it: the regiment's just back from the West Indies, I must have a little fling, and then when I'm married I'll reform; I will upon my honour, now. And – I say – Dob – don't be angry with me, and I'll give you a hundred next month, when I know my father will stand something handsome; and I'll ask Heavytop for leave, and I'll go to town, and see Amelia to-morrow – there now, will *that* satisfy you?'

'It's impossible to be long angry with you, George,' said the good-natured captain; 'and as for the money, old boy, you know if I wanted it you'd share your last shilling with me.'

'That I would, by Jove, Dobbin,' George said, with the greatest generosity, though by the way he never had any money to spare.

'Only I wish you had sown those wild oats of yours, George. If you could have seen poor little Miss Emmy's face when she asked me about you the other day, you would have pitched those billiard-balls to the deuce. Go and comfort her, you rascal. Go and write her a long letter. Do something to make her happy; a very little will.'

'I believe she's d–d fond of me,' the lieutenant said, with a self-satisfied air; and went off to finish the evening with some jolly fellows in the mess-room.

Amelia meanwhile, in Russell Square, was looking at the moon, which was shining upon that peaceful spot, as well as upon the square of the Chatham barracks, where Lieutenant Osborne was quartered, and thinking to herself how her hero was employed. Perhaps he is visiting the sentries, thought she; perhaps he is bivouacking; perhaps he is attending the couch of a wounded comrade, or studying the art of war up in his own desolate chamber. And her kind thoughts sped away as if they were angels and had wings, and flying down the river to Chatham and Rochester, strove to peep into the barracks where George was. . . . All things considered, I think it was as well the gates were shut, and the sentry allowed no one to pass; so that the poor little white-robed angel could not hear the songs those young fellows were roaring over the whisky-punch.

The day after the little conversation at Chatham barracks, young Osborne, to show that he would be as good as his word, prepared to go to town, thereby incurring Captain Dobbin's applause. 'I should have liked to make her a little present,' Osborne said to his friend in confidence, 'only I am quite out of cash until my father tips up.' But Dobbin would not allow this good nature and generosity to be balked, and so accommodated Mr. Osborne with a few pound notes, which the latter took after a little faint scruple.

And I dare say he would have bought something very handsome for Amelia; only, getting off the coach in Fleet Street, he was attracted by a handsome shirt-pin in a jeweller's window, which he could not resist; and having paid for that, had very little money to spare for indulging in any further exercise of kindness. Never mind: you may be sure it was not his presents Amelia wanted. When he came to Russell Square, her face lighted up as if he had been sunshine. The little cares, fears, tears, timid misgivings, sleepless fancies of I don't know how many days and nights, were forgotten, under one moment's influence of that familiar, irresistible smile. He beamed on her from the drawing-room door — magnificent with ambrosial whiskers, like a god. Sambo, whose face as he announced Captain Osbin (having conferred a brevet rank on that young officer) blazed with a sympathetic grin, saw the little girl start, and flush, and jump up from her watching-place in the window; and Sambo retreated: and as soon as the door was shut, she went fluttering to Lieutenant George Osborne's heart as if it was the only natural home for her to nestle in. Oh, thou poor panting little soul! The very finest tree in the whole forest, with the straightest stem, and the strongest arms, and the thickest foliage, wherein you choose to build and coo, may be marked, for what you know, and may be down with a crash ere long. What an old, old simile that is, between man and timber!

In the meanwhile, George kissed her very kindly on her forehead and glistening eyes, and was very gracious and good; and she thought his diamond shirt-pin (which she had not known him to wear before) the prettiest ornament ever seen.

The observant reader, who has marked our young lieutenant's previous behaviour, and has preserved our report of the brief conversation which he has just had with Captain Dobbin, has possibly come to certain conclusions regarding the character of Mr. Osborne. Some cynical Frenchman has said that there are two parties to a love-transaction: the one who loves and the other who condescends to be so treated. Perhaps the love is occasionally on the man's side: perhaps on the lady's. Perhaps some infatuated swain has ere this mistaken insensibility for modesty, dullness for maiden-reserve, mere vacuity for sweet bashfulness, and a goose, in a word, for a swan. Perhaps some beloved female subscriber has arrayed an ass in the splendour and glory of her imagination; admired his dullness as manly simplicity; worshipped his selfishness as manly superiority; treated his stupidity as majestic gravity, and used him as the brilliant fairy Titania did a certain weaver at Athens. I think I have seen such comedies of errors going on in the world. But this is certain, that Amelia believed her lover to be one of the most gallant and brilliant men in the empire: and it is possible Lieutenant Osborne thought so too.

He was a little wild: how many young men are; and don't girls like a rake better than a milksop? He hadn't sown his wild oats as yet, but he would soon: and quit the army now that peace was proclaimed; the Corsican monster locked up at Elba; promotion by consequence over; and no chance left for the display of his undoubted military talents and valour: and his allowance, with Amelia's settlement, would enable them to take a snug place in the country somewhere, in a good sporting neighbourhood; and he would hunt a little, and farm a little; and they would be very happy. As for remaining in the army as a married man, that was impossible. Fancy Mrs. George Osborne in lodgings in a county town; or, worse still, in the East or West Indies, with a society of officers, and patronized by Mrs. Major O'Dowd! Amelia died with laughing at Osborne's stories about Mrs. Major O'Dowd. He loved her much too fondly to subject her to that horrid woman and her vulgarities, and the rough treat-ment of a soldier's wife. He didn't care for himself – not he; but his dear little girl should take the place in society to which, as his wife, she was entitled: and to these proposals you may be sure she acceded, as she would to any other from the same author.

Holding this kind of conversation, and building number-less castles in the air (which Amelia adorned with all sorts of flower-gardens, rustic walks, country churches, Sunday schools, and the like; while George had his mind's eye directed to the stables, the kennel, and the cellar), this young pair passed away a couple of hours very pleasantly; and as the lieutenant had only that single day in town, and a great deal of most important business to transact, it was proposed that Miss Emmy should dine with her future sisters-in-law. This invitation was accepted joyfully. He conducted her to his sisters; where he left her talking and prattling in a way that astonished those ladies, who thought that George might make something of her; and he then went off to transact his business.

In a word, he went out and ate ices at a pastrycook's shop in Charing Cross; tried a new coat in Pall Mall; dropped in at the Old Slaughters', and called for Captain Cannon; played eleven games at billiards with the captain, of which he won eight, and returned to Russell Square half an hour late for dinner, but in very good humour.

It was not so with old Mr. Osborne. When that gentleman came from the City, and was welcomed in the drawing-room by his daughters and the elegant Miss Wirt, they saw at once by his face – which was puffy, solemn, and yellow at the best of times – and by the scowl and twitching of his black eyebrows, that the heart within his large white waistcoat was disturbed and uneasy. When Amelia stepped forward to salute him, which she always did with great trembling and timidity, he gave a surly grunt of recognition, and dropped the little hand out of his great hirsute paw without any attempt to hold it there. He looked round gloomily at his eldest daughter; who, comprehending the meaning of his look, which asked unmistakably, 'Why the devil is *she* here?' said at once:–

'George is in town, papa; and has gone to the Horse Guards, and will be back to dinner.'

'Oh, he is, is he? I won't have the dinner kept waiting for *him*, Jane;' with which this worthy man lapsed into his particular chair, and then the utter silence in his genteel, well-furnished drawing-room was only interrupted by the alarmed ticking of the great French clock.

When that chronometer, which was surmounted by a cheerful brass group of the sacrifice of Iphigenia, tolled five in a heavy cathedral tone, Mr. Osborne pulled the bell at his right hand violently, and the butler rushed up.

'Dinner!' roared Mr. Osborne.

'Mr. George isn't come in, sir,' interposed the man.

'Damn Mr. George, sir. Am I master of the house? DINNER!' Mr. Osborne scowled. Amelia trembled. A telegraphic communication of eyes passed between the other three ladies. The obedient bell in the lower regions began ringing the announcement of the meal. The tolling over, the head of the family thrust his hands into the great tail-pockets of his great blue coat and brass buttons, and without waiting for a further announcement, strode downstairs alone, scowling over his shoulder at the four females.

'What's the matter now, my dear?' asked one of the other, as they rose and tripped gingerly behind the sire.

'I suppose the funds are falling,' whispered Miss Wirt;

and so, trembling and in silence, this hushed female company followed their dark leader. They took their places in silence. He growled out a blessing, which sounded as gruffly as a curse. The great silver dish-covers were removed. Amelia trembled in her place, for she was next to the awful Osborne, and alone on her side of the table – the gap being occasioned by the absence of George.

'Soup?' says Mr. Osborne, clutching the ladle, fixing his eyes on her, in a sepulchral tone; and having helped her and the rest, did not speak for a while.

'Take Miss Sedley's plate away,' at last he said. 'She can't eat the soup – no more can I. It's beastly. Take away the soup, Hicks, and to-morrow turn the cook out of the house, Jane.'

Having concluded his observations upon the soup, Mr. Osborne made a few curt remarks respecting the fish, also of a savage and satirical tendency, and cursed Billingsgate with an emphasis quite worthy of the place. Then he lapsed into silence, and swallowed sundry glasses of wine, looking more and more terrible, till a brisk knock at the door told of George's arrival, when everybody began to rally.

'He could not come before. General Daguilet had kept him waiting at the Horse Guards. Never mind soup or fish. Give him anything – he didn't care what. Capital mutton – capital everything.' His good humour contrasted with his father's severity; and he rattled on unceasingly during dinner, to the delight of all – of one especially, who need not be mentioned.

As soon as the young ladies had discussed the orange and the glass of wine which formed the ordinary conclusion of the dismal banquets at Mr. Osborne's house, the signal to make sail for the drawing-room was given, and they all arose and departed. Amelia hoped George would soon join them there. She began playing some of his favourite waltzes (then newly imported) at the great carved-legged, leather-cased grand piano in the drawing-room overhead. This little artifice did not bring him. He was deaf to the waltzes; they grew fainter and fainter; the discomfited performer left the huge instrument presently; and though her three friends performed some of the loudest and most brilliant new pieces of their répertoire, she did not hear a single note, but sat thinking, and boding evil. Old Osborne's scowl, terrific always, had never before looked so deadly to her. His eyes followed her out of the room, as if she had been guilty of something. When they brought her coffee, she started as though it were a cup of poison which Mr. Hicks, the butler, wished to propose to her. What mystery was there lurking? Oh, those women! They nurse and cuddle their presentiments, and make darlings of their ugliest thoughts, as they do of their deformed children.

The gloom on the paternal countenance had also impressed George Osborne with anxiety. With such eyebrows, and a look so decidedly bilious, how was he to extract that money from the governor, of which George was consumedly in want? He began praising his father's wine. That was generally a successful means of cajoling the old gentleman.

'We never got such madeira in the West Indies, sir, as yours. Colonel Heavytop took off three bottles of that you sent me down, under his belt the other day.'

'Did he?' said the old gentleman. 'It stands me in eight shillings a bottle.'

'Will you take six guineas a dozen for it, sir?' said George, with a laugh. 'There's one of the greatest men in the kingdom wants some.'

'Does he?' growled the senior. 'Wish he may get it.'

'When General Daguilet was at Chatham, sir, Heavytop gave him a breakfast, and asked me for some of the wine. The general liked it just as well – wanted a pipe for the commander-in-chief. He's His Royal Highness's righthand man.'

'It *is* devilish fine wine,' said the Eyebrows, and they looked more good-humoured; and George was going to take advantage of this complacency, and bring the supply question on the mahogany; when the father, relapsing into solemnity, though rather cordial in manner, bade him ring the bell for claret. 'And we'll see if that's as good as the madeira, George, to which His Royal Highness is welcome, I'm sure. And as we are drinking it, I'll talk to you about a matter of importance.'

Amelia heard the claret bell ringing as she sat nervously upstairs. She thought, somehow, it was a mysterious and presentimental bell. Of the presentiments which some people are always having, *some* surely must come right.

'What I want to know, George,' the old gentleman said,

after slowly smacking his first bumper. 'What I want to know is, how you and – ah – that little thing upstairs, are carrying on?'

'I think, sir, it's not hard to see,' George said, with a self-satisfied grin. 'Pretty clear, sir. – What capital wine!'

'What d'you mean, pretty clear, sir?'

'Why, hang it, sir, don't push me too hard. I'm a modest man. I – ah – I don't set up to be a lady-killer; but I do own that she's as devilish fond of me as she can be. Anybody can see that with half an eye.'

'And you, yourself?'

'Why, sir, didn't you order me to marry her, and ain't I a good boy? Haven't our papas settled it ever so long?'

'A pretty boy, indeed. Haven't I heard of your doings, sir, with Lord Tarquin, Captain Crawley of the Guards, the Honourable Mr. Deuceace and that set? Have a care, sir, have a care.'

The old gentleman pronounced these aristocratic names with the greatest gusto. Whenever he met a great man he grovelled before him, and my-lorded him as only a freeborn Briton can do. He came home and looked out his history in the *Peerage:* he introduced his name into his daily conversation; he bragged about his lordship to his daughters. He fell down prostrate and basked in him as a Neapolitan beggar does in the sun. George was alarmed when he heard the names. He feared his father might have been informed of certain transactions at play. But the old moralist eased him by saying serenely:–

'Well, well, young men will be young men. And the comfort to me is, George, that living in the best society in England, as I hope you do; as I think you do; as my means will allow you to do —'

'Thank you, sir,' says George, making his point at once. 'One can't live with these great folks for nothing; and my purse, sir, look at it;' and he held up a little token which had been netted by Amelia, and contained the very last of Dobbin's pound notes.

'You shan't want, sir. The British merchant's son shan't want, sir. My guineas are as good as theirs, George, my boy; and I don't grudge 'em. Call on Mr. Chopper as you go through the City to-morrow; he'll have something for you. I don't grudge money when I know you're in good society, because I know that good society can never go wrong. There's no pride in me. I was a humbly born man – but you have had advantages. Make a good use of 'em. Mix with the young nobility. There's many of 'em who can't spend a dollar to your guinea, my boy. And as for the pink bonnets' (here from under the heavy eyebrows there came a knowing and not very pleasing leer) – 'why, boys will be boys. Only there's one thing I order you to avoid, which, if you do not, I'll cut you off with a shilling, by Jove; and that's gambling, sir.'

'Oh, of course, sir,' said George.

'But to return to the other business about Amelia: why shouldn't you marry higher than a stockbroker's daughter. George – that's what I want to know?'

'It's a family business, sir,' says George, cracking filberts. 'You and Mr. Sedley made the match a hundred years ago.'

'I don't deny it; but people's positions alter, sir. I don't deny that Sedley made my fortune, or rather put me in the way of acquiring, by my own talents and genius, that proud position, which, I may say, I occupy in the tallow trade and the City of London. I've shown my gratitude to Sedley; and he's tried it of late, sir, as my cheque-book can show. George! I tell you in confidence I don't like the looks of Mr. Sedley's affairs. My chief clerk, Mr. Chopper, does not like the looks of 'em, and he's an old file, and knows 'Change as well as any man in London.

Hulker & Bullock are looking shy at him. He's been dabbling on his own account, I fear. They say the *Jeune Amélie* was his, which was taken by the Yankee privateer *Molasses*. And that's flat, – unless I see Amelia's ten thousand down you don't marry her. I'll have no lame duck's daughter in my family. Pass the wine, sir – or ring for coffee.'

With which Mr. Osborne spread out the evening paper, and George knew from this signal that the colloquy was ended, and that his papa was about to take a nap.

He hurried upstairs to Amelia in the highest spirits. What was it that made him more attentive to her on that night than he had been for a long time – more eager to amuse her, more tender, more brilliant in talk? Was it that his generous heart warmed to her at the prospect of misfortune; or that the idea of losing the dear little prize made him value it more?

She lived upon the recollections of that happy evening for many days afterwards, remembering his words; his looks; the song he sang; his attitude, as he leant over her or looked at her from a distance. As it seemed to her, no night ever passed so quickly at Mr. Osborne's house before; and for once this young person was almost provoked to be angry by the premature arrival of Mr. Sambo with her shawl.

George came and took a tender leave of her the next morning; and then hurried off to the City, where he visited Mr. Chopper, his father's head man, and received from that gentleman a document which he exchanged at Hulker's & Bullock's for a whole pocketful of money. As George entered the house, old John Sedley was passing out of the banker's parlour, looking very dismal. But his godson was much too elated to mark the worthy stockbroker's depression, or the dreary eyes which the kind old gentleman cast upon him. Young Bullock did not come grinning out of the parlour with him as had been his wont in former years.

And as the swinging doors of Hulker, Bullock & Co. closed upon Mr. Sedley, Mr. Quill, the cashier (whose benevolent occupation it is to hand out crisp bank-notes from a drawer and dispense sovereigns out of a copper shovel), winked at Mr. Driver, the clerk at the desk on his right. Mr. Driver winked again.

'No go,' Mr. D. whispered.

'Not at no price,' Mr. Q. said. 'Mr. George Osborne, sir, how will you take it?' George crammed eagerly a quantity of notes into his pockets, and paid Dobbin fifty pounds that very evening at mess.

That very evening Amelia wrote him the tenderest of long letters. Her heart was overflowing with tenderness, but it still foreboded evil. What was the cause of Mr. Osborne's dark looks? she asked. Had any difference arisen between him and her papa? Her poor papa returned so melancholy from the City, that all were alarmed about him at home – in fine, there were four pages of loves and fears and hopes and forebodings.

'Poor little Emmy – dear little Emmy. How fond she is of me,' George said, as he perused the missive – 'and Gad, what a headache that mixed punch has given me!' Poor little Emmy, indeed.

CHAPTER XIV

MISS CRAWLEY AT HOME

ABOUT this time there drove up to an exceedingly snug and well-appointed house in Park Lane, a travelling chariot with a lozenge on the panels, a discontented female in a green veil and crimped curls on the rumble, and a large and confidential man on the box. It was the equipage of our friend Miss Crawley, returning from Hants. The carriage-windows were shut; the fat spaniel, whose head and tongue ordinarily lolled out of one of them, reposed on the lap of the discontented female. When the vehicle stopped, a large round bundle of shawls was taken out of the carriage by the aid of various domestics and a young lady who accompanied the heap of cloaks. That bundle contained Miss Crawley, who was conveyed upstairs forthwith, and put into a bed and chamber warmed properly as for the reception of an invalid. Messengers went off for her physician and medical man. They came, consulted, prescribed, vanished. The young companion of Miss Crawley, at the conclusion of their interview, came in to receive their instructions, and administered those antiphlogistic medicines which the eminent men ordered.

Captain Crawley of the Life Guards rode up from Knights-bridge Barracks the next day; his black charger pawed the straw before his invalid aunt's door. He was most affectionate in his inquiries regarding that amiable relative. There seemed to be much source of apprehension. He found Miss Crawley's maid (the discontented female) unusually sulky and despondent; he found Miss Briggs, her *dame de compagnie*, in tears alone in the drawing-room. She had hastened home, hearing of her beloved friend's illness. She wished to fly to her couch, that couch which she, Briggs, had so often smoothed in the hour of sickness. She was denied admission to Miss Crawley's apartment. A stranger was administering her medicines – a stranger from the country – an odious Miss . . . – tears choked the utterance of the *dame de compagnie*, and she buried her crushed affections and her poor old red nose in her pocket-handkerchief.

Rawdon Crawley sent up his name by the sulky *femme de*

chambre, and Miss Crawley's new companion, coming tripping down from the sick-room, put a little hand into his as
he stepped forward eagerly to meet her, gave a glance of
great scorn at the bewildered Briggs, and, beckoning the
young Guardsman out of the back drawing-room, led him
downstairs into that now desolate dining-parlour, where so
many a good dinner had been celebrated.

Here these two talked for ten minutes, discussing, no
doubt, the symptoms of the old invalid above stairs; at the
end of which period the parlour-bell was rung briskly, and
answered on that instant by Mr. Bowls, Miss Crawley's large
confidential butler (who, indeed, happened to be at the
keyhole during the most part of the interview); and the captain
coming out, curling his moustachios, mounted the black
charger pawing among the straw, to the admiration of the
little blackguard boys collected in the street. He looked in
at the dining-room window, managing his horse, which
curveted and capered beautifully – for one instant the young
person might be seen at the window, then her figure vanished, and, doubtless, she went upstairs again to resume the
affecting duties of benevolence.

Who could this young woman be, I wonder? That evening
a little dinner for two persons was laid in the dining-room
– when Mrs. Firkin, the lady's maid, pushed into her
mistress's apartment, and bustled about there during the
vacancy occasioned by the departure of the new nurse – and
the latter and Miss Briggs sat down to the neat little meal.

Briggs was so much choked by emotion that she could
hardly take a morsel of meat. The young person carved a
fowl with the utmost delicacy, and asked so distinctly for
egg-sauce, that poor Briggs, before whom that delicious
condiment was placed, started, made a great clattering with
the ladle, and once more fell back in the most gushing
hysterical state.

'Had you not better give Miss Briggs a glass of wine?'
said the person to Mr. Bowls, the large confidential man.
He did so. Briggs seized it mechanically, gasped it down
convulsively, moaned a little, and began to play with the
chicken on her plate.

'I think we shall be able to help each other,' said the
person, with great suavity: 'and shall have no need of Mr.
Bowls's kind services. Mr. Bowls, if you please, we will ring

when we want you.' He went downstairs, where, by the way, he vented the most horrid curses upon the unoffending footman, his subordinate.

'It is a pity you take on so, Miss Briggs,' the young lady said, with a cool, slightly sarcastic air.

'My dearest friend is so ill, and wo-o-o-on't see me,' gurgled out Briggs in an agony of renewed grief.

'She's not very ill any more. Console yourself, dear Miss Briggs. She has only overeaten herself – that is all. She is greatly better. She will soon be quite restored again. She is weak from being cupped and from medical treatment, but she will rally immediately. Pray console yourself, and take a little more wine.'

'But why, why won't she see me again?' Miss Briggs bleated out. 'Oh, Matilda, Matilda, after three-and-twenty years' tenderness! is this the return to your poor, poor Arabella?'

'Don't cry too much, poor Arabella,' the other said (with ever so little of a grin); 'she only won't see you, because she says you don't nurse her as well as I do. It's no pleasure to me to sit up all night. I wish you might do it instead.'

'Have I not tended that dear couch for years?' Arabella said, 'and now —'

'Now she prefers somebody else. Well, sick people have these fancies, and must be humoured. When she's well I shall go.'

'Never, never,' Arabella exclaimed, madly inhaling her salts-bottle.

'Never be well or never go, Miss Briggs?' the other said, with the same provoking good nature. 'Pooh – she will be well in a fortnight, when I shall go back to my little pupils at Queen's Crawley, and to their mother, who is a great deal more sick than our friend. You need not be jealous about me, my dear Miss Briggs. I am a poor little girl without any friends, or any harm in me. I don't want to supplant you in Miss Crawley's good graces. She will forget me a week after I am gone: and her affection for you has been the work of years. Give me a little wine if you please, my dear Miss Briggs, and let us be friends. I'm sure I want friends.'

The placable and soft-hearted Briggs speechlessly pushed out her hand at this appeal; but she felt the desertion most

keenly for all that, and bitterly, bitterly moaned the fickle-
ness of her Matilda. At the end of half an hour, the meal
over, Miss Rebecca Sharp (for such, astonishing to state, is
the name of her who has been described ingeniously as 'the
person' hitherto) went upstairs again to her patient's rooms,
from which, with the most engaging politeness, she elimi-
nated poor Firkin. 'Thank you, Mrs. Firkin, that will quite
do; how nicely you make it! I will ring when anything is
wanted.' 'Thank you;' and Firkin came downstairs in a
tempest of jealousy, only the more dangerous because she
was forced to confine it in her own bosom.

Could it be the tempest which, as she passed the landing
of the first floor, blew open the drawing-room door? No; it
was stealthily opened by the hand of Briggs. Briggs had been
on the watch. Briggs too well heard the creaking Firkin
descend the stairs, and the clink of the spoon and gruel-basin
the neglected female carried.

'Well, Firkin?' says she, as the other entered the apartment. 'Well, Jane?'

'Wuss and wuss, Miss B.,' Firkin said, wagging her head.

'Is she not better then?'

'She never spoke but once, and I asked her if she felt a
little more easy, and she told me to hold my stupid tongue.
Oh, Miss B., I never thought to have seen *this* day!' And
the waterworks again began to play.

'What sort of a person is this Miss Sharp, Firkin? I little
thought, while enjoying my Christmas revels in the elegant
home of my firm friends, the Reverend Lionel Delamere and
his amiable lady, to find a stranger had taken my place in
the affections of my dearest, my still dearest Matilda!' Miss
Briggs, it will be seen by her language, was of a literary and
sentimental turn, and had once published a volume of poems
– *Trills of the Nightingale* – by subscription.

'Miss B., they are all infatyated about that young woman,'
Firkin replied. 'Sir Pitt wouldn't have let her go, but
he daredn't refuse Miss Crawley anything. Mrs. Bute at the
Rectory just as bad – never happy out of her sight. The
capting quite wild about her. Mr. Crawley mortial jealous.
Since Miss C. was took ill, she won't have nobody near her
but Miss Sharp, I can't tell for where nor for why; and I
think somethink has bewidged everybody.'

Rebecca passed that night in constant watching upon Miss

Crawley; the next night the old lady slept so comfortably, that Rebecca had time for several hours' comfortable repose herself on the sofa, at the foot of her patroness's bed; very soon, Miss Crawley was so well that she sat up and laughed heartily at a perfect imitation of Miss Briggs and her grief, which Rebecca described to her. Briggs's weeping snuffle, and her manner of using the handkerchief, were so completely rendered, that Miss Crawley became quite cheerful, to the admiration of the doctors when they visited her, who usually found this worthy woman of the world, when the least sickness attacked her, under the most abject depression and terror of death.

Captain Crawley came every day, and received bulletins from Miss Rebecca respecting his aunt's health. This improved so rapidly, that poor Briggs was allowed to see her patroness; and persons with tender hearts may imagine the smothered emotions of that sentimental female, and the affecting nature of the interview.

Miss Crawley liked to have Briggs in a good deal soon. Rebecca used to mimic her to her face with the most admirable gravity, thereby rendering the imitation doubly piquant to her worthy patroness.

The causes which had led to the deplorable illness of Miss Crawley, and her departure from her brother's house in the country, were of such an unromantic nature that they are hardly fit to be explained in this genteel and sentimental novel. For how is it possible to hint of a delicate female, living in good society, that she ate and drank too much, and that a hot supper of lobsters profusely enjoyed at the Rectory was the reason of an indisposition which Miss Crawley herself persisted was solely attributable to the dampness of the weather? The attack was so sharp that Matilda – as his reverence expressed it – was very nearly 'off the hooks'; all the family was in a fever of expectation regarding the will, and Rawdon Crawley was making sure of at least forty thousand pounds before the commencement of the London season. Mr. Crawley sent over a choice parcel of tracts, to prepare her for the change from Vanity Fair and Park Lane for another world; but a good doctor from Southampton being called in in time, vanquished the lobster which was so nearly fatal to her, and gave her sufficient strength to enable her to return to London. The baronet did not disguise his exceeding mortification at the turn which affairs took.

While everybody was attending on Miss Crawley, and messengers every hour from the Rectory were carrying news of her health to the affectionate folks there, there was a lady in another part of the house being exceedingly ill, of whom no one took any notice at all; and this was the lady of Crawley herself. The good doctor shook his head after seeing her; to which visit Sir Pitt consented, as it could be paid without a fee; and she was left fading away in her lonely chamber, with no more heed paid to her than to a weed in the park.

The young ladies, too, lost much of the inestimable benefit of their governess's instruction. So affectionate a nurse was Miss Sharp, that Miss Crawley would take her medicines from no other hand. Firkin had been deposed long before her mistress's departure from the country. That faithful attendant found a gloomy consolation on returning to London, in seeing Miss Briggs suffer the same pangs of jealousy and undergo the same faithless treatment to which she herself had been subject.

Captain Rawdon got an extension of leave on his aunt's illness, and remained dutifully at home. He was always in her antechamber. (She lay sick in the state bedroom, into which you entered by the little blue saloon.) His father was always meeting him there; or if he came down the corridor ever so quietly, his father's door was sure to open, and the hyena face of the old gentleman to glare out. What was it set one to watch the other so? A generous rivalry, no doubt, as to which should be most attentive to the dear sufferer in the state bedroom. Rebecca used to come out and comfort both of them; or one or the other of them, rather. Both of these worthy gentlemen were most anxious to have news of the invalid from her little confidential messenger.

At dinner – to which meal she descended for half an hour – she kept the peace between them, after which she disappeared for the night; when Rawdon would ride over to the depôt of the 150th at Mudbury, leaving his papa to the society of Mr. Horrocks and his rum-and-water. She passed as weary a fortnight as ever mortal spent in Miss Crawley's sick-room; but her little nerves seemed to be of iron, and she was quite unshaken by the duty and the tedium of the sick-chamber.

She never told until long afterwards how painful that duty was; how peevish a patient was the jovial old lady; how angry; how sleepless; in what horrors of death; during what long nights she lay moaning, and in almost delirious agonies respecting that future world which she quite ignored when she was in good health. – Picture to yourself, O fair young reader, a worldly, selfish, graceless, thankless, religionless old woman, writhing in pain and fear, and without her wig. Picture her to yourself, and ere you be old, learn to love and pray!

Sharp watched this graceless bedside with indomitable patience. Nothing escaped her; and, like a prudent steward, she found a use for everything. She told many a good story about Miss Crawley's illness in after-days, – stories which made the lady blush through her artificial carnations. During the illness she was never out of temper; always alert; she slept light, having a perfectly clear conscience; and could take that refreshment at almost any minute's warning. And so you saw few traces of fatigue in her appearance. Her face might be a trifle paler, and the circles round her eyes a little blacker than usual; but whenever she came out from the sick-room she was always smiling, fresh, and neat, and looked as trim in her little dressing-gown and cap, as in her smartest evening suit.

The captain thought so, and raved about her in uncouth convulsions. The barbed shaft of love had penetrated his dull hide. Six weeks – appropinquity – opportunity – had victimized him completely. He made a confidant of his aunt at the Rectory, of all persons in the world. She rallied him about it; she had perceived his folly; she warned him; she finished by owning that little Sharp was the most clever, droll, odd, good-natured, simple, kindly creature in England. Rawdon must not trifle with her affections, though – dear Miss Crawley would never pardon him for that; for she, too, was quite overcome by the little governess, and loved Sharp like a daughter. Rawdon must go away – go back to his regiment and naughty London, and not play with a poor artless girl's feelings.

Many and many a time this good-natured lady, compassionating the forlorn life-guardsman's condition, gave him an opportunity of seeing Miss Sharp at the Rectory, and of walking home with her, as we have seen. When men of a certain sort, ladies, are in love, though they see the hook and the string, and the whole apparatus with which they are to be taken, they gorge the bait nevertheless – they must come to it – they must swallow it – and are presently struck and landed gasping. Rawdon saw there was a manifest intention on Mrs. Bute's part to captivate him with Rebecca. He was not very wise; but he was a man about town, and had seen several seasons. A light dawned upon his dusky soul, as he thought, through a speech of Mrs. Bute's.

'Mark my words, Rawdon,' she said. 'You will have Miss Sharp one day for your relation.'

'What relation, – my cousin, hey, Mrs. Bute? Francis sweet on her, hey?' inquired the waggish officer.

'More than that,' Mrs. Bute said, with a flash from her black eyes.

'Not Pitt? – He sha'n't have her. The sneak a'n't worthy of her. He's booked to Lady Jane Sheepshanks.'

'You men perceive nothing. You silly, blind creature – if anything happens to Lady Crawley, Miss Sharp will be your mother-in-law; and *that's* what will happen.'

Rawdon Crawley, Esquire, gave vent to a prodigious whistle, in token of astonishment at this announcement. He couldn't deny it. His father's evident liking for Miss Sharp had not escaped him. He knew the old gentleman's character well; and a more unscrupulous old – whyou – he did not conclude the sentence, but walked home, curling his moustachios, and convinced he had found a clue to Mrs. Bute's mystery.

'By Jove, it's too bad,' thought Rawdon, 'too bad, by Jove! I do believe the woman wants the poor girl to be ruined, in order that she shouldn't come into the family as Lady Crawley.'

When he saw Rebecca alone, he rallied her about his father's attachment in his graceful way. She flung up her head scornfully, looked him full in the face, and said, –

'Well, suppose he *is* fond of me. I know he is, and others too. You don't think I am afraid of him, Captain Crawley? You don't suppose I can't defend my own honour,' said the little woman, looking as stately as a queen.

'Oh, ah, why – give you fair warning – look out, you know – that's all,' said the moustachio-twiddler.

'You hint at something not honourable, then?' said she, flashing out.

'Oh – Gad – really – Miss Rebecca,' the heavy dragoon interposed.

'Do you suppose I have no feeling of self-respect, because I am poor and friendless, and because rich people have none? Do you think, because I am a governess, I have not as much sense, and feeling, and good breeding as you gentlefolks in Hampshire? I'm a Montmorency. Do you suppose a Montmorency is not as good as a Crawley?'

When Miss Sharp was agitated, and alluded to her maternal relatives, she spoke with ever so slight a foreign accent, which gave a great charm to her clear ringing voice. 'No,' she continued, kindling as she spoke to the captain; 'I can endure poverty, but not shame – neglect, but not insult; and insult from – from *you*.'

Her feelings gave way, and she burst into tears.

'Hang it, Miss Sharp – Rebecca – by Jove – upon my soul, I wouldn't for a thousand pounds. Stop, Rebecca!'

She was gone. She drove out with Miss Crawley that day. It was before the latter's illness. At dinner she was unusually brilliant and lively; but she would take no notice of the hints, or the nods, or the clumsy expostulations of the humiliated, infatuated guardsman. Skirmishes of this sort passed perpetually during the little campaign – tedious to relate, and similar in result. The Crawley heavy cavalry was maddened by defeat, and routed every day.

If the baronet of Queen's Crawley had not had the fear of losing his sister's legacy before his eyes, he never would have permitted his dear girls to lose the educational blessings which their invaluable governess was conferring upon them. The old house at home seemed a desert without her, so useful and pleasant had Rebecca made herself there. Sir Pitt's letters were not copied and corrected; his books not made up; his household business and manifold schemes neglected, now that his little secretary was away. And it was easy to see how necessary such an amanuensis was to him, by the tenor and spelling of the numerous letters which he sent to her, entreating her and commanding her to return. Almost every day brought a frank from the baronet, enclosing the most urgent prayers to Becky for her return, or conveying pathetic statements to Miss Crawley, regarding the neglected state of his daughters' education; of which documents Miss Crawley took very little heed.

Miss Briggs was not formally dismissed, but her place as companion was a sinecure and a derision; and her company was the fat spaniel in the drawing-room, or occasionally the discontented Firkin in the housekeeper's closet. Nor though the old lady would by no means hear of Rebecca's departure, was the latter regularly installed in office in Park Lane. Like many wealthy people, it was Miss Crawley's habit to accept as much service as she could get from her inferiors; and good-naturedly to take leave of them when she no longer found them useful. Gratitude among certain rich folks is scarcely natural or to be thought of. They take needy people's services as their due. Nor have you, O poor parasite and humble hanger-on, much reason to complain! Your friendship for Dives is about as sincere as the return which it usually gets. It is money you love, and not the man; and were Croesus and his footman to change places, you know, you poor rogue, who would have the benefit of your allegiance.

And I am not sure that, in spite of Rebecca's simplicity and activity, and gentleness and untiring good humour, the shrewd old London lady, upon whom these treasures of friendship were lavished, had not a lurking suspicion all the while of her affectionate nurse and friend. It must have often crossed Miss Crawley's mind that nobody does anything for nothing. If she measured her own feeling towards the world, she must have been pretty well able to gauge those of the world towards herself; and perhaps she reflected, that it is the ordinary lot of people to have no friends if they themselves care for nobody.

Well, meanwhile, Becky was the greatest comfort and convenience to her, and she gave her a couple of new gowns, and an old necklace and shawl, and showed her friendship by abusing all her intimate acquaintances to her new confidante (than which there can't be a more touching proof of regard), and meditated vaguely some great future benefit – to marry her perhaps to Clump, the apothecary, or to settle her in some advantageous way of life; or, at any rate, to send her back to Queen's Crawley when she had done with her, and the full London season had begun.

When Miss Crawley was convalescent and descended to

the drawing-room, Becky sang to her, and otherwise amused her; when she was well enough to drive out, Becky accompanied her. And amongst the drives which they took, whither, of all places in the world, did Miss Crawley's admirable good nature and friendship actually induce her to penetrate, but to Russell Square, Bloomsbury, and the house of John Sedley, Esquire.

Ere that event, many notes had passed, as may be imagined, between the two dear friends. During the months of Rebecca's stay in Hampshire, the eternal friendship had (must it be owned?) suffered considerable diminution, and grown so decrepit and feeble with old age as to threaten demise altogether. The fact is, both girls had their own real affairs to think of: Rebecca her advance with her employers – Amelia her own absorbing topic. When the two girls met, and flew into each other's arms with that impetuosity which distinguishes the behaviour of young ladies towards each other, Rebecca performed her part of the embrace with the most perfect briskness and energy. Poor little Amelia blushed as she kissed her friend, and thought she had been guilty of something very like coldness towards her.

Their first interview was but a very short one. Amelia was just ready to go out for a walk. Miss Crawley was waiting in her carriage below, her people wondering at the locality in which they found themselves, and gazing upon honest Sambo, the black footman of Bloomsbury, as one of the queer natives of the place. But when Amelia came down with her kind smiling looks (Rebecca must introduce her to her friend, Miss Crawley was longing to see her, and was too ill to leave her carriage) – when, I say, Amelia came down, the Park Lane shoulder-knot aristocracy wondered more and more that such a thing could come out of Bloomsbury; and Miss Crawley was fairly captivated by the sweet blushing face of the young lady who came forward so timidly and so gracefully to pay her respects to the protector of her friend.

'What a complexion, my dear. What a sweet voice!' Miss Crawley said, as they drove away westward after the little interview. 'My dear Sharp, your young friend is charming. Send for her to Park Lane, do you hear?' Miss Crawley had a good taste. She liked natural manners – a little timidity only set them off. She liked pretty faces near her; as she liked pretty pictures and nice china. She talked of Amelia with rapture half a dozen times that day. She mentioned her to Rawdon Crawley, who came dutifully to partake of his aunt's chicken.

Of course, on this Rebecca instantly stated, that Amelia was engaged to be married – to a Lieutenant Osborne – a very old flame.

'Is he a man in a line-regiment?' Captain Crawley asked, remembering after an effort, as became a guardsman, the number of the regiment, the –th.

Rebecca thought that was the regiment. 'The captain's name,' she said, 'was Captain Dobbin.'

'A lanky gawky fellow,' said Crawley, 'tumbles over everybody. I know him; and Osborne's a goodish-looking fellow, with large black whiskers?'

'Enormous,' Miss Rebecca Sharp said, 'and enormously proud of them, I assure you.'

Captain Rawdon Crawley burst into a hoarse laugh by way of reply; and being pressed by the ladies to explain, did so when the explosion of hilarity was over. 'He fancies he can play at billiards,' said he. 'I won two hundred of him at the "Cocoa-Tree." *He* play, the young flat! He'd have played for anything that day, but his friend Captain Dobbin carried him off, hang him!'

'Rawdon, Rawdon, don't be so wicked,' Miss Crawley remarked, highly pleased.

'Why, ma'am, of all the young fellows I've seen out of the line, I think this fellow's the greenest. Tarquin and Deuceace get what money they like out of him. He'd go to the deuce to be seen with a lord. He pays their dinners at Greenwich, and they invite the company.'

'And very pretty company too, I dare say.'

'Quite right, Miss Sharp. Right, as usual, Miss Sharp. Uncommon pretty company, – haw, haw!' and the captain laughed more and more, thinking he had made a good joke.

'Rawdon, don't be naughty!' his aunt exclaimed.

'Well, his father's a City man – immensely rich, they say. Hang those City fellows, they must bleed; and I've not done with him yet, I can tell you. Haw, haw!'

'Fie, Captain Crawley; I shall warn Amelia. A gambling husband!'

'Horrid, ain't he, hey?' the captain said with great solem-

nity; and then added, a sudden thought having struck him:
– 'Gad, I say, ma'am, we'll have him here.'

'Is he a presentable sort of a person?' the aunt inquired.

'Presentable? – oh, very well. You wouldn't see any
difference,' Captain Crawley answered. 'Do let's have him,
when you begin to see a few people; and his whatdyecallem
– his inamorato – eh, Miss Sharp; that's what you call it –
comes. Gad, I'll write him a note, and have him; and I'll
try if he can play piquet as well as billiards. Where does he
live, Miss Sharp?'

Miss Sharp told Crawley the lieutenant's town address;
and a few days after this conversation, Lieutenant Osborne
received a letter, in Captain Rawdon's schoolboy hand, and
enclosing a note of invitation from Miss Crawley.

Rebecca dispatched also an invitation to her darling Amelia, who, you may be sure, was ready enough to accept it
when she heard that George was to be of the party. It was
arranged that Amelia was to spend the morning with the
ladies of Park Lane, where all were very kind to her. Rebecca
patronized her with calm superiority: she was so much the
cleverer of the two, and her friend so gentle and unassuming,
that she always yielded when anybody chose to command,
and so took Rebecca's orders with perfect meekness and good
humour. Miss Crawley's graciousness was also remarkable.
She continued her raptures about little Amelia, talked about
her before her face as if she were a doll, or a servant, or a
picture, and admired her with the most benevolent wonder
possible. I admire that admiration which the genteel world
sometimes extends to the commonalty. There is no more
agreeable object in life than to see May Fair folks condescending. Miss Crawley's prodigious benevolence rather
fatigued poor little Amelia, and I am not sure that of the
three ladies in Park Lane she did not find honest Miss Briggs
the most agreeable. She sympathized with Briggs as with all
neglected or gentle people: she wasn't what you call a woman
of spirit.

George came to dinner – a repast *en garçon* with Captain
Crawley.

The great family coach of the Osbornes transported him
to Park Lane from Russell Square; where the young ladies,
who were not themselves invited, and professed the greatest
indifference at that slight, nevertheless looked at Sir Pitt

Crawley's name in the *Baronetage;* and learned everything which that work had to teach about the Crawley family and their pedigree, and the Binkies, their relatives, &c. &c. Rawdon Crawley received George Osborne with great frankness and graciousness: praised his play at billiards: asked him when he would have his revenge: was interested about Osborne's regiment: and would have proposed piquet to him that very evening, but Miss Crawley absolutely forbade any gambling in her house; so that the young lieutenant's purse was not lightened by his gallant patron, for that day at least. However, they made an engagement for the next, somewhere: to look at a horse that Crawley had to sell, and to try him in the Park; and to dine together, and to pass the evening with some jolly fellows. 'That is, if you're not on duty to that pretty Miss Sedley,' Crawley said, with a knowing wink. 'Monstrous nice girl, 'pon my honour, though, Osborne,' he was good enough to add. 'Lots of tin, I suppose, eh?'

Osborne wasn't on duty; he would join Crawley with pleasure: and the latter, when they met the next day, praised his new friend's horsemanship – as he might with perfect honesty – and introduced him to three or four young men of the first fashion, whose acquaintance immensely elated the simple young officer.

'How's little Miss Sharp, by the by,' Osborne inquired of his friend over their wine, with a dandified air. 'Good-natured little girl that. Does she suit you well at Queen's Crawley? Miss Sedley liked her a good deal last year.'

Captain Crawley looked savagely at the lieutenant out of his little blue eyes, and watched him when he went up to resume his acquaintance with the fair governess. Her conduct must have relieved Crawley if there was any jealously in the bosom of that life-guardsman.

When the young men went upstairs, and after Osborne's introduction to Miss Crawley, he walked up to Rebecca with a patronizing, easy swagger. He was going to be kind to her and protect her. He would even shake hands with her, as a friend of Amelia's; and saying, 'Ah, Miss Sharp! how-dy-doo?' held out his left hand towards her, expecting that she would be quite confounded at the honour.

Miss Sharp put out her right forefinger, – and gave him a little nod, so cool and killing, that Rawdon Crawley, watching the operations from the other room, could hardly

restrain his laughter as he saw the lieutenant's entire discomfiture; the start he gave, the pause, and the perfect
clumsiness with which he at length condescended to take the
finger which was offered for his embrace.

'She'd beat the devil, by Jove!' the captain said, in a
rapture: and the lieutenant, by way of beginning the conversation, agreeably asked Rebecca how she liked her new
place.

'My place?' said Miss Sharp, coolly, 'how kind of you to
remind me of it! It's a tolerably good place: the wages are
pretty good – not so good as Miss Wirt's, I believe, with
your sisters in Russell Square. How are those young ladies?
– not that I ought to ask.'

'Why not?' Mr. Osborne said, amazed.

'Why, they never condescended to speak to me, or to ask
me into their house, whilst I was staying with Amelia; but
we poor governesses, you know, are used to slights of this
sort.'

'My dear Miss Sharp!' Osborne ejaculated.

'At least in some families,' Rebecca continued. 'You can't
think what a difference there is though. We are not so
wealthy in Hampshire as you lucky folks of the City. But
then I am in a gentleman's family – good old English stock.
I suppose you know Sir Pitt's father refused a peerage. And
you see how I am treated. I am pretty comfortable. Indeed,
it is rather a good place. But how *very* good of you to
inquire!'

Osborne was quite savage. The little governess patronized
him and *persiflé*'d him until this young British Lion felt
quite uneasy; nor could he muster sufficient presence of
mind to find a pretext for backing out of this most delectable
conversation.

'I thought you liked the City families pretty well,' he
said, haughtily.

'Last year you mean, when I was fresh from that horrid
vulgar school? Of course I did. Doesn't every girl like to
come home for the holidays? And how was I to know any
better? But oh, Mr. Osborne, what a difference eighteen
months' experience makes! – eighteen months spent, pardon
me for saying so, with gentlemen. As for dear Amelia, she,
I grant you, is a pearl, and would be charming anywhere.
There now, I see you are beginning to be in a good humour;

but oh, these queer odd City people! And Mr. Jos – how is that wonderful Mr. Joseph?'

'It seems to me you didn't dislike that wonderful Mr. Joseph last year,' Osborne said, kindly.

'How severe of you! Well, *entre nous*, I didn't break my heart about him; yet if he had asked me to do what you mean by your looks (and very expressive and kind they are, too), I wouldn't have said no.'

Mr. Osborne gave a look as much as to say, 'Indeed, how very obliging!'

'What an honour to have had you for a brother-in-law, you are thinking? To be sister-in-law to George Osborne, Esquire, son of John Osborne, Esquire, son of – what was your grandpapa, Mr. Osborne? Well, don't be angry. You can't help your pedigree, and I quite agree with you that I would have married Mr. Joe Sedley; for could a poor penniless girl do better? Now you know the whole secret. *I'm* frank and open; and, considering all things, it was very kind of you to allude to the circumstance – very kind and polite. Amelia dear, Mr. Osborne and I were talking about your poor brother Joseph. How is he?'

Thus was George utterly routed. Not that Rebecca was in the right; but she had managed most successfully to put him in the wrong. And he now shamefully fled, feeling, if he stayed another minute, that he would have been made to look foolish in the presence of Amelia.

Though Rebecca had had the better of him, George was above the meanness of tale-bearing or revenge upon a lady, – only he could not help cleverly confiding to Captain Crawley, next day, some notions of his regarding Miss Rebecca – that she was a sharp one, a dangerous one, a desperate flirt, &c.; in all of which opinions Crawley agreed laughingly, and with every one of which Miss Rebecca was made acquainted before twenty-four hours were over. They added to her original regard for Mr. Osborne. Her woman's instinct had told her that it was George who had interrupted the success of her first love-passage, and she esteemed him accordingly.

'I only just warn you,' he said to Rawdon Crawley, with a knowing look – he had bought the horse, and lost some score of guineas after dinner, 'I just warn you – I know women, and counsel you to be on the look-out.'

'Thank you, my boy,' said Crawley, with a look of peculiar gratitude. 'You're wide awake, I see.' And George went off, thinking Crawley was quite right.

He told Amelia of what he had done, and how he had counselled Rawdon Crawley – a devilish good, straight-forward fellow – to be on his guard against that little sly, scheming Rebecca.

'Against *whom?*' Amelia cried.

'Your friend the governess. – Don't look so astonished.'

'Oh, George, what *have* you done?' Amelia said. For her woman's eyes, which Love had made sharp-sighted, had in one instant discovered a secret which was invisible to Miss Crawley, to poor virgin Briggs, and, above all, to the stupid peepers of that young whiskered prig, Lieutenant Osborne.

For as Rebecca was shawling her in an upper apartment, where these two friends had an opportunity for a little of that secret talking and conspiring which forms the delight of female life; Amelia, coming up to Rebecca, and taking her two little hands in hers, said, 'Rebecca, I see it all.'

Rebecca kissed her.

And regarding this delightful secret, not one syllable more was said by either of the young women. But it was destined to come out before long.

Some short period after the above events, and Miss Rebecca Sharp still remaining at her patroness's house in Park Lane, one more hatchment might have been seen in Great Gaunt Street, figuring amongst the many which usually ornament that dismal quarter. It was over Sir Pitt Crawley's house; but it did not indicate the worthy baronet's demise. It was a feminine hatchment, and indeed a few years back had served as a funeral compliment to Sir Pitt's old mother, the late dowager Lady Crawley. Its period of service over, the hatchment had come down from the front of the house, and lived in retirement somewhere in the back premises of Sir Pitt's mansion. It reappeared now for poor Rose Dawson. Sir Pitt was a widower again. The arms quartered on the shield along with his own were not, to be sure, poor Rose's. She had no arms. But the cherubs painted on the scutcheon answered as well for her as for Sir Pitt's mother, and *Resurgam* was written under the coat, flanked by the Crawley

Dove and Serpent. Arms and Hatchments, Resurgam. – Here is an opportunity for moralizing!

Mr. Crawley had tended that otherwise friendless bedside. She went out of the world strengthened by such words and comfort as he could give her. For many years his was the only kindness she ever knew; the only friendship that solaced in any way that feeble, lonely soul. Her heart was dead long before her body. She had sold it to become Sir Pitt Crawley's wife. Mothers and daughters are making the same bargain every day in Vanity Fair.

When the demise took place, her husband was in London attending to some of his innumerable schemes, and busy with his endless lawyers. He had found time, nevertheless, to call often in Park Lane, and to dispatch many notes to Rebecca, entreating her, enjoining her, commanding her to return to her young pupils in the country, who were now utterly without companionship during their mother's illness. But Miss Crawley would not hear of her departure; for though there was no lady of fashion in London who would desert her friends more complacently as soon as she was tired of their society, and though few tired of them sooner, yet as long as her *engouement* lasted her attachment was prodigious, and she clung still with the greatest energy to Rebecca.

The news of Lady Crawley's death provoked no more grief or comment than might have been expected in Miss Crawley's family circle. 'I suppose I must put off my party for the 3rd,' Miss Crawley said; and added, after a pause, 'I hope my brother will have the decency not to marry again.' 'What a confounded rage Pitt will be in if he does,' Rawdon remarked, with his usual regard for his elder brother. Rebecca said nothing. She seemed by far the gravest and most impressed of the family. She left the room before Rawdon went away that day; but they met by chance below, as he was going away after taking leave, and had a parley together.

On the morrow, as Rebecca was gazing from the window, she startled Miss Crawley, who was placidly occupied with a French novel, by crying out in an alarmed tone, 'Here's Sir Pitt, ma'am!' and the baronet's knock followed this announcement.

'My dear, I can't see him. I won't see him. Tell Bowls

not at home, or go downstairs and say I'm too ill to receive any one. My nerves really won't bear my brother at this moment;' cried out Miss Crawley, and resumed the novel.

'She's too ill to see you, sir,' Rebecca said, tripping down to Sir Pitt, who was preparing to ascend.

'So much the better,' Sir Pitt answered. 'I want to see *you*, Miss Becky. Come along a me into the parlour,' and they entered that apartment together.

'I wawnt you back at Queen's Crawley, miss,' the baronet said, fixing his eyes upon her, and taking off his black gloves and his hat with its great crape hatband. His eyes had such a strange look, and fixed upon her so steadfastly, that Rebecca Sharp began almost to tremble.

'I hope to come soon,' she said in a low voice, 'as soon as Miss Crawley is better – and return to – to the dear children.'

'You've said so these three months, Becky,' replied Sir Pitt, 'and still you go hanging on to my sister, who'll fling you off like an old shoe, when she's wore you out. I tell you I *want* you. I'm going back to the Vuneral. Will you come back? Yes or no.'

'I daren't – I don't think – it would be right – to be alone – with you, sir,' Becky said, seemingly in great agitation.

'I say agin, I want you,' Sir Pitt said, thumping the table. 'I can't git on without you. I didn't see what it was till you went away. The house all goes wrong. It's not the same place. All my accounts has got muddled agin. You *must* come back. Do come back. Dear Becky, do come.'

'Come – as what, sir?' Rebecca gasped out.

'Come as Lady Crawley, if you like,' the baronet said, grasping his crape hat. 'There! will that zatusfy you? Come back and be my wife. Your vit vor't. Birth be hanged. Your as good as a lady as ever I see. You've got more brains in your little vinger than any baronet's wife in the country. Will you come? Yes or no?'

'Oh, Sir Pitt!' Rebecca said, very much moved.

'Say yes, Becky,' Sir Pitt continued. 'I'm an old man, but a good'n. I'm good for twenty years. I'll make you happy, zee if I don't. You shall do what you like; spend what you like; and 'av it all your own way. I'll make you a zettlement. I'll do everything reglar. Look year!' and the old man fell down on his knees and leered at her like a satyr.

Rebecca started back a picture of consternation. In the course of this history we have never seen her lose her presence of mind; but she did now, and wept some of the most genuine tears that ever fell from her eyes.

'Oh, Sir Pitt!' she said. 'Oh, sir – I – I'm *married already.*'

CHAPTER XV

IN WHICH REBECCA'S HUSBAND APPEARS FOR A SHORT TIME

E VERY reader of a sentimental turn (and we desire no other) must have been pleased with the tableau with which the last act of our little drama concluded; for what can be prettier than an image of Love on his knees before Beauty?

But when Love heard that awful confession from Beauty that she was married already, he bounced up from his attitude of humility on the carpet, uttering exclamations which caused poor little Beauty to be more frightened than she was when she made her avowal. 'Married; you're joking,' the baronet cried, after the first explosion of rage and wonder. 'You're making vun of me, Becky. Who'd ever go to marry you without a shilling to your vortune?'

'Married! married!' Rebecca said, in an agony of tears – her voice choking with emotion, her handkerchief up to her ready eyes, fainting against the mantelpiece – a figure of woe fit to melt the most obdurate heart. 'Oh, Sir Pitt, dear Sir Pitt, do not think me ungrateful for all your goodness to me. It is only your generosity that has extorted my secret.'

'Generosity be hanged!' Sir Pitt roared out. 'Who is it tu, then, you're married? Where was it?'

'Let me come back with you to the country, sir! Let me watch over you as faithfully as ever! Don't, don't separate me from dear Queen's Crawley!'

'The feller has left you, has he?' the baronet said, beginning, as he fancied, to comprehend. 'Well, Becky – come back if you like. You can't eat your cake and have it. Any ways I made you a vair offer. Coom back as governess – you shall have it all your own way.' She held out one hand. She cried fit to break her heart; her ringlets fell over her face, and over the marble mantelpiece where she laid it.

'So the rascal ran off, eh?' Sir Pitt said, with a hideous attempt at consolation. 'Never mind, Becky, *I'll* take care of 'ee.'

'Oh, sir! it would be the pride of my life to go back to Queen's Crawley, and take care of the children, and of you as formerly, when you said you were pleased with the services of your little Rebecca. When I think of what you have just offered me, my heart fills with gratitude – indeed it does. I can't be your wife, sir; let me – let me be your daughter.'

Saying which, Rebecca went down on *her* knees in a most tragical way, and taking Sir Pitt's horny black hand between her own two (which were very pretty and white, and as soft as satin), looked up in his face with an expression of exquisite pathos and confidence, when – when the door opened, and Miss Crawley sailed in.

Mrs. Firkin and Miss Briggs, who happened by chance to be at the parlour-door soon after the baronet and Rebecca entered the apartment, had also seen accidentally through the keyhole the old gentleman prostrate before the governess, and had heard the generous proposal which he made her. It was scarcely out of his mouth, when Mrs. Firkin and Miss Briggs had streamed up the stairs, had rushed into the drawing-room where Miss Crawley was reading the French novel, and had given that old lady the astounding intelligence that Sir Pitt was on his knees, proposing to Miss Sharp. And if you calculate the time for the above dialogue to take place – the time for Briggs and Firkin to fly to the drawing-room – the time for Miss Crawley to be astonished, and to drop her volume of Pigault le Brun – and the time for her to come downstairs – you will see how exactly accurate this history is, and how Miss Crawley *must* have appeared at the very instant when Rebecca had assumed the attitude of humility.

'It is the lady on the ground, and not the gentleman,' Miss Crawley said, with a look and voice of great scorn. 'They told me that *you* were on your knees, Sir Pitt: do kneel once more, and let me see this pretty couple!'

'I have thanked Sir Pitt Crawley, ma'am,' Rebecca said, rising, 'and have told him that – that I never can become Lady Crawley.'

'Refused him!' Miss Crawley said, more bewildered than

ever. Briggs and Firkin at the door opened the eyes of astonishment and the lips of wonder.

'Yes – refused,' Rebecca continued, with a sad, tearful voice.

'And am I to credit my ears that you absolutely proposed to her, Sir Pitt?' the old lady asked.

'Ees,' said the baronet, 'I did.'

'And she refused you as she says?'

'Ees,' Sir Pitt said, his features on a broad grin.

'It does not seem to break your heart at any rate,' Miss Crawley remarked.

'Nawt a bit,' answered Sir Pitt, with a coldness and good humour which set Miss Crawley almost mad with bewilderment. That an old gentleman of station should fall on his knees to a penniless governess, and burst out laughing because she refused to marry him – that a penniless governess should refuse a baronet with four thousand a year, – these were mysteries which Miss Crawley could never comprehend. It surpassed any complications of intrigue in her favourite Pigault le Brun.

'I'm glad you think it good sport, brother,' she continued, groping wildly through this amazement.

'Vamous,' said Sir Pitt. 'Who'd ha' thought it! what a sly little devil! what a little fox it waws!' he muttered to himself, chuckling with pleasure.

'Who'd have thought what?' cries Miss Crawley, stamping with her foot. 'Pray, Miss Sharp, are you waiting for the Prince Regent's divorce, that you don't think our family good enough for you?'

'My attitude,' Rebecca said, 'when you came in, ma'am, did not look as if I despised such an honour as this good – this noble man has deigned to offer me. Do you think I have no heart? Have you all loved me, and been so kind to the poor orphan – deserted – girl, and am *I* to feel nothing? O my friends! O my benefactors! may not my love, my life, my duty, try to repay the confidence you have shown me? Do you grudge me even gratitude, Miss Crawley? It is too much – my heart is too full;' and she sank down in a chair so pathetically, that most of the audience present were perfectly melted with her sadness.

'Whether you marry me or not, you're a good little girl, Becky, and I'm your vriend, mind,' said Sir Pitt, and putting on his crape-bound hat, he walked away – greatly to Rebecca's relief; for it was evident that her secret was unrevealed to Miss Crawley, and she had the advantage of a brief reprieve.

Putting her handkerchief to her eyes, and nodding away honest Briggs, who would have followed her upstairs, she went up to her apartment; while Briggs and Miss Crawley, in a high state of excitement, remained to discuss the strange event, and Firkin, not less moved, dived down into the kitchen regions, and talked of it with all the male and female company there. And so impressed was Mrs. Firkin with the news, that she thought proper to write off by that very night's post, 'with her humble duty to Mrs. Bute Crawley and the family at the Rectory, and Sir Pitt has been and proposed for to marry Miss Sharp, wherein she has refused him, to the wonder of all.'

The two ladies in the dining-room (where worthy Miss Briggs was delighted to be admitted once more to a confidential conversation with her patroness) wondered to their hearts' content at Sir Pitt's offer, and Rebecca's refusal; Briggs very acutely suggesting that there must have been some obstacle in the shape of a previous attachment, otherwise no young woman in her senses would ever have refused so advantageous a proposal.

'You would have accepted it yourself, wouldn't you, Briggs?' Miss Crawley said, kindly.

'Would it not be a privilege to be Miss Crawley's sister?' Briggs replied, with meek evasion.

'Well, Becky would have made a good Lady Crawley, after all,' Miss Crawley remarked (who was mollified by the girl's refusal, and very liberal and generous now there was no call for her sacrifices). 'She has brains in plenty (much more wit in her little finger than you have, my poor dear Briggs, in all your head). Her manners are excellent, now I have formed her. She's a Montmorency, Briggs, and blood *is* something, though I despise it for my part; and she would have held her own amongst those pompous stupid Hampshire people much better than that unfortunate ironmonger's daughter.'

Briggs coincided as usual, and the 'previous attachment' was then discussed in conjectures. 'You poor friendless creatures are always having some foolish *tendre*,' Miss Crawley said. 'You yourself, you know, were in love with a writing-master (don't cry, Briggs – you're always crying, and it won't bring him to life again), and I suppose this unfortunate Becky has been silly and sentimental too – some apothecary, or house-steward, or painter, or young curate, or something of that sort.'

'Poor thing, poor thing!' says Briggs (who was thinking of twenty-four years back, and that hectic young writing-master, whose lock of yellow hair, and whose letters, beautiful in their illegibility, she cherished in her old desk upstairs). 'Poor thing, poor thing!' says Briggs. Once more she was a fresh-cheeked lass of eighteen; she was at evening church, and the hectic writing-master and she were quavering out of the same psalm-book.

'After such conduct on Rebecca's part,' Miss Crawley said enthusiastically, 'our family should do something. Find out who is the *objet*, Briggs. I'll set him up in a shop; or order my portrait of him, you know; or speak to my cousin, the bishop – and I'll *doter* Becky, and we'll have a wedding, Briggs, and you shall make the breakfast, and be a brides-maid.'

Briggs declared that it would be delightful, and vowed that her dear Miss Crawley was always kind and generous, and went up to Rebecca's bedroom to console her and prattle about the offer, and the refusal, and the cause thereof; and to hint at the generous intentions of Miss Crawley, and to find out who was the gentleman that had the mastery of Miss Sharp's heart.

Rebecca was very kind, very affectionate and affected – responded to Briggs's offers of tenderness with grateful fervour – owned there was a secret attachment – a delicious mystery – what a pity Miss Briggs had not remained half a minute longer at the keyhole! Rebecca might perhaps, have told more: but five minutes after Miss Briggs's arrival in Rebecca's apartment, Miss Crawley actually made her appearance there – an unheard-of honour; – her impatience had overcome her; she could not wait for the tardy operations of her ambassadress: so she came in person, and ordered Briggs out of the room. And expressing her approval of Rebecca's conduct, she asked particulars of the interview, and the previous transactions which had brought about the astonishing offer of Sir Pitt.

Rebecca said she had long had some notion of the partiality with which Sir Pitt honoured her (for he was in the habit of making his feelings known in a very frank and unreserved manner), but, not to mention private reasons with which she would not for the present trouble Miss Crawley, Sir Pitt's age, station, and habits were such as to render a marriage quite impossible; and could a woman with any feeling of self-respect and any decency listen to proposals at such a moment, when the funeral of the lover's deceased wife had not actually taken place?

'Nonsense, my dear, you would never have refused him had there not been some one else in the case,' Miss Crawley said, coming to her point at once. 'Tell me the private reasons: what are the private reasons? There *is* some one; who is it that has touched your heart?'

Rebecca cast down her eyes, and owned there was. 'You have guessed right, dear lady,' she said, with a sweet simple faltering voice. 'You wonder at one so poor and friendless having an attachment, don't you? I have never heard that poverty was any safeguard against it. I wish it were.'

'My poor dear child,' cried Miss Crawley, who was always quite ready to be sentimental, 'is our passion unrequited, then? Are we pining in secret? Tell me all, and let me console you.'

'I wish you could, dear madam,' Rebecca said in the same tearful tone. 'Indeed, indeed, I need it.' And she laid her head upon Miss Crawley's shoulder and wept there so naturally that the old lady, surprised into sympathy, embraced her with an almost maternal kindness, uttered many soothing protests of regard and affection for her, vowed that she loved her as a daughter, and would do everything in her power to serve her. 'And now who is it, my dear? Is it that pretty Miss Sedley's brother? You said something about an affair with him. I'll ask him here, my dear. And you shall have him: indeed you shall.'

'Don't ask me now,' Rebecca said. 'You shall know all soon. Indeed you shall. Dear kind Miss Crawley — dear friend, may I say so?'

'That you may, my child,' the old lady replied, kissing her.

'I can't tell you now,' sobbed out Rebecca, 'I am very miserable. But oh! love me always — promise you will love me always.' And in the midst of mutual tears – for the emotions of the younger woman had awakened the sympathies of the elder – this promise was solemnly given by Miss Crawley, who left her little protégée, blessing and admiring her as a dear, artless, tender-hearted, affectionate, incomprehensible creature.

And now she was left alone to think over the sudden and wonderful events of the day, and of what had been and what might have been. What think you were the private feelings of Miss, no (begging her pardon), of Mrs. Rebecca? If, a few pages back, the present writer claimed the privilege of peeping into Miss Amelia Sedley's bedroom, and understanding with the omniscience of the novelist all the gentle pains and passions which were tossing upon that innocent pillow, why should he not declare himself to be Rebecca's confidant too, master of her secrets, and seal-keeper of that young woman's conscience?

Well then, in the first place, Rebecca gave way to some very sincere and touching regrets that a piece of marvellous good fortune should have been so near her, and she actually obliged to decline it. In this natural emotion every properly regulated mind will certainly share. What good mother is there that would not commiserate a penniless spinster, who might have been my lady, and have shared four thousand a year? What well-bred young person is there in all Vanity Fair, who will not feel for a hard-working, ingenious, meritorious girl, who gets such an honourable, advantageous, provoking offer, just at the very moment when it is out of her power to accept it? I am sure our friend Becky's disappointment deserves and will command every sympathy.

I remember one night being in the Fair myself, at an evening party. I observed old Miss Toady there also present, single out for her special attentions and flattery little Mrs. Briefless, the barrister's wife, who is of a good family certainly, but, as we all know, is as poor as poor can be.

What, I asked in my own mind, can cause this obsequiousness on the part of Miss Toady; has Briefless got a county court, or has his wife had a fortune left her? Miss Toady explained presently, with that simplicity which distinguishes all her conduct. 'You know,' she said, 'Mrs. Briefless is grand-daughter of Sir John Redhand, who is so ill at Cheltenham that he can't last six months. Mrs.

Briefless's papa succeeds; so you see she *will* be a baronet's daughter.' And Toady asked Briefless and his wife to dinner the very next week.

If the mere chance of becoming a baronet's daughter can procure a lady such homage in the world, surely, surely we may respect the agonies of a young woman who has lost the opportunity of becoming a baronet's wife. Who would have dreamed of Lady Crawley dying so soon? She was one of those sickly women that might have lasted these ten years – Rebecca thought to herself, in all the woes of repentance – and I might have been my lady! I might have led that old man whither I would. I might have thanked Mrs. Bute for her patronage, and Mr. Pitt for his insufferable condescension. I would have had the townhouse newly furnished and decorated. I would have had the handsomest carriage in London, and a box at the opera; and I would have been presented next season. All this *might* have been; and now – now all was doubt and mystery.

But Rebecca was a young lady of too much resolution and energy of character to permit herself much useless and unseemly sorrow for the irrevocable past; so, having devoted only the proper portion of regret to it, she wisely turned her whole attention towards the future, which was now vastly more important to her. And she surveyed her position, and its hopes, doubts, and chances.

In the first place, she was *married*; – that was a great fact. Sir Pitt knew it. She was not so much surprised into the avowal, as induced to make it by a sudden calculation. It must have come some day: and why not now as at a later period? He who would have married her himself must at least be silent with regard to her marriage. How Miss Crawley would bear the news – was the great question. Misgivings Rebecca had; but she remembered all Miss Crawley had said; the old lady's avowed contempt for birth; her daring liberal opinions; her general romantic propensities; her almost doting attachment to her nephew, and her repeatedly-expressed fondness for Rebecca herself. She is so fond of him, Rebecca thought, that she will forgive him anything: she is so used to me that I don't think she could be comfortable without me: when the *éclaircissement* comes there will be a scene, and hysterics, and a great quarrel, and then a great reconciliation. At all events, what use was there in delaying? the die was thrown, and now or to-morrow the issue must be the same. And so, resolved that Miss Crawley should have the news, the young person debated in her mind as to the best means of conveying it to her; and whether she should face the storm that must come, or fly and avoid it until its first fury was blown over. In this state of meditation she wrote the following letter: —

DEAREST FRIEND, — The great crisis which we have debated about so often is *come*. Half of my secret is known, and I have thought and thought, until I am quite sure that now is the time to reveal *the whole of the mystery*. Sir Pitt came to me this morning, and made — what do you think? — *a declaration in form*. Think of that! Poor little me! I might have been Lady Crawley. How pleased Mrs. Bute would have been; and *ma tante* if I had taken precedence of her! I might have been somebody's mamma, instead of — Oh, I tremble, I tremble, when I think how soon we must tell all! —

Sir Pitt knows I am married, and not knowing to whom, is not very much displeased as yet. *Ma tante* is *actually angry* that I should have refused him. But she is all kindness and graciousness. She condescends to say I would have made him a good wife; and vows that she will be a mother to your little Rebecca. She will be shaken when she first hears the news. But need we fear anything beyond a momentary anger? I think not: *I am sure* not. She dotes upon you so (you naughty, good-for-nothing man), that she would pardon you *anything*: and, indeed, I believe, the next place in her heart is mine: and that she would be miserable without me. Dearest! something *tells me* we shall conquer. You shall leave that odious regiment: quit gaming, racing, and *be a good boy*; and we shall all live in Park Lane, and *ma tante* shall leave us all her money.

I shall try and walk to-morrow at 3 in the usual place. If Miss B. accompanies me, you must come to dinner, and bring an answer, and put it in the third volume of Porteus's *Sermons*. But, at all events, come to your own   R.

To Miss ELIZA STYLES,
     At Mr. Barnet's, Saddler, Knightsbridge.

And I trust there is no reader of this little story who has not discernment enough to perceive that the Miss Eliza Styles (an old schoolfellow, Rebecca said, with whom she had resumed an active correspondence of late), and who used to fetch these letters from the saddler's, wore brass spurs, and large curling moustachios, and was indeed no other than Captain Rawdon Crawley.

CHAPTER XVI

THE LETTER ON THE PINCUSHION

How they were married is not of the slightest consequence to anybody. What is to hinder a Captain who is a major, and a young lady who is of age, from purchasing a licence, and uniting themselves at any church in this town? Who needs to be told, that if a woman has a will, she will assuredly find a way? – My belief is, that one day, when Miss Sharp had gone to pass the forenoon with her dear friend Miss Amelia Sedley in Russell Square, a lady very like her might have been seen entering a church in the city, in company with a gentleman with dyed moustachios, who, after a quarter of an hour's interval, escorted her back to the hackney-coach in waiting, and that this was a quiet bridal party.

And who on earth, after the daily experience we have, can question the probability of a gentleman marrying anybody? How many of the wise and learned have married their cooks? Did not Lord Eldon himself, the most prudent of men, make a runaway match? Were not Achilles and Ajax both in love with their servant-maids? And are we to expect a heavy dragoon with strong desires and small brains, who had never controlled a passion in his life, to become prudent all of a sudden, and to refuse to pay any price for an indulgence to which he had a mind? If people only made prudent marriages, what a stop to population there would be!

It seems to me, for my part, that Mr. Rawdon's marriage was one of the honestest actions which we shall have to record in any portion of that gentleman's biography which has to do with the present history. No one will say it is unmanly to be captivated by a woman, or, being captivated, to marry her; and the admiration, the delight, the passion, the wonder, the unbounded confidence, and frantic adoration with which, by degrees, this big warrior got to regard the little Rebecca, were feelings which the ladies at least will pronounce were not altogether discreditable to him. When she sang, every note thrilled in his dull soul, and tingled through his huge frame. When she spoke, he brought all the force of his brains to listen and wonder. If she was jocular, he used to revolve her jokes in his mind, and explode over them half an hour afterwards in the street, to the surprise of the groom in the tilbury by his side, or the comrade riding with him in Rotten Row. Her words were oracles to him, her smallest actions marked by an infallible grace and wisdom. 'How she sings – how she paints,' thought he. 'How she rode that kicking mare at Queen's Crawley!' And he would say to her in confidential moments, 'By Jove, Beck, you're fit to be Commander-in-Chief, or Archbishop of Canterbury, by Jove.' Is his case a rare one? and don't we see every day in the world many an honest Hercules at the apronstrings of Omphale, and great whiskered Samsons prostrate in Delilah's lap?

When, then, Becky told him that the great crisis was near, and the time for action had arrived, Rawdon expressed himself as ready to act under her orders, as he would be to charge with his troop at the command of his colonel. There was no need for him to put his letter into the third volume of Porteus. Rebecca easily found a means to get rid of Briggs, her companion, and met her faithful friend in 'the usual place' on the next day. She had thought over matters at night, and communicated to Rawdon the result of her determinations. He agreed, of course, to everything; was quite sure that it was all right: that what she proposed was best; that Miss Crawley would infallibly relent, or 'come round', as he said, after a time. Had Rebecca's resolutions been entirely different, he would have followed them as implicitly. 'You have head enough for both of us, Beck,' said he. 'You're sure to get us out of the scrape. I never saw your equal, and I've met with some clippers in my time too.' And with this simple confession of faith, the love-stricken dragoon left her to execute his part of the project which she had formed for the pair.

It consisted simply in the hiring of quiet lodgings at Brompton, or in the neighbourhood of the barracks, for Captain and Mrs. Crawley. For Rebecca had determined, and very prudently, we think, to fly. Rawdon was only too happy at her resolve; he had been entreating her to take this measure any time for weeks past. He pranced off to engage the lodgings with all the impetuosity of love. He agreed to pay two guineas a week so readily, that the landlady regretted she had asked him so little. He ordered in a piano; and half a nursery-house full of flowers: and a heap of good things. As for shawls, kid gloves, silk stockings, gold French watches, bracelets and perfumery, he sent them in with the profusion of blind love and unbounded credit. And having relieved his mind by this outpouring of generosity, he went and dined nervously at the club, waiting until the great moment of his life should come.

The occurrences of the previous day; the admirable conduct of Rebecca in refusing an offer so advantageous to her, the secret unhappiness preying upon her, the sweetness and silence with which she bore her affliction, made Miss Crawley much more tender than usual. An event of this nature, a marriage, or a refusal, or a proposal, thrills through a whole houseful of women, and sets all their hysterical sympathies at work. As an observer of human nature, I regularly frequent St. George's, Hanover Square, during the genteel marriage season; and though I have never seen the bridegroom's male friends give way to tears, or the beadles and officiating clergy any way affected, yet it is not at all uncommon to see women who are not in the least concerned in the operations going on – old ladies who are long past marrying, stout middle-aged females with plenty of sons and daughters, let alone pretty young creatures in pink bonnets, who are on their promotion, and may naturally take an interest in the ceremony, – I say it is quite common to see the women present piping, sobbing, sniffling; hiding their little faces in their little useless pocket-handkerchiefs; and heaving, old and young, with emotion. When my friend, the fashionable John Pimlico, married the lovely Lady Belgravia Green Parker, the excitement was so general, that even the little snuffy old pew-opener who let me into the seat, was in tears. And wherefore? I inquired of my own soul: *she* was not going to be married.

Miss Crawley and Briggs in a word, after the affair of Sir Pitt, indulged in the utmost luxury of sentiment, and Rebecca became an object of the most tender interest to them. In her absence Miss Crawley solaced herself with the most sentimental of the novels in her library. Little Sharp, with her secret griefs, was the heroine of the day.

That night Rebecca sang more sweetly and talked more pleasantly than she had ever been heard to do in Park Lane.

She twined herself round the heart of Miss Crawley. She spoke lightly and laughingly of Sir Pitt's proposal, ridiculed it as the foolish fancy of an old man; and her eyes filled with tears, and Briggs's heart with unutterable pangs of defeat, as she said she desired no other lot than to remain for ever with her dear benefactress. 'My dear little creature,' the old lady said, 'I don't intend to let you stir for years, that you may depend upon it. As for going back to that odious brother of mine after what has passed, it is out of the question. Here you stay with me and Briggs. Briggs wants to go to see her relations very often. Briggs, you may go when you like. But as for you, my dear, you must stay and take care of the old woman.'

If Rawdon Crawley had been then and there present, instead of being at the club nervously drinking claret, the pair might have gone down on their knees before the old spinster, avowed all, and been forgiven in a twinkling. But that good chance was denied to the young couple, doubtless in order that this story might be written, in which numbers of their wonderful adventures are narrated – adventures which could never have occurred to them if they had been housed and sheltered under the comfortable uninteresting forgiveness of Miss Crawley.

Under Mrs. Firkin's orders, in the Park Lane establishment, was a young woman from Hampshire, whose business it was, among other duties, to knock at Miss Sharp's door with that jug of hot water, which Firkin would rather have perished than have presented to the intruder. This girl, bred on the family estate, had a brother in Captain Crawley's troop, and if the truth were known, I dare say it would come out that she was aware of certain arrangements, which have a great deal to do with this history. At any rate she purchased a yellow shawl, a pair of green boots, and a light blue hat with a red feather, with three guineas which Rebecca gave her, and as little Sharp was by no means too liberal with her money, no doubt it was for services rendered that Betty Martin was so bribed.

On the second day after Sir Pitt Crawley's offer to Miss Sharp, the sun rose as usual, and at the usual hour Betty Martin, the upstairs maid, knocked at the door of the governess's bed-chamber.

No answer was returned, and she knocked again. Silence was still uninterrupted; and Betty, with the hot water, opened the door and entered the chamber.

The little white dimity bed was as smooth and trim as on the day previous, when Betty's own hands had helped to make it. Two little trunks were corded in one end of the room; and on the table before the window – on the pin-cushion – the great fat pincushion lined with pink inside, and twilled like a lady's nightcap – lay a letter. It had been reposing there probably all night.

Betty advanced towards it on tiptoe, as if she were afraid to awake it – looked at it, and round the room, with an air of great wonder and satisfaction; took up the letter, and grinned intensely as she turned it round and over, and finally carried it in to Miss Briggs's room below.

How could Betty tell that the letter was for Miss Briggs, I should like to know? All the schooling Betty had was at Mrs. Bute Crawley's Sunday School, and she could no more read writing than Hebrew.

'La, Miss Briggs,' the girl exclaimed, 'oh, miss, something must have happened – there's nobody in Miss Sharp's room; the bed ain't been slep in, and she've run away, and left this letter for you, miss.'

'*What!*' cries Briggs, dropping her comb, the thin wisp of faded hair falling over her shoulders; 'an elopement! Miss Sharp a fugitive! What, what is this?' and she eagerly broke the neat seal, and, as they say, 'devoured the contents' of the letter addressed to her.

DEAR MISS BRIGGS (the refugee wrote), the kindest heart in the world as yours is, will pity and sympathize with me and excuse me. With tears, and prayers, and blessings, I leave the home where the poor orphan has ever met with kindness and affection. Claims even superior to those of my benefactress call me hence. I go to my duty – to my *husband*. Yes, I am married. My husband *commands* me to seek the *humble home* which we call ours. Dearest Miss Briggs, break the news as your delicate sympathy will know how to do it – to my dear, my beloved friend and benefactress. Tell her, ere I went, I shed tears on her dear pillow – that pillow that I have so often soothed in sickness – that I long *again* to watch – Oh, with what joy shall I return to dear Park Lane! How I tremble for the answer which is to *seal my fate!* When Sir Pitt deigned to offer me his hand, an honour of which my beloved Miss Crawley said I was *deserving* (my blessings go with her for judging the poor orphan worthy to be *her sister!*), I told Sir Pitt that I was *already a wife*. Even he forgave me. But my courage failed me, when I should have told him all – that I could not be his wife, for I *was his daughter!* I am wedded to the best and most generous of men – Miss Crawley's Rawdon is *my* Rawdon. At his *command* I open my lips, and follow him to our humble home, as I would *through the world*. Oh, my excellent and kind friend, intercede with my Rawdon's beloved aunt for him and the poor girl to whom all *his noble race* have shown such *unparalleled affection*. Ask Miss Crawley to receive *her children*. I can say no more, but blessings, blessings on all in the dear house I leave, prays

Your affectionate and *grateful*,
REBECCA CRAWLEY .

Midnight.

Just as Briggs had finished reading this affecting and interesting document which reinstated her in her position as first confidante of Miss Crawley, Mrs. Firkin entered the room. 'Here's Mrs. Bute Crawley just arrived by the mail from Hampshire, and wants some tea: will you come down and make breakfast, miss?'

And to the surprise of Firkin, clasping her dressing-gown around her, the wisp of hair floating dishevelled behind her, the little curl-papers still sticking in bunches round her forehead, Briggs sailed down to Mrs. Bute with the letter in her hand containing the wonderful news.

'Oh, Mrs. Firkin,' gasped Betty, 'sech a business. Miss Sharp have a gone and run away with the capting, and they're off to Gretny Green!' We would devote a chapter to describe the emotions of Mrs. Firkin, did not the passions of her mistresses occupy our genteeler muse.

When Mrs. Bute Crawley, numbed with midnight travelling, and warming herself at the newly-crackling parlour fire, heard from Miss Briggs the intelligence of the clandestine marriage, she declared it was quite providential that she should have arrived at such a time to assist poor dear Miss Crawley in supporting the shock – that Rebecca was an artful little hussy of whom she had always had her suspicions; and that as for Rawdon Crawley, she never could account for his aunt's infatuation regarding him, and had long considered him a profligate, lost, and abandoned being. And this awful conduct, Mrs. Bute said, will have at least *this* good effect, it will open poor dear Miss Crawley's eyes to the real

character of this wicked man. Then Mrs. Bute had a comfortable hot toast and tea; and as there was a vacant room
in the house now, there was no need for her to remain at
the 'Gloster' Coffee-house where the Portsmouth mail had
set her down, and whence she ordered Mr. Bowls's aide de
camp, the footman, to bring away her trunks.

Miss Crawley, be it known, did not leave her room until
near noon – taking chocolate in bed in the morning, while
Becky Sharp read the *Morning Post* to her, or otherwise
amusing herself or dawdling. The conspirators below agreed
that they would spare the dear lady's feelings until she
appeared in her drawing-room: meanwhile it was announced
to her, that Mrs. Bute Crawley had come up from Hampshire
by the mail, was staying at the 'Gloster', sent her love to
Miss Crawley, and asked for breakfast with Miss Briggs. The
arrival of Mrs. Bute, which would not have caused any
extreme delight at another period, was hailed with pleasure
now; Miss Crawley being pleased at the notion of a gossip
with her sister-in-law regarding the late Lady Crawley, the
funeral arrangements pending, and Sir Pitt's abrupt proposals to Rebecca.

It was not until the old lady was fairly ensconced in her
usual arm-chair in the drawing-room, and the preliminary
embraces and inquiries had taken place between the ladies,
that the conspirators thought it advisable to submit her to
the operation. Who has not admired the artifices and delicate
approaches with which women 'prepare' their friends for bad
news? Miss Crawley's two friends made such an apparatus
of mystery before they broke the intelligence to her, that
they worked her up to the necessary degree of doubt and
alarm.

'And she refused Sir Pitt, my dear, dear Miss Crawley,
prepare yourself for it,' Mrs. Bute said, 'because – because
she couldn't help herself.'

'Of course there was a reason,' Miss Crawley answered.
'She liked somebody else. I told Briggs so yesterday.'

'*Likes* somebody else!' Briggs gasped. 'Oh, my dear friend,
she is married already.'

'Married already,' Mrs. Bute chimed in; and both sat with
clasped hands looking from each other at their victim.

'Send her to me, the instant she comes in. The little sly
wretch: how dared she not tell me?' cried out Miss Crawley.

'She won't come in soon. Prepare yourself, dear friend – she's gone out for a long time – she's – she's gone altogether.'

'Gracious goodness, and who's to make my chocolate? Send for her and have her back; I desire that she come back,' the old lady said.

'She decamped last night, ma'am,' cried Mrs. Bute.

'She left a letter for me,' Briggs exclaimed. 'She's married to —'

'Prepare her, for heaven's sake. Don't torture her, my dear Miss Briggs.'

'She's married to whom?' cries the spinster in a nervous fury.

'To – to a relation of —'

'She refused Sir Pitt,' cried the victim. 'Speak at once. Don't drive me mad.'

'Oh, ma'am – prepare her, Miss Briggs – she's married to Rawdon Crawley.'

'Rawdon married – Rebecca – governess – nobod – Get out of my house, you fool, you idiot – you stupid old Briggs – how dare you? You're in the plot – you made him marry, thinking that I'd leave my money from him – you did, Martha,' the poor old lady screamed in hysteric sentences.

'I, ma'am, ask a member of this family to marry a drawing-master's daughter?'

'Her mother was a Montmorency,' cried out the old lady, pulling at the bell with all her might.

'Her mother was an opera-girl, and she has been on the stage or worse herself,' said Mrs. Bute.

Miss Crawley gave a final scream, and fell back in a faint. They were forced to take her back to the room which she had just quitted. One fit of hysterics succeeded another. The doctor was sent for – the apothecary arrived. Mrs. Bute took up the post of nurse by her bedside. 'Her relations ought to be round about her,' that amiable woman said.

She had scarcely been carried up to her room, when a new person arrived to whom it was also necessary to break the news. This was Sir Pitt. 'Where's Becky?' he said, coming in. 'Where's her traps? She's coming with me to Queen's Crawley.'

'Have you not heard the astonishing intelligence regarding her surreptitious union?' Briggs asked.

'What's that to me?' Sir Pitt asked. 'I know she's married. That makes no odds. Tell her to come down at once, and not keep me.'

'Are you not aware, sir,' Miss Briggs asked, 'that she has left our roof, to the dismay of Miss Crawley, who is nearly killed by the intelligence of Captain Rawdon's union with her?'

When Sir Pitt Crawley heard that Rebecca was married to his son, he broke out into a fury of language, which it would do no good to repeat in this place, as indeed it sent poor Briggs shuddering out of the room; and with her we will shut the door upon the figure of the frenzied old man, wild with hatred and insane with baffled desire.

One day after he went to Queen's Crawley, he burst like a madman into the room she had used when there – dashed open her boxes with his foot, and flung about her papers, clothes, and other relics. Miss Horrocks, the butler's daughter, took some of them. The children dressed themselves and acted plays in the others. It was but a few days after the poor mother had gone to her lonely burying-place; and was laid, unwept and disregarded, in a vault full of strangers.

'Suppose the old lady doesn't come to,' Rawdon said to his little wife, as they sat together in the snug little Brompton lodgings. She had been trying the new piano all the morning. The new gloves fitted her to a nicety; the new shawls became her wonderfully; the new rings glittered on her little hands, and the new watch ticked at her waist; 'suppose she don't come round, eh, Becky?'

'*I'll* make your fortune,' she said; and Delilah patted Samson's cheek.

'You can do anything,' he said, kissing the little hand. 'By Jove, you can; and we'll drive down to the "Star and Garter", and dine, by Jove.'

CHAPTER XVII

HOW CAPTAIN DOBBIN BOUGHT A PIANO

IF there is any exhibition in all Vanity Fair which Satire and Sentiment can visit arm-in-arm together; where you light on the strangest contrasts laughable and tearful: where you may be gentle and pathetic, or savage and cynical with perfect propriety: it is at one of those public assemblies, a crowd of which are advertised every day in the last page of the *Times* newspaper, and over which the late Mr. George Robins used to preside with so much dignity. There are very few London people, as I fancy, who have not attended at these meetings, and all with a taste for moralizing must have thought, with a sensation and interest not a little startling and queer, of the day when their turn shall come too, and Mr. Hammerdown will sell by the orders of Diogenes's assignees, or will be instructed by the executors, to offer to public competition, the library, furniture, plate, wardrobe, and choice cellar of wines of Epicurus deceased.

Even with the most selfish disposition, the Vanity-Fairian, as he witnesses this sordid part of the obsequies of a departed friend, can't but feel some sympathies and regret. My Lord Dives's remains are in the family vault: the statuaries are cutting an inscription veraciously commemorating his virtues, and the sorrows of his heir, who is disposing of his goods. What guest at Dives's table can pass the familiar house without a sigh? – the familiar house of which the lights used to shine so cheerfully at seven o'clock, of which the hall-doors opened so readily, of which the obsequious servants, as you passed up the comfortable stair, sounded your name from landing to landing, until it reached the apartment where jolly old Dives welcomed his friends! What a number of them he had; and what a noble way of entertaining them. How witty people used to be here, who were morose when they got out of the door; and how courteous and friendly men who slandered and hated each other everywhere else! He was pompous, but with such a cook what would one not swallow? he was rather dull, perhaps, but would not such wine make any conversation pleasant? We must get some of his burgundy at any price, the mourners cry at his club. 'I got this box at old Dives's sale,' Pincher says, handing it round, 'one of Louis XV's mistresses – pretty thing, is it not – sweet miniature,' and they talked of the way in which young Dives is dissipating his fortune.

How changed the house is, though! The front is patched over with bills, setting forth the particulars of the furniture in staring capitals. They have hung a shred of carpet out of an upstairs window – a half-dozen of porters are lounging on the dirty steps – the hall swarms with dingy guests of oriental countenance, who thrust printed cards into your hand and offer to bid. Old women and amateurs have invaded the upper apartments, pinching the bed-curtains, poking into the feathers, shampooing the mattresses, and clapping the wardrobe drawers to and fro. Enterprising young housekeepers are measuring the looking-glasses and hangings to see if they will suit the new *ménage* (Snob will brag for years that he has purchased this or that at Dives's sale), and Mr. Hammerdown is sitting on the great mahogany dining-tables, in the dining-room below, waving the ivory hammer, and employing all the artifices of eloquence, enthusiasm, entreaty, reason, despair; shouting to his people; satirizing Mr. Davids for his sluggishness; inspiriting Mrs. Moss into action; imploring, commanding, bellowing, until down comes the hammer like fate, and we pass to the next lot. O Dives, who would ever have thought, as we sat round the broad table sparkling with plate and spotless linen, to have seen such a dish at the head of it as that roaring auctioneer?

It was rather late in the sale. The excellent drawing-room furniture by the best makers; the rare and famous wines selected, regardless of cost, and with the well-known taste of the purchaser; the rich and complete set of family plate had been sold on the previous days. Certain of the best wines (which all had a great character among amateurs in the neighbourhood) had been purchased for his master, who knew them very well, by the butler of our friend John Osborne, Esquire, of Russell Square. A small portion of the most useful articles of the plate had been bought by some young stockbrokers from the City. And now the public being invited to the purchase of minor objects, it happened that the orator on the table was expatiating on the merits of a picture, which he sought to recommend to his audience: it was by no means so select or numerous a company as had attended the previous days of the auction.

'No. 369,' roared Mr. Hammerdown. 'Portrait of a gentleman on an elephant. Who'll bid for the gentleman on the elephant? Lift up the picture, Blowman, and let the company examine this lot.' A long, pale, military-looking gentleman, seated demurely at the mahogany table, could not help grinning as this valuable lot was shown by Mr. Blowman.

'Turn the elephant to the captain, Blowman. What shall we say, sir, for the elephant?' but the captain, blushing in a very hurried and discomfited manner, turned away his head, and the auctioneer respected his discomposure.

'Shall we say twenty guineas for this work of art? – fifteen, five, name your own price. The gentleman without the elephant is worth five pound.'

'I wonder it ain't come down with him,' said a professional wag, 'he's anyhow a precious big one;' at which (for the elephant-rider was represented as of a very stout figure) there was a general giggle in the room.

'Don't be trying to deprecate the value of the lot, Mr. Moss,' Mr. Hammerdown said; 'let the company examine it as a work of art – the attitude of the gallant animal quite according to natur'; the gentleman in a nankeen jacket, his gun in his hand, is going to the chase; in the distance a banyanntree and a pagody, most likely resemblances of some interesting spot in our famous Eastern possessions. How much for this lot? Come, gentlemen, don't keep me here all day.'

Some one bid five shillings, at which the military gentleman looked towards the quarter from which this splendid offer had come, and there saw another officer with a young lady on his arm, who both appeared to be highly amused with the scene, and to whom, finally, this lot was knocked down for half a guinea. He at the table looked more surprised and discomposed than ever when he spied this pair, and his head sank into his military collar, and he turned his back upon them, so as to avoid them altogether.

Of all the other articles which Mr. Hammerdown had the honour to offer for public competition that day it is not our purpose to make mention, save of one only, a little square piano, which came down from the upper regions of the house (the state grand piano having been disposed of previously); this the young lady tried with a rapid and skilful hand (making the officer blush and start again), and for it, when its turn came, her agent began to bid.

But there was an opposition here. The Hebrew aide de camp in the service of the officer at the table bid against the Hebrew gentleman employed by the elephant purchasers, and a brisk battle ensued over this little piano, the combatants being greatly encouraged by Mr. Hammerdown.

At last, when the competition had been prolonged for some time, the elephant captain and lady desisted from the race; and the hammer coming down, the auctioneer said:— 'Mr. Lewis, twenty-five,' and Mr. Lewis's chief thus became the proprietor of the little square piano. Having effected the purchase, he sat up as if he was greatly relieved, and the unsuccessful competitors catching a glimpse of him at this moment, the lady said to her friend,

'Why, Rawdon, it's Captain Dobbin.'

I suppose Becky was discontented with the new piano her husband had hired for her, or perhaps the proprietors of that instrument had fetched it away, declining farther credit, or perhaps she had a particular attachment for the one which she had first tried to purchase, recollecting it in old days, when she used to play upon it, in the little sitting-room of our dear Amelia Sedley.

The sale was at the old house in Russell Square, where we passed some evenings together at the beginning of this story. Good old John Sedley was a ruined man. His name had been proclaimed as a defaulter on the Stock Exchange, and his bankruptcy and commercial extermination had followed. Mr. Osborne's butler came to buy some of the famous port wine to transfer to the cellars over the way. As for one dozen well-manufactured silver spoons and forks at per oz., and one dozen dessert ditto ditto, there were three young stock-brokers (Messrs. Dale, Spiggot, and Dale, of Threadneedle Street, indeed), who, having had dealings with the old man, and kindnesses from him in days when he was kind to everybody with whom he dealt, sent this little spar out of the wreck with their love to good Mrs. Sedley; and with respect to the piano, as it had been Amelia's, and as she might miss it and want one now, and as Captain William Dobbin could no more play upon it than he could dance on the tight-rope, it is probable that he did not purchase the instrument for his own use.

In a word, it arrived that evening, at a wonderful small cottage in a street leading from the Fulham Road – one of those streets which have the finest romantic names – (this was called St. Adelaide Villas, Anna-Maria Road, West), where the houses look like baby-houses; where the people, looking out of the first-floor windows, must infallibly, as you think, sit with their feet in the parlours; where the shrubs in the little gardens in front, bloom with a perennial display of little children's pinafores, little red socks, caps, &c. (polyandria polygynia); whence you hear the sound of jingling spinets and women singing; where little porter pots hang on the railings sunning themselves; whither of evenings you see city clerks padding wearily: here it was that Mr. Clapp, the clerk of Mr. Sedley, had his domicile, and in this asylum the good old gentleman hid his head with his wife and daughter when the crash came.

Jos Sedley had acted as a man of his disposition would, when the announcement of the family-misfortune reached him. He did not come to London, but he wrote to his mother to draw upon his agents for whatever money was wanted, so that his kind broken-spirited old parents had no present poverty to fear. This done, Jos went on at the boarding-house at Cheltenham pretty much as before. He drove his curricle; he drank his claret; he played his rubber; he told his Indian stories, and the Irish widow consoled and flattered him as usual. His present of money, needful as it was, made little impression on his parents; and I have heard Amelia say, that the first day on which she saw her father lift up his head after the failure, was on the receipt of the packet of forks and spoons with the young stockbrokers' love, over which he burst out crying like a child, being greatly more affected than even his wife, to whom the present was addressed. Edward Dale, the junior of the house, who purchased the spoons for the firm, was, in fact, very sweet upon Amelia, and offered for her in spite of all. He married Miss Louisa Cutts (daughter of Higham and Cutts, the eminent corn-factors), with a handsome fortune in 1820; and is now living in splendour, and with a numerous family, at his elegant villa, Muswell Hill. But we must not let the recollections of this good fellow cause us to diverge from the principal history.

I hope the reader has much too good an opinion of Captain and Mrs. Crawley to suppose that they ever would have dreamed of paying a visit to so remote a district as Blooms-bury, if they thought the family whom they proposed to honour with a visit were not merely out of fashion, but out of money, and could be serviceable to them in no possible manner. Rebecca was entirely surprised at the sight of the comfortable old house where she had met with no small kindness, ransacked by brokers and bargainers, and its quiet family treasures given up to public desecration and plunder. A month after her flight, she had bethought her of Amelia, and Rawdon, with a horse laugh, had expressed a perfect willingness to see young George Osborne again. 'He's a very agreeable acquaintance, Beck,' the wag added. 'I'd like to sell him another horse, Beck. I'd like to play a few more games at billiards with him. He'd be what I call *useful* just now, Mrs. C.– ha, ha!' by which sort of speech it is not to be supposed that Rawdon Crawley had a deliberate desire to cheat Mr. Osborne at play, but only wished to take that fair advantage of him which almost every sporting gentleman in Vanity Fair considers to be his due from his neighbour.

The old aunt was long in 'coming-to'. A month had elapsed. Rawdon was denied the door by Mr. Bowls; his servants could not get a lodgement in the house at Park Lane; his letters were sent back unopened. Miss Crawley never stirred out – she was unwell – and Mrs. Bute remained still and never left her. Crawley and his wife both of them augured evil from the continued presence of Mrs. Bute.

'Gad, I begin to perceive now why she was always bringing us together at Queen's Crawley,' Rawdon said.

'What an artful little woman!' ejaculated Rebecca.

'Well, *I* don't regret it, if you don't,' the captain cried, still in an amorous rapture with his wife, who rewarded him with a kiss by way of reply, and was indeed not a little gratified by the generous confidence of her husband.

'If he had but a little more brains,' she thought to herself, 'I might make something of him;' but she never let him perceive the opinion she had of him; listened with indefatigable complacency to his stories of the stable and the mess; laughed at all his jokes; felt the greatest interest in Jack Spatterdash, whose cab-horse had come down, and Bob Martingale, who had been taken up in a gambling-house, and Tom Cinqbars, who was going to ride the steeplechase. When he came home she was alert and happy: when he went out she pressed him to go: when he stayed at home, she played and sang for him, made him good drinks, superintended his dinner, warmed his slippers, and steeped his soul in comfort. The best of women (I have heard my grandmother say) are hypocrites. We don't know how much they hide from us: how watchful they are when they seem most artless and confidential: how often those frank smiles which they wear so easily, are traps to cajole or elude or disarm – I don't mean in your mere coquettes, but your domestic models, and paragons of female virtue. Who has not seen a woman hide the dullness of a stupid husband, or coax the fury of a savage one? We accept this amiable slavishness, and praise a woman for it: we call this pretty treachery truth. A good housewife is of necessity a humbug; and Cornelia's husband was hoodwinked, as Potiphar was – only in a different way.

By these attentions that veteran rake, Rawdon Crawley, found himself converted into a very happy and submissive married man. His former haunts knew him not. They asked about him once or twice at his clubs, but did not miss him much: in those booths of Vanity Fair people seldom do miss each other. His secluded wife ever smiling and cheerful, his little comfortable lodgings, snug meals, and homely evenings, had all the charms of novelty and secrecy. The marriage was not yet declared to the world, or published in the *Morning Post*. All his creditors would have come rushing on him in a body, had they known that he was united to a woman without fortune. 'My relations won't cry fie upon me,' Becky said, with rather a bitter laugh; and she was quite contented to wait until the old aunt should be reconciled, before she claimed her place in society. So she lived at Brompton, and meanwhile saw no one, or only those few of her husband's male companions who were admitted into her little dining-room. These were all charmed with her. The little dinners, the laughing and chatting, the music afterwards, delighted all who participated in these enjoyments. Major Martingale never thought about asking to see the marriage licence. Captain Cinqbars was perfectly enchanted with her skill in making punch. And young Lieutenant Spatterdash (who was fond of piquet, and whom Crawley would often invite) was evidently and quickly smitten by Mrs. Crawley; but her own circumspection and modesty never forsook her for a moment, and Crawley's reputation as a fire-eating and jealous warrior, was a further and complete defence to his little wife.

There are gentlemen of very good blood and fashion in this city who never have entered a lady's drawing-room; so that though Rawdon Crawley's marriage might be talked about in his county, where, of course, Mrs. Bute had spread the news, in London it was doubted, or not heeded, or not talked about at all. He lived comfortably on credit. He had a large capital of debts, which, laid out judiciously, will carry a man along for many years, and on which certain men about town contrive to live a hundred times better than even men with ready money can do. Indeed who is there that walks London streets, but can point out a half-dozen of men riding by him splendidly, while he is on foot, courted by fashion, bowed into their carriages by tradesmen, denying themselves nothing, and living on who knows what? We see Jack Thriftless prancing in the Park, or darting in his brougham down Pall Mall: we eat his dinners served on his miraculous plate. 'How did this begin,' we say, 'or where will it end?' 'My dear fellow,' I heard Jack once say, 'I owe money in every capital in Europe.' The end must come some day, but in the mean time Jack thrives as much as ever; people are glad enough to shake him by the hand, ignore the little dark stories that are whispered every now and then against him, and pronounce him a good-natured, jovial, reckless fellow.

Truth obliges us to confess that Rebecca had married a gentleman of this order. Everything was plentiful in his house but ready money, of which their *ménage* pretty early felt the want; and reading the *Gazette* one day, and coming upon the announcement of 'Lieutenant G. Osborne to be captain by purchase, vice Smith, who exchanges,' Rawdon uttered that sentiment regarding Amelia's lover, which ended in the visit to Russell Square.

When Rawdon and his wife wished to communicate with Captain Dobbin at the sale, and to know particulars of the catastrophe which had befallen Rebecca's old acquaintances, the captain had vanished; and such information as they got was from a stray porter or broker at the auction.

'Look at them with their hooked beaks,' Becky said, getting into the buggy, her picture under her arm in great glee. 'They're like vultures after a battle.'

'Don't know. Never was in action, my dear. Ask Martingale; he was in Spain, aide de camp to General Blazes.'

'He was a very kind old man, Mr. Sedley,' Rebecca said; 'I'm really sorry he's gone wrong.'

'Oh, stockbrokers – bankrupts – used to it, you know.' Rawdon replied, cutting a fly off the horse's ear.

'I wish we could have afforded some of the plate, Rawdon,' the wife continued sentimentally. 'Five-and-twenty guineas was monstrously dear for that little piano. We chose it at Broadwood's for Amelia, when she came from school. It only cost five-and-thirty then.'

'What-d'ye-call-'em – "Osborne" – will cry off now, I suppose, since the family is smashed. How cut up your pretty little friend will be; hey, Becky?'

'I dare say she'll recover it,' Becky said, with a smile – and they drove on and talked about something else.

CHAPTER XVIII

WHO PLAYED ON THE PIANO CAPTAIN DOBBIN BOUGHT?

OUR surprised story now finds itself for a moment among very famous events and personages, and hanging on to the skirts of history. When the eagles of Napoleon Bonaparte, the Corsican upstart, were flying from Provence, where they had perched after a brief sojourn in Elba, and from steeple to steeple until they reached the towers of Notre Dame, I wonder whether the Imperial birds had any eye for a little corner of the parish of Bloomsbury, London, which you might have thought so quiet, that even the whirring and flapping of those mighty wings would pass unobserved there?

'Napoleon has landed at Cannes.' Such news might create a panic at Vienna, and cause Russia to drop his cards, and take Prussia into a corner, and Talleyrand and Metternich to wag their heads together, while Prince Hardenberg, and even the present Marquis of Londonderry, were puzzled; but how was this intelligence to affect a young lady in Russell Square, before whose door the watchman sang the hours when she was asleep: who, if she strolled in the square, was guarded there by the railings and the beadle: who, if she walked ever so short a distance to buy a ribbon in Southampton Row, was followed by black Sambo with an enormous cane: who was always cared for, dressed, put to bed, and watched over by ever so many guardian angels, with and without wages. *Bon Dieu*, I say, is it not hard that the fateful rush of the great Imperial struggle can't take place without affecting a poor little harmless girl of eighteen, who is occupied in billing and cooing, or working muslin collars in Russell Square? You, too, kindly, homely flower! – is the great roaring war tempest coming to sweep you down, here, although cowering under the shelter of Holborn? Yes; Napoleon is flinging his last stake, and poor little Emmy Sedley's happiness forms, somehow, part of it.

In the first place, her father's fortune was swept down with that fatal news. All his speculations had of late gone wrong with the luckless old gentleman. Ventures had failed; merchants had broken; funds had risen when he calculated they would fall. What need to particularize? If success is rare and slow, everybody knows how quick and easy ruin is. Old Sedley had kept his own sad counsel. Everything seemed to go on as usual in the quiet, opulent house; the good-natured mistress pursuing, quite unsuspiciously, her bustling idleness, and daily easy avocations; the daughter absorbed still in one selfish, tender thought, and quite regardless of all the world besides, when that final crash came, under which the worthy family fell.

One night Mrs. Sedley was writing cards for a party; the Osbornes had given one, and she must not be behindhand; John Sedley, who had come home very late from the City, sat silent at the chimney side, while his wife was prattling to him; Emmy had gone up to her room ailing and low-spirited. 'She's not happy,' the mother went on. 'George Osborne neglects her. I've no patience with the airs of those people. The girls have not been in the house these three weeks; and George has been twice in town without coming. Edward Dale saw him at the opera. Edward would marry her, I'm sure: and there's Captain Dobbin who, I think, would – only I hate all army men. Such a dandy as George has become. With his military airs, indeed! We must show some folks that we're as good as they. Only give Edward Dale any encouragement, and you'll see. We must have a party, Mr. S. Why don't you speak, John? Shall I say Tuesday fortnight? Why don't you answer? Good God, John, what has happened?'

John Sedley sprang up out of his chair to meet his wife, who ran to him. He seized her in his arms, and said, with a hasty voice, 'We're ruined, Mary. We've got the world to begin over again, dear. It's best that you should know all, and at once.' As he spoke, he trembled in every limb, and almost fell. He thought the news would have overpowered his wife – his wife, to whom he had never said a hard word. But it was he that was the most moved, sudden as the shock was to her. When he sank back into his seat, it was the wife that took the office of consoler. She took his trembling hand, and kissed it, and put it round her neck: she called him her John – her dear John – her old man – her kind old man; she poured out a hundred words of incoherent love and tenderness; her faithful voice and simple caresses wrought this sad heart up to an inexpressible delight and anguish, and cheered and solaced his overburdened soul.

Only once in the course of the long night as they sat together, and poor Sedley opened his pent-up soul, and told the story of his losses and embarrassments – the treason of some of his oldest friends, the manly kindness of some, from whom he never could have expected it – in a general confession – only once did the faithful wife give way to emotion.

'My God, my God, it will break Emmy's heart,' she said.

The father had forgotten the poor girl. She was lying, awake and unhappy, overhead. In the midst of friends, home, and kind parents, she was alone. To how many people can any one tell all? Who will be open where there is no sympathy, or has call to speak to those who never can understand? Our gentle Amelia was thus solitary. She had no confidante, so to speak, ever since she had anything to confide. She could not tell the old mother her doubts and cares; the would-be sisters seemed every day more strange to her. And she had misgivings and fears which she dared not acknowledge to herself, though she was always secretly brooding over them.

Her heart tried to persist in asserting that George Osborne was worthy and faithful to her, though she knew otherwise. How many a thing had she said, and got no echo from him. How many suspicions of selfishness and indifference had she to encounter and obstinately overcome. To whom could the poor little martyr tell these daily struggles and tortures? Her hero himself only half understood her. She did not dare to own that the man she loved was her inferior; or to feel that she had given her heart away too soon. Given once, the pure bashful maiden was too modest, too tender, too trustful, too weak, too much woman to recall it. We are Turks with the affections of our women; and have made them subscribe to our doctrine too. We let their bodies go abroad liberally enough, with smiles and ringlets and pink bonnets to disguise them instead of veils and yakmaks. But their souls must be seen by only one man, and they obey not unwillingly, and consent to remain at home as our slaves – ministering to us and doing drudgery for us.

So imprisoned and tortured was this gentle little heart, when in the month of March, Anno Domini 1815, Napoleon landed at Cannes, and Louis XVIII fled, and all Europe was in alarm, and the funds fell, and old John Sedley was ruined.

We are not going to follow the worthy old stockbroker through those last pangs and agonies of ruin through which he passed before his commercial demise befell. They declared him at the Stock Exchange; he was absent from his house of business: his bills were protested: his act of bankruptcy formal. The house and furniture of Russell Square were seized and sold up, and he and his family were thrust away, as we have seen, to hide their heads where they might.

John Sedley had not the heart to review the domestic establishment who have appeared now and anon in our pages, and of whom he was now forced by poverty to take leave. The wages of those worthy people were discharged with that punctuality which men frequently show who only owe in great sums – they were sorry to leave good places – but they did not break their hearts at parting from their adored master and mistress. Amelia's maid was profuse in condolences, but went off quite resigned to better herself in a genteeler quarter of the town. Black Sambo, with the infatuation of his profession, determined on setting up a public-house. Honest old Mrs. Blenkinsop indeed, who had seen the birth of Jos and Amelia, and the wooing of John Sedley and his wife, was for staying by them without wages, having amassed a considerable sum in their service: and she accompanied the fallen people into their new and humble place of refuge, where she tended them and grumbled against them for a while.

Of all Sedley's opponents in his debates with his creditors which now ensued, and harassed the feelings of the humiliated old gentleman so severely, that in six weeks he oldened more than he had done for fifteen years before – the most determined and obstinate seemed to be John Osborne, his old friend and neighbour – John Osborne, whom he had set up in life – who was under a hundred obligations to him – and whose son was to marry Sedley's daughter. Any one of these circumstances would account for the bitterness of Osborne's opposition.

When one man has been under very remarkable obligations to another, with whom he subsequently quarrels, a common sense of decency, as it were, makes of the former a much severer enemy than a mere stranger would be. To account for your own hard-heartedness and ingratitude in such a case, you are bound to prove the other party's crime. It is not that you are selfish, brutal, and angry at the failure of a speculation – no, no – it is that your partner has led you into it by the basest treachery and with the most sinister motives. From a mere sense of consistency, a persecutor is bound to show that the fallen man is a villain – otherwise he, the persecutor, is a wretch himself.

And as a general rule, which may make all creditors who are inclined to be severe, pretty comfortable in their minds, no men embarrassed are altogether honest, very likely. They conceal something; they exaggerate chances of good luck; hide away the real state of affairs; say that things are flourishing when they are hopeless; keep a smiling face (a dreary smile it is) upon the verge of bankruptcy – are ready to lay hold of any pretext for delay or of any money, so as to stave off the inevitable ruin a few days longer. 'Down with such dishonesty,' says the creditor in triumph, and reviles his sinking enemy. 'You fool, why do you catch at a straw?' calm good sense says to the man that is drowning. 'You villain, why do you shrink from plunging into the irretrievable *Gazette*?' says prosperity to the poor devil battling in that black gulf. Who has not remarked the readiness with which the closest of friends and honestest of men suspect and accuse each other of cheating when they fall out on money matters? Everybody does it. Everybody is right, I suppose, and the world is a rogue.

Then Osborne had the intolerable sense of former benefits to goad and irritate him: these are always a cause of hostility aggravated. Finally, he had to break off the match between Sedley's daughter and his son; and as it had gone very far indeed, and as the poor girl's happiness and perhaps character were compromised, it was necessary to show the strongest reasons for the rupture, and for John Osborne to prove John Sedley to be a very bad character indeed.

At the meetings of creditors, then, he comported himself with a savageness and scorn towards Sedley, which almost succeeded in breaking the heart of that ruined bankrupt man. On George's intercourse with Amelia he put an instant veto – menacing the youth with maledictions if he broke his commands, and vilipending the poor innocent girl as the basest and most artful of vixens. One of the great conditions of anger and hatred is, that you must tell and believe lies against the hated object, in order, as we said, to be consistent.

When the great crash came – the announcement of ruin, and the departure from Russell Square, and the declaration that all was over between her and George – all over between her and love, her and happiness, her and faith in the world – a brutal letter from John Osborne told her in a few curt lines that her father's conduct had been of such a nature that all engagements between the families were at an end – when the final award came, it did not shock her so much as her parents, as her mother rather expected (for John Sedley himself was entirely prostrate in the ruins of his own affairs and shattered honour). Amelia took the news very palely and calmly. It was only the confirmation of the dark presages which had long gone before. It was the mere reading of the sentence – of the crime she had long ago been guilty – the crime of loving wrongly, too violently, against reason. She told no more of her thoughts now than she had before. She seemed scarcely more unhappy now when convinced all hope was over, than before when she felt but dared not confess that it was gone. So she changed from the large house to the small one without any mark or difference; remained in her little room for the most part; pined silently; and died away day by day. I do not mean to say that all females are so. My dear Miss Bullock, I do not think *your* heart would break in this way. You are a strong-minded young woman with proper principles. I do not venture to say that mine would; it has suffered, and, it must be confessed, survived. But there are some souls thus gently constituted, thus frail, and delicate, and tender.

Whenever old John Sedley thought of the affair between

George and Amelia, or alluded to it, it was with bitterness almost as great as Mr. Osborne himself had shown. He cursed Osborne and his family as heartless, wicked, and ungrateful. No power on earth, he swore, would induce him to marry his daughter to the son of such a villain, and he ordered Emmy to banish George from her mind, and to return all the presents and letters which she had ever had from him.

She promised acquiescence, and tried to obey. She put up the two or three trinkets: and, as for the letters, she drew them out of the place where she kept them; and read them over – as if she did not know them by heart already: but she could not part with them. That effort was too much for her; she placed them back in her bosom again – as you have seen a woman nurse a child that is dead. Young Amelia felt that she would die or lose her senses outright, if torn away from this last consolation. How she used to blush and lighten up when those letters came! How she used to trip away with a beating heart, so that she might read unseen! If they were cold, yet how perversely this fond little soul interpreted them into warmth. If they were short or selfish, what excuses she found for the writer!

It was over these few worthless papers that she brooded and brooded. She lived in her past life – every letter seemed to recall some circumstance of it. How well she remembered them all! His looks and tones, his dress, what he said and how – these relics and remembrances of dead affection were all that were left her in the world. And the business of her life was – to watch the corpse of Love.

To death she looked with inexpressible longing. Then, she thought, I shall always be able to follow him. I am not praising her conduct or setting her up as a model for Miss Bullock to imitate. Miss B. knows how to regulate her feelings better than this poor little creature. Miss B. would never have committed herself as that imprudent Amelia had done; pledged her love irretrievably; confessed her heart away, and got back nothing – only a brittle promise which was snapped and worthless in a moment. A long engagement is a partnership which one party is free to keep or to break, but which involves all the capital of the other.

Be cautious then, young ladies; be wary how you engage. Be shy of loving frankly; never tell all you feel, or (a better way still) feel very little. See the consequences of being prematurely honest and confiding, and mistrust yourselves and everybody. Get yourselves married as they do in France, where the lawyers are the bridesmaids and confidantes. At any rate, never have any feelings which may make you uncomfortable, or make any promises which you cannot at any required moment command and withdraw. That is the way to get on, and be respected, and have a virtuous character in Vanity Fair.

If Amelia could have heard the comments regarding her which were made in the circle from which her father's ruin had just driven her, she would have seen what her own crimes were, and how entirely her character was jeopardied. Such criminal imprudence Mrs. Smith never knew of; such horrid familiarities Mrs. Brown had always condemned, and the end might be a warning to *her* daughters. 'Captain Osborne, of course, could not marry a bankrupt's daughter,' the Miss Dobbins said. 'It was quite enough to have been swindled by the father. As for that little Amelia, her folly had really passed all —'

'All what?' Captain Dobbin roared out. 'Haven't they been engaged ever since they were children? Wasn't it as good as a marriage? Dare any soul on earth breathe a word against the sweetest, the purest, the tenderest, the most angelical of young women?'

'La, William, don't be so highty-tighty with *us*. We're not men. We can't fight you,' Miss Jane said. 'We've said nothing against Miss Sedley: but that her conduct throughout was *most imprudent*, not to call it by any worse name; and that her parents are people who certainly merit their misfortunes.'

'Hadn't you better, now that Miss Sedley is free, propose for her yourself, William?' Miss Ann asked sarcastically. 'It would be a most eligible family connexion. He! he!'

'I marry her!' Dobbin said, blushing very much, and talking quick. 'If you are so ready, young ladies, to chop and change, do you suppose that *she* is? Laugh and sneer at that angel. She can't hear it; and she's miserable and unfortunate, and deserves to be laughed at. Go on joking, Ann. You're the wit of the family, and the others like to hear it.'

'I must tell you again we're not in a barrack, William,' Miss Ann remarked.

'In a barrack, by Jove – I wish anybody in a barrack would say what you do,' cried out this uproused British lion. 'I should like to hear a man breathe a word against her, by Jupiter. But men don't talk in this way, Ann: it's only women, who get together and hiss, and shriek and cackle. There, get away – don't begin to cry. I only said you were a couple of geese,' Will Dobbin said, perceiving Miss Ann's pink eyes were beginning to moisten as usual. 'Well, you're not geese, you're swans – anything you like, only do, do leave Miss Sedley alone.'

Anything like William's infatuation about that silly little flirting, ogling thing was never known, the mamma and sisters agreed together in thinking: and they trembled lest, her engagement being off with Osborne, she should take up immediately her other admirer and captain. In which forebodings these worthy young women no doubt judged according to the best of their experience; or rather (for as yet they had had no opportunities of marrying or of jilting) according to their own notions of right and wrong.

'It is a mercy, mamma, that the regiment is ordered abroad,' the girls said. '*This* danger, at any rate, is spared our brother.'

Such, indeed, was the fact; and so it is that the French Emperor comes in to perform a part in this domestic comedy of Vanity Fair which we are now playing, and which would never have been enacted without the intervention of this august mute personage. It was he that ruined the Bourbons and Mr. John Sedley. It was he whose arrival in his capital called up all France in arms to defend him there; and all Europe to oust him. While the French nation and army were swearing fidelity round the eagles in the Champ de Mai, four mighty European hosts were getting in motion for the great *chasse à l'aigle*; and one of these was a British army, of which two heroes of ours, Captain Dobbin and Captain Osborne, formed a portion.

The news of Napoleon's escape and landing was received by the gallant –th with a fiery delight and enthusiasm, which everybody can understand who knows that famous corps. From the colonel to the smallest drummer in the regiment, all were filled with hope and ambition and patriotic fury; and thanked the French Emperor as for a personal kindness in coming to disturb the peace of Europe. Now was the time the –th had so long panted for, to show their comrades in arms that they could fight as well as the Peninsular veterans, and that all the pluck and valour of the –th had not been killed by the West Indies and the yellow fever. Stubble and Spooney looked to get their companies without purchase. Before the end of the campaign (which she resolved to share), Mrs. Major O'Dowd hoped to write herself Mrs. Colonel O'Dowd, C. B. Our two friends (Dobbin and Osborne) were quite as much excited as the rest: and each in his way – Mr. Dobbin very quietly, Mr. Osborne very loudly and energetically – was bent upon doing his duty, and gaining his share of honour and distinction.

The agitation thrilling through the country and army in consequence of this news was so great, that private matters were little heeded: and hence probably George Osborne, just gazetted to his company, busy with preparations for the march, which must come inevitably, and panting for further promotion – was not so much affected by other incidents which would have interested him at a more quiet period. He was not, it must be confessed, very much cast down by good old Mr. Sedley's catastrophe. He tried his new uniform, which became him very handsomely, on the day when the first meeting of the creditors of the unfortunate gentleman took place. His father told him of the wicked, rascally, shameful conduct of the bankrupt, reminded him of what he had said about Amelia, and that their connexion was broken off for ever; and gave him that evening a good sum of money to pay for the new clothes and epaulets in which he looked so well. Money was always useful to this free-handed young fellow, and he took it without many words. The bills were up in the Sedley house, where he had passed so many, many happy hours. He could see them as he walked from home that night (to the Old Slaughter's, where he put up when in town), shining white in the moon. That comfortable home was shut, then, upon Amelia and her parents: where had they taken refuge? The thought of their ruin affected him not a little. He was very melancholy that night in the coffee-room at the Slaughter's; and drank a good deal, as his comrades remarked there.

Dobbin came in presently, cautioned him about the drink, which he only took, he said, because he was deuced low;

but when his friend began to put to him clumsy inquiries, and asked him for news in a significant manner, Osborne declined entering into conversation with him; avowing, however, that he was devilish disturbed and unhappy.

Three days afterwards, Dobbin found Osborne in his room at the barracks:– his head on the table, a number of papers about, the young captain evidently in a state of great despondency. 'She – she's sent me back some things I gave her – some damned trinkets. Look here!' There was a little packet directed in the well-known hand to Captain George Osborne, and some things lying about – a ring, a silver knife he had bought, as a boy, for her at a fair; a gold chain, and a locket with hair in it. 'It's all over,' said he, with a groan of sickening remorse. 'Look, Will, you may read it if you like.'

There was a little letter of a few lines, to which he pointed, which said:–

My papa has ordered me to return to you these presents, which you made in happier days to me; and I am to write to you for the last time. I think, I know you feel as much as I do the blow which has come upon us. It is I that absolve you from an engagement which is impossible in our present misery. I am sure you had no share in it, or in the cruel suspicions of Mr. Osborne, which are the hardest of all our griefs to bear. Farewell. Farewell. I pray God to strengthen me to bear this and other calamities, and to bless you always.   A.

I shall often play upon the piano – your piano. It was like you to send it.

Dobbin was very soft-hearted. The sight of women and children in pain always used to melt him. The idea of Amelia broken-hearted and lonely, tore that good-natured soul with anguish. And he broke out into an emotion, which anybody who likes may consider unmanly. He swore that Amelia was an angel, to which Osborne said aye with all his heart. He, too, had been reviewing the history of their lives, – and had seen her from her childhood to her present age, so sweet, so innocent, so charmingly simple, and artlessly fond and tender.

What a pang it was to lose all that: to have had it and not prized it! A thousand homely seenes and recollections crowded on him – in which he always saw her good and beautiful. And for himself, he blushed with remorse and shame, as the remembrance of his own selfishness and indifference contrasted with that perfect purity. For a while, glory, war, everything was forgotten, and the pair of friends talked about her only.

'Where are they?' Osborne asked, after a long talk, and a long pause, – and, in truth, with no little shame at thinking that he had taken no steps to follow her. 'Where are they? There's no address to the note.'

Dobbin knew. He had not merely sent the piano; but had written a note to Mrs. Sedley, and asked permission to come and see her, – and he had seen her, and Amelia too, yesterday, before he came down to Chatham; and, what is more, he had brought that farewell letter and packet which had so moved them.

The good-natured fellow had found Mrs. Sedley only too willing to receive him, and greatly agitated by the arrival of the piano, which, as she. conjectured, *must* have come from George, and was a signal of amity on his part. Captain Dobbin did not correct this error of the worthy lady, but listened to all her story of complaints and misfortunes with great sympathy – condoled with her losses and privations, and agreed in reprehending the cruel conduct of Mr. Osborne towards his first benefactor. When she had eased her overflowing bosom somewhat, and poured forth many of her sorrows, he had the courage to ask actually to see Amelia, who was above in her room as usual, and whom her mother led trembling downstairs.

Her appearance was so ghastly, and her look of despair so pathetic, that honest William Dobbin was frightened as he beheld it; and read the most fatal forebodings in that pale fixed face. After sitting in his company a minute or two, she put the packet into his hand, and said, 'Take this to Captain Osborne, if you please, and – and I hope he's quite well – and it was very kind of you to come and see us – and we like our new house very much. And I – I think I'll go upstairs, mamma, for I'm not very strong.' And with this, and a curtsy and a smile, the poor child went her way. The mother, as she led her up, cast back looks of anguish towards Dobbin. The good fellow wanted no such appeal. He loved her himself too fondly for that. Inexpressible grief, and pity, and terror pursued him, and he came away as if he was a criminal after seeing her.

When Osborne heard that his friend had found her, he made hot and anxious inquiries regarding the poor child. How was she? How did she look? What did she say? His comrade took his hand, and looked him in the face.

'George, she's dying,' William Dobbin said, – and could speak no more.

There was a buxom Irish servant-girl, who performed all the duties of the little house where the Sedley family had found refuge; and this girl had in vain, on many previous days, striven to give Amelia aid or consolation. Emmy was much too sad to answer, or even to be aware of the attempts the other was making in her favour.

Four hours after the talk between Dobbin and Osborne, this servant-maid came into Amelia's room, where she sat as usual, brooding silently over her letters – her little treasures. The girl, smiling, and looking arch and happy, made many trials to attract poor Emmy's attention, who, however, took no heed of her.

'Miss Emmy,' said the girl.

'I'm coming,' Emmy said, not looking round.

'There's a message,' the maid went on. 'There's some-thing – somebody – sure, here's a new letter for you – don't be reading them old ones any more.' And she gave her a letter, which Emmy took, and read.

'I must see you,' the letter said. 'Dearest Emmy – dearest love – dearest wife, come to me.'

George and her mother were outside, waiting until she had read the letter.

CHAPTER XIX

MISS CRAWLEY AT NURSE

W E have seen how Mrs. Firkin, the lady's-maid, as soon as any event of importance to the Crawley family came to her knowledge, felt bound to communicate it to Mrs. Bute Crawley, at the Rectory; and have before mentioned how particularly kind and attentive that good-natured lady was to Miss Crawley's confidential servant. She had been a gracious friend to Mrs. Briggs, the companion, also; and had secured the latter's goodwill by a number of those attentions and promises, which cost so little in the making, and are yet so valuable and agreeable to the recipient. Indeed, every good economist and manager of a household must know how cheap and yet how amiable these professions are, and what a flavour they give to the most homely dish in life. Who was the blundering idiot who said that 'fine words butter no parsnips'? Half the parsnips of society are served and rendered palatable with no other sauce. As the immortal Alexis Soyer can make more delicious soup for a halfpenny than an ignorant cook can concoct with pounds of vegetables and meat, so a skilful artist will make a few simple and pleasing phrases go farther than ever so much substantial benefit-stock in the hands of a mere bungler. Nay, we know that substantial benefits often sicken some stomachs; whereas, most will digest any amount of fine words, and be always eager for more of the same food. Mrs. Bute had told Briggs and Firkin so often of the depth of her affection for them; and what *she* would do, if she had Miss Crawley's fortune, for friends so excellent and attached, that the ladies in question had the deepest regard for her; and felt as much gratitude and confidence as if Mrs. Bute had loaded them with the most expensive favours.

Rawdon Crawley, on the other hand, like a selfish heavy dragoon as he was, never took the least trouble to conciliate his aunt's aides de camp, showed his contempt for the pair with entire frankness – made Firkin pull of his boots on one occasion – sent her out in the rain on ignominious messages – and if he gave her a guinea, flung it to her as if it were a box on the ear. As his aunt, too, made a butt of Briggs, the captain followed the example, and levelled his jokes at her – jokes about as delicate as a kick from his charger. Whereas, Mrs. Bute consulted her in matters of taste or difficulty, admired her poetry, and by a thousand acts of kindness and politeness, showed her appreciation of Briggs; and if she made Firkin a twopenny-halfpenny present, accompanied it with so many compliments, that the two-pence-halfpenny was transmuted into gold in the heart of the grateful waiting-maid, who, besides, was looking forwards quite contentedly to some prodigious benefit which must happen to her on the day when Mrs. Bute came into her fortune.

The different conduct of these two people is pointed out respectfully to the attention of persons commencing the world. Praise everybody, I say to such: never be squeamish, but speak out your compliment both point-blank in a man's face, and behind his back, when you know there is a reasonable chance of his hearing it again. Never lose a chance of saying a kind word. As Collingwood never saw a vacant place in his estate but he took an acorn out of his pocket and popped it in; so deal with your compliments through life. An acorn costs nothing; but it may sprout into a prodigious bit of timber.

In a word, during Rawdon Crawley's prosperity, he was only obeyed with sulky acquiescence; when his disgrace came, there was nobody to help or pity him. Whereas, when Mrs. Bute took the command at Miss Crawley's house, the garrison there were charmed to act under such a leader, expecting all sorts of promotion from her promises, her generosity, and her kind words.

That he would consider himself beaten, after one defeat, and make no attempt to regain the position he had lost, Mrs. Bute Crawley never allowed herself to suppose. She knew Rebecca to be too clever and spirited and desperate a woman to submit without a struggle; and felt that she must prepare for that combat, and be incessantly watchful against assault, or mine, or surprise.

In the first place, though she held the town, was she sure of the principal inhabitant? Would Miss Crawley herself hold out; and had she not a secret longing to welcome back the ousted adversary? The old lady liked Rawdon, and Rebecca, who amused her. Mrs. Bute could not disguise from herself the fact that none of her party could so contribute to the pleasures of the town-bred lady. 'My girls' singing, after that little odious governess's, I know is unbearable,' the candid rector's wife owned to herself. 'She always used to go to sleep when Martha and Louisa played their duets. Jim's stiff college manners and poor dear Bute's talk about his dogs and horses always annoyed her. If I took her to the Rectory, she would grow angry with us all, and fly, I know she would; and might fall into that horrid Rawdon's clutches again, and be the victim of that little viper of a Sharp. Meanwhile, it is clear to me that she is exceedingly unwell, and cannot move for some weeks, at any rate; during which we must think of some plan to protect her from the arts of those unprincipled people.'

In the very best of moments, if anybody told Miss Crawley that she was, or looked ill, the trembling old lady sent off for her doctor; and I daresay she *was* very unwell after the sudden family event, which might serve to shake stronger nerves than hers. At least, Mrs. Bute thought it was her duty to inform the physician, and the apothecary, and the *dame de compagnie*, and the domestics, that Miss Crawley was in a most critical state, and that they were to act accordingly. She had the street laid knee-deep with straw; and the knocker put by with Mr. Bowls's plate. She insisted that the doctor should call twice a day; and deluged her patient with draughts every two hours. When anybody entered the room, she uttered a *shshshsh* so sibilant and ominous, that it frightened the poor old lady in her bed, from which she could not look without seeing Mrs. Bute's beady eyes eagerly fixed on her, as the latter sat steadfast in the arm-chair by the bedside. They seemed to lighten in the dark (for she kept the curtains closed) as she moved about the room on velvet paws like a cat. There Miss Crawley lay for days — ever so many days — Mrs. Bute reading books of devotion to her: for nights, long nights, during which she had to hear the watchman sing, the night-light sputter; visited at midnight, the last thing, by the stealthy apothecary; and then left to look at Mrs. Bute's twinkling eyes, or the flicks of yellow that the rushlight threw on the dreary darkened ceiling. Hygeia herself would have fallen sick under such a regimen; and how much more this poor old nervous victim? It has been said that when she was in health and good spirits, this venerable inhabitant of Vanity Fair had as free notions about religion and morals as Monsieur de Voltaire himself could desire, but when illness overtook her, it was aggravated by the most dreadful terrors of death, and an utter cowardice took possession of the prostrate old sinner.

Sick-bed homilies and pious reflections are, to be sure, out of place in mere story-books, and we are not going (after the fashion of some novelists of the present day) to cajole the public into a sermon, when it is only a comedy that the reader pays his money to witness. But, without preaching, the truth may surely be borne in mind, that the bustle, and triumph, and laughter, and gaiety which Vanity Fair exhibits in public, do not always pursue the performer into private life, and that the most dreary depression of spirits and dismal repentances sometimes overcome him. Recollection of the best ordained banquets will scarcely cheer sick epicures. Reminiscences of the most becoming dresses and brilliant ball-triumphs will go very little way to console faded beauties. Perhaps statesmen, at a particular period of existence, are not much gratified at thinking over the most triumphant divisions; and the success or the pleasure of yesterday become of very small account when a certain (albeit uncertain) morrow is in view, about which all of us must some day or other be speculating. O brother wearers of motley! Are there not moments when one grows sick of grinning and tumbling, and the jingling of cap and bells? This, dear friends and companions, is my amiable object – to walk with you through the Fair, to examine the shops and the shows there; and that we should all come home after the flare, and the noise, and the gaiety, and be perfectly miserable in private.

'If that poor man of mine had a head on his shoulders.' Mrs. Bute Crawley thought to herself, 'how useful he might be, under present circumstances, to this unhappy old lady! He might make her repent of her shocking free-thinking ways; he might urge her to do her duty, and cast off that odious reprobate who has disgraced himself and his family; and he might induce her to do justice to my dear girls and the two boys, who require and deserve, I am sure, every assistance which their relatives can give them.'

And, as the hatred of vice is always a progress towards virtue, Mrs. Bute Crawley endeavoured to instil into her sister-in-law a proper abhorrence for all Rawdon Crawley's manifold sins: of which his uncle's wife brought forward such a catalogue as indeed would have served to condemn a whole regiment of young officers. If a man has committed wrong in life, I don't know any moralist more anxious to point his errors out to the world than his own relations; so Mrs. Bute showed a perfect family interest and knowledge of Rawdon's history. She had all the particulars of that ugly quarrel with Captain Marker, in which Rawdon, wrong from the beginning, ended in shooting the captain. She knew how the unhappy Lord Dovedale, whose mamma had taken a house at Oxford, so that he might be educated there, and who had never touched a card in his life till he came to London, was perverted by Rawdon at the 'Cocoa-Tree,'

made helplessly tipsy by this abominable seducer and per-
verter of youth, and fleeced of four thousand pounds. She
described with the most vivid minuteness the agonies of the
country families whom he had ruined – the sons whom he
had plunged into dishonour and poverty – the daughters
whom he had inveigled into perdition. She knew the poor
tradesmen who were bankrupt by his extravagance – the
mean shifts and rogueries with which he had ministered to
it – the astounding falsehoods by which he had imposed
upon the most generous of aunts, and the ingratitude and
ridicule by which he had repaid her sacrifices. She imparted
these stories gradually to Miss Crawley; gave her the whole
benefit of them; felt it to be her bounden duty as a Christian
woman and mother of a family to do so; had not the smallest
remorse or compunction for the victim whom her tongue
was immolating; nay, very likely thought her act was quite
meritorious, and plumed herself upon her resolute manner
of performing it. Yes, if a man's character is to be abused,
say what you will, there's nobody like a relation to do the
business. And one is bound to own, regarding this unfortunate wretch of a Rawdon Crawley, that the mere truth was
enough to condemn him, and that all inventions of scandal
were quite superfluous pains on his friends' parts.

Rebecca, too, being now a relative, came in for the fullest
share of Mrs. Bute's kind inquiries. This indefatigable pur-
suer of truth (having given strict orders that the door was
to be denied to all emissaries or letters from Rawdon), took
Miss Crawley's carriage, and drove to her old friend Miss
Pinkerton, at Minerva House, Chiswick Mall, to whom she
announced the dreadful intelligence of Captain Rawdon's
seduction by Miss Sharp, and from whom she got sundry
strange particulars regarding the ex-governess's birth and
early history. The friend of the Lexicographer had plenty
of information to give. Miss Jemima was made to fetch the
drawing-master's receipts and letters. This one was from a
spunging-house: that entreated an advance: another was full
of gratitude for Rebecca's reception by the ladies of Chiswick: and the last document from the unlucky artist's pen
was that in which, from his dying bed, he recommended his
orphan child to Miss Pinkerton's protection. There were
juvenile letters and petitions from Rebecca, too, in the
collection, imploring aid for her father, or declaring her own

gratitude. Perhaps in Vanity Fair there are no better satires than letters. Take a bundle of your dear friend's of ten years back – your dear friend whom you hate now. Look at a file of your sister's: how you clung to each other till you quarrelled about the twenty-pound legacy! Get down the roundhand scrawls of your son who has half broken your heart with selfish undutifulness since; or a parcel of your own, breathing endless ardour and love eternal, which were sent back by your mistress when she married the nabob – your mistress for whom you now care no more than for Queen Elizabeth. Vows, love, promises, confidences, gratitude, how queerly they read after a while! There ought to be a law in Vanity Fair ordering the destruction of every written document (except receipted tradesmen's bills) after a certain brief and proper interval. Those quacks and misanthropes who advertise indelible Japan ink, should be made to perish along with their wicked discoveries. The best ink for Vanity Fair use would be one that faded utterly in a couple of days, and left the paper clean and blank, so that you might write on it to somebody else.

From Miss Pinkerton's the indefatigable Mrs. Bute followed the track of Sharp and his daughter back to the lodgings in Greek Street, which the defunct painter had occupied; and where portraits of the landlady in white satin, and of the husband in brass buttons, done by Sharp in lieu of a quarter's rent, still decorated the parlour walls. Mrs. Stokes was a communicative person, and quickly told all she knew about Mr. Sharp; how dissolute and poor he was; how good-natured and amusing; how he was always hunted by bailiffs and duns; how, to the landlady's horror, though she never could abide the woman, he did not marry his wife till a short time before her death; and what a queer little wild vixen his daughter was; how she kept them all laughing with her fun and mimicry; how she used to fetch the gin from the public-house, and was known in all the studios in the quarter – in brief, Mrs. Bute got such a full account of her new niece's parentage, education, and behaviour as would scarcely have pleased Rebecca, had the latter known that such inquiries were being made concerning her.

Of all these industrious researches Miss Crawley had the full benefit. Mrs. Rawdon Crawley was the daughter of an opera-girl. She had danced herself. She had been a model to the painters. She was brought up as became her mother's daughter. She drank gin with her father, &c. &c. It was a lost woman who was married to a lost man; and the moral to be inferred from Mrs. Bute's tale was, that the knavery of the pair was irremediable, and that no properly-conducted person should ever notice them again.

These were the materials which prudent Mrs. Bute gathered together in Park Lane, the provisions and ammunition as it were with which she fortified the house against the siege which she knew that Rawdon and his wife would lay to Miss Crawley.

But if a fault may be found with her arrangements, it is this, that she was too eager: she managed rather too well; undoubtedly she made Miss Crawley more ill than was necessary; and though the old invalid succumbed to her authority, it was so harassing and severe, that the victim would be inclined to escape at the very first chance which fell in her way. Managing women, the ornaments of their sex – women who order everything for everybody, and know so much better than any person concerned what is good for their neighbours, don't sometimes speculate upon the possibility of a domestic revolt, or upon other extreme consequences resulting from their overstrained authority.

Thus, for instance, Mrs. Bute, with the best intentions no doubt in the world, and wearing herself to death as she did by forgoing sleep, dinner, fresh air, for the sake of her invalid sister-in-law, carried her conviction of the old lady's illness so far that she almost managed her into her coffin. She pointed out her sacrifices and their results one day to the constant apothecary, Mr. Clump.

'I am sure, my dear Mr. Clump,' she said, 'no efforts of mine have been wanting to restore our dear invalid, whom the ingratitude of her nephew has laid on the bed of sickness. *I* never shrink from personal discomfort: *I* never refuse to sacrifice myself.'

'Your devotion, it must be confessed, is admirable,' Mr. Clump says, with a low bow; 'but —'

'I have scarcely closed my eyes since my arrival: I give up sleep, health, every comfort, to my sense of duty. When my poor James was in the small-pox, did I allow any hireling to nurse him? No.'

'You did what became an excellent mother, my dear madam – the best of mothers; but —'

'As the mother of a family and the wife of an English clergyman, I humbly trust that my principles are good,' Mrs. Bute said, with a happy solemnity of conviction; 'and, as long as Nature supports me, never, never, Mr. Clump, will I desert the post of duty. Others may bring that grey head with sorrow to the bed of sickness' (here Mrs. Bute, waving her hand, pointed to one of old Miss Crawley's coffee-coloured fronts, which was perched on a stand in the dressing-room), 'but *I* will never quit it. Ah, Mr. Clump! I fear, I know, that that couch needs spiritual as well as medical consolation.'

'What I was going to observe, my dear madam,' – here the resolute Clump once more interposed with a bland air – 'what I was going to observe when you gave utterance to sentiments which do you so much honour, was that I think you alarm yourself needlessly about our kind friend, and sacrifice your own health too prodigally in her favour.'

'I would lay down my life for my duty, or for any member of my husband's family,' Mrs. Bute interposed.

'Yes, madam, if need were; but we don't want Mrs. Bute Crawley to be a martyr,' Clump said gallantly. 'Dr. Squills and myself have both considered Miss Crawley's case with every anxiety and care, as you may suppose. We see her low-spirited and nervous; family events have agitated her.'

'Her nephew will come to perdition,' Mrs. Crawley cried.

'Have agitated her: and you arrived like a guardian angel, my dear madam, a positive guardian angel, I assure you, to soothe her under the pressure of calamity. But Dr. Squills and I were thinking that our amiable friend is not in such a state as renders confinement to her bed necessary. She is depressed, but this confinement perhaps adds to her depression. She should have change, fresh air, gaiety; the most delightful remedies in the pharmacopoeia,' Mr. Clump said, grinning and showing his handsome teeth. 'Persuade her to rise, dear madam; drag her from her couch and her low spirits; insist upon her taking little drives. They will restore the roses too to *your* cheeks, if I may so speak to Mrs. Bute Crawley.'

'The sight of her horrid nephew casually in the Park, where I am told the wretch drives with the brazen partner of his crimes,' Mrs. Bute said (letting the cat of selfishness out of the bag of secrecy), 'would cause her such a shock, that we should have to bring her back to bed again. She must not go out, Mr. Clump. She shall not go out as long as I remain to watch over her. And as for *my* health, what matters it? I give it cheerfully, sir. I sacrifice it at the altar of my duty.'

'Upon my word, madam,' Mr. Clump now said bluntly, 'I won't answer for her life if she remains locked up in that dark room. She is so nervous that we may lose her any day; and if you wish Captain Crawley to be her heir, I warn you frankly, madam, that you are doing your very best to serve him.'

'Gracious mercy! is her life in danger?' Mrs. Bute cried. 'Why, why, Mr. Clump, did you not inform me sooner?'

The night before, Mr. Clump and Dr. Squills had had a consultation (over a bottle of wine at the house of Sir Lapin Warren, whose lady was about to present him with a thirteenth blessing), regarding Miss Crawley and her case.

'What a little harpy that woman from Hampshire is, Clump,' Squills remarked, 'that has seized upon old Tilly Crawley. Devilish good madeira.'

'What a fool Rawdon Crawley has been,' Clump replied, 'to go and marry a governess! There was something about the girl, too.'

'Green eyes, fair skin, pretty figure, famous frontal development,' Squills remarked. 'There is something about her; and Crawley *was* a fool, Squills.'

'A d— fool – always was,' the apothecary replied.

'Of course the old girl will fling him over,' said the physician, and after a pause added, 'She'll cut up well, I suppose.'

'Cut up,' says Clump with a grin; 'I wouldn't have her cut up for two hundred a year.'

'That Hampshire woman will kill her in two months, Clump, my boy, if she stops about her,' Dr. Squills said. 'Old woman; full feeder; nervous subject; palpitation of the heart; pressure on the brain; apoplexy; off she goes. Get her up, Clump; get her out: or I wouldn't give many weeks purchase for your two hundred a year.' And it was acting upon this hint that the worthy apothecary spoke with so much candour to Mrs. Bute Crawley.

Having the old lady under her hand: in bed: with nobody near, Mrs. Bute had made more than one assault upon her, to induce her to alter her will. But Miss Crawley's usual terrors regarding death increased greatly when such dismal propositions were made to her, and Mrs. Bute saw that she must get her patient into cheerful spirits and health before she could hope to attain the pious object which she had in view. Whither to take her was the next puzzle. The only place where she is not likely to meet those odious Rawdons is at church, and that won't amuse her, Mrs. Bute justly felt. 'We must go and visit our beautiful suburbs of London,' she then thought. 'I hear they are the most picturesque in the world;' and so she had a sudden interest for Hampstead, and Hornsey, and found that Dulwich had great charms for her, and getting her victim into her carriage, drove her to those rustic spots, beguiling the little journeys with conversations about Rawdon and his wife, and telling every story to the old lady which could add to her indignation against this pair of reprobates.

Perhaps Mrs. Bute pulled the string unnecessarily tight. For though she worked up Miss Crawley to a proper dislike of her disobedient nephew, the invalid had a great hatred and secret terror of her victimizer, and panted to escape from her. After a brief space, she rebelled against Highgate and Hornsey utterly. She would go into the Park. Mrs. Bute knew they would meet the abominable Rawdon there, and she was right. One day in the ring, Rawdon's stanhope came in sight; Rebecca was seated by him. In the enemy's equipage Miss Crawley occupied her usual place, with Mrs. Bute on her left, the poodle and Miss Briggs on the back seat. It was a nervous moment, and Rebecca's heart beat quick as she recognized the carriage; and as the two vehicles crossed each other in the line, she clasped her hands, and looked towards the spinster with a face of agonized attachment and devotion. Rawdon himself trembled, and his face grew purple behind his dyed moustachios. Only old Briggs was moved in the other carriage, and cast her great eyes nervously towards her old friends. Miss Crawley's bonnet was resolutely turned towards the Serpentine. Mrs. Bute happened to be in ecstacies with the poodle, and was calling him a little darling, and a sweet little zoggy, and a pretty pet. The carriages moved on, each in his line.

'Done, by Jove,' Rawdon said to his wife.

'Try once more, Rawdon,' Rebecca answered. 'Could not you lock your wheels into theirs, dearest?'

Rawdon had not the heart for that manœuvre. When the carriages met again, he stood up in his stanhope; he raised his hand ready to doff his hat; he looked with all his eyes. But this time Miss Crawley's face was not turned away; she and Mrs. Bute looked him full in the face, and cut their nephew pitilessly. He sank back in his seat with an oath, and striking out of the ring, dashed away desperately homewards.

It was a gallant and decided triumph for Mrs. Bute. But she felt the danger of many such meetings, as she saw the evident nervousness of Miss Crawley; and she determined that it was most necessary for her dear friend's health, that they should leave town for a while, and recommended Brighton very strongly.

CHAPTER XX

IN WHICH CAPTAIN DOBBIN ACTS AS THE MESSENGER OF HYMEN

WITHOUT knowing how, Captain William Dobbin found himself the great promoter, arranger, and manager of the match between George Osborne and Amelia. But for him it never would have taken place: he could not but confess as much to himself, and smiled rather bitterly as he thought that he of all men in the world should be the person upon whom the care of this marriage had fallen. But though indeed the conducting of this negotiation was about as painful a task as could be set to him, yet when he had a duty to perform, Captain Dobbin was accustomed to go through it without many words or much hesitation: and, having made up his mind completely, that if Miss Sedley was balked of her husband she would die of the disappointment, he was determined to use all his best endeavours to keep her alive.

I forbear to enter into minute particulars of the interview between George and Amelia, when the former was brought back to the feet (or should we venture to say the arms?) of his young mistress by the intervention of his friend honest William. A much harder heart than George's would have melted at the sight of that sweet face so sadly ravaged by grief and despair, and at the simple tender accents in which she told her little broken-hearted story: but as she did not faint when her mother, trembling, brought Osborne to her; and as she only gave relief to her overcharged grief, by laying her head on her lover's shoulder and there weeping for a while the most tender, copious, and refreshing tears – old Mrs. Sedley, too greatly relieved, thought it was best to leave the young persons to themselves; and so quitted Emmy crying over George's hand, and kissing it humbly, as if he were her supreme chief and master, and as if she were quite a guilty and unworthy person needing every favour and grace from him.

This prostration and sweet unrepining obedience exquisitely touched and flattered George Osborne. He saw a slave before him in that simple yielding faithful creature, and his soul within him thrilled secretly somehow at the knowledge of his power. He would be generous-minded, Sultan as he was, and raise up this kneeling Esther and make a queen of her: besides, her sadness and beauty touched him as much as her submission, and so he cheered her, and raised her up and forgave her, so to speak. All her hopes and feelings, which were dying and withering, this her sun having been removed from her, bloomed again and at once, its light being restored. You would scarcely have recognized the beaming little face upon Amelia's pillow that night as the one that was laid there the night before, so wan, so lifeless, so careless of all round about. The honest Irish maid-servant, delighted with the change, asked leave to kiss the face that had grown all of a sudden so rosy. Amelia put her arms round the girl's neck and kissed her with all her heart, like a child. She was little more. She had that night a sweet refreshing sleep, like one – and what a spring of inexpressible happiness as she woke in the morning sunshine!

'He will be here again to-day,' Amelia thought. 'He is the greatest and best of men.' And the fact is, that George thought he was one of the generousest creatures alive; and that he was making a tremendous sacrifice in marrying this young creature.

While she and Osborne were having their delightful *tête-à-tête* above-stairs, old Mrs. Sedley and Captain Dobbin were conversing below upon the state of the affairs, and the chances and future arrangements of the young people. Mrs. Sedley having brought the two lovers together and left them embracing each other with all their might, like a true woman, was of opinion that no power on earth would induce Mr. Sedley to consent to the match between his daughter and the son of a man who had so shamefully, wickedly, and monstrously treated him. And she told a long story about happier days and their earlier splendours, when Osborne lived in a very humble way in the New Road, and his wife was *too glad* to receive some of Jos's little baby things, with which Mrs. Sedley accommodated her at the birth of one of Osborne's own children. The fiendish ingratitude of that man, she was sure, had broken Mr. S.'s heart: and as for a marriage, he would never, never, never, *never* consent.

'They must run away together, ma'am,' Dobbin said, laughing, 'and follow the example of Captain Rawdon Crawley, and Miss Emmy's friend the little governess.' Was it possible? Well she never! Mrs. Sedley was all excitement about this news. She wished that Blenkinsop were here to hear it: Blenkinsop always mistrusted that Miss Sharp. – What an escape Jos had had! and she described the already well-known love-passages between Rebecca and the collector of Boggley Wollah.

It was not, however, Mr. Sedley's wrath which Dobbin feared, so much as that of the other parent concerned, and he owned that he had a very considerable doubt and anxiety respecting the behaviour of the black-browed old tyrant of a Russia merchant in Russell Square. He has forbidden the match peremptorily, Dobbin thought. He knew what a savage determined man Osborne was, and how he stuck by his word. 'The only chance George has of reconcilement,' argued his friend, 'is by distinguishing himself in the coming campaign. If he dies they both go together. If he fails in distinction – what then? He has some money from his mother, I have heard – enough to purchase his majority – or he must sell out and go and dig in Canada, or rough it in a cottage in the country.' With such a partner Dobbin thought he would not mind Siberia – and, strange to say, this absurd and utterly imprudent young fellow never for a moment considered that the want of means to keep a nice carriage and horses, and of an income which should enable its possessors to entertain their friends genteelly, ought to operate as bars to the union of George and Miss Sedley.

It was these weighty considerations which made him think too that the marriage should take place as quickly as possible. Was he anxious himself, I wonder, to have it over? – as people, when death has occurred, like to press forward the funeral, or when a parting is resolved upon, hasten it. It is certain that Mr. Dobbin, having taken the matter in hand, was most extraordinarily eager in the conduct of it. He urged on George the necessity of immediate action: he showed the chances of reconciliation with his father, which a favourable mention of his name in the *Gazette* must bring about. If need were he would go himself and brave both the fathers in the business. At all events, he besought George to go through with it before the orders came, which everybody expected, for the departure of the regiment from England on foreign service.

Bent upon these hymeneal projects, and with the applause and consent of Mrs. Sedley, who did not care to break the matter personally to her husband. Mr. Dobbin went to seek John Sedley at his house of call in the City, the 'Tapioca' Coffee-house, where, since his own offices were shut up, and fate had overtaken him, the poor broken-down old gentleman used to betake himself daily, and write letters and receive them, and tie them up into mysterious bundles, several of which he carried in the flaps of his coat. I don't know anything more dismal than that business and bustle and mystery of a ruined man: those letters from the wealthy which he shows you: those worn greasy documents promising support and offering condolence which he places wistfully before you, and on which he builds his hopes of restoration and future fortune. My beloved reader has no doubt in the course of his experience been waylaid by many such a luckless companion. He takes you into the corner; he has his bundle of papers out of his gaping coat pocket; and the tape off, and the string in his mouth, and the favourite letters selected and laid before you; and who does not know the sad eager half-crazy look which he fixes on you with his hopeless eyes?

Changed into a man of this sort, Dobbin found the once florid, jovial, and prosperous John Sedley. His coat, that used to be so glossy and trim, was white at the seams, and the buttons showed the copper. His face had fallen in, and was unshorn; his frill and neckcloth hung limp under his bagging waistcoat. When he used to treat the boys in old days at a coffee-house, he would shout and laugh louder than anybody there, and have all the waiters skipping round him; it was quite painful to see how humble and civil he was to John of the 'Tapioca', a blear-eyed old attendant in dingy stockings and cracked pumps, whose business it was to serve glasses of wafers, and bumpers of ink in pewter, and slices of paper to the frequenters of this dreary house of entertainment, where nothing else seemed to be consumed. As for William Dobbin, whom he had tipped repeatedly in his youth, and who had been the old gentleman's butt on a thousand occasions, old Sedley gave his hand to him in a very hesitating humble manner now, and called him 'sir'. A feeling of shame and remorse took possession of William Dobbin as the broken old man so received and addressed him, as if he himself had been somehow guilty of the misfortunes which had brought Sedley so low.

'I am very glad to see you, Captain Dobbin, sir,' says he, after a skulking look or two at his visitor (whose lanky figure and military appearance caused some excitement likewise to twinkle in the blear eyes of the waiter in the cracked dancing-pumps, and awakened the old lady in black, who dozed among the mouldy old coffee-cups in the bar). 'How is the worthy alderman, and my lady, your excellent mother, sir?' He looked round at the waiter as he said 'My lady', as much as to say, 'Hark ye, John, I have friends still, and persons of rank and reputation, too.' 'Are you come to do anything in my way, sir? My young friends, Dale and Spiggot, do all my business for me now, until my new offices are ready; for I'm only here temporarily, you know, captain. What can we do for you, sir? Will you like to take anything?'

Dobbin, with a great deal of hesitation and stuttering, protested that he was not in the least hungry or thirsty; that he had no business to transact; that he only came to ask if Mr. Sedley was well, and to shake hands with an old friend; and, he added, with a desperate perversion of truth, 'My mother is very well – that is, she's been very unwell, and is only waiting for the first fine day to go out and call upon Mrs. Sedley. How is Mrs. Sedley, sir? I hope she's quite well.' And here he paused, reflecting on his own consummate hypocrisy; for the day was as fine, and the sunshine as bright as it ever is in Coffin Court, where the 'Tapioca' Coffee-house is situated: and Mr. Dobbin remembered that he had seen Mrs. Sedley himself only an hour before, having driven Osborne down to Fulham in his gig, and left him there *tête à tête* with Miss Amelia.

'My wife will be very happy to see her ladyship,' Sedley replied, pulling out his papers. 'I've a very kind letter here from your father, sir, and beg my respectful compliments to him. Lady D. will find us in rather a smaller house than we were accustomed to receive our friends in; but it's snug, and the change of air does good to my daughter, who was suffering in town rather – you remember little Emmy, sir? – yes, suffering a good deal.' The old gentleman's eyes were wandering as he spoke, and he was thinking of something else, as he sat thrumming on his papers and fumbling at the worn red tape.

'You're a military man,' he went on; 'I ask you, Bill Dobbin, could any man ever have speculated upon the return of that Corsican scoundrel from Elba? When the allied sovereigns were here last year, and we gave 'em that dinner in the City, sir, and we saw the Temple of Concord, and the fireworks, and the Chinese bridge in St. James's Park, could any sensible man suppose that peace wasn't really concluded, after we'd actually sung *Te Deum* for it, sir? I ask you, William, could I suppose that the Emperor of Austria was a damned traitor – a traitor, and nothing more? I don't mince words – a double-faced infernal traitor and schemer, who meant to have his son-in-law back all along. And I say that the escape of Boney from Elba was a damned imposition and plot, sir, in which half the powers of Europe were concerned, to bring the funds down, and to ruin this country. That's why I'm here, William. That's why my name is in the *Gazette*. Why, sir? – because I trusted the Emperor of Russia and the Prince Regent. Look here. Look at my papers. Look what the funds were on the 1st of March – what the French fives were when I bought for the account. And what they're at now. There was collusion, sir, or that villain never would have escaped. Where was the English Commissioner who allowed him to get away? He ought to be shot, sir – brought to a court martial, and shot, by Jove.'

'We're going to hunt Boney out, sir,' Dobbin said, rather

alarmed at the fury of the old man, the veins of whose forehead began to swell, and who sat drumming his papers with his clenched fist. 'We are going to hunt him out, sir – the Duke's in Belgium already, and we expect marching-orders every day.'

'Give him no quarter. Bring back the villain's head, sir. Shoot the coward down, sir,' Sedley roared. 'I'd enlist myself, by —; but I'm a broken old man – ruined by that damned scoundrel – and by a parcel of swindling thieves in this country whom I made, sir, and who are rolling in their carriages now,' he added, with a break in his voice.

Dobbin was not a little affected by the sight of this once kind old friend, crazed almost with misfortune and raving with senile anger. Pity the fallen gentleman: you to whom money and fair repute are the chiefest good; and so, surely, are they in Vanity Fair.

'Yes,' he continued, 'there are some vipers that you warm, and they sting you afterwards. There are some beggars that you put on horseback, and they're the first to ride you down. You know whom I mean, William Dobbin, my boy. I mean a purse-proud villain in Russell Square, whom I knew without a shilling, and whom I pray and hope to see a beggar as he was when I befriended him.'

'I have heard something of this, sir, from my friend, George,' Dobbin said, anxious to come to his point. 'The quarrel between you and his father has cut him up a great deal, sir. Indeed, I'm the bearer of a message from him.'

'Oh, *that's* your errand, is it?' cried the old man, jumping up. 'What! perhaps he condoles with me, does he? Very kind of him, the stiff-backed prig, with his dandified airs and West End swagger. He's hankering about my house, is he still? If my son had the courage of a man, he'd shoot him. He's as big a villain as his father. I won't have his name mentioned in my house. I curse the day that ever I let him into it; and I'd rather see my daughter dead at my feet than married to him.'

'His father's harshness is not George's fault, sir. Your daughter's love for him is as much your doing as his. Who are you, that you are to play with two young people's affections and break their hearts at your will?'

'Recollect it's not his father that breaks the match off,' old Sedley cried out. 'It's I that forbid it. That family and mine are separated for ever. I'm fallen low, but not so low as that: no, no. And so you may tell the whole race – son, and father, and sisters, and all.'

'It's my belief, sir, that you have not the power or the right to separate those two,' Dobbin answered in a low voice; 'and that if you don't give your daughter your consent, it will be her duty to marry without it. There's no reason she should die or live miserably because you are wrong-headed. To my thinking she's just as much married as if the banns had been read in all the churches in London. And what better answer can there be to Osborne's charges against you, as charges there are, than that his son claims to enter your family and marry your daughter?'

A light of something like satisfaction seemed to break over old Sedley as this point was put to him: but he still persisted that with his consent the marriage between Amelia and George should never take place.

'We must do it without,' Dobbin said, smiling, and told Mr. Sedley, as he had told Mrs. Sedley in the day, before, the story of Rebecca's elopement with Captain Crawley. It evidently amused the old gentleman. 'You're terrible fellows, you captains,' said he, tying up his papers; and his face wore something like a smile upon it, to the astonishment of the blear-eyed waiter who now entered, and had never seen such as expression upon Sedley's countenance since he had used the dismal coffee-house.

The idea of hitting his enemy Osborne such a blow soothed, perhaps, the old gentleman: and, their colloquy presently ending, he and Dobbin parted pretty good friends.

'My sisters say she has diamonds as big as pigeons' eggs,' George said, laughing. 'How they must set off her complexion! A perfect illumination it must be when her jewels are on her neck. Her jet-black hair is as curly as Sambo's. I dare say she wore a nose-ring when she went to Court; and with a plume of feathers in her top-knot she would look a perfect Belle Sauvage.'

George, in conversation with Amelia, was rallying the appearance of a young lady of whom his father and sisters had lately made the acquaintance, and who was an object of vast respect to the Russell Square family. She was reported to have I don't know how many plantations in the West

Indies; a deal of money in the funds; and three stars to her
name in the East India stockholders' list. She had a mansion
in Surrey, and a house in Portland Place. The name of the
rich West India heiress had been mentioned with applause
in the *Morning Post*. Mrs. Haggistoun, Colonel Haggistoun's
widow, her relative, 'chaperoned' her, and kept her house.
She was just from school, where she had completed her
education, and George and his sisters had met her at an
evening party at old Hulker's house, Devonshire Place (Hulker, Bullock, & Co. were long the correspondents of her house
in the West Indies), and the girls had made the most cordial
advances to her, which the heiress had received with great
good humour. An orphan in her position – with her money
– so interesting! the Misses Osborne said. They were full of
their new friend when they returned from the Hulker ball to
Miss Wirt, their companion: they had made arrangements for
continually meeting, and had the carriage and drove to see
her the very next day. Mrs. Haggistoun, Colonel Haggistoun's
widow, a relation of Lord Binkie, and always talking of him,
struck the dear unsophisticated girls as rather haughty, and
too much inclined to talk about her great relations: but Rhoda
was everything they could wish – the frankest, kindest, most
agreeable creature – wanting a little polish, but so good-
natured. The girls Christian-named each other at once.

'You should have seen her dress for court, Emmy.'
Osborne cried, laughing. 'She came to my sisters to show it
off, before she was presented in state by my Lady Binkie,
the Haggistoun's kinswoman. She's related to every one, that
Haggistoun. Her diamonds blazed out like Vauxhall on the
night we were there. (Do you remember Vauxhall, Emmy,
and Jos singing to his dearest diddle-diddle-darling?) Diamonds and mahogany, my dear! think what an advantageous
contrast – and the white feathers in her hair – I mean in
her wool. She had ear-rings like chandeliers; you might have
lighted 'em up, by Jove – and a yellow satin train that
streeled after her like the tail of a comet.'

'How old is she?' asked Emmy, to whom George was
rattling away regarding this dark paragon, on the morning
of their re-union – rattling away as no other man in the
world surely could.

'Why, the Black Princess, though she has only just left
school, must be two- or three-and-twenty. And you should

see the hand she writes! Mrs. Colonel Haggistoun usually writes her letters, but in a moment of confidence, she put pen to paper for my sisters; she spelt satin satting, and Saint James's, Saint Jams.'

'Why, surely it must be Miss Swartz, the parlour boarder,' Emmy said, remembering that good-natured young mulatto girl, who had been so hysterically affected when Amelia left Miss Pinkerton's academy.

'The very name,' George said. 'Her father was a German Jew – a slave-owner they say – connected with the Cannibal Islands in some way or other. He died last year, and Miss Pinkerton has finished her education. She can play two pieces on the piano; she knows three songs; she can write when Mrs. Haggistoun is by to spell for her; and Jane and Maria already have got to love her as a sister.'

'I wish they would have loved me,' said Emmy, wistfully. 'They were always very cold to me.'

'My dear child, they would have loved you if you had had two hundred thousand pounds,' George replied. 'That is the way in which they have been brought up. Ours is a ready-money society. We live among bankers and city big-wigs, and be hanged to them, and every man, as he talks to you, is jingling his guineas in his pocket. There is that jackass Fred Bullock, is going to marry Maria – there's Goldmore, the East India Director, there's Dipley, in the tallow trade – *our* trade,' George said, with an uneasy laugh and a blush. 'Curse the whole pack of money-grubbing vulgarians! I fall asleep at their great heavy dinners. I feel ashamed in my father's great stupid parties. I've been accustomed to live with gentlemen, and men of the world and fashion, Emmy, not with a parcel of turtle-fed tradesmen. Dear little woman, you are the only person of our set who ever looked, or thought, or spoke like a lady: and you do it because you're an angel and can't help it. Don't remonstrate. You *are* the only lady. Didn't Miss Crawley remark it, who has lived in the best company in Europe? And as for Crawley, of the Life Guards, hang it, he's a fine fellow: and I like him for marrying the girl he had chosen.'

Amelia admired Mr. Crawley very much, too, for this; and trusted Rebecca would be happy with him, and hoped (with a laugh) Jos would be consoled. And so the pair went on prattling, as in quite early days, Amelia's confidence being perfectly restored to her, though she expressed a great deal of pretty jealousy about Miss Swartz, and professed to be dreadfully frightened – like a hypocrite as she was – lest George should forget her for the heiress and her money and her estates in St. Kitts. But the fact is, she was a great deal too happy to have fears or doubts or misgivings of any sort: and having George at her side again, was not afraid of any heiress or beauty, or indeed of any sort of danger.

When Captain Dobbin came back in the afternoon to these people – which he did with a great deal of sympathy for them – it did his heart good to see how Amelia had grown young again – how she laughed, and chirped, and sang familiar old songs at the piano, which were only interrupted by the bell from without proclaiming Mr. Sedley's return from the City, before whom George received a signal to retreat.

Beyond the first smile of recognition – and even that was an hypocrisy, for she thought his arrival rather provoking – Miss Sedley did not once notice Dobbin during his visit. But he was content, so that he saw her happy; and thankful to have been the means of making her so.

CHAPTER XXI

A QUARREL ABOUT AN HEIRESS

L OVE may be felt for any young lady endowed with such qualities as Miss Swartz possessed; and a great dream of ambition entered into old Mr. Osborne's soul, which she was to realize. He encouraged, with the utmost enthusiasm and friendliness, his daughters' amiable attachment to the young heiress, and protested that it gave him the sincerest pleasure as a father to see the love of his girls so well disposed.

'You won't find,' he would say to Miss Rhoda, 'that splendour and rank to which you are accustomed at the West End, my dear miss, at our humble mansion in Russell Square. My daughters are plain, disinterested girls, but their hearts are in the right place, and they've conceived an attachment for you which does them honour – I say, which does them honour. I'm a plain, simple, humble British merchant – an honest one, as my respected friends Hulker

& Bullock will vouch, who were the correspondents of your
late lamented father. You'll find us a united, simple, happy,
and I think I may say respected, family – a plain table, a
plain people, but a warm welcome, my dear Miss Rhoda –
Rhoda, let me say, for my heart warms to you, it does really.
I'm a frank man, and I like you. A glass of champagne!
Hicks, champagne to Miss Swartz.'

There is little doubt that old Osborne believed all he said,
and that the girls were quite earnest in their protestations
of affection for Miss Swartz. People in Vanity Fair fasten
on to rich folks quite naturally. If the simplest people are
disposed to look not a little kindly on great Prosperity (for
I defy any member of the British public to say that the
notion of Wealth has not something awful and pleasing to
him; and you, if you are told that the man next you at dinner
has got half a million, not to look at him with a certain
interest) – if the simple look benevolently on money, how
much more do your old worldlings regard it! Their affections
rush out to meet and welcome money. Their kind sentiments
awaken spontaneously towards the interesting possessors of
it. I know some respectable people who don't consider
themselves at liberty to indulge in friendship for any individual who has not a certain competency, or place in society.
They give a loose to their feelings on proper occasions. And
the proof is, that the major part of the Osborne family, who
had not, in fifteen years, been able to get up a hearty regard
for Amelia Sedley, became as fond of Miss Swartz in the
course of a single evening as the most romantic advocate of
friendship at first sight could desire.

What a match for George she'd be (the sister and Miss
Wirt agreed), and how much better than that insignificant
little Amelia! Such a dashing young fellow as he is, with his
good looks, rank, and accomplishments, would be the very
husband for her. Visions of balls in Portland Place, presentations at Court, and introductions to half the peerage, filled
the minds of the young ladies; who talked of nothing but
George and his grand acquaintances to their beloved new
friend.

Old Osborne thought she would be a great match, too,
for his son. He should leave the army; he should go into
Parliament; he should cut a figure in the fashion and in the
state. His blood boiled with honest British exultation, as he

saw the name of Osborne ennobled in the person of his son, and thought that he might be the progenitor of a glorious line of baronets. He worked in the City and on 'Change, until he knew everything relating to the fortune of the heiress, how her money was placed, and where her estates lay. Young Fred Bullock, one of his chief informants, would have liked to make a bid for her himself (it was so the young banker expressed it), only he was booked to Maria Osborne. But not being able to secure her as a wife, the disinterested Fred quite approved of her as a sister-in-law. 'Let George cut in directly and win her,' was his advice. 'Strike while the iron's hot, you know – while she's fresh to the town: in a few weeks some d— fellow from the West End will come in with a title and a rotten rent-roll and cut all us City men out, as Lord Fitzrufus did last year with Miss Grogram, who was actually engaged to Podder, of Podder & Brown's. The sooner it is done the better, Mr. Osborne; them's my sentiments,' the wag said: though, when Osborne had left the bank parlour, Mr. Bullock remembered Amelia, and what a pretty girl she was, and how attached to George Osborne; and he gave up at least ten seconds of his valuable time to regretting the misfortune which had befallen that unlucky young woman.

While thus George Osborne's good feelings, and his good friend and genius, Dobbin, were carrying back the truant to Amelia's feet, George's parent and sisters were arranging this splendid match for him, which they never dreamed he would resist.

When the elder Osborne gave what he called 'a hint', there was no possibility for the most obtuse to mistake his meaning. He called kicking a footman downstairs, a hint to the latter to leave his service. With his usual frankness and delicacy he told Mrs. Haggistoun that he would give her a cheque for five thousand pounds on the day his son was married to her ward: and called that proposal a hint, and considered it a very dexterous piece of diplomacy. He gave George finally such another hint regarding the heiress; and ordered him to marry her out of hand, as he would have ordered his butler to draw a cork, or his clerk to write a letter.

This imperative hint disturbed George a good deal. He was in the very first enthusiasm and delight of his second courtship of Amelia, which was inexpressibly sweet to him.

The contrast of her manners and appearance with those of the heiress, made the idea of a union with the latter appear doubly ludicrous and odious. Carriages and opera-boxes, thought he; fancy being seen in them by the side of such a mahogany charmer as that! Add to all, that the Junior Osborne was quite as obstinate as the Senior: when he wanted a thing, quite as firm in his resolution to get it: and quite as violent when angered, as his father in his most stern moments.

On the first day when his father formally gave him the hint that he was to place his affections at Miss Swartz's feet, George temporized with the old gentleman. 'You should have thought of the matter sooner, sir,' he said. 'It can't be done now, when we're expecting every day to go on foreign service. Wait till my return, if I do return;' and then he represented, that the time when the regiment was daily expecting to quit England, was exceedingly ill-chosen: that the few days or weeks during which they were still to remain at home, must be devoted to business and not to love-making: time enough for that when he came home with his majority; 'for, I promise you,' said he, with a satisfied air, 'that one way or other you shall read the name of George Osborne in the *Gazette.*'

The father's reply to this was founded upon the infor-mation which he had got in the City: that the West End chaps would infallibly catch hold of the heiress if any delay took place: that if he didn't marry Miss S., he might at least have an engagement in writing, to come into effect when he returned to England: and that a man who could get ten thousand a year by staying at home, was a fool to risk his life abroad.

'So that you would have me shown up as a coward, sir, and our name dishonoured for the sake of Miss Swartz's money,' George interposed.

This remark staggered the old gentleman; but as he had to reply to it, and as his mind was nevertheless made up, he said, 'You will dine here to-morrow, sir, and every day Miss Swartz comes, you will be here to pay your respects to her. If you want for money, call upon Mr. Chopper.' Thus a new obstacle was in George's way, to interfere with his plans regarding Amelia; and about which he and Dobbin had more than one confidential consultation. His friend's opinion respecting the line of conduct which he ought to pursue, we know already. And as for Osborne, when he was once bent on a thing, a fresh obstacle or two only rendered him the more resolute.

The dark object of the conspiracy into which the chiefs of the Osborne family had entered, was quite ignorant of all their plans regarding her (which, strange to say, her friend and chaperon did not divulge), and, taking all the young ladies' flattery for genuine sentiment, and being, as we have before had occasion to show, of a very warm and impetuous nature, responded to their affection with quite a tropical ardour. And if the truth may be told, I dare say that she too had some selfish attraction in the Russell Square house; and, in a word, thought George Osborne a very nice young man. His whiskers had made an impression upon her, on the very first night she beheld them at the ball at Messrs. Hulkers; and, as we know, she was not the first woman who had been charmed by them. George had an air at once swaggering and melancholy, languid and fierce. He looked like a man who had passions, secrets, and private harrowing griefs and adventures. His voice was rich and deep. He would say it was a warm evening, or ask his partner to take an ice, with a tone as sad and confidential as if he were breaking her mother's death to her, or preluding a declaration of love. He trampled over all the young bucks of his father's circle, and was the hero among those third-rate men. Some few sneered at him and hated him. Some, like Dobbin, fanatically admired him. And his whiskers had began to do their work, and to curl themselves round the affections of Miss Swartz.

Whenever there was a chance of meeting him in Russell Square, that simple and good-natured young woman was quite in a flurry to see her dear Miss Osbornes. She went to great expenses in new gowns, and bracelets, and bonnets, and in prodigious feathers. She adorned her person with her utmost skill to please the Conqueror, and exhibited all her simple accomplishments to win his favour. The girls would ask her, with the greatest gravity, for a little music, and she would sing her three songs and play her two little pieces as often as ever they asked, and with an always increasing pleasure to herself. During these delectable entertainments,

Miss Wirt and the chaperon sat by, and conned over the *Peerage*, and talked about the nobility.

The day after George had his hint from his father, and a short time before the hour of dinner, he was lolling upon a sofa in the drawing-room in a very becoming and perfectly natural attitude of melancholy. He had been, at his father's request, to Mr. Chopper in the City (the old gentleman, though he gave great sums to his son, would never specify any fixed allowance for him, and rewarded him only as he was in the humour). He had then been to pass three hours with Amelia, his dear little Amelia, at Fulham; and he came home to find his sisters spread in starched muslin in the drawing-room, the dowagers cackling in the background, and honest Swartz in her favourite amber-coloured satin, with turquoise-bracelets, countless rings, flowers, feathers, and all sorts of tags and gimcracks, about as elegantly decorated as a she chimney-sweep on May Day.

The girls, after vain attempts to engage him in conversation, talked about fashions and the last Drawing-room until he was perfectly sick of their chatter. He contrasted their behaviour with little Emmy's — their shrill voices with her tender ringing tones; their attitudes and their elbows and their starch, with her humble soft movements and modest graces. Poor Swartz was seated in a place where Emmy had been accustomed to sit. Her bejewelled hands lay sprawling in her amber satin lap. Her tags and ear-rings twinkled, and her big eyes rolled about. She was doing nothing with perfect contentment, and thinking herself charming. Anything so becoming as the satin the sisters had never seen.

'Dammy,' George said to a confidential friend, 'she looked like a China doll, which has nothing to do all day but to grin and wag its head. By Jove, Will, it was all I could to do prevent myself from throwing the sofa-cushion at her.' He restrained that exhibition of sentiment, however.

The sisters began to play the Battle of Prague. 'Stop that d— thing,' George howled out in a fury from the sofa. 'It makes me mad. *You* play us something, Miss Swartz, do. Sing something, anything but the Battle of Prague.'

'Shall I sing *Blue Eyed Mary*, or the air from the Cabinet?' Miss Swartz asked.

'That sweet thing from the Cabinet,' the sisters said.

'We've had that,' replied the misanthrope on the sofa.

'I can sing *Fluvy du Tajy*,' Swartz said, in a meek voice, 'if I had the words.' It was the last of the worthy young woman's collection.

'Oh, *Fleuve du Tage*,' Miss Maria cried; 'we have the song,' and went to fetch the book in which it was.

Now it happened that this song, then in the height of the fashion, had been given to the young ladies by a young friend of theirs, whose name was on the title, and Miss Swartz, having concluded the ditty with George's applause (for he remembered that it was a favourite of Amelia's), was hoping for an encore perhaps, and fiddling with the leaves of the music, when her eye fell upon the title, and she saw 'Amelia Sedley' written in the corner.

'Lor!' cried Miss Swartz, spinning swiftly round on the music-stool, 'is it *my* Amelia? Amelia that was at Miss P.'s at Hammersmith? I know it is. It's her, and – Tell me about her – where is she?'

'Don't mention her,' Miss Maria Osborne said hastily. 'Her family has disgraced itself. Her father cheated papa, and as for her, she is never to be mentioned *here*.' This was Miss Maria's return for George's rudeness about the Battle of Prague.

'Are you a friend of Amelia's?' George said, bouncing up. 'God bless you for it, Miss Swartz. Don't believe what the girls say. *She's* not to blame at any rate. She's the best —'

'You know you're not to speak about her, George,' cried Jane. 'Papa forbids it.'

'Who's to prevent me?' George cried out. 'I *will* speak of her. I say she's the best, the kindest, the gentlest, the sweetest girl in England; and that, bankrupt or no, my sisters are not fit to hold candles to her. If you like her, go and see her, Miss Swartz; she wants friends now; and I say, God bless everybody who befriends her. Anybody who speaks kindly of her is my friend; anybody who speaks against her is my enemy. Thank you, Miss Swartz;' and he went up and wrung her hand.

'George! George!' one of the sisters cried imploringly.

'I say,' George said fiercely, 'I thank everybody who loves Amelia Sed —.' He stopped. Old Osborne was in the room with a face livid with rage, and eyes like hot coals.

Though George had stopped in his sentence, yet, his blood being up, he was not to be cowed by all the generations of Osborne; rallying instantly, he replied to the bullying look

of his father, with another so indicative of resolution and
defiance, that the elder man quailed in his turn, and looked
away. He felt that the tussle was coming. 'Mrs. Haggistoun,
let me take you down to dinner,' he said. 'Give your arm
to Miss Swartz, George,' and they marched.

'Miss Swartz, I love Amelia, and we've been engaged
almost all our lives,' Osborne said to his partner; and during
all the dinner, George rattled on with a volubility which
surprised himself, and made his father doubly nervous for the
fight which was to take place as soon as the ladies were gone.

The difference between the pair was, that while the father
was violent and a bully, the son had thrice the nerve and
courage of the parent, and could not merely make an attack,
but resist it; and finding that the moment was now come
when the contest between him and his father was to be
decided, he took his dinner with perfect coolness and appetite before the engagement began. Old Osborne, on the
contrary, was nervous, and drank much. He floundered in
his conversation with the ladies, his neighbours: George's
coolness only rendering him more angry. It made him half
mad to see the calm way in which George, flapping his
napkin, and with a swaggering bow, opened the door for the
ladies to leave the room; and filling himself a glass of wine,
smacked it, and looked his father full in the face, as if to
say, 'Gentlemen of the Guard, fire first.' The old man also
took a supply of ammunition, but his decanter clinked
against the glass as he tried to fill it.

After giving a great heave, and with a purple choking face,
he then began. 'How dare you, sir, mention that person's
name before Miss Swartz to-day, in my drawing-room? I ask
you, sir, how dare you do it?'

'Stop, sir,' says George, 'don't say dare, sir. Dare isn't a
word to be used to a captain in the British Army.'

'I shall say what I like to my son, sir. I can cut him off
with a shilling if I like. I can make him a beggar if I like.
I *will* say what I like,' the elder said.

'I'm a gentleman though I *am* your son, sir,' George
answered haughtily. 'Any communications which you have
to make to me, or any orders which you may please to give,
I beg may be couched in that kind of language which I am
accustomed to hear.'

Whenever the lad assumed his haughty manner, it always

created either great awe or great irritation in the parent. Old Osborne stood in secret terror of his son as a better gentleman than himself; and perhaps my readers may have remarked in their experience of this Vanity Fair of ours, that there is no character which a low-minded man so much mistrusts, as that of a gentleman.

'My father didn't give me the education you have had, nor the advantages you have had, nor the money you have had. If I had kept the company *some folks* have had through *my means*, perhaps my son wouldn't have any reason to brag, sir, of his *superiority* and *West End airs*' (these words were uttered in the elder Osborne's most sarcastic tones). 'But it wasn't considered the part of a gentleman, in *my* time, for a man to insult his father. If I'd done any such thing, mine would have kicked me downstairs, sir.'

'I never insulted you, sir. I said I begged you to remember your son was a gentleman as well as yourself. I know very well that you give me plenty of money,' said George (fingering a bundle of notes which he had got in the morning from Mr. Chopper). 'You tell it me often enough, sir. There's no fear of my forgetting it.'

'I wish you'd remember other things as well, sir,' the sire answered. 'I wish you'd remember that in this house – so long as you choose to *honour* it with your *company*, captain – I'm the master, and that name, and that that – that you – that I say —'

'That what, sir?' George asked, with scarcely a sneer, filling another glass of claret.

'—— !' burst out his father with a screaming oath – 'that the name of those Sedleys never be mentioned here, sir – not one of the whole damned lot of 'em, sir.'

'It wasn't I, sir, that introduced Miss Sedley's name. It was my sisters who spoke ill of her to Miss Swartz; and by Jove I'll defend her wherever I go. Nobody shall speak lightly of that name in my presence. Our family has done her quite enough injury already, I think, and may leave off reviling her now she's down. I'll shoot any man but you who says a word against her.'

'Go on, sir, go on,' the old gentleman said, his eyes starting out of his head.

'Go on about what, sir? about the way in which we've treated that angel of a girl? Who told me to love her? It was your doing. I might have chosen elsewhere, and looked higher, perhaps, than your society: but I obeyed you. And now that her heart's mine you give me orders to fling it away, and punish her, kill her perhaps – for the faults of other people. It's a shame, by Heavens,' said George, working himself up into passion and enthusiasm as he proceeded, 'to play at fast and loose with a young girl's affections – and with such an angel as that – one so superior to the people amongst whom she lived that she might have excited envy, only she was so good and gentle that it's a wonder anybody dared to hate her. If I desert her, sir, do you suppose she forgets me?'

'I ain't going to have any of this dam sentimental non-sense and humbug here, sir,' the father cried out. 'There shall be no beggar-marriages in my family. If you choose to fling away eight thousand a year, which you may have for the asking, you may do it: but by Jove you take your pack and walk out of this house, sir. Will you do as I tell you, once for all, sir, or will you not?'

'Marry that mulatto woman?' George said, pulling up his shirt-collars. 'I don't like the colour, sir. Ask the black that sweeps opposite Fleet Market, sir. *I'm* not going to marry a Hottentot Venus.'

Mr. Osborne pulled frantically at the cord by which he was accustomed to summon the butler when he wanted wine – and, almost black in the face, ordered that functionary to call a coach for Captain Osborne.

'I've done it,' said George, coming into the Slaughter's an hour afterwards, looking very pale.

'What, my boy?' says Dobbin.

George told what had passed between his father and himself.

'I'll marry her to-morrow,' he said with an oath. 'I love her more every day, Dobbin.'

CHAPTER XXII

A MARRIAGE AND PART OF A HONEYMOON

ENEMIES the most obstinate and courageous can't hold out against starvation; so the elder Osborne felt himself pretty easy about his adversary in the encounter we have just described: and as soon as George's supplies fell short, confidently expected his unconditional submission. It was unlucky, to be sure, that the lad should have secured a stock of provisions on the very day when the first encounter took place; but this relief was only temporary, old Osborne thought, and would but delay George's surrender. No communication passed between father and son for some days. The former was sulky at this silence, but not disquieted; for, as he said, he knew where he could put the screw upon George, and only waited the result of that operation. He told the sisters the upshot of the dispute between them, but ordered them to take no notice of the matter, and welcome George on his return as if nothing had happened. His cover was laid as usual every day, and perhaps the old gentleman rather anxiously expected him; but he never came. Some one inquired at the Slaughter's regarding him, where it was said that he and his friend Captain Dobbin had left town.

One gusty, raw day at the end of April, – the rain whipping the pavement of that ancient street where the old Slaughter's Coffee-house was once situated – George Osborne came into the coffee-room, looking very haggard and pale; although dressed rather smartly in a blue coat and brass buttons, and a neat buff waistcoat of the fashion of those days. Here was his friend Captain Dobbin, in blue and brass too, having abandoned the military frock and French-grey trousers, which were the usual coverings of his lanky person.

Dobbin had been in the coffee-room for an hour or more. He had tried all the papers, but could not read them. He had looked at the clock many scores of times; and at the street, where the rain was pattering down, and the people as they clinked by in pattens, left long reflections on the shining stones: he tattooed at the table: he bit his nails most completely, and nearly to the quick (he was accustomed to ornament his great big hands in this way): he balanced the teaspoon dexterously on the milk jug: upset it, &c. &c.; and in fact showed those signs of disquietude, and practised those desperate attempts at amusement, which men are accustomed to employ when very anxious, and expectant, and perturbed in mind.

Some of his comrades, gentlemen who used the room, joked him about the splendour of his costume and his agitation of manner. One asked him if he was going to be married? Dobbin laughed, and said he would send his acquaintance (Major Wagstaff, of the Engineers) a piece of cake when that event took place. At length Captain Osborne made his appearance, very smartly dressed, but very pale and agitated, as we have said. He wiped his pale face with a large yellow bandanna pocket-handkerchief that was prodigiously scented. He shook hands with Dobbin, looked at the clock, and told John, the waiter, to bring him some curaçoa. Of this cordial he swallowed off a couple of glasses with nervous eagerness. His friend asked with some interest about his health.

'Couldn't get a wink of sleep till daylight, Dob,' said he. 'Infernal headache and fever. Got up at nine, and went down to the Hummums for a bath. I say, Dob, I feel just as I did on the morning I went out with Rocket at Quebec.'

'So do I,' William responded. 'I was a deuced deal more nervous than you were that morning. You made a famous breakfast, I remember. Eat something now.'

'You're a good old fellow, Will. I'll drink your health, old boy, and farewell to —'

'No, no; two glasses are enough,' Dobbin interrupted him. 'Here, take away the liqueurs, John. Have some cayenne-pepper with your fowl. Make haste though, for it is time we were there.'

It was about half an hour from twelve when this brief meeting and colloquy took place between the two captains. A coach, into which Captain Osborne's servant put his master's desk and dressing-case, had been in waiting for some time; and into this the two gentlemen hurried under an umbrella, and the valet mounted on the box, cursing the rain and the dampness of the coachman who was steaming beside him. 'We shall find a better trap than this at the church-door,' says he; 'that's a comfort.' And the carriage drove on, taking the road down Piccadilly; where Apsley House and St. George's Hospital wore red jackets still; where there were oil-lamps; where Achilles was not yet born; nor the Pimlico arch raised; nor the hideous equestrian monster which pervades it and the neighbourhood; – and so they drove down by Brompton to a certain chapel near the Fulham Road there.

A chariot was in waiting with four horses; likewise a coach

of the kind called glass coaches. Only a very few idlers were collected on account of the dismal rain.

'Hang it!' said George, 'I said only a pair.'

'My master would have four,' said Mr. Joseph Sedley's servant, who was in waiting; and he and Mr. Osborne's man agreed, as they followed George and William into the church, that it was a 'reg'lar shabby turn hout; and with scarce so much as a breakfast or a wedding faviour.'

'Here you are,' said our old friend, Jos Sedley, coming forward. 'You're five minutes late, George, my boy. What a day, eh? Demmy, it's like the commencement of the rainy season in Bengal. But you'll find my carriage is watertight. Come along, my mother and Emmy are in the vestry.'

Jos Sedley was splendid. He was fatter than ever. His shirt-collars were higher; his face was redder; his shirt-frill flaunted gorgeously out of his variegated waistcoat. Varnished boots were not invented as yet; but the Hessians on his beautiful legs shone so, that they must have been the identical pair in which the gentleman in the old picture used to shave himself; and on his light-green coat there bloomed a fine wedding-favour, like a great white spreading magnolia.

In a word, George had thrown the great cast. He was going to be married. Hence his pallor and nervousness – his sleepless night and agitation in the morning. I have heard people who have gone through the same thing own to the same emotion. After three or four ceremonies, you get accustomed to it, no doubt; but the first dip, everybody allows, is awful.

The bride was dressed in a brown silk pelisse (as Captain Dobbin has since informed me), and wore a straw bonnet with a pink ribbon; over the bonnet she had a veil of white Chantilly lace, a gift from Mr. Joseph Sedley, her brother. Captain Dobbin himself had asked leave to present her with a gold chain and watch, which she sported on this occasion; and her mother gave her her diamond brooch – almost the only trinket which was left to the old lady. As the service went on, Mrs. Sedley sat and whimpered a great deal in a pew, consoled by the Irish maidservant and Mrs. Clapp from the lodgings. Old Sedley would not be present. Jos acted for his father, giving away the bride, whilst Captain Dobbin stepped up as groomsman to his friend George.

There was nobody in the church besides the officiating

persons and the small marriage party and their attendants. The two valets sat aloof superciliously. The rain came rattling down on the windows. In the intervals of the service you heard it, and the sobbing of old Mrs. Sedley in the pew. The parson's tones echoed sadly through the empty walls. Osborne's 'I will' was sounded in very deep bass. Emmy's response came fluttering up to her lips from her heart, but was scarcely heard by anybody except Captain Dobbin.

When the service was completed, Jos Sedley came forward and kissed his sister, the bride, for the first time for many months; George's look of gloom had gone, and he seemed quite proud and radiant. 'It's your turn, William,' says he, putting his hand fondly upon Dobbin's shoulder; and Dobbin went up and touched Amelia on the cheek.

Then they went into the vestry and signed the register. 'God bless you, Old Dobbin,' George said, grasping him by the hand, with something very like moisture glistening in his eyes. William replied only by nodding his head. His heart was too full to say much.

'Write directly, and come down as soon as you can, you know,' Osborne said. After Mrs. Sedley had taken an hysterical adieu of her daughter, the pair went off to the carriage. 'Get out of the way, you little devils,' George cried to a small crowd of damp urchins, that were hanging about the chapel-door. The rain drove into the bride and bridegroom's faces as they passed to the chariot. The postilions' favours draggled on their dripping jackets. The few children made a dismal cheer, as the carriage, splashing mud, drove away.

William Dobbin stood in the church-porch, looking at it, a queer figure. The small crew of spectators jeered him. He was not thinking about them or their laughter.

'Come home and have some tiffin, Dobbin,' a voice cried behind him; as a pudgy hand was laid on his shoulder, and the honest fellow's reverie was interrupted. But the captain had no heart to go a-feasting with Jos Sedley. He put the weeping old lady and her attendants into the carriage along with Jos, and left them without any farther words passing. This carriage, too, drove away, and the urchins gave another sarcastical cheer.

'Here, you little beggars,' Dobbin said, giving some sixpences amongst them, and then went off by himself through the rain. It was all over. They were married, and happy, he prayed God. Never since he was a boy had he felt so miserable and so lonely. He longed with a heartsick yearning for the first few days to be over, that he might see her again.

Some ten days after the above ceremony, three young men of our acquaintance were enjoying that beautiful prospect of bow-windows on the one side and blue sea on the other, which Brighton affords to the traveller. Sometimes it is towards the ocean – smiling with countless dimples, speckled with white sails, with a hundred bathing-machines kissing the skirt of his blue garment – that the Londoner looks enraptured: sometimes, on the contrary, a lover of human nature rather than of prospects of any kind, it is towards the bow-windows that he turns, and that swarm of human life which they exhibit. From one issue the notes of a piano, which a young lady in ringlets practises six hours daily, to the delight of the fellow lodgers: at another, lovely Polly, the nursemaid, may be seen dandling Master Omnium in her arms: whilst Jacob, his papa, is beheld eating prawns, and devouring the *Times* for breakfast, at the window below. Yonder are the Misses Leery, who are looking out for the young officers of the Heavies, who are pretty sure to be pacing the cliff; or again it is a City man, with a nautical turn, and a telescope, the size of a six-pounder, who has his instrument pointed seawards, so as to command every pleasure-boat, herring-boat, or bathing-machine that comes to, or quits, the shore, &c., &c. But have we any leisure for a description of Brighton? – for Brighton, a clean Naples with genteel lazzaroni – for Brighton, that always looks brisk, gay, and gaudy, like a harlequin's jacket – for Brighton, which used to be seven hours' distant from London at the time of our story; which is now only a hundred minutes off; and which may approach who knows how much nearer, unless Joinville comes and untimely bombards it?

'What a monstrous fine girl that is in the lodgings over the milliner's,' one of these three promenaders remarked to the other; 'Gad, Crawley, did you see what a wink she gave me as I passed?'

'Don't break her heart, Jos, you rascal,' said another. 'Don't trifle with her affections, you Don Juan!'

'Get away,' said Jos Sedley, quite pleased, and leering up at the maidservant in question with a most killing ogle. Jos was even more splendid at Brighton than he had been at his sister's marriage. He had brilliant under-waistcoats, any one of which would have set up a moderate buck. He sported a military frock-coat, ornamented with frogs, knobs, black buttons, and meandering embroidery. He had affected a military appearance and habits of late; and he walked with his two friends, who were of that profession, clinking his boot-spurs, swaggering prodigiously, and shooting death-glances at all the servant girls who were worthy to be slain.

'What shall we do, boys, till the ladies return?' the buck asked. The ladies were out to Rottingdean in his carriage on a drive. 'Let's have a game at billiards,' one of his friends said – the tall one, with lacquered moustachios.

'No, dammy; no, captain,' Jos replied, rather alarmed. 'No billiards to-day, Crawley, my boy; yesterday was enough.'

'You play very well,' said Crawley, laughing. 'Don't he, Osborne? How well he made that five stroke, eh?'

'Famous,' Osborne said. 'Jos is a devil of a fellow at billiards, and at everything else, too. I wish there were any tiger-hunting about here; we might go and kill a few before dinner. (There goes a fine girl! what an ankle, eh, Jos?) Tell us that story about the tiger-hunt, and the way you did for him in the jungle – it's a wonderful story that, Crawley.' Here George Osborne gave a yawn. 'It's rather slow work,' said he, 'down here; what *shall* we do?'

'Shall we go and look at some horses that Snaffler's just brought from Lewes fair?' Crawley said.

'Suppose we go and have some jellies at Dutton's,' said the rogue Jos, willing to kill two birds with one stone. 'Devilish fine gal at Dutton's.'

'Suppose we go and see the *Lightning* come in, it's just about time?' George said. This advice prevailing over the stables and the jelly, they turned towards the coach-office to witness the *Lightning*'s arrival.

As they passed, they met the carriage – Jos Sedley's open carriage, with its magnificent armorial bearings – that splen-did conveyance in which he used to drive about at Cheltenham, majestic and solitary, with his arms folded, and his hat cocked; or, more happy, with ladies by his side.

Two were in the carriage now: one a little person, with

light hair, and dressed in the height of the fashion; the other in a brown silk pelisse, and a straw bonnet with pink ribbons, with a rosy, round, happy face, that did you good to behold. She checked the carriage as it neared the three gentlemen, after which exercise of authority she looked rather nervous, and then began to blush most absurdly. 'We have had a delightful drive, George,' she said, 'and – and we're so glad to come back; and Joseph, don't let him be late.'

'Don't be leading our husbands into mischief, Mr. Sedley, you wicked, wicked man you,' Rebecca said, shaking at Jos a pretty little finger covered with the neatest French kid glove. 'No billiards, no smoking, no naughtiness!'

'My dear Mrs. Crawley – Ah now! upon my honour!' was all Jos could ejaculate by way of reply; but he managed to fall into a tolerable attitude, with his head lying on his shoulder, grinning upwards at his victim, with one hand at his back, which he supported on his cane, and the other hand (the one with the diamond ring) fumbling in his shirtfrill and among his under-waistcoats. As the carriage drove off he kissed the diamond hand to the fair ladies within. He wished all Cheltenham, all Chowringhee, all Calcutta, could see him in that position, waving his hand to such a beauty, and in company with such a famous buck as Rawdon Crawley of the Guards.

Our young bride and bridegroom had chosen Brighton as the place where they would pass the first few days after their marriage; and having engaged apartments at the 'Ship' Inn, enjoyed themselves there in great comfort and quietude, until Jos presently joined them. Nor was he the only companion they found there. As they were coming into the hotel from a seaside walk one afternoon, on whom should they light but Rebecca and her husband. The recognition was immediate. Rebecca flew into the arms of her dearest friend. Crawley and Osborne shook hands together cordially enough: and Becky, in the course of a very few hours, found means to make the latter forget that little unpleasant passage of words which had happened between them. 'Do you remember the last time we met at Miss Crawley's, when I was so rude to you, dear Captain Osborne? I thought you seemed careless about dear Amelia. It was that made me angry: and so pert: and so unkind: and so ungrateful. Do forgive me!' Rebecca said, and she held out her hand with so frank and winning a grace, that Osborne could not but take it. By humbly and frankly acknowledging yourself to be in the wrong, there is no knowing, my son, what good you may do. I knew once a gentleman, and very worthy practitioner in Vanity Fair, who used to do little wrongs to his neighbours on purpose, and in order to apologize for them in an open and manly way afterwards — and what ensued? My friend Crocky Doyle was liked everywhere, and deemed to be rather impetuous — but the honestest fellow. Becky's humility passed for sincerity with George Osborne.

These two young couples had plenty of tales to relate to each other. The marriages of either were discussed; and their prospects in life canvassed with the greatest frankness and interest on both sides. George's marriage was to be made known to his father by his friend Captain Dobbin; and young Osborne trembled rather for the result of that communication. Miss Crawley, on whom all Rawdon's hopes depended, still held out. Unable to make an entry into her house in Park Lane, her affectionate nephew and niece had followed her to Brighton, where they had emissaries continually planted at her door.

'I wish you could see some of Rawdon's friends who are always about *our* door,' Rebecca said, laughing. 'Did you ever see a dun, my dear; or a bailiff and his man? Two of the abominable wretches watched all last week at the greengrocer's opposite, and we could not get away until Sunday. If aunty does not relent, what *shall* we do?'

Rawdon, with roars of laughter, related a dozen amusing anecdotes of his duns, and Rebecca's adroit treatment of them. He vowed with a great oath, that there was no woman in Europe who could talk a creditor over as she could. Almost immediately after their marriage, her practice had begun, and her husband found the immense value of such a wife. They had credit in plenty, but they had bills also in abundance, and laboured under a scarcity of ready money. Did these debt-difficulties affect Rawdon's good spirits? No. Everybody in Vanity Fair must have remarked how well those live who are comfortably and thoroughly in debt: how they deny themselves nothing; how jolly and easy they are in their minds. Rawdon and his wife had the very best apartments at the inn at Brighton; the landlord, as he brought in the first dish, bowed before them as to his greatest customers: and Rawdon abused the dinners and wine with an audacity which no grandee in the land could surpass. Long custom, a manly appearance, faultless boots and clothes, and a happy fierceness of manner, will often help a man as much as a great balance at the banker's.

The two wedding parties met constantly in each other's apartments. After two or three nights the gentlemen of an evening had a little piquet, as their wives sat and chatted apart. This pastime, and the arrival of Jos Sedley, who made his appearance in his grand open carriage, and who played a few games at billiards with Captain Crawley, replenished Rawdon's purse somewhat, and gave him the benefit of that ready money for which the greatest spirits are sometimes at a standstill.

So the three gentlemen walked down to see the *Lightning* coach come in. Punctual to the minute, the coach crowded inside and out, the guard blowing his accustomed tune on the horn – the *Lightning* came tearing down the street, and pulled up at the coach-office.

'Hullo! there's old Dobbin,' George cried, quite delighted to see his old friend perched on the roof; and whose promised visit to Brighton had been delayed until now. 'How are you, old fellow? Glad you're come down. Emmy'll be delighted to see you,' Osborne said, shaking his comrade warmly by the hand as soon as his descent from the vehicle was effected – and then he added, in a lower and agitated voice, 'What's the news. Have you been in Russell Square? What does the governor say? Tell me everything.'

Dobbin looked very pale and grave. 'I've seen your father,' said he. 'How's Amelia – Mrs. George? I'll tell you all the news presently: but I've brought the great news of all: and that is —'

'Out with it, old fellow,' George said.

'We're ordered to Belgium. All the army goes – Guards and all. Heavytop's got the gout, and is mad at not being able to move. O'Dowd goes in command, and we embark from Chatham next week.'

This news of war could not but come with a shock upon our lovers, and caused all these gentlemen to look very serious.

CHAPTER XXIII

CAPTAIN DOBBIN PROCEEDS ON HIS CANVASS

WHAT is the secret mesmerism which friendship possesses, and under the operation of which a person ordinarily sluggish, or cold, or timid, becomes wise, active, and resolute, in another's behalf? As Alexis, after a few passes from Dr. Elliotson, despises pain, reads with the back of his head, sees miles off, looks into next week, and performs other wonders, of which, in his own private normal condition, he is quite incapable; so you see, in the affairs of the world, and under the magnetism of friendship, the modest man become bold, the shy confident, the lazy active, or the impetuous prudent and peaceful. What is it, on the other hand, that makes the lawyer eschew his own cause, and call in his learned brother as an adviser? And what causes the doctor, when ailing, to send for his rival, and not sit down and examine his own tongue in the chimney-glass, or write his own prescription at his study-table? I throw out these queries for intelligent readers to answer, who know, at once, how credulous we are, and how sceptical, how soft and how obstinate, how firm for others and how diffident about ourselves: meanwhile, it is certain that our friend William Dobbin, who was personally of so complying a disposition that if his parents had pressed him much, it is probable he would have stepped down into the kitchen and married the cook, and who, to further his own interests, would have found the most insuperable difficulty in walking across the street, found himself as busy and eager in the conduct of George Osborne's affairs, as the most selfish tactician could be in the pursuit of his own.

Whilst our friend George and his young wife were enjoying the first blushing days of the honeymoon at Brighton, honest William was left as George's plenipotentiary in London, to transact all the business part of the marriage. His duty it was to call upon old Sedley and his wife, and to keep the former in good humour: to draw Jos and his brother-in-law nearer together, so that Jos's position and dignity, as collector of Boggley Wollah, might compensate for his father's loss of station, and tend to reconcile old

Osborne to the alliance: and finally, to communicate it to the latter in such a way as should least irritate the old gentleman.

Now, before he faced the head of the Osborne house with the news which it was his duty to tell, Dobbin bethought him that it would be politic to make friends of the rest of the family, and, if possible, have the ladies on his side. They can't be angry in their hearts, thought he. No woman ever was really angry at a romantic marriage. A little crying out, and they must come round to their brother; when the three of us will lay siege to old Mr. Osborne. So this Machiavellian captain of infantry cast about him for some happy means or stratagem by which he could gently and gradually bring the Miss Osbornes to a knowledge of their brother's secret.

By a little inquiry regarding his mother's engagements, he was pretty soon able to find out by whom of her ladyship's friends parties were given at that season; where he would be likely to meet Osborne's sisters; and, though he had that abhorrence of routs and evening parties, which many sensible men, alas! entertain, he soon found one where the Miss Osbornes were to be present. Making his appearance at the ball, where he danced a couple of sets with both of them, and was prodigiously polite, he actually had the courage to ask Miss Osborne for a few minutes' conversation at an early hour the next day, when he had, he said, to communicate to her news of the very greatest interest.

What was it that made her start back, and gaze upon him for a moment, and then on the ground at her feet, and make as if she would faint on his arm, had he not by opportunely treading on her toes, brought the young lady back to self-control? Why was she so violently agitated at Dobbin's request? This can never be known. But when he came the next day, Maria was not in the drawing-room with her sister, and Miss Wirt went off for the purpose of fetching the latter, and the captain and Miss Osborne were left together. They were both so silent that the tick-tock of the Sacrifice of Iphigenia clock on the mantelpiece became quite rudely audible.

'What a nice party it was last night,' Miss Osborne at length began, encouragingly; 'and – and how you're improved in your dancing, Captain Dobbin. Surely somebody has taught you,' she added, with amiable archness.

'You should see me dance a reel with Mrs. Major O'Dowd of ours; and a jig – did you ever see a jig? But I think anybody could dance with *you*, Miss Osborne, who dance so well.'

'Is the major's lady young and beautiful, captain?' the fair questioner continued. 'Ah, what a terrible thing it must be to be a soldier's wife! I wonder they have any spirits to dance, and in these dreadful times of war, too! Oh, Captain Dobbin, I tremble sometimes when I think of our dearest George, and the dangers of the poor soldier. Are there many married officers of the –th, Captain Dobbin?'

'Upon my word, she's playing her hand rather too openly,' Miss Wirt thought; but this observation is merely paren-thetic, and was not heard through the crevice of the door at which the governess uttered it.

'One of our young men is just married,' Dobbin said, now coming to the point. 'It was a very old attachment, and the young couple are as poor as church mice.'

'Oh, how delightful! Oh, how romantic!' Miss Osborne cried, as the captain said 'old attachment' and 'poor'. Her sympathy encouraged him.

'The finest young fellow in the regiment,' he continued. 'Not a braver or handsomer officer in the army; and such a charming wife! How you would like her! how you *will* like her when you know her, Miss Osborne.' The young lady thought the actual moment had arrived, and that Dobbin's nervousness which now came on and was visible in many twitchings of his face, in his manner of beating the ground with his great feet, in the rapid buttoning and unbuttoning of his frock-coat, &c. – Miss Osborne, I say, thought that when he had given himself a little air, he would unbosom himself entirely, and prepared eagerly to listen. And the clock, in the altar on which Iphigenia was situated, begin-ning, after a preparatory convulsion, to toll twelve, the mere tolling seemed as if it would last until one – so prolonged was the knell to the anxious spinster.

'But it's not about marriage that I came to speak – that is that marriage – that is – no, I mean – my dear Miss Osborne, it's about our dear friend George,' Dobbin said.

'About George?' she said in a tone so discomfited that Maria and Miss Wirt laughed at the other side of the door, and even that abandoned wretch of a Dobbin felt inclined to smile himself; for he was not altogether unconscious of the state of affairs: George having often bantered him gracefully and said 'Hang it, Will, why don't you take old Polly? She'll have you if you ask her. I'll bet you five to two she will.'

'Yes, about George, then,' he continued. 'There has been a difference between him and Mr. Osborne. And I regard him so much – for you know we have been like brothers – that I hope and pray the quarrel may be settled. We must go abroad, Miss Osborne. We may be ordered off at a day's warning. Who knows what may happen in the campaign? Don't be agitated, dear Miss Osborne; and those two at least should part friends.'

'There has been no quarrel, Captain Dobbin, except a little usual scene with papa,' the lady said. 'We are expecting George back daily. What papa wanted was only for his good. He has but to come back, and I'm sure all will be well; and dear Rhoda, who went away from here in sad, sad anger, I know will forgive him. Woman forgives but too readily, captain.'

'Such an angel as *you* I am sure would,' Mr. Dobbin said, with atrocious astuteness. 'And no man can pardon himself for giving a woman pain. What would you feel, if a man were faithless to you?'

'I should perish – I should throw myself out of window – I should take poison – I should pine and die. I know I should,' Miss cried, who had nevertheless gone through one or two affairs of the heart without any idea of suicide.

'And there are others,' Dobbin continued, 'as true and as kind-hearted as yourself. I'm not speaking about the West India heiress, Miss Osborne, but about a poor girl whom George once loved, and who was bred from her childhood to think of nobody but him. I've seen her in her poverty uncomplaining, broken-hearted, without a fault. It is of Miss Sedley I speak. Dear Miss Osborne, can your generous heart quarrel with your brother for being faithful to her? Could his own conscience ever forgive him if he deserted her? Be her friend – she always loved you – and – and I am come here charged by George to tell you that he holds his engagement to her as the most sacred duty he has; and to entreat *you*, at least, to be on his side.'

When any strong emotion took possession of Mr. Dobbin,

and after the first word or two of hesitation, he could speak with perfect fluency, and it was evident that his eloquence on this occasion made some impression upon the lady whom he addressed.

'Well,' said she, 'this is – most surprising – most painful – most extraordinary – what will papa say? – that George should fling away such a superb establishment as was offered to him, – but at any rate he has found a very brave champion in you, Captain Dobbin. It is of no use, however,' she continued, after a pause; 'I feel for poor Miss Sedley, most certainly – most sincerely, you know. We never thought the match a good one, though we were always very kind to her here – very. But papa will never consent, I am sure. And a well-brought-up young woman, you know, – with a well-regulated mind must – George must give her up, dear Captain Dobbin, indeed he must.'

'Ought a man to give up the woman he loved, just when misfortune befell her?' Dobbin said, holding out his hand. 'Dear Miss Osborne, is this the counsel I hear from *you*? My dear young lady! you must befriend her. He can't give her up. He must not give her up. Would a man, think you, give *you* up if you were poor?'

This adroit question touched the heart of Miss Jane Osborne not a little. 'I don't know whether we poor girls ought to believe what you men say, captain,' she said. 'There is that in woman's tenderness which induces her to believe too easily. I'm afraid you are cruel, cruel deceivers,' – and Dobbin certainly thought he felt a pressure of the hand which Miss Osborne had extended to him.

He dropped it in some alarm. 'Deceivers!' said he. 'No, dear Miss Osborne, all men are not; your brother is not; George has loved Amelia Sedley ever since they were children; no wealth would make him marry any but her. Ought he to forsake her? Would you counsel him to do so?'

What could Miss Jane say to such a question, and with her own peculiar views? She could not answer it, so she parried it by saying, 'Well, if you are not a deceiver, at least you are *very* romantic;' and Captain William let this observation pass without challenge.

At length when, by the help of further polite speeches, he deemed that Miss Osborne was sufficiently prepared to receive the whole news, he poured it into her ear. 'George could not give up Amelia – George was married to her' – and then he related the circumstances of the marriage as we know them already: how the poor girl would have died had not her lover kept his faith: how Old Sedley had refused all consent to the match, and a licence had been got: and Jos Sedley had come from Cheltenham to give away the bride: how they had gone to Brighton in Jos's chariot-and-four to pass the honeymoon: and how George counted on his dear kind sisters to befriend him with their father, as women – so true and tender as they were – assuredly would do. And so, asking permission (readily granted) to see her again, and rightly conjecturing that the news he had brought would be told in the next five minutes to the other ladies, Captain Dobbin made his bow and took his leave.

He was scarcely out of the house, when Miss Maria and Miss Wirt rushed in to Miss Osborne, and the whole wonderful secret was imparted to them by that lady. To do them justice, neither of the sisters were very much displeased. There is something about a runaway match with which few ladies can be seriously angry, and Amelia rather rose in their estimation, from the spirit which she had displayed in consenting to the union. As they debated the story, and prattled about it, and wondered what papa would do and say, came a loud knock, as of an avenging thunderclap at the door, which made these conspirators start. It must be papa, they thought. But it was not he. It was only Mr. Frederick Bullock, who had come from the City according to appointment, to conduct the ladies to a flower-show.

This gentleman, as may be imagined, was not kept long in ignorance of the secret. But his face, when he heard it, showed an amazement which was very different to that look of sentimental wonder which the countenances of the sisters wore. Mr. Bullock was a man of the world, and a junior partner of a wealthy firm. He knew what money was, and the value of it: and a delightful throb of expectation lighted up his little eyes, and caused him to smile on his Maria, as he thought that by this piece of folly of Mr. George's she might be worth thirty thousand pounds more than he had ever hoped to get with her.

'Gad! Jane,' said he, surveying even the elder sister with some interest, 'Eels will be sorry he cried off. You may be a fifty thousand pounder yet.'

The sisters had never thought of the money question up to that moment, but Fred Bullock bantered them with graceful gaiety about it during their forenoon's excursion; and they had risen not a little in their own esteem by the time when, the morning amusement over, they drove back to dinner. And do not let my respected reader exclaim against this selfishness as unnatural. It was but this present morning, as he rode on the omnibus from Richmond; while it changed horses, this present chronicler, being on the roof, marked three little children playing in a puddle below, very dirty and friendly and happy. To these three presently came another little one. '*Polly*,' says she, '*your sister's got a penny*.' At which the children got up from the puddle instantly, and ran off to pay their court to Peggy. And as the omnibus drove off I saw Peggy with the infantine procession at her tail, marching with great dignity towards the stall of a neighbouring lollipop-woman.

CHAPTER XXIV

IN WHICH MR. OSBORNE TAKES DOWN
THE FAMILY BIBLE

So having prepared the sisters, Dobbin hastened away to the City to perform the rest and more difficult part of the task which he had undertaken. The idea of facing old Osborne rendered him not a little nervous, and more than once he thought of leaving the young ladies to communicate the secret, which, as he was aware they could not long retain. But he had promised to report to George upon the manner in which the elder Osborne bore the intelligence; so going into the City to the paternal counting-house in Thames Street, he dispatched thence a note to Mr. Osborne begging for a half-hour's conversation relative to the affairs of his son George. Dobbin's messenger returned from Mr. Osborne's house of business, with the compliments of the latter, who would be very happy to see the captain immediately, and away accordingly Dobbin went to confront him.

The captain, with a half-guilty secret to confess, and with the prospect of a painful and stormy interview before him, entered Mr. Osborne's offices with a most dismal countenance and abashed gait, and, passing through the outer room

where Mr. Chopper presided, was greeted by that functionary from his desk with a waggish air which farther discomfited him. Mr. Chopper winked and nodded and pointed his
pen towards his patron's door, and said, 'You'll find the
governor all right,' with the most provoking good humour.

Osborne rose too, and shook him heartily by the hand,
and said, 'How do, my dear boy?' with a cordiality that made
poor George's ambassador feel doubly guilty. His hand lay
as if dead in the old gentleman's grasp. He felt that he,
Dobbin, was more or less the cause of all that had happened.
It was he had brought back George to Amelia: it was he had
applauded, encouraged, transacted almost the marriage which
he was come to reveal to George's father: and the latter was
receiving him with smiles of welcome; patting him on the
shoulder, and calling him 'Dobbin, my dear boy'. The envoy
had indeed good reason to hang his head.

Osborne fully believed that Dobbin had come to announce
his son's surrender. Mr. Chopper and his principal were
talking over the matter between George and his father, at
the very moment when Dobbin's messenger arrived. Both
agreed that George was sending in his submission. Both had
been expecting it for some days – and 'Lord! Chopper, what
a marriage we'll have!' Mr. Osborne said to his clerk,
snapping his big fingers, and jingling all the guineas and
shillings in his great pockets as he eyed his subordinate with
a look of triumph.

With similar operations conducted in both pockets, and
a knowing jolly air, Osborne from his chair regarded Dobbin
seated blank and silent opposite to him. 'What a bumpkin
he is for a captain in the army,' old Osborne thought. 'I
wonder George hasn't taught him better manners.'

At last Dobbin summoned courage to begin. 'Sir,' said
he, 'I've brought you some very grave news. I have been at
the Horse Guards this morning, and there's no doubt that
our regiment will be ordered abroad, and on its way to
Belgium before the week is over. And you know, sir, that
we shan't be home again before a tussle which may be fatal
to many of us.'

Osborne looked grave. 'My s—, the regiment will do its
duty, sir, I dare say,' he said.

'The French are very strong, sir,' Dobbin went on. 'The
Russians and Austrians will be a long time before they can

bring their troops down. We shall have the first of the fight, sir; and depend on it Boney will take care that it shall be a hard one.'

'What are you driving at, Dobbin?' his interlocutor said, uneasy and with a scowl. 'I suppose no Briton's afraid of any d— Frenchman, hay?'

'I only mean, that before we go, and considering the great and certain risk that hangs over every one of us – if there are any differences between you and George – it would be as well, sir, that – that you should shake hands: wouldn't it? Should anything happen to him, I think you would never forgive yourself if you hadn't parted in charity.'

As he said this, poor William Dobbin blushed crimson, and felt and owned that he himself was a traitor. But for him, perhaps, this severance need never have taken place. Why had not George's marriage been delayed? What call was there to press it on so eagerly? He felt that George would have parted from Amelia at any rate without a mortal pang. Amelia, too, *might* have recovered the shock of losing him. It was his counsel had brought about this marriage, and all that was to ensue from it. And why was it? Because he loved her so much that he could not bear to see her unhappy: or because his own sufferings of suspense were so unendurable that he was glad to crush them at once – as we hasten a funeral after a death, or, when a separation from those we love is imminent, cannot rest until the parting be over.

'You are a good fellow, William,' said Mr. Osborne in a softened voice; 'and me and George shouldn't part in anger, that is true. Look here. I've done for him as much as any father ever did. He's had three times as much money from me, as I warrant your father ever gave you. But I don't brag about that. How I've toiled for him, and worked and employed my talents and energy, *I* won't say. Ask Chopper. Ask himself. Ask the City of London. Well, I propose to him such a marriage as any nobleman in the land might be proud of – the only thing in life I ever asked him – and he refuses me. Am *I* wrong? Is the quarrel of *my* making? What do I seek but his good, for which I've been toiling like a convict ever since he was born? Nobody can say there's anything selfish in *me*. Let him come back. I say, here's my hand. I say, forget and forgive. As for marrying now, it's out of the question. Let him and Miss S. make it up, and make out the marriage afterwards, when he comes back a colonel; for he shall be a colonel, by G— he shall, if money can do it. I'm glad you've brought him round. I know it's you, Dobbin. You've took him out of many a scrape before. Let him come. *I* shan't be hard. Come along, and dine in Russell Square to-day: both of you. The old shop, the old hour. You'll find a neck of venison, and no questions asked.'

This praise and confidence smote Dobbin's heart very keenly. Every moment the colloquy continued in this tone, he felt more and more guilty. 'Sir,' said he, 'I fear you deceive yourself. I am sure you do. George is much too high-minded a man ever to marry for money. A threat on your part that you would disinherit him in case of disobedience would only be followed by resistance on his.'

'Why, hang it, man, you don't call offering him eight or ten thousand a year, threatening him?' Mr. Osborne said, with still provoking good humour. ' 'Gad, if Miss S. will have me, I'm her man. *I* ain't particular about a shade or so of tawny.' And the old gentleman gave his knowing grin and coarse laugh.

'You forget, sir, previous engagements into which Captain Osborne had entered,' the ambassador said, gravely.

'What engagements? What the devil do you mean? You don't mean,' Mr. Osborne continued, gathering wrath and astonishment as the thought now first came upon him; 'you don't mean that he's such a d— fool as to be still hankering after that swindling old bankrupt's daughter? You've not come here for to make me suppose that he wants to marry *her?* Marry *her*, that *is* a good one. My son and heir marry a beggar's girl out of a gutter. D— him, if he does, let him buy a broom and sweep a crossing. She was always dangling and ogling after him, I recollect now; and I've no doubt she was put on by her old sharper of a father.'

'Mr. Sedley was your very good friend, sir,' Dobbin interposed, almost pleased at finding himself growing angry. 'Time was you called him better names than rogue and swindler. The match was of your making. George had no right to play fast and loose —'

'Fast and loose!' howled out old Osborne. 'Fast and loose! Why, hang me, those are the very words my gentleman used himself when he gave himself airs, last Thursday was a fortnight, and talked about the British army to his father who made him. What, it's you who have been a setting of him up – is it? and my service to you, *captain*. It's you who want to introduce beggars into my family. Thank you for nothing, captain. Marry *her* indeed – he, he! why should he? I warrant you she'd go to him fast enough without.'

'Sir,' said Dobbin, starting up in undisguised anger; 'no man shall abuse that lady in my hearing, and you least of all.'

'Oh, you're a going to call me out, are you? Stop, let me ring the bell for pistols for two. Mr. George sent you here to insult his father, did he?' Osborne said, pulling at the bell-cord.

'Mr. Osborne,' said Dobbin, with a faltering voice, 'it's you who are insulting the best creature in the world. You had best spare her, sir, for she's your son's wife.'

And with this, feeling that he could say no more, Dobbin went away, Osborne sinking back in his chair, and looking wildly after him. A clerk came in, obedient to the bell; and the captain was scarcely out of the court where Mr. Osborne's offices were, when Mr. Chopper the chief clerk came rushing hatless after him.

'For God's sake, what is it?' Mr. Chopper said, catching the captain by the skirt. 'The governor's in a fit. What has Mr. George been doing?'

'He married Miss Sedley five days ago,' Dobbin replied. 'I was his groomsman, Mr. Chopper, and you must stand his friend.'

The old clerk shook his head. 'If that's your news, captain, it's bad. The governor will never forgive him.'

Dobbin begged Chopper to report progress to him at the hotel where he was stopping, and walked off moodily westwards, greatly perturbed as to the past and the future.

When the Russell Square family came to dinner that evening, they found the father of the house seated in his usual place, but with that air of gloom on his face, which, whenever it appeared there, kept the whole circle silent. The ladies, and Mr. Bullock who dined with them, felt that the news had been communicated to Mr. Osborne. His dark looks affected Mr. Bullock so far as to render him still and quiet: but he was unusually bland and attentive to Miss Maria, by whom he sat, and to her sister presiding at the head of the table.

Miss Wirt, by consequence, was alone on her side of the board, a gap being left between her and Miss Jane Osborne. Now this was George's place when he dined at home; and his cover, as we said, was laid for him in expectation of that truant's return. Nothing occurred during dinner-time except smiling Mr. Frederick's flagging confidential whispers, and the clinking of plate and china, to interrupt the silence of the repast. The servants went about stealthily doing their duty. Mutes at funerals could not look more glum than the domestics of Mr. Osborne. The neck of venison of which he had invited Dobbin to partake, was carved by him in perfect silence; but his own share went away almost untasted, though he drank much, and the butler assiduously filled his glass.

At last, just at the end of the dinner, his eyes, which had been staring at everybody in turn, fixed themselves for a while upon the plate laid for George. He pointed to it presently with his left hand. His daughters looked at him and did not comprehend, or choose to comprehend, the signal; nor did the servants at first understand it.

'Take that plate away,' at last he said, getting up with an oath – and with this pushing his chair back, he walked into his own room.

Behind Mr. Osborne's dining-room was the usual apartment which went in his house by the name of the study; and was sacred to the master of the house. Hither Mr. Osborne would retire of a Sunday forenoon when not minded to go to church; and here pass the morning in his crimson leather chair, reading the paper. A couple of glazed bookcases were here, containing standard works in stout gilt bindings. The *Annual Register*, the *Gentleman's Magazine*, Blair's *Sermons*, and Hume and Smollett. From year's end to year's end he never took one of these volumes from the shelf; but there was no member of the family that would dare for his life to touch one of the books, except upon those rare Sunday evenings when there was no dinner party, and when the great scarlet Bible and Prayer-book were taken out from the corner where they stood beside his copy of the *Peerage*, and the servants being rung up to the dining parlour, Osborne read the evening service to his family in a loud grating pompous voice. No member of the household, child or domestic, ever entered that room without a certain terror.

Here he checked the housekeeper's accounts, and overhauled the butler's cellar-book. Hence he could command, across the clean gravel courtyard, the back entrance of the stables with which one of his bells communicated, and into this yard the coachman issued from his premises as into a dock, and Osborne swore at him from the study window. Four times a year Miss Wirt entered this apartment to get her salary; and his daughters to receive their quarterly allowance. George as a boy had been horsewhipped in this room many times; his mother sitting sick on the stair listening to the cuts of the whip. The boy was scarcely ever known to cry under the punishment; the poor woman used to fondle and kiss him secretly, and give him money to soothe him when he came out.

There was a picture of the family over the mantelpiece, removed thither from the front room after Mrs. Osborne's death – George was on a pony, the elder sister holding him up a bunch of flowers; the younger led by her mother's hand; all with red cheeks and large red mouths, simpering on each other in the approved family-portrait manner. The mother lay under ground now, long since forgotten – the sisters and brother had a hundred different interests of their own, and, familiar still, were utterly estranged from each other. Some few score of years afterwards, when all the parties represented are grown old, what bitter satire there is in those flaunting childish family-portraits, with their farce of sentiment and smiling lies, and innocence so self-conscious and self-satisfied. Osborne's own state portrait, with that of his great silver inkstand and armchair, had taken the place of honour in the dining-room, vacated by the family-piece.

To this study old Osborne retired then, greatly to the relief of the small party whom he left. When the servants had withdrawn, they began to talk for a while volubly but very low; then they went upstairs quietly, Mr. Bullock accompanying them stealthily on his creaking shoes. He had no heart to sit alone drinking wine, and so close to the terrible old gentleman in the study hard at hand.

An hour at least after dark, the butler, not having received any summons, ventured to tap at his door and take him in wax candles and tea. The master of the house sat in his chair, pretending to read the paper, and when the servant,

placing the lights and refreshment on the table by him,
retired, Mr. Osborne got up and locked the door after him.
This time there was no mistaking the matter; all the household knew that some great catastrophe was going to happen
which was likely direly to affect Master George.

In the large shining mahogany escritoire Mr. Osborne had
a drawer especially devoted to his son's affairs and papers.
Here he kept all the documents relating to him ever since
he had been a boy: here were his prize copy-books and
drawing-books, all bearing George's hand, and that of the
master: here were his first letters in large roundhand sending
his love to papa and mamma, and conveying his petitions
for a cake. His dear godpapa Sedley was more than once
mentioned in them. Curses quivered on old Osborne's livid
lips, and horrid hatred and disappointment writhed in his
heart, as looking through some of these papers he came on
that name. They were all marked and docketed, and tied
with red tape. It was – 'From Georgy, requesting 5s., April
23, 18– ; answered April 25,' – or 'Georgy about a pony,
October 13,' – and so forth. In another packet were 'Dr.
S.'s accounts' – 'G.'s tailor's bills and outfits, drafts on me
by G. Osborne, jun.' &c., – his letters from the West Indies
– his agent's letters, and the newspapers containing his
commissions: here was a whip he had when a boy, and in a
paper a locket containing his hair, which his mother used
to wear.

Turning one over after another, and musing over these
memorials, the unhappy man passed many hours. His dearest
vanities, ambitious hopes, had all been here. What pride he
had in his boy! He was the handsomest child ever seen.
Everybody said he was like a nobleman's son. A royal
princess had remarked him, and kissed him, and asked his
name in Kew Gardens. What City man could show such
another? Could a prince have been better cared for? Anything
that money could buy had been his son's. He used to go
down on speech-days with four horses and new liveries, and
scatter new shillings among the boys at the school where
George was: when he went with George to the depôt of his
regiment, before the boy embarked for Canada, he gave the
officers such a dinner as the Duke of York might have sat
down to. Had he ever refused a bill when George drew one?
There they were – paid without a word. Many a general in

the army couldn't ride the horses he had! He had the child before his eyes, on a hundred different days when he remembered George – after dinner, when he used to come in as bold as a lord and drink off his glass by his father's side, at the head of the table – on the pony at Brighton, when he cleared the hedge and kept up with the huntsman – on the day when he was presented to the Prince Regent at the levée, when all St. James's couldn't produce a finer young fellow. And this, this was the end of all! – to marry a bankrupt and fly in the face of duty and fortune! What humiliation and fury: what pangs of sickening rage, balked ambition and love; what wounds of outraged vanity, tenderness even, had this old worldling now to suffer under!

Having examined these papers, and pondered over this one and the other, in that bitterest of all helpless woe, with which miserable men think of happy past times – George's father took the whole of the documents out of the drawer in which he had kept them so long, and locked them into a writing-box, which he tied, and sealed with his seal. Then he opened the bookcase, and took down the great red Bible we have spoken of – a pompous book, seldom looked at, and shining all over with gold. There was a frontispiece to the volume, representing Abraham sacrificing Isaac. Here according to custom, Osborne had recorded on the fly-leaf, and in his large clerk-like hand, the dates of his marriage and his wife's death, and the births and Christian names of his children. Jane came first, then George Sedley Osborne, then Maria Frances, and the days of the christening of each. Taking a pen, he carefully obliterated George's name from the page; and when the leaf was quite dry, restored the volume to the place from which he had moved it. Then he took a document out of another drawer, where his own private papers were kept; and having read it, crumpled it up and lighted it at one of the candles, and saw it burn entirely away in the grate. It was his will; which being burned, he sat down and wrote off a letter, and rang for his servant, whom he charged to deliver it in the morning. It was morning already: as he went up to bed: the whole house was alight with the sunshine; and the birds were singing among the fresh green leaves in Russell Square.

Anxious to keep all Mr. Osborne's family and dependants in good humour, and to make as many friends as possible for George in his hour of adversity, William Dobbin, who knew the effect which good dinners and good wines have upon the soul of man, wrote off immediately on his return to his inn the most hospitable of invitations to Thomas Chopper, Esquire, begging that gentleman to dine with him at the Slaughter's next day. The note reached Mr. Chopper before he left the City, and the instant reply was, that 'Mr. Chopper presents his respectful compliments, and will have the honour and pleasure of waiting on Captain D.' The invitation and the rough draft of the answer were shown to Mrs. Chopper and her daughters on his return to Somers Town that evening, and they talked about military gents and West End men with great exultation as the family sat and partook of tea. When the girls had gone to rest, Mr. and Mrs. C. discoursed upon the strange events which were occurring in the governor's family. Never had the clerk seen his principal so moved. When he went in to Mr. Osborne, after Captain Dobbin's departure, Mr. Chopper found his chief black in the face, and all but in a fit: some dreadful quarrel, he was certain, had occurred between Mr. O. and the young captain. Chopper had been instructed to make out an account of all sums paid to Captain Osborne within the last three years. 'And a precious lot of money he has had too,' the chief clerk said, and respected his old and young master the more, for the liberal way in which the guineas had been flung about. The dispute was something about Miss Sedley. Mrs. Chopper vowed and declared she pitied that poor young lady to lose such a handsome young fellow as the capting. As the daughter of an unlucky speculator, who had paid a very shabby dividend, Mr. Chopper had no great regard for Miss Sedley. He respected the house of Osborne before all others in the City of London: and his hope and wish was that Captain George should marry a nobleman's daughter. The clerk slept a great deal sounder than his principal that night; and, cuddling his children after breakfast (of which he partook with a very hearty appetite, though his modest cup of life was only sweetened with brown sugar), he set off in his best Sunday suit and frilled shirt for business, promising his admiring wife not to punish Captain D.'s port too severely that evening.

Mr. Osborne's countenance, when he arrived in the City at his usual time, struck those dependants who were accus-

tomed, for good reasons, to watch its expression, as peculiarly ghastly and worn. At twelve o'clock Mr. Higgs (of the
firm of Higgs & Blatherwick, solicitors, Bedford Row) called
by appointment, and was ushered into the governor's private
room, and closeted there for more than an hour. At about
one Mr. Chopper received a note brought by Captain Dobbin's man, and containing an inclosure for Mr. Osborne,
which the clerk went in and delivered. A short time afterwards Mr. Chopper and Mr. Birch, the next clerk, were
summoned, and requested to witness a paper. 'I've been
making a new will,' Mr. Osborne said, to which these
gentlemen appended their names accordingly. No conversation passed. Mr. Higgs looked exceedingly grave as he came
into the outer rooms, and very hard in Mr. Chopper's face;
but there were not any explanations. It was remarked that
Mr. Osborne was particularly quiet and gentle all day, to
the surprise of those who had augured ill from his darkling
demeanour. He called no man names that day, and was not
heard to swear once. He left business early; and before going
away, summoned his chief clerk once more, and having given
him general instructions, asked him, after some seeming
hesitation and reluctance to speak, if he knew whether
Captain Dobbin was in town?

Chopper said he believed he was. Indeed both of them
knew the fact perfectly.

Osborne took a letter directed to that officer, and, giving
it to the clerk, requested the latter to deliver it into Dobbin's
own hands immediately.

'And now, Chopper,' says he, taking his hat, and with a
strange look, 'my mind will be easy.' Exactly as the clock
struck two (there was no doubt an appointment between the
pair), Mr. Frederick Bullock called, and he and Mr. Osborne
walked away together.

The colonel of the –th regiment, in which Messieurs
Dobbin and Osborne had companies, was an old general who
had made his first campaign under Wolfe at Quebec, and
was long since quite too old and feeble for command; but
he took some interest in the regiment of which he was the
nominal head, and made certain of his young officers welcome at his table, a kind of hospitality which I believe is
not now common amongst his brethren. Captain Dobbin was

an especial favourite of this old general. Dobbin was versed
in the literature of his profession, and could talk about the
great Frederic, and the Empress Queen, and their wars,
almost as well as the general himself, who was indifferent
to the triumphs of the present day, and whose heart was
with the tacticians of fifty years back. This officer sent a
summons to Dobbin to come and breakfast with him, on the
morning when Mr. Osborne altered his will, and Mr. Chopper put on his best shirt-frill, and then informed his young
favourite, a couple of days in advance, of that which they
were all expecting – a marching order to go to Belgium. The
order for the regiment to hold itself in readiness would leave
the Horse Guards in a day or two; and as transports were
in plenty, they would get their route before the week was
over. Recruits had come in during the stay of the regiment
at Chatham; and the old general hoped that the regiment
which had helped to beat Montcalm in Canada, and to rout
Mr. Washington on Long Island, would prove itself worthy
of its historical reputation on the oft-trodden battle-grounds
of the Low Countries. 'And so my good friend, if you have
any *affaire là*,' said the old general, taking a pinch of snuff
with his trembling white old hand, and then pointing to the
spot of his *robe de chambre* under which his heart was still
feebly beating, 'if you have any Phillis to console, or to bid
farewell to papa and mamma, or any will to make, I recommend you to set about your business without delay.' With
which the general gave his young friend a finger to shake,
and a good-natured nod of his powdered and pigtailed head;
and the door being closed upon Dobbin, sat down to pen a
poulet (he was exceedingly vain of his French) to Mademoiselle Aménaide of His Majesty's Theatre.

This news made Dobbin grave, and he thought of our
friends at Brighton, and then he was ashamed of himself
that Amelia was always the first thing in his thoughts (always
before anybody – before father and mother, sisters and duty
– always at waking and sleeping indeed, and all day long);
and returning to his hotel, he sent off a brief note to Mr.
Osborne acquainting him with the information which he had
received, and which might tend further, he hoped, to bring
about a reconciliation with George.

This note, dispatched by the same messenger who had
carried the invitation to Chopper on the previous day,

alarmed the worthy clerk not a little. It was enclosed to him, and as he opened the letter he trembled lest the dinner should be put off on which he was calculating. His mind was inexpressibly relieved when he found that the envelope was only a reminder for himself. ('I shall expect you at half-past five,' Captain Dobbin wrote.) He was very much interested about his employer's family; but *que voulez-vous?* a grand dinner was of more concern to him than the affairs of any other mortal.

Dobbin was quite justified in repeating the general's information to any officers of the regiment whom he should see in the course of his peregrinations; accordingly he imparted it to Ensign Stubble, whom he met at the agent's, and who – such was his military ardour – went off instantly to purchase a new sword at the accoutrement-makers. Here this young fellow, who, though only seventeen years of age, and about sixty-five inches high, with a constitution natur-ally rickety and much impaired by premature brandy-and-water, had an undoubted courage and a lion's heart, poised, tried, bent, and balanced a weapon such as he thought would do execution amongst Frenchmen. Shouting 'Ha, ha!' and stamping his little feet with tremendous energy, he delivered the point twice or thrice at Captain Dobbin, who parried the thrust laughingly with his bamboo walking-stick.

Mr. Stubble, as may be supposed from his size and slenderness, was of the Light Bobs. Ensign Spooney, on the contrary, was a tall youth and belonged to (Captain Dobbin's) the Grenadier Company, and he tried on a new bearskin cap, under which he looked savage beyond his years. Then these two lads went off to the Slaughter's, and having ordered a famous dinner, sat down and wrote off letters to the kind anxious parents at home – letters full of love and heartiness, and pluck and bad spelling. Ah! there were many anxious hearts beating through England at that time; and mothers' prayers and tears flowing in many homesteads.

Seeing young Stubble engaged in composition at one of the coffee-room tables at the Slaughter's, and the tears trickling down his nose on to the paper (for the youngster was thinking of his mamma, and that he might never see her again), Dobbin, who was going to write off a letter to George Osborne, relented, and locked up his desk. 'Why should I?' said he. 'Let her have this night happy. I'll go and see my parents early in the morning, and go down to Brighton myself to-morrow.'

So he went up and laid his big hand on young Stubble's shoulder, and backed up that young champion, and told him if he would leave off brandy-and-water he would be a good soldier, as he always was a gentlemanly good-hearted fellow. Young Stubble's eyes brightened up at this, for Dobbin was greatly respected in the regiment, as the best officer and the cleverest man in it.

'Thank you, Dobbin,' he said, rubbing his eyes with his knuckles, 'I was just – just telling her I would. And, oh, sir, she's so *dam* kind to me.' The waterpumps were at work again, and I am not sure that the soft-hearted captain's eyes did not also twinkle.

The two ensigns, the captain, and Mr. Chopper, dined together in the same box. Chopper brought the letter from Mr. Osborne, in which the latter briefly presented his compliments to Captain Dobbin, and requested him to forward the enclosed to Captain George Osborne. Chopper knew nothing further; he described Mr. Osborne's appearance, it is true, and his interview with his lawyer, wondered how the governor had sworn at nobody, and – especially as the wine circled round – abounded in speculations and conjectures. But these grew more vague with every glass, and at length became perfectly unintelligible. At a late hour Captain Dobbin put his guest into a hackney-coach, in a hiccupping state, and swearing that he would be the kick – the kick – captain's friend for ever and ever.

When Captain Dobbin took leave of Miss Osborne we have said that he asked leave to come and pay her another visit, and the spinster expected him for some hours the next day, when, perhaps, had he come, and had he asked her that question which she was prepared to answer, she would have declared herself as her brother's friend, and a reconciliation might have been effected between George and his angry father. But though she waited at home the captain never came. He had his own affairs to pursue; his own parents to visit and console; and at an early hour of the day to take his place on the *Lightning* coach, and go down to his friends at Brighton. In the course of the day Miss Osborne heard her father give orders that that meddling scoundrel, Captain Dobbin, should never be admitted within his doors again, and any hopes in which she may have indulged privately were thus abruptly brought to an end. Mr. Frederick Bullock came, and was particularly affectionate to Maria, and attentive to the broken-spirited old gentleman. For though he said his mind would be easy, the means which he had taken to secure quiet did not seem to have succeeded as yet, and the events of the past two days had visibly shattered him.

CHAPTER XXV

IN WHICH ALL THE PRINCIPAL PERSONAGES THINK FIT TO LEAVE BRIGHTON

CONDUCTED to the ladies, at the Ship Inn, Dobbin assumed a jovial and rattling manner, which proved that this young officer was becoming a more consummate hypocrite every day of his life. He was trying to hide his own private feelings, first upon seeing Mrs. George Osborne in her new condition, and secondly to mask the apprehensions he entertained as to the effect which the dismal news brought down by him would certainly have upon her.

'It is my opinion, George,' he said, 'that the French Emperor will be upon us, horse and foot, before three weeks are over, and will give the duke such a dance as shall make the Peninsula appear mere child's play. But you need not say that to Mrs. Osborne, you know. There mayn't be any fighting on our side after all, and our business in Belgium may turn out to be a mere military occupation. Many persons think so; and Brussels is full of fine people and ladies of fashion.' So it was agreed to represent the duty of the British army in Belgium in this harmless light to Amelia.

This plot being arranged, the hypocritical Dobbin saluted Mrs. George Osborne quite gaily, tried to pay her one or two compliments relative to her new position as a bride (which compliments, it must be confessed, were exceedingly clumsy and hung fire wofully), and then fell to talking about Brighton, and the sea-air, and the gaieties of the place, and the beauties of the road and the merits of the *Lightning* coach and horses, – all in a manner quite incomprehensible to Amelia, and very amusing to Rebecca, who was watching the captain, as indeed she watched every one near whom she came.

Little Amelia, it must be owned, had rather a mean opinion of her husband's friend, Captain Dobbin. He lisped – he was very plain and homely-looking: and exceedingly awkward and ungainly. She liked him for his attachment to her husband (to be sure there was very little merit in that), and she thought George was most generous and kind in extending his friendship to his brother officer. George had mimicked Dobbin's lisp and queer manners many times to her, though to do him justice, he always spoke most highly of his friend's good qualities. In her little day of triumph, and not knowing him intimately as yet, she made light of honest William – and he knew her opinions of him quite well, and acquiesced in them very humbly. A time came when she knew him better, and changed her notions regarding him: but that was distant as yet.

As for Rebecca, Captain Dobbin had not been two hours in the ladies' company before she understood his secret perfectly. She did not like him, and feared him privately; nor was he very much prepossessed in her favour. He was so honest, that her arts and cajoleries did not affect him, and he shrank from her with instinctive repulsion. And, as she was by no means so far superior to her sex as to be above jealousy, she disliked him the more for his adoration of Amelia. Nevertheless, she was very respectful and cordial in her manner towards him. A friend to the Osbornes! a friend to her dearest benefactors! She vowed she should always love him sincerely: she remembered him quite well on the Vauxhall night, as she told Amelia archly, and she made a little fun of him when the two ladies went to dress for dinner. Rawdon Crawley paid scarcely any attention to Dobbin, looking upon him as a good-natured nincompoop, and under-bred City man. Jos patronized him with much dignity.

When George and Dobbin were alone in the latter's room, to which George had followed him, Dobbin took from his desk the letter which he had been charged by Mr. Osborne to deliver to his son. 'It's not in my father's handwriting,' said George, looking rather alarmed; nor was it: the letter was from Mr. Osborne's lawyer, and to the following effect:–

BEDFORD ROW, May 7, 1815.

SIR, – I am commissioned by Mr. Osborne to inform you, that he abides by the determination which he before expressed to you, and that in consequence of the marriage which you have been pleased to contract, he ceases to consider you henceforth as a member of his family. This determination is final and irrevocable.

Although the moneys expended upon you in your minority, and the bills which you have drawn upon him so unsparingly of late years, far exceed in amount the sum to which you are entitled in your own right (being the third part of the fortune of your mother, the late Mrs. Osborne, and which reverted to you at her decease, and to Miss Jane Osborne and Miss Maria Frances Osborne); yet I am instructed by Mr. Osborne to say, that he waives all claim upon your estate, and that the sum of 2,000*l*., 4 per cent annuities, at the value of the day (being your one-third share of the sum of 6,000*l*.), shall be paid over to yourself or your agents upon your receipt for the same, by

Your obedient Servt., S. HIGGS.

PS. – Mr. Osborne desires me to say, once for all, that he declines to receive any messages, letters, or communications from you on this or any other subject.

'A pretty way you have managed the affair,' said George, looking savagely at William Dobbin. 'Look there, Dobbin,' and he flung over to the latter his parent's letter. 'A beggar, by Jove, and all in consequence of my d–d sentimentality. Why couldn't we have waited? A ball might have done for me in the course of the war, and may still, and how will Emmy be bettered by being left a beggar's widow? It was all your doing. You were never easy until you had got me married and ruined. What the deuce am I to do with two thousand pounds? Such a sum won't last two years. I've lost a hundred and forty to Crawley at cards and billiards since I've been down here. A pretty manager of a man's matters *you* are, forsooth.'

'There's no denying that the position is a hard one,' Dobbin replied, after reading over the letter with a blank countenance; 'and, as you say, it is partly of my making. There are some men that wouldn't mind changing with you,' he added, with a bitter smile. 'How many captains in the regiment have two thousand pounds to the fore, think you? You must live on your pay till your father relents, and if you die, you leave your wife a hundred a year.'

'Do you suppose a man of my habits can live on his pay and a hundred a year?' George cried out in great anger. 'You must be a fool to talk so, Dobbin. How the deuce am I to keep up my position in the world upon such a pitiful pittance? I can't change my habits. I *must* have my comforts. *I* wasn't brought up on porridge like MacWhirter, or on potatoes, like old O'Dowd. Do you expect my wife to take in soldiers' washing, or ride after the regiment in a baggage-wagon?'

'Well, well,' said Dobbin, still good-naturedly, 'we'll get her a better conveyance. But try and remember that you are only a dethroned prince now, George, my boy; and be quiet whilst the tempest lasts. It won't be for long. Let your name be mentioned in the *Gazette*, and I'll engage the old father relents towards you.'

'Mentioned in the *Gazette!*' George answered. 'And in what part of it? Among the killed and wounded returns, and at the top of the list, very likely.'

'Psha! It will be time enough to cry out when we are hurt,' Dobbin said. 'And if anything happens, you know, George, I have got a little, and I am not a marrying man, and I shall not forget my godson in my will,' he added, with a smile. Whereupon the dispute ended, – as many scores of such conversations between Osborne and his friend had concluded previously – by the former declaring there was no possibility of being angry with Dobbin long, and forgiving him very generously after abusing him without cause.

'I say, Becky,' cried Rawdon Crawley out of his dressing-room, to his lady, who was attiring herself for dinner in her own chamber.

'What?' said Becky's shrill voice. She was looking over her shoulder in the glass. She had put on the neatest and freshest white frock imaginable, and with bare shoulders and a little necklace, and a light-blue sash, she looked the image of youthful innocence and girlish happiness.

'I say, what'll Mrs. O. do, when O. goes out with the regiment?' Crawley said, coming into the room, performing a duet on his head with two huge hair-brushes, and looking out from under his hair with admiration on his pretty little wife.

'I suppose she'll cry her eyes out,' Becky answered. 'She has been whimpering half a dozen of times at the very notion of it, already to me.'

'*You* don't care, I suppose,' Rawdon said, half angry at his wife's want of feeling.

'You wretch! don't you know that I intend to go with you,' Becky replied. 'Besides, you're different. You go as General Tufto's aide de camp. *We* don't belong to the line,' Mrs. Crawley said, throwing up her head with an air that so enchanted her husband that he stooped down and kissed it.

'Rawdon, dear – don't you think – you'd better get that – money from Cupid, before he goes?' Becky continued, fixing on a killing bow. She called George Osborne, Cupid. She had flattered him about his good looks a score of times already. She watched over him kindly at écarté of a night when he would drop into Rawdon's quarters for a half-hour before bedtime.

She had often called him a horrid dissipated wretch, and threatened to tell Emmy of his wicked ways and naughty extravagant habits. She brought his cigar and lighted it for him; she knew the effect of that manœuvre, having practised it in former days upon Rawdon Crawley. He thought her gay, brisk, arch, distinguée, delightful. In their little drives and dinners, Becky, of course, quite outshone poor Emmy, who remained very mute and timid while Mrs. Crawley and her husband rattled away together, and Captain Crawley (and Jos after he joined the young married people) gobbled in silence.

Emmy's mind somehow misgave her about her friend. Rebecca's wit, spirits, and accomplishments troubled her with a rueful disquiet. They were only a week married, and here was George already suffering ennui, and eager for others' society! She trembled for the future. How shall I be a companion for him, she thought, – so clever and so brilliant, and I such a humble foolish creature? How noble it was of him to marry me – to give up everything and stoop down to me! I ought to have refused him, only I had not the heart. I ought to have stopped at home and taken care of poor papa. And her neglect of her parents (and indeed there was some foundation for this charge which the poor child's uneasy conscience brought against her) was now remembered for the first time, and caused her to blush with humiliation. Oh! thought she, I have been very wicked and selfish – selfish in forgetting them in their sorrows – selfish in forcing George to marry me. I know I'm not worthy of him – I know he would have been happy without me – and yet – I tried, I tried to give him up.

It is hard when, before seven days of marriage are over, such thoughts and confessions as these force themselves on a little bride's mind. But so it was, and the night before Dobbin came to join these young people – on a fine brilliant moonlight night of May – so warm and balmy that the windows were flung open to the balcony, from which George and Mrs. Crawley were gazing upon the calm ocean spread shining before them, while Rawdon and Jos were engaged at backgammon within – Amelia couched in a great chair quite neglected, and watching both these parties, felt a despair and remorse such as were bitter companions for that tender lonely soul. Scarce a week was past, and it was come to this! The future, had she regarded it, offered a dismal prospect; but Emmy was too shy, so to speak, to look to that, and embark alone on that wide sea, and unfit to navigate it without a guide and protector. I know Miss Smith has a mean opinion of her. But how many, my dear madam, are endowed with your prodigious strength of mind?

'Gad, what a fine night, and how bright the moon is!' George said, with a puff of his cigar, which went soaring up skywards.

'How delicious they smell in the open air! I adore them. Who'd think the moon was two hundred and thirty-six thousand eight hundred and forty-seven miles off?' Becky added, gazing at that orb with a smile. 'Isn't it clever of me to remember that? Pooh! we learned it all at Miss Pinkerton's! How calm the sea is, and how clear everything. I declare I can almost see the coast of France!' and her bright green eyes streamed out, and shot into the night as if they *could* see through it.

'Do you know what I intend to do one morning?' she said; 'I find I can swim beautifully, and some day, when my Aunt Crawley's companion – old Briggs, you know – you remember her – that hook-nosed woman, with the long wisps of hair – when Briggs goes out to bathe, I intend to dive under her awning, and insist on a reconciliation in the water. Isn't that a stratagem?'

George burst out laughing at the idea of this aquatic meeting. 'What's the row there, you two?' Rawdon shouted out, rattling the box. Amelia was making a fool of herself in an absurd hysterical manner, and retired to her own room to whimper in private.

Our history is destined in this chapter to go backwards and forwards in a very irresolute manner seemingly, and having conducted our story to to-morrow presently, we shall immediately again have occasion to step back to yesterday, so that the whole of the tale may get a hearing. As you behold at Her Majesty's drawing-room, the ambassadors' and high dignitaries' carriages whisk off from a private door, while Captain Jones's ladies are waiting for their fly: as you see in the Secretary of the Treasury's antechamber, a half-dozen of petitioners waiting patiently for their audience, and called out one by one, when suddenly an Irish member or some eminent personage enters the apartment, and instantly walks into Mr. Under-Secretary over the heads of all the people present: so in the conduct of a tale, the romancer is obliged to exercise this most partial sort of justice. Although all the little incidents must be heard, yet they must be put off when the great events make their appearance; and surely such a circumstance as that which brought Dobbin to Brighton, viz., the ordering out of the Guards and the line to Belgium, and the mustering of the allied armies in that country under the command of his Grace the Duke of Wellington – such a dignified circumstance as that, I say, was entitled to the *pas* over all minor occurrences whereof this history is composed mainly, and hence a little trifling disarrangement and disorder was excusable and becoming. We have only now advanced in time so far beyond Chapter XXII as to have got our various characters up into their dressing-rooms before the dinner, which took place as usual on the day of Dobbin's arrival.

George was too humane or too much occupied with the tie of his neckcloth to convey at once all the news to Amelia which his comrade had brought with him from London. He came into her room, however, holding the attorney's letter in his hand, and with so solemn and important an air that his wife, always ingeniously on the watch for calamity, thought the worst was about to befall, and running up to her husband, besought her dearest George to tell her every-thing – he was ordered abroad; there would be a battle next week – she knew there would.

Dearest George parried the question about foreign service,

and with a melancholy shake of the head said, 'No, Emmy; it isn't that: it's not myself I care about: it's you. I have had bad news from my father. He refuses any communication with me; he has flung us off; and leaves us to poverty. *I* can rough it well enough; but you, my dear, how will you bear it? read here.' And he handed her over the letter.

Amelia, with a look of tender alarm in her eyes, listened to her noble hero as he uttered the above generous sentiments, and sitting down on the bed, read the letter which George gave her with such a pompous martyr-like air. Her face cleared up as she read the document, however. The idea of sharing poverty and privation in company with the beloved object, is, as we have before said, far from being disagreeable to a warm-hearted woman. The notion was actually pleasant to little Amelia. Then, as usual, she was ashamed of herself for feeling happy at such an indecorous moment, and checked her pleasure, saying demurely, 'Oh, George, how your poor heart must bleed at the idea of being separated from your papa.'

'It does,' said George, with an agonized countenance.

'But he can't be angry with you long,' she continued. 'Nobody could, I'm sure. He must forgive you, my dearest, kindest husband. Oh, I shall never forgive myself if he does not.'

'What vexes me, my poor Emmy, is not *my* misfortune, but yours,' George said. 'I don't care for a little poverty; and I think, without vanity, I've talents enough to make my own way.'

'That you have,' interposed his wife, who thought that war should cease, and her husband should be made a general instantly.

'Yes, I shall make my way as well as another,' Osborne went on; 'but you, my dear girl, how can I bear your being deprived of the comforts and station in society which my wife had a right to expect? My dearest girl in barracks; the wife of a soldier in a marching regiment; subject to all sorts of annoyance and privation! It makes me miserable.'

Emmy, quite at ease, as this was her husband's only cause of disquiet, took his hand, and with a radiant face and smile began to warble that stanza from the favourite song of 'Wapping Old Stairs', in which the heroine after rebuking her Tom for inattention, promises 'his trousers to mend, and his grog too to make', if he will be constant and kind, and not forsake her. 'Besides,' she said, after a pause, during which she looked as pretty and happy as any young woman need, 'isn't two thousand pounds an immense deal of money, George?'

George laughed at her *naïveté*; and finally they went down to dinner, Amelia clinging on George's arm, still warbling the tune of 'Wapping Old Stairs', and more pleased and light of mind than she had been for some days past.

Thus the repast, which at length came off, instead of being dismal, was an exceedingly brisk and merry one. The excitement of the campaign counteracted in George's mind the depression occasioned by the disinheriting letter. Dobbin still kept up his character of rattle. He amused the company with accounts of the army in Belgium, where nothing but fêtes and gaiety and fashion were going on. Then, having a particular end in view, this dexterous captain proceeded to describe Mrs. Major O'Dowd, packing her own and her major's wardrobe, and how his best epaulets had been stowed into a tea canister, whilst her own famous yellow turban, with the bird of paradise wrapped in brown paper, was locked up in the major's tin cocked-hat case, and wondered what effect it would have at the French king's court at Ghent, or the great military balls at Brussels.

'Ghent! Brussels!' cried out Amelia with a sudden shock and start. 'Is the regiment ordered away, George, – is it ordered away?' A look of terror came over the sweet smiling face, and she clung to George as by an instinct.

'Don't be afraid, dear,' he said good-naturedly; 'it is but a twelve hours' passage. It won't hurt you. You shall go, too, Emmy.'

'*I* intend to go,' said Becky, 'I'm on the staff. General Tufto is a great flirt of mine. Isn't he, Rawdon?'

Rawdon laughed out with his usual roar. William Dobbin flushed up quite red. 'She can't go,' he said; 'think of the – of the danger,' he was going to add; but had not all his conversation during dinner-time tended to prove there was none? He became very confused and silent.

'I must and will go,' Amelia cried with the greatest spirit; and George, applauding her resolution, patted her under the chin, and asked all the persons present if they ever saw such a termagant of a wife, and agreed that the lady should bear him company. 'We'll have Mrs. O'Dowd to chaperon you,' he said. What cared she so long as her husband was near her? Thus somehow the bitterness of a parting was juggled away. Though war and danger were in store, war and danger might not befall for months to come. There was a respite at any rate, which made the timid little Amelia almost as happy as a full reprieve would have done, and which even Dobbin owned in his heart was very welcome. For, to be permitted to see her was now the greatest privilege and hope of his life, and he thought with himself secretly how he would watch and protect her. I wouldn't have let her go if I had been married to her, he thought. But George was the master, and his friend did not think fit to remonstrate.

Putting her arm round her friend's waist, Rebecca at length carried Amelia off from the dinner-table where so much business of importance had been discussed, and left the gentlemen in a highly exhilarated state drinking and talking very gaily.

In the course of the evening Rawdon got a little family-note from his wife, which although he crumpled it up and burnt it instantly in the candle, we had the good luck to read over Rebecca's shoulder. 'Great news,' she wrote. 'Mrs. Bute is gone. Get the money from Cupid to-night, as he'll be off to-morrow most likely. Mind this. – R.' So when the little company was about adjourning to coffee in the women's apartment, Rawdon touched Osborne on the elbow, and said gracefully, 'I say, Osborne, my boy, if quite convenient, I'll trouble you for that 'ere small trifle.' It was not quite convenient, but nevertheless George gave him a considerable present instalment in bank-notes from his pocket-book, and a bill on his agents at a week's date, for the remaining sum.

This matter arranged, George, and Jos, and Dobbin, held a council of war over their cigars, and agreed that a general move should be made for London in Jos's open carriage the next day. Jos, I think, would have preferred staying until Rawdon Crawley quitted Brighton, but Dobbin and George overruled him, and he agreed to carry the party to town, and ordered four horses, as became his dignity. With these they set off in state, after breakfast, the next day. Amelia had risen very early in the morning, and packed her little trunks with the greatest alacrity, while Osborne lay in bed deploring that she had not a maid to help her. She was only too glad, however, to perform this office for herself. A dim uneasy sentiment about Rebecca filled her mind already; and although they kissed each other most tenderly at parting, yet we know what jealousy is; and Mrs. Amelia possessed that among other virtues of her sex.

Besides these characters who are coming and going away, we must remember that there were some other old friends of ours at Brighton; Miss Crawley, namely, and the suite in attendance upon her. Now, although Rebecca and her husband were but at a few stones' throw of the lodgings which the invalid Miss Crawley occupied, the old lady's door remained as pitilessly closed to them as it had been heretofore in London. As long as she remained by the side of her sister-in-law, Mrs. Bute Crawley took care that her beloved Matilda should not be agitated by a meeting with her nephew. When the spinster took her drive, the faithful Mrs. Bute sat beside her in the carriage. When Miss Crawley took the air in a chair, Mrs. Bute marched on one side of the vehicle, whilst honest Briggs occupied the other wing. And if they met Rawdon and his wife by chance – although the former constantly and obsequiously took off his hat, the Miss-Crawley party passed him by with such a frigid and killing indifference, that Rawdon began to despair.

'We might as well be in London as here,' Captain Rawdon often said, with a downcast air.

'A comfortable inn in Brighton is better than a spunging-house in Chancery Lane,' his wife answered, who was of a more cheerful temperament. 'Think of those two aides de camp of Mr. Moses, the sheriff's officer, who watched our lodging for a week. Our friends here are very stupid, but Mr. Jos and Captain Cupid are better companions than Mr. Moses's men, Rawdon, my love.'

'I wonder the writs haven't followed me down here,' Rawdon continued, still desponding.

'When they do, we'll find means to give them the slip,' said dauntless little Becky, and further pointed out to her husband the great comfort and advantage of meeting Jos and Osborne, whose acquaintance had brought to Rawdon Crawley a most timely little supply of ready money.

'It will hardly be enough to pay the inn bill,' grumbled the Guardsman.

'Why need we pay it?' said the lady, who had an answer for everything.

Through Rawdon's valet, who still kept up a trifling acquaintance with the male inhabitants of Miss Crawley's servants' hall, and was instructed to treat the coachman to drink whenever they met, old Miss Crawley's movements were pretty well known by our young couple; and Rebecca luckily bethought herself of being unwell, and of calling in the same apothecary who was in attendance upon the spinster, so that their information was on the whole tolerably complete. Nor was Miss Briggs, although forced to adopt a hostile attitude, secretly inimical to Rawdon and his wife. She was naturally of a kindly and forgiving disposition. Now that the cause of jealousy was removed, her dislike for Rebecca disappeared also, and she remembered the latter's invariable good words and good humour. And, indeed, she and Mrs. Firkin, the lady's-maid, and the whole of Miss Crawley's household, groaned under the tyranny of the triumphant Mrs. Bute.

As often will be the case, that good but imperious woman pushed her advantages too far, and her successes quite unmercifully. She had in the course of a few weeks brought the invalid to such a state of helpless docility, that the poor soul yielded herself entirely to her sister's orders, and did not even dare to complain of her slavery to Briggs or Firkin. Mrs. Bute measured out the glasses of wine which Miss Crawley was daily allowed to take, with irresistible accuracy, greatly to the annoyance of Firkin and the butler, who found themselves deprived of control over even the sherry-bottle. She apportioned the sweetbreads, jellies, chickens; their quantity and order. Night and noon and morning she brought the abominable drinks ordained by the doctor, and made her patient swallow them with so affecting an obedience, that Firkin said my poor missus du take her physic like a lamb. She prescribed the drive in the carriage or the ride in the chair, and, in a word, ground down the old lady in her convalescence in such a way as only belongs to your proper-managing, motherly, moral woman. If ever the patient faintly resisted, and pleaded for a little bit more dinner or a little drop less medicine, the nurse threatened her with instantaneous death, when Miss Crawley instantly gave in. 'She's no spirit left in her,' Firkin remarked to Briggs; 'she ain't

'ave called me a fool these three weeks.' Finally, Mrs. Bute
had made up her mind to dismiss the aforesaid honest
lady's-maid, Mr. Bowls the large confidential man, and
Briggs herself, and to send for her daughters from the
Rectory, previous to removing the dear invalid bodily to
Queen's Crawley, when an odious accident happened which
called her away from duties so pleasing. The Reverend Bute
Crawley, her husband, riding home one night, fell with his
horse and broke his collar-bone. Fever and inflammatory
symptoms set in, and Mrs. Bute was forced to leave Sussex
for Hampshire. As soon as ever Bute was restored, she
promised to return to her dearest friend, and departed,
leaving the strongest injunctions with the household regarding their behaviour to their mistress; and as soon as she got
into the Southampton coach, there was such a jubilee and
sense of relief in all Miss Crawley's house, as the company
of persons assembled there had not experienced for many a
week before. That very day Miss Crawley left off her
afternoon dose of medicine: that afternoon Bowls opened an
independent bottle of sherry for himself and Mrs. Firkin:
that night Miss Crawley and Miss Briggs indulged in a game
of piquet instead of one of Porteus's sermons. It was as in
the old nursery-story, when the stick forgot to beat the dog,
and the whole course of events underwent a peaceful and
happy revolution.

At a very early hour in the morning, twice or thrice a
week, Miss Briggs used to betake herself to a bathing-
machine, and disport in the water in a flannel gown and an
oilskin cap. Rebecca, as we have seen, was aware of this
circumstance, and though she did not attempt to storm
Briggs as she had threatened, and actually dive into that
lady's presence and surprise her under the sacredness of the
awning, Mrs. Rawdon determined to attack Briggs as she
came away from her bath, refreshed and invigorated by her
dip, and likely to be in good humour.

So, getting up very early the next morning, Becky brought
the telescope in their sitting-room, which faced the sea, to
bear upon the bathing-machines on the beach; saw Briggs
arrive, enter her box, and put out to sea; and was on the
shore just as the nymph of whom she came in quest stepped
out of the little caravan on to the shingles. It was a pretty
picture: the beach; the bathing women's faces; the long line

of rocks and building were blushing and bright in the sunshine. Rebecca wore a kind, tender smile on her face, and was holding out her pretty white hand as Briggs emerged from the box. What could Briggs do but accept the salutation?

'Miss Sh–. Mrs. Crawley,' she said.

Mrs. Crawley seized her hand, pressed it to her heart, and with a sudden impulse, flinging her arms round Briggs, kissed her affectionately. 'Dear, dear friend!' she said, with a touch of such natural feeling, that Miss Briggs of course at once began to melt, and even the bathing-woman was mollified.

Rebecca found no difficulty in engaging Briggs in a long, intimate, and delightful conversation. Everything that had passed since the morning of Becky's sudden departure from Miss Crawley's house in Park Lane up to the present day, and Mrs. Bute's happy retreat, was discussed and described by Briggs. All Miss Crawley's symptoms, and the particulars of her illness and medical treatment, were narrated by the confidante with that fullness and accuracy which women delight in. About their complaints and their doctors do ladies ever tire of talking to each other? Briggs did not on this occasion; nor did Rebecca weary of listening. She was thankful, truly thankful, that the dear kind Briggs, that the faithful, the invaluable Firkin, had been permitted to remain with their benefactress through her illness. Heaven bless her! though she, Rebecca, had seemed to act undutifully towards Miss Crawley; yet was not her fault a natural and excusable one? Could she help giving her hand to the man who had won her heart? Briggs, the sentimental, could only turn up her eyes to heaven at this appeal, and heave a sympathetic sigh, and think that she, too, had given away her affections long years ago, and own that Rebecca was no very great criminal.

'Can I ever forget her who so befriended the friendless orphan? No, though she has cast me off,' the latter said, 'I shall never cease to love her, and I would devote my life to her service. As my own benefactress, as my beloved Rawdon's adored relative, I love and admire Miss Crawley, dear Miss Briggs, beyond any woman in the world, and next to her I love all those who are faithful to her. *I* would never have treated Miss Crawley's faithful friends as that odious designing Mrs. Bute had done. Rawdon, who was all heart,'

Rebecca continued, 'although his outward manners might seem rough and careless, had said a hundred times, with tears in his eyes, that he blessed Heaven for sending his dearest aunty two such admirable nurses as her attached Firkin and her admirable Miss Briggs. Should the machinations of the horrible Mrs. Bute end, as she too much feared they would, in banishing everybody that Miss Crawley loved from her side, and leaving that poor lady a victim to those harpies at the Rectory, Rebecca besought her (Miss Briggs) to remember that her own home, humble as it was, was always open to receive Briggs. Dear friend,' she exclaimed, in a transport of enthusiasm, '*some* hearts can *never* forget benefits; *all* women are not Bute Crawleys! Though why should I complain of her,' Rebecca added; 'though I have been her tool and the victim to her arts, do I not owe my dearest Rawdon to her?' And Rebecca unfolded to Briggs all Mrs. Bute's conduct at Queen's Crawley, which, though unintelligible to her then, was clearly enough explained by the events now, – now that the attachment had sprung up which Mrs. Bute had encouraged by a thousand artifices, – now that two innocent people had fallen into the snares which she had laid for them, and loved and married and been ruined through her schemes.

It was all very true. Briggs saw the stratagems as clearly as possible. Mrs. Bute had made the match between Rawdon and Rebecca. Yet, though the latter was a perfectly innocent victim, Miss Briggs could not disguise from her friend her fear that Miss Crawley's affections were hopelessly estranged from Rebecca, and that the old lady would never forgive her nephew for making so imprudent a marriage.

On this point Rebecca had her own opinion, and still kept up a good heart. If Miss Crawley did not forgive them at present, she might at least relent on a future day. Even now, there was only that puling, sickly Pitt Crawley between Rawdon and a baronetey; and should anything happen to the former, all would be well. At all events, to have Mrs. Bute's designs exposed, and herself well abused, was a satisfaction, and might be advantageous to Rawdon's interest; and Rebecca, after an hour's chat with her recovered friend, left her with the most tender demonstrations of regard, and quite assured that the conversation they had had together would be reported to Miss Crawley before many hours were over.

This interview ended, it became full time for Rebecca to return to her inn, where all the party of the previous day were assembled at a farewell breakfast. Rebecca took such a tender leave of Amelia as became two women who loved each other as sisters; and having used her handkerchief plentifully, and hung on her friend's neck as if they were parting for ever, and waved the handkerchief (which was quite dry, by the way) out of the window, as the carriage drove off; she came back to the breakfast-table, and ate some prawns with a good deal of appetite, considering her emotion; and while she was munching these delicacies, explained to Rawdon what had occurred in her morning walk between herself and Briggs. Her hopes were very high: she made her husband share them. She generally succeeded in making her husband share all her opinions, whether melancholy or cheerful.

'You will now, if you please, my dear, sit down at the writing-table and pen me a pretty little letter to Miss Crawley, in which you'll say that you are a good boy, and that sort of thing.' So Rawdon sat down, and wrote off, 'Brighton, Thursday,' and 'My dear Aunt,' with great rapidity: but there the gallant officer's imagination failed him. He mumbled the end of his pen, and looked up in his wife's face. She could not help laughing at his rueful countenance, and, marching up and down the room with her hands behind her, the little woman began to dictate a letter, which he took down.

'Before quitting the country and commencing a campaign, which very possibly may be fatal –'

'What?' said Rawdon, rather surprised, but took the humour of the phrase, and presently wrote it down with a grin.

'Which very possibly may be fatal, I have come hither –'

'Why not say come here, Becky; come here's grammar,' the dragoon interposed.

'I have come hither,' Rebecca insisted, with a stamp of her foot, 'to say farewell to my dearest and earliest friend. I beseech you before I go, not perhaps to return, once more to let me press the hand from which I have received nothing but kindnesses all my life.'

'Kindnesses all my life,' echoed Rawdon, scratching down the words, and quite amazed at his own facility of composition.

'I ask nothing from you but that we should part not in anger. I have the pride of my family on some points, though not on all. I married a painter's daughter, and am not ashamed of the union.'

'No, run me through the body if I am!' Rawdon ejaculated.

'You old booby,' Rebecca said, pinching his ear, and looking over to see that he made no mistakes in spelling – 'beseech is not spelt with an *a*, and earliest is.' So he altered these words, bowing to the superior knowledge of his little missis.

'I thought that you were aware of the progress of my attachment,' Rebecca continued: 'I knew that Mrs. Bute Crawley confirmed and encouraged it. But I make no reproaches. I married a poor woman, and am content to abide by what I have done. Leave your property, dear aunt, as you will. *I* shall never complain of the way in which you dispose of it. I would have you believe that I love you for yourself, and not for money's sake. I want to be reconciled to you ere I leave England. Let me, let me see you before I go. A few weeks or months hence it may be too late, and I cannot bear the notion of quitting the country without a kind word of farewell from you.'

'She won't recognize my style in *that*,' said Becky. 'I made the sentences short and brisk on purpose.' And this authentic missive was dispatched under cover to Miss Briggs.

Old Miss Crawley laughed when Briggs, with great mystery, handed her over this candid and simple statement. 'We may read it now Mrs. Bute is away,' she said. 'Read it to me, Briggs.'

When Briggs had read the epistle out, her patroness laughed more. 'Don't you see, you goose,' she said to Briggs, who professed to be much touched by the honest affection which pervaded the composition – 'don't you see that Rawdon never wrote a word of it. He never wrote to me without asking for money in his life, and all his letters are full of bad spelling, and dashes, and bad grammar. It is that little serpent of a governess who rules him.' They are all alike, Miss Crawley thought in her heart. They all want me dead, and are hankering for my money.

'I don't mind seeing Rawdon,' she added, after a pause, and in a tone of perfect indifference. 'I had just as soon shake hands with him as not. Provided there is no scene, why shouldn't we meet? I don't mind. But human patience has its limits; and mind, my dear, I respectfully decline to

receive Mrs. Rawdon – I can't support *that* quite' – and
Miss Briggs was fain to be content with this half-message
of conciliation; and thought that the best method of bringing
the old lady and her nephew together, was to warn Rawdon
to be in waiting on the Cliff, when Miss Crawley went out
for her air in her chair.

There they met. I don't know whether Miss Crawley had
any private feeling of regard or emotion upon seeing her old
favourite; but she held out a couple of fingers to him with
as smiling and good-humoured an air as if they had met
only the day before. And as for Rawdon, he turned as red
as scarlet, and wrung off Briggs's hand, so great was his
rapture and his confusion at the meeting. Perhaps it was
interest that moved him: or perhaps affection: perhaps he
was touched by the change which the illness of the last weeks
had wrought in his aunt.

'The old girl has always acted like a trump to me,' he
said to his wife, as he narrated the interview, 'and I felt,
you know, rather queer, and that sort of thing. I walked by
the side of the what-d'ye-call-'em, you know, and to her
own door, where Bowls came to help her in. And I wanted
to go in very much, only —'

'*You didn't go in*, Rawdon!' screamed his wife.

'No, my dear; I'm hanged if I wasn't afraid when it came
to the point.'

'You fool! you ought to have gone in, and never come
out again,' Rebecca said.

'Don't call me names,' said the big guardsman, sulkily;
'Perhaps I *was* a fool, Becky, but you shouldn't say so;' and
he gave his wife a look, such as his countenance could wear
when angered, and such as was not pleasant to face.

'Well, dearest, to-morrow you must be on the look-out,
and go and see her, mind, whether she asks you or no.'
Rebecca said, trying to soothe her angry yoke-mate. On
which he replied, that he would do exactly as he liked, and
would just thank her to keep a civil tongue in her head –
and the wounded husband went away, and passed the forenoon at the billiard-room, sulky, silent, and suspicious.

But before the night was over he was compelled to give
in, and own, as usual, to his wife's superior prudence and
foresight, by the most melancholy confirmation of the

presentiments which she had regarding the consequences of the mistake which he had made. Miss Crawley *must* have had some emotion upon seeing him and shaking hands with him after so long a rupture. She mused upon the meeting a considerable time. 'Rawdon is getting very fat and old, Briggs,' she said to her companion. 'His nose has become red, and he is exceedingly coarse in appearance. His marriage to that woman has hopelessly vulgarized him. Mrs. Bute always said they drank together; and I have no doubt they do. Yes: he smelt of gin abominably. I remarked it. Didn't you?'

In vain Briggs interposed that Mrs. Bute spoke ill of everybody: and, as far as a person in *her* humble position could judge, was an—

'An artful designing woman? Yes, so she is, and she does speak ill of every one – but I am certain that woman has made Rawdon drink. All those low people do —'

'He was very much affected at seeing you, ma'am,' the companion said; 'and I am sure, when you remember that he is going to the field of danger —'

'How much money has he promised you, Briggs?' the old spinster cried out, working herself into a nervous rage – 'there now, of course you begin to cry. I hate scenes. Why am I always to be worried? Go and cry up in your own room, and send Firkin to me, – no, stop, sit down and blow your nose, and leave off crying, and write a letter to Captain Crawley.' Poor Briggs went and placed herself obediently at the writing-book. Its leaves were blotted all over with the relics of the firm, strong, rapid handwriting of the spinster's late amanuensis, Mrs. Bute Crawley.

'Begin "My dear sir", or "Dear sir", that will be better, and say you are desired by Miss Crawley – no, by Miss Crawley's medical man, by Mr. Creamer, to state, that my health is such that all strong emotions would be dangerous in my present delicate condition – and that I must decline any family discussions or interviews whatever. And thank him for coming to Brighton, and so forth, and beg him not to stay any longer on my account. And, Miss Briggs, you may add that I wish him a *bon voyage*, and that if he will take the trouble to call upon my lawyer's in Gray's Inn Square, he will find there a communication for him. Yes, that will do; and that will make him leave Brighton.' The benevolent Briggs penned this sentence with the utmost satisfaction.

'To seize upon me the very day after Mrs. Bute was gone,' the old lady prattled on; 'it was too indecent. Briggs, my dear, write to Mrs. Crawley, and say *she* needn't come back. No – she needn't – and she shan't – and I won't be a slave in my own house – and I won't be starved and choked with poison. They all want to kill me – all – all —' and with this the lonely old woman burst into a scream of hysterical tears.

The last scene of her dismal Vanity Fair comedy was fast approaching; the tawdry lamps were going out one by one; and the dark curtain was almost ready to descend.

That final paragraph, which referred Rawdon to Miss Crawley's solicitor in London, and which Briggs had written so good-naturedly, consoled the dragoon and his wife somewhat, after their first blank disappointment on reading the spinster's refusal of a reconciliation. And it effected the purpose for which the old lady had caused it to be written, by making Rawdon very eager to get to London.

Out of Jos's losings and George Osborne's bank-notes, he paid his bill at the inn, the landlord whereof does not probably know to this day how doubtfully his account once stood. For, as a general sends his baggage to the rear before an action, Rebecca had wisely packed up all their chief valuables and sent them off under care of George's servant, who went in charge of the trunks on the coach back to London. Rawdon and his wife returned by the same conveyance next day.

'I should have liked to see the old girl before we went,' Rawdon said. 'She looks so cut up and altered that I'm sure she can't last long. I wonder what sort of a cheque I shall have at Waxy's. Two hundred – it can't be less than two hundred – hey, Becky?'

In consequence of the repeated visits of the gentlemen whose portraits have been taken in a preceding page, Rawdon and his wife did not go back to their lodgings at Brompton, but put up at an inn. Early the next morning, Rebecca had an opportunity of seeing them as she skirted that suburb on her road to old Mrs. Sedley's house at Fulham, whither she went to look for her dear Amelia and her Brighton friends. They were all off to Chatham, thence to Harwich, to take shipping for Belgium with the regiment – kind old Mrs.

Sedley very much depressed and tearful, solitary. Returning from this visit, Rebecca found her husband, who had been off to Gray's Inn, and learnt his fate. He came back furious.

'By Jove, Becky,' says he, 'she's only given me twenty pound!'

Though it told against themselves, the joke was too good, and Becky burst out laughing at Rawdon's discomfiture.

CHAPTER XXVI

BETWEEN LONDON AND CHATHAM

O N quitting Brighton, our friend George, as became a person of rank and fashion, travelling in a barouche with four horses, drove in state to a fine hotel in Cavendish Square, where a suite of splendid rooms, and a table magnificently furnished with plate and surrounded by a half-dozen of black and silent waiters, was ready to receive the young gentleman and his bride. George did the honours of the place with a princely air to Jos and Dobbin; and Amelia, for the first time, and with exceeding shyness and timidity, presided at what George called her own table.

George pooh-poohed the wine and bullied the waiters royally, and Jos gobbled the turtle with immense satisfaction. Dobbin helped him to it; for the lady of the house, before whom the tureen was placed, was so ignorant of the contents, that she was going to help Mr. Sedley without bestowing upon him either calipash or calipee.

The splendour of the entertainment, and the apartments in which it was given, alarmed Mr. Dobbin, who remonstrated after dinner, when Jos was asleep in the great chair. But in vain he cried out against the enormity of turtle and champagne that was fit for an archbishop. 'I've always been accustomed to travel like a gentleman,' George said, 'and, damme, my wife shall travel like a lady. As long as there's a shot in the locker, *she* shall want for nothing,' said the generous fellow, quite pleased with himself for his magnificence of spirit. Nor did Dobbin try and convince him that Amelia's happiness was not centred in turtle-soup.

A while after dinner, Amelia timidly expressed a wish to go and see her mamma, at Fulham: which permission George granted her with some grumbling. And she tripped away to

her enormous bedroom, in the centre of which stood the
enormous funereal bed, 'that the Emperor Halixander's sister
slep in when the allied sufferings was here,' and put on her
little bonnet and shawl with the utmost eagerness and pleasure. George was still drinking claret when she returned to
the dining-room, and made no signs of moving. 'Aren't you
coming with me, dearest?' she asked him. No; the 'dearest'
had 'business' that night. His man should get her a coach,
and go with her. And the coach being at the door of the
hotel, Amelia made George a little disappointed curtsy after
looking vainly into his face once or twice, and went sadly
down the great staircase, Captain Dobbin after, who handed
her into the vehicle, and saw it drive away to its destination.
The very valet was ashamed of mentioning the address to
the hackney-coachman before the hotel-waiters, and promised
to instruct him when they got farther on.

Dobbin walked home to his old quarters at the Slaughter's,
thinking very likely that it would be delightful to be in that
hackney-coach, along with Mrs. Osborne. George was evidently of quite a different taste; for when he had taken wine
enough, he went off to half-price at the play, to see Mr.
Kean perform in Shylock. Captain Osborne was a great lover
of the drama, and had himself performed high-comedy
characters with great distinction in several garrison theatrical
entertainments. Jos slept on until long after dark, when he
woke up with a start at the motions of his servant, who was
removing and emptying the decanters on the table; and the
hackney-coach stand was again put into requisition for a
carriage to convey this stout hero to his lodgings and bed.

Mrs. Sedley, you may be sure, clasped her daughter to
her heart with all maternal eagerness and affection, running
out of the door as the carriage drew up before the little
garden-gate, to welcome the weeping, trembling, young bride.
Old Mr. Clapp, who was in his shirt-sleeves, trimming the
garden-plot, shrank back alarmed. The Irish servant-lass
rushed up from the kitchen, and smiled a 'God bless you'.
Amelia could hardly walk along the flags and up the steps
into the parlour.

How the floodgates were opened and mother and daughter
wept, when they were together embracing each other in this
sanctuary, may readily be imagined by every reader who

possesses the least sentimental turn. When don't ladies weep? At what occasion of joy, sorrow, or other business of life? and, after such an event as a marriage, mother and daughter were surely at liberty to give way to a sensibility which is as tender as it is refreshing. About a question of marriage I have seen women who hate each other kiss and cry together quite fondly. How much more do they feel when they love! Good mothers are married over again at their daughters' weddings: and as for subsequent events, who does not know how ultra-maternal grandmothers are? – in fact a woman, until she is a grandmother, does not often really know what to be a mother is. Let us respect Amelia and her mamma whispering and whimpering and laughing and crying in the parlour and the twilight. Old Mr. Sedley did. *He* had not divined who was in the carriage when it drove up. He had not flown out to meet his daughter, though he kissed her very warmly when she entered the room (where he was occupied, as usual, with his papers and tapes and statements of accounts), and after sitting with the mother and daughter for a short time, he very wisely left the little apartment in their possession.

George's valet was looking on in a very supercilious manner at Mr. Clapp in his shirt-sleeves, watering his rose-bushes. He took off his hat, however, with much condescension to Mr. Sedley, who asked news about his son-in-law, and about Jos's carriage, and whether his horses had been down to Brighton, and about that infernal traitor Bonaparty, and the war; until the Irish maidservant came with a plate and a bottle of wine, from which the old gentleman insisted upon helping the valet. He gave him a half-guinea too, which the servant pocketed with a mixture of wonder and contempt. 'To the health of your master and mistress, Trotter,' Mr. Sedley said, 'and here's something to drink your health when you get home, Trotter.'

There were but nine days past since Amelia had left that little cottage and home – and yet how far off the time seemed since she had bidden it farewell. What a gulf lay between her and that past life. She could look back to it from her present standing-place, and contemplate, almost as another being, the young unmarried girl absorbed in her love, having no eyes but for one special object, receiving parental affection if not ungratefully, at least indifferently, and as if it were her due – her whole heart and thoughts bent on the accomplishment of one desire. The review of those days, so lately gone yet so far away, touched her with shame; and the aspect of the kind parents filled her with tender remorse. Was the prize gained – the heaven of life – and the winner still doubtful and unsatisfied? As his hero and heroine pass the matrimonial barrier, the novelist generally drops the curtain, as if the drama were over then: the doubts and struggles of life ended: as if, once landed in the marriage country, all were green and pleasant there: and wife and husband had nothing but to link each other's arms together, and wander gently downwards towards old age in happy and perfect fruition. But our little Amelia was just on the bank of her new country, and was already looking anxiously back towards the sad friendly figures waving farewell to her across the stream, from the other distant shore.

In honour of the young bride's arrival, her mother thought it necessary to prepare I don't know what festive entertainment, and after the first ebullition of talk, took leave of Mrs. George Osborne for a while, and dived down to the lower regions of the house to a sort of kitchen-parlour (occupied by Mr. and Mrs. Clapp, and in the evening, when her dishes were washed, and her curl-papers removed, by Miss Flannigan, the Irish servant), there to take measures for the preparing of a magnificent ornamented tea. All people have their ways of expressing kindness, and it seemed to Mrs. Sedley that a muffin and a quantity of orange marmalade spread out in a little cut-glass saucer would be peculiarly agreeable refreshments to Amelia in her most interesting situation.

While these delicacies were being transacted below, Amelia, leaving the drawing-room, walked upstairs and found herself, she scarce knew how, in the little room which she had occupied before her marriage, and in that very chair in which she had passed so many bitter hours. She sank back in its arms as if it were an old friend; and fell to thinking over the past week, and the life beyond it. Already to be looking sadly and vaguely back: always to be pining for something which, when obtained, brought doubt and sadness rather than pleasure: here was the lot of our poor little creature, and harmless lost wanderer in the great struggling crowds of Vanity Fair.

Here she sat, and recalled to herself fondly that image of George to which she had knelt before marriage. Did she own to herself how different the real man was from that superb young hero whom she had worshipped? It requires many, many years – and a man must be very bad indeed – before a woman's pride and vanity will let her own to such a confession. Then Rebecca's twinkling green eyes and baleful smile lighted upon her, and filled her with dismay. And so she sat for a while indulging in her usual mood of selfish brooding, in that very listless melancholy attitude in which the honest maidservant had found her, on the day when she brought up the letter in which George renewed his offer of marriage.

She looked at the little white bed, which had been hers a few days before, and thought she would like to sleep in it that night, and wake, as formerly, with her mother smiling over her in the morning. Then she thought with terror of the great funeral damask pavilion in the vast and dingy state bedroom, which was awaiting her at the grand hotel in Cavendish Square. Dear little white bed! how many a long night had she wept on its pillow! How she had despaired and hoped to die there; and now were not all her wishes accomplished, and the lover of whom she had despaired her own for ever? Kind mother! how patiently and tenderly she had watched round that bed! She went and knelt down by the bedside; and there this wounded and timorous, but gentle and loving soul, sought for consolation, where as yet, it must be owned, our little girl had but seldom looked for it. Love had been her faith hitherto; and the sad, bleeding, disappointed heart began to feel the want of another consoler.

Have we a right to repeat or to overhear her prayers? These, brother, are secrets, and out of the domain of Vanity Fair, in which our story lies.

But this may be said, that when the tea was finally announced, our young lady came downstairs a great deal more cheerful; that she did not despond, or deplore her fate, or think about George's coldness, or Rebecca's eyes, as she had been wont to do of late. She went downstairs and kissed her father and mother, and talked to the old gentleman, and made him more merry than he had been for many a day. She sat down at the piano which Dobbin had bought for her, and sang over all her father's favourite old songs. She pronounced the tea to be excellent, and praised the exquisite taste in which the marmalade was arranged in the saucers. And in determining to make everybody else happy, she found herself so; and was sound asleep in the great funereal pavilion, and only woke up with a smile when George arrived from the theatre.

For the next day, George had more important 'business' to transact than that which took him to see Mr. Kean in Shylock. Immediately on his arrival in London he had written off to his father's solicitors, signifying his royal pleasure that an interview should take place between them on the morrow. His hotel losses at billiards and cards to Captain Crawley had almost drained the young man's purse, which wanted replenishing before he set out on his travels, and he had no resource but to infringe upon the two thousand pounds which the attorneys were commissioned to pay over to him. He had a perfect belief in his own mind that his father would relent before very long. How could any parent be obdurate for a length of time against such a paragon as he was? If his mere past and personal merits did not succeed in mollifying the father, George determined that he would distinguish himself so prodigiously in the ensuing campaign that the old gentleman must give in to him. And if not? Bah! the world was before him. His luck might change at cards, and there was a deal of spending in two thousand pounds.

So he sent off Amelia once more in a carriage to her mamma, with strict orders and carte blanche to the two ladies to purchase everything requisite for a lady of Mrs. George Osborne's fashion, who was going on a foreign tour. They had but one day to complete the outfit, and it may be imagined that their business therefore occupied them pretty fully. In a carriage once more, bustling about from milliner to linen-draper, escorted back to the carriage by obsequious shopmen or polite owners, Mrs. Sedley was herself again almost, and sincerely happy for the first time since their misfortunes. Nor was Mrs. Amelia at all above the pleasure of shopping, and bargaining, and seeing and buying pretty things. (Would any man, the most philosophic, give two-pence for a woman who was?) She gave herself a little treat, obedient to her husband's orders, and purchased a quantity of lady's gear, showing a great deal of taste and elegant discernment, as all the shop-folks said.

And about the war that was ensuing, Mrs. Osborne was not much alarmed; Bonaparty was to be crushed almost without a struggle. Margate packets were sailing every day, filled with men of fashion and ladies of note, on their way to Brussels and Ghent. People were going not so much to a war as to a fashionable tour. The newspapers laughed the wretched upstart and swindler to scorn. Such a Corsican wretch as that withstand the armies of Europe and the genius of the immortal Wellington! Amelia held him in utter contempt; for it needs not to be said that this soft and gentle creature took her opinions from those people who surrounded her, such fidelity being much too humble-minded to think for itself. Well, in a word, she and her mother performed a great day's shopping, and she acquitted herself with considerable liveliness and credit on this her first appearance in the genteel world of London.

George meanwhile, with his hat on one side, his elbows squared, and his swaggering martial air, made for Bedford Row, and stalked into the attorney's offices as if he was lord of every pale-faced clerk who was scribbling there. He ordered somebody to inform Mr. Higgs that Captain Osborne was waiting, in a fierce and patronizing way, as if the *pékin* of an attorney, who had thrice his brains, fifty times his money, and a thousand times his experience, was a wretched underling who should instantly leave all his business in life to attend on the captain's pleasure. He did not see the sneer of contempt which passed all round the room, from the first clerk to the articled gents, from the articled gents to the ragged writers and white-faced runners, in clothes too tight for them, as he sat there tapping his boot with his cane, and thinking what a parcel of miserable poor devils these were. The miserable poor devils knew all about his affairs. They talked about them over their pints of beer at their public-house clubs to other clerks of a night. Ye gods, what do not attorneys and attorneys' clerks know in London! Nothing is hidden from their inquisition, and their familiars mutely rule our city.

Perhaps George expected, when he entered Mr. Higgs's apartment, to find that gentleman commissioned to give him some message of compromise or conciliation from his father;

perhaps his haughty and cold demeanour was adopted as a sign of his spirit and resolution: but if so, his fierceness was met by a chilling coolness and indifference on the attorney's part, that rendered swaggering absurd. He pretended to be writing at a paper, when the captain entered. 'Pray, sit down, sir,' said he, 'and I will attend to your little affair in a moment. Mr. Poe, get the release papers, if you please;' and then he fell to writing again.

Poe having produced those papers, his chief calculated the amount of two thousand pounds stock at the rate of the day; and asked Captain Osborne whether he would take the sum in a cheque upon the bankers, or whether he should direct the latter to purchase stock to that amount. 'One of the late Mrs. Osborne's trustees is out of town,' he said indifferently, 'but my client wishes to meet your wishes, and have done with the business as quick as possible.'

'Give me a cheque, sir,' said the captain very surlily. 'Damn the shillings and halfpence, sir,' he added, as the lawyer was making out the amount of the draft; and, flattering himself that by this stroke of magnanimity he had put the old quiz to the blush, he stalked out of his office with the paper in his pocket.

'That chap will be in gaol in two years,' Mr. Higgs said to Mr. Poe.

'Won't O. come round, sir, don't you think?'

'Won't the Monument come round,' Mr. Higgs replied.

'He's going it pretty fast,' said the clerk. 'He's only married a week, and I saw him and some other military chaps handing Mrs. Highflyer to her carriage after the play.' And then another case was called, and Mr. George Osborne thenceforth dismissed from these worthy gentlemen's memory.

The draft was upon our friends Hulker and Bullock of Lombard Street, to whose house, still thinking he was doing business, George bent his way, and from whom he received his money. Frederick Bullock, Esq., whose yellow face was over a ledger, at which sat a demure clerk, happened to be in the banking-room when George entered. His yellow face turned to a more deadly colour when he saw the captain, and he slunk back guiltily into the inmost parlour. George was too busy gloating over the money (for he had never had such a sum before), to mark the countenance or flight of the cadaverous suitor of his sister.

Fred Bullock told old Osborne of his son's appearance and conduct, 'He came in as bold as brass,' said Frederick. 'He has drawn out every shilling. How long will a few hundred pounds last such a chap as that?' Osborne swore with a great oath that he little cared when or how soon he spent it. Fred dined every day in Russell Square now. But altogether, George was highly pleased with his day's business. All his own baggage and outfit was put into a state of speedy preparation, and he paid Amelia's purchases with cheques on his agents, and with the splendour of a lord.

CHAPTER XXVII

IN WHICH AMELIA JOINS HER REGIMENT

WHEN Jos's fine carriage drove up to the inn door at Chatham, the first face which Amelia recognized was the friendly countenance of Captain Dobbin, who had been pacing the street for an hour past in expectation of his friends' arrival. The captain, with shells on his frock-coat, and a crimson sash and sabre, presented a military appearance, which made Jos quite proud to be able to claim such an acquaintance, and the stout civilian hailed him with a cordiality very different from the reception which Jos vouchsafed to his friend in Brighton and Bond Street.

Along with the captain was Ensign Stubble; who, as the barouche neared the inn, burst out with an exclamation of 'By Jove! what a pretty girl;' highly applauding Osborne's choice. Indeed, Amelia dressed in her wedding-pelisse and pink ribbons, with a flush in her face, occasioned by rapid travel through the open air, looked so fresh and pretty, as fully to justify the ensign's compliment. Dobbin liked him for making it. As he stepped forward to help the lady out of the carriage, Stubble saw what a pretty little hand she gave him, and what a sweet pretty little foot came tripping down the step. He blushed profusely, and made the very best bow of which he was capable; to which Amelia, seeing the number of the –th regiment embroidered on the ensign's cap, replied with a blushing smile, and a curtsy on her part; which finished the young ensign on the spot. Dobbin took most kindly to Mr. Stubble from that day, and encouraged him to talk about Amelia in their private walks, and at each

other's quarters. It became the fashion, indeed, among all
the honest young fellows of the –th to adore and admire
Mrs. Osborne. Her simple artless behaviour, and modest
kindness of demeanour, won all their unsophisticated hearts;
all which simplicity and sweetness are quite impossible to
describe in print. But who has not beheld these among
women, and recognized the presence of all sorts of qualities
in them, even though they say no more to you than that
they are engaged to dance the next quadrille, or that it is
very hot weather? George, always the champion of his
regiment, rose immensely in the opinion of the youth of the
corps, by his gallantry in marrying this portionless young
creature, and by his choice of such a pretty kind partner.

In the sitting-room which was awaiting the travellers.
Amelia, to her surprise, found a letter addressed to Mrs.
Captain Osborne. It was a triangular billet, on pink paper,
and sealed with a dove and an olive branch, and a profusion
of light-blue sealing-wax, and it was written in a very large,
though undecided female hand.

'It's Peggy O'Dowd's fist,' said George, laughing. 'I know
it by the kisses on the seal.' And in fact, it was a note
from Mrs. Major O'Dowd, requesting the pleasure of Mrs.
Osborne's company that very evening to a small friendly
party. 'You must go,' George said. 'You will make acquaintance with the regiment there. O'Dowd goes in command of
the regiment, and Peggy goes in command of O'Dowd.'

But they had not been for many minutes in the enjoyment
of Mrs. O'Dowd's letter, when the door was flung open,
and a stout jolly lady, in a riding-habit, followed by a couple
of officers of Ours, entered the room.

'Sure, I couldn't stop till tay-time. Present me, Garge,
my dear fellow, to your lady. Madam, I'm deloighted to see
ye; and to present to you me husband, Meejor O'Dowd;'
and with this, the jolly lady in the riding-habit grasped
Amelia's hand very warmly, and the latter knew at once that
the lady was before her whom her husband had so often
laughed at. 'You've often heard of me from that husband of
yours,' said the lady, with great vivacity.

'You've often heard of her,' echoed her husband, the Major.

Amelia answered, smiling, 'that she had.'

'And small good he's told you of me,' Mrs. O'Dowd
replied; adding that 'George was a wicked divvle'.

'That I'll go bail for,' said the major, trying to look knowing, at which George laughed; and Mrs. O'Dowd, with a tap of her whip, told the major to be quite; and then requested to be presented in form to Mrs. Captain Osborne.

'This, my dear,' said George with great gravity, 'is my very good, kind, and excellent friend, Auralia Margaretta otherwise called Peggy.'

'Faith, you're right,' interposed the major.

'Otherwise called Peggy, lady of Major Michael O'Dowd, of our regiment, and daughter of Fitzjurld Ber'sford de Burgo Malony of Glenmalony, County Kildare.'

'And Muryan Squeer, Doblin,' said the lady, with calm superiority.

'And Muryan Square, sure enough,' the major whispered.

' 'Twas there ye coorted me, meejor dear,' the lady said; and the major assented to this as to every other proposition which was made generally in company.

Major O'Dowd, who had served his sovereign in every quarter of the world, and had paid for every step in his profession by some more than equivalent act of daring and gallantry, was the most modest, silent, sheep-faced, and meek of little men, and as obedient to his wife as if he had been her tay-boy. At the mess-table he sat silently, and drank a great deal. When full of liquor, he reeled silently home. When he spoke, it was to agree with everybody on every conceivable point; and he passed through life in perfect case and good humour. The hottest suns of India never heated his temper; and the Walcheren ague never shook it. He walked up to a battery with just as much indifference as to a dinner-table; had dined on horseflesh and turtle with equal relish and appetite; and had an old mother, Mrs. O'Dowd of O'Dowdstown indeed, whom he had never disobeyed but when he ran away and enlisted, and when he persisted in marrying that odious Peggy Malony.

Peggy was one of five sisters, and eleven children of the noble house of Glenmalony; but her husband, though her own cousin, was of the mother's side, and so had not the inestimable advantage of being allied to the Malonies, whom she believed to be the most famous family in the world. Having tried nine seasons at Dublin and two at Bath and Cheltenham, and not finding a partner for life, Miss Malony ordered her cousin Mick to marry her when she was about thirty-three years of age; and the honest fellow obeying, carried her off to the West Indies, to preside over the ladies of the –th regiment, into which he had just exchanged.

Before Mrs. O'Dowd was half an hour in Amelia's (or indeed in anybody else's) company, this amiable lady told all her birth and pedigree to her new friend. 'My dear,' said she, good-naturedly, 'it was my intention that Garge should be a brother of my own, and my sister Glorvina would have suited him entirely. But as bygones are bygones, and he was engaged to yourself, why, I'm determined to take you as a sister instead, and to look upon you as such, and to love you as one of the family. Faith, you've got such a nice good-natured face and way widg you, that I'm sure we'll agree; and that you'll be an addition to our family anyway.'

' 'Deed and she will,' said O'Dowd, with an approving air, and Amelia felt herself not a little amused and grateful to be thus suddenly introduced to so large a party of relations.

'We're all good fellows here,' the major's lady continued. 'There's not a regiment in the service where you'll find a more united society nor a more agreeable mess-room. There's no quarrelling, bickering, slandthering, nor small talk amongst *us*. We all love each other.'

'Especially Mrs. Magenis,' said George, laughing.

'Mrs. Captain Magenis and me has made up, though her treatment of me would bring me grey hairs with sorrow to the grave.'

'And you with such a beautiful front of black, Peggy, my dear,' the major cried.

'Hould your tongue, Mick, you booby. Them husbands are always in the way, Mrs. Osborne, my dear; and as for my Mick, I often tell him he should never open his mouth but to give the word of command, or to put meat and drink into it. I'll tell you about the regiment, and warn you when we're alone. Introduce me to your brother now; sure he's a mighty fine man, and reminds me of me cousin, Dan Malony (Malony of Ballymalony, my dear, you know, who mar'ied Ophalia Scully, of Oystherstown, own cousin to Lord Poldoody). Mr. Sedley, sir, I'm deloighted to be made known te ye. I suppose you'll dine at the mess to-day. (Mind that divvle of a docther, Mick, and whatever ye du, keep yourself sober for me party this evening.)'

'It's the 150th gives us a farewell dinner, my love,' interposed the major, 'but we'll easy get a card for Mr. Sedley.'

'Run, Simple (Ensign Simple, of Ours, my dear Amelia. I forgot to introjuice him to ye). Run in a hurry, with Mrs. Major O'Dowd's compliments to Colonel Tavish, and Captain Osborne has brought his brothernlaw down, and will bring him to the 150th mess at five o'clock sharp – when you and I, my dear, will take a snack here, if you like.' Before Mrs. O'Dowd's speech was concluded, the young ensign was trotting downstairs on his commission.

'Obedience is the soul of the army. We will go to our duty while Mrs. O'Dowd will stay and enlighten you, Emmy,' Captain Osborne said; and the two captains, taking each a wing of the major, walked out with that officer, grinning at each other over his head.

And, now having her new friend to herself, the impetuous Mrs. O'Dowd proceeded to pour out such a quantity of information as no poor little woman's memory could ever tax itself to bear. She told Amelia a thousand particulars relative to the very numerous family of which the amazed young lady found herself a member. 'Mrs. Heavytop, the colonel's wife, died in Jamaica of the yellow faver and a broken heart comboined, for the horrud old colonel, with a head as bald as a cannon-ball, was making sheep's eyes at a half-caste girl there. Mrs. Magenis, though without education, was a good woman, but she had the divvle's tongue, and would cheat her own mother at whist. Mrs. Captain Kirk must turn up her lobster eyes forsooth at the idea of an honest round game (wherein me fawther, as pious a man as ever went to church, me uncle Dane Malony, and our cousin the bishop, took a hand at loo, or whist, every night of their lives). Nayther of 'em's goin' with the regiment this time,' Mrs. O'Dowd added. 'Fanny Magenis stops with her mother, who sells small coal and potatoes, most likely, in Islington-town, hard by London, though she's always bragging of her father's ships, and pointing them out to us as they go up the river: and Mrs. Kirk and her children will stop here in Bethesda Place, to be nigh to her favourite preacher, Dr. Ramshorn. Mrs. Bunny's in an interesting

situation – faith, and she always is, then – and has given
the lieutenant seven already. And Ensign Posky's wife, who
joined two months before you, my dear, has quarl'd with
Tom Posky a score of times, till you can hear 'em all over
the bar'ck (they say they're come to broken pleets, and Tom
never accounted for his black oi), and she'll go back to her
mother, who keeps a ladies' siminary at Richmond, – bad
luck to her for running away from it! Where did ye get your
finishing, my dear? I had moin, and no expince speered, at
Madame Flanahan's, at Ilyssus Grove, Booterstown, near
Dublin, wid a marchioness to teach us the true Parisian
pronunciation, and a retired mejor-general of the French
service to put us through the exercise.'

Of this incongruous family our astonished Amelia found
herself all of a sudden a member: with Mrs. O'Dowd as an
elder sister. She was presented to her other female relations
at tea-time, on whom, as she was quiet, good-natured, and
not too handsome she made rather an agreeable impression
until the arrival of the gentlemen from the mess of the 150th,
who all admired her so, that her sisters began, of course, to
find fault with her.

'I hope Osborne has sown his wild oats,' said Mrs.
Magenis to Mrs. Bunny. 'If a reformed rake makes a good
husband, sure it's she will have the fine chance with Garge,'
Mrs. O'Dowd remarked to Posky, who had lost her position
as bride in the regiment, and was quite angry with the
usurper. And as for Mrs. Kirk, the disciple of Dr. Ramshorn
put one or two leading professional questions to Amelia, to
see whether she was awakened, whether she was a professing
Christian and so forth, and finding from the simplicity of
Mrs. Osborne's replies that she was yet in utter darkness,
put into her hands three little penny books with pictures,
viz., the *Howling Wilderness*, the *Washerwoman of Wandsworth
Common*, and the *British Soldier's Best Bayonet*, which, bent
upon awakening her before she slept, Mrs. Kirk begged
Amelia to read that night ere she went to bed.

But all the men, like good fellows as they were, rallied
round their comrade's pretty wife, and paid her their court
with soldierly gallantry. She had a little triumph, which
flushed her spirits and made her eyes sparkle. George was
proud of her popularity, and pleased with the manner (which
was very gay and graceful, though naïve and a little timid)

with which she received the gentlemen's attentions, and answered their compliments. And he in his uniform – how much handsomer he was than any man in the room! She felt that he was affectionately watching her, and glowed with pleasure at his kindness. 'I will make all his friends welcome,' she resolved in her heart. 'I will love all who love him. I will always try and be gay and good-humoured and make his home happy.'

The regiment indeed adopted her with acclamation. The captains approved, the lieutenants applauded, the ensigns admired. Old Cutler, the doctor, made one or two jokes, which, being professional, need not be repeated; and Cackle, the Assistant M.D. of Edinburgh, condescended to examine her upon leeterature, and tried her with his three best French quotations. Young Stubble went about from man to man whispering, 'Jove, isn't she a pretty gal?' and never took his eyes off her except when the negus came in.

As for Captain Dobbin, he never so much as spoke to her during the whole evening. But he and Captain Porter of the 150th took home Jos to the hotel, who was in a very maudlin state, and had told his tiger-hunt story with great effect, both at the mess-table, and at the soirée to Mrs. O'Dowd in her turban and bird of paradise. Having put the collector into the hands of his servant, Dobbin loitered about, smoking his cigar before the inn door. George had meanwhile very carefully shawled his wife, and brought her away from Mrs. O'Dowd's after a general hand-shaking from the young officers, who accompanied her to the fly, and cheered that vehicle as it drove off. So Amelia gave Dobbin her little hand as she got out of the carriage, and rebuked him smilingly for not having taken any notice of her all night.

The captain continued that deleterious amusement of smoking, long after the inn and the street were gone to bed. He watched the lights vanish from George's sitting-room windows, and shine out in the bedroom close at hand. It was almost morning when he returned to his own quarters. He could hear the cheering from the ships in the river, where the transports were already taking in their cargoes preparatory to dropping down the Thames.

CHAPTER XXVIII

IN WHICH AMELIA INVADES THE LOW COUNTRIES

THE regiment with its officers was to be transported in ships provided by His Majesty's government for the occasion: and in two days after the festive assembly at Mrs. O'Dowd's apartments, in the midst of cheering from all the East India ships in the river, and the military on shore, the band playing 'God save the King', the officers waving their hats, and the crews hurrahing gallantly, the transports went down the river and proceeded under convoy to Ostend. Meanwhile the gallant Jos had agreed to escort his sister and the major's wife, the bulk of whose goods and chattels, including the famous bird of paradise and turban, were with the regimental baggage: so that our two heroines drove pretty much unencumbered to Ramsgate, where there were plenty of packets plying, in one of which they had a speedy passage to Ostend.

That period of Jos's life which now ensued was so full of incident, that it served him for conversation for many years after, and even the tiger-hunt story was put aside for more stirring narratives which he had to tell about the great campaign of Waterloo. As soon as he had agreed to escort his sister abroad, it was remarked that he ceased shaving his upper lip. At Chatham he followed the parades and drills with great assiduity. He listened with the utmost attention to the conversation of his brother officers (as he called them in afterdays sometimes), and learned as many military names as he could. In these studies the excellent Mrs. O'Dowd was of great assistance to him; and on the day finally when they embarked on board the *Lovely Rose* which was to carry them to their destination, he made his appearance in a braided frock-coat and duck trousers, with a foraging cap ornamented with a smart gold band. Having his carriage with him, and informing everybody on board confidentially that he was going to join the Duke of Wellington's army, folks mistook him for a great personage, a commissary-general, or a government courier at the very least.

He suffered hugely on the voyage, during which the ladies were likewise prostrate; but Amelia was brought to life again as the packet made Ostend, by the sight of the transports conveying her regiment, which entered the harbour almost at the same time with the *Lovely Rose*. Jos went in a collapsed state to an inn, while Captain Dobbin escorted the ladies, and then busied himself in freeing Jos's carriage and luggage from the ship and the custom-house, for Mr. Jos was at present without a servant, Osborne's man and his own pampered menial having conspired together at Chatham, and refused point-blank to cross the water. This revolt, which came very suddenly, and on the last day, so alarmed Mr. Sedley, junior, that he was on the point of giving up the expedition, but Captain Dobbin (who made himself immensely officious in the business, Jos said), rated him and laughed at him soundly: the moustachios were grown in advance, and Jos finally was persuaded to embark. In place of the well bred and well-fed London domestics, who could only speak English, Dobbin procured for Jos's party a swarthy little Belgian servant who could speak no language at all; but who, by his bustling behaviour, and by invariably addressing Mr. Sedley as 'My lord', speedily acquired that gentleman's favour. Times are altered at Ostend now; of the Britons who go thither, very few look like lords, or act like those members of our hereditary aristocracy. They seem for the most part shabby in attire, dingy of linen, lovers of billiards and brandy, and cigars and greasy ordinaries.

But it may be said as a rule, that every Englishman in the Duke of Wellington's army paid his way. The remembrance of such a fact surely becomes a nation of shopkeepers. It was a blessing for a commerce-loving country to be overrun by such an army of customers: and to have such creditable warriors to feed. And the country which they came to protect is not military. For a long period of history they have let other people fight there. When the present writer went to survey with eagle glance the field of Waterloo, we asked the conductor of the diligence, a portly warlike-looking veteran, whether he had been at the battle. '*Pas si bête*' – such an answer and sentiment as no Frenchman would own to – was his reply. But on the other hand, the postilion who drove us was a *viscount*, a son of some bankrupt imperial general, who accepted a pennyworth of beer on the road. The moral is surely a good one.

This flat, flourishing, easy country never could have

looked more rich and prosperous, than in that opening summer of 1815, when its green fields and quiet cities were enlivened by multiplied red-coats: when its wide *chaussées* swarmed with brilliant English equipages; when its great canal-boats, gliding by rich pastures and pleasant quaint old villages, by old châteaux lying amongst old trees, were all crowded with well-to-do English travellers: when the soldier who drank at the village inn, not only drank, but paid his score; and Donald, the Highlander,* billeted in the Flemish farm-house, rocked the baby's cradle, while Jean and Jeannette were out getting in the hay. As our painters are bent on military subjects just now, I throw out this as a good subject for the pencil, to illustrate the principle of an honest English war. All looked as brilliant and harmless as a Hyde Park review. Meanwhile, Napoleon, screened behind his curtain of frontier-fortresses, was preparing for the outbreak which was to drive all these orderly people into fury and blood; and lay so many of them low.

Everybody had such a perfect feeling of confidence in the leader (for the resolute faith which the Duke of Wellington had inspired in the whole English nation was as intense as that more frantic enthusiasm with which at one time the French regarded Napoleon), the country seemed in so perfect a state of orderly defence, and the help at hand in case of need so near and overwhelming, that alarm was unknown, and that our travellers, among whom two were naturally of a very timid sort, were, like all the other multiplied English tourists, entirely at ease. The famous regiment, with so many of whose officers we have made acquaintance, was drafted in canal-boats to Bruges and Ghent, thence to march to Brussels. Jos accompanied the ladies in the public boats; the which all old travellers in Flanders must remember for the luxury and accommodation they afforded. So prodigiously good was the eating and drinking on board these sluggish but most comfortable vessels, that there are legends extant of an English traveller, who, coming to Belgium for a week, and travelling in one of these boats, was so delighted with the fare there that he went backwards and forwards from Ghent to Bruges perpetually until the railroads were

---

* This incident is mentioned in Mr. Gleig's *Story of the Battle of Waterloo*.

invented, when he drowned himself on the last trip of the passage-boat. Jos's death was not to be of this sort, but his comfort was exceeding, and Mrs. O'Dowd insisted that he only wanted her sister Glorvina to make his happiness complete. He sat on the roof of the cabin all day drinking Flemish beer, shouting for Isidor, his servant, and talking gallantly to the ladies.

His courage was prodigious. 'Boney attack *us*!' he cried. 'My dear creature, my poor Emmy, don't be frightened. There's no danger. The allies will be in Paris in two months, I tell you; when I'll take you to dine in the Palais Royal, by Jove! There are three hundred thousand Rooshians, I tell you, now entering France by Mayence and the Rhine – three hundred thousand under Wittgenstein and Barclay de Tolly, my poor love. You don't know military affairs, my dear. I do, and I tell you there's no infantry in France can stand against Rooshian infantry, and no general of Boney's that's fit to hold a candle to Wittgenstein. Then there are the Austrians, they are five hundred thousand if a man, and they are within ten marches of the frontier by this time, under Schwartzenberg and Prince Charles. Then there are the Prooshians under the gallant Prince Marshal. Show me a cavalry chief like him now that Murat is gone. Hey, Mrs. O'Dowd? Do you think our little girl here need be afraid? Is there any cause for fear, Isidor? Hey, sir? Get some more beer.'

Mrs. O'Dowd said that her 'Glorvina was not afraid of any man alive, let alone a Frenchman,' and tossed off a glass of beer with a wink which expressed her liking for the beverage.

Having frequently been in presence of the enemy, or, in other words, faced the ladies at Cheltenham and Bath, our friend, the collector, had lost a great deal of his pristine timidity, and was now, especially when fortified with liquor, as talkative as might be. He was rather a favourite with the regiment, treating the young officers with sumptuosity, and amusing them by his military airs. And as there is one well-known regiment of the army which travels with a goat heading the column, whilst another is led by a deer, George said with respect to his brother-in-law, that his regiment marched with an elephant.

Since Amelia's introduction to the regiment, George

began to be rather ashamed of some of the company to which he had been forced to present her; and determined, as he told Dobbin (with what satisfaction to the latter it need not be said), to exchange into some better regiment soon, and to get his wife away from those damned vulgar women. But this vulgarity of being ashamed of one's society is much more common among men than women (except very great ladies of fashion, who, to be sure, indulge in it); and Mrs. Amelia, a natural and unaffected person, had none of that artificial shamefacedness which her husband mistook for delicacy on his own part. Thus Mrs. O'Dowd had a cock's plume in her hat, and a very large 'repayther' on her stomach, which she used to ring on all occasions, narrating how it had been presented to her by her fawther, as she stipt into the car'ge after her mar'ge; and these ornaments, with other outward peculiarities of the major's wife, gave excruciating agonies to Captain Osborne, when his wife and the major's came in contact; whereas Amelia was only amused by the honest lady's eccentricities, and not in the least ashamed of her company.

As they made that well-known journey, which almost every Englishman of middle rank has travelled since, there might have been more instructive, but few more entertaining, companions than Mrs. Major O'Dowd. 'Talk about kenal boats, my dear! Ye should see the kenal boats between Dublin and Ballinasloe. It's there the rapid travelling is; and the beautiful cattle. Sure my fawther got a goold medal (and his Excellency himself eat a slice of it, and said never was finer mate in his loif) for a four-year-old heifer, the like of which ye never saw in *this* country any day.' And Jos owned with a sigh, 'that for good streaky beef, really mingled with fat and lean, there was no country like England.'

'Except Ireland, where all your best mate comes from,' said the major's lady; proceeding, as is not unusual with patriots of her nation, to make comparisons greatly in favour of her own country. The idea of comparing the market of Bruges with those of Dublin, although she had suggested it herself, caused immense scorn and derision on her part. 'I'll thank ye tell me what they mean by that old gazabo on the top of the market-place,' said she, in a burst of ridicule fit to have brought the old tower down. The place was full of English soldiery as they passed. English bugles woke them

in the morning; at nightfall they went to bed to the note
of the British fife and drum: all the country and Europe
was in arms, and the greatest event of history pending:
and honest Peggy O'Dowd, whom it concerned as well as
another, went on prattling about Ballinafad, and the horses
in the stables at Glenmalony, and the clar't drunk there; and
Jos Sedley interposed about curry and rice at Dumdum;
and Amelia thought about her husband, and how best she
should show her love for him; as if these were the great
topics of the world.

Those who like to lay down the history-book, and to
speculate upon what *might* have happened in the world but
for the fatal occurrence of what actually did take place (a
most puzzling, amusing, ingenious, and profitable kind of
meditation), have no doubt often thought to themselves what
a specially bad time Napoleon took to come back from Elba,
and to let loose his eagle from Gulf San Juan to Notre Dame.
The historians on our side tell us that the armies of the
allied powers were all providentially on a war-footing, and
ready to bear down at a moment's notice upon the Elban
Emperor. The august jobbers assembled at Vienna, and
carving out the kingdoms of Europe according to their
wisdom, had such causes of quarrel among themselves as
might have set the armies which had overcome Napoleon to
fight against each other, but for the return of the object of
unanimous hatred and fear. This monarch had an army in
full force because he had jobbed to himself Poland, and was
determined to keep it: another had robbed half Saxony, and
was bent upon maintaining his acquisition: Italy was the
object of a third's solicitude. Each was protesting against the
rapacity of the other; and could the Corsican but have waited
in his prison until all these parties were by the ears, he
might have returned and reigned unmolested. But what
would have become of our story and all our friends, then?
If all the drops in it were dried up, what would become of
the sea?
    In the meanwhile the business of life and living, and the
pursuits of pleasure especially, went on as if no end were
to be expected to them, and no enemy in front. When our
travellers arrived at Brussels, in which their regiment was
quartered, a great piece of good fortune, as all said, they

found themselves in one of the gayest and most brilliant
little capitals in Europe, and where all the Vanity Fair booths
were laid out with the most tempting liveliness and splendour. Gambling was here in profusion, and dancing in
plenty: feasting was there to fill with delight that great
gourmand of a Jos: there was a theatre where a miraculous
Catalani was delighting all hearers; beautiful rides, all enlivened
with martial splendour; a rare old city, with strange costumes
and wonderful architecture, to delight the eyes of little
Amelia, who had never before seen a foreign country, and
fill her with charming surprises: so that now and for a few
weeks' space, in a fine handsome lodging, whereof the
expenses were borne by Jos and Osborne, who was flush of
money and full of kind attentions to his wife – for about a
fortnight, I say, during which her honeymoon ended, Mrs.
Amelia was as pleased and happy as any little bride out of
England.

Every day during this happy time there was novelty and
amusement for all parties. There was a church to see, or a
picture-gallery – there was a ride, or an opera. The bands
of the regiments were making music at all hours. The
greatest folks of England walked in the Park, there was a
perpetual military festival. George, taking out his wife to a
new jaunt or junket every night, was quite pleased with
himself as usual, and swore he was becoming quite a domestic character. And a jaunt or a junket with *him!* Was it not
enough to set this little heart beating with joy? Her letters
home to her mother were filled with delight and gratitude
at this season. Her husband bade her buy laces, millinery,
jewels, and gimcracks of all sorts. Oh, he was the kindest,
best, and most generous of men!

The sight of the very great company of lords and ladies
and fashionable persons who thronged the town, and appeared
in every public place, filled George's truly British soul with
intense delight. They flung off that happy frigidity and
insolence of demeanour which occasionally characterizes the
great at home, and appearing in numberless public places,
condescended to mingle with the rest of the company whom
they met there. One night at a party given by the general
of the division to which George's regiment belonged, he had
the honour of dancing with Lady Blanche Thistlewood, Lord
Bareacres's daughter; he bustled for ices and refreshments

for the two noble ladies; he pushed and squeezed for Lady
Bareacres's carriage; he bragged about the countess when
he got home, in a way which his own father could not
have surpassed. He called upon the ladies the next day; he
rode by their side in the Park; he asked their party to a
great dinner at a restaurateur's, and was quite wild with
exultation when they agreed to come. Old Bareacres, who
had not much pride and a large appetite, would go for a
dinner anywhere.

'I hope there will be no women besides our own party,'
Lady Bareacres said, after reflecting upon the invitation
which had been made, and accepted with too much pre-
cipitancy.

'Gracious Heaven, mamma – you don't suppose the man
would bring his wife,' shrieked Lady Blanche, who had been
languishing in George's arms in the newly-imported waltz
for hours the night before. 'The men are bearable, but their
women —'

'Wife, just married, dev'lish pretty woman, I hear,' the
old earl said.

'Well, my dear Blanche,' said the mother, 'I suppose, as
papa wants to go, we must go; but we needn't know them
in England, you know.' And so, determined to cut their new
acquaintance in Bond Street, these great folks went to eat
his dinner at Brussels, and condescending to make him pay
for their pleasure, showed their dignity by making his wife
uncomfortable, and carefully excluding her from the conversation. This is a species of dignity in which the high-bred
British female reigns supreme. To watch the behaviour of a
fine lady to other and humbler women is a very good sport
for a philosophical frequenter of Vanity Fair.

This festival, on which honest George spent a great deal
of money, was the very dismallest of all the entertainments
which Amelia had in her honeymoon. She wrote the most
piteous accounts of the feast home to her mamma: how the
Countess of Bareacres would not answer when spoken to;
how Lady Blanche stared at her with her eyeglass; and what
a rage Captain Dobbin was in at their behaviour; and how
my lord, as they came away from the feast, asked to see the
bill, and pronounced it a d— bad dinner, and d— dear. But
though Amelia told all these stories, and wrote home regarding her guests' rudeness, and her own discomfiture; old Mrs.

Sedley was mightily pleased nevertheless, and talked about Emmy's friend, the Countess of Bareacres, with such assiduity that the news how his son was entertaining peers and peeresses actually came to Osborne's ears in the City.

Those who know the present Lieutenant-General Sir George Tufto, K.C.B., and have seen him, as they may on most days in the season, padded and in stays, strutting down Pall Mall with a rickety swagger on his high-heeled lacquered boots, leering under the bonnets of passers-by, or riding a showy chestnut, and ogling broughams in the Parks – those who know the present Sir George Tufto would hardly recognize the daring Peninsular and Waterloo officer. He has thick curling brown hair and black eyebrows now, and his whiskers are of the deepest purple. He was light-haired and bald in 1815, and stouter in the person and in the limbs, which especially have shrunk very much of late. When he was about seventy years of age (he is now nearly eighty), his hair, which was very scarce and quite white, suddenly grew thick, and brown, and curly, and his whiskers and eyebrows took their present colour. Ill-natured people say that his chest is all wool, and that his hair, because it never grows, is a wig. Tom Tufto, with whose father he quarrelled ever so many years ago, declares that Mademoiselle de Jaisey, of the French theatre, pulled his grandpapa's hair off in the green-room; but Tom is notoriously spiteful and jealous; and the general's wig has nothing to do with our story.

One day, as some of our friends of the –th were sauntering in the flower-market of Brussels, having been to see the Hotel de Ville, which Mrs. Major O'Dowd declared was not near so large or handsome as her fawther's mansion of Glenmalony, an officer of rank, with an orderly behind him, rode up to the market, and descending from his horse, came amongst the flowers, and selected the very finest bouquet which money could buy. The beautiful bundle being tied up in a paper, the officer remounted, giving the nosegay into the charge of his military groom, who carried it with a grin, following his chief, who rode away in great state and self-satisfaction.

'You should see the flowers at Glenmalony,' Mrs. O'Dowd was remarking. 'Me fawther has three Scotch garners with nine helpers. We have an acre of hot-houses, and pines as common as pays in the sayson. Our greeps weighs six pounds every bunch of 'em, and upon me honour and conscience I think our magnolias is as big as taykettles.'

Dobbin, who never used to 'draw out' Mrs. O'Dowd as that wicked Osborne delighted in doing (much to Amelia's terror, who implored him to spare her), fell back in the crowd, crowing and sputtering until he reached a safe distance, when he exploded amongst the astonished market-people with shrieks of yelling laughter.

'Hwhat's that gawky guggling about?' said Mrs. O'Dowd. 'Is it his nose bleedn? He always used to say 'twas his nose bleedn, till he must have pomped all the blood out of um. An't the magnolias at Glenmalony as big as taykettles, O'Dowd?'

'Deed then they are, and bigger, Peggy,' the major said. When the conversation was interrupted in the manner stated by the arrival of the officer who purchased the bouquet.

'Devlish fine horse – who is it?' George asked.

'You should see me brother Molloy Moloney's horse, Molasses, that won the cop at the Curragh,' the major's wife was exclaiming, and was continuing the family history, when her husband interrupted her by saying,

'It's General Tufto, who commands the — cavalry division;' adding quietly, 'he and I were both shot in the same leg at Talavera.'

'Where you got your step,' said George with a laugh. 'General Tufto! Then, my dear, the Crawleys are come.'

Amelia's heart fell – she knew not why. The sun did not seem to shine so bright. The tall old roofs and gables looked less picturesque all of a sudden, though it was a brilliant sunset, and one of the brightest and most beautiful days at the end of May.

CHAPTER XXIX

BRUSSELS

M r. Jos had hired a pair of horses for his open carriage, with which cattle, and the smart London vehicle, he made a very tolerable figure in the drives about Brussels. George purchased a horse for his private riding, and he and Captain Dobbin would often accompany the carriage in which Jos and his sister took daily excursions of pleasure.

They went out that day in the park for their accustomed diversion, and there, sure enough, George's remark with regard to the arrival of Rawdon Crawley and his wife proved to be correct. In the midst of a little troop of horsemen, consisting of some of the very greatest persons in Brussels, Rebecca was seen in the prettiest and tightest of riding-habits, mounted on a beautiful little Arab, which she rode to perfection (having acquired the art at Queen's Crawley, where the baronet, Mr. Pitt, and Rawdon himself had given her many lessons), and by the side of the gallant General Tufto.

'Sure it's the juke himself,' cried Mrs. Major O'Dowd to Jos, who began to blush violently; 'and that's Lord Uxbridge on the bay. How elegant he looks! Me brother, Molloy Moloney, is as like him as two peas.'

Rebecca did not make for the carriage; but as soon as she perceived her old acquaintance, Amelia, seated in it, acknowledged her presence by a gracious word and smile, and by kissing and shaking her fingers playfully in the direction of the vehicle. Then she resumed her conversation with General Tufto, who asked 'who the fat officer was in the gold-laced cap?' on which Becky replied, 'that he was an officer in the East Indian service.' But Rawdon Crawley rode out of the ranks of his company, and came up and shook hands heartily with Amelia, and said to Jos, 'Well, old boy, how are you?' and stared in Mrs. O'Dowd's face and black cock's feathers until she began to think she had made a conquest of him.

George, who had been delayed behind, rode up almost immediately with Dobbin, and they touched their caps to the august personages, among whom Osborne at once perceived Mrs. Crawley. He was delighted to see Rawdon leaning over his carriage familiarly and talking to Amelia, and met the aide de camp's cordial greeting with more than corresponding warmth. The nods between Rawdon and Dobbin were of the very faintest specimens of politeness.

Crawley told George where they were stopping with General Tufto at the Hotel du Parc, and George made his friend promise to come speedily to Osborne's own residence. 'Sorry I hadn't seen you three days ago,' George said. 'Had a dinner at the restaurateur's – rather a nice thing. Lord Bareacres, and the countess, and Lady Blanche, were good enough to dine with us – wish we'd had you.' Having thus let his friend know his claims to be a man of fashion, Osborne parted from Rawdon, who followed the august squadron down an alley into which they cantered, while George and Dobbin resumed their places, one on each side of Amelia's carriage.

'How well the juke looked,' Mrs. O'Dowd remarked. 'The Wellesleys and Moloneys are related; but, of course, poor *I* would never dream of introjuicing myself unless his Grace thought proper to remember our family-tie.'

'He's a great soldier,' Jos said, much more at ease now the great man was gone. 'Was there ever a battle won like Salamanca? Hey, Dobbin? But where was it he learnt his art? In India, my boy! The jungle's the school for a general, mark me that. I knew him myself, too, Mrs. O'Dowd: we both of us danced the same evening with Miss Cutler, daughter of Cutler of the Artillery, and a devilish fine girl, at Dumdum.'

The apparition of the great personages held them all in talk during the drive; and at dinner; and until the hour came when they were all to go to the opera.

It was almost like Old England. The house was filled with familiar British faces, and those toilettes for which the British female has long been celebrated. Mrs. O'Dowd's was not the least splendid amongst these; and she had a curl on her forehead, and a set of Irish diamonds and Cairngorms, which outshone all the decorations in the house, in her notion. Her presence used to excruciate Osborne; but go she would upon all parties of pleasure on which she heard her young friends were bent. It never entered into her thought but that they must be charmed with her company.

'She's been useful to you, my dear,' George said to his wife, whom he could leave alone with less scruple when she had this society. 'But what a comfort it is that Rebecca's come: you will have her for a friend, and we may get rid now of this damn'd Irishwoman.' To this Amelia did not answer, yes or no: and how do we know what her thoughts were?

The *coup d'œil* of the Brussels opera-house did not strike Mrs. O'Dowd as being so fine as the theatre in Fishamble Street, Dublin, nor was French music at all equal, in her opinion, to the melodies of her native country. She favoured her friends with these and other opinions in a very loud

tone of voice, and tossed about a great clattering fan she
sported, with the most splendid complacency.

'Who is that wonderful woman with Amelia, Rawdon,
love?' said a lady in an opposite box (who, almost always
civil to her husband in private, was more fond than ever of
him in company). 'Don't you see that creature with a yellow
thing in her turban, and a red satin gown, and a great watch?'

'Near the pretty little woman in white?' asked a middle-
aged gentleman seated by the querist's side, with orders in
his button, and several under-waistcoats, and a great, choky,
white stock.

'That pretty woman in white is Amelia, general: you are
remarking all the pretty women, you naughty man.'

'Only one, begad, in the warld!' said the general, delighted,
and the lady gave him a tap with a large bouquet which
she had.

'Bedad it's him,' said Mrs. O'Dowd; 'and that's the very
bokay he bought in the Marshy aux Flures!' and when
Rebecca, having caught her friend's eye, performed the little
hand-kissing operation once more, Mrs. Major O'D., taking
the compliment to herself, returned the salute with a gracious smile, which sent that unfortunate Dobbin shrieking
out of the box again.

At the end of the act, George was out of the box in a
moment, and he was even going to pay his respects to
Rebecca in her *loge*. He met Crawley in the lobby, however,
where they exchanged a few sentences upon the occurrences
of the last fortnight.

'You found my cheque all right at the agent's?' George
said, with a knowing air.

'All right, my boy,' Rawdon answered. 'Happy to give
you your revenge. Governor come round?'

'Not yet,' said George, 'but he will; and you know I've
some private fortune through my mother. Has aunty relented?'

'Sent me twenty pound, damned old screw. When shall
we have a meet? The general dines out on Tuesday. Can't
you come Tuesday? I say, make Sedley cut off his moustache. What the devil does a civilian mean with a moustache
and those infernal frogs to his coat! By-bye. Try and come
on Tuesday;' and Rawdon was going off with two brilliant
young gentlemen of fashion, who were, like himself, on the
staff of a general officer.

George was only half pleased to be asked to dinner on that particular day when the general was *not* to dine. 'I will go in and pay my respects to your wife,' said he; at which Rawdon said, 'Hm, as you please,' looking very glum, and at which the two young officers exchanged knowing glances. George parted from them, and strutted down the lobby to the general's box, the number of which he had carefully counted.

'*Entrez*,' said a clear little voice, and our friend found himself in Rebecca's presence; who jumped up, clapped her hands together, and held out both of them to George, so charmed was she to see him. The general, with the orders in his button, stared at the newcomer with a sulky scowl, as much as to say, who the devil are you?

'My dear Captain George!' cried little Rebecca in an ecstasy. 'How good of you to come. The general and I were moping together *tête à tête*. General, this is my Captain George of whom you heard me talk.'

'Indeed,' said the general, with a very small bow, 'of what regiment is Captain George?'

George mentioned the –th: how he wished he could have said it was a crack cavalry corps.

'Come home lately from the West Indies, I believe. Not seen much service in the late war. Quartered here, Captain George?' – the general went on with killing haughtiness.

'Not Captain George, you stupid man; Captain Osborne,' Rebecca said. The general all the while was looking savagely from one to the other.

'Captain Osborne, indeed! Any relation to the L— Osbornes?'

'We bear the same arms,' George said, as indeed was the fact; Mr. Osborne having consulted with a herald in Long Acre, and picked the L— arms out of the *Peerage*, when he set up his carriage fifteen years before. The general made no reply to this announcement; but took up his opera-glass – the double-barrelled lorgnon was not invented in those days – and pretended to examine the house: but Rebecca saw that his disengaged eye was working round in her direction, and shooting out bloodshot glances at her and George.

She redoubled in cordiality. 'How is dearest Amelia? But I needn't ask: how pretty she looks! And who is that nice good-natured looking creature with her — a flame of yours? Oh, you wicked men! And there is Mr. Sedley eating ices, I declare: how he seems to enjoy it! General, why have we not had any ices?'

'Shall I go and fetch you some?' said the general, bursting with wrath.

'Let *me* go, I entreat you,' George said.

'No, I will go to Amelia's box. Dear, sweet girl! Give me your arm, Captain George;' and so saying, and with a nod to the general, she tripped into the lobby. She gave George the queerest, knowingest look, when they were together, a look which might have been interpreted, 'Don't you see the state of affairs, and what a fool I'm making of him?' But he did not perceive it. He was thinking of his own plans, and lost in pompous admiration of his own irresistible powers of pleasing.

The curses to which the general gave a low utterance, as soon as Rebecca and her conqueror had quitted him, were so deep, that I am sure no compositor in Messrs. Bradbury and Evans's establishment would venture to print them were they written down. They came from the general's heart; and a wonderful thing it is to think that the human heart is capable of generating such produce, and can throw out, as occasion demands, such a supply of lust and fury, rage and hatred.

Amelia's gentle eyes, too, had been fixed anxiously on the pair, whose conduct had so chafed the jealous general: but when Rebecca entered her box, she flew to her friend with an affectionate rapture which showed itself, in spite of the publicity of the place; for she embraced her dearest friend in the presence of the whole house, at least in full view of the general's glass, now brought to bear upon the Osborne party. Mrs. Rawdon saluted Jos, too, with the kindliest greeting: she admired Mrs. O'Dowd's large Cairngorm brooch and superb Irish diamonds, and wouldn't believe that they were not from Golconda direct. She bustled, she chattered, she turned and twisted, and smiled upon one, and smirked on another, all in full view of the jealous opera-glass opposite. And when the time for the ballet came (in which there was no dancer that went through her grimaces or performed her comedy of action better), she skipped back to her own box, leaning on Captain Dobbin's arm this time.

No, she would not have George's: he must stay and talk to his dearest, best, little Amelia.

'What a humbug that woman is,' honest old Dobbin mumbled to George, when he came back from Rebecca's box, whither he had conducted her in perfect silence, and with a countenance as glum as an undertaker's. 'She writhes and twists about like a snake. All the time she was here, didn't you see, George, how she was acting at the general over the way?'

'Humbug – acting? Hang it, she's the nicest little woman in England,' George replied, showing his white teeth, and giving his ambrosial whiskers a twirl. 'You ain't a man of the world, Dobbin. Dammy, look at her now, she's talked over Tufto in no time. Look how he's laughing! Gad, what a shoulder she has! Emmy, why didn't you have a bouquet? Everybody has a bouquet.'

'Faith, then, why didn't you *boy* one?' Mrs. O'Dowd said; and both Amelia and William Dobbin thanked her for this timely observation. But beyond this neither of the ladies rallied. Amelia was overpowered by the flash and the dazzle and the fashionable talk of her worldly rival. Even the O'Dowd was silent and subdued after Becky's brilliant apparition, and scarcely said a word more about Glenmalony all the evening.

'When do you intend to give up play, George, as you have promised me, any time these hundred years?' Dobbin said to his friend a few days after the night at the opera. 'When do you intend to give up sermonizing?' was the other's reply. 'What the deuce, man, are you alarmed about? We play low; I won last night. You don't suppose Crawley cheats? With fair play it comes to pretty much the same thing at the year's end.'

'But I don't think he could pay if he lost,' Dobbin said; and his advice met with the success which advice usually commands. Osborne and Crawley were repeatedly together now. General Tufto dined abroad almost constantly. George was always welcome in the apartments (very close indeed to those of the general), which the aide de camp and his wife occupied in the hotel.

Amelia's manners were such when she and George visited Crawley and his wife at these quarters, that they had very

nearly come to their first quarrel; that is, George scolded
his wife violently for her evident unwillingness to go, and
the high and mighty manner in which she comported herself
towards Mrs. Crawley, her old friend; and Amelia did not
say one single word in reply; but with her husband's eye
upon her, and Rebecca scanning her as she felt, was, if
possible, more bashful and awkward on the second visit
which she paid to Mrs. Rawdon, than on her first call.

Rebecca was doubly affectionate, of course, and would
not take notice, in the least, of her friend's coolness. 'I think
Emmy has become prouder since her father's name was in
the ——, since Mr. Sedley's *misfortunes*,' Rebecca said, soften-
ing the phrase charitably for George's ear. 'Upon my word,
I thought when we were at Brighton she was doing me the
honour to be jealous of me; and now I suppose she is
scandalized because Rawdon, and I, and the general live
together. Why, my dear creature, how could we, with our
means, live at all, but for a friend to share expenses? And
do you suppose that Rawdon is not big enough to take care
of my honour? But I'm very much obliged to Emmy, very,'
Mrs. Rawdon said.

'Pooh, jealousy!' answered George, 'all women are jealous.'

'And all men too. Weren't you jealous of General Tufto,
and the general of you, on the night of the opera? Why, he
was ready to eat me for going with you to visit that foolish
little wife of yours; as if I care a pin for either of you,'
Crawley's wife said, with a pert toss of her head. 'Will you
dine here? The dragon dines with the commander-in-chief.
Great news is stirring. They say the French have crossed
the frontier. We shall have a quiet dinner.'

George accepted the invitation, although his wife was a
little ailing. They were now not quite six weeks married.
Another woman was laughing or sneering at her expense,
and he not angry. He was not even angry with himself, this
good-natured fellow. It is a shame, he owned to himself; but
hang it, if a pretty woman *will* throw herself into your way,
why, what can a fellow do, you know? I *am* rather free about
women, he had often said, smiling and nodding knowingly
to Stubble and Spooney, and other comrades of the mess-
table; and they rather respected him than otherwise for this
prowess. Next to conquering in war, conquering in love has
been a source of pride, time out of mind, amongst men in

Vanity Fair, or how should schoolboys brag of their amours, or Don Juan be popular?

So Mr. Osborne, having a firm conviction in his own mind that he was a woman-killer and destined to conquer, did not run counter to his fate, but yielded himself up to it quite complacently. And as Emmy did not say much or plague him with her jealousy, but merely became unhappy and pined over it miserably in secret, he chose to fancy that she was not suspicious of what all his acquaintance were perfectly aware – namely, that he was carrying on a desperate flirtation with Mrs. Crawley. He rode with her whenever she was free. He pretended regimental business to Amelia (by which falsehood she was not in the least deceived), and consigning his wife to solitude or her brother's society, passed his evenings in the Crawleys' company; losing money to the husband and flattering himself that the wife was dying in love for him. It is very likely that this worthy couple never absolutely conspired and agreed together in so many words: the one to cajole the young gentleman, whilst the other won his money at cards: but they understood each other perfectly well, and Rawdon let Osborne come and go with entire good humour.

George was so occupied with his new acquaintances that he and William Dobbin were by no means so much together as formerly. George avoided him in public and in the regiment, and, as we see, did not like those sermons which his senior was disposed to inflict upon him. If some parts of his conduct made Captain Dobbin exceedingly grave and cool; of what use was it to tell George that though his whiskers were large, and his own opinion of his knowingness great, he was as green as a schoolboy? that Rawdon was making a victim of him as he had done of many before, and as soon as he had used him would fling him off with scorn? He would not listen: and so, as Dobbin, upon those days when he visited the Osborne house, seldom had the advantage of meeting his old friend, much painful and unavailing talk between them was spared. Our friend George was in the full career of the pleasures of Vanity Fair.

There never was, since the days of Darius, such a brilliant train of camp-followers as hung round the train of the Duke of Wellington's army in the Low Countries, in 1815; and led it dancing and feasting, as it were, up to the very brink of battle. A certain ball which a noble duchess gave at Brussels, on the 15th of June in the above-named year, is historical. All Brussels had been in a state of excitement about it, and I have heard from ladies who were in that town at the period, that the talk and interest of persons of their own sex regarding the ball was much greater even than in respect of the enemy in their front. The struggles, intrigues, and prayers to get tickets were such as only English ladies will employ, in order to gain admission to the society of the great of their own nation.

Jos and Mrs. O'Dowd, who were panting to be asked, strove in vain to procure tickets; but others of our friends were more lucky. For instance, through the interest of my Lord Bareacres, and as a set-off for the dinner at the restaurateur's, George got a card for Captain and Mrs. Osborne; which circumstance greatly elated him. Dobbin, who was a friend of the general commanding the division in which their regiment was, came laughing one day to Mrs. Osborne, and displayed a similar invitation, which made Jos envious, and George wonder how the deuce he should be getting into society. Mr. and Mrs. Rawdon, finally, were of course invited; as became the friends of a general commanding a cavalry brigade.

On the appointed night, George, having commanded new dresses and ornaments of all sorts for Amelia, drove to the famous ball, where his wife did not know a single soul. After looking about for Lady Bareacres, who cut him, thinking the card was quite enough – and after placing Amelia on a bench, he left her to her own cogitations there, thinking, on his own part, that he had behaved very handsomely in getting her new clothes, and bringing her to the ball, where she was free to amuse herself as she liked. Her thoughts were not of the pleasantest, and nobody except honest Dobbin came to disturb them.

Whilst her appearance was an utter failure (as her husband felt with a sort of rage), Mrs. Rawdon Crawley's début was, on the contrary, very brilliant. She arrived very late. Her face was radiant; her dress perfection. In the midst of the great persons assembled, and the eyeglasses directed to her, Rebecca seemed to be as cool and collected as when she used to marshal Miss Pinkerton's little girls to church.

Numbers of the men she knew already, and the dandies
thronged round her. As for the ladies, it was whispered
among them that Rawdon had run away with her from out
of a convent, and that she was a relation of the Montmorency
family. She spoke French so perfectly that there might be
some truth in this report, and it was agreed that her manners
were fine, and her air *distingué*. Fifty would-be partners
thronged round her at once, and pressed to have the honour
to dance with her. But she said she was engaged, and only
going to dance very little; and made her way at once to the
place where Emmy sat quite unnoticed, and dismally
unhappy. And so, to finish the poor child at once, Mrs.
Rawdon ran and greeted affectionately her dearest Amelia,
and began forthwith to patronize her. She found fault with
her friend's dress, and her hairdresser, and wondered how
she could be so *chaussée*, and vowed that she must send her
corsetière the next morning. She vowed that it was a delightful ball; that there was everybody that every one knew, and
only a *very* few nobodies in the whole room. It is a fact,
that in a fortnight, and after three dinners in general society,
this young woman had got up the genteel jargon so well,
that a native could not speak it better; and it was only from
her French being so good, that you could know she was not
a born woman of fashion.

George, who had left Emmy on her bench on entering
the ball-room, very soon found his way back when Rebecca
was by her dear friend's side. Becky was just lecturing Mrs.
Osborne upon the follies which her husband was committing.
'For God's sake, stop him from gambling, my dear,' she
said, 'or he will ruin himself. He and Rawdon are playing
at cards every night, and you know he is very poor, and
Rawdon will win every shilling from him if he does not take
care. Why don't you prevent him, you little careless creature?
Why don't you come to us of an evening, instead of moping
at home with that Captain Dobbin? I dare say he is *très
aimable*; but how could one love a man with feet of such
size? Your husband's feet are darlings — Here he comes.
Where have you been, wretch? Here is Emmy crying her
eyes out for you. Are you coming to fetch me for the
quadrille?' And she left her bouquet and shawl by Amelia's
side, and tripped off with George to dance. Women only
know how to wound so. There is a poison on the tips of

their little shafts, which stings a thousand times more than a man's blunter weapon. Our poor Emmy, who had never hated, never sneered all her life, was powerless in the hands of her remorseless little enemy.

George danced with Rebecca twice or thrice – how many times Amelia scarcely knew. She sat quite unnoticed in her corner, except when Rawdon came up with some words of clumsy conversation: and later in the evening, when Captain Dobbin made so bold as to bring her refreshments and sit beside her. He did not like to ask her why she was so sad; but as a pretext for the tears which were filling in her eyes, she told him that Mrs. Crawley had alarmed her by telling her that George would go on playing.

'It is curious, when a man is bent upon play, by what clumsy rogues he will allow himself to be cheated,' Dobbin said; and Emmy said, 'Indeed.' She was thinking of something else. It was not the loss of the money that grieved her.

At last George came back for Rebecca's shawl and flowers. She was going away. She did not even condescend to come back and say good-bye to Amelia. The poor girl let her husband come and go without saying a word, and her head fell on her breast. Dobbin had been called away, and was whispering deep in conversation with the general of the division, his friend, and had not seen this last parting. George went away then with the bouquet; but when he gave it to the owner, there lay a note, coiled like a snake among the flowers. Rebecca's eye caught it at once. She had been used to deal with notes in early life. She put out her hand and took the nosegay. He saw by her eyes as they met, that she was aware what she should find there. Her husband hurried her away, still too intent upon his own thoughts, seemingly, to take note of any marks of recognition which might pass between his friend and his wife. These were, however, but trifling. Rebecca gave George her hand with one of her usual quick knowing glances, and made a curtsy and walked away. George bowed over the hand, said nothing in reply to a remark of Crawley's, did not hear it even, his brain was so throbbing with triumph and excitement, and allowed them to go away without a word.

His wife saw the one part at least of the bouquet-scene. It was quite natural that George should come at Rebecca's

request to get her her scarf and flowers: it was no more than
he had done twenty times before in the course of the last
few days; but now it was too much for her. 'William,' she
said, suddenly clinging to Dobbin, who was near her, 'you've
always been very kind to me – I'm – I'm not well. Take me
home.' She did not know she called him by his Christian
name, as George was accustomed to do. He went away with
her quickly. Her lodgings were hard by; and they threaded
through the crowd without, where everything seemed to be
more astir than even in the ball-room within.

George had been angry twice or thrice at finding his
wife up on his return from the parties which he frequented: so she went straight to bed now; but although she
did not sleep, and although the din and clatter, and the
galloping of horsemen was incessant, she never heard any of
these noises, having quite other disturbances to keep her
awake.

Osborne meanwhile, wild with elation, went off to a
play-table, and began to bet frantically. He won repeatedly.
'Everything succeeds with me to-night,' he said. But his
luck at play even did not cure him of his restlessness,
and he started up after a while, pocketing his winnings,
and went to a buffet, where he drank off many bumpers of
wine.

Here, as he was rattling away to the people around,
laughing loudly and wild with spirits, Dobbin found him.
He had been to the card-tables to look there for his friend.
Dobbin looked as pale and grave as his comrade was flushed
and jovial.

'Hullo, Dob! Come and drink, old Dob! The duke's wine
is famous. Give me some more, you sir;' and he held out a
trembling glass for the liquor.

'Come out, George,' said Dobbin, still gravely; 'don't
drink.'

'Drink! there's nothing like it. Drink yourself, and light
up your lantern jaws, old boy. Here's to you.'

Dobbin went up and whispered something to him, at
which George, giving a start and a wild hurray, tossed off
his glass, clapped it on the table, and walked away speedily
on his friend's arm. 'The enemy has passed the Sambre,'
William said, 'and our left is already engaged. Come away.
We are to march in three hours.'

Away went George, his nerves quivering with excitement at the news so long looked for, so sudden when it came. What were love and intrigue now? He thought about a thousand things but these in his rapid walk to his quarters – his past life and future chances – the fate which might be before him – the wife, the child perhaps, from whom unseen he might be about to part. Oh, how he wished that night's work undone! and that with a clear conscience at least he might say farewell to the tender and guileless being by whose love he had set such little store!

He thought over his brief married life. In those few weeks he had frightfully dissipated his little capital. How wild and reckless he had been! Should any mischance befall him: what was then left for her? How unworthy he was of her. Why had he married her? He was not fit for marriage. Why had he disobeyed his father, who had been always so generous to him? Hope, remorse, ambition, tenderness, and selfish regret filled his heart. He sat down and wrote to his father, remembering what he had said once before, when he was engaged to fight a duel. Dawn faintly streaked the sky as he closed this farewell letter. He sealed it, and kissed the superscription. He thought how he had deserted that generous father, and of the thousand kindnesses which the stern old man had done him.

He had looked into Amelia's bedroom when he entered; she lay quiet, and her eyes seemed closed, and he was glad that she was asleep. On arriving at his quarters from the ball, he had found his regimental servant already making preparations for his departure: the man had understood his signal to be still, and these arrangements were very quickly and silently made. Should he go in and wake Amelia, he thought, or leave a note for her brother to break the news of departure to her? He went in to look at her once again.

She had been awake when he first entered her room, but had kept her eyes closed, so that even her wakefulness should not seem to reproach him. But when he had returned, so soon after herself, too, this timid little heart had felt more at ease, and turning towards him as he stepped softly out of the room, she had fallen into a light sleep. George came in and looked at her again, entering still more softly. By the pale night-lamp he could see her sweet, pale face – the purple eyelids were fringed and closed, and one round arm, smooth and white, lay outside of the coverlet. Good God! how pure she was; how gentle, how tender, and how friendless! and he, how selfish, brutal, and black with crime! Heart-stained, and shame-stricken, he stood at the bed's foot, and looked at the sleeping girl. How dared he – who was he, to pray for one so spotless! God bless her! God bless her! He came to the bedside, and looked at the hand, the little soft hand, lying asleep; and he bent over the pillow noiselessly towards the gentle pale face.

Two fair arms closed tenderly round his neck as he stooped down. 'I am awake, George,' the poor child said, with a sob fit to break the little heart that nestled so closely by his own. She was awake, poor soul, and to what? At that moment a bugle from the Place of Arms began sounding clearly, and was taken up through the town; and amidst the drums of the infantry, and the shrill pipes of the Scotch, the whole city awoke.

CHAPTER XXX

'THE GIRL I LEFT BEHIND ME'

WE do not claim to rank among the military novelists. Our place is with the non-combatants. When the decks are cleared for action we go below and wait meekly. We should only be in the way of the manœuvres that the gallant fellows are performing overhead. We shall go no farther with the –th than to the city gate: and, leaving Major O'Dowd to his duty, come back to the major's wife, and the ladies and the baggage.

Now, the major and his lady, who had not been invited to the ball at which in our last chapter other of our friends figured, had much more time to take their wholesome natural rest in bed, than was accorded to people who wished to enjoy pleasure as well as to do duty. 'It's my belief, Peggy, my dear,' said he, as he placidly pulled his nightcap over his ears, 'that there will be such a ball danced in a day or two as some of 'em has never heard the chune of;' and he was much more happy to retire to rest after partaking of a quiet tumbler, than to figure at any other sort of amusement. Peggy, for her part, would have liked to have shown her turban and bird of paradise at the ball, but for the information which her husband had given her, and which made her very grave.

'I'd like ye wake me about half an hour before the assembly beats,' the major said to his lady. 'Call me at half-past one, Peggy dear, and see me things is ready. Maybe I'll not come back to breakfast, Mrs. O'D.' With which words, which signified his opinion that the regiment would march the next morning, the major ceased talking, and fell asleep.

Mrs. O'Dowd, the good housewife, arrayed in curl-papers and a camisole, felt that her duty was to act, and not to sleep, at this juncture. 'Time enough for that,' she said, 'when Mick's gone;' and so she packed his travelling-valise ready for the march, brushed his cloak, his cap, and other warlike habiliments, set them out in order for him; and stowed away in the cloak-pockets a light package of portable refreshments, and a wicker-covered flask or pocket-pistol, containing near a pint of a remarkably sound Cognac brandy, of which she and the major approved very much; and as soon as the hands of the 'repayther' pointed to half-past one, and its interior arrangements (it had a tone quite aqual to a cathaydral, its fair owner considered) knelled forth that fatal hour, Mrs. O'Dowd woke up her major, and had as comfortable a cup of coffee prepared for him as any made that morning in Brussels. And who is there will deny that this worthy lady's preparations betokened affection as much as the fits of tears and hysterics by which more sensitive females exhibited their love, and that their partaking of this coffee, which they drank together while the bugles were sounding the turn-out and the drums beating in the various quarters of the town, was not more useful and to the purpose than the outpouring of any mere sentiment could be? The consequence was, that the major appeared on parade quite trim, fresh, and alert, his well-shaved rosy countenance, as he sat on horseback, giving cheerfulness and confidence to the whole corps. All the officers saluted her when the regiment marched by the balcony on which this brave woman stood and waved them a cheer as they passed; and I daresay it was not from want of courage, but from a sense of female delicacy and propriety, that she refrained from leading the gallant –th personally into action.

On Sundays, and at periods of a solemn nature, Mrs.

O'Dowd used to read with great gravity out of a large volume of her uncle the dean's sermons. It had been of great comfort to her on board the transport as they were coming home, and were very nearly wrecked, on their return from the West Indies. After the regiment's departure she betook herself to this volume for meditation; perhaps she did not understand much of what she was reading, and her thoughts were elsewhere: but the sleep project, with poor Mick's nightcap there on the pillow, was quite a vain one. So it is in the world. Jack or Donald marches away to glory with his knapsack on his shoulder, stepping out briskly to the tune of *The Girl I left behind me*. It is she who remains and suffers, – and has the leisure to think, and brood, and remember.

Knowing how useless regrets are, and how the indulgence of sentiment only serves to make people more miserable, Mrs. Rebecca wisely determined to give way to no vain feelings of sorrow, and bore the parting from her husband with quite a Spartan equanimity. Indeed Captain Rawdon himself was much more affected at the leave-taking than the resolute little woman to whom he bade farewell. She had mastered this rude coarse nature; and he loved and worshipped her with all his faculties of regard and admiration. In all his life he had never been so happy, as, during the past few months, his wife had made him. All former delights of turf, mess, hunting-field, and gambling-table; all previous loves and courtships of milliners, opera-dancers, and the like easy triumphs of the clumsy military Adonis, were quite insipid when compared to the lawful matrimonial pleasures which of late he had enjoyed. She had known perpetually how to divert him; and he had found his house and her society a thousand times more pleasant than any place or company which he had ever frequented from his childhood until now. And he cursed his past follies and extravagances, and bemoaned his vast outlying debts above all, which must remain for ever as obstacles to prevent his wife's advancement in the world. He had often groaned over these in midnight conversations with Rebecca, although as a bachelor they had never given him any disquiet. He himself was struck with this phenomenon. 'Hang it,' he would say (or perhaps use a still stronger expression out of his simple vocabulary), 'before I was married I didn't care what bills I put my name to, and so long as Moses would wait or Levy would renew for three months, I kept on never minding. But since I'm married, except renewing, of course, I give you my honour I've not touched a bit of stamped paper.'

Rebecca always knew how to conjure away these moods of melancholy. 'Why, my stupid love,' she would say, 'we have not done with your aunt yet. If she fails us, isn't there what you call the *Gazette?* or, stop, when your uncle Bute's life drops, I have another scheme. The living has always belonged to the younger brother, and why shouldn't you sell out and go into the Church?' The idea of this conversion set Rawdon into roars of laughter: you might have heard the explosion through the hotel at midnight, and the haw-haws of the great dragoon's voice. General Tufto heard him from his quarters on the first floor above them; and Rebecca acted the scene with great spirit, and preached Rawdon's first sermon, to the immense delight of the general at breakfast.

But these were mere bygone days and talk. When the final news arrived that the campaign was opened, and the troops were to march, Rawdon's gravity became such that Becky rallied him about it in a manner which rather hurt the feelings of the Guardsman. 'You don't suppose I'm afraid, Becky, I should think,' he said, with a tremor in his voice. 'But I'm a pretty good mark for a shot, and you see if it brings me down, why I leave one and perhaps two behind me whom I should wish to provide for, as I brought 'em into the scrape. It is no laughing matter *that*, Mrs. C., anyways.'

Rebecca by a hundred caresses and kind words tried to soothe the feelings of the wounded lover. It was only when her vivacity and sense of humour got the better of this sprightly creature (as they would do under most circumstances of life indeed), that she would break out with her satire, but she could soon put on a demure face. 'Dearest love,' she said, 'do you suppose I feel nothing?' and, hastily dashing something from her eyes, she looked up in her husband's face with a smile.

'Look here,' said he. 'If I drop, let us see what there is for you. I have had a pretty good run of luck here, and here's two hundred and thirty pounds. I have got ten napoleons in my pocket. That is as much as I shall want; for the general pays everything like a prince; and if I'm hit, why you know I cost nothing. Don't cry, little woman; I may live to vex you yet. Well, I shan't take either of my horses, but shall ride the general's grey charger: it's cheaper, and I told him mine was lame. If I'm done, those two ought to fetch you something. Grigg offered ninety for the mare yesterday, before this confounded news came, and like a fool I wouldn't let her go under the two o's. Bulfinch will fetch his price any day, only you'd better sell him in this country, because the dealers have so many bills of mine, and so I'd rather he shouldn't go back to England. Your little mare the general gave you will fetch something, and there's no d–d livery stable bills here as there are in London,' Rawdon added, with a laugh. 'There's that dressing-case cost me two hundred, – that is, I owe two for it; and the gold tops and bottles must be worth thirty or forty. Please to put *that* up the spout, ma'am, with my pins, and rings, and watch and chain, and things. They cost a precious lot of money. Miss Crawley, I know, paid a hundred down for the chain and ticker. Gold tops and bottles, indeed! dammy, I'm sorry I didn't take more now. Edwards pressed on me a silver-gilt boot-jack, and I might have had a dressing-case fitted up with a silver warming-pan, and a service of plate. But we must make the best of what we've got, Becky, you know.'

And so, making his last dispositions, Captain Crawley, who had seldom thought about anything but himself, until the last few months of his life, when Love had obtained the mastery over the dragoon, went through the various items of his little catalogue of effects, striving to see how they might be turned into money for his wife's benefit, in case any accident should befall him. He pleased himself by noting down with a pencil, in his big schoolboy hand-writing, the various items of his portable property which might be sold for his widow's advantage – as, for example. 'My double-barril by Manton, say 40 guineas; my driving-cloak, lined with sable fur, 50*l*.; my duelling pistols in rosewood case (same which I shot Captain Marker), 20*l*.; my regulation saddle-holsters and housings; my Laurie ditto, and so forth, over all of which articles he made Rebecca the mistress.

Faithful to his plan of economy, the captain dressed himself in his oldest and shabbiest uniform and epaulets, leaving the newest behind, under his wife's (or it might be his widow's) guardianship. And this famous dandy of

Windsor and Hyde Park went off on his campaign with a kit as modest as that of a sergeant, and with something like a prayer on his lips for the woman he was leaving. He took her up from the ground, and held her in his arms for a minute, tight pressed against his strong beating heart. His face was purple and his eyes dim, as he put her down and left her. He rode by his general's side, and smoked his cigar in silence as they hastened after the troops of the general's brigade, which preceded them; and it was not until they were some miles on their way that he left off twirling his moustache and broke silence.

And Rebecca, as we have said, wisely determined not to give way to unavailing sentimentality on her husband's departure. She waved him an adieu from the window, and stood there for a moment looking out after he was gone. The cathedral towers and the full gables of the quaint old houses were just beginning to blush in the sunrise. There had been no rest for her that night. She was still in her pretty ball-dress, her fair hair hanging somewhat out of curl on her neck, and the circles round her eyes dark with watching. 'What a fright I seem,' she said, examining herself in the glass, 'and how pale this pink makes one look!' So she divested herself of this pink raiment; in doing which a note fell out from her corsage, which she picked up with a smile, and locked into her dressing-box. And then she put her bouquet of the ball into a glass of water, and went to bed, and slept very comfortably.

The town was quite quiet when she woke up at ten o'clock, and partook of coffee, very requisite and comfortable after the exhaustion and grief of the morning's occurrences.

This meal over, she resumed honest Rawdon's calculations of the night previous, and surveyed her position. Should the worst befall, all things considered, she was pretty well-to-do. There were her own trinkets and trousseau, in addition to those which her husband had left behind. Rawdon's generosity, when they were first married, has already been described and lauded. Besides these, and the little mare, the general, her slave and worshipper, had made her many very handsome presents, in the shape of cashmere shawls bought at the auction of a bankrupt French general's lady, and numerous tributes from the jewellers' shops, all of which betokened her admirer's taste and wealth. As for 'tickers',

as poor Rawdon called watches, her apartments were alive
with their clicking. For, happening to mention one night
that hers, which Rawdon had given to her, was of English
workmanship, and went ill, on the very next morning there
came to her a little bijou marked Leroy, with a chain and
cover charmingly set with turquoises, and another signed
Breguet, which was covered with pearls, and yet scarcely
bigger than a half-crown. General Tufto had bought one,
and Captain Osborne had gallantly presented the other. Mrs.
Osborne had no watch, though, to do George justice, she
might have had one for the asking, and the Honourable Mrs.
Tufto in England had an old instrument of her mother's
that might have served for the plate warming-pan which
Rawdon talked about. If Messrs. Howell and James were to
publish a list of the purchasers of all the trinkets which they
sell, how surprised would some families be: and if all these
ornaments went to gentlemen's lawful wives and daughters,
what a profusion of jewellery there would be exhibited in
the genteelest homes of Vanity Fair!

Every calculation made of these valuables Mrs. Rebecca
found, not without a pungent feeling of triumph and self-
satisfaction, that should circumstances occur, she might
reckon on six or seven hundred pounds at the very least, to
begin the world with; and she passed the morning disposing,
ordering, looking out, and locking up her properties in the
most agreeable manner. Among the notes in Rawdon's pocket-
book, was a draft for twenty pounds on Osborne's banker.
This made her think about Mrs. Osborne. 'I will go and get
the draft cashed,' she said. 'and pay a visit afterwards to
poor little Emmy.' If this is a novel without a hero, at least
let us lay claim to a heroine. No man in the British army
which has marched away, not the great duke himself, could
be more cool or collected in the presence of doubts and
difficulties, than the indomitable little aide de camp's wife.

And there was another of our acquaintances who was also
to be left behind, a non-combatant, and whose emotions and
behaviour we have therefore a right to know. This was our
friend the ex-collector of Boggley Wollah, whose rest was
broken, like other people's, by the sounding of the bugles
in the early morning. Being a great sleeper, and fond of his
bed, it is possible he would have snoozed on until his usual

hour of rising in the forenoon, in spite of all the drums, bugles, and bagpipes in the British army, but for an interruption, which did not come from George Osborne, who shared Jos's quarters with him, and was as usual occupied too much with his own affairs, or with grief at parting with his wife, to think of taking leave of his slumbering brother-in-law – it was not George, we say, who interposed between Jos Sedley and sleep, but Captain Dobbin, who came and roused him up, insisting on shaking hands with him before his departure.

'Very kind of you,' said Jos, yawning, and wishing the captain at the deuce.

'I – I didn't like to go off without saying good-bye, you know,' Dobbin said, in a very incoherent manner; 'because you know some of us mayn't come back again, and I like to see you all well, and – and that sort of thing, you know.'

'What do you mean?' Jos asked, rubbing his eyes. The captain did not in the least hear him or look at the stout gentleman in the nightcap, about whom he professed to have such a tender interest. The hypocrite was looking and listening with all his might in the direction of George's apartments, striding about the room, upsetting the chairs, beating the tattoo, biting his nails, and showing other signs of great inward emotion.

Jos had always had rather a mean opinion of the captain, and now began to think his courage was somewhat equivocal. 'What is it I can do for you, Dobbin?' he said, in a sarcastic tone.

'I tell you what you can do,' the captain replied, coming up to the bed; 'we march in a quarter of an hour, Sedley, and neither George nor I may ever come back. Mind you, you are not to stir from this town until you ascertain how things go. You are to stay here and watch over your sister, and comfort her, and see that no harm comes to her. If anything happens to George, remember she has no one but you in the world to look to. If it goes wrong with the army, you'll see her safe back to England; and you will promise me on your word that you will never desert her. I know you won't: as far as money goes, you were always free enough with that. Do you want any? I mean, have you enough gold to take you back to England in case of a misfortune?'

'Sir,' said Jos majestically, 'when I want money, I know

where to ask for it. And as for my sister, *you* needn't tell me how I ought to behave to her.'

'You speak like a man of spirit, Jos,' the other answered good-naturedly, 'and I am glad that George can leave her in such good hands. So I may give him your word of honour, may I, that in case of extremity you will stand by her?'

'Of course, of course,' answered Mr. Jos, whose generosity in money matters Dobbin estimated quite correctly.

'And you'll see her safe out of Brussels in the event of a defeat?'

'A defeat! D— it, sir, it's impossible. Don't try and frighten *me*,' the hero cried from his bed; and Dobbin's mind was thus perfectly set at ease now that Jos had spoken out so resolutely respecting his conduct to his sister. 'At least,' thought the captain, 'there will be a retreat secured for her in case the worst should ensue.'

If Captain Dobbin expected to get any personal comfort and satisfaction from having one more view of Amelia before the regiment marched away, his selfishness was punished just as such odious egotism deserved to be. The door of Jos's bedroom opened into the sitting-room which was common to the family party, and opposite this door was that of Amelia's chamber. The bugles had wakened everybody: there was no use in concealment now. George's servant was packing in this room: Osborne coming in and out of the contiguous bedroom, flinging to the man such articles as he thought fit to carry on the campaign. And presently Dobbin had the opportunity which his heart coveted, and he got sight of Amelia's face once more. But what a face it was! So white, so wild and despair-stricken, that the remembrance of it haunted him afterwards like a crime, and the sight smote him with inexpressible pangs of longing and pity.

She was wrapped in a white morning dress, her hair falling on her shoulders, and her large eyes fixed and without light. By way of helping on the preparations for the departure, and showing that she too could be useful at a moment so critical, this poor soul had taken up a sash of George's from the drawers whereon it lay, and followed him to and fro with the sash in her hand, looking on mutely as his packing proceeded. She came out and stood, learning at the wall, holding this sash against her bosom, from which the heavy net of crimson dropped like a large stain of blood.

Our gentle-hearted captain felt a guilty shock as he looked
at her. 'Good God,' thought he, 'and is it grief like this I
dared to pry into?' And there was no help: no means to
soothe and comfort this helpless, speechless misery. He stood
for a moment and looked at her, powerless and torn with
pity, as a parent regards an infant in pain.

At last, George took Emmy's hand, and led her back into
the bedroom, from whence he came out alone. The parting
had taken place in that moment, and he was gone.

'Thank Heaven that is over,' George thought, bounding
down the stair, his sword under his arm, and as he ran
swiftly to the alarm-ground, where the regiment was mus-
tered, and whither trooped men and officers hurrying from
their billets, his pulse was throbbing and his cheeks flushed:
the great game of war was going to be played, and he one
of the players. What a fierce excitement of doubt, hope, and
pleasure! What tremendous hazards of loss or gain! What
were all the games of chance he had ever played compared
to this one? Into all contests requiring athletic skill and
courage, the young man, from his boyhood upwards, had
flung himself with all his might. The champion of his school
and his regiment, the bravos of his companions had followed
him everywhere; from the boys' cricket-match to the gar-
rison-races, he had won a hundred of triumphs; and wherever
he went, women and men had admired and envied him.
What qualities are there for which a man gets so speedy a
return of applause, as those of bodily superiority, activity,
and valour? Time out of mind strength and courage have
been the theme of bards and romances; and from the story
of Troy down to to-day, poetry has always chosen a soldier
for a hero. I wonder is it because men are cowards in heart
that they admire bravery so much, and place military valour
so far beyond every other quality for reward and worship?

So, at the sound of that stirring call to battle, George
jumped away from the gentle arms in which he had been
dallying; not without a feeling of shame (although his wife's
hold on him had been but feeble), that he should have been
detained there so long. The same feeling of eagerness and
excitement was amongst all those friends of his of whom we
have had occasional glimpses, from the stout senior major,
who led the regiment into action, to little Stubble, the
ensign, who was to bear its colours on that day.

The sun was just rising as the march began – it was a gallant sight – the band led the column, playing the regimental march – then came the major in command, riding upon Pyramus, his stout charger – then marched the grenadiers, their captain at their head; in the centre were the colours, borne by the senior and junior ensigns – then George came marching at the head of his company. He looked up, and smiled at Amelia, and passed on; and even the sound of the music died away.

CHAPTER XXXI

IN WHICH JOS SEDLEY TAKES CARE OF HIS SISTER

THUS all the superior officers being summoned on duty elsewhere, Jos Sedley was left in command of the little colony at Brussels, with Amelia invalided, Isidor, his Belgian servant, and the *bonne*, who was maid-of-all-work for the establishment, as a garrison under him. Though he was disturbed in spirit, and his rest destroyed by Dobbin's interruption and the occurrences of the morning, Jos nevertheless remained for many hours in bed, wakeful and rolling about there until his usual hour of rising had arrived. The sun was high in the heavens, and our gallant friends of the –th miles on their march, before the civilian appeared in his flowered dressing-gown at breakfast.

About George's absence, his brother-in-law was very easy in mind. Perhaps Jos was rather pleased in his heart that Osborne was gone, for during George's presence, the other had played but a very secondary part in the household, and Osborne did not scruple to show his contempt for the stout civilian. But Emmy had always been good and attentive to him. It was she who ministered to his comforts, who superintended the dishes that he liked, who walked or rode with him (as she had many, too many, opportunities of doing, for where was George?) and who interposed her sweet face between his anger and her husband's scorn. Many timid remonstrances had she uttered to George in behalf of her brother, but the latter in his trenchant way cut these entreaties short. 'I'm an honest man,' he said, 'and if I have a feeling I show it, as an honest man will. How the deuce, my dear, would you have me behave respectfully to such a fool as your brother?' So Jos was pleased with George's absence. His plain hat and gloves on a sideboard, and the idea that the owner was away, caused Jos I don't know what secret thrill of pleasure. '*He* won't be troubling me this morning,' Jos thought, 'with his dandified airs and his impudence.'

'Put the captain's hat into the ante-room,' he said to Isidor, the servant.

'Perhaps he won't want it again,' replied the lackey, looking knowingly at his master. He hated George too, whose insolence towards him was quite of the English sort.

'And ask if madam is coming to breakfast,' Mr. Sedley said with great majesty, ashamed to enter with a servant upon the subject of his dislike for George. The truth is, he had abused his brother to the valet a score of times before.

Alas! madam could not come to breakfast, and cut the *tartines* that Mr. Jos liked. Madam was a great deal too ill, and had been in a frightful state ever since her husband's departure, so her *bonne* said. Jos showed his sympathy, by pouring her out a large cup of tea. It was his way of exhibiting kindness: and he improved on this; he not only sent her breakfast, but he bethought him what delicacies she would most like for dinner.

Isidor, the valet, had looked on very sulkily, while Osborne's servant was disposing of his master's baggage previous to the captain's departure: for in the first place he hated Mr. Osborne, whose conduct to him, and to all inferiors, was generally overbearing (nor does the continental domestic like to be treated with insolence as our own better-tempered servants do): and secondly, he was angry that so many valuables should be removed from under his hands, to fall into other people's possession when the English discomfiture should arrive. Of this defeat he and a vast number of other persons in Brussels and Belgium did not make the slightest doubt. The almost universal belief was, that the emperor would divide the Prussian and English armies, annihilate one after the other, and march into Brussels before three days were over: when all the movables of his present masters, who would be killed, or fugitives, or prisoners, would lawfully become the property of Monsieur Isidor.

As he helped Jos through his toilsome and complicated

daily toilette, this faithful servant would calculate what he should do with the very articles with which he was decorating his master's person. He would make a present of the silver essence-bottles and toilette knicknacks to a young lady of whom he was fond; and keep the English cutlery and the large ruby pin for himself. It would look very smart upon one of the fine frilled shirts, which, with the gold-laced cap and the frogged frock coat, that might easily be cut down to suit his shape, and the captain's gold-headed cane, and the great double ring with the rubies, which he would have made into a pair of beautiful ear-rings, he calculated would make a perfect Adonis of himself, and render Mademoiselle Reine an easy prey. 'How those sleeve-buttons will suit me,' thought he, as he fixed a pair on the fat pudgy wrists of Mr. Sedley. 'I long for sleeve-buttons; and the captain's boots with brass spurs, in the next room, *corbleu*, what an effect they will make in the Allée Verte!' So while Monsieur Isidor with bodily fingers was holding on to his master's nose, and shaving the lower part of Jos's face, his imagination was rambling along the Green Avenue, dressed out in a frogged coat and lace, and in company with Mademoiselle Reine; he was loitering in spirit on the banks, and examining the barges sailing slowly under the cool shadows of the trees by the canal, or refreshing himself with a mug of Faro at the bench of a beer-house on the road to Laeken.

But Mr. Joseph Sedley, luckily for his own peace, no more knew what was passing in his domestic's mind than the respected reader and I suspect what John or Mary, whose wages we pay, think of ourselves. What our servants think of us! – Did we know what our intimates and dear relations thought of us, we should live in a world that we should be glad to quit, and in a frame of mind and a constant terror, that would be perfectly unbearable. So Jos's man was marking his victim down, as you see one of Mr. Paynter's assistants in Leadenhall Street ornament an unconscious turtle with a placard on which is written, 'Soup to-morrow.'

Amelia's attendant was much less selfishly disposed. Few dependants could come near that kind and gentle creature without paying their usual tribute of loyalty and affection to her sweet and affectionate nature. And it is a fact that Pauline, the cook, consoled her mistress more than anybody whom she saw on this wretched morning; for when she found

how Amelia remained for hours, silent, motionless, and haggard, by the windows in which she had placed herself to
watch the last bayonets of the column as it marched away,
the honest girl took the lady's hand, and said, '*Tenez, madame,
est-ce qu'il n'est pas aussi à l'armée, mon homme à moi?*' with
which she burst into tears, and Amelia falling into her arms,
did likewise, and so each pitied and soothed the other.

Several times during the forenoon Mr. Jos's Isidor went
from his lodgings into the town, and to the gates of the
hotels and lodging-houses round about the Parc, where the
English were congregated, and there mingling with other
valets, couriers, and lackeys, gathered such news as was
abroad, and brought back bulletins for his master's information. Almost all these gentlemen were in heart partisans of
the emperor, and had their opinions about the speedy end
of the campaign. The emperor's proclamation from Avesnes
had been distributed everywhere plentifully in Brussels.
'Soldiers!' it said, 'this is the anniversary of Marengo and
Friedland, by which the destinies of Europe were twice
decided. Then, as after Austerlitz, as after Wagram, we were
too generous. We believed in the oaths and promises of
princes whom we suffered to remain upon their thrones. Let
us march once more to meet them. We and they, are we not
still the same men? Soldiers! these same Prussians who are
so arrogant to-day, were three to one against you at Jena,
and six to one at Montmirail. Those among you who were
prisoners in England can tell their comrades what frightful
torments they suffered on board the English hulks. Madmen!
a moment of prosperity has blinded them, and if they enter
into France it will be to find a grave there!' But the partisans
of the French prophesied a more speedy extermination of
the Emperor's enemies than this; and it was agreed on all
hands that Prussians and British would never return except
as prisoners in the rear of the conquering army.

These opinions in the course of the day were brought to
operate upon Mr. Sedley. He was told that the Duke of
Wellington had gone to try and rally his army, the advance
of which had been utterly crushed the night before.

'Crushed, psha!' said Jos, whose heart was pretty stout at
breakfast-time. 'The duke has gone to beat the emperor as
he has beaten all his generals before.'

'His papers are burned, his effects are removed, and his

quarters are being got ready for the Duke of Dalmatia.' Jos's informant replied. 'I had it from his own *maitre d'hôtel*. Milor Due de Richemont's people are packing up everything. His grace has fled already, and the duchess is only waiting to see the plate packed to join the King of France at Ostend.'

'The King of France is at Ghent, fellow,' replied Jos, affecting incredulity.

'He fled last night to Bruges, and embarks to-day from Ostend. The Duke de Berri is taken prisoner. Those who wish to be safe had better go soon, for the dykes will be open to-morrow, and who can fly when the whole country is under water?'

'Nonsense, sir, we are three to one, sir, against any force Boney can bring in the field,' Mr. Sedley objected; 'the Austrians and the Russians are on their march. He must, he shall be crushed,' Jos said, slapping his hand on the table.

'The Prussians were three to one at Jena, and he took their army and kingdom in a week. They were six to one at Montmirail, and he scattered them like sheep. The Austrian army *is* coming, but with the empress and the King of Rome at its head; and the Russians, bah! the Russians will withdraw. No quarter is to be given to the English, on account of their cruelty to our braves on board the infamous pontoons. Look here, here it is in black and white. Here's the proclamation of his majesty the emperor and king,' said the now declared partisan of Napoleon, and taking the document from his pocket, Isidor sternly thrust it into his master's face, and already looked upon the frogged coat and valuables as his own spoil.

Jos was, if not seriously alarmed as yet, at least considerably disturbed in mind. 'Give me my coat and cap sir,' said he, 'and follow me. I will go myself and learn the truth of these reports.' Isidor was furious as Jos put on the braided frock. 'Milor had better not wear that military coat,' said he; 'the Frenchmen have sworn not to give quarter to a single British soldier.'

'Silence, sirrah!' said Jos, with a resolute countenance still and thrust his arm into the sleeve with indomitable resolution, in the performance of which heroic act he was found by Mrs. Rawdon Crawley, who at this juncture came up to visit Amelia, and entered without ringing at the ante-chamber door.

Rebecca was dressed very neatly and smartly, as usual: her quiet sleep after Rawdon's departure had refreshed her, and her pink smiling cheeks were quite pleasant to look at, in a town and on a day when everybody else's countenance wore the appearance of the deepest anxiety and gloom. She laughed at the attitude in which Jos was discovered, and the struggles and convulsions with which the stout gentleman thrust himself into the braided coat.

'Are you preparing to join the army, Mr. Joseph?' she said. 'Is there to be nobody left in Brussels to protect us poor women?' Jos succeeded in plunging into the coat, and came forward blushing and stuttering out excuses to his fair visitor. 'How was she after the events of the morning – after the fatigues of the ball the night before?' Monsieur Isidor disappeared into his master's adjacent bedroom, bearing off the flowered dressing-gown.

'How good of you to ask,' said she, pressing one of his hands in both her own. 'How cool and collected you look when everybody else is frightened! How is our dear little Emmy? It must have been an awful, awful parting.'

'Tremendous,' Jos said.

'You men can bear anything,' replied the lady. 'Parting or danger are nothing to you. Own now that you were going to join the army and leave us to our fate. I know you were – something tells me you were. I was so frightened, when the thought came into my head (for I do sometimes think of you when I'm alone, Mr. Joseph!), that I ran off immediately to beg and entreat you not to fly from us.'

This speech might be interpreted, 'My dear sir, should an accident befall the army, and a retreat be necessary, you have a very comfortable carriage, in which I propose to take a seat.' I don't know whether Jos understood the words in this sense. But he was profoundly mortified by the lady's inattention to him during their stay at Brussels. He had never been presented to any of Rawdon Crawley's great acquaintances: he had scarcely been invited to Rebecca's parties; for he was too timid to play much, and his presence bored George and Rawdon equally, who neither of them, perhaps, liked to have a witness of the amusements in which the pair chose to indulge. 'Ah!' thought Jos, 'now she wants me she comes to me. When there is nobody else in the way she can think about old Joseph Sedley!' But besides these doubts he felt flattered at the idea Rebecca expressed of his courage.

He blushed a good deal, and put on an air of importance. 'I should like to see the action,' he said. 'Every man of any spirit would, you know. I've seen a little service in India, but nothing on this grand scale.'

'You men would sacrifice anything for a pleasure,' Rebecca answered. 'Captain Crawley left me this morning as gay as if he were going to a hunting-party. What does he care? What do any of you care for the agonies and tortures of a poor forsaken woman? (I wonder whether he *could* really have been going to the troops, this great lazy gourmand?) Oh! dear Mr. Sedley, I have come to you for comfort – for consolation. I have been on my knees all the morning. I tremble at the frightful danger into which our husbands, our friends, our brave troops and allies, are rushing. And I come here for shelter, and find another of my friends – the last remaining to me – bent upon plunging into the dreadful scene!'

'My dear madam,' Jos replied, now beginning to be quite soothed. 'Don't be alarmed. I only said I should like to go – what Briton would not? But my duty keeps me here: I can't leave that poor creature in the next room.' And he pointed with his finger to the door of the chamber in which Amelia was.

'Good noble brother!' Rebecca said, putting her handkerchief to her eyes, and smelling the eau-de-Cologne with which it was scented. 'I have done you injustice: you have got a heart. I thought you had not.'

'Oh, upon my honour!' Jos said, making a motion as if he would lay his hand upon the spot in question. 'You do me injustice, indeed you do – my dear Mrs. Crawley.'

'I do, now your heart is true to your sister. But I remember two years ago – when it was false to me!' Rebecca said, fixing her eyes upon him for an instant, and then turning away into the window.

Jos blushed violently. That organ which he was accused by Rebecca of not possessing began to thump tumultuously. He recalled the days when he had fled from her, and the passion which had once inflamed him – the days when he had driven her in his curricle: when she had knit the green purse for him: when he had sat enraptured gazing at her white arms and bright eyes.

'I know you think me ungrateful,' Rebecca continued, coming out of the window, and once more looking at him and addressing him in a low tremulous voice. 'Your coldness, your averted looks, your manner when we have met of late – when I came in just now, all proved it to me. But were there no reasons why I should avoid you? Let your own heart answer that question. Do you think my husband was too much inclined to welcome you? The only unkind words I have ever had from him (I will do Captain Crawley that justice) have been about you – and most cruel, cruel words they were.'

'Good gracious! what have I done?' asked Jos in a flurry of pleasure and perplexity; 'what have I done – to – to —?'

'Is jealousy nothing?' said Rebecca. 'He makes me miserable about you. And whatever it might have been once – my heart is all his. I am innocent now. Am I not, Mr. Sedley?'

All Jos's blood tingled with delight, as he surveyed this victim to his attractions. A few adroit words, one or two knowing tender glances of the eyes, and his heart was inflamed again and his doubts and suspicious forgotten. From Solomon downwards, have not wiser men than he been cajoled and befooled by women? 'If the worst comes to the worst,' Becky thought, 'my retreat is secure; and I have a right-hand seat in the barouche.'

There is no knowing into what declarations of love and ardour the tumultuous passions of Mr. Joseph might have led him, if Isidor the valet had not made his reappearance at this minute, and begun to busy himself about the domestic affairs. Jos, who was just going to gasp out an avowal, choked almost with the emotion that he was obliged to restrain. Rebecca too bethought her that it was time she should go in and comfort her dearest Amelia. '*Au revoir*,' she said, kissing her hand to Mr. Joseph, and tapped gently at the door of his sister's apartment. As she entered and closed the door on herself, he sank down in a chair, and gazed and sighed and puffed portentously. 'That coat is very tight for Milor,' Isidor said, still having his eye on the frogs; but his master heard him not: his thoughts were elsewhere: now glowing, maddening, upon the contemplation of the enchanting Rebecca: anon shrinking guiltily before the vision of the jealous Rawdon Crawley, with his curling, fierce moustachios, and his terrible duelling pistols loaded and cocked.

Rebecca's appearance struck Amelia with terror, and made her shrink back. It recalled her to the world and the remembrance of yesterday. In the overpowering fears about to-morrow she had forgotten Rebecca, – jealousy – everything except that her husband was gone and was in danger. Until this dauntless worldling came in and broke the spell, and lifted the latch, we too have forborne to enter into that sad chamber. How long had that poor girl been on her knees! what hours of speechless prayer and bitter prostration had she passed there! The war-chroniclers who write brilliant stories of fight and triumph scarcely tell us of these. These are too mean parts of the pageant: and you don't hear widows' cries or mothers' sobs in the midst of the shouts and jubilation in the great Chorus of Victory. And yet when was the time, that such have not cried out: heart-broken, humble protestants, unheard in the uproar of the triumph!

After the first movement of terror in Amelia's mind – when Rebecca's green eyes lighted upon her, and rustling in her fresh silks and brilliant ornaments, the latter tripped up with extended arms to embrace her – a feeling of anger succeeded, and from being deadly pale before, her face flushed up red, and she returned Rebecca's look after a moment with a steadiness which surprised and somewhat abashed her rival.

'Dearest Amelia, you are very unwell,' the visitor said, putting forth her hand to take Amelia's. 'What is it? I could not rest until I knew how you were.'

Amelia drew back her hand – never since her life began had that gentle soul refused to believe or to answer any demonstration of goodwill or affection. But she drew back her hand, and trembled all over. 'Why are *you* here, Rebecca?' she said, still looking at her solemnly with her large eyes. These glances troubled her visitor.

'She must have seen him give me the letter at the ball,' Rebecca thought. 'Don't be agitated, dear Amelia,' she said, looking down. 'I came but to see if I could – if you were well.'

'Are you well?' said Amelia. 'I dare say you are. You don't love your husband. You would not be here if you did. Tell me, Rebecca, did I ever do you anything but kindness?'

'Indeed, Amelia, no,' the other said, still hanging down her head.

'When you were quite poor, who was it that befriended you? Was I not a sister to you? You saw us all in happier days before he married me. I was all in all then to him; or would he have given up his fortune, his family, as he nobly did to make me happy? Why did you come between my love and me? Who sent you to separate those whom God joined, and take my darling's heart from me – my own husband? Do you think you could love him as I did? His love was everything to me. You knew it, and wanted to rob me of it. For shame, Rebecca; bad and wicked woman – false friend and false wife.'

'Amelia, I protest before God, I have done my husband no wrong,' Rebecca said, turning from her.

'Have you done *me* no wrong, Rebecca? You did not succeed, but you tried. Ask your heart if you did not?'

She knows nothing, Rebecca thought.

'He came back to me. I knew he would. I knew that no falsehood, no flattery, could keep him from me long. I knew he would come. I prayed so that he should.'

The poor girl spoke these words with a spirit and volubility which Rebecca had never before seen in her, and before which the latter was quite dumb. 'But what have I done to you,' she continued in a more pitiful tone, 'that you should try and take him from me? I had him but for six weeks. You might have spared me those, Rebecca. And yet, from the very first day of our wedding, you came and blighted it. Now he is gone, are you come to see how unhappy I am?' She continued, 'You made me wretched enough for the past fortnight: you might have spared me to-day.'

'I – I never came here,' interposed Rebecca, with unlucky truth.

'No. You didn't come. You took him away. Are you come to fetch him from me?' she continued in a wilder tone. 'He was here, but he is gone now. There on that very sofa he sat. Don't touch it. We sat and talked there. I was on his knee, and my arms were round his neck, and we said, "Our Father." Yes, he was here: and they came and took him away, but he promised me to come back.'

'He will come back, my dear,' said Rebecca, touched in spite of herself.

'Look,' said Amelia, 'this is his sash – isn't it a pretty colour?' and she took up the fringe and kissed it. She had tied it round her waist at some part of the day. She had forgotten her anger, her jealousy, the very presence of her rival seemingly. For she walked silently and almost with a smile on her face, towards the bed, and began to smooth down George's pillow.

Rebecca walked, too, silently away. 'How is Amelia?' asked Jos, who still held his position in the chair.

'There should be somebody with her,' said Rebecca. 'I think she is very unwell:' and she went away with a very grave face, refusing Mr. Sedley's entreaties that she would stay and partake of the early dinner which he had ordered.

Rebecca was of a good-natured and obliging disposition; and she liked Amelia rather than otherwise. Even her hard words, reproachful as they were, were complimentary – the groans of a person stinging under defeat. Meeting Mrs. O'Dowd, whom the dean's sermons had by no means comforted, and who was walking very disconsolately in the Parc, Rebecca accosted the latter, rather to the surprise of the major's wife, who was not accustomed to such marks of politeness from Mrs. Rawdon Crawley, and informing her that poor little Mrs. Osborne was in a desperate condition, and almost mad with grief, sent off the good-natured Irishwoman straight to see if she could console her young favourite.

'I've cares of my own enough,' Mrs. O'Dowd said, gravely, 'and I thought poor Amelia would be little wanting for company this day. But if she's so bad as you say, and you can't attend to her, who used to be so fond of her, faith I'll see if I can be of service. And so good marning to ye, madam;' with which speech and a toss of her head, the lady of the repayther took a farewell of Mrs. Crawley, whose company she by no means courted.

Becky watched her marching off, with a smile on her lip. She had the keenest sense of humour, and the Parthian look which the retreating Mrs. O'Dowd flung over her shoulder almost upset Mrs. Crawley's gravity. 'My service to ye, me fine madam, and I'm glad to see ye so cheerful,' thought Peggy. 'It's not *you* that will cry your eyes out with grief, anyway.' And with this she passed on, and speedily found her way to Mrs. Osborne's lodgings.

The poor soul was still at the bedside, where Rebecca had left her, and stood almost crazy with grief. The major's wife, a stronger-minded woman, endeavoured her best to comfort her young friend. 'You must bear up, Amelia, dear,' she said kindly, 'for he mustn't find you ill when he sends for you after the victory. It's not you are the only woman that are in the hands of God this day.'

'I know that. I am very wicked, very weak,' Amelia said. She knew her own weakness well enough. The presence of the more resolute friend checked it, however; and she was the better of this control and company. They went on till two o'clock; their hearts were with the column as it marched farther and farther away. Dreadful doubt and anguish – prayers and fears and griefs unspeakable – followed the regiment. It was the women's tribute to the war. It taxes both alike, and takes the blood of the men, and the tears of the women.

At half-past two an event occurred of daily importance to Mr. Joseph: the dinner hour arrived. Warriors may fight and perish, but he must dine. He came into Amelia's room to see if he could coax her to share that meal. 'Try,' said he; 'the soup is very good. Do try, Emmy,' and he kissed her hand. Except when she was married, he had not done so much for years before. 'You are very good and kind, Joseph,' she said. 'Everybody is, but, if you please, I will stay in my room to-day.'

The savour of the soup, however, was agreeable to Mrs. O'Dowd's nostrils: and she thought she would bear Mr. Jos company. So the two sat down to their meal. 'God bless the meat,' said the major's wife, solemnly: she was thinking of her honest Mick, riding at the head of his regiment: ' 'Tis but a bad dinner those poor boys will get to-day,' she said, with a sigh, and then, like a philosopher, fell to.

Jos's spirits rose with his meal. He would drink the regiment's health; or, indeed, take any other excuse to indulge in a glass of champagne. 'We'll drink to O'Dowd and the brave –th,' said he, bowing gallantly to his guest. 'Hey, Mrs. O'Dowd. Fill Mrs. O'Dowd's glass, Isidor.'

But all of a sudden, Isidor started, and the major's wife laid down her knife and fork. The windows of the room were open, and looked southward, and a dull distant sound came over the sun-lighted roofs from that direction. 'What is it?' said Jos. 'Why don't you pour, you rascal?'

'*C'est le feu!*' said Isidor, running to the balcony.

'God defend us; it's cannon!' Mrs. O'Dowd cried, starting up, and followed too to the window. A thousand pale and anxious faces might have been seen looking from other casements. And presently it seemed as if the whole population of the city rushed into the streets.

CHAPTER XXXII

IN WHICH JOS TAKES FLIGHT, AND THE WAR IS BROUGHT TO A CLOSE

W E of peaceful London City have never beheld – and please God never shall witness – such a scene of hurry and alarm, as that which Brussels presented. Crowds rushed to the Namur gate, from which direction the noise proceeded, and many rode along the level *chaussée*, to be in advance of any intelligence from the army. Each man asked his neighbour for news; and even great English lords and ladies condescended to speak to persons whom they did not know. The friends of the French went abroad, wild with excitement, and prophesying the triumph of their emperor. The merchants closed their shops, and came out to swell the general chorus of alarm and clamour. Women rushed to the churches, and crowded the chapels, and knelt and prayed on the flags and steps. The dull sound of the cannon went on rolling, rolling. Presently carriages with travellers began to leave the town, galloping away by the Ghent barrier. The prophecies of the French partisans began to pass for facts. 'He has cut the armies in two,' it was said. 'He is marching straight on Brussels. He will overpower the English, and be here to-night.' 'He will overpower the English,' shrieked Isidor to his master, 'and will be here to-night.' The man bounded in and out from the lodgings to the street, always returning with some fresh particulars of disaster. Jos's face grew paler and paler. Alarm began to take entire possession of the stout civilian. All the champagne he drank brought no courage to him. Before sunset he was worked up to such a pitch of nervousness as gratified his friend Isidor to behold, who now counted surely upon the spoils of the owner of the laced coat.

The women were away all this time. After hearing the firing for a moment, the stout major's wife bethought her of her friend in the next chamber, and ran in to watch, and if possible to console, Amelia. The idea that she had that helpless and gentle creature to protect, gave additional strength to the natural courage of the honest Irishwoman. She passed five hours by her friend's side, sometimes in remonstrance, sometimes talking cheerfully, oftener in silence, and terrified mental supplication. 'I never let go her hand once,' said the stout lady afterwards, 'until after sunset, when the firing was over.' Pauline, the *bonne*, was on her knees at church hard by, praying for *son homme à elle*.

When the noise of the cannonading was over, Mrs. O'Dowd issued out of Amelia's room into the parlour adjoining, where Jos sat with two emptied flasks, and courage entirely gone. Once or twice he had ventured into his sister's bedroom, looking very much alarmed, and as if he would say something. But the major's wife kept her place, and he went away without disburthening himself of his speech. He was ashamed to tell her that he wanted to fly.

But when she made her appearance in the dining-room, where he sat in the twilight in the cheerless company of his empty champagne-bottles, he began to open his mind to her.

'Mrs. O'Dowd,' he said, 'hadn't you better get Amelia ready?'

'Are you going to take her out a walk?' said the major's lady; 'sure she's too weak to stir.'

'I – I've ordered the carriage,' he said, 'and – and post-horses; Isidor is gone for them,' Jos continued.

'What do you want with driving to-night?' answered the lady. 'Isn't she better on her bed? I've just got her to lie down.'

'Get her up,' said Jos; 'she must get up, I say:' and he stamped his foot energetically. 'I say the horses are ordered – yes, the horses are ordered. It's all over, and —'

'And what?' asked Mrs. O'Dowd.

'I'm off for Ghent,' Jos answered. 'Everybody is going; there's a place for you! We shall start in half an hour.'

The major's wife looked at him with infinite scorn. 'I don't move till O'Dowd gives me the route,' said she. 'You may go if you like, Mr. Sedley; but, faith, Amelia and I stop here.'

'She *shall* go,' said Jos, with another stamp of his foot.

Mrs. O'Dowd put herself with arms akimbo before the bedroom door.

'Is it her mother you're going to take her to?' she said; 'or do you want to go to mamma yourself, Mr. Sedley? Good marning – a pleasant journey to ye, sir. *Bon voyage*, as they say, and take my counsel, and shave off them moustachios, or they'll bring you into mischief.'

'D–n!' yelled out Jos, wild with fear, rage, and mortification; and Isidor came in at this juncture, swearing in his turn. '*Pas de chevaux, sacrebleu!*' hissed out the furious domestic. All the horses were gone. Jos was not the only man in Brussels seized with panic that day.

But Jos's fears, great and cruel as they were already, were destined to increase to an almost frantic pitch before the night was over. It has been mentioned how Pauline, the *bonne*, had *son homme à elle*, also in the ranks of the army that had gone out to meet the Emperor Napoleon, This lover was a native of Brussels, and a Belgian hussar. The troops of his nation signalized themselves in this war for anything but courage, and young Van Cutsum, Pauline's admirer, was too good a soldier to disobey his colonel's orders to run away. Whilst in garrison at Brussels young Regulus (he had been born in the revolutionary times) found his great comfort, and passed almost all his leisure moments in Pauline's kitchen; and it was with pockets and holsters crammed full of good things from her larder, that he had taken leave of his weeping sweetheart, to proceed upon the campaign a few days before.

As far as his regiment was concerned, this campaign was over now. They had formed a part of the division under the command of his sovereign apparent, the Prince of Orange, and as respected length of swords and moustachios, and the richness of uniform and equipments, Regulus and his comrades looked to be as gallant a body of men as ever trumpets sounded for.

When Ney dashed upon the advance of the allied troops, carrying one position after the other, until the arrival of the great body of the British army from Brussels changed the aspect of the combat of Quatre Bras, the squadrons among which Regulus rode showed the greatest activity in retreating before the French, and were dislodged from one post and another which they occupied with perfect alacrity on their part. Their movements were only checked by the advance of the British in their rear. Thus forced to halt, the enemy's cavalry (whose bloodthirsty obstinacy cannot be too severely reprehended) had at length an opportunity of coming to close quarters with the brave Belgians before them; who preferred to encounter the British rather than the French, and at once turning tail, rode through the English regiments that were behind them, and scattered in all directions. The regiment, in fact, did not exist any more. It was nowhere. It had no head-quarters. Regulus found himself galloping many miles from the field of action, entirely alone; and whither should he fly for refuge so naturally as to that kitchen and those faithful arms in which Pauline had so often welcomed him?

At some ten o'clock the clinking of a sabre might have been heard up the stair of the house where the Osbornes occupied a story in the Continental fashion. A knock might have been heard at the kitchen door; and poor Pauline, come back from church, fainted almost with terror as she opened it and saw before her her haggard hussar. He looked as pale as the midnight dragoon who came to disturb Leonora. Pauline would have screamed, but that her cry would have called her masters, and discovered her friend. She stifled her scream, then, and leading her hero into the kitchen, gave him beer, and the choice bits from the dinner, which Jos had not had the heart to taste. The hussar showed he was no ghost by the prodigious quantity of flesh and beer which he devoured – and during the mouthfuls he told his tale of disaster.

His regiment had performed prodigies of courage, and had withstood for a while the onset of the whole French army. But they were overwhelmed at last, as was the whole British army by this time. Ney destroyed each regiment as it came up. The Belgians in vain interposed to prevent the butchery of the English. The Brunswickers were routed and had fled – their duke was killed. It was a general *débâcle*. He sought to drown his sorrow for the defeat in floods of beer.

Isidor, who had come into the kitchen, heard the conversation and rushed out to inform his master. 'It is all over,' he shrieked to Jos. 'Milor duke is a prisoner; the Duke of Brunswick is killed; the British army is in full flight; there is only one man escaped, and he is in the kitchen now –

come and hear him.' So Jos tottered into that apartment
where Regulus still sat on the kitchen-table, and clung fast
to his flagon of beer. In the best French which he could
muster, and which was in sooth of a very ungrammatical
sort, Jos besought the hussar to tell his tale. The disasters
deepened as Regulus spoke. He was the only man of his
regiment not slain on the field. He had seen the Duke of
Brunswick fall, the black hussars fly, the Écossais pounded
down by the cannon.

'And the –th?' gasped Jos.

'Cut in pieces,' said the hussar – upon which Pauline
crying out, 'Oh, my mistress, *ma bonne petite dame*,' went
off fairly into hysterics, and filled the house with her
screams.

Wild with terror, Mr. Sedley knew not how or where to
seek for safety. He rushed from the kitchen back to the
sitting-room, and cast an appealing look at Amelia's door,
which Mrs. O'Dowd had closed and locked in his face; but
he remembered how scornfully the latter had received him,
and after pausing and listening for a brief space at the door,
he left it, and resolved to go into the street, for the first
time that day. So, seizing a candle, he looked about for his
gold-laced cap, and found it lying in its usual place, on a
console-table, in the ante-room, placed before a mirror at
which Jos used to coquet, always giving his side-locks a twirl,
and his cap the proper cock over his eye, before he went
forth to make appearance in public. Such is the force of habit,
that even in the midst of his terror he began mechanically
to twiddle with his hair, and arrange the cock of his hat.
Then he looked amazed at the pale face in the glass before
him, and especially at his moustachios, which had attained
a rich growth in the course of near seven weeks, since they
had come into the world. They *will* mistake me for a military
man, thought he, remembering Isidor's warning, as to the
massacre with which all the defeated British army was
threatened; and staggering back to his bedchamber, he began
wildly pulling the bell which summoned his valet.

Isidor answered that summons. Jos had sunk in a chair
– he had torn off his neck-cloths, and turned down his
collars, and was sitting with both his hands lifted to his
throat.

'*Coupez-moi*, Isidor,' shouted he; '*vite! coupez-moi!*'

Isidor thought for a moment he had gone mad, and that he wished his valet to cut his throat.

'*Les moustaches*,' gasped Jos; '*les moustaches – coupy, rasy, vite!*' – his French was of this sort – voluble, as we have said, but not remarkable for grammar.

Isidor swept off the moustachios in no time with the razor, and heard with inexpressible delight his master's orders that he should fetch a hat and a plain coat. '*Ne porty ploo – habit militair – bonny – donny à voo, prenny dehors*' – were Jos's words, – the coat and cap were at last his property.

This gift being made, Jos selected a plain black coat and waistcoat from his stock, and put on a large white neck-cloth, and a plain beaver. If he could have got a shovel-hat he would have worn it. As it was, you would have fancied he was a flourishing, large parson of the Church of England.

'*Venny maintenong*,' he continued, '*sweevy – ally – party – dong la roo.*' And so having said, he plunged swiftly down the stairs of the house, and passed into the street.

Although Regulus had vowed that he was the only man of his regiment or of the allied army, almost, who had escaped being cut to pieces by Ney, it appeared that his statement was incorrect, and that a good number more of the supposed victims had survived the massacre. Many scores of Regulus's comrades had found their way back to Brussels, and – all agreeing that they had run away – filled the whole town with an idea of the defeat of the allies. The arrival of the French was expected hourly; the panic continued, and preparations for flight went on everywhere. No horses! thought Jos, in terror. He made Isidor inquire of scores of persons, whether they had any to lend or sell, and his heart sank within him, at the negative answers returned everywhere. Should he take the journey on foot? Even fear could not render that ponderous body so active.

Almost all the hotels occupied by the English in Brussels face the Parc, and Jos wandered irresolutely about in this quarter, with crowds of other people, oppressed as he was by fear and curiosity. Some families he saw more happy than himself, having discovered a team of horses, and rattling through the streets in retreat; others again there were whose case was like his own, and who could not for any bribes or entreaties procure the necessary means of flight. Amongst these would-be fugitives, Jos remarked the Lady Bareacres and her daughter, who sat in their carriage in the *porte-cochère* of their hotel, all their imperials packed, and the only drawback to whose flight was the same want of motive power which kept Jos stationary.

Rebecca Crawley occupied apartments in this hotel; and had before this period had sundry hostile meetings with the ladies of the Bareacres family. My Lady Bareacres cut Mrs. Crawley on the stairs when they met by chance; and in all places where the latter's name was mentioned, spoke perseveringly ill of her neighbour. The countess was shocked at the familiarity of General Tufto with the aide de camp's wife. The Lady Blanche avoided her as if she had been an infectious disease. Only the earl himself kept up a sly occasional acquaintance with her, when out of the jurisdiction of his ladies.

Rebecca had her revenge now upon these insolent enemies. It became known in the hotel that Captain Crawley's horses had been left behind, and when the panic began, Lady Bareacres condescended to send her maid to the captain's wife with her ladyship's compliments, and a desire to know the price of Mrs. Crawley's horses. Mrs. Crawley returned a note with her compliments, and an intimation that it was not her custom to transact bargains with ladies' maids.

This curt reply brought the earl in person to Becky's apartment; but he could get no more success than the first ambassador. 'Send a lady's maid to *me!*' Mrs. Crawley cried in great anger; 'why didn't my Lady Bareacres tell me to go and saddle the horses! Is it her ladyship that wants to escape, or her ladyship's *femme de chambre?*' And this was all the answer that the earl bore back to his countess.

What will not necessity do? The countess herself actually came to wait upon Mrs. Crawley on the failure of her second envoy. She entreated her to name her own price; she even offered to invite Becky to Bareacres House, if the latter would but give her the means of returning to that residence. Mrs. Crawley sneered at her.

'I don't want to be waited on by bailiffs in livery.' she said; 'you will never get back though most probably – at least not you and your diamonds together. The French will have those. They will be here in two hours, and I shall be half-way to Ghent by that time. I would not sell you my horses, no, not for the two largest diamonds that your ladyship wore at the ball.' Lady Bareacres trembled with rage and terror. The diamonds were sewed into her habit, and secreted in my lord's padding and boots. 'Woman, the diamonds are at the banker's, and I *will* have the horses,' she said. Rebecca laughed in her face. The infuriate countess went below, and sat in her carriage; her maid, her courier, and her husband were sent once more through the town, each to look for cattle; and woe betide those who came last! Her ladyship was resolved on departing the very instant the horses arrived from any quarter – with her husband or without him.

Rebecca had the pleasure of seeing her ladyship in the horseless carriage, and keeping her eyes fixed upon her, and bewailing, in the loudest tone of voice, the countess's perplexities. 'Not to be able to get horses!' she said, 'and to have all those diamonds sewed into the carriage cushions! What a prize it will be for the French when they come! – the carriage and the diamonds I mean; not the lady!' She gave this information to the landlord, to the servants, to the guests, and the innumerable stragglers about the courtyard. Lady Bareacres could have shot her from the carriage-window.

It was while enjoying the humiliation of her enemy that Rebecca caught sight of Jos, who made towards her directly he perceived her.

That altered, frightened, fat face, told his secret well enough. He too wanted to fly, and was on the look-out for the means of escape. '*He* shall buy my horses,' thought Rebecca, 'and I'll ride the mare.'

Jos walked up to his friend, and put the question for the hundredth time during the past hour, 'Did she know where horses were to be had?'

'What, *you* fly?' said Rebecca, with a laugh. 'I thought you were the champion of all the ladies, Mr. Sedley.'

'I – I'm not a military man.' gasped he.

'And Amelia? – Who is to protect that poor little sister of yours?' asked Rebecca. 'You surely would not desert her?'

'What good can I do her, suppose – suppose the enemy arrive?' Jos answered. 'They'll spare the women; but my man tells me that they have taken an oath to give no quarter to the men – the dastardly cowards.'

'Horrid!' cried Rebecca, enjoying his perplexity.

'Besides, I don't want to desert her,' cried the brother. 'She *shan't* be deserted. There is a seat for her in my carriage, and one for you, dear Mrs. Crawley, if you will come; and if we can get horses —' sighed he –

'I have two to sell,' the lady said. Jos could have flung himself into her arms at the news. 'Get the carriage, Isidor,' he cried; 'we've found them – we have found them.'

'My horses never were in harness,' added the lady. 'Bulfinch would kick the carriage to pieces, if you put him in the traces.'

'But he is quiet to ride?' asked the civilian.

'As quiet as a lamb, and as fast as a hare,' answered Rebecca.

'Do you think he is up to my weight?' Jos said. He was already on his back, in imagination, without ever so much as a thought for poor Amelia. What person who loved a horse-speculation could resist such a temptation?

In reply, Rebecca asked him to come into her room, whither he followed her quite breathless to conclude the bargain. Jos seldom spent a half-hour in his life which cost him so much money. Rebecca, measuring the value of the goods which she had for sale by Jos's eagerness to purchase, as well as by the scarcity of the article, put upon her horses a price so prodigious as to make even the civilian draw back. 'She would sell both or neither,' she said resolutely. Rawdon had ordered her not to part with them for a price less than that which she specified. Lord Bareacres below would give her the same money – and with all her love and regard for the Sedley family, her dear Mr. Joseph must conceive that poor people must live – nobody, in a word, could be more affectionate, but more firm about the matter of business.

Jos ended by agreeing, as might be supposed of him. The sum he had to give her was so large that he was obliged to ask for time; so large as to be a little fortune to Rebecca, who rapidly calculated that with this sum, and the sale of the residue of Rawdon's effects, and her pension as a widow should he fall, she would now be absolutely independent of the world, and might look her weeds steadily in the face.

Once or twice in the day she certainly had herself thought about flying. But her reason gave her better counsel. 'Suppose the French do come,' thought Becky, 'what can they do to a poor officer's widow? Bah! the times of sacks and sieges are over. We shall be let to go home quietly, or I may live pleasantly abroad with a snug little income.'

Meanwhile Jos and Isidor went off to the stables to inspect the newly-purchased cattle. Jos bade his man saddle the horses at once. He would ride away that very night, that very hour. And he left the valet busy in getting the horses ready, and went homewards himself to prepare for his departure. It must be secret. He would go to his chamber by the back entrance. He did not care to face Mrs. O'Dowd and Amelia, and own to them that he was about to run.

By the time Jos's bargain with Rebecca was completed, and his horses had been visited and examined, it was almost morning once more. But though midnight was long passed, there was no rest for the city; the people were up, the lights in the houses flamed, crowds were still about the doors, and the streets were busy. Rumours of various natures went still from mouth to mouth: one report averred that the Prussians had been utterly defeated; another that it was the English who had been attacked and conquered: a third that the latter had held their ground. This last rumour gradually got strength. No Frenchmen had made their appearance. Stragglers had come in from the army bringing reports more and more favourable: at last an aide de camp actually reached Brussels with dispatches for the commandant of the place, who placarded presently through the town an official announcement of the success of the allies at Quatre Bras, and the entire repulse of the French under Ney after a six hours' battle. The aide de camp must have arrived some time while Jos and Rebecca were making their bargain together, or the latter was inspecting his purchase. When he reached his own hotel, he found a score of its numerous inhabitants on the threshold discoursing of the news; there was no doubt as to its truth. And he went up to communicate it to the ladies under his charge. He did not think it was necessary to tell them how he had intended to take leave of them, how he had bought horses, and what a price he had paid for them.

But success or defeat was a minor matter to them, who had only thought for the safety of those they loved. Amelia, at the news of the victory, became still more agitated even than before. She was for going that moment to the army. She besought her brother with tears to conduct her thither. Her doubts and terrors reached their paroxysm; and the poor girl, who for many hours had been plunged into stupor, raved and ran hither and thither in hysteric insanity – a piteous sight. No man writhing in pain on the hard-fought field fifteen miles off, where lay, after their struggles, so many of the brave – no man suffered more keenly than this poor harmless victim of the war. Jos could not bear the sight of her pain. He left his sister in the charge of her stouter female companion, and descended once more to the threshold of the hotel, where everybody still lingered, and talked, and waited for more news.

It grew to be broad daylight as they stood here, and fresh news began to arrive from the war, brought by men who had been actors in the scene. Wagons and long country carts laden with wounded came rolling into the town; ghastly groans came from within them, and haggard faces looked up sadly from out of the straw. Jos Sedley was looking at one of these carriages with a painful curiosity – the moans of the people within were frightful – the wearied horses could hardly pull the cart. 'Stop! stop!' a feeble voice cried from the straw, and the carriage stopped opposite Mr. Sedley's hotel.

'It is George, I know it is!' cried Amelia, rushing in a moment to the balcony, with a pallid face and loose flowing hair. It was not George, however, but it was the next best thing: it was news of him.

It was poor Tom Stubble, who had marched out of Brussels so gallantly twenty-four hours before, bearing the colours of the regiment, which he had defended very gallantly upon the field. A French lancer had speared the young ensign in the leg, who fell, still bravely holding to his flag. At the conclusion of the engagement, a place had been found for the poor boy in a cart, and he had been brought back to Brussels.

'Mr. Sedley, Mr. Sedley!' cried the boy, faintly, and Jos came up almost frightened at the appeal. He had not at first distinguished who it was that called him.

Little Tom Stubble held out his hot and feeble hand. 'I'm to be taken in here,' he said. 'Osborne – and – and Dobbin said I was; and you are to give the man two napoleons: my mother will pay you.' This young fellow's thoughts, during the long feverish hours passed in the cart, had been wandering to his father's parsonage which he had

quitted only a few months before, and he had sometimes
forgotten his pain in that delirium.

The hotel was large, and the people kind, and all the
inmates of the cart were taken in and placed on various
couches. The young ensign was conveyed upstairs to Osborne's
quarters. Amelia and the major's wife had rushed down to
him, when the latter had recognized him from the balcony.
You may fancy the feelings of these women when they were
told that the day was over, and both their husbands were
safe; in what mute rapture Amelia fell on her good friend's
neck, and embraced her; in what a grateful passion of prayers
she fell on her knees, and thanked the Power which had
saved her husband.

Our young lady, in her fevered and nervous condition,
could have had no more salutary medicine prescribed for her
by any physician than that which chance put in her way.
She and Mrs. O'Dowd watched incessantly by the wounded
lad, whose pains were very severe, and in the duty thus
forced upon her, Amelia had not time to brood over her
personal anxieties, or to give herself up to her own fears and
forebodings after her wont. The young patient told in his
simple fashion the events of the day, and the actions of
our friends of the gallant –th. They had suffered severely.
They had lost very many officers and men. The major's
horse had been shot under him as the regiment charged, and
they all thought that O'Dowd was gone, and that Dobbin
had got his majority, until on their return from the charge
to their old ground, the major was discovered seated on
Pyramus's carcass, refreshing himself from a case-bottle. It
was Captain Osborne that cut down the French lancer who
had speared the ensign. Amelia turned so pale at the notion
that Mrs. O'Dowd stopped the young ensign in this story.
And it was Captain Dobbin who at the end of the day,
though wounded himself, took up the lad in his arms and
carried him to the surgeon, and thence to the cart which
was to bring him back to Brussels. And it was he who
promised the driver two louis if he would make his way to
Mr. Sedley's hotel in the city; and tell Mrs. Captain Osborne
that the action was over, and that her husband was unhurt
and well.

'Indeed, but he has a good heart that William Dobbin,'
Mrs. O'Dowd said, 'though he is always laughing at me.'

Young Stubble vowed there was not such another officer in the army, and never ceased his praises of the senior captain, his modesty, his kindness, and his admirable coolness in the field. To these parts of the conversation, Amelia lent a very distracted attention: it was only when George was spoken of that she listened, and when he was not mentioned, she thought about him.

In tending her patient, and in thinking of the wonderful escapes of the day before, her second day passed away not too slowly with Amelia. There was only one man in the army for her: and as long as he was well, it must be owned that its movements interested her little. All the reports which Jos brought from the streets fell very vaguely on her ears; though they were sufficient to give that timorous gentleman, and many other people then in Brussels, every disquiet. The French had been repulsed certainly, but it was after a severe and doubtful struggle, and with only a division of the French army. The emperor, with the main body, was away at Ligny, where he had utterly annihilated the Prussians, and was now free to bring his whole force to bear upon the allies. The Duke of Wellington was retreating upon the capital, and a great battle must be fought under its walls probably, of which the chances were more than doubtful. The Duke of Wellington had but twenty thousand British troops on whom he could rely, for the Germans were raw militia, the Belgians disaffected; and with this handful his Grace had to resist a hundred and fifty thousand men that had broken into Belgium under Napoleon. Under Napoleon! What warrior was there, however famous and skilful, that could fight at odds with him?

Jos thought of all these things, and trembled. So did all the rest of Brussels – where people felt that the fight of the day before was but the prelude to the greater combat which was imminent. One of the armies opposed to the emperor was scattered to the winds already. The few English that could be brought to resist him would perish at their posts, and the conqueror would pass over their bodies into the city. Woe be to those whom he found there! Addresses were prepared, public functionaries assembled and debated secretly, apartments were got ready, and tricoloured banners and triumphal emblems manufactured, to welcome the arrival of his majesty the emperor and king.

The emigration still continued, and wherever families could find means of departure, they fled. When Jos, on the afternoon of the 17th of June, went to Rebecca's hotel, he found that the great Bareacres's carriage had at length rolled away from the *porte-cochère*. The earl had procured a pair of horses somehow, in spite of Mrs. Crawley, and was rolling on the road to Ghent. Louis the Desired was getting ready his portmanteau in that city, too. It seemed as if Misfortune was never tired of worrying into motion that unwieldy exile.

Jos felt that the delay of yesterday had been only a respite, and that his dearly bought horses must of a surety be put into requisition. His agonies were very severe all this day. As long as there was an English army between Brussels and Napoleon, there was no need of immediate flight; but he had his horses brought from their distant stables, to the stables in the courtyard of the hotel where he lived; so that they might be under his own eyes, and beyond the risk of violent abduction. Isidor watched the stable-door constantly, and had the horses saddled, to be ready for the start. He longed intensely for that event.

After the reception of the previous day, Rebecca did not care to come near her dear Amelia. She clipped the bouquet which George had brought her, and gave fresh water to the flowers, and read over the letter which he had sent her. 'Poor wretch,' she said, twirling round the little bit of paper in her fingers, 'how I could crush her with this! – and it is for a thing like this that she must break her heart, forsooth – for a man who is stupid – a coxcomb – and who does not care for her. My poor good Rawdon is worth ten of this creature.' And then she fell to thinking what she should do if – if anything happened to poor good Rawdon, and what a great piece of luck it was that he had left his horses behind.

In the course of this day, too, Mrs. Crawley, who saw not without anger the Bareacres party drive off, bethought her of the precaution which the countess had taken, and did a little needlework for her own advantage; she stitched away the major part of her trinkets, bills, and bank-notes about her person, and so prepared, was ready for any event – to fly if she thought fit, or to stay and welcome the conqueror, were he Englishman or Frenchman. And I am not sure that

she did not dream that night of becoming a duchess and
madame la maréchale, while Rawdon wrapped in his cloak,
and making his bivouac under the rain at Mount St. John,
was thinking, with all the force of his heart, about the little
wife whom he had left behind him.

The next day was a Sunday. And Mrs. Major O'Dowd
had the satisfaction of seeing both her patients refreshed in
health and spirits by some rest which they had taken during
the night. She herself had slept on a great chair in Amelia's
room, ready to wait upon her poor friend or the ensign,
should either need her nursing. When morning came, this
robust woman went back to the house where she and her
major had their billet; and here performed an elaborate
and splendid toilette, befitting the day. And it is very
possible that whilst alone in that chamber, which her husband had inhabited, and where his cap still lay on the pillow,
and his cane stood in the corner, one prayer at least was
sent up to Heaven for the welfare of the brave soldier
Michael O'Dowd.

When she returned she brought her Prayer-book with her,
and her uncle the dean's famous book of sermons, out of
which she never failed to read every Sabbath; not understanding all, haply, not pronouncing many of the words
aright, which were long and abstruse – for the dean was a
learned man, and loved long Latin words – but with great
gravity, vast emphasis, and with tolerable correctness in the
main. How often has my Mick listened to these sermons,
she thought, and me reading in the cabin of a calm! She
proposed to resume this exercise on the present day, with
Amelia and the wounded ensign for a congregation. The
same service was read on that day in twenty thousand
churches at the same hour; and millions of British men and
women, on their knees, implored protection of the Father
of all.

They did not hear the noise which disturbed our little
congregation at Brussels. Much louder than that which had
interrupted them two days previously, as Mrs. O'Dowd was
reading the service in her best voice, the cannon of Waterloo
began to roar.

When Jos heard that dreadful sound, he made up his
mind that he would bear this perpetual recurrence of terrors
no longer, and would fly at once. He rushed into the sick

man's room, where our three friends had paused in their prayers, and further interrupted them by a passionate appeal to Amelia.

'I can't stand it any more, Emmy,' he said; 'I won't stand it; and you must come with me. I have bought a horse for you – never mind at what price – and you must dress and come with me, and ride behind Isidor.'

'God forgive me, Mr. Sedley, but you are no better than a coward,' Mrs. O'Dowd said, laying down the book.

'I say come, Amelia,' the civilian went on; 'never mind what she says; why are we to stop here and be butchered by the Frenchmen?'

'You forget the –th, my boy,' said the little Stubble, the wounded hero from his bed – 'and – and you won't leave me, will you, Mrs. O'Dowd?'

'No, my dear fellow,' said she, going up and kissing the boy. 'No harm shall come to you while I stand by. I don't budge till I get the word from Mick. A pretty figure I'd be, wouldn't I, stuck behind that chap on a pillion?'

This image caused the young patient to burst out laughing in his bed, and even made Amelia smile. 'I don't ask her,' Jos shouted out – 'I don't ask that – that Irishwoman, but you, Amelia; once for all, will you come?'

'Without my husband, Joseph?' Amelia said, with a look of wonder, and gave her hand to the major's wife. Jos's patience was exhausted.

'Good-bye, then,' he said, shaking his fist in a rage, and slamming the door by which he retreated. And this time he really gave his order for march: and mounted in the court-yard. Mrs. O'Dowd heard the clattering hoofs of the horses as they issued from the gate; and looking on, made many scornful remarks on poor Joseph as he rode down the street with Isidor after him in the laced cap. The horses, which had not been exercised for some days, were lively, and sprang about the street. Jos, a clumsy and timid horseman, did not look to advantage in the saddle. 'Look at him, Amelia dear, driving into the parlour window. Such a bull in a china-shop I never saw.' And presently the pair of riders disappeared at a canter down the street leading in the direction of the Ghent road, Mrs. O'Dowd pursuing them with a fire of sarcasm so long as they were in sight.

All that day from morning until past sunset, the cannon

never ceased to roar. It was dark when the cannonading stopped all of a sudden.

All of us have read of what occurred during that interval. The tale is in every Englishman's mouth; and you and I, who were children when the great battle was won and lost, are never tired of hearing and recounting the history of that famous action. Its remembrance rankles still in the bosoms of millions of the countrymen of those brave men who lost the day. They pant for an opportunity of revenging that humiliation; and if a contest, ending in a victory on their part, should ensue, elating them in their turn, and leaving its cursed legacy of hatred and rage behind to us, there is no end to the so-called glory and shame, and to the alternations of successful and unsuccessful murder, in which two high-spirited nations might engage. Centuries hence, we Frenchmen and Englishmen might be boasting and killing each other still, carrying out' bravely the Devil's code of honour.

All our friends took their share and fought like men in the great field. All day long, whilst the women were praying ten miles away, the lines of the dauntless English infantry were receiving and repelling the furious charges of the French horsemen. Guns which were heard at Brussels were ploughing up their ranks, and comrades falling, and the resolute survivors closing in. Towards evening, the attack of the French, repeated and resisted so bravely, slackened in its fury. They had other foes besides the British to engage, or were preparing for a final onset. It came at last: the columns of the Imperial Guard marched up the hill of St. Jean, at length and at once to sweep the English from the height which they had maintained all day, and spite of all: unscared by the thunder of the artillery, which hurled death from the English line – the dark rolling column pressed on and up the hill. It seemed almost to crest the eminence, when it began to wave and falter. Then it stopped, still facing the shot. Then at last the English troops rushed from the post from which no enemy had been able to dislodge them, and the Guard turned and fled.

No more firing was heard at Brussels – the pursuit rolled miles away. Darkness came down on the field and city: and Amelia was praying for George, who was lying on his face, dead, with a bullet through his heart.

CHAPTER XXXIII

IN WHICH MISS CRAWLEY'S RELATIONS ARE VERY ANXIOUS ABOUT HER

THE kind reader must please to remember – while the army is marching from Flanders, and, after its heroic actions there, is advancing to take the fortifications on the frontiers of France, previous to an occupation of that country – that there are a number of persons living peaceably in England who have to do with the history at present in hand, and must come in for their share of the chronicle. During the time of these battles and dangers, old Miss Crawley was living at Brighton, very moderately moved by the great events that were going on. The great events rendered the newspapers rather interesting, to be sure, and Briggs read out the *Gazette*, in which Rawdon Crawley's gallantry was mentioned with honour, and his promotion was presently recorded.

'What a pity that young man has taken such an irretrievable step in the world!' his aunt said; 'with his rank and distinction he might have married a brewer's daughter with a quarter of a million – like Miss Grains; or have looked to ally himself with the best families in England. He would have had my money some day or other; or his children would – for I'm not in a hurry to go, Miss Briggs, although you may be in a hurry to be rid of me; and instead of that, he is a doomed pauper, with a dancing-girl for a wife.'

'Will my dear Miss Crawley not cast an eye of compassion upon the heroic soldier, whose name is inscribed in the annals of his country's glory?' said Miss Briggs, who was greatly excited by the Waterloo proceedings, and loved speaking romantically when there was an occasion. 'Has not the captain – or the colonel as I may now style him – done deeds which make the name of Crawley illustrious?'

'Briggs, you are a fool,' said Miss Crawley: 'Colonel Crawley has dragged the name of Crawley through the mud, Miss Briggs. Marry a drawing-master's daughter indeed! – marry a *dame de compagnie* – for she was no better, Briggs; no, she was just what you are – only younger, and a great deal prettier and cleverer. Were you an accomplice of that abandoned wretch, I wonder, of whose vile arts he became a victim, and of whom you used to be such an admirer? Yes, I dare say you were an accomplice. But you will find yourself disappointed in my will, I can tell you: and you will have the goodness to write to Mr. Waxy, and say that I desire to see him immediately.' Miss Crawley was now in the habit of writing to Mr. Waxy her solicitor almost every day in the week, for her arrangements respecting her property were all revoked, and her perplexity was great as to the future disposition of her money.

The spinster had, however, rallied considerably; as was proved by the increased vigour and frequency of her sarcasms upon Miss Briggs, all which attacks the poor companion bore with meekness, with cowardice, with a resignation that was half generous and half hypocritical – with the slavish submission, in a word, that women of her disposition and station are compelled to show. Who has not seen how women bully women? What tortures have men to endure, comparable to those daily-repeated shafts of scorn and cruelty with which poor women are riddled by the tyrants of their sex? Poor victims! But we are starting from our proposition, which is, that Miss Crawley was always particularly annoying and savage when she was rallying from illness – as they say wounds tingle most when they are about to heal.

While thus approaching, as all hoped, to convalescence, Miss Briggs was the only victim admitted into the presence of the invalid; yet Miss Crawley's relatives afar off did not forget their beloved kinswoman, and by a number of tokens, presents, and kind affectionate messages, strove to keep themselves alive in her recollection.

In the first place, let us mention her nephew, Rawdon Crawley. A few weeks after the famous fight of Waterloo, and after the *Gazette* had made known to her the promotion and gallantry of that distinguished officer, the Dieppe packet brought over to Miss Crawley at Brighton, a box containing presents, and a dutiful letter, from the colonel, her nephew. In the box were a pair of French epaulets, a Cross of the Legion of Honour, and the hilt of a sword – relics from the field of battle: and the letter described with a good deal of humour how the latter belonged to a commanding-officer of the Guard, who having sworn that 'the Guard died but never surrendered', was taken prisoner the next minute by a private soldier, who broke the Frenchman's sword with the butt of his musket, when Rawdon made himself master of the shattered weapon. As for the cross and epaulets they came from a colonel of French cavalry, who had fallen under the aide de camp's arm in the battle: and Rawdon Crawley did not know what better to do with the spoils than to send them to his kindest and most affectionate old friend. Should he continue to write to her from Paris, whither the army was marching? He might be able to give her interesting news from that capital, and of some of Miss Crawley's old friends of the emigration, to whom she had shown so much kindness during their distress.

The spinster caused Briggs to write back to the colonel a gracious and complimentary letter, encouraging him to continue his correspondence. His first letter was so excessively lively and amusing that she should look with pleasure for its successors. 'Of course, I know,' she explained to Miss Briggs, 'that Rawdon could not write such a good letter any more than you could, my poor Briggs, and that it is that clever little wretch of a Rebecca, who dictates every word to him; but that is no reason why my nephew should not amuse me; and so I wish to let him understand that I am in high good humour.'

I wonder whether she knew that it was not only Becky who wrote the letters, but that Mrs. Rawdon actually took and sent home the trophies – which she bought for a few francs, from one of the innumerable pedlars who immediately began to deal in relics of the war. The novelist, who knows everything, knows this also. Be this, however, as it may, Miss Crawley's gracious reply greatly encouraged our young friends, Rawdon and his lady, who hoped for the best from their aunt's evidently pacified humour: and they took care to entertain her with many delightful letters from Paris, whither, as Rawdon said, they had the good luck to go in the track of the conquering army.

To the rector's lady, who went off to tend her husband's broken collar-bone at the Rectory at Queen's Crawley, the spinster's communications were by no means so gracious. Mrs. Bute, that brisk, managing, lively, imperious woman, had committed the most fatal of all errors with regard to her sister-in-law. She had not merely oppressed her and her household – she had bored Miss Crawley; and if poor Miss

Briggs had been a woman of any spirit, she might have been made happy by the commission which her principal gave her to write a letter to Mrs. Bute Crawley, saying that Miss Crawley's health was greatly improved since Mrs. Bute had left her, and begging the latter on no account to put herself to trouble, or quit her family for Miss Crawley's sake. This triumph over a lady who had been very haughty and cruel in her behaviour to Miss Briggs, would have rejoiced most women; but the truth is. Briggs was a woman of no spirit at all, and the moment her enemy was discomfited, she began to feel compassion in her favour.

'How silly I was,' Mrs. Bute thought, and with reason, 'ever to hint that I was coming, as I did, in that foolish letter when we sent Miss Crawley the guinea-fowls. I ought to have gone without a word to the poor dear doting old creature, and taken her out of the hands of that ninny Briggs, and that harpy of a *femme de chambre*. Oh! Bute, Bute, why did you break your collar-bone?'

Why, indeed? We have seen how Mrs. Bute, having the game in her hands, had really played her cards too well. She had ruled over Miss Crawley's household utterly and completely, to be utterly and completely routed when a favourable opportunity for rebellion came. She and her household, however, considered that she had been the victim of horrible selfishness and treason, and that her sacrifices in Miss Crawley's behalf had met with the most savage ingratitude. Rawdon's promotion, and the honourable mention made of his name in the *Gazette*, filled this good Christian lady also with alarm. Would his aunt relent towards him now that he was a lieutenant-colonel and a C.B.? and would that odious Rebecca once more get into favour? The rector's wife wrote a sermon for her husband about the vanity of military glory and the prosperity of the wicked, which the worthy parson read in his best voice and without understanding one syllable of it. He had Pitt Crawley for one of his auditors – Pitt, who had come with his two half-sisters to church, which the old baronet could now by no means be brought to frequent.

Since the departure of Becky Sharp, that old wretch had given himself up entirely to his bad courses, to the great scandal of the county and the mute horror of his son. The ribbons in Miss Horrocks's cap became more splendid than ever. The polite families fled the Hall and its owner in terror.

Sir Pitt went about tippling at his tenants' houses; and drank rum-and-water with the farmers at Mudbury and the neighbouring places on market-days. He drove the family coach-and-four to Southampton with Miss Horrocks inside: and the county people expected, every week, as his son did in speechless agony, that his marriage with her would be announced in the provincial paper. It was indeed a rude burden for Mr. Crawley to bear. His eloquence was palsied at the missionary meetings, and other religious assemblies in the neighbourhood, where he had been in the habit of presiding, and of speaking for hours; for he felt, when he rose, that the audience said, 'That is the son of the old reprobate Sir Pitt, who is very likely drinking at the public-house at this very moment.' And once, when he was speaking of the benighted condition of the King of Timbuctoo, and the number of his wives who were likewise in darkness, some tipsy miscreant from the crowd asked, 'How many is there at Queen's Crawley, Young Squaretoes?' to the surprise of the platform, and the ruin of Mr. Pitt's speech. And the two daughters of the house of Queen's Crawley would have been allowed to run utterly wild (for Sir Pitt swore that no governess should ever enter into his doors again), had not Mr. Crawley, by threatening the old gentleman, forced the latter to send them to school.

Meanwhile, as we have said, whatever individual differences there might be between them all, Miss Crawley's dear nephews and nieces were unanimous in loving her and sending her tokens of affection. Thus Mrs. Bute sent guinea-fowls, and some remarkably fine cauliflowers, and a pretty purse or pincushion worked by her darling girls, who begged to keep a *little* place in the recollection of their dear aunt, while Mr. Pitt sent peaches and grapes and venison from the Hall. The Southampton coach used to carry these tokens of affection to Miss Crawley at Brighton: it used sometimes to convey Mr. Pitt thither too: for his differences with Sir Pitt caused Mr. Crawley to absent himself a good deal from home now: and besides, he had an attraction at Brighton in the person of the Lady Jane Sheepshanks, whose engagement to Mr. Crawley has been formerly mentioned in this history. Her ladyship and her sisters lived at Brighton with their mamma, the Countess Southdown, that strong-minded woman so favourably known in the serious world.

A few words ought to be said regarding her ladyship and her noble family, who are bound by ties of present and future relationship to the house of Crawley. Respecting the chief of the Southdown family, Clement William, fourth Earl of Southdown, little need be told, except that his lordship came into Parliament (as Lord Wolsey) under the auspices of Mr. Wilberforce, and for a time was a credit to his political sponsor, and decidedly a serious young man. But words cannot describe the feelings of his admirable mother, when she learned, very shortly after her noble husband's demise, that her son was a member of several worldly clubs, had lost largely at play at Wattier's and the 'Cocoa-Tree'; that he had raised money on post-obits, and encumbered the family estate; that he drove four-in-hand, and patronized the ring; and that he actually had an opera-box, where he entertained the most dangerous bachelor company. His name was only mentioned with groans in the dowager's circle.

The Lady Emily was her brother's senior by many years; and took considerable rank in the serious world as author of some of the delightful tracts before-mentioned, and of many hymns and spiritual pieces. A mature spinster, and having but faint ideas of marriage, her love for the blacks occupied almost all her feelings. It is to her, I believe, we owe that beautiful poem –

> Lead us to some sunny isle,
> Yonder in the western deep;
> Where the skies for ever smile,
> And the blacks for ever weep, &c.

She had correspondences with clerical gentlemen in most of our East and West India possessions; and was secretly attached to the Reverend Silas Hornblower, who was tattooed in the South Sea Islands.

As for the Lady Jane, on whom, as it has been said, Mr. Pitt Crawley's affection had been placed, she was gentle, blushing, silent, and timid. In spite of his falling away, she wept for her brother, and was quite ashamed of loving him still. Even yet she used to send him little hurried smuggled notes, and pop them in the post in private. The one dreadful secret which weighed upon her life was, that she and the old housekeeper had been to pay Southdown a furtive visit at his chambers in the Albany; and found him – Oh, the naughty dear abandoned wretch! – smoking a cigar with a bottle of curaçao before him. She admired her sister, she adored her mother, she thought Mr. Crawley the most delightful and accomplished of men, after Southdown, that fallen angel: and her mamma and sister, who were ladies of the most superior sort, managed everything for her, and regarded her with that amiable pity, of which your really superior woman always has such a share to give away. Her mamma ordered her dresses, her books, her bonnets, and her ideas for her. She was made to take pony-riding, or piano-exercise, or any other sort of bodily medicament, according as my Lady Southdown saw meet; and her lady-ship would have kept her daughter in pinafores up to her present age of six-and-twenty, but that they were thrown off when Lady Jane was presented to Queen Charlotte.

When these ladies first came to their house at Brighton, it was to them alone that Mr. Crawley paid his personal visits, contenting himself by leaving a card at his aunt's house, and making a modest inquiry of Mr. Bowls or his assistant footman, with respect to the health of the invalid. When he met Miss Briggs coming home from the library with a cargo of novels under her arm, Mr. Crawley blushed in a manner quite unusual to him, as he stepped forward and shook Miss Crawley's companion by the hand. He introduced Miss Briggs to the lady with whom he happened to be walking, the Lady Jane Sheepshanks, saying, 'Lady Jane, permit me to introduce to you my aunt's kindest friend and most affectionate companion, Miss Briggs, whom you know under another title, as authoress of the delightful *Lyrics of the Heart*, of which you are so fond.' Lady Jane blushed too as she held out a kind little hand to Miss Briggs, and said something very civil and incoherent about mamma, and proposing to call on Miss Crawley, and being glad to be made known to the friends and relatives of Mr. Crawley; and with soft dove-like eyes saluted Miss Briggs as they separated, while Pitt Crawley treated her to a profound courtly bow, such as he had used to H.H. the Duchess of Pumpernickel, when he was attaché at that court.

The artful diplomatist and disciple of the Machiavellian Binkie! It was he who had given Lady Jane that copy of poor Briggs's early poems, which he remembered to have seen at Queen's Crawley, with a dedication from the poetess to his father's late wife; and he brought the volume with him to Brighton, reading it in the Southampton coach and marking it with his own pencil, before he presented it to the gentle Lady Jane.

It was he, too, who laid before Lady Southdown the great advantages which might occur from an intimacy between her family and Miss Crawley, – advantages both worldly and spiritual, he said: for Miss Crawley was now quite alone; the monstrous dissipation and alliance of his brother Rawdon had estranged her affections from that reprobate young man; the greedy tyranny and avarice of Mrs. Bute Crawley had caused the old lady to revolt against the exorbitant pretensions of that part of the family; and though he himself had held off all his life from cultivating Miss Crawley's friendship, with perhaps an improper pride, he thought now that every becoming means should be taken, both to save her soul from perdition, and to secure her fortune to himself as the head of the house of Crawley.

The strong-minded Lady Southdown quite agreed in both proposals of her son-in-law, and was for converting Miss Crawley off-hand. At her own home, both at Southdown and at Trottermore Castle, this tall and awful missionary of the truth rode about the country in her barouche with outriders, launched packets of tracts among the cottagers and tenants, and would order Gaffer Jones to be converted, as she would order Goody Hicks to take a James's powder, without appeal, resistance, or benefit of clergy. My Lord Southdown, her late husband, an epileptic and simple-minded nobleman, was in the habit of approving of everything which his Matilda did and thought. So that whatever changes her own belief might undergo (and it accommodated itself to a prodigious variety of opinion, taken from all sorts of doctors among the Dissenters) she had not the least scruple in ordering all her tenants and inferiors to follow and believe after her. Thus, whether she received the Reverend Saunders McNitre, the Scotch divine; or the Reverend Luke Waters, the mild Wesleyan; or the Reverend Giles Jowls, the illuminated cobbler, who dubbed himself reverend as Napoleon crowned himself emperor – the household, children, tenantry of my Lady Southdown were expected to go down on their knees with her ladyship, and say Amen to the prayers of either doctor. During these exercises old Southdown, on account of his invalid condition, was allowed to sit in his own room, and have negus and the paper read to him. Lady Jane was the old earl's favourite daughter, and tended him and loved him sincerely: as for Lady Emily, the authoress of the *Washerwoman of Finchley Common*, her denunciation of future punishments (at this period, for her opinions modified afterwards) were so awful that they used to frighten the timid old gentleman her father, and the physicians declared his fits always occurred after one of her ladyship's sermons.

'I will certainly call,' said Lady Southdown then, in reply to the exhortation of her daughter's *prétendu*, Mr. Pitt Crawley – 'Who is Miss Crawley's medical man?'

Mr. Crawley mentioned the name of Mr. Creamer.

'A most dangerous and ignorant practitioner, my dear Pitt. I have providentially been the means of removing him from several houses; though in one or two instances I did not arrive in time. I could not save poor dear General Glanders, who was dying under the hands of that ignorant man – dying. He rallied a little under the Podgers pills which I administered to him; but alas! it was too late. His death was delightful, however; and his change was only for the better: Creamer, my dear Pitt, must leave your aunt.'

Pitt expressed his perfect acquiescence. He, too, had been carried along by the energy of his noble kinswoman, and future mother-in-law. He had been made to accept Saunders McNitre, Luke Waters, Giles Jowls, Podgers's Pills, Rodgers's Pills, Pokey's Elixir, every one of her ladyship's remedies spiritual or temporal. He never left her house without carrying respectfully away with him piles of her quack theology and medicine. Oh, my dear brethren and fellow-sojourners in Vanity Fair, which among you does not know and suffer under such benevolent despots? It is in vain you say to them, 'Dear madam, I took Podger's specific at your orders last year, and believe in it. Why, why, am I to recant and accept the Rodgers's articles now?' There is no help for it; the faithful proselytizer, if she cannot convince by argument, bursts into tears, and the recusant finds himself, at the end of the contest, taking down the bolus, and saying, 'Well, well, Rodger's be it.'

'And as for her spiritual state,' continued the lady, 'that

of course must be looked to immediately; with Creamer about her, she may go off any day: and in what a condition, my dear Pitt, in what a dreadful condition! I will send the Reverend Mr. Irons to her instantly. Jane, write a line to the Reverend Bartholomew Irons, in the third person, and say that I desire the pleasure of his company this evening at tea at half-past six. He is an awakening man; he ought to see Miss Crawley before she rests this night. And Emily, my love, get ready a packet of books for Miss Crawley. Put up *A Voice from the Flames, A Trumpet-warning to Jericho*, and the *Fleshpots Broken; or, the Converted Cannibal.*'

'And the *Washerwoman of Finchley Common*, mamma,' said Lady Emily. 'It is as well to begin soothingly at first.'

'Stop, my dear ladies,' said Pitt the diplomatist. 'With every deference to the opinion of my beloved and respected Lady Southdown, I think it would be quite unadvisable to commence so early upon serious topics with Miss Crawley. Remember her delicate condition, and how little, how *very* little accustomed she has hitherto been to considerations connected with her immortal welfare.'

'Can we then begin too early, Pitt?' said Lady Emily, rising with six little books already in her hand.

'If you begin abruptly, you will frighten her altogether. I know my aunt's worldly nature so well as to be sure that any abrupt attempt at conversion will be the very worst means that can be employed for the welfare of that unfortunate lady. You will only frighten and annoy her. She will very likely fling the books away, and refuse all acquaintance with the givers.'

'You are as worldly as Miss Crawley, Pitt,' said Lady Emily, tossing out of the room, her books in her hand.

'And I need not tell you, my dear Lady Southdown,' Pitt continued, in a low voice, and without heeding the interruption, 'how fatal a little want of gentleness and caution may be to any hopes which we may entertain with regard to the worldly possessions of my aunt. Remember she has seventy thousand pounds; think of her age, and her highly nervous and delicate condition; I know that she has destroyed the will which was made in my brother's (Colonel Crawley's) favour: it is by soothing that wounded spirit that we must lead it into the right path, and not by frightening it; and so I think you will agree with me that – that —'

'Of course, of course,' Lady Southdown remarked. 'Jane, my love, you need not send that note to Mr. Irons. If her health is such that discussions fatigue her, we will wait her amendment. I will call upon Miss Crawley to-morrow.'

'And if I might suggest, my sweet lady,' Pitt said in a bland tone, 'it would be as well not to take our precious Emily, who is too enthusiastic; but rather that you should be accompanied by our sweet and dear Lady Jane.'

'Most certainly, Emily would ruin everything,' Lady Southdown said; and this time agreed to forgo her usual practice, which was, as we have said, before she bore down personally upon any individual whom she proposed to subjugate, to fire in a quantity of tracts upon the menaced party (as a charge of the French was always preceded by a furious cannonade). Lady Southdown, we say, for the sake of the invalid's health, or for the sake of her soul's ultimate welfare, or for the sake of her money, agreed to temporize.

The next day the great Southdown female family carriage, with the earl's coronet and the lozenge (upon which the three lambs trottant argent upon the field vert of the Southdowns, were quartered with sable on a bend or, three snuffmulls gules, the cognizance of the house of Binkie), drove up in state to Miss Crawley's door, and the tall serious footman handed in to Mr. Bowls her ladyship's cards for Miss Crawley, and one likewise for Miss Briggs. By way of compromise Lady Emily sent in a packet in the evening for the latter lady, containing copies of the *Washerwoman*, and other mild and favourite tracts for Miss B.'s own perusal; and a few for the servants' hall, viz.: *Crumbs from the Pantry, The Frying-Pan and the Fire*, and *The Livery of Sin*, of a much stronger kind.

CHAPTER XXXIV

JAMES CRAWLEY'S PIPE IS PUT OUT

T HE amiable behaviour of Mr. Crawley, and Lady Jane's kind reception of her, highly flattered Miss Briggs, who was enabled to speak a good word for the latter, after the cards of the Southdown family had been presented to Miss Crawley. A countess's card left personally too for her, Briggs, was not a little pleasing to the poor friendless companion.

'What could Lady Southdown mean by leaving a card upon *you*, I wonder, Miss Briggs?' said the republican Miss Crawley; upon which the companion meekly said 'that she hoped there could be no harm in a lady of rank taking notice of a poor gentlewoman', and she put away this card in her work-box amongst her most cherished personal treasures. Furthermore, Miss Briggs explained how she had met Mr. Crawley walking with his cousin and long-affianced bride the day before: and she told how kind and gentle-looking the lady was, and what a plain, not to say common, dress she had, all the articles of which, from the bonnet down to the boots, she described and estimated with female accuracy.

Miss Crawley allowed Briggs to prattle on without interrupting her too much. As she got well, she was pining for society. Mr. Creamer, her medical man, would not hear of her returning to her old haunts and dissipation in London. The old spinster was too glad to find any companionship at Brighton, and not only were the cards acknowledged the very next day, but Pitt Crawley was graciously invited to come and see his aunt. He came, bringing with him Lady Southdown and her daughter. The dowager did not say a word about the state of Miss Crawley's soul; but talked with much discretion about the weather: about the war and the downfall of the monster Bonaparte: and above all, about doctors, quacks, and the particular merits of Dr. Podgers, whom she then patronized.

During their interview Pitt Crawley made a great stroke, and one which showed that, had his diplomatic career not been blighted by early neglect, he might have risen to a high rank in his profession. When the Countess Dowager of Southdown fell foul of the Corsican upstart, as the fashion was in those days, and showed that he was a monster stained with every conceivable crime, a coward and a tyrant not fit to live, one whose fall was predicted, &c., Pitt Crawley suddenly took up the cudgels in favour of the man of Destiny. He described the First Consul as he saw him at Paris at the Peace of Amiens; when he, Pitt Crawley, had the gratification of making the acquaintance of the great and good Mr. Fox, a statesman whom, however much he might differ with him, it was impossible not to admire fervently – a statesman who had always had the highest opinion of the Emperor Napoleon. And he spoke in terms of the strongest

indignation of the faithless conduct of the allies towards this
dethroned monarch, who, after giving himself generously up
to their mercy, was consigned to an ignoble and cruel
banishment, while a bigoted Popish rabble was tyrannizing
over France in his stead.

This orthodox horror of Romish superstition saved Pitt
Crawley in Lady Southdown's opinion, whilst his admiration
for Fox and Napoleon raised him immeasurably in Miss
Crawley's eyes. Her friendship with that defunct British
statesman was mentioned when we first introduced her in
this history. A true Whig, Miss Crawley had been in opposition all through the war, and though, to be sure, the
downfall of the emperor did not very much agitate the old
lady, or his ill-treatment tend to shorten her life or natural
rest, yet Pitt spoke to her heart when he lauded both her
idols; and by that single speech made immense progress in
her favour.

'And what do you think, my dear?' Miss Crawley said to
the young lady, for whom she had taken a liking at first
sight, as she always did for pretty and modest young people;
though it must be owned her affections cooled as rapidly as
they rose.

Lady Jane blushed very much, and said, 'that she did not
understand politics, which she left to wiser heads than hers;
but though mamma was, no doubt, correct, Mr. Crawley
had spoken beautifully.' And when the ladies were retiring
at the conclusion of their visit, Miss Crawley hoped Lady
Southdown would be so kind as to send her Lady Jane
sometimes, if she could be spared to come down and console
a poor sick lonely old woman.' This promise was graciously
accorded, and they separated upon great terms of amity.

'Don't let Lady Southdown come again, Pitt,' said the
old lady. 'She is stupid and pompous like all your mother's
family, whom I never could endure. But bring that nice
good-natured little Lady Jane as often as ever you please.'
Pitt promised that he would do so. He did not tell the
Countess of Southdown what opinion his aunt had formed
of her ladyship, who, on the contrary, thought that she had
made a most delightful and majestic impression on Miss
Crawley.

And so, nothing loath to comfort a sick lady, and perhaps
not sorry in her heart to be freed now and again from the

dreary spouting of the Reverend Bartholomew Irons, and the serious toadies who gathered round the footstool of the pompous countess, her mamma, Lady Jane became a pretty constant visitor to Miss Crawley, accompanied her in her drives, and solaced many of her evenings. She was so naturally good and soft, that even Firkin was not jealous of her; and the gentle Briggs thought her friend was less cruel to her, when kind Lady Jane was by. Towards her ladyship Miss Crawley's manners were charming. The old spinster told her a thousand anecdotes about her youth, talking to her in a very different strain from that in which she had been accustomed to converse with the godless little Rebecca; for there was that in Lady Jane's innocence which rendered light talking impertinence before her, and Miss Crawley was too much of a gentlewoman to offend such purity. The young lady herself had never received kindness except from this old spinster, and her brother and father: and she repaid Miss Crawley's *engouement* by artless sweetness and friendship.

In the autumn evenings (when Rebecca was flaunting at Paris, the gayest among the gay conquerors there, and our Amelia, our dear wounded Amelia, ah! where was she?) Lady Jane would be sitting in Miss Crawley's drawing-room singing sweetly to her, in the twilight, her little simple songs and hymns, while the sun was setting and the sea was roaring on the beach. The old spinster used to wake up when these ditties ceased, and ask for more. As for Briggs, and the quantity of tears of happiness which she now shed as she pretended to knit, and looked out at the splendid ocean darkling before the windows, and the lamps of heaven beginning more brightly to shine – who, I say, can measure the happiness and sensibility of Briggs?

Pitt meanwhile in the dining-room, with a pamphlet of the Corn Laws or a Missionary Register by his side, took that kind of recreation which suits romantic and unromantic men after dinner. He sipped madeira: built castles in the air: thought himself a fine fellow: felt himself much more in love with Jane than he had been any time these seven years, during which their *liaison* had lasted without the slightest impatience on Pitt's part – and slept a good deal. When the time for coffee came, Mr. Bowls used to enter in a noisy manner, and summon Squire Pitt, who would be found in the dark very busy with his pamphlet.

'I wish, my love, I could get somebody to play piquet with me,' Miss Crawley said, one night, when this functionary made his appearance with the candles and the coffee. 'Poor Briggs can no more play than an owl, she is so stupid' (the spinster always took an opportunity of abusing Briggs before the servants); 'and I think I should sleep better if I had my game.'

At this Lady Jane blushed to the tips of her little ears, and down to the ends of her pretty fingers; and when Mr. Bowls had quitted the room, and the door was quite shut, she said:

'Miss Crawley, I can play a little. I used to – to play a little with poor dear papa.'

'Come and kiss me. Come and kiss me this instant, you dear good little soul,' cried Miss Crawley in an ecstasy: and in this picturesque and friendly occupation Mr. Pitt found the old lady and the young one, when he came upstairs with his pamphlet in his hand. How she did blush all the evening, that poor Lady Jane!

It must not be imagined that Mr. Pitt Crawley's artifices escaped the attention of his dear relations at the Rectory at Queen's Crawley. Hampshire and Sussex lie very close together, and Mrs. Bute had friends in the latter county who took care to inform her of all, and a great deal more than all, that passed at Miss Crawley's house at Brighton. Pitt was there more and more. He did not come for months together to the Hall, where his abominable old father abandoned himself completely to rum-and-water, and the odious society of the Horrocks family. Pitt's success rendered the rector's family furious, and Mrs. Bute regretted more (though she confessed less) than ever her monstrous fault in so insulting Miss Briggs, and in being so haughty and parsimonious to Bowls and Firkin, that she had not a single person left in Miss Crawley's household to give her information of what took place there. 'It was all Bute's collar-bone,' she persisted in saying; 'if that had not broke, I never would have left her. I am a martyr to duty and to your odious unclerical habit of hunting, Bute.'

'Hunting; nonsense! It was you that frightened her, Barbara,' the divine interposed. 'You're a clever woman, but you've got a devil of a temper; and you're a screw with your money, Barbara.'

'You'd have been screwed in gaol, Bute, if I had not kept your money.'

'I know I would, my dear,' said the rector, good-naturedly. 'You *are* a clever woman, but you manage too well, you know:' and the pious man consoled himself with a big glass of port.

'What the deuce can she find in that spooney of a Pitt Crawley?' he continued. 'The fellow has not pluck enough to say Bo to a goose. I remember when Rawdon, who *is* a man, and be hanged to him, used to flog him round the stables as if he was a whipping-top: and Pitt would go howling home to his ma – ha, ha! Why, either of my boys would wap him with one hand. Jim says he's remembered at Oxford as Miss Crawley still – the spooney.'

'I say, Barbara,' his reverence continued, after a pause.

'What!' said Barbara, who was biting her nails and drubbing the table.

'I say, why not send Jim over to Brighton to see if he can do anything with the old lady. He's very near getting his degree, you know. He's only been plucked twice – so was I – but he's had the advantages of Oxford and a university education. He knows some of the best chaps there. He pulls stroke in the Boniface boat. He's a handsome feller. D– it, ma'am, let's put him on the old woman, hey; and tell him to thrash Pitt if he says anythink. Ha, ha, ha!'

'Jim might go down and see her, certainly,' the housewife said, adding, with a sigh, 'If we could but get one of the girls into the house; but she could never endure them, because they are not pretty!' Those unfortunate and well-educated women made themselves heard from the neighbouring drawing-room, where they were thrumming away, with hard fingers, an elaborate music-piece on the pianoforte, as their mother spoke; and indeed they were at music, or at backboard, or at geography, or at history, the whole day long. But what avail all these accomplishments, in Vanity Fair, to girls who are short, poor, plain, and have a bad complexion? Mrs. Bute could think of nobody but the curate to take one of them off her hands; and Jim coming in from the stable at this minute, through the parlour window, with a short pipe stuck in his oilskin cap, he and his father fell to talking about odds on the St. Leger, and the colloquy between the rector and his wife ended.

Mrs. Bute did not augur much good to the cause from the sending of her son James as an ambassador, and saw him depart in rather a despairing mood. Nor did the young fellow himself, when told what his mission was to be, expect much pleasure or benefit from it; but he was consoled by the thought that possibly the old lady would give him some handsome remembrance of her, which would pay a few of his most pressing bills at the commencement of the ensuing Oxford term, and so took his place by the coach from Southampton, and was safely landed at Brighton on the same evening, with his portmanteau, his favourite bull-dog Towzer, and an immense basket of farm and garden produce, from the dear Rectory folks to the dear Miss Crawley. Considering it was too late to disturb the invalid lady on the first night of his arrival, he put up at an inn, and did not wait upon Miss Crawley until a late hour in the noon of next day.

James Crawley, when his aunt had last beheld him, was a gawky lad, at that uncomfortable age when the voice varies between an unearthly treble and a preternatural bass; when the face not uncommonly blooms out with appearances for which Rowland's Kalydor is said to act as a cure; when boys are seen to shave furtively with their sister's scissors, and the sight of other young women produces intolerable sensations of terror in them; when the great hands and ankles protrude a long way from garments which have grown too tight for them; when their presence after dinner is at once frightful to the ladies, who are whispering in the twilight in the drawing-room, and inexpressibly odious to the gentlemen over the mahogany, who are restrained from freedom of intercourse and delightful interchange of wit by the presence of that gawky innocence; when, at the conclusion of the second glass, papas say, 'Jack, my boy, go out and see if the evening holds up,' and the youth, willing to be free, yet hurt at not being yet a man, quits the incomplete banquet. James, then a hobbledehoy, was now become a young man, having had the benefits of a university education, and acquired the inestimable polish, which is gained by living in a fast set at a small college, and contracting debts, and being rusticated, and being plucked.

He was a handsome lad, however, when he came to present himself to his aunt at Brighton, and good looks were

always a title to the fickle old lady's favour. Nor did his
blushes and awkwardness take away from it: she was pleased
with these healthy tokens of the young gentleman's ingenu-
ousness.

He said 'he had come down for a couple of days to see
a man of his college, and – and to pay my respects to you,
ma'am, and my father's and mother's, who hope you are
well'.

Pitt was in the room with Miss Crawley when the lad
was announced, and looked very blank when his name was
mentioned. The old lady had plenty of humour, and enjoyed
her correct nephew's perplexity. She asked after all the
people at the Rectory with great interest; and said she was
thinking of paying them a visit. She praised the lad to his
face, and said he was well-grown and very much improved,
and that it was a pity his sisters had not some of his good
looks; and finding, on inquiry, that he had taken up his
quarters at an hotel, would not hear of his stopping there,
but bade Mr. Bowls send for Mr. James Crawley's things
instantly; 'and hark ye, Bowls,' she added, with great graciousness, 'you will have the goodness to pay Mr. James's
bill.'

She flung Pitt a look of arch triumph, which caused that
diplomatist almost to choke with envy. Much as he had
ingratiated himself with his aunt, she had never yet invited
him to stay under her roof, and here was a young whipper-
snapper, who at first sight was made welcome there.

'I beg your pardon, sir,' says Bowls, advancing with a
profound bow; 'what otel, sir, shall Thomas fetch the luggage
from?'

'Oh, dam,' said young James, starting up, as if in some
alarm, 'I'll go.'

'What!' said Miss Crawley.

'The "Tom Cribb's Arms",' said James, blushing deeply.

Miss Crawley burst out laughing at this title. Mr. Bowls
gave one abrupt guffaw, as a confidential servant of the
family, but choked the rest of the volley; the diplomatist
only smiled.

'I – I didn't know any better,' said James, looking down.
'I've never been here before; it was the coachman told me.'
The young story-teller! The fact is, that on the Southampton
coach, the day previous, James Crawley had met the Tutbury

Pet, who was coming to Brighton to make a match with the Rottingdean Fibber; and enchanted by the Pet's conversation, had passed the evening in company with that scientific man and his friends, at the inn in question.

'I – I'd best go and settle the score,' James continued. 'Couldn't think of asking you, ma'am,' he added, generously.

This delicacy made his aunt laugh the more.

'Go and settle the bill, Bowls,' she said, with a wave of her hand, 'and bring it to me.'

Poor lady, she did not know what she had done! 'There – there's a little *dawg*,' said James, looking frightfully guilty. 'I'd best go for him. He bites footmen's calves.'

All the party cried out with laughing at this description; even Briggs and Lady Jane, who was sitting mute during the interview between Miss Crawley and her nephew: and Bowls, without a word, quitted the room.

Still, by way of punishing her elder nephew, Miss Crawley persisted in being gracious to the young Oxonian. There were no limits to her kindness or her compliments when they once began. She told Pitt he might come to dinner, and insisted that James should accompany her in her drive, and paraded him solemnly up and down the cliff, on the back seat of the barouche. During all this excursion, she condescended to say civil things to him: she quoted Italian and French poetry to the poor bewildered lad, and persisted that he was a fine scholar, and was perfectly sure he would gain a gold medal, and be a Senior Wrangler.

'Haw, haw,' laughed James, encouraged by these compliments; 'Senior Wrangler, indeed; that's at the other shop.'

'What is the other shop, my dear child?' said the lady.

'Senior Wranglers at Cambridge, not Oxford,' said the scholar, with a knowing air; and would probably have been more confidential, but that suddenly there appeared on the cliff in a tax-cart, drawn by a bang-up pony, dressed in white flannel coats, with mother-of-pearl buttons, his friends the Tutbury Pet and the Rottingdean Fibber, with three other gentlemen of their acquaintance, who all saluted poor James there in the carriage as he sat. This incident damped the ingenuous youth's spirits, and no word of yea or nay could he be induced to utter during the rest of the drive.

On his return he found his room prepared, and his portmanteau ready, and might have remarked that Mr.

Bowls's countenance, when the latter conducted him to his apartment, wore a look of gravity, wonder, and compassion. But the thought of Mr. Bowls did not enter his head. He was deploring the dreadful predicament in which he found himself, in a house full of old women, jabbering French and Italian, and talking poetry to him. 'Reglarly up a tree, by jingo!' exclaimed the modest boy, who could not face the gentlest of her sex – not even Briggs – when she began to talk to him; whereas, put him at Iffley Lock, and he could out-slang the boldest bargeman.

At dinner, James appeared choking in a white neckcloth, and had the honour of handing my Lady Jane downstairs, while Briggs and Mr. Crawley followed afterwards, conducting the old lady, with her apparatus of bundles, and shawls, and cushions. Half of Briggs's time at dinner was spent in superintending the invalid's comfort, and in cutting up chicken for her fat spaniel. James did not talk much, but he made a point of asking all the ladies to drink wine, and accepted Mr. Crawley's challenge, and consumed the greater part of a bottle of champagne which Mr. Bowls was ordered to produce in his honour. The ladies having withdrawn, and the two cousins being left together, Pitt, the ex-diplomatist, became very communicative and friendly. He asked after James's career at college – what his prospects in life were – hoped heartily he would get on; and, in a word, was frank and amiable. James's tongue unloosed with the port, and he told his cousin his life, his prospects, his debts, his troubles at the Little-go, and his rows with the proctors, filling rapidly from the bottles before him, and flying from Port to Madeira with joyous activity.

'The chief pleasure which my aunt has,' said Mr. Crawley, filling his glass, 'is that people should do as they like in her house. This is Liberty Hall, James, and you can't do Miss Crawley a greater kindness than to do as you please, and ask for what you will. I know you have all sneered at me in the country for being a Tory. Miss Crawley is liberal enough to suit any fancy. She is a Republican in principle, and despises everything like rank or title.'

'Why are you going to marry an earl's daughter?' said James.

'My dear friend, remember it is not poor Lady Jane's fault that she is well born,' Pitt replied, with a courtly air.

'She cannot help being a lady. Besides, I am a Tory, you know.'

'Oh, as for that,' said Jim, 'there's nothing like old blood; no, dammy, nothing like it. I'm none· of your Radicals. I know what it is to be a gentleman, dammy. See the chaps in a boat-race; look at the fellers in a fight; aye, look at a dawg killing rats, – which is it wins? the good blooded ones. Get some more port, Bowls, old boy, whilst I buzz this bottle here. What was I a-saying?'

'I think you were speaking of dogs killing rats,' Pitt remarked mildly, handling his cousin the decanter to 'buzz'.

'Killing rats was I? Well, Pitt, are you a sporting man? Do you want to see a dawg as *can* kill a rat? If you do, come down with me to Tom Corduroy's, in Castle Street Mews, and I'll show you such a bull-terrier as — Pooh! gammon,' cried James, bursting out laughing at his own absurdity, – '*you* don't care about a dawg or rat; it's all nonsense. I'm blest if I think you know the difference between a dog and a duck.'

'No; by the way,' Pitt continued with increased blandness, 'it was about blood you were talking, and the personal advantages which people derive from patrician birth. Here's the fresh bottle.'

'Blood's the word,' said James, gulping the ruby fluid down. 'Nothing like blood, sir, in hosses, dawgs, *and* men. Why, only last term, just before I was rusticated, that is, I mean just before I had the measles, ha, ha, – there was me and Ringwood of Christchurch, Bob Ringwood, Lord Cinqbar's son, having our beer at the "Bell" at Blenheim, when the Banbury bargeman offered to fight either of us for a bowl of punch. I couldn't. My arm was in a sling; couldn't even take the drag down, – a brute of a mare of mine had fell with me only two days before, out with the Abingdon, and I thought my arm was broke. Well, sir, I couldn't finish him, but Bob had his coat off at once – he stood up to the Banbury man for three minutes, and polished him off in four rounds easy. Gad, how he did drop, sir, and what was it? Blood, sir, all blood.'

'You don't drink, James,' the ex-attaché continued. 'In my time at Oxford, the men passed round the bottle a little quicker than you young fellows seem to do.'

'Come, come,' said James, putting his hand to his nose

and winking at his cousin with a pair of vinous eyes, 'no jokes, old boy; no trying it on on me. You want to trot me out, but it's no go. *In vino veritas*, old boy. Mars, Bacchus, Apollo *virorum*, hey? I wish my aunt would send down some of this to the governor; it's a precious good tap.'

'You had better ask her,' Machiavel continued, 'or make the best of your time now. What says the bard, *Nunc vino pellite curas, Cras ingens iterabimus aequor*,' and the Bacchanalian, quoting the above with a House of Commons air, tossed off nearly a thimbleful of wine with an immense flourish of his glass.

At the Rectory, when the bottle of port wine was opened after dinner, the young ladies had each a glass from a bottle of currant wine. Mrs. Bute took one glass of port, honest James had a couple commonly, but as his father grew very sulky if he made further inroads on the bottle, the good lad generally refrained from trying for more, and subsided either into the currant wine, or to some private gin-and-water in the stables, which he enjoyed in the company of the coachman and his pipe. At Oxford, the quantity of wine was unlimited, but the quality was inferior: but when quantity and quality united, as at his aunt's house, James showed that he could appreciate them indeed; and hardly needed any of his cousin's encouragement in draining off the second bottle supplied by Mr. Bowls.

When the time for coffee came, however, and for a return to the ladies, of whom he stood in awe, the young gentleman's agreeable frankness left him, and he relapsed into his usual surly timidity: contenting himself by saying yes and no, by scowling at Lady Jane, and by upsetting one cup of coffee during the evening.

If he did not speak he yawned in a pitiable manner, and his presence threw a damp upon the modest proceedings of the evening, for Miss Crawley and Lady Jane at their piquet, and Miss Briggs at her work, felt that his eyes were wildly fixed on them, and were uneasy under that maudlin look.

'He seems a very silent, awkward, bashful lad,' said Miss Crawley to Mr. Pitt.

'He is more communicative in men's society than with ladies,' Machiavel drily replied: perhaps rather disappointed that the port wine had not made Jim speak more.

He had spent the early part of the next morning in writing

home to his mother a most flourishing account of his reception by Miss Crawley. But ah! he little knew what evils the day was bringing for him, and how short his reign of favour was destined to be. A circumstance which Jim had forgotten – a trivial but fatal circumstance – had taken place at the 'Cribb's Arms' on the night before he had come to his aunt's house. It was no other than this – Jim, who was always of a generous disposition, and when in his cups especially hospitable, had in the course of the night treated the Tutbury champion and the Rottingdean man, and their friends, twice or thrice to the refreshment of gin-and-water – so that no less than eighteen glasses of that fluid at eightpence per glass were charged in Mr. James Crawley's bill. It was not the amount of eightpences, but the quantity of gin which told fatally against poor James's character, when his aunt's butler, Mr. Bowls, went down at his mistress's request to pay the young gentleman's bill. The landlord, fearing lest the account should be refused altogether, swore solemnly that the young gent had consumed personally every farthing's worth of the liquor: and Bowls paid the bill finally, and showed it on his return home to Mrs. Firkin, who was shocked at the frightful prodigality of gin; and took the bill to Miss Briggs as accountant-general; who thought it her duty to mention the circumstance to her principal, Miss Crawley.

Had he drunk a dozen bottles of claret the old spinster could have pardoned him. Mr. Fox and Mr. Sheridan drank claret. Gentlemen drank claret. But eighteen glasses of gin consumed among boxers in an ignoble pot-house – it was an odious crime and not to be pardoned readily. Everything went against the lad: he came home perfumed from the stables, whither he had been to pay his dog Towzer a visit – and whence he was going to take his friend out for an airing, when he met Miss Crawley and her wheezy Blenheim spaniel, which Towzer would have eaten up had not the Blenheim fled squealing to the protection of Miss Briggs, while the atrocious master of the bulldog stood laughing at the horrible persecution.

This day too the unlucky boy's modesty had likewise forsaken him. He was lively and facetious at dinner. During the repast he levelled one or two jokes against Pitt Crawley: he drank as much wine as upon the previous day; and going quite unsuspiciously to the drawing-room, began to entertain the ladies there with some choice Oxford stories. He described the different pugilistic qualities of Molyneux and Dutch Sam, offered playfully to give Lady Jane the odds upon the Tutbury Pet against the Rottingdean man, or take them, as her ladyship chose: and crowned the pleasantry by proposing to back himself against his cousin Pitt Crawley, either with or without the gloves. 'And that's a fair offer, my buck,' he said with a loud laugh, slapping Pitt on the shoulder, 'and my father told me to make it too, and he'll go halves in the bet, ha, ha!' So saying, the engaging youth nodded knowingly at poor Miss Briggs, and pointed his thumb over his shoulder at Pitt Crawley in a jocular and exulting manner.

Pitt was not pleased altogether perhaps, but still not unhappy in the main. Poor Jim had his laugh out: and staggered across the room with his aunt's candle, when the old lady moved to retire, and offered to salute her with the blandest tipsy smile: and he took his own leave and went upstairs to his bedroom perfectly satisfied with himself, and with a pleased notion that his aunt's money would be left to him in preference to his father and all the rest of the family.

Once up in the bedroom, one would have thought he could not make matters worse; and yet this unlucky boy did. The moon was shining very pleasantly out on the sea, and Jim, attracted to the window by the romantic appearance of the ocean, and the heavens, thought he would farther enjoy them while smoking. Nobody would smell the tobacco, he thought, if he cunningly opened the window and kept his head and pipe in the fresh air. This he did: but being in an excited state, poor Jim had forgotten that his door was open all this time, so that the breeze blowing inwards and a fine thorough draught being established, the clouds of tobacco were carried downstairs, and arrived with quite undiminished fragrance to Miss Crawley and Miss Briggs.

That pipe of tobacco finished the business: and the Bute-Crawleys never knew how many thousand pounds it cost them. Firkin rushed downstairs to Bowls, who was reading out the *Fire and the Frying-Pan* to his aide de camp in a loud and ghostly voice. The dreadful secret was told to him by Firkin with so frightened a look, that for the first moment Mr. Bowls and his young man thought that robbers were in the house; the legs of whom had probably been discovered by the woman under Miss Crawley's bed. When made aware of the fact however – to rush upstairs at three steps at a time – to enter the unconscious James's apartment, calling out, 'Mr. James,' in a voice stifled with alarm, and to cry, 'For Gawd's sake, sir, stop that 'ere pipe,' was the work of a minute with Mr. Bowls. 'Oh, Mr. James, what *'ave* you done,' he said in a voice of the deepest pathos, as he threw the implement out of the window. 'What 'ave you done, sir, missis can't abide 'em.'

'Missis needn't smoke,' said James with a frantic misplaced laugh, and thought the whole matter an excellent joke. But his feelings were very different in the morning, when Mr. Bowls's young man who operated upon Mr. James's boots, and brought him his hot water to shave that beard which he was so anxiously expecting, handed a note in to Mr. James in bed, in the handwriting of Miss Briggs.

'Dear sir,' it said, 'Miss Crawley has passed an exceedingly disturbed night, owing to the shocking manner in which the house has been polluted by tobacco; Miss Crawley bids me say she regrets that she is too unwell to see you before you go – and above all that she ever induced you to remove from the ale-house, where she is sure you will be much more comfortable during the rest of your stay at Brighton.'

And herewith honest James's career as a candidate for his aunt's favour ended. He *had* in fact, and without knowing it, done what he menaced to do. He had fought his cousin Pitt with the gloves.

Where meanwhile was he who had been once first favourite for this race for money? Becky and Rawdon, as we have seen, were come together after Waterloo, and were passing the winter of 1815 at Paris in great splendour and gaiety. Rebecca was a good economist, and the price poor Jos Sedley had paid for her two horses was in itself sufficient to keep their little establishment afloat for a year, at the least; there was no occasion to turn into money 'my pistols, the same which I shot Captain Marker,' or the gold dressing-case, or the cloak lined with sable. Becky had it made into a pelisse for herself, in which she rode in the Bois de Boulogne to the admiration of all: and you should have seen the scene between her and her delighted husband, whom she rejoined after the army had entered Cambray, and when she unsewed herself, and let out of her dress all those watches, knick-knacks, bank-notes, cheques, and valuables, which she had secreted in the wadding, previous to her meditated flight from Brussels! Tufto was charmed, and Rawdon roared with delightful laughter, and swore that she was better than any play he ever saw, by Jove. And the way in which she jockeyed Jos, and which she described with infinite fun, carried up his delight to a pitch of quite insane enthusiasm. He believed in his wife as much as the French soldiers in Napoleon.

Her success in Paris was remarkable. All the French ladies voted her charming. She spoke their language admirably. She adopted at once their grace, their liveliness, their manner. Her husband was stupid certainly – all English are stupid – and, besides, a dull husband at Paris is always a point in a lady's favour. He was the heir of the rich and *spirituelle* Miss Crawley, whose house had been open to so many of the French noblesse during the emigration. They received the colonel's wife in their own hotels – 'Why,' wrote a great lady to Miss Crawley, who had bought her lace and trinkets at the duchess's own price, and given her many a dinner during the pinching times after the Revolution – 'Why does not our dear miss come to her nephew and niece, and her attached friends in Paris? All the world *raffoles* of the charming mistress and her *espiègle* beauty. Yes, we see in her the grace, the charm, the wit of our dear friend Miss Crawley! The King took notice of her yesterday at the Tuileries, and we are all jealous of the attention which Monsieur pays her. If you could have seen the spite of a certain stupid Miladi Bareacres (whose eagle-beak and toque and feathers may be seen peering over the heads of all assemblies), when Madame the Duchess of Angoulême, the august daughter and companion of kings, desired especially to be presented to Mrs. Crawley, as your dear daughter and protégée, and thanked her in the name of France, for all your benevolence towards our unfortunates during their exile! She is of all the societies, of all the balls – of the balls – yes – of the dances, no; and yet how interesting and pretty this fair creature looks surrounded by the homage of the men, and so soon to be a mother! To hear her speak of you, her protectress, her mother, would bring tears to the eyes

of ogres. How she loves you! how we all love our admirable,
our respectable Miss Crawley!'

It is to be feared that this letter of the Parisian great lady
did not by any means advance Mrs. Becky's interest with
her admirable, her respectable, relative. On the contrary, the
fury of the old spinster was beyond bounds, when she found
what was Rebecca's situation, and how audaciously she had
made use of Miss Crawley's name, to get an entrée into
Parisian society. Too much shaken in mind and body to
compose a letter in the French language in reply to that of
her correspondent, she dictated to Briggs a furious answer
in her own native tongue, repudiating Mrs. Rawdon Crawley
altogether, and warning the public to beware of her as a
most artful and dangerous person. But as Madame the
Duchess of X — had only been twenty years in England,
she did not understand a single word of the language, and
contented herself by informing Mrs. Rawdon Crawley at
their next meeting, that she had received a charming letter
from that *chère Mees*, and that it was full of benevolent things
for Mrs. Crawley, who began seriously to have hopes that
the spinster would relent.

Meanwhile, she was the gayest and most admired of
Englishwomen: and had a little European congress on her
reception night. Prussians, and Cossacks, Spaniards and
English – all the world was at Paris during this famous
winter: to have seen the stars and cordons in Rebecca's
humble saloon would have made all Baker Street pale with
envy. Famous warriors rode by her carriage in the Bois, or
crowded her modest little box at the Opera. Rawdon was in
the highest spirits. There were no duns in Paris as yet: there
were parties every day at Vérey's or Beauvilliers'; play was
plentiful and his luck good. Tufto perhaps was sulky. Mrs.
Tufto had come over to Paris at her own invitation, and
besides this *contretemps*, there were a score of generals now
round Becky's chair, and she might take her choice of a
dozen bouquets when she went to the play. Lady Bareacres
and the chiefs of the English society, stupid and irreproachable females, writhed with anguish at the success of the little
upstart Becky, whose poisoned jokes quivered and rankled
in their chaste breasts. But she had all the men on her side.
She fought the women with indomitable courage, and they
could not talk scandal in any tongue but their own.

So in *fêtes*, pleasures, and prosperity, the winter of 1815–16 passed away with Mrs. Rawdon Crawley, who accommodated herself to polite life as if her ancestors had been people of fashion for centuries past – and who from her wit, talent, and energy, indeed merited a place of honour in Vanity Fair. In the early spring of 1816, Galignani's journal contained the following announcement in an interesting corner of the paper: 'On the 26th of March – the lady of Lieutenant-Colonel Crawley, of the Life Guards Green – of a son and heir.'

This event was copied into the London papers, out of which Miss Briggs read the statement to Miss Crawley, at breakfast, at Brighton. The intelligence, expected as it might have been, caused a crisis in the affairs of the Crawley family. The spinster's rage rose to its height, and sending instantly for Pitt, her nephew, and for the Lady Southdown, from Brunswick Square, she requested an immediate celebration of the marriage which had been so long pending between the two families. And she announced that it was her intention to allow the young couple a thousand a year during her lifetime, at the expiration of which the bulk of her property would be settled upon her nephew and her dear niece, Lady Jane Crawley. Waxy came down to ratify the deeds – Lord Southdown gave away his sister – she was married by a bishop, and not by the Rev. Bartholomew Irons – to the disappointment of the irregular prelate.

When they were married, Pitt would have liked to take a hymeneal tour with his bride, as became people of their condition. But the affection of the old lady towards Lady Jane had grown so strong, that she fairly owned she could not part with her favourite. Pitt and his wife came therefore, and lived with Miss Crawley: and (greatly to the annoyance of poor Pitt, who conceived himself a most injured character – being subject to the humours of his aunt on one side, and of his mother-in-law on the other) Lady Southdown, from her neighbouring house, reigned over the whole family – Pitt, Lady Jane, Miss Crawley, Briggs, Bowls, Firkin, and all. She pitilessly dosed them with her tracts and her medicine: she dismissed Creamer, she installed Rodgers, and soon stripped Miss Crawley of even the semblance of authority. The poor soul grew so timid that she actually left off bullying Briggs any more, and clung to her niece, more fond and more terrified every day. Peace to thee, kind and selfish, vain and generous old heathen! – We shall see thee no more. Let us hope that Lady Jane supported her kindly, and led her with gentle hand out of the busy struggle of Vanity Fair.

CHAPTER XXXV

WIDOW AND MOTHER

THE news of the great fights of Quatre Bras and Waterloo reached England at the same time. The *Gazette* first published the result of the two battles; at which glorious intelligence all England thrilled with triumph and fear. Particulars then followed; and after the announcement of the victories came the list of the wounded and the slain. Who can tell the dread with which that catalogue was opened and read! Fancy, at every village and homestead almost through the three kingdoms, the great news coming of the battles of Flanders, and the feelings of exultation and gratitude, bereavement and sickening dismay, when the lists of the regimental losses were gone through, and it became known whether the dear friend and relative had escaped or had fallen. Anybody who will take the trouble of looking back to a file of the newspapers of the time, must, even now, feel at second-hand this breathless pause of expectation. The lists of casualties are carried on from day to day: you stop in the midst as in a story which is to be continued in our next. Think what the feelings must have been as those papers followed each other fresh from the press; and if such an interest could be felt in our country, and about a battle where but twenty thousand of our people were engaged, think of the condition of Europe for twenty years before, where people were fighting, not by thousands, but by millions; each one of whom as he struck his enemy wounded horribly some other innocent heart far away.

The news which that famous *Gazette* brought to the Osbornes gave a dreadful shock to the family and its chief. The girls indulged unrestrained in their grief. The gloom-stricken old father was still more borne down by his fate and sorrow. He strove to think that a judgement was on the boy for his disobedience. He dared not own that the severity of the sentence frightened him, and that its fulfilment had

come too soon upon his curses. Sometimes a shuddering
terror struck him, as if he had been the author of the doom
which he had called down on his son. There was a chance
before of reconciliation. The boy's wife might have died; or
he might have come back and said, Father, I have sinned.
But there was no hope now. He stood on the other side of
the gulf impassable, haunting his parent with sad eyes. He
remembered them once before so in a fever, when every one
thought the lad was dying, and he lay on his bed speechless,
and gazing with a dreadful gloom. Good God! how the father
clung to the doctor then; and with what a sickening anxiety
he followed him: what a weight of grief was off his mind
when, after the crisis of the fever, the lad recovered, and
looked at his father once more with eyes that recognized
him. But now there was no help or cure, or chance of
reconcilement: above all, there were no humble words to
soothe vanity outraged and furious, or bring to its natural
flow the poisoned, angry blood. And it is hard to say which
pang it was that tore the proud father's heart most keenly
– that his son should have gone out of the reach of his
forgiveness, or that the apology which his own pride expected
should have escaped him.

Whatever his sensations might have been, however, the
stern old man would have no confidant. He never mentioned
his son's name to his daughters; but ordered the elder to
place all the females of the establishment in mourning; and
desired that the male servants should be similarly attired in
deep black. All parties and entertainments, of course, were
to be put off. No communications were made to his future
son-in-law, whose marriage-day had been fixed; but there
was enough in Mr. Osborne's appearance to prevent Mr.
Bullock from making any inquiries, or in any way pressing
forward that ceremony. He and the ladies whispered about
it under their voices in the drawing-room sometimes, whither
the father never came. He remained constantly in his own
study; the whole front part of the house being closed until
some time after the completion of the general mourning.

About three weeks after the 18th of June, Mr. Osborne's
acquaintance, Sir William Dobbin, called at Mr. Osborne's
house in Russell Square, with a very pale and agitated face,
and insisted upon seeing that gentleman. Ushered into his
room, and after a few words, which neither the speaker nor

the host understood, the former produced from an enclosure a letter sealed with a large red seal. 'My son, Major Dobbin,' the alderman said, with some hesitation, 'dispatched me a letter by an officer of the –th, who arrived in town to-day. My son's letter contains one for you, Osborne.' The alderman placed the letter on the table, and Osborne stared at him for a moment or two in silence. His looks frightened the ambassador, who after looking guiltily for a little time at the grief-stricken man, hurried away without a farther word.

The letter was in George's well-known bold handwriting. It was that one which he had written before daybreak on the 16th of June, and just before he took leave of Amelia. The great red seal was emblazoned with the sham coat of arms which Osborne had assumed from the *Peerage*, with '*Pax in bello*' for a motto; that of the ducal house with which the vain old man tried to fancy himself connected. The hand that signed it would never hold pen or sword more. The very seal that sealed it had been robbed from George's dead body as it lay on the field of battle. The father knew nothing of this, but sat and looked at the letter in terrified vacancy. He almost fell when he went to open it.

Have you ever had a difference with a dear friend? How his letters, written in the period of love and confidence, sicken and rebuke you! What a dreary mourning it is to dwell upon those vehement protests of dead affection! What lying epitaphs they make over the corpse of love! What dark, cruel comments upon Life and Vanities! Most of us have got or written drawers full of them. They are closet-skeletons which we keep and shun. Osborne trembled long before the letter from his dead son.

The poor boy's letter did not say much. He had been too proud to acknowledge the tenderness which his heart felt. He only said, that on the eve of a great battle, he wished to bid his father farewell, and solemnly to implore his good offices for the wife – it might be for the child – whom he left behind him. He owned with contrition that his irregularities and extravagance had already wasted a large part of his mother's little fortune. He thanked his father for his former generous conduct; and he promised him, that if he fell on the field or survived it, he would act in a manner worthy of the name of George Osborne.

His English habit, pride, awkwardness perhaps, had

prevented him from saying more. His father could not see the kiss George had placed on the superscription of his letter. Mr. Osborne dropped it with the bitterest, deadliest pang of balked affection and revenge. His son was still beloved and unforgiven.

About two months afterwards, however, as the young ladies of the family went to church with their father, they remarked how he took a different seat from that which he usually occupied when he chose to attend divine worship; and that from his cushion opposite, he looked up at the wall over their heads. This caused the young women likewise to gaze in the direction towards which the father's gloomy eyes pointed: and they saw an elaborate monument upon the wall, where Britannia was represented weeping over an urn, and a broken sword, and a couchant lion, indicated that the piece of sculpture had been erected in honour of a deceased warrior. The sculptors of those days had stocks of such funereal emblems in hand; as you may see still on the walls of St. Paul's, which are covered with hundreds of these braggart heathen allegories. There was a constant demand for them during the first fifteen years of the present century.

Under the memorial in question were emblazoned the well-known and pompous Osborne arms; and the inscription said, that the monument was 'Sacred to the memory of George Osborne, Junior, Esq., late a Captain in His Majesty's –th regiment of foot, who fell on the 18th of June, 1815, aged 28 years, while fighting for his king and country in the glorious victory of Waterloo. *Dulce et decorum est pro patria mori.*'

The sight of that stone agitated the nerves of the sisters so much that Miss Maria was compelled to leave the church. The congregation made way respectfully for those sobbing girls clothed in deep black, and pitied the stern old father seated opposite the memorial of the dead soldier. 'Will he forgive Mrs. George?' the girls said to themselves as soon as their ebullition of grief was over. Much conversation passed too among the acquaintances of the Osborne family, who knew of the rupture between the son and father caused by the former's marriage, as to the chance of a reconciliation with the young widow. There were bets among the gentlemen both about Russell Square and in the City.

If the sisters had any anxiety regarding the possible

recognition of Amelia as a daughter of the family, it was increased presently, and towards the end of the autumn, by their father's announcement that he was going abroad. He did not say whither, but they knew at once that his steps would be turned towards Belgium, and were aware that George's widow was still in Brussels. They had pretty accurate news indeed of poor Amelia from Lady Dobbin and her daughters. Our honest captain had been promoted in consequence of the death of the second major of the regiment of the field; and the brave O'Dowd, who had distinguished himself greatly here as upon all occasions where he had a chance to show his coolness and valour, was a colonel and Companion of the Bath.

Very many of the brave –th, who had suffered severely upon both days of action, were still at Brussels in the autumn, recovering of their wounds. The city was a vast military hospital for months after the great battles; and as men and officers began to rally from their hurts, the gardens and places of public resort swarmed with maimed warriors old and young, who, just rescued out of death, fell to gambling, and gaiety, and love-making, as people of Vanity Fair will do. Mr. Osborne found out some of the –th easily. He knew their uniform quite well, and had been used to follow all the promotions and exchanges in the regiment, and loved to talk about it and its officers as if he had been one of the number. On the day after his arrival at Brussels, and as he issued from his hotel, which faced the park, he saw a soldier in the well-known facings, reposing on a stone bench in the garden, and went and sat down trembling by the wounded convalescent man.

'Were you in Captain Osborne's company?' he said, and added, after a pause, 'he was my son, sir.'

The man was not of the captain's company, but he lifted up his unwounded arm and touched his cap sadly and respectfully to the haggard broken-spirited gentleman who questioned him. 'The whole army didn't contain a finer or a better officer,' the soldier said. 'The sergeant of the captain's company (Captain Raymond had it now) was in town, though, and was just well of a shot in the shoulder. His honour might see him if he liked, who could tell him anything he wanted to know about – about the –th's actions. But his honour had seen Major Dobbin, no doubt, the brave captain's great friend; and Mrs. Osborne, who was here too, and had been very bad, he heard everybody say. They say she was out of her mind like for six weeks or more. But your honour knows all about that – and asking your pardon' – the man added.

Osborne put a guinea into the soldier's hand, and told him he should have another if he would bring the sergeant to the Hotel du Parc; a promise which very soon brought the desired officer to Mr. Osborne's presence. And the first soldier went away; and after telling a comrade or two how Captain Osborne's father was arrived, and what a free-handed generous gentleman he was, they went and made good cheer with drink and feasting, as long as the guineas lasted which had come from the proud purse of the mourning old father.

In the sergeant's company, who was also just convalescent, Osborne made the journey of Waterloo and Quatre Bras, a journey which thousands of his countrymen were then taking. He took the sergeant with him in his carriage, and went through both fields under his guidance. He saw the point of the road where the regiment marched into action on the 16th, and the slope down which they drove the French cavalry who were pressing on the retreating Belgians. There was the spot where the noble captain cut down the French officer who was grappling with the young ensign for the colours, the colour-sergeants having been shot down. Along this road they retreated on the next day, and here was the bank at which the regiment bivouacked under the rain of the night of the 17th. Further on was the position which they took and held during the day, forming time after time to receive the charge of the enemy's horsemen, and lying down under shelter of the bank from the furious French cannonade. And it was at this declivity when at evening the whole English line received the order to advance, as the enemy fell back after his last charge, that the captain, hurraying and rushing down the hill waving his sword, received a shot and fell dead. 'It was Major Dobbin who took back the captain's body to Brussels,' the sergeant said, in a low voice, 'and had him buried as your honour knows.' The peasants and relic-hunters about the place were screaming round the pair, as the soldier told his story, offering for sale all sorts of mementoes of the fight, crosses, and epaulets, and shattered cuirasses, and eagles.

Osborne gave a sumptuous reward to the sergeant when he parted with him, after having visited the scenes of his son's last exploits. His burial-place he had already seen. Indeed, he had driven thither immediately after his arrival at Brussels. George's body lay in the pretty burial-ground of Laeken, near the city; in which place, having once visited it on a party of pleasure, he had lightly expressed a wish to have his grave made. And there the young officer was laid by his friend, in the unconsecrated corner of the garden, separated by a little hedge from the temples and towns and plantations of flowers and shrubs, under which the Roman Catholic dead repose. It seemed a humiliation to old Osborne to think that his son, an English gentleman, a captain in the famous British army, should not be found worthy to lie in ground where mere foreigners were buried. Which of us is there can tell how much vanity lurks in our warmest regard for others, and how selfish our love is? Old Osborne did not speculate much upon the mingled nature of his feelings, and how his instinct and selfishness were combating together. He firmly believed that everything he did was right, that he ought on all occasions to have his own way – and like the sting of a wasp or serpent his hatred rushed out armed and poisonous against anything like opposition. He was proud of his hatred as of everything else. Always to be right, always to trample forward, and never to doubt, are not these the great qualities with which dullness takes the lead in the world?

As after the drive to Waterloo, Mr. Osborne's carriage was nearing the gates of the city at sunset, they met another open barouche, in which were a couple of ladies and a gentleman, and by the side of which an officer was riding. Osborne gave a start back, and the sergeant, seated with him, cast a look of surprise at his neighbour, as he touched his cap to the officer, who mechanically returned the salute. It was Amelia, with the lame young ensign by her side, and opposite to her her faithful friend Mrs. O'Dowd. It was Amelia, but how changed from the fresh and comely girl Osborne knew. Her face was white and thin. Her pretty brown hair was parted under a widow's cap – the poor child. Her eyes were fixed, and looking nowhere. They stared blank in the face of Osborne, as the carriages crossed each other, but she did not know him; nor did he recognize her, until looking up, he saw Dobbin riding by her; and then he knew who it was. He hated her. He did not know how much until he saw her there. When her carriage had passed on, he turned and stared at the sergeant, with a curse and defiance in his eye, cast at his companion, who could not help looking at him – as much as to say, 'How dare *you* look at me? Damn you! I *do* hate her. It is she who has tumbled my hopes and all my pride down.' 'Tell the scoundrel to drive on quick,' he shouted with an oath, to the lackey on the box. A minute afterwards, a horse came clattering over the pavement behind Osborne's carriage, and Dobbin rode up. His thoughts had been elsewhere as the carriages passed each other, and it was not until he had ridden some paces forward, that he remembered it was Osborne who had just passed him. Then he turned to examine if the sight of her father-in-law had made any impression on Amelia, but the poor girl did not know who had passed. Then William, who daily used to accompany her in his drives, taking out his watch, made some excuse about an engagement which he suddenly recollected, and so rode off. She did not remark that either: but sat looking before her, over the homely landscape towards the woods in the distance, by which George marched away.

'Mr. Osborne, Mr. Osborne!' cried Dobbin, as he rode up and held out his hand. Osborne made no motion to take it, but shouted out once more and with another curse to his servant to drive on.

Dobbin laid his hand on the carriage side. 'I will see you, sir,' he said. 'I have a message for you.'

'From that woman?' said Osborne, fiercely.

'No,' replied the other, 'from your son;' at which Osborne fell back into the corner of his carriage, and Dobbin allowing it to pass on, rode close behind it, and so through the town until they reached Mr. Osborne's hotel, and without a word. There he followed Osborne up to his apartments. George had often been in the rooms; they were the lodgings which the Crawleys had occupied during their stay in Brussels.

'Pray, have you any commands for me, Captain Dobbin, or, I beg your pardon, I should say, *Major* Dobbin, since better men than you are dead, and you step into their *shoes*,' said Mr. Osborne, in that sarcastic tone which he sometimes was pleased to assume.

'Better men *are* dead,' Dobbin replied. 'I want to speak to you about one.'

'Make it short, sir,' said the other with an oath, scowling at his visitor.

'I am here as his closest friend,' the major resumed, 'and the executor of his will. He made it before we went into action. Are you aware how small his means are, and of the straitened circumstances of his widow?'

'I don't know his widow, sir,' Osborne said. 'Let her go back to her father.' But the gentleman whom he addressed was determined to remain in good temper, and went on without heeding the interruption.

'Do you know, sir, Mrs. Osborne's condition? Her life and her reason almost have been shaken by the blow which has fallen on her. It is very doubtful whether she will rally. There is a chance left for her, however, and it is about this I came to speak to you. She will be a mother soon. Will you visit the parent's offence upon the child's head? or will you forgive the child for poor George's sake?'

Osborne broke out into a rhapsody of self-praise and imprecations; by the first, excusing himself to his own conscience for his conduct; by the second, exaggerating the undutifulness of George. No father in all England could have behaved more generously to a son, who had rebelled against him wickedly. He had died without even so much as confessing he was wrong. Let him take the consequences of his undutifulness and folly. As for himself, Mr. Osborne, he was a man of his word. He had sworn never to speak to that woman, or to recognize her as his son's wife. 'And that's what you may tell her,' he concluded with an oath; 'and that's what I will stick to to the last day of my life.'

There was no hope from that quarter then. The widow must live on her slender pittance, or on such aid as Jos could give her. 'I might tell her, and she would not heed it,' thought Dobbin, sadly: for the poor girl's thoughts were not here at all since her catastrophe, and, stupefied under the pressure of her sorrow, good and evil were alike indifferent to her. So, indeed, were even friendship and kindness. She received them both uncomplainingly, and having accepted them, relapsed into her grief.

Suppose some twelve months after the above conversation took place to have passed in the life of our poor Amelia. She has spent the first portion of that time in a sorrow so profound and pitiable, that we who have been watching and describing some of the emotions of that weak and tender heart, must draw back in the presence of the cruel grief under which it is bleeding. Tread silently round the hapless couch of the poor prostrate soul. Shut gently the door of the dark chamber wherein she suffers, as those kind people did who nursed her through the first months of her pain, and never left her until heaven had sent her consolation. A day came – of almost terrified delight and wonder – when the poor widowed girl pressed a child upon her breast – a child, with the eyes of George who was gone – a little boy, as beautiful as a cherub. What a miracle it was to hear its first cry! How she laughed and wept over it – how love, and hope, and prayer woke again in her bosom as the baby nestled there. She was safe. The doctors who attended her, and had feared for her life or for her brain, had waited anxiously for this crisis before they could pronounce that either was secure. It was worth the long months of doubt and dread which the persons who had constantly been with her had passed, to see her eyes once more beaming tenderly upon them.

Our friend Dobbin was one of them. It was he who brought her back to England and to her mother's house; when Mrs. O'Dowd, receiving a peremptory summons from her colonel, had been forced to quit her patient. To see Dobbin holding the infant, and to hear Amelia's laugh of triumph as she watched him, would have done any man good who had a sense of humour. William was the god-father of the child, and exerted his ingenuity in the pur-chase of cups, spoons, pap-boats, and corals for this little Christian.

How his mother nursed him, and dressed him, and lived upon him; how she drove away all nurses, and would scarce allow any hand but her own to touch him; how she con-sidered that the greatest favour she could confer upon his godfather, Major Dobbin, was to allow the major occasionally to dandle him, need not be told here. This child was her being. Her existence was a maternal caress. She enveloped the feeble and unconscious creature with love and wor-ship. It was her life which the baby drank in from her bosom. Of nights, and when alone, she had stealthy and intense raptures of motherly love, such as God's marvellous care has awarded to the female instinct – joys how far higher and lower than reason – blind beautiful devotions which only women's hearts know. It was William Dobbin's task to muse upon these movements of Amelia's, and to watch her heart; and if his love made him divine almost all the feelings which agitated it, alas! he could see with a fatal perspicuity that there was no place there for him. And so, gently, he bore his fate, knowing it, and content to bear it.

I suppose Amelia's father and mother saw through the intentions of the major, and were not ill-disposed to encourage him; for Dobbin visited their house daily, and stayed for hours with them, or with Amelia, or with the honest landlord, Mr. Clapp, and his family. He brought, on one pretext or another, presents to everybody, and almost every day; and went, with the landlord's little girl, who was rather a favourite with Amelia, by the name of Major Sugarplums. It was this little child who commonly acted as mistress of the ceremonies to introduce him to Mrs. Osborne. She laughed one day when Major Sugarplums's cab drove up to Fulham, and he descended from it, bringing out a wooden horse, a drum, a trumpet, and other warlike toys, for little Georgy, who was scarcely six months old, and for whom the articles in question were entirely premature.

The child was asleep. 'Hush,' said Amelia, annoyed, perhaps, at the creaking of the major's boots; and she held out her hand; smiling because William could not take it until he had rid himself of his cargo of toys. 'Go downstairs, little Mary,' said he presently to the child, 'I want to speak to Mrs. Osborne.' She looked up rather astonished, and laid down the infant on its bed.

'I am come to say good-bye, Amelia,' said he, taking her slender little white hand gently.

'Good-bye? and where are you going?' she said, with a smile.

'Send the letters to the agents,' he said; 'they will forward them; for you will write to me, won't you? I shall be away a long time.'

'I'll write to you about Georgy,' she said. 'Dear William, how good you have been to him and to me! Look at him. Isn't he like an angel?'

The little pink hands of the child closed mechanically round the honest soldier's finger, and Amelia looked up in his face with bright maternal pleasure. The cruellest looks could not have wounded him more than that glance of hopeless kindness. He bent over the child and mother. He could not speak for a moment. And it was with all his strength that he could force himself to say a God bless you. 'God bless you,' said Amelia, and held up her face and kissed him.

'Hush! Don't wake Georgy!' she added, as William Dobbin went to the door with heavy steps. She did not hear the noise of his cab-wheels as he drove away: she was looking at the child, who was laughing in his sleep.

CHAPTER XXXVI

HOW TO LIVE WELL ON NOTHING A YEAR

I SUPPOSE there is no man in this Vanity Fair of ours so little observant as not to think sometimes about the worldly affairs of his acquaintances, or so extremely charitable as not to wonder how his neighbour Jones, or his neighbour Smith, can make both ends meet at the end of the year. With the utmost regard for the family, for instance (for I dine with them twice or thrice in the season), I cannot but own that the appearance of the Jenkinses in the Park, in the large barouche with the grenadier footmen, will surprise and mystify me to my dying day: for though I know the equipage is only jobbed, and all the Jenkins people are on board-wages, yet those three men and the carriage must represent an expense of six hundred a year at the very least – and then there are the splendid dinners, the two boys at Eton, the prize governess and masters for the girls, the trip abroad, or to Eastbourne or Worthing in the autumn, the annual ball with a supper from Gunter's (who, by the way, supplies most of the *first-rate* dinners which J. gives, as I know very well, having been invited to one of them to fill a vacant place, when I saw at once that these repasts are very superior to the *common* run of entertainments for which the *humbler* sort of J.'s acquaintances get cards) – who, I say, with the most good-natured feelings in the world, can help wondering how the Jenkinses make out matters? What *is* Jenkins? – we all know – Commissioner of the Tape and Sealing-Wax Office, with 1,200*l.* a year for a salary. Had his wife a private fortune? Pooh! – Miss Flint – one of eleven children of a small squire in Buckinghamshire. All she ever gets from her family is a turkey at Christmas, in exchange for which she has to board two or three of her sisters in the off season; and lodge and feed her brothers when they come to town. How does Jenkins balance his income? I say, as every friend of his must say, How is it that he has not been outlawed long since; and that he ever came back (as he did to the surprise of everybody) last year from Boulogne?

'I' is here introduced to personify the world in general – the Mrs. Grundy of each respected reader's private circle – every one of whom can point to some families of his acquaintance who live nobody knows how. Many a glass of wine have we all of us drunk, I have very little doubt, hob-and-nobbing with the hospitable giver, and wondering how the deuce he paid for it.

Some three or four years after his stay in Paris, when Rawdon Crawley and his wife were established in a very small comfortable house in Curzon Street, Mayfair, there was scarcely one of the numerous friends whom they entertained at dinner, that did not ask the above question regarding them. The novelist, it has been said before, knows everything, and as I am in a situation to be able to tell the public how Crawley and his wife lived without any income, may I entreat the public newspapers which are in the habit of extracting portions of the various periodical works now published, *not* to reprint the following exact narrative and calculations – of which I ought, as the discoverer (and at some expense, too), to have the benefit. My son, I would say, were I blessed with a child – you may by deep inquiry and constant intercourse with him, learn how a man lives comfortably on nothing a year. But it is best not to be intimate with gentlemen of this profession, and to take the calculations at second-hand, as you do logarithms, for to work them yourself, depend upon it, will cost you something considerable.

On nothing per annum, then, and during a course of some two or three years, of which we can afford to give but a very brief history, Crawley and his wife lived very happily and comfortably at Paris. It was in this period that he quitted the Guards, and sold out of the army. When we find him again, his moustachios and the title of colonel on his card are the only relics of his military profession.

It has been mentioned that Rebecca, soon after her arrival in Paris, took a very smart and leading position in the society of that capital, and was welcomed at some of the most distinguished houses of the restored French nobility. The English men of fashion in Paris courted her, too, to the disgust of the ladies their wives, who could not bear the parvenue. For some months the salons of the Faubourg St. Germain, in which her place was secured, and the splendours of the new Court, where she was received with much distinction, delighted, and perhaps a little intoxicated Mrs. Crawley, who may have been disposed during this period of elation to slight the people – honest young military men mostly – who formed her husband's chief society.

But the colonel yawned sadly among the duchesses and great ladies of the Court. The old women who played écarté made such a noise about a five-franc piece, that it was not worth Colonel Crawley's while to sit down at a card-table. The wit of their conversation he could not appreciate, being ignorant of their language. And what good could his wife get, he urged, by making curtsies every night to a whole circle of princesses? He left Rebecca presently to frequent these parties alone; resuming his own simple pursuits and amusements amongst the amiable friends of his own choice.

The truth is, when we say of a gentleman that he lives elegantly on nothing a year, we use the word 'nothing' to signify something unknown; meaning, simply, that we don't know how the gentleman in question defrays the expenses of his establishment. Now, our friend the colonel had a great aptitude for all games of chance: and exercising himself, as he continually did, with the cards, the dice-box, or the cue, it is natural to suppose that he attained a much greater skill in the use of these articles than men can possess who only occasionally handle them. To use a cue at billiards well is like using a pencil, or a German flute, or a small-sword – you cannot master any one of these implements at first, and it is only by repeated study and perseverance, joined to a natural taste, that a man can excel in the handling of either. Now, Crawley, from being only a brilliant amateur had grown to be a consummate master of billiards. Like a great general, his genius used to rise with the danger, and when the luck had been unfavourable to him for a whole game, and the bets were consequently against him, he would, with consummate skill and boldness, make some prodigious hits which would restore the battle, and come in a victor at the end, to the astonishment of everybody – of everybody, that is, who was a stranger to his play. Those who were accustomed to see it were cautious how they staked their money against a man of such sudden resources, and brilliant and overpowering skill.

At games of cards he was equally skilful; for though he would constantly lose money at the commencement of an evening, playing so carelessly and making such blunders, that new-comers were often inclined to think meanly of his talent; yet when roused to action, and awakened to caution by repeated small losses, it was remarked that Crawley's play became quite different, and that he was pretty sure of beating his enemy thoroughly before the night was over. Indeed, very few men could say that they ever had the better of him.

His successes were so repeated that no wonder the envious and the vanquished spoke sometimes with bitterness regarding them. And as the French say of the Duke of Wellington, who never suffered a defeat, that only an astonishing series of lucky accidents enabled him to be an invariable winner; yet even they allow that he cheated at Waterloo, and was enabled to win the last great trick: – so it was hinted at head quarters in England, that some foul play must have taken place in order to account for the continuous successes of Colonel Crawley.

Though Frascati's and the Salon were open at that time in Paris, the mania for play was so widely spread, that the public gambling-rooms did not suffice for the general ardour, and gambling went on in private houses as much as if there had been no public means for gratifying the passion. At Crawley's charming little *réunions* of an evening this fatal amusement commonly was practised – much to good-natured little Mrs. Crawley's annoyance. She spoke about her husband's passion for dice with the deepest grief; she bewailed it to everybody who came to her house. She besought the young fellows never, never to touch a box; and when young Green, of the Rifles, lost a very considerable sum of money, Rebecca passed a whole night in tears, as the servant told the unfortunate young gentleman, and actually went on her knees to her husband to beseech him to remit the debt, and burn the acknowledgement. How could he? He had lost just as much himself to Blackstone of the Hussars, and Count Punter of the Hanoverian Cavalry. Green might have any decent time; but pay? – of course he must pay; – to talk of burning I O U's was child's play.

Other officers, chiefly young – for the young fellows gathered round Mrs. Crawley – came from her parties with long faces, having dropped more or less money at her fatal card-tables. Her house began to have an unfortunate reputation. The old hands warned the less experienced of their danger. Colonel O'Dowd, of the – th regiment, one of those occupying in Paris, warned Lieutenant Spooney of that corps. A loud and violent fracas took place between the infantry-colonel and his lady, who were dining at the Café de Paris, and Colonel and Mrs. Crawley, who were also taking their meal there. The ladies engaged on both sides. Mrs. O'Dowd snapped her fingers in Mrs. Crawley's face, and called her husband 'no betther than a blackleg'. Colonel Crawley challenged Colonel O'Dowd, C.B. The commander-in-chief hearing of the dispute sent for Colonel Crawley, who was getting ready the same pistols, 'which he shot Captain Marker,' and had such a conversation with him that no duel took place. If Rebecca had not gone on her knees to General Tufto, Crawley would have been sent back to England; and he did not play, except with civilians, for some weeks after.

But in spite of Rawdon's undoubted skill and constant successes, it became evident to Rebecca, considering these things, that their position was but a precarious one, and that, even although they paid scarcely anybody, their little capital would end one day by dwindling into zero. 'Gambling,' she would say, 'dear, is good to help your income, but not as an income itself. Some day people may be tired of play, and then where are we?' Rawdon acquiesced in the justice of her opinion; and in truth he had remarked that after a few nights of his little suppers, &c., gentlemen *were* tired of play with him, and, in spite of Rebecca's charms, did not present themselves very eagerly.

Easy and pleasant as their life at Paris was, it was after all only an idle dalliance and amiable trifling; and Rebecca saw that she must push Rawdon's fortune in their own country. She must get him a place or appointment at home or in the colonies; and she determined to make a move upon England as soon as the way could be cleared for her. As a first step she had made Crawley sell out of the Guards, and go on half-pay. His function as aide de camp to General Tufto had ceased previously. Rebecca laughed in all companies at that officer, at his toupee (which he mounted on coming to Paris), at his waistband, at his false teeth, at his pretensions to be a lady-killer above all, and his absurd vanity in fancying every woman whom he came near was in love with him. It was Mrs. Brent, the beetle-browed wife of Mr. Commissary Brent, to whom the general transferred his attentions now — his bouquets, his dinners at the restaurateurs', his opera-boxes, and his knick-knacks. Poor Mrs. Tufto was no more happy than before, and had still to pass long evenings alone with her daughters, knowing that her general was gone off scented and curled to stand behind Mrs. Brent's chair at the play. Becky had a dozen admirers in his place to be sure; and could cut her rival to pieces with her wit. But as we have said, she was growing tired of this idle social life: opera-boxes and restaurateur dinners palled upon her: nosegays could not be laid by as a provision for future years: and she could not live upon knick-knacks, laced handkerchiefs, and kid gloves. She felt the frivolity of pleasure, and longed for more substantial benefits.

At this juncture news arrived which was spread among the many creditors of the colonel at Paris, and which caused them great satisfaction. Miss Crawley, the rich aunt from whom he expected his immense inheritance, was dying; the colonel must haste to her bedside. Mrs. Crawley and her child would remain behind until he came to reclaim them. He departed for Calais, and having reached that place in safety, it might have been supposed that he went to Dover; but instead he took the diligence to Dunkirk, and thence travelled to Brussels, for which place he had a former predilection. The fact is, he owed more money at London than at Paris; and he preferred the quiet little Belgian city to either of the more noisy capitals.

Her aunt was dead. Mrs. Crawley ordered the most intense mourning for herself and little Rawdon. The colonel was busy arranging the affairs of the inheritance. They could take the premier now, instead of the little entresol of the

hotel which they occupied. Mrs. Crawley and the landlord
had a consultation about the new hangings, an amicable
wrangle about the carpets, and a final adjustment of everything except the bill. She went off in one of his carriages;
her French *bonne* with her; the child by her side; the
admirable landlord and landlady smiling farewell to her from
the gate. General Tufto was furious when he heard she was
gone, and Mrs. Brent furious with him for being furious;
Lieutenant Spooney was cut to the heart; and the landlord
got ready his best apartments previous to the return of the
fascinating little woman and her husband. He *serré*'d the
trunks which she left in his charge with the greatest care.
They had been especially recommended to him by Madame
Crawley. They were not, however, found to be particularly
valuable when opened some time after.

But before she went to join her husband in the Belgic
capital, Mrs. Crawley made an expedition into England,
leaving behind her little son upon the Continent, under the
care of her French maid.

The parting between Rebecca and the little Rawdon did
not cause either party much pain. She had not, to say truth,
seen much of the young gentleman since his birth. After the
amiable fashion of French mothers, she had placed him out
at nurse in a village in the neighbourhood of Paris, where
little Rawdon passed the first months of his life, not unhappily, with a numerous family of foster-brothers, in wooden
shoes. His father would ride over many a time to see him
here, and the elder Rawdon's paternal heart glowed to see
him rosy and dirty, shouting lustily, and happy in the
making of mud-pies under the superintendence of the gardener's wife, his nurse.

Rebecca did not care much to go and see the son and
heir. Once he spoiled a new dove-coloured pelisse of hers.
He preferred his nurse's caresses to his mamma's, and when
finally he quitted that jolly nurse and almost parent, he cried
loudly for hours. He was only consoled by his mother's
promise that he should return to his nurse the next day;
indeed the nurse herself, who probably would have been
pained at the parting too, was told that the child would
immediately be restored to her, and for some time awaited
quite anxiously his return.

In fact, our friends may be said to have been among the

first of that brood of hardy English adventurers who have
subsequently invaded the Continent, and swindled in all the
capitals of Europe. The respect in those happy days of
1817–18 was very great for the wealth and honour of Britons.
They had not then learned, as I am told, to haggle for
bargains with the pertinacity which now distinguishes them.
The great cities of Europe had not been as yet open to the
enterprise of our rascals. And whereas, there is now hardly
a town of France or Italy in which you shall not see some
noble countryman of our own, with that happy swagger and
insolence of demeanour which we carry everywhere, swindling inn-landlords, passing fictitious cheques upon credulous
bankers, robbing coach-makers of their carriages, goldsmiths
of their trinkets, easy travellers of their money at cards, –
even public libraries of their books: – thirty years ago you
needed but to be a Milor Anglais, travelling in a private
carriage, and credit was at your hand wherever you chose
to seek it, and gentlemen, instead of cheating, were cheated.
It was not for some weeks after the Crawleys' departure that
the landlord of the hotel which they occupied during their
residence at Paris, found out the losses which he had sus-
tained: not until Madame Marabou, the milliner, made
repeated visits with her little bill for articles supplied to
Madame Crawley; not until Monsieur Didelot from the
Boule d'Or in the Palais Royal had asked half a dozen times
whether *cette charmante miladi* who had bought watches and
bracelets of him was *de retour*. It is a fact that even the poor
gardener's wife, who had nursed madame's child, was never
paid after the first six months for that supply of the milk
of human kindness with which she had furnished the lusty
and healthy little Rawdon. No, not even the nurse was paid
– the Crawleys were in too great a hurry to remember their
trifling debt to her. As for the landlord of the hotel, his
curses against the English nation were violent for the rest
of his natural life. He asked all travellers whether they knew
a certain Colonel Lor Crawley – *avec sa femme* – *une petite
dame, très spirituelle*. '*Ah, monsieur!*' he would add – '*ils m'ont
affreusement volé*.' It was melancholy to hear his accents as
he spoke of that catastrophe.

Rebecca's object in her journey to London was to effect
a kind of compromise with her husband's numerous creditors, and by offering them a dividend of ninepence or a

shilling in the pound, to secure a return for him into his own country. It does not become us to trace the steps which she took in the conduct of this most difficult negotiation; but, having shown them to their satisfaction, that the sum which she was empowered to offer was all her husband's available capital, and having convinced them that Colonel Crawley would prefer a perpetual retirement on the Continent to a residence in this country with his debts unsettled; having proved to them that there was no possibility of money accruing to him from other quarters, and no earthly chance of their getting a larger dividend than that which she was empowered to offer, she brought the colonel's creditors unanimously to accept her proposals, and purchased with fifteen hundred pounds of ready money, more than ten times that amount of debts.

Mrs. Crawley employed no lawyer in the transaction. The matter was so simple, to have or to leave, as she justly observed, that she made the lawyers of the creditors themselves do the business. And Mr. Lewis representing Mr. Davids, of Red Lion Square, and Mr. Moss acting for Mr. Manasseh of Cursitor Street (chief creditors of the colonel's), complimented his lady upon the brilliant way in which she did business, and declared that there was no professional man who could beat her.

Rebecca received their congratulations with perfect modesty; ordered a bottle of sherry and a bread cake to the little dingy lodgings where she dwelt, while conducting the business, to treat the enemy's lawyers: shook hands with them at parting, in excellent good humour, and returned straightway to the Continent, to rejoin her husband and son, and acquaint the former with the glad news of his entire liberation. As for the latter, he had been considerably neglected during his mother's absence by Mademoiselle Genevieve, her French maid; for that young woman, contracting an attachment for a soldier in the garrison of Calais, forgot her charge in the society of this *militaire*, and little Rawdon very narrowly escaped drowning on Calais sands at this period, where the absent Genevieve had left and lost him.

And so, Colonel and Mrs. Crawley came to London: and it is at their house in Curzon Street, Mayfair, that they really showed the skill which must be possessed by those who would live on the resources above-named.

CHAPTER XXXVII

THE SUBJECT CONTINUED

I N the first place, and as a matter of the greatest necessity, we are bound to describe how a house may be got for nothing a year. These mansions are to be had either unfurnished, where, if you have credit with Messrs. Gillows or Bantings, you can get them splendidly *montées* and decorated entirely according to your own fancy; or they are to be let furnished; a less troublesome and complicated arrangement to most parties. It was so that Crawley and his wife preferred to hire their house.

Before Mr. Bowls came to preside over Miss Crawley's house and cellar in Park Lane, that lady had had for a butler a Mr. Raggles, who was born on the family estate of Queen's Crawley, and indeed was a younger son of a gardener there. By good conduct, a handsome person and calves, and a grave demeanour, Raggles rose from the knife-board to the foot-board of the carriage; from the foot-board to the butler's pantry. When he had been a certain number of years at the head of Miss Crawley's establishment, where he had had good wages, fat perquisites, and plenty of opportunities of saving, he announced that he was about to contract a matrimonial alliance with a late cook of Miss Crawley's, who had subsisted in an honourable manner by the exercise of a mangle, and the keeping of a small greengrocer's shop in the neighbourhood. The truth is, that the ceremony had been clandestinely performed some years back; although the news of Mr. Raggles's marriage was first brought to Miss Crawley by a little boy and girl of seven and eight years of age, whose continual presence in the kitchen had attracted the attention of Miss Briggs.

Mr. Raggles then retired and personally undertook the superintendence of the small shop and the greens. He added milk and cream, eggs and country-fed pork to his stores, contenting himself, whilst other retired butlers were vending spirits in public-houses, by dealing in the simplest country produce. And having a good connexion amongst the butlers in the neighbourhood, and a snug back parlour where he and Mrs. Raggles received them, his milk, cream, and eggs got to be adopted by many of the fraternity, and his profits increased every year. Year after year he quietly and modestly amassed money, and when at length that snug and complete bachelor's residence at No. 201, Curzon Street, May Fair, lately the residence of the Honourable Frederick Deuceace, gone abroad, with its rich and appropriate furniture by the first makers, was brought to the hammer, who should go in and purchase the lease and furniture of the house but Charles Raggles? A part of the money he borrowed, it is true, and at rather a high interest, from a brother butler, but the chief part he paid down, and it was with no small pride that Mrs. Raggles found herself sleeping in a bed of carved mahogany, with silk curtains, with a prodigious cheval-glass opposite to her, and a wardrobe which would contain her, and Raggles, and all the family.

Of course, they did not intend to occupy permanently an apartment so splendid. It was in order to let the house again that Raggles purchased it. As soon as a tenant was found, he subsided into the greengrocer's shop once more; but a happy thing it was for him to walk out of that tenement and into Curzon Street, and there survey his house – his own house – with geraniums in the window and a carved bronze knocker. The footman occasionally lounging at the area railing treated him with respect; the cook took her green stuff at his house and called him Mr. Landlord; and there was not one thing the tenants did, or one dish which they had for dinner, that Raggles might not know of, if he liked.

He was a good man; good and happy. The house brought him in so handsome a yearly income, that he was determined to send his children to good schools, and accordingly, regardless of expense, Charles was sent to boarding at Dr. Swishtail's, Sugarcane Lodge, and little Matilda to Miss Peckover's, Laurentinum House, Clapham.

Raggles loved and adored the Crawley family as the author of all his prosperity in life. He had a silhouette of his mistress in his back shop, and a drawing of the porter's lodge at Queen's Crawley, done by that spinster herself in India ink – and the only addition he made to the decorations of the Curzon Street house was a print of Queen's Crawley in Hampshire, the seat of Sir Walpole Crawley, Baronet, who was represented in a gilded car drawn by six white horses, and passing by a lake covered with swans, and barges containing ladies in hoops, and musicians with flags and periwigs. Indeed Raggles thought there was no such palace in all the world, and no such august family.

As luck would have it, Raggles's house in Curzon Street was to let when Rawdon and his wife returned to London. The colonel knew it and its owner quite well; the latter's connexion with the Crawley family had been kept up constantly, for Raggles helped Mr. Bowls whenever Miss Crawley received friends. And the old man not only let his house to the colonel, but officiated as his butler whenever he had company; Mrs. Raggles operating in the kitchen below, and sending up dinners of which old Miss Crawley herself might have approved. This was the way, then, Crawley got his house for nothing; for though Raggles had to pay taxes and rates, and the interest of the mortgage to the brother butler; and the insurance of his life; and the charges for his children at school; and the value of the meat and drink which his own family – and for a time that of Colonel Crawley too – consumed; and though the poor wretch was utterly ruined by the transaction, his children being flung on the streets, and himself driven into the Fleet Prison: yet somebody must pay even for gentlemen who live for nothing a year – and so it was this unlucky Raggles was made the representative of Colonel Crawley's defective capital.

I wonder how many families are driven to roguery and to ruin by great practitioners in Crawley's way? – how many great noblemen rob their petty tradesmen, condescend to swindle their poor retainers out of wretched little sums, and cheat for a few shillings? When we read that a noble nobleman has left for the Continent, or that another noble nobleman has an execution in his house – and that one or other owe six or seven millions, the defeat seems glorious even, and we respect the victim in the vastness of his ruin. But who pities a poor barber who can't get his money for powdering the footmen's heads; or a poor carpenter who has ruined himself by fixing up ornaments and pavilions for my lady's *déjeuner;* or the poor devil of a tailor whom the steward patronizes, and who has pledged all he is worth, and more, to get the liveries ready, which my lord has done him the honour to bespeak? – When the great house tumbles down, these miserable wretches fall under it unnoticed: as they say in the old legends, before a man goes to the devil himself, he sends plenty of other souls thither.

Rawdon and his wife generously gave their patronage to all such of Miss Crawley's tradesmen and purveyors as chose to serve them. Some were willing enough, especially the poor ones. It was wonderful to see the pertinacity with which the washerwoman from Tooting brought the cart every Saturday, and her bills week after week. Mr. Raggles himself had to supply the greengroceries. The bill for servants' porter at the 'Fortune of War' public-house is a curiosity in the chronicles of beer. Every servant also was owed the greater part of his wages, and thus kept up perforce an interest in the house. Nobody in fact was paid. Not the blacksmith who opened the lock; nor the glazier who mended the pane; nor the jobber who let the carriage; nor the groom who drove it; nor the butcher who provided the leg of mutton; nor the coals which roasted it; nor the cook who basted it; nor the servants who ate it: and this I am given to understand is not unfrequently the way in which people live elegantly on nothing a year.

In a little town such things cannot be done without remark. We know there the quantity of milk our neighbour takes, and espy the joint or the fowls which are going in for his dinner. So, probably, 200 and 202 in Curzon Street might know what was going on in the house between them, the servants communicating through the area-railings; but Crawley and his wife and his friends did not know 200 and 202. When you came to 201 there was a hearty welcome, a kind smile, a good dinner, and a jolly shake of the hand from the host and hostess there, just for all the world as if they had been undisputed masters of three or four thousand a year – and so they were, not in money, but in produce and labour – if they did not pay for the mutton, they had it: if they did not give bullion in exchange for their wine, how should we know? Never was better claret at any man's table than at honest Rawdon's; dinners more gay and neatly served. His drawing-rooms were the prettiest little modest salons conceivable: they were decorated with the greatest taste, and a thousand knick-knacks from Paris, by Rebecca: and when she sat at her piano trilling songs with a lightsome heart, the stranger voted himself in a little paradise of domestic comfort, and agreed that if the husband was rather stupid, the wife was charming, and the dinners the pleasantest in the world.

Rebecca's wit, cleverness, and flippancy made her speedily the vogue in London among a certain class. You saw demure chariots at her door, out of which stepped very great people. You beheld her carriage in the Park, surrounded by dandies of note. The little box in the third tier of the Opera was crowded with heads constantly changing; but it must be confessed that the ladies held aloof from her, and that their doors were shut to our little adventurer.

With regard to the world of female fashion and its customs, the present writer of course can only speak at second-hand. A man can no more penetrate or understand those mysteries than he can know what the ladies talk about when they go upstairs after dinner. It is only by inquiry and perseverance, that one sometimes gets hints of those secrets; and by a similar diligence every person who treads the Pall Mall pavement and frequents the clubs of this metropolis, knows, either through his own experience or through some acquaintance with whom he plays at billiards or shares the joint, something about the genteel world of London, and how, as there are men (such as Rawdon Crawley, whose position we mentioned before), who cut a good figure to the eyes of the ignorant world and to the apprentices in the Park, who behold them consorting with the most notorious dandies there, so there are ladies, who may be called men's women, being welcomed entirely by all the gentlemen, and cut or slighted by all their wives. Mrs. Firebrace is of this sort; the lady with the beautiful fair ringlets whom you see every day in Hyde Park, surrounded by the greatest and most famous dandies of this empire. Mrs. Rockwood is another, whose parties are announced laboriously in the fashionable newspapers, and with whom you see that all sorts of ambassadors and great noblemen dine; and many more might be mentioned had they to do with the history at present in hand. But while simple folks who are out of the world, or country people with a taste for the genteel, behold these ladies in their seeming glory in public places, or envy them from afar off, persons who are better instructed could inform them that these envied ladies have no more chance of establishing themselves in 'society', than the benighted squire's wife in Somersetshire, who reads of their doings in the *Morning Post*. Men living about London are aware of these awful truths. You hear how pitilessly many ladies of seeming rank and wealth are excluded from this 'society'. The frantic efforts which they make to enter this circle, the meannesses to which they submit, the insults which they undergo, are matters of wonder to those who take human- or womankind for a study; and the pursuit of fashion under difficulties would be a fine theme for any very great person who had the wit, the leisure, and the knowledge of the English language necessary for the compiling of such a history.

Now the few female acquaintances whom Mrs. Crawley had known abroad, not only declined to visit her when she came to this side of the Channel, but cut her severely when they met in public places. It was curious to see how the great ladies forgot her, and no doubt not altogether a pleasant study to Rebecca. When Lady Bareacres met her in the waiting-room at the Opera, she gathered her daughters about her as if they would be contaminated by a touch of Becky, and retreating a step or two, placed herself in front of them, and stared at her little enemy. To stare Becky out of countenance required a severer glance than even the frigid old Bareacres could shoot out of her dismal eyes. When Lady de la Mole, who had ridden a score of times by Becky's side at Brussels, met Mrs. Crawley's open carriage in Hyde Park, her ladyship was quite blind, and could not in the least recognize her former friend. Even Mrs. Blenkinsop, the banker's wife, cut her at church. Becky went regularly to church now; it was edifying to see her enter there with Rawdon by her side, carrying a couple of large gilt Prayer-books, and afterwards going through the ceremony with the gravest resignation.

Rawdon at first felt very acutely the slights which were passed upon his wife, and was inclined to be gloomy and savage. He talked of calling out the husbands or brothers of every one of the insolent women who did not pay a proper respect to his wife; and it was only by the strongest com-mands and entreaties on her part, that he was brought into keeping a decent behaviour. 'You can't shoot me into society,' she said, good-naturedly. 'Remember, my dear, that I was but a governess, and you, you poor silly old man, have the worst reputation for debt, and dice, and all sorts of wickedness. We shall get quite as many friends as we want by and by, and in the meanwhile you must be a good boy, and obey your schoolmistress in everything she tells you to do. When we heard that your aunt had left almost everything to Pitt and his wife, do you remember what a rage you were in? You would have told all Paris, if I had not made you keep your temper, and where would you have been now? – in prison at Sainte-Pélagie for debt, and not established in London in a handsome house, with every comfort about you – you were in such a fury you were ready to murder your brother, you wicked Cain you, and what good would have come of remaining angry? All the rage in the world won't get us your aunt's money; and it is much better that we should be friends with your brother's family than enemies, as those foolish Butes are. When your father dies, Queen's Crawley will be a pleasant house for you and me to pass the winter in. If we are ruined, you can carve and take charge of the stable, and I can be a governess to Lady Jane's children. Ruined! fiddlededee! I will get you a good place before that; or Pitt and his little boy will die, and we will be Sir Rawdon and my lady. While there is life, there is hope, my dear, and I intend to make a man of you yet. Who sold your horses for you? Who paid your debts for you?' Rawdon was obliged to confess that he owed all these benefits to his wife, and to trust himself to her guidance for the future.

Indeed, when Miss Crawley quitted the world, and that money for which all her relatives had been fighting so eagerly was finally left to Pitt, Bute Crawley, who found that only five thousand pounds had been left to him instead of the twenty upon which he calculated, was in such a fury at his disappointment, that he vented it in savage abuse upon his nephew; and the quarrel always rankling between them ended in an utter breach of intercourse. Rawdon Crawley's conduct, on the other hand, who got but a hundred pounds, was such as to astonish his brother and delight his sister-in-law, who was disposed to look kindly upon all the members of her husband's family. He wrote to his brother a very frank, manly, good-humoured letter from Paris. He was aware, he said, that by his own marriage he had forfeited his aunt's favour; and though he did not disguise his disappointment that she should have been so entirely relentless towards him, he was glad that the money was still kept in their branch of the family, and heartily congratulated his brother on his good fortune. He sent his affectionate remembrances to his sister, and hoped to have her goodwill for Mrs. Rawdon; and the letter concluded with a postscript to Pitt in the latter lady's own handwriting. She, too, begged to join in her husband's congratulations. She should ever remember Mr. Crawley's kindness to her in early days when she was a friendless orphan, the instructress of his little sisters, in whose welfare she still took the tenderest interest. She wished him every happiness in his married life, and, asking his permission to offer her remembrances to Lady Jane (of whose goodness all the world informed her), she hoped that one day she might be allowed to present her little boy to his uncle and aunt, and begged to bespeak for him their goodwill and protection.

Pitt Crawley received this communication very graciously – more graciously than Miss Crawley had received some of Rebecca's previous compositions in Rawdon's handwriting; and as for Lady Jane, she was so charmed with the letter, that she expected her husband would instantly divide her aunt's legacy into two equal portions, and send off one-half to his brother at Paris.

To her ladyship's surprise, however, Pitt declined to accommodate his brother with a cheque for thirty thousand pounds. But he made Rawdon a handsome offer of his hand whenever the latter should come to England and choose to take it; and, thanking Mrs. Crawley for her good opinion of himself and Lady Jane, he graciously pronounced his willingness to take any opportunity to serve her little boy.

Thus an almost reconciliation was brought about between the brothers. When Rebecca came to town Pitt and his wife were not in London. Many a time she drove by the old door in Park Lane to see whether they had taken possession of Miss Crawley's house there. But the new family did not make its appearance; it was only through Raggles that she heard of their movements – how Miss Crawley's domestics had been dismissed with decent gratuities, and how Mr. Pitt had only once made his appearance in London, when he stopped for a few days at the house, did business with his lawyers there, and sold off all Miss Crawley's French novels to a bookseller out of Bond Street. Becky had reasons of her own which caused her to long for the arrival of her new relation. 'When Lady Jane comes,' thought she, 'she shall be my sponsor in London society; and as for the women! bah! the women will ask me when they find the men want to see me.'

An article as necessary to a lady in this position as her brougham or her bouquet, is her companion. I have always admired the way in which the tender creatures, who cannot exist without sympathy, hire an exceedingly plain friend of their own sex from whom they are almost inseparable. The sight of that inevitable woman in her faded gown seated behind her dear friend in the opera-box, or occupying the back seat of the barouche, is always a wholesome and moral one to me, as jolly a reminder as that of the death's-head which figured in the repasts of Egyptian *bon-vivants*, a strange sardonic memorial of Vanity Fair. What? – even battered, brazen, beautiful, conscienceless, heartless Mrs. Firebrace, whose father died of her shame: even lovely, daring Mrs. Mantrap, who will ride at any fence which any man in England will take, and who drives her greys in the Park, while her mother keeps a huxter's stall in Bath still; – even those who are so bold, one might fancy they could face anything, dare not face the world without a female friend. They must have somebody to cling to, the affectionate creatures! And you will hardly see them in any public place without a shabby companion in a dyed silk, sitting somewhere in the shade close behind them.

'Rawdon,' said Becky, very late one night, as a party of gentlemen were seated round her crackling drawing-room fire (for the men came to her house to finish the night; and she had ice and coffee for them, the best in London): 'I must have a sheep-dog.'

'A what?' said Rawdon, looking up from an écarté table.

'A sheep-dog!' said young Lord Southdown. 'My dear Mrs. Crawley, what a fancy! Why not have a Danish dog? I know of one as big as a camelopard, by Jove. It would almost pull your brougham. Or a Persian grey-hound, eh? (I propose, if you please); or a little pug that would go into one of Lord Steyne's snuff-boxes? There's a man at Bayswater got one with such a nose that you might, – I mark the king and play, – that you might hang your hat on it.'

'I mark the trick,' Rawdon gravely said. He attended to his game commonly, and didn't much meddle with the conversation except when it was about horses and betting.

'What *can* you want with a shepherd's dog?' the lively little Southdown continued.

'I mean a *moral* shepherd's dog,' said Becky, laughing, and looking up at Lord Steyne.

'What the devil's that?' said his lordship.

'A dog to keep the wolves off me,' Rebecca continued. 'A companion.'

'Dear little innocent lamb, you want one,' said the marquis; and his jaw thrust out, and he began to grin hideously, his little eyes leering towards Rebecca.

The great Lord of Steyne was standing by the fire sipping coffee. The fire crackled and blazed pleasantly. There was a score of candles sparkling round the mantelpiece, in all sorts of quaint sconces, of gilt and bronze and porcelain. They lighted up Rebecca's figure to admiration, as she sat on a sofa covered with a pattern of gaudy flowers. She was in a pink dress, that looked as fresh as a rose; her dazzling white arms and shoulders were half covered with a thin hazy scarf through which they sparkled; her hair hung in curls round her neck; one of her little feet peeped out from the fresh crisp folds of the silk: the prettiest little foot in the prettiest little sandal in the finest silk stocking in the world.

The candles lighted up Lord Steyne's shining bald head, which was fringed with red hair. He had thick bushy eyebrows, with little twinkling bloodshot eyes, surrounded by a thousand wrinkles. His jaw was underhung, and when he laughed, two white buck-teeth protruded themselves and glistened savagely in the midst of the grin. He had been dining with royal personages, and wore his garter and ribbon. A short man was his lordship, broad-chested, and bow-legged, but proud of the fineness of his foot and ankle, and always caressing his garter-knee.

'And so the Shepherd is not enough,' said he, 'to defend his lambkin?'

'The Shepherd is too fond of playing at cards and going to his clubs,' answered Becky, laughing.

'Gad, what a debauched Corydon!' said my lord – 'what a mouth for a pipe!'

'I take your three to two,' here said Rawdon, at the card-table.

'Hark at Meliboeus,' snarled the noble marquis; 'he's pastorally occupied too: he's shearing a Southdown. What an innocent mutton, hey? Damme, what a snowy fleece!'

Rebecca's eyes shot out gleams of scornful humour. 'My lord,' she said, 'you are a knight of the Order.' He had the collar round his neck, indeed – a gift of the restored princes of Spain.

Lord Steyne in early life had been notorious for his daring and his success at play. He had sat up two days and two nights with Mr. Fox at hazard. He had won money of the most august personages of the realm: he had won his marquisate, it was said, at the gaming-table; but he did not like an allusion to those bygone *fredaines*. Rebecca saw the scowl gathering over his heavy brow.

She rose up from her sofa, and went and took his coffee-cup out of his hand with a little curtsy. 'Yes,' she said, 'I must get a watch-dog. But he won't bark at *you*.' And, going into the other drawing-room, she sat down to the piano, and began to sing little French songs in such a charming, thrilling voice, that the mollified nobleman speedily followed her into that chamber, and might be seen nodding his head and bowing time over her.

Rawdon and his friend meanwhile played écarté until they had enough. The colonel won; but, say that he won ever so much and often, nights like these, which occurred many times in the week – his wife having all the talk and all the admiration, and he sitting silent without the circle, not comprehending a word of the jokes, the allusions, the mystical language within – must have been rather wearisome to the ex-dragoon.

'How is Mrs. Crawley's husband?' Lord Steyne used to say to him by way of a good day when they met: and indeed that was now his avocation in life. He was Colonel Crawley no more. He was Mrs. Crawley's husband.

About the little Rawdon, if nothing has been said all this while, it is because he is hidden upstairs in a garret somewhere, or has crawled below into the kitchen for companionship. His mother scarcely ever took notice of him. He passed the days with his French *bonne* as long as that domestic remained in Mr. Crawley's family, and when the Frenchwoman went away, the little fellow, howling in the loneliness of the night, had compassion taken on him by a housemaid, who took him out of his solitary nursery into her bed in the garret hard by, and comforted him.

Rebecca, my Lord Steyne, and one or two more were in the drawing-room taking tea after the Opera, when this shouting was heard overhead. 'It's my cherub crying for his nurse,' she said. She did not offer to move to go and see the child. 'Don't agitate your feelings by going to look for him,' said Lord Steyne, sardonically. 'Bah!' replied the other, with a sort of blush, 'he'll cry himself to sleep;' and they fell to talking about the Opera.

Rawdon had stolen off though, to look after his son and heir; and came back to the company when he found that honest Dolly was consoling the child. The colonel's dressing-room was in those upper regions. He used to see the boy there in private. They had interviews together every morning when he shaved; Rawdon minor sitting on a box by his father's side and watching the operation with never-ceasing pleasure. He and the sire were great friends. The father would bring him sweetmeats from the dessert, and hide them in a certain old epaulet box, where the child went to seek them, and laughed with joy on discovering the treasure: laughed, but not too loud: for mamma was below asleep and must not be disturbed. She did not go to rest till very late, and seldom rose till after noon.

Rawdon bought the boy plenty of picture-books, and crammed his nursery with toys. Its walls were covered with pictures pasted up by the father's own hand, and purchased by him for ready money. When he was off duty with Mrs. Rawdon in the Park, he would sit up here, passing hours with the boy; who rode on his chest, who pulled his great moustachios as if they were driving-reins, and spent days with him in indefatigable gambols. The room was a low room, and once, when the child was not five years old his father, who was tossing him wildly up in his arms, hit the poor little chap's skull so violently against the ceiling, that he almost dropped the child, so terrified was he at the disaster.

Rawdon minor had made up his face for a tremendous howl – the severity of the blow indeed authorized that indulgence: but just as he was going to begin, the father interposed.

'For God's sake, Rawdy, don't wake mamma,' he cried. And the child looking in a very hard and piteous way at his father, bit his lips, clenched his hands, and didn't cry a bit. Rawdon told that story at the clubs, at the mess, to everybody in town. 'By Gad, sir,' he explained to the public in general, 'what a good plucked one that boy of mine is – what a trump he is! I half sent his head through the ceiling, by Gad, and he wouldn't cry for fear of disturbing his mother.'

Sometimes – once or twice in a week – that lady visited the upper regions in which the child lived. She came in like a vivified figure out of the *Magasin des Modes* – blandly smiling in the most beautiful new clothes and little gloves and boots. Wonderful scarfs, laces, and jewels glittered about her. She had always a new bonnet on: and flowers bloomed perpetually in it: or else magnificent curling ostrich feathers, soft and snowy as camellias. She nodded twice or thrice patronizingly to the little boy, who looked up from his dinner or from the pictures of soldiers he was painting. When she left the room an odour of rose, or some other magical fragrance lingered about the nursery. She was an unearthly being in his eyes, superior to his father – to all the world: to be worshipped and admired at a distance. To drive with that lady in the carriage was an awful rite: he sat up in the back seat, and did not dare to speak: he gazed with all his eyes at the beautifully-dressed princess opposite to him. Gentlemen on splendid prancing horses came up, and smiled and talked with her. How her eyes beamed upon all of them! Her hand used to quiver and wave gracefully as they passed. When he went out with her he had his new red dress on. His old brown holland was good enough when he stayed at home. Sometimes, when she was away, and Dolly his maid was making his bed, he came into his mother's room. It was as the abode of a fairy to him – a mystic chamber of splendour and delights. There in the wardrobe hung those wonderful robes – pink and blue, and many-tinted. There was the jewel-case, silver-clasped: and the wondrous bronze hand on the dressing-table, glistening all over with a hundred rings. There was the cheval-glass, that miracle of art, in which he could just see his own wondering head, and the reflection of Dolly (queerly distorted, and as if up in the ceiling), plumping and patting the pillows of the bed. O thou poor lonely little benighted boy! Mother is the name for God in the lips and hearts of little children; and here was one who was worshipping a stone!

Now Rawdon Crawley, rascal as the colonel was, had certain manly tendencies of affection in his heart, and could love a child and a woman still. For Rawdon minor he had a great secret tenderness then, which did not escape Rebecca, though she did not talk about it to her husband. It did not annoy her: she was too good-natured. It only increased her scorn for him. He felt somehow ashamed of this paternal softness, and hid it from his wife – only indulging in it when alone with the boy.

He used to take him out of mornings, when they would go to the stables together and to the Park. Little Lord Southdown, the best-natured of men, who would make you a present of the hat from his head, and whose main occupation in life was to buy knick-knacks that he might give them away afterwards, bought the little chap a pony not much bigger than a large rat, the donor said, and on this little black Shetland pygmy young Rawdon's great father was pleased to mount the boy, and to walk by his side in the Park. It pleased him to see his old quarters, and his old fellow-guardsmen at Knightsbridge: he had begun to think of his bachelorhood with something like regret. The old troopers were glad to recognize their ancient officer, and dandle the little colonel. Colonel Crawley found dining at mess and with his brother-officers very pleasant. 'Hang it, I ain't clever enough for her – I know it. She won't miss me,' he used to say: and he was right: his wife did not miss him.

Rebecca was fond of her husband. She was always perfectly good-humoured and kind to him. She did not even show her scorn much for him; perhaps she liked him the better for being a fool. He was her upper servant and *maître d'hôtel*. He went on her errands: obeyed her orders without question: drove in the carriage in the ring with her without repining; took her to the opera-box; solaced himself at his club during the performance, and came punctually back to fetch her when due. He would have liked her to be a little fonder of the boy: but even to that he reconciled himself. 'Hang it, you know she's so clever,' he said, 'and I'm not literary and that, you know.' For, as we have said before, it requires no great wisdom to be able to win at cards and billiards, and Rawdon made no pretensions to any other sort of skill.

When the companion came, his domestic duties became very light. His wife encouraged him to dine abroad: she would let him off duty at the Opera. 'Don't stay and stupefy yourself at home to-night, my dear,' she would say. 'Some men are coming who will only bore you. I would not ask them, but you know it's for your good, and now I have a sheep-dog, I need not be afraid to be alone.'

'A sheep-dog – a companion! Becky Sharp with a companion! Isn't it good fun?' thought Mrs. Crawley to herself. The notion tickled hugely her sense of humour.

One Sunday morning, as Rawdon Crawley, his little son, and the pony, were taking their accustomed walk in the Park, they passed by an old acquaintance of the colonel's, Corporal Clink, of the regiment, who was in conversation with a friend, an old gentleman, who held a boy in his arms about the age of little Rawdon. This other youngster had seized hold of the Waterloo medal which the corporal wore, and was examining it with delight.

'Good morning, your honour,' said Clink, in reply to the 'How-do, Clink?' of the colonel. 'This 'ere young gentleman is about the little colonel's age, sir,' continued the corporal.

'His father was a Waterloo man, too,' said the old gentleman who carried the boy. 'Wasn't he, Georgy?'

'Yes,' said Georgy. He and the little chap on the pony were looking at each other with all their might – solemnly scanning each other as children do.

'In a line regiment,' Clink said, with a patronizing air.

'He was a captain in the – th Regiment,' said the old gentleman, rather pompously. 'Captain George Osborne, sir – perhaps you knew him. He died the death of a hero, sir, fighting against the Corsican tyrant.'

Colonel Crawley blushed quite red. 'I knew him very well, sir,' he said, 'and his wife, his dear little wife, sir – how is she?'

'She is my daughter, sir,' said the old gentleman, pulling down the boy, and taking out a card with great solemnity, which he handed to the colonel. On it was written –

'Mr. Sedley, Sole Agent for the Black Diamond and Anti-Cinder Coal Association, Bunker's Wharf, Thames Street, and Anna-Maria Cottages, Fulham Road West.'

Little Georgy went up and looked at the Shetland pony.

'Should you like to have a ride?' said Rawdon minor from the saddle.

'Yes,' said Georgy. The colonel, who had been looking at him with some interest, took up the child and put him on the pony behind Rawdon minor.

'Take hold of him, Georgy,' he said, 'take my little boy round the waist – his name is Rawdon.' And both the children began to laugh.

'You won't see a prettier pair, I think, *this* summer's day, sir,' said the good-natured corporal; and the colonel, the corporal, and old Mr. Sedley with his umbrella, walked by the side of the children.

CHAPTER XXXVIII

A FAMILY IN A VERY SMALL WAY

W E must suppose little George Osborne has ridden from Knightsbridge towards Fulham, and will stop and make inquiries at that village regarding some friends whom we have left there. How is Mrs. Amelia after the storm of Waterloo? Is she living and thriving? What has come of Major Dobbin, whose cab was always hankering about her premises? and are there any news of the collector of Boggley Wollah? The facts concerning the latter are briefly these:–

Our worthy fat friend Joseph Sedley returned to India not long after his escape from Brussels. Either his furlough was up, or he dreaded to meet any witnesses of his Waterloo flight. However it might be, he went back to his duties in Bengal, very soon after Napoleon had taken up his residence at St. Helena, where Jos saw the ex-Emperor. To hear Mr. Sedley talk on board ship you would have supposed that it was not the first time he and the Corsican had met, and that the civilian had bearded the French general at Mount St. John. He had a thousand anecdotes about the famous battles; he knew the position of every regiment, and the loss which each had incurred. He did not deny that he had been concerned in those victories – that he had been with the army, and carried dispatches for the Duke of Wellington. And he described what the duke did and said on every conceivable moment of the day of Waterloo, with such an accurate knowledge of his grace's sentiments and proceedings, that it was clear he must have been by the conqueror's side throughout the day; though, as a non-combatant, his name was not mentioned in the public documents relative to the battle. Perhaps he actually worked himself up to believe that he had been engaged with the army; certain it is that he made a prodigious sensation for some time at Calcutta, and was called Waterloo Sedley during the whole of his subsequent stay in Bengal.

The bills which Jos had given for the purchase of those unlucky horses were paid without question by him and his agents. He never was heard to allude to the bargain, and nobody knows for a certainty what became of the horses, or how he got rid of them, or of Isidor, his Belgian servant, who sold a grey horse, very like the one which Jos rode, at Valenciennes some time during the autumn of 1815.

Jos's London agents had orders to pay one hundred and twenty pounds yearly to his parents at Fulham. It was the chief support of the old couple; for Mr. Sedley's speculations in life subsequent to his bankruptcy did not by any means retrieve the broken old gentleman's fortune. He tried to be a wine-merchant, a coal-merchant, a commission-lottery agent, &c. &c. He sent round prospectuses to his friends whenever he took a new trade, and ordered a new brass plate for the door, and talked pompously about making his fortune still. But Fortune never came back to the feeble and stricken old man. One by one his friends dropped off, and were weary of buying dear coals and bad wine from him; and there was only his wife in all the world who fancied, when he tottered off to the City of a morning, that he was still doing any business there. At evening he crawled slowly back; and he used to go of nights to a little club at a tavern, where he disposed of the finances of the nation. It was wonderful to hear him talk about millions, and agios, and discounts, and what Rothschild was doing, and Baring Brothers. He talked of such vast sums that the gentlemen of the club (the apothecary, the undertaker, the great carpenter and builder, the parish clerk, who was allowed to come stealthily, and

Mr. Clapp, our old acquaintance) respected the old gentleman. 'I was better off once, sir,' he did not fail to tell
everybody who 'used the room'. 'My son, sir, is at this
minute chief magistrate of Ramgunge in the Presidency of
Bengal, and touching his four thousand rupees *per mensem*.
My daughter might be a colonel's lady if she liked. I might
draw upon my son, the first magistrate, sir, for two thousand
pound to-morrow, and Alexander would cash my bill, down
sir, down on the counter, sir. But the Sedleys were always
a proud family.' You and I, my dear reader, may drop into
this condition one day: for have not many of our friends
attained it? Our luck may fail: our powers forsake us: our
place on the boards be taken by better and younger mimes
– the chance of life roll away and leave us shattered and
stranded. Then men will walk across the road when they
meet you – or, worse still, hold you out a couple of fingers
and patronize you in a pitying way – then you will know,
as soon as your back is turned, that your friend begins with
a 'Poor devil, what imprudences he has committed, what
chances *that* chap has thrown away!' Well, well – a carriage
and three thousand a year is not the summit of the reward
nor the end of God's judgement of men. If quacks prosper
as often as they go to the wall – if zanies succeed and knaves
arrive at fortune, and, vice versa, sharing ill luck and
prosperity for all the world like the ablest and most honest
amongst us – I say, brother, the gifts and pleasures of Vanity
Fair cannot be held of any great account, and that it is
probable . . . but we are wandering out of the domain of the
story.

Had Mrs. Sedley been a woman of energy, she would
have exerted it after her husband's ruin, and, occupying a
large house, would have taken in boarders. The broken
Sedley would have acted well as the boarding-house landlady's husband; the Munoz of private life; the titular lord
and master: the carver, house-steward, and humble husband
of the occupier of the dingy throne. I have seen men of good
brains and breeding, and of good hopes and vigour once,
who feasted squires and kept hunters in their youth, meekly
cutting up legs of mutton for rancorous old harridans, and
pretending to preside over their dreary tables – but Mrs.
Sedley, we say, had not spirit enough to bustle about for 'a
few select inmates to join a cheerful musical family', such

as one reads of in the *Times*. She was content to lie on the
shore where fortune had stranded her – and you could see
that the career of this old couple was over.

I don't think they were unhappy. Perhaps they were a
little prouder in their downfall than in their prosperity. Mrs.
Sedley was always a great person for her landlady, Mrs.
Clapp, when she descended and passed many hours with her
in the basement or ornamented kitchen. The Irish maid Betty
Flanagan's bonnets and ribbons, her sauciness, her idleness,
her reckless prodigality of kitchen candles, her consumption
of tea and sugar, and so forth, occupied and amused the old
lady almost as much as the doings of her former household,
when she had Sambo and the coachman, and a groom, and
a footboy, and a housekeeper with a regiment of female
domestics – her former household, about which the good
lady talked a hundred times a day. And besides Betty
Flanagan, Mrs. Sedley had all the maids-of-all-work in the
street to superintend. She knew how each tenant of the
cottages paid or owed his little rent. She stepped aside
when Mrs. Rougemont the actress passed with her dubious
family. She flung up her head when Mrs. Pestler, the
apothecary's lady, drove by in her husband's professional
one-horse chaise. She had colloquies with the greengrocer
about the penn'orth of turnips which Mr. Sedley loved:
she kept an eye upon the milkman, and the baker's boy;
and made visitations to the butcher, who sold hundreds of
oxen very likely with less ado than was made about Mrs.
Sedley's loin of mutton: and she counted the potatoes under
the joint on Sundays, on which days, dressed in her best,
she went to church twice and read Blair's sermons in the
evening.

On that day, for 'business' prevented him on week-days
from taking such a pleasure, it was old Sedley's delight to
take out his little grandson Georgy to the neighbouring parks
or Kensington Gardens, to see the soldiers or to feed the
ducks. Georgy loved the red-coats, and his grandpapa told
him how his father had been a famous soldier, and introduced him to many sergeants and others with Waterloo
medals on their breasts, to whom the old grandfather pompously presented the child as the son of Captain Osborne of
the –th, who died gloriously on the glorious 18th. He has
been known to treat some of these non-commissioned gentle-

men to a glass of porter, and, indeed, in their first Sunday walks, was disposed to spoil little Georgy, sadly gorging the boy with apples and parliament, to the detriment of his health – until Amelia declared that George should never go out with his grandpapa, unless the latter promised solemnly, and on his honour, not to give the child any cakes, lollipops, or stall produce whatever.

Between Mrs. Sedley and her daughter there was a sort of coolness about this boy, and a secret jealousy – for one evening in George's very early days, Amelia, who had been seated at work in their little parlour scarcely remarking that the old lady had quitted the room, ran upstairs instinctively to the nursery at the cries of the child, who had been asleep until that moment – and there found Mrs. Sedley in the act of surreptitiously administering Daffy's Elixir to the infant. Amelia, the gentlest and sweetest of every-day mortals, when she found this meddling with her maternal authority, thrilled and trembled all over with anger. Her cheeks, ordinarily pale, now flushed up, until they were as red as they used to be when she was a child of twelve years old. She seized the baby out of her mother's arms, and then grasped at the bottle, leaving the old lady gaping at her, furious, and holding the guilty teaspoon.

Amelia flung the bottle crashing into the fireplace. 'I will *not* have baby poisoned, mamma,' cried Emmy, rocking the infant about violently with both her arms round him, and turning with flashing eyes at her mother.

'Poisoned, Amelia!' said the old lady; 'this language to me?'

'He shall not have any medicine but that which Mr. Pestler sends for him. He told me that Daffy's Elixir was poison.'

'Very good: you think I'm a murderess then,' replied Mrs. Sedley. 'This is the language you use to your mother. I have met with misfortunes: I have sunk low in life: I have kept my carriage, and now walk on foot: but I did not know I was a murderess before, and thank you for the *news*.'

'Mamma,' said the poor girl, who was always ready for tears – 'you shouldn't be hard upon me. I – I didn't mean – I mean, I did not wish to say you would do any wrong to this dear child: only —'

'Oh, no, my love – only that I was a murderess; in which

case, I had better go to the Old Bailey. Though I didn't
poison *you*, when you were a child; but gave you the best
of education, and the most expensive masters money could
procure. Yes; I've nursed five children, and buried three:
and the one I loved the best of all, and tended through
croup, and teething, and measles, and whooping-cough, and
brought up with foreign masters, regardless of expense, and
with accomplishments at Minerva House – which I never
had when I was a girl – when I was too glad to honour my
father and mother, that I might live long in the land, and
to be useful, and not to mope all day in my room and act
the fine lady – says I'm a murderess. Ah, Mrs. Osborne! may
you never nourish a viper in your bosom, that's *my* prayer.'

'Mamma, mamma!' cried the bewildered girl: and the
child in her arms set up a frantic chorus of shouts.

'A murderess, indeed! Go down on your knees and pray
to God to cleanse your wicked ungrateful heart, Amelia, and
may He forgive you as I do;' and Mrs. Sedley tossed out of
the room, hissing out the word 'poison' once more, and so
ending her charitable benediction.

Till the termination of her natural life, this breach between
Mrs. Sedley and her daughter was never thoroughly mended.
The quarrel gave the elder lady numberless advantages
which she did not fail to turn to account with female
ingenuity and perseverance. For instance, she scarcely spoke
to Amelia for many weeks afterwards. She warned the
domestics not to touch the child, as Mrs. Osborne might be
offended. She asked her daughter to see and satisfy herself
that there was no poison prepared in the little daily messes
that were concocted for Georgy. When neighbours asked
after the boy's health, she referred them pointedly to Mrs.
Osborne. *She* never ventured to ask whether the baby was
well or not. *She* would not touch the child although he was
her grandson, and own precious darling, for she was not *used*
to children, and might kill it. And whenever Mr. Pestler
came upon his healing inquisition, she received the doctor
with such a sarcastic and scornful demeanour, as made the
surgeon declare that not Lady Thistlewood herself, whom
he had the honour of attending professionally, could give
herself greater airs than old Mrs. Sedley, from whom he
never took a fee. And very likely Emmy was jealous too,
upon her own part, as what mother is not, of those who

would manage her children for her, or become candidates for the first place in their affections? It is certain that when anybody nursed the child, she was uneasy, and that she would no more allow Mrs. Clapp or the domestic to dress or tend him, than she would have let them wash her husband's miniature which hung up over her little bed; – the same little bed from which the poor girl had gone to his; and to which she retired now for many long, silent, tearful, but happy years.

In this room was all Amelia's heart and treasure. Here it was that she tended her boy, and watched him through the many ills of childhood, with a constant passion of love. The elder George returned in him somehow, only improved, and as if come back from heaven. In a hundred little tones, looks, and movements, the child was so like his father, that the widow's heart thrilled as she held him to it; and he would often ask the cause of her tears. It was because of his likeness to his father, she did not scruple to tell him. She talked constantly to him about this dead father, and spoke of her love for George to the innocent and wondering child; much more than she ever had done to George himself, or to any confidante of her youth. To her parents she never talked about this matter; shrinking from baring her heart to them. Little George very likely could understand no better than they; but into his ears she poured her sentimental secrets unreservedly, and into his only. The very joy of this woman was a sort of grief, or so tender, at least, that its expression was tears. Her sensibilities were so weak and tremulous, that perhaps they ought not to be talked about in a book. I was told by Dr. Pestler (now a most flourishing lady's physician, with a sumptuous dark-green carriage, a prospect of speedy knighthood, and a house in Manchester Square), that her grief at weaning the child was a sight that would have unmanned a Herod. He was very soft-hearted many years ago, and his wife was mortally jealous of Mrs. Amelia, then and long afterwards.

Perhaps the doctor's lady had good reason for her jealousy: most women shared it, of those who formed the small circle of Amelia's acquaintance, and were quite angry at the enthusiasm with which the other sex regarded her. For almost all men who came near her loved her; though no doubt they would be at a loss to tell you why. She was not brilliant, nor witty, nor wise overmuch, nor extraordinarily handsome. But wherever she went she touched and charmed every one of the male sex, as invariably as she awakened the scorn and incredulity of her own sisterhood. I think it was her weakness which was her principal charm: – a kind of sweet submission and softness, which seemed to appeal to each man she met for his sympathy and protection. We have seen how in the regiment, though she spoke but to few of George's comrades there, all the swords of the young fellows at the mess-table would have leapt from their scabbards to fight round her; and so it was in the little narrow lodging-house and circle of Fulham, she interested and pleased everybody. If she had been Mrs. Mango herself, of the great house of Mango, Plantain, & Co., Crutched Friars, and the magnificent proprietress of the Pineries, Fulham, who gave summer *déjeuners* frequented by dukes and earls, and drove about the parish with magnificent yellow liveries and bay horses, such as the royal stables at Kensington themselves could not turn out – I say had she been Mrs. Mango herself, or her son's wife, Lady Mary Mango (daughter of the Earl of Castlemouldy, who condescended to marry the head of the firm), the tradesmen of the neighbourhood could not pay her more honour than they invariably showed to the gentle young widow, when she passed by their doors, or made her humble purchases at their shops.

Thus it was not only Mr. Pestler, the medical man, but Mr. Linton the young assistant, who doctored the servant-maids and small tradesmen, and might be seen any day reading the *Times* in the surgery, who openly declared himself the slave of Mrs. Osborne. He was a personable young gentleman, more welcome at Mrs. Sedley's lodgings than his principal; and if anything went wrong with Georgy, he would drop in twice or thrice in the day, to see the little chap, and without so much as the thought of a fee. He would abstract lozenges, tamarinds, and other produce from the surgery drawers for little Georgy's benefit, and compounded draughts and mixtures for him of miraculous sweetness, so that it was quite a pleasure to the child to be ailing. He and Pestler, his chief, sat up two whole nights by the boy in that momentous and awful week when Georgy had the measles; and when you would have thought, from the mother's terror, that there had never been measles in the world before.

Would they have done as much for other people? Did they sit up for the folks at the Pineries, when Ralph Plantagenet, and Gwendoline, and Guinever Mango had the same juvenile complaint? Did they sit up for little Mary Clapp, the landlord's daughter, who actually caught the disease of little Georgy? Truth compels one to say, no. They slept quite undisturbed, at least as far as she was concerned – pronounced hers to be a slight case, which would almost cure itself, sent her in a draught or two, and threw in bark when the child rallied, with perfect indifference, and just for form's sake.

Again, there was the little French chevalier opposite, who gave lessons in his native tongue at various schools in the neighbourhood, and who might be heard in his apartment of nights playing tremulous old gavottes and minuets, on a wheezy old fiddle. Whenever this powdered and courteous old man, who never missed a Sunday at the convent chapel at Hammersmith, and who was in all respects, thoughts, conduct, and bearing, utterly unlike the bearded savages of his nation, who curse perfidious Albion, and scowl at you from over their cigars, in the Quadrant arcades at the present day – whenever the old Chevalier de Talonrouge spoke of Mistress Osborne, he would first finish his pinch of snuff, flick away the remaining particles of dust with a graceful wave of his hand, gather up his fingers again into a bunch, and, bringing them up to his mouth, blow them open with a kiss, exclaiming, '*Ah! la divine créature!*' He vowed and protested that when Amelia walked in the Brompton Lanes flowers grew in profusion under her feet. He called little Georgy Cupid, and asked him news of Venus, his mamma; and told the astonished Betty Flanagan that she was one of the Graces, and the favourite attendant of the *Reine des Amours*.

Instances might be multiplied of this easily gained and unconscious popularity. Did not Mr. Binney, the mild and genteel curate of the district chapel, which the family attended, call assiduously upon the widow, dandle the little boy on his knee, and offer to teach him Latin, to the anger of the elderly virgin, his sister, who kept house for him? 'There is nothing in her, Beilby,' the latter lady would say. 'When she comes to tea here she does not speak a word during the whole evening. She is but a poor lackadaisical creature, and it is my belief has no heart at all. It is only her pretty face which all you gentlemen admire so. Miss Grits, who has five thousand pounds, and expectations besides, has twice as much character, and is a thousand times more agreeable to *my* taste; and if she were good-looking I know that you would think her perfection.'

Very likely Miss Binney was right to a great extent. It *is* the pretty face which creates sympathy in the hearts of men, those wicked rogues. A woman may possess the wisdom and chastity of Minerva, and we give no heed to her, if she has a plain face. What folly will not a pair of bright eyes make pardonable? What dullness may not red lips and sweet accents render pleasant? And so, with their usual sense of justice, ladies argue that because a woman is handsome, therefore she is a fool. O ladies, ladies! there are some of you who are neither handsome nor wise.

These are but trivial incidents to recount in the life of our heroine. Her tale does not deal in wonders, as the gentle reader has already no doubt perceived; and if a journal had been kept of her proceedings during the seven years after the birth of her son, there would be found few incidents more remarkable in it than that of the measles, recorded in the foregoing page. Yes, one day, and greatly to her wonder, the Reverend Mr. Binney, just mentioned, asked her to change her name of Osborne for his own; when, with deep blushes, and tears in her eyes and voice, she thanked him for his regard for her, expressed gratitude for his attentions to her and to her poor little boy, but said that she never, never could think of any but – but the husband whom she had lost.

On the twenty-fifth of April, and the eighteenth of June, the days of her marriage and widowhood, she kept her room entirely, consecrating them (and we do not know how many hours of solitary night-thought, her little boy sleeping in his crib by her bedside) to the memory of that departed friend. During the day she was more active. She had to teach George to read and to write, and a little to draw. She read books, in order that she might tell him stories from them. As his eyes opened, and his mind expanded, under the influence of the outward nature round about him, she taught the child, to the best of her humble power, to acknowledge the Maker of all; and every night and every morning he and

she – (in that awful and touching communion which I think
must bring a thrill to the heart of every man who witnesses
or who remembers it) – the mother and the little boy –
prayed to Our Father together, the mother pleading with all
her gentle heart, the child lisping after her as she spoke.
And each time they prayed to God to bless dear papa, as if
he were alive and in the room with them.

To wash and dress this young gentleman – to take him
for a run of the mornings, before breakfast, and the retreat
of grandpapa for 'business' – to make for him the most
wonderful and ingenious dresses, for which end the thrifty
widow cut up and altered every available little bit of finery
which she possessed out of her wardrobe during her marriage
– for Mrs. Osborne herself (greatly to her mother's vexation,
who preferred fine clothes, especially since her misfortunes)
always wore a black gown, and a straw bonnet with a black
ribbon – occupied her many hours of the day. Others she
had to spare, at the service of her mother and her old father.
She had taken the pains to learn, and used to play cribbage
with this gentleman on the nights when he did not go to
his club. She sang for him when he was so minded, and it
was a good sign, for he invariably fell into a comfortable
sleep during the music. She wrote out his numerous memorials, letters, prospectuses, and projects. It was in her handwriting that most of the old gentleman's former acquaintances
were informed that he had become an agent for the Black
Diamond and Anti-Cinder Coal Company, and could supply
his friends and the public with the best coals at –s. per
chaldron. All he did was to sign the circulars with his
flourish and signature, and direct them in a shaky, clerklike
hand. One of these papers was sent to Major Dobbin, –
Regt., care of Messrs. Cox and Greenwood; but the major
being in Madras at the time, had no particular call for coals.
He knew, though, the hand which had written the prospectus. Good God! what would he not have given to hold it in
his own! A second prospectus came out, informing the major
that J. Sedley and Company, having established agencies
at Oporto, Bordeaux, and St. Mary's, were enabled to offer
to their friends and the public generally, the finest and
most celebrated growths of ports, sherries, and claret wines
at reasonable prices, and under extraordinary advantages.
Acting upon this hint, Dobbin furiously canvassed the

governor, the commander-in-chief, the judges, the regiments, and everybody whom he knew in the Presidency, and
sent home to Sedley and Co. orders for wine which perfectly
astonished Mr. Sedley and Mr. Clapp, who was the Co. in
the business. But no more orders came after that first burst
of good fortune, on which poor old Sedley was about to
build a house in the City, a regiment of clerks, a dock to
himself, and correspondents all over the world. The old
gentleman's former taste in wine had gone: the curses of the
mess-room assailed Major Dobbin for the vile drinks he had
been the means of introducing there; and he bought back a
great quantity of the wine, and sold it at public outcry, at
an enormous loss to himself. As for Jos, who was by this
time promoted to a seat at the Revenue Board at Calcutta,
he was wild with rage when the post brought him out a
bundle of these bacchanalian prospectuses, with a private
note from his father, telling Jos that his senior counted upon
him in this enterprise, and had consigned a quantity of select
wines to him, as per invoice, drawing bills upon him for the
amount of the same. Jos, who would no more have it
supposed that his father, Jos Sedley's father, of the Board
of Revenue, was a wine merchant asking for orders, than
that he was Jack Ketch, refused the bills with scorn, wrote
back contumeliously to the old gentleman, bidding him to
mind his own affairs; and the protested paper coming back,
Sedley and Co. had to take it up, with the profits which
they had made out of the Madras venture, and with a little
portion of Emmy's savings.

Besides her pension of fifty pounds a year, there had been
five hundred pounds, as her husband's executor stated, left
in the agent's hands at the time of Osborne's demise, which
sum, as George's guardian, Dobbin proposed to put out at
8 per cent in an Indian house of agency. Mr. Sedley, who
thought the major had some roguish intentions of his own
about the money, was strongly against this plan; and he went
to the agents to protest personally against the employment
of the money in question, when he learned, to his surprise,
that there had been no such sum in their hands, that all the
late captain's assets did not amount to a hundred pounds,
and that the five hundred pounds in question must be a
separate sum, of which Major Dobbin knew the particulars.
More than ever convinced that there was some roguery, old

Sedley pursued the major. As his daughter's nearest friend, he demanded with a high hand, a statement of the late captain's accounts. Dobbin's stammering, blushing, and awkwardness added to the other's convictions that he had a rogue to deal with; and in a majestic tone he told that officer a piece of his mind, as he called it, simply stating his belief that the major was unlawfully detaining his late son-in-law's money.

Dobbin at this lost all patience, and if his accuser had not been so old and so broken, a quarrel might have ensued between them at the Slaughters' Coffee-house, in a box of which place of entertainment the gentlemen had their colloquy. 'Come upstairs, sir,' lisped out the major. 'I insist on your coming upstairs, and I will show which is the injured party, poor George or I;' and, dragging the old gentleman up to his bedroom, he produced from his desk Osborne's accounts, and a bundle of I O U's which the latter had given, who, to do him justice, was always ready to give an I O U. 'He paid his bills in England,' Dobbin added, 'but he had not a hundred pounds in the world when he fell. I and one or two of his brother-officers made up the little sum, which was all that we could spare, and you dare tell us that we are trying to cheat the widow and the orphan.' Sedley was very contrite and humbled, though the fact is, that William Dobbin had told a great falsehood to the old gentleman; having himself given every shilling of the money, having buried his friend, and paid all the fees and charges incident upon the calamity and removal of poor Amelia.

About these expenses old Osborne had never given himself any trouble to think, nor any other relative of Amelia, nor Amelia herself, indeed. She trusted to Major Dobbin as an accountant, took his somewhat confused calculations for granted: and never once suspected how much she was in his debt.

Twice or thrice in the year, according to her promise, she wrote him letters to Madras, letters all about little Georgy. How he treasured these papers! Whenever Amelia wrote he answered, and not until then. But he sent over endless remembrances of himself to his godson and to her. He ordered and sent a box of scarfs, and a grand ivory set of chess-men from China. The pawns were little green and white men, with real swords and shields; the knights were on horseback, the castles were on the backs of elephants. 'Mrs. Mango's own set at the Pineries was not so fine,' Mr. Pestler remarked. These chess-men were the delight of Georgy's life, who printed his first letter in acknowledgement of this gift of his godpapa. He sent over preserves and pickles, which latter the young gentleman tried surreptitiously in the sideboard, and half-killed himself with eating. He thought it was a judgement upon him for stealing, they were so hot. Emmy wrote a comical little account of this mishap to the major: it pleased him to think that her spirits were rallying, and that she could be merry sometimes now. He sent over a pair of shawls, a white one for her, and a black one with palm-leaves for her mother, and a pair of red scarfs, as winter wrappers, for old Mr. Sedley and George. The shawls were worth fifty guineas a piece at the very least, as Mrs. Sedley knew. She wore hers in state at church at Brompton, and was congratulated by her female friends upon the splendid acquisition. Emmy's, too, became prettily her modest black gown. 'What a pity it is she won't think of him,' Mrs. Sedley remarked to Mrs. Clapp, and to all her friends of Brompton. 'Jos never sent us such presents, I am sure, and grudges us everything. It is evident that the major is over head and ears in love with her: and yet, whenever I so much as hint it, she turns red and begins to cry, and goes and sits upstairs with her miniature. I'm sick of that miniature. I wish we had never seen those odious purse-proud Osbornes.'

Amidst such humble scenes and associates George's early youth was passed, and the boy grew up delicate, sensitive, imperious, woman-bred – domineering the gentle mother whom he loved with passionate affection. He ruled all the rest of the little world round about him. As he grew, the elders were amazed at his haughty manner and his constant likeness to his father. He asked questions about everything, as inquiring youth will do. The profundity of his remarks and interrogatories astonished his old grandfather, who perfectly bored the club at the tavern with stories about the little lad's learning and genius. He suffered his grandmother with a good-humoured indifference. The small circle round about him believed that the equal of the boy did not exist upon the earth. Georgy inherited his father's pride, and perhaps thought they were not wrong.

When he grew to be about six years old, Dobbin began to write to him very much. The major wanted to hear that Georgy was going to a school, and hoped he would acquit himself with credit there: or would he have a good tutor at home? it was time that he should begin to learn; and his godfather and guardian hinted that he hoped to be allowed to defray the charges of the boy's education, which would fall heavily upon his mother's straitened income. The major, in a word, was always thinking about Amelia and her little boy, and by orders to his agents kept the latter provided with picture-books, paint-boxes, desks, and all conceivable implements of amusement and instruction. Three days before George's sixth birthday, a gentleman in a gig, accompanied by a servant, drove up to Mr. Sedley's house, and asked to see Master George Osborne: it was Mr. Woolsey, military tailor, of Conduit Street, who came at the major's order to measure the young gentleman for a suit of cloth clothes. He had had the honour of making for the captain, the young gentleman's father.

Sometimes, too, and by the major's desire no doubt, his sisters, the Misses Dobbin, would call in the family carriage to take Amelia and the little boy a drive if they were so inclined. The patronage and kindness of these ladies was very uncomfortable to Amelia, but she bore it meekly enough, for her nature was to yield; and, besides, the carriage and its splendours gave little Georgy immense pleasure. The ladies begged occasionally that the child might pass a day with them, and he was always glad to go to that fine garden-house at Denmark Hill, where they lived, and where there were such fine grapes in the hot-houses and peaches on the walls.

One day they kindly came over to Amelia with news which they were *sure* would delight her – something *very* interesting about their dear William.

'What was it: was he coming home?' she asked with pleasure beaming in her eyes.

'Oh, no – not the least – but they had very good reason to believe that dear William was about to be married – and to a relation of a very dear friend of Amelia's – to Miss Glorvina O'Dowd, Sir Michael O'Dowd's sister, who had gone out to join Lady O'Dowd at Madras – a very beautiful and accomplished girl, everybody said.'

Amelia said 'Oh!' Amelia was very, *very* happy indeed.
But she supposed Glorvina could not be like her old
acquaintance, who was most kind – but – but she was very
happy indeed. And by some impulse, of which I cannot
explain the meaning, she took George in her arms and kissed
him with an extraordinary tenderness. Her eyes were quite
moist when she put the child down; and she scarcely spoke
a word during the whole of the drive – though she was so
very happy indeed.

CHAPTER XXXIX

A CYNICAL CHAPTER

O UR duty now takes us back for a brief space to some
old Hampshire acquaintances of ours, whose hopes
respecting the disposal of their rich kinswoman's property
were so wofully disappointed. After counting upon thirty
thousand pounds from his sister, it was a heavy blow to
Bute Crawley to receive but five; out of which sum, when
he had paid his own debts and those of Jim, his son at
college, a very small fragment remained to portion off his
four plain daughters. Mrs. Bute never knew, or at least never
acknowledged, how far her own tyrannous behaviour had
tended to ruin her husband. All that woman could do, she
vowed and protested she had done. Was it her fault if she
did not possess those sycophantic arts which her hypocritical
nephew, Pitt Crawley, practised? She wished him all the
happiness which he merited out of his ill-gotten gains. 'At
least the money will remain in the family,' she said, charitably. 'Pitt will never spend it, my dear, that is quite certain;
for a greater miser does not exist in England, and he is as
odious, though in a different way, as his spendthrift brother,
the abandoned Rawdon.'

So Mrs. Bute, after the first shock of rage and disappointment, began to accommodate herself as best she could
to her altered fortunes, and to save and retrench with all
her might. She instructed her daughters how to bear poverty
cheerfully, and invented a thousand notable methods to
conceal or evade it. She took them about to balls and public
places in the neighbourhood, with praise-worthy energy: nay,
she entertained her friends in a hospitable comfortable man-

ner at the Rectory, and much more frequently than before dear Miss Crawley's legacy had fallen in. From her outward bearing nobody would have supposed that the family had been disappointed in their expectations: or have guessed from her frequent appearance in public how she pinched and starved at home. Her girls had more milliner's furniture than they had ever enjoyed before. They appeared perseveringly at the Winchester and Southampton assemblies; they penetrated to Cowes for the race-balls and regatta-gaieties there; and their carriage, with the horses taken from the plough, was at work perpetually, until it began almost to be believed that the four sisters had had fortunes left them by their aunt, whose name the family never mentioned in public but with the most tender gratitude and regard. I know no sort of lying which is more frequent in Vanity Fair than this; and it may be remarked how people who practise it take credit to themselves for their hypocrisy, and fancy that they are exceedingly virtuous and praiseworthy, because they are able to deceive the world with regard to the extent of their means.

Mrs. Bute certainly thought herself one of the most virtuous women in England, and the sight of her happy family was an edifying one to strangers. They were so cheerful, so loving, so well-educated, so simple! Martha painted flowers exquisitely, and furnished half the charity-bazaars in the county. Emma was a regular County Bulbul, and her verses in the *Hampshire Telegraph* were the glory of its Poet's Corner. Fanny and Matilda sang duets together, mamma playing the piano, and the other two sisters sitting with their arms round each other's waists, and listening affectionately. Nobody saw the poor girls drumming at the duets in private. No one saw mamma drilling them rigidly hour after hour. In a word, Mrs. Bute put a good face against fortune, and kept up appearances in the most virtuous manner.

Everything that a good and respectable mother could do Mrs. Bute did. She got over yachting men from Southampton, parsons from the Cathedral Close at Winchester, and officers from the barracks there. She tried to inveigle the young barristers at assizes, and encouraged Jim to bring home friends with whom he went out hunting with the H.H. What will not a mother do for the benefit of her beloved ones?

Between such a woman and her brother-in-law, the odious baronet at the Hall, it is manifest that there could be very little in common. The rupture between Bute and his brother Sir Pitt was complete; indeed, between Sir Pitt and the whole county, to which the old man was a scandal. His dislike for respectable society increased with age, and the lodge-gates had not opened to a gentleman's carriage-wheels since Pitt and Lady Jane came to pay their visit of duty after their marriage.

That was an awful and unfortunate visit, never to be thought of by the family without horror. Pitt begged his wife, with a ghastly countenance, never to speak of it; and it was only through Mrs. Bute herself, who still knew everything which took place at the Hall, that the circumstances of Sir Pitt's reception of his son and daughter-in-law were ever known at all.

As they drove up the avenue of the park in their neat and well-appointed carriage, Pitt remarked with dismay and wrath great gaps among the trees – his trees, – which the old baronet was felling entirely without licence. The park wore an aspect of utter dreariness and ruin. The drives were ill kept, and the neat carriage splashed and foundered in muddy pools along the road. The great sweep in front of the terrace and entrance stair was black and covered with mosses; the once trim flower-beds rank and weedy. Shutters were up along almost the whole line of the house; the great hall-door was unbarred after much ringing of the bell; an individual in ribbons was seen flitting up the black oak stair, as Horrocks at length admitted the heir of Queen's Crawley and his bride into the halls of their fathers. He led the way into Sir Pitt's 'Library', as it was called, the fumes of tobacco growing stronger as Pitt and Lady Jane approached that apartment. 'Sir Pitt ain't very well,' Horrocks remarked apologetically, and hinted that his master was afflicted with lumbago.

The library looked out on the front walk and park. Sir Pitt had opened one of the windows, and was bawling out thence to the postilion and Pitt's servant, who seemed to be about to take the baggage down.

'Don't move none of them trunks,' he cried, pointing with a pipe which he held in his hand. 'It's only a morning visit, Tucker, you fool. Lor, what cracks that off hoss has in his heels! Ain't there no one at the "King's Head" to rub 'em a little? How do, Pitt? How do, my dear? Come to see the old man, hey? Gad – you've a pretty face, too. You ain't like that old horse-godmother, your mother. Come and give old Pitt a kiss, like a good little gal.'

The embrace disconcerted the daughter-in-law somewhat, as the caresses of the old gentleman, unshorn and perfumed with tobacco, might well do. But she remembered that her brother Southdown had moustachios, and smoked cigars, and submitted to the baronet with a tolerable grace.

'Pitt has got vat,' said the baronet, after this mark of affection. 'Does he read ee very long zermons, my dear? Hundredth Psalm, Evening Hymn – hey, Pitt? Go and get a glass of malmsey and a cake for my Lady Jane, Horrocks, you great big booby, and don't stand stearing there like a fat pig. I won't ask you to stop, my dear; you'll find it too stoopid, and so should I too along a Pitt. I'm an old man now, and like my own ways, and my pipe and backgammon of a night.'

'I can play at backgammon, sir,' said Lady Jane, laughing. 'I used to play with papa and Miss Crawley, didn't I, Mr. Crawley?'

'Lady Jane can play, sir, at the game to which you state that you are so partial,' Pitt said haughtily.

'But she wawn't stop for all that. Naw, naw, goo back to Mudbury and give Mrs. Rincer a benefit: or drive down to the Rectory, and ask Buty for a dinner. He'll be charmed to see you, you know; he's so much obliged to you for gittin the old woman's money. Ha, ha! Some of it will do to patch up the Hall when I'm gone.'

'I perceive, sir,' said Pitt, with a heightened voice, 'that your people will cut down the timber.'

'Yees, yees, very fine weather, and seasonable for the time of year,' Sir Pitt answered, who had suddenly grown deaf. 'But I'm gittin old, Pitt, now. Law bless you, you ain't far from fifty yourself. But he wears well, my pretty Lady Jane, don't he? It's all godliness, sobriety, and a moral life. Look at me, I'm not very fur from fowr-score – he, he;' and he laughed, and took snuff, and leered at her and pinched her hand.

Pitt once more brought the conversation back to the timber; but the baronet was deaf again in an instant.

'I'm gittin very old, and have been cruel bad this year
with the lumbago. I shan't be here now for long; but I'm
glad ee've come, daughter-in-law. I like your face, Lady Jane:
it's got none of the damned high-boned Binkie look in it;
and I'll give ee something pretty, my dear, to go to Court
in.' And he shuffled across the room to a cupboard, from
which he took a little old case containing jewels of some
value. 'Take that,' said he, 'my dear; it belonged to my
mother, and afterwards to the first Lady Crawley. Pretty
pearls – never gave 'em the ironmonger's daughter. No, no.
Take 'em and put 'em up quick,' said he, thrusting the case
into his daughter's hand, and clapping the door of the cabinet
to, as Horrocks entered with a salver and refreshments.

'What have you a been and given Pitt's wife?' said the
individual in ribbons, when Pitt and Lady Jane had taken
leave of the old gentleman. It was Miss Horrocks, the
butler's daughter – the cause of the scandal throughout the
country – the lady who reigned now almost supreme at
Queen's Crawley.

The rise and progress of those Ribbons had been marked
with dismay by the county and family. The Ribbons opened
an account at the Mudbury Branch Savings Bank; the Ribbons drove to church, monopolizing the pony-chaise, which
was for the use of the servants at the Hall. The domestics
were dismissed at her pleasure. The Scotch gardener, who
still lingered on the premises, taking a pride in his walls and
hothouses, and indeed making a pretty good livelihood by
the garden, which he farmed, and of which he sold the
produce at Southampton, found the Ribbons eating peaches
in a sunshiny morning at the south wall, and had his ears
boxed when he remonstrated about this attack on his property.
He and his Scotch wife and his Scotch children, the only
respectable inhabitants of Queen's Crawley, were forced to
migrate, with their goods and their chattels, and left the
stately comfortable gardens to go to waste, and the flower-
beds to run to seed. Poor Lady Crawley's rose-garden
became the dreariest wilderness. Only two or three domestics
shuddered in the bleak old servants' hall. The stables and
offices were vacant, and shut up, and half ruined. Sir Pitt
lived in private, and boozed nightly with Horrocks, his butler
or house-steward (as he now began to be called), and the
abandoned Ribbons. The times were very much changed

since the period when she drove to Mudbury in the spring-cart, and called the small tradesmen 'sir'. It may have been shame, or it may have been dislike of his neighbours, but the old Cynic of Queen's Crawley hardly issued from his park-gates at all now. He quarrelled with his agents, and screwed his tenants by letter. His days were passed in conducting his own correspondence; the lawyers and farm-bailiffs who had to do business with him, could not reach him but through the Ribbons, who received them at the door of the housekeeper's room, which commanded the back entrance by which they were admitted; and so the baronet's daily perplexities increased, and his embarrassments multi-plied round him.

The horror of Pitt Crawley may be imagined, as these reports of his father's dotage reached the most exemplary and correct of gentlemen. He trembled daily lest he should hear that the Ribbons was proclaimed his second legal mother-in-law. After that first and last visit, his father's name was never mentioned in Pitt's polite and genteel establishment. It was the skeleton in his house, and all the family walked by it in terror and silence. The Countess Southdown kept on dropping per coach at the lodge-gate the most exciting tracts, tracts which ought to frighten the hair off your head. Mrs. Bute at the parsonage nightly looked out to see if the sky was red over the elms behind which the Hall stood, and the mansion was on fire. Sir G. Wapshot and Sir H. Fuddlestone, old friends of the house, wouldn't sit on the bench with Sir Pitt at Quarter Sessions, and cut him dead in the High Street of Southampton, where the reprobate stood offering his dirty old hands to them. Noth-ing had any effect upon him; he put his hands into his pockets, and burst out laughing, as he scrambled into his carriage-and-four; he used to burst out laughing at Lady Southdown's tracts; and he laughed at his sons, and at the world, and at the Ribbons when she was angry, which was not seldom.

Miss Horrocks was installed as housekeeper at Queen's Crawley, and ruled all the domestics there with great majesty and rigour. All the servants were instructed to address her as 'mum', or 'madam', – and there was one little maid, on her promotion, who persisted in calling her 'my lady', without any rebuke on the part of the housekeeper. 'There

has been better ladies, and there has been worser, Hester,'
was Miss Horrock's reply to this compliment of her inferior:
so she ruled, having supreme power over all except her
father, whom, however, she treated with considerable haughtiness, warning him not to be too familiar in his behaviour to
one 'as was to be a baronet's lady'. Indeed, she rehearsed
that exalted part in life with great satisfaction to herself, and
to the amusement of old Sir Pitt, who chuckled at her airs
and graces, and would laugh by the hour together at her
assumptions of dignity and imitations of genteel life. He
swore it was as good as a play to see her in the character
of a fine dame, and he made her put on one of the first Lady
Crawley's courtdresses, swearing (entirely to Miss Horrocks's
own concurrence) that the dress became her prodigiously,
and threatening to drive her off that very instant to Court
in a coach-and-four. She had the ransacking of the wardrobes
of the two defunct ladies, and cut and hacked their posthu-
mous finery so as to suit her own tastes and figure. And she
would have liked to take possession of their jewels and
trinkets too; but the old baronet had locked them away in
his private cabinet, nor could she coax or wheedle him out
of the keys. And it is a fact, that some time after she left
Queen's Crawley a copybook belonging to this lady was
discovered, which showed that she had taken great pains in
private to learn the art of writing in general, and especially
of writing her own name as Lady Crawley, Lady Betsy
Horrocks, Lady Elizabeth Crawley, &c.

Though the good people of the parsonage never went to
the Hall, and shunned the horrid old dotard its owner, yet
they kept a strict knowledge of all that happened there, and
were looking out every day for the catastrophe for which
Miss Horrocks was also eager. But Fate intervened enviously,
and prevented her from receiving the reward due to such
immaculate love and virtue.

One day the baronet surprised 'her ladyship', as he
jocularly called her, seated at that old and tuneless piano in
the drawing-room, which had scarcely been touched since
Becky Sharp played quadrilles upon it. Seated at the piano
with the utmost gravity, and squalling to the best of her
power in imitation of the music which she had sometimes
heard. The little kitchenmaid on her promotion was standing
at her mistress's side, quite delighted during the operation,

and wagging her head up and down, and crying, 'Lor, mum, 'tis bittiful,' – just like a genteel sycophant in a real drawing-room.

This incident made the old baronet roar with laughter, as usual. He narrated the circumstance a dozen times to Horrocks in the course of the evening, and greatly to the discomfiture of Miss Horrocks. He thrummed on the table as if it had been a musical instrument and squalled in imitation of her manner of singing. He vowed that such a beautiful voice ought to be cultivated, and declared she ought to have singing-masters, in which proposals she saw nothing ridiculous. He was in great spirits that night; and drank with his friend and butler an extraordinary quantity of rum-and-water – at a very late hour the faithful friend and domestic conducted his master to his bedroom.

Half an hour afterwards there was a great hurry and bustle in the house. Lights went about from window to window in the lonely desolate old Hall, whereof but two or three rooms were ordinarily occupied by its owner. Presently a boy on a pony went galloping off to Mudbury, to the doctor's house there. And in another hour (by which fact we ascertain how carefully the excellent Mrs. Bute Crawley had always kept up an understanding with the great house), that lady in her clogs and calash, the Reverend Bute Crawley, and James Crawley her son, had walked over from the Rectory through the park, and had entered the mansion by the open hall-door.

They passed through the hall and the small oak parlour, on the table of which stood the three tumblers and the empty rum-bottle which had served for Sir Pitt's carouse, and through that apartment into Sir Pitt's study, where they found Miss Horrocks, of the guilty ribbons, with a wild air, trying at the presses and escritoires with a bunch of keys. She dropped them with a scream of terror, as little Mrs. Bute's eyes flashed out at her from under her black calash.

'Look at that, James and Mr. Crawley,' cried Mrs. Bute, pointing at the scared figure of the black-eyed, guilty wench.

'He gave 'em me; he gave 'em me!' she cried.

'Gave them you, you abandoned creature!' screamed Mrs. Bute. 'Bear witness, Mr. Crawley, we found this good-for-nothing woman in the act of stealing your brother's property; and she will be hanged, as I always said she would.'

Betsy Horrocks quite daunted, flung herself down on her knees, bursting into tears. But those who know a really good woman are aware that she is not in a hurry to forgive, and that the humiliation of an enemy is a triumph to her soul.

'Ring the bell, James,' Mrs. Bute said. 'Go on ringing it till the people come.' The three or four domestics resident in the deserted old house came presently at that jangling and continued summons.

'Put that woman in the strong-room,' she said. 'We caught her in the act of robbing Sir Pitt. Mr. Crawley, you'll make out her committal – and, Beddoes, you'll drive her over in the spring-cart, in the morning, to Southampton Gaol.'

'My dear,' interposed the magistrate and rector – 'she's only —'

'Are there no handcuffs?' Mrs. Bute continued, stamping in her clogs. 'There used to be handcuffs. Where's the creature's abominable father?'

'He *did* give 'em me,' still cried poor Betsy; 'didn't he, Hester? You saw Sir Pitt – you know you did – give 'em me, ever so long ago – the day after Mudbury fair: not that I want 'em. Take 'em if you think they ain't mine.' And here the unhappy wretch pulled out from her pocket a large pair of paste shoe-buckles which had excited her admiration, and which she had just appropriated out of one of the bookcases in the study, where they had lain.

'Law, Betsy, how could you go for to tell such a wicked story!' said Hester, the little kitchenmaid late on her promotion – 'and to Madam Crawley, so good and kind, and his rev'rince' (with a curtsy) 'and you may search all *my* boxes, mum, I'm sure, and here's my keys as I'm an honest girl though of pore parents and workhouse bred – and if you find so much as a beggarly bit of lace or a silk stocking out of all the gownds as *you've* had the picking of may I never go to church again.'

'Give up your keys, you hardened hussy,' hissed out the virtuous little lady in the calash.

'And here's a candle, mum, and if you please, mum, I can show you her room, mum, and the press in the housekeeper's room, mum, where she keeps heaps and heaps of things, mum,' cried out the eager little Hester with a profusion of curtsies.

'Hold your tongue, if you please. I know the room which the creature occupies perfectly well. Mrs. Brown, have the goodness to come with me, and Beddoes, don't you lose sight of that woman,' said Mrs. Bute, seizing the candle. – 'Mr. Crawley, you had better go upstairs, and see that they are not murdering your unfortunate brother' – and the calash, escorted by Mrs. Brown, walked away to the apartment, which, as she said truly, she knew perfectly well.

Bute went upstairs, and found the doctor from Mudbury, with the frightened Horrocks over his master in a chair. They were trying to bleed Sir Pitt Crawley.

With the early morning an express was sent off to Mr. Pitt Crawley by the rector's lady, who assumed the command of everything, and had watched the old baronet through the night. He had been brought back to a sort of life; he could not speak, but seemed to recognize people. Mrs. Bute kept resolutely by his bedside. She never seemed to want to sleep, that little woman, and did not close her fiery black eyes once, though the Doctor snored in the arm-chair. Horrocks made some wild efforts to assert his authority and assist his master: but Mrs. Bute called him a tipsy old wretch, and bade him never show his face again in that house or he should be transported like his abominable daughter.

Terrified by her manner he slunk down to the oak parlour where Mr. James was, who, having tried the bottle standing there and found no liquor in it, ordered Mr. Horrocks to get another bottle of rum, which he fetched, with clean glasses, and to which the rector and his son sat down: ordering Horrocks to put down the keys at that instant and never to show his face again.

Cowed by this behaviour Horrocks gave up the keys: and he and his daughter slunk off silently through the night, and gave up possession of the house of Queen's Crawley.

CHAPTER XL

IN WHICH BECKY IS RECOGNIZED BY THE FAMILY

THE heir of Crawley arrived at home, in due time, after this catastrophe, and henceforth may be said to have reigned in Queen's Crawley. For though the old baronet survived many months, he never recovered the use of his intellect or his speech completely, and the government of the estate devolved upon his elder son. In a strange condition Pitt found it. Sir Pitt was always buying and mortgaging: he had twenty men of business, and quarrels with each; quarrels with all his tenants, and lawsuits with them; lawsuits with the lawyers; lawsuits with the Mining and Dock Companies in which he was proprietor; and with every person with whom he had business. To unravel these difficulties, and to set the estate clear was a task worthy of the orderly and persevering diplomatist of Pumpernickel: and he set himself to work with prodigious assiduity. His whole family, of course, was transported to Queen's Crawley, whither Lady Southdown, of course, came too; and she set about converting the parish under the rector's nose, and brought down her irregular clergy to the dismay of the angry Mrs. Bute. Sir Pitt had concluded no bargain for the sale of the living of Queen's Crawley; when it should drop, her ladyship proposed to take the patronage into her own hands, and present a young protégé to the Rectory; on which subject the diplomatic Pitt said nothing.

Mrs. Bute's intentions with regard to Miss Betsy Horrocks were not carried into effect: and she paid no visit to Southampton Gaol. She and her father left the Hall, when the latter took possession of the 'Crawley Arms' in the village, of which he had got a lease from Sir Pitt. The ex-butler had obtained a small freehold there likewise, which gave him a vote for the borough. The rector had another of these votes, and these and four others formed the representative body which returned the two members for Queen's Crawley.

There was a show of courtesy kept up between the Rectory and the Hall ladies, between the younger ones at least, for Mrs. Bute and Lady Southdown never could meet without battles, and gradually ceased seeing each other. Her ladyship kept her room when the ladies from the Rectory visited their cousins at the Hall. Perhaps Mr. Pitt was not very much displeased at these occasional absences of his mamma-in-law. He believed the Binkie family to be the greatest and wisest, and most interesting in the world, and her ladyship and his aunt had long held ascendancy over him; but sometimes he felt that she commanded him too

much. To be considered young was complimentary doubtless; but at six-and-forty to be treated as a boy was sometimes mortifying. Lady Jane yielded up everything, however,
to her mother. She was only fond of her children in private;
and it was lucky for her that Lady Southdown's multifarious
business, her conferences with ministers, and her correspondence with all the missionaries of Africa, Asia, and
Australasia, &c., occupied the venerable countess a great deal,
so that she had but little time to devote to her granddaughter, the little Matilda, and her grandson, Master Pitt
Crawley. The latter was a feeble child: and it was only by
prodigious quantities of calomel that Lady Southdown was
able to keep him in life at all.

As for Sir Pitt he retired into those very apartments where
Lady Crawley had been previously extinguished, and here
was tended by Miss Hester, the girl upon her promotion,
with constant care and assiduity. What love, what fidelity,
what constancy is there equal to that of a nurse with good
wages? They smooth pillows: and make arrowroot: they get
up at nights: they bear complaints and querulousness: they
see the sun shining out of doors and don't want to go abroad:
they sleep on arm-chairs, and eat their meals in solitude:
they pass long, long evenings doing nothing, watching the
embers, and the patient's drink simmering in the jug: they
read the weekly paper the whole week through; and Law's
Serious Call or the *Whole Duty of Man* suffices them for
literature for the year – and we quarrel with them because,
when their relations come to see them once a week, a little
gin is smuggled in in their linen-basket. Ladies, what man's
love is there that would stand a year's nursing of the object
of his affection? Whereas a nurse will stand by you for ten
pounds a quarter, and we think her too highly paid. At least
Mr. Crawley grumbled a good deal about paying half as
much to Miss Hester for her constant attendance upon the
baronet his father.

Of sunshiny days this old gentleman was taken out in a
chair on the terrace – the very chair which Miss Crawley
had had at Brighton, and which had been transported thence
with a number of Lady Southdown's effects to Queen's
Crawley. Lady Jane always walked by the old man; and was
an evident favourite with him. He used to nod many times
to her and smile when she came in, and utter inarticulate

deprecatory moans when she was going away. When the door
shut upon her he would cry and sob – whereupon Hester's
face and manner, which was always exceedingly bland and
gentle while her lady was present, would change at once and
she would make faces at him, and clench her fist, and scream
out, 'Hold your tongue, you stoopid old fool,' and twirl away
his chair from the fire which he loved to look at – at which
he would cry more. For this was all that was left after more
than seventy years of cunning and struggling, and drinking,
and scheming, and sin, and selfishness – a whimpering old
idiot put in and out of bed and cleaned and fed like a baby.

At last a day came when the nurse's occupation was over.
Early one morning as Pitt Crawley was at his steward's and
bailiff's books in the study, a knock came to the door, and
Hester presented herself dropping a curtsy, and said –

'If you please, Sir Pitt, Sir Pitt died this morning, Sir
Pitt. I was a-making of his toast, Sir Pitt, for his gruel, Sir
Pitt, which he took every morning reglar at six, Sir Pitt,
and – I thought I heard a moan like, Sir Pitt – and – and
– and –' She dropped another curtsy.

What was it that made Pitt's pale face flush quite red?
Was it because he was Sir Pitt at last, with a seat in
Parliament, and perhaps future honours in prospect? 'I'll
clear the estate now with the ready money,' he thought, and
rapidly calculated its incumbrances and the improvements
which he would make. He would not use his aunt's money
previously lest Sir Pitt should recover and his outlay be in
vain.

All the blinds were pulled down at the Hall and Rectory:
the church bell was tolled, and the chancel hung in black;
and Bute Crawley didn't go to a coursing meeting, but went
and dined quietly at Fuddlestone, where they talked about
his deceased brother and young Sir Pitt over their port. Miss
Betsy, who was by this time married to a saddler at Mudbury, cried a good deal. The family surgeon rode over and
paid his respectful compliments, and inquiries for the health
of their ladyships. The death was talked about at Mudbury
and at the 'Crawley Arms'; the landlord whereof had become
reconciled with the rector of late, who was occasionally known
to step into the parlour and taste Mr. Horrocks's mild beer.

'Shall I write to your brother – or will you?' asked Lady
Jane of her husband, Sir Pitt.

'I will write, of course,' Sir Pitt said, 'and invite him to the funeral: it will be but becoming.'

'And – and – Mrs. Rawdon,' said Lady Jane, timidly.

'Jane!' said Lady Southdown, 'how can you think of such a thing?'

'Mrs. Rawdon must of course be asked,' said Sir Pitt resolutely.

'Not whilst *I* am in the house!' said Lady Southdown.

'Your ladyship will be pleased to recollect that I am the head of this family,' Sir Pitt replied. 'If you please, Lady Jane, you will write a letter to Mrs. Rawdon Crawley, requesting her presence upon this melancholy occasion.'

'Jane, I forbid you to put pen to paper!' cried the countess.

'I believe I am the head of this family,' Sir Pitt repeated; 'and however much I may regret any circumstance which may lead to your ladyship quitting this house, must, if you please, continue to govern it as I see fit.'

Lady Southdown rose up as magnificent as Mrs. Siddons in Lady Macbeth, and ordered that horses might be put to her carriage. If her son and daughter turned her out of their house, she would hide her sorrows somewhere in loneliness, and pray for their conversion to better thoughts.

'We don't turn you out of our house, mamma,' said the timid Lady Jane, imploringly.

'You invite such company to it as no Christian lady should meet, and I will have my horses to-morrow morning.'

'Have the goodness to write, Jane, under my dictation,' said Sir Pitt, rising, and throwing himself into an attitude of command, like the Portrait of a Gentleman in the Exhibition, 'and begin. "Queen's Crawley, September 14, 1822. – My dear brother —" '

Hearing these decisive and terrible words, Lady Macbeth, who had been waiting for a sign of weakness or vacillation on the part of her son-in-law, rose, and with a scared look, left the library. Lady Jane looked up to her husband, as if she would fain follow and soothe her mamma; but Pitt forbade his wife to move.

'She won't go away,' he said. 'She has let her house at Brighton and has spent her last half-year's dividends. A countess living at an inn is a ruined woman. I have been waiting long for an opportunity to take this – this decisive step, my love; for, as you must perceive, it is impossible that there should be two chiefs in a family: and now, if you please, we will resume the dictation. "My dear brother, the melancholy intelligence which it is my duty to convey to my family must have long been anticipated by," ' &c.

In a word, Pitt having come to his kingdom, and having by good luck, or desert rather, as he considered, assumed almost all the fortune which his other relatives had expected, was determined to treat his family kindly and respectably, and make a house of Queen's Crawley once more. It pleased him to think that he should be its chief. He proposed to use the vast influence that his commanding talents and position must speedily acquire for him in the county to get his brother placed and his cousins decently provided for, and perhaps had a little sting of repentance as he thought that he was the proprietor of all that they had hoped for. In the course of three or four days' reign his bearing was changed, and his plans quite fixed: he determined to rule justly and honestly, to depose Lady Southdown, and to be on the friendliest possible terms with all the relations of his blood.

So he dictated a letter to his brother Rawdon – a solemn and elaborate letter, containing the profoundest observations, couched in the longest words, and filling with wonder the simple little secretary, who wrote under her husband's order. 'What an orator this will be,' thought she, 'when he enters the House of Commons' (on which point, and on the tyranny of Lady Southdown, Pitt had sometimes dropped hints to his wife in bed); 'how wise and good, and what a genius my husband is! I fancied him a little cold; but how good, and what a genius!'

The fact is, Pitt Crawley had got every word of the letter by heart, and had studied it with diplomatic secrecy, deeply and perfectly, long before he thought fit to communicate it to his astonished wife.

This letter, with a huge black border and seal, was accordingly dispatched by Sir Pitt Crawley to his brother the colonel, in London. Rawdon Crawley was but half-pleased at the receipt of it. 'What's the use of going down to that stupid place?' thought he. 'I can't stand being alone with Pitt after dinner, and horses there and back will cost us twenty pound.'

He carried the letter, as he did all difficulties, to Becky, upstairs in her bedroom – with her chocolate, which he always made and took to her of a morning.

He put the tray with the breakfast and the letter on the dressing-table, before which Becky sat combing her yellow hair. She took up the black-edged missive, and having read it, she jumped up from the chair, crying 'Hurray!' and waving the note round her head.

'Hurray?' said Rawdon, wondering at the little figure capering about in a streaming flannel dressing-gown, with tawny locks dishevelled. 'He's not left us anything, Becky. I had my share when I came of age.'

'You'll never be of age, you silly old man,' Becky replied. 'Run out now to Madam Brunoy's, for I must have some mourning: and get a crape on your hat, and a black waistcoat – I don't think you've got one; order it to be brought home to-morrow, so that we may be able to start on Thursday.'

'You don't mean to go?' Rawdon interposed.

'Of course I mean to go. I mean that Lady Jane shall present me at Court next year. I mean that your brother shall give you a seat in Parliament, you stupid old creature. I mean that Lord Steyne shall have your vote and his, my dear, old, silly man; and that you shall be an Irish Secretary, or a West Indian Governor: or a Treasurer, or a Consul, or some such thing.'

'Posting will cost a dooce of a lot of money,' grumbled Rawdon.

'We might take Southdown's carriage, which ought to be present at the funeral, as he is a relation of the family: but, no – I intend that we shall go by the coach. They'll like it better. It seems more humble —'

'Rawdy goes of course?' the colonel asked.

'No such thing; why pay an extra place? He's too big to travel bodkin between you and me. Let him stay here in the nursery, and Briggs can make him a black frock. Go you: and do as I bid you. And you had best tell Sparks, your man, that old Sir Pitt is dead, and that you will come in for something considerable when the affairs are arranged. He'll tell this to Raggles, who has been pressing for money, and it will console poor Raggles.' And so Becky began sipping her chocolate.

When the faithful Lord Steyne arrived in the evening, he

found Becky and her companion, who was no other than
our friend Briggs, busy cutting, ripping, snipping, and tearing all sorts of black stuffs available for the melancholy
occasion.

'Miss Briggs and I are plunged in grief and despondency
for the death of our papa,' Rebecca said. 'Sir Pitt Crawley
is dead, my lord. We have been tearing our hair all the
morning, and now we are tearing up our old clothes.'

'Oh, Rebecca, how can you —' was all that Briggs could
say as she turned up her eyes.

'Oh, Rebecca, how can you —' echoed my lord. 'So that
old scoundrel's dead, is he? He might have been a peer if
he had played his cards better. Mr. Pitt had very nearly
made him; but he ratted always at the wrong time. What an
old Silenus it was.'

'I might have been Silenus's widow,' said Rebecca. 'Don't
you remember, Miss Briggs, how you peeped in at the door,
and saw old Sir Pitt on his knees to me?' Miss Briggs, our
old friend, blushed very much at this reminiscence; and was
glad when Lord Steyne ordered her to go downstairs and
make him a cup of tea.

Briggs was the house-dog whom Rebecca had provided
as guardian of her innocence and reputation. Miss Crawley
had left her a little annuity. She would have been content
to remain in the Crawley family with Lady Jane, who was
good to her and to everybody; but Lady Southdown dismissed poor Briggs as quickly as decency permitted; and Mr.
Pitt (who thought himself much injured by the uncalled-for
generosity of his deceased relative towards a lady who had
only been Miss Crawley's faithful retainer a score of years)
made no objections to that exercise of the dowager's authority. Bowls and Firkin likewise received their legacies, and
their dismissals; and married and set up a lodging-house,
according to the custom of their kind.

Briggs tried to live with her relations in the country, but
found that attempt was vain after the better society to which
she had been accustomed. Briggs's friends, small tradesmen
in a country town, quarrelled over Miss Briggs's forty pounds
a year, as eagerly and more openly than Miss Crawley's
kinsfolk had for that lady's inheritance. Briggs's brother, a
Radical hatter and grocer, called his sister a purse-proud

aristocrat, because she would not advance a part of her capital to stock his shop: and she would have done so most likely, but that their sister, a Dissenting shoemaker's lady, at variance with the hatter and grocer who went to another chapel, showed how their brother was on the verge of bankruptcy, and took possession of Briggs for a while. The Dissenting shoemaker wanted Miss Briggs to send his son to college, and make a gentleman of him. Between them the two families got a great portion of her private savings out of her: and finally she fled to London followed by the anathemas of both, and determined to seek for servitude again as infinitely less onerous than liberty. And advertising in the papers that a 'Gentlewoman of agreeable manners, and accustomed to the best society, was anxious to,' &c., she took up her residence with Mr. Bowls in Half Moon Street, and waited the result of the advertisement.

So it was that she fell in with Rebecca. Mrs. Rawdon's dashing little carriage and ponies was whirling down the street one day, just as Miss Briggs, fatigued, had reached Mr. Bowls's door, after a weary walk to the *Times* office in the City, to insert her advertisement for the sixth time. Rebecca was driving, and at once recognized the gentlewoman with agreeable manners, and being a perfectly good-humoured woman, as we have seen, and having a regard for Briggs, she pulled up the ponies at the doorsteps, gave the reins to the groom, and jumping out had hold of both Briggs's hands, before she of the agreeable manners had recovered from the shock of seeing an old friend.

Briggs cried, and Becky laughed a great deal, and kissed the gentlewoman as soon as they got into the passage; and thence into Mrs. Bowls's front parlour, with the red moreen curtains, and the round looking-glass, with the chained eagle above, gazing upon the back of the ticket in the window which announced 'Apartments to Let'.

Briggs told all her history amidst those perfectly uncalled-for sobs and ejaculations of wonder with which women of her soft nature salute an old acquaintance, or regard a rencontre in the street; for though people meet other people every day, yet some there are who insist upon discovering miracles; and women, even though they have disliked each other, begin to cry when they meet, deploring and remembering the time when they last quarrelled. So, in a word,

Briggs told all her history, and Becky gave a narrative of her own life, with her usual artlessness and candour.

Mrs. Bowls, late Firkin, came and listened grimly in the passage to the hysterical sniffling and giggling which went on in the front parlour. Becky had never been a favourite of hers. Since the establishment of the married couple in London they had frequented their former friends of the house of Raggles, and did not like the latter's account of the colonel's *ménage*. '*I* wouldn't trust him, Ragg, my boy,' Bowls remarked: and his wife, when Mrs. Rawdon issued from the parlour, only saluted the lady with a very sour curtsy; and her fingers were like so many sausages, cold and lifeless, when she held them out in deference to Mrs. Rawdon, who persisted in shaking hands with the retired lady's-maid. She whirled away into Piccadilly, nodding, with the sweetest of smiles towards Miss Briggs, who hung nodding at the window close under the advertisement-card, and at the next moment was in the Park with a half-dozen of dandies cantering after her carriage.

When she found how her friend was situated, and how having a snug legacy from Miss Crawley, salary was no object to our gentlewoman, Becky instantly formed some benevolent little domestic plans concerning her. This was just such a companion as would suit her establishment, and she invited Briggs to come to dinner with her that very evening, when she should see Becky's dear little darling Rawdon.

Mrs. Bowls cautioned her lodger against venturing into the lion's den, 'wherein you will rue it, Miss B., mark my words, and as sure as my name is Bowls.' And Briggs promised to be very cautious. The upshot of which caution was that she went to live with Mrs. Rawdon the next week, and had lent Rawdon Crawley six hundred pounds upon annuity before six more months were over.

CHAPTER XLI

IN WHICH BECKY REVISITS THE HALLS
OF HER ANCESTORS

S o the mourning being ready, and Sir Pitt Crawley warned of their arrival, Colonel Crawley and his wife took a couple of places in the same old 'Highflyer' coach, by which Rebecca had travelled in the defunct baronet's company, on her first journey into the world some nine years before. How well she remembered the inn yard, and the ostler to whom she refused money, and the insinuating Cambridge lad who wrapped her in his coat on the journey! Rawdon took his place outside, and would have liked to drive, but his grief forbade him. He sat by the coachman, and talked about horses and the road the whole way; and who kept the inns, and who horsed the coach by which he had travelled so many a time, when he and Pitt were boys going to Eton. At Mudbury a carriage and a pair of horses received them, with a coachman in black. 'It's the old drag, Rawdon,' Rebecca said, as they got in. 'The worms have eaten the cloth a good deal – there's the stain which Sir Pitt – ha! I see Dawson the ironmonger has his shutters up – which Sir Pitt made such a noise about. It was a bottle of cherry brandy he broke which we went to fetch for your aunt from Southampton. How time flies, to be sure! that can't be Polly Talboys, that bouncing girl standing by her mother at the cottage there. I remember her a mangy little urchin picking weeds in the garden.'

'Fine gal,' said Rawdon, returning the salute which the cottage gave him, by two fingers applied to his crape hatband. Becky bowed and saluted, and recognized people here and there graciously. These recognitions were inexpressibly pleasant to her. It seemed as if she was not an impostor any more, and was coming to the home of her ancestors. Rawdon was rather abashed, and cast down on the other hand. What recollections of boyhood and innocence might have been flitting across his brain? What pangs of dim remorse and doubt and shame?

'Your sisters must be young women now,' Rebecca said, thinking of those girls for the first time perhaps since she had left them.

'Don't know, I'm shaw,' replied the colonel. 'Hullo! here's old Mother Lock. How-dy-do, Mrs. Lock? Remember me, don't you? Master Rawdon, hey? Dammy, how those old women last; she was a hundred when I was a boy.'

They were going through the lodge-gates kept by old Mrs. Lock, whose hand Rebecca insisted upon shaking, as she flung open the creaking old iron gate, and the carriage

passed between the two moss-grown pillars surmounted by
the dove and serpent.

'The governor has cut into the timber,' Rawdon said,
looking about, and then was silent – so was Becky. Both of
them were rather agitated, and thinking of old times. He
about Eton, and his mother, whom he remembered, a frigid
demure woman, and a sister who died, of whom he had been
passionately fond; and how he used to thrash Pitt; and about
little Rawdy at home. And Rebecca thought about her own
youth, and the dark secrets of those early tainted days; and
of her entrance into life by yonder gates; and of Miss
Pinkerton, and Joe, and Amelia.

The gravel walk and terrace had been scraped quite clean.
A grand painted hatchment was already over the great
entrance, and two very solemn and tall personages in black
flung open each a leaf of the door as the carriage pulled up
at the familiar steps. Rawdon turned red, and Becky somewhat pale, as they passed through the old hall, arm in arm.
She pinched her husband's arm as they entered the oak
parlour, where Sir Pitt and his wife were ready to receive
them. Sir Pitt in black, Lady Jane in black, and my Lady
Southdown with a large black headpiece of bugles and
feathers, which waved on her ladyship's head like an undertaker's tray.

Sir Pitt had judged correctly, that she would not quit the
premises. She contented herself by preserving a solemn and
stony silence, when in company of Pitt and his rebellious
wife, and by frightening the children in the nursery by the
ghastly gloom of her demeanour. Only a very faint bending
of the head-dress and plumes welcomed Rawdon and his
wife, as those prodigals returned to their family.

To say the truth, they were not affected very much one
way or other by this coolness. Her ladyship was a person
only of secondary consideration in their minds just then –
they were intent upon the reception which the reigning
brother and sister would afford them.

Pitt, with rather a heightened colour, went up and shook
his brother by the hand; and saluted Rebecca with a hand-
shake and a very low bow. But Lady Jane took both the
hands of her sister-in-law and kissed her affectionately. The
embrace somehow brought tears into the eyes of the little
adventuress – which ornaments, as we know, she wore very

seldom. The artless mark of kindness and confidence touched and pleased her; and Rawdon, encouraged by this demonstration on his sister's part, twirled up his moustachios, and took leave to salute Lady Jane with a kiss, which caused her ladyship to blush exceedingly.

'Dev'lish nice little woman, Lady Jane,' was his verdict, when he and his wife were together again. 'Pitt's got fat, too, and is doing the thing handsomely.' 'He can afford it,' said Rebecca, and agreed in her husband's farther opinion, 'that the mother-in-law was a tremendous old Guy – and that the sisters were rather well-looking young women.'

They, too, had been summoned from school to attend the funeral ceremonies. It seemed Sir Pitt Crawley, for the dignity of the house and family, had thought right to have about the place as many persons in black as could possibly be assembled. All the men and maids of the house, the old women of the almshouse, whom the elder Sir Pitt had cheated out of a great portion of their due, the parish clerk's family, and the special retainers of both Hall and Rectory were habited in sable; added to these, the undertaker's men, at least a score, with crapes and hatbands, and who made a goodly show when the great burying show took place – but these are mute personages in our drama; and, having nothing to do or say, need occupy a very little space here.

With regard to her sisters-in-law Rebecca did not attempt to forget her former position of governess towards them, but recalled it frankly and kindly, and asked them about their studies with great gravity, and told them that she had thought of them many and many a day, and longed to know of their welfare. In fact you would have supposed that ever since she had left them she had not ceased to keep them uppermost in her thoughts, and to take the tenderest interest in their welfare. So supposed Lady Crawley herself and her young sisters.

'She's hardly changed since eight years,' said Miss Rosalind to Miss Violet, as they were preparing for dinner.

'Those red-haired women look wonderfully well,' replied the other.

'Hers is much darker than it was; I think she must dye it,' Miss Rosalind added. 'She is stouter, too, and altogether improved,' continued Miss Rosalind, who was disposed to be very fat.

'At least she gives herself no airs, and remembers that she was our governess once,' Miss Violet said, intimating that it befitted all governesses to keep their proper place, and forgetting altogether that she was granddaughter not only of Sir Walpole Crawley, but of Mr. Dawson of Mudbury, and so had a coal-scuttle in her scutcheon. There are other very well-meaning people whom one meets every day in Vanity Fair, who are surely equally oblivious.

'It can't be true what the girls at the Rectory said, that her mother was an opera-dancer —'

'A person can't help their birth,' Rosalind replied with great liberality. 'And I agree with our brother, that as she is in the family, of course we are bound to notice her. I am sure Aunt Bute need not talk: she wants to marry Kate to young Hooper, the wine-merchant, and absolutely asked him to come to the Rectory for orders.'

'I wonder whether Lady Southdown will go away; she looked very glum upon Mrs. Rawdon,' the other said.

'I wish she would. *I* won't read the *Washerwoman of Finchley Common*,' vowed Violet; and so saying, and avoiding a passage at the end of which a certain coffin was placed with a couple of watchers, and lights perpetually burning in the closed room, these young women came down to the family dinner, for which the bell rang as usual.

But before this, Lady Jane conducted Rebecca to the apartments prepared for her, which, with the rest of the house, had assumed a very much improved appearance of order and comfort during Pitt's regency, and here beholding that Mrs. Rawdon's modest little trunks had arrived, and were placed in the bedroom and dressing-room adjoining, helped her to take off her neat black bonnet and cloak, and asked her sister-in-law in what more she could be useful.

'What I should like best,' said Rebecca, 'would be to go to the nursery; and see your dear little children': on which the two ladies looked very kindly at each other, and went to that apartment hand in hand.

Becky admired little Matilda, who was not quite four years old, as the most charming little love in the world; and the boy, a little fellow of two years – pale, heavy-eyed, and large-headed, she pronounced to be a perfect prodigy in point of size, intelligence, and beauty.

'I wish mamma would not insist on giving him so much

medicine,' Lady Jane said, with a sigh. 'I often think we should all be better without it.' And then Lady Jane and her new-found friend had one of those confidential medical conversations about the children, which all mothers, and most women, as I am given to understand, delight in. Fifty years ago, and when the present writer, being an interesting little boy, was ordered out of the room with the ladies after dinner, I remember quite well that their talk was chiefly about their ailments; and putting this question directly to two or three since, I have always got from them the acknowledgement that times are not changed. Let my fair readers remark for themselves this very evening when they quit the dessert-table, and assemble to celebrate the drawing-room mysteries. Well – in half an hour Becky and Lady Jane were close and intimate friends – and in the course of the evening her ladyship informed Sir Pitt that she thought her new sister-in-law was a kind, frank, unaffected, and affectionate young woman.

And so having easily won the daughter's goodwill, the indefatigable little woman bent herself to conciliate the august Lady Southdown. As soon as she found her ladyship alone, Rebecca attacked her on the nursery question at once, and said that her own little boy was saved, actually saved, by calomel, freely administered, when all the physicians in Paris had given the dear child up. And then she mentioned how often she had heard of Lady Southdown from that excellent man the Reverend Lawrence Grills, minister of the chapel in May Fair, which she frequented; and how her views were very much changed by circumstances and misfortunes; and how she hoped that a past life spent in worldliness and error might not incapacitate her from *more serious* thought for the future. She described how in former days she had been indebted to Mr. Crawley for religious instruction, touched upon the *Washerwoman of Finchley Common*, which she had read with the greatest profit, and asked about Lady Emily, its gifted author, now Lady Emily Hornblower, at Cape Town, where her husband had strong hopes of becoming Bishop of Caffraria.

But she crowned all, and confirmed herself in Lady Southdown's favour, by feeling very much agitated and unwell after the funeral, and requesting her ladyship's medical advice, which the dowager not only gave, but, wrapped up in a bed-gown, and looking more like Lady Macbeth than ever, came privately in the night to Becky's room, with a parcel of favourite tracts, and a medicine of her own composition, which she insisted that Mrs. Rawdon should take.

Becky first accepted the tracts, and began to examine them with great interest, engaging the dowager in a conversation concerning them and the welfare of her soul, by which means she hoped that her body might escape medication. But after the religious topics were exhausted, Lady Macbeth would not quit Becky's chamber until her cup of night-drink was emptied too; and poor Mrs. Rawdon was compelled actually to assume a look of gratitude, and to swallow the medicine under the unyielding old dowager's nose, who left her victim finally with a benediction.

It did not much comfort Mrs. Rawdon; her countenance was very queer when Rawdon came in and heard what had happened; and his explosions of laughter were as loud as usual, when Becky, with a fun which she could not disguise, even though it was at her own expense, described the occurrence, and how she had been victimized by Lady Southdown. Lord Steyne, and her son in London, had many a laugh over the story, when Rawdon and his wife returned to their quarters in May Fair. Becky acted the whole scene for them. She put on a nightcap and gown. She preached a great sermon in the true serious manner: she lectured on the virtue of the medicine which she pretended to administer, with a gravity of imitation so perfect, that you would have thought it was the countess's own Roman nose through which she snuffled. 'Give us Lady Southdown and the black dose,' was a constant cry amongst the folks in Becky's little drawing-room in May Fair. And for the first time in her life the Dowager Countess of Southdown was made amusing.

Sir Pitt remembered the testimonies of respect and veneration which Rebecca had paid personally to himself in early days, and was tolerably well disposed towards her. The marriage, ill-advised as it was, had improved Rawdon very much – that was clear from the colonel's altered habits and demeanour – and had it not been a lucky union as regarded Pitt himself? The cunning diplomatist smiled inwardly as he owned that he owed his fortune to it, and acknowledged that he at least ought not to cry out against it. His satisfaction was not removed by Rebecca's own statements, behaviour, and conversation.

She doubled the deference which before had charmed him, calling out his conversational powers in such a manner as quite to surprise Pitt himself, who, always inclined to respect his own talents, admired them the more when Rebecca pointed them out to him. With her sister-in-law, Rebecca was satisfactorily able to prove, that it was Mrs. Bute Crawley who brought about the marriage which she afterwards so calumniated: that it was Mrs. Bute's avarice – who hoped to gain all Miss Crawley's fortune, and deprive Rawdon of his aunt's favour – which caused and invented all the wicked reports against Rebecca. 'She succeeded in making us poor,' Rebecca said, with an air of angelical patience; 'but how can I be angry with a woman who has given me one of the best husbands in the world? And has not her own avarice been sufficiently punished by the ruin of her own hopes, and the loss of the property by which she set so much store? Poor!' she cried. 'Dear Lady Jane, what care we for poverty? I am used to it from childhood, and I am often thankful that Miss Crawley's money has gone to restore the splendour of the noble old family of which I am so proud to be a member. I am sure Sir Pitt will make a much better use of it than Rawdon would.'

All these speeches were reported to Sir Pitt by the most faithful of wives, and increased the favourable impression which Rebecca made; so much so, that when on the third day after the funeral the family party were at dinner, Sir Pitt Crawley, carving fowls at the head of the table, actually said to Mrs. Rawdon, 'Ahem! *Rebecca*, may I give you a wing?' – a speech which made the little woman's eyes sparkle with pleasure.

While Rebecca was prosecuting the above schemes and hopes, and Pitt Crawley arranging the funeral ceremonial and other matters connected with his future progress and dignity, and Lady Jane busy with her nursery, as far as her mother would let her, and the sun rising and setting, and the clock-tower bell of the Hall ringing to dinner and to prayers as usual, the body of the late owner of Queen's Crawley lay in the apartment which he had occupied, watched unceasingly by the professional attendants who were engaged for that rite. A woman or two, and three or four undertaker's men, the best whom Southampton could furnish, dressed in black, and of a proper stealthy and tragical demeanour, had charge of the remains which they watched turn about, having the housekeeper's room for their place of rendezvous when off duty, where they played at cards in privacy and drank their beer.

The members of the family and servants of the house kept away from the gloomy spot, where the bones of the descendant of an ancient line of knights and gentlemen lay, awaiting their final consignment to the family crypt. No regrets attended them, save those of the poor woman who had hoped to be Sir Pitt's wife and widow, and who had fled in disgrace from the Hall over which she had so nearly been a ruler. Beyond her and a favourite old pointer he had, and between whom and himself an attachment subsisted during the period of his imbecility, the old man had not a single friend to mourn him, having indeed, during the whole course of his life, never taken the least pains to secure one. Could the best and kindest of us who depart from the earth, have an opportunity of revisiting it, I suppose he or she (assuming that any Vanity Fair feelings subsist in the sphere whither we are bound) would have a pang of mortification at finding how soon our survivors were consoled. And so Sir Pitt was forgotten — like the kindest and best of us — only a few weeks sooner.

Those who will may follow his remains to the grave, whither they were borne on the appointed day, in the most becoming manner, the family in black coaches, with their handkerchiefs up to their noses, ready for the tears which did not come: the undertaker and his gentlemen in deep tribulation: the select tenantry mourning out of compliment to the new landlord: the neighbouring gentry's carriages at three miles an hour, empty, and in profound affliction: the parson speaking out the formula about 'our dear brother departed'. As long as we have a man's body, we play our Vanities upon it, surrounding it with humbug and cere-monies, laying it in state, and packing it up in gilt nails and velvet: and we finish our duty by placing over it a stone, written all over with lies. Bute's curate, a smart young fellow from Oxford, and Sir Pitt Crawley, composed between them an appropriate Latin epitaph for the late lamented baronet:

and the former preached a classical sermon, exhorting the survivors not to give way to grief, and informing them in the most respectful terms that they also would be one day called upon to pass that gloomy and mysterious portal which had just closed upon the remains of their lamented brother. Then the tenantry mounted on horseback again, or stayed and refreshed themselves at the 'Crawley Arms'. Then, after a lunch in the servants' hall at Queen's Crawley, the gentry's carriages wheeled off to their different destinations: then the undertaker's men, taking the ropes, palls, velvets, ostrich feathers, and other mortuary properties, clambered up on the roof of the hearse, and rode off to Southampton. Their faces relapsed into a natural expression as the horses, clearing the lodge gates, got into a brisker trot on the open road; and squads of them might have been seen, speckling with black the public-house entrances, with pewter pots flashing in the sunshine. Sir Pitt's invalid-chair was wheeled away into a tool-house in the garden: the old pointer used to howl sometimes at first, but these were the only accents of grief which were heard in the Hall of which Sir Pitt Crawley, Baronet, had been master for some threescore years.

As the birds were pretty plentiful, and partridge-shooting is as it were the duty of an English gentleman of statesman-like propensities, Sir Pitt Crawley, the first shock of grief over, went out a little and partook of that diversion in a white hat with a crape round it. The sight of those fields of stubble and turnips, now his own, gave him many secret joys. Sometimes, and with an exquisite humility, he took no gun, but went out with a peaceful bamboo cane; Rawdon, his big brother, and the keepers blazing away at his side. Pitt's money and acres had a great effect upon his brother. The penniless colonel became quite obsequious and respectful to the head of his house, and despised the milksop Pitt no longer. Rawdon listened with sympathy to his senior's prospects of planting and draining: gave his advice about the stables and cattle, rode over to Mudbury to look at a mare which he thought would carry Lady Jane, and offered to break her, &c.; the rebellious dragoon was quite humbled and subdued, and became a most creditable younger brother. He had constant bulletins from Miss Briggs in London respecting little Rawdon, who was left behind there: who

sent messages of his own. 'I am very well,' he wrote. 'I hope
you are very well. I hope mamma is very well. The pony is
very well. Grey takes me to ride in the Park. I can canter.
I met the little boy who rode before. He cried when he
cantered. I do not cry.' Rawdon read these letters to his
brother, and Lady Jane, who was delighted with them. The
baronet promised to take charge of the lad at school; and
his kind-hearted wife gave Rebecca a bank-note, begging her
to buy a present with it for her little nephew.

One day followed another, and the ladies of the house
passed their life in those calm pursuits and amusements
which satisfy country ladies. Bells rang to meals, and to
prayers. The young ladies took exercise on the pianoforte
every morning after breakfast, Rebecca giving them the
benefit of her instruction. Then they put on thick shoes and
walked in the park or shrubberies, or beyond the palings
into the village, descending upon the cottages, with Lady
Southdown's medicine, and tracts for the sick people there.
Lady Southdown drove out in a pony-chaise, when Rebecca
would take her place by the dowager's side, and listen to
her solemn talk with the utmost interest. She sang Handel
and Haydn to the family of evenings, and engaged in a large
piece of worsted work, as if she had been born to the
business, and as if this kind of life was to continue with her
until she should sink to the grave in a polite old age, leaving
regrets and a great quantity of Consols behind her – as if
there were not cares and duns, schemes, shifts, and poverty,
waiting outside the park gates, to pounce upon her when
she issued into the world again.

'It isn't difficult to be a country gentleman's wife,'
Rebecca thought. 'I think I could be a good woman if I had
five thousand a year. I could dawdle about in the nursery,
and count the apricots on the wall. I could water plants in
a greenhouse, and pick off dead leaves from the geraniums.
I could ask old women about their rheumatisms, and order
half a crown's worth of soup for the poor. I shouldn't miss
it much, out of five thousand a year. I could even drive out
ten miles to dine at a neighbour's, and dress in the fashions
of the year before last. I could go to church and keep awake
in the great family pew: or go to sleep behind the curtains,
with my veil down, if I only had practice. I could pay
everybody, if I had but the money. This is what the con-

jurers here pride themselves upon doing. They look down with pity upon us miserable sinners who have none. They think themselves generous if they give our children a five-pound note, and us contemptible if we are without one.' And who knows but Rebecca was right in her speculations – and that it was only a question of money and fortune which made the difference between her and an honest woman? If you take temptations into account, who is to say that he is better than his neighbour? A comfortable career of prosperity, if it does not make people honest, at least keeps them so. An alderman coming from a turtle feast will not step out of his carriage to steal a leg of mutton; but put him to starve, and see if he will not purloin a loaf. Becky consoled herself by so balancing the chances and equalizing the distribution of good and evil in the world.

The old haunts, the old fields and woods, the copses, ponds, and gardens, the rooms of the old house where she had spent a couple of years seven years ago, were all carefully revisited by her. She had been young there, or comparatively so, for she forgot the time when she ever *was* young – but she remembered her thoughts and feelings seven years back, and contrasted them with those which she had at present, now that she had seen the world and lived with great people, and raised herself far beyond her original humble station.

'I have passed beyond it, because I have brains,' Becky thought, 'and almost all the rest of the world are fools. I could not go back, and consort with those people now, whom I used to meet in my father's studio. Lords come up to my door with stars and garters instead of poor artists with screws of tobacco in their pockets. I have a gentleman for my husband, and an earl's daughter for my sister in the very house where I was little better than a servant a few years ago. But am I much better to do now in the world than I was when I was the poor painter's daughter, and wheedled the grocer round the corner for sugar and tea? Suppose I had married Francis who was so fond of me – I couldn't have been much poorer than I am now. Heigho! I wish I could exchange my position in society, and all my relations for a snug sum in the Three per Cent Consols;' for so it was that Becky felt the Vanity of human affairs, and it was in those securities that she would have liked to cast anchor.

It may perhaps have struck her that to have been honest

and humble, to have done her duty, and to have marched straightforward on her way, would have brought her as near happiness as that path by which she was striving to attain it. But, – just as the children at Queen's Crawley went round the room, where the body of their father lay; – if ever Becky had these thoughts, she was accustomed to walk round them, and not look in. She eluded them, and despised them – or at least she was committed to the other path from which retreat was now impossible. And for my part I believe that remorse is the least active of all a man's moral senses – the very easiest to be deadened when wakened: and in some never wakened at all. We grieve at being found out, and at the idea of shame or punishment; but the mere sense of wrong makes very few people unhappy in Vanity Fair.

So Rebecca, during her stay at Queen's Crawley, made as many friends of the Mammon of Unrighteousness as she could possibly bring under control. Lady Jane and her husband bade her farewell with the warmest demonstrations of goodwill. They looked forward with pleasure to the time when the family-house in Gaunt Street being repaired and beautified, they were to meet again in London. Lady Southdown made her up a packet of medicine, and sent a letter by her to the Rev. Lawrence Grills, exhorting that gentleman to save the brand who 'honoured' the letter from the burning. Pitt accompanied them with four horses in the carriage to Mudbury, having sent on their baggage in a cart previously, accompanied with loads of game.

'How happy you will be to see your darling little boy again!' Lady Crawley said, taking leave of her kinswoman.

'Oh, so happy!' said Rebecca, throwing up the green eyes. She was immensely happy to be free of the place, and yet loath to go. Queen's Crawley was abominably stupid; and yet the air there was somehow purer than that which she had been accustomed to breathe. Everybody had been dull, but had been kind in their way. 'It is all the influence of a long course of Three per Cents,' Becky said to herself, and was right very likely.

However, the London lamps flashed joyfully as the stage rolled into Piccadilly, and Briggs had made a beautiful fire in Curzon Street, and little Rawdon was up to welcome back his papa and mamma.

CHAPTER XLII

WHICH TREATS OF THE OSBORNE FAMILY

CONSIDERABLE time has elapsed since we have seen our respectable friend, old Mr. Osborne of Russell Square. He has not been the happiest of mortals since last we met him. Events have occurred which have not improved his temper, and in more instances than one he has not been allowed to have his own way. To be thwarted in this reasonable desire was always very injurious to the old gentleman; and resistance became doubly exasperating when gout, age, loneliness, and the force of many disappointments combined to weigh him down. His stiff black hair began to grow quite white soon after his son's death; his face grew redder; his hands trembled more and more as he poured out his glass of port wine. He led his clerks a dire life in the City; his family at home were not much happier. I doubt if Rebecca, whom we have seen piously praying for Consols, would have exchanged her poverty and the daredevil excitement and chances of her life, for Osborne's money and the humdrum gloom which enveloped him. He had proposed for Miss Swartz, but had been rejected scornfully by the partisans of that lady, who married her to a young sprig of Scotch nobility. He was a man to have married a woman out of low life, and bullied her dreadfully afterwards: but no person presented herself suitable to his taste; and, instead, he tyrannized over his unmarried daughter, at home. She had a fine carriage and fine horses, and sat at the head of a table loaded with the grandest plate. She had a cheque-book, a prize footman to follow her when she walked, unlimited credit, and bows and compliments from all the tradesmen, and all the appurtenances of an heiress; but she spent a woful time. The little charity-girls at the Founding, the sweeperess at the crossing, the poorest under-kitchenmaid in the servants' hall, was happy compared to that unfortunate and now middle-aged young lady.

Frederick Bullock, Esq., of the house of Bullock, Hulker, and Bullock, had married Maria Osborne, not without a great deal of difficulty and grumbling on Mr. Bullock's part. George being dead and cut out of his father's will, Frederick

insisted that the half of the old gentleman's property should
be settled upon his Maria, and indeed, for a long time,
refused 'to come to the scratch' (it was Mr. Frederick's own
expression) on any other terms. Osborne said Fred had
agreed to take his daughter with twenty thousand, and he
should bind himself to no more. 'Fred might take it, and
welcome, or leave it, and go and be hanged.' Fred, whose
hopes had been raised when George had been disinherited,
thought himself infamously swindled by the old merchant,
and for some time made as if he would break off the match
altogether. Osborne withdrew his account from Bullock and
Hulker's, went on 'Change with a horsewhip which he swore
he would lay across the back of a certain scoundrel that
should be nameless, and demeaned himself in his usual
violent manner. Jane Osborne condoled with her sister Maria
during this family feud. 'I always told you, Maria, that it
was your money he loved, and not you,' she said, soothingly.

'He selected *me* and my money at any rate: he didn't
choose you and yours,' replied Maria, tossing up her head.

The rupture was, however, only temporary. Fred's father
and senior partners counselled him to take Maria, even with
the twenty thousand settled, half down, and half at the death
of Mr. Osborne, with the chances of the further division of
the property. So he 'knuckled down', again to use his own
phrase; and sent old Hulker with peaceable overtures to
Osborne. It was his father, he said, who would not hear of
the match, and had made the difficulties; he was most anxious
to keep the engagement. The excuse was sulkily accepted by
Mr. Osborne. Hulker and Bullock were a high family of the
City aristocracy, and connected with the 'nobs' at the West
End. It was something for the old man to be able to say,
'My son, sir, of the house of Hulker, Bullock and Co., sir;
my daughter's cousin, Lady Mary Mango, sir, daughter of
the Right Honourable the Earl of Castlemouldy.' In his
imagination he saw his house peopled by the 'nobs'. So he
forgave young Bullock, and consented that the marriage
should take place.

It was a grand affair – the bridegroom's relatives giving
the breakfast, their habitations being near St. George's,
Hanover Square, where the business took place. The 'nobs
of the West End' were invited, and many of them signed
the book. Mr. Mango and Lady Mary Mango were there,

with the dear young Gwendoline and Gwinever Mango as bridesmaids; Colonel Bludyer of the Dragoon Guards (eldest son of the house of Bludyer Brothers, Mincing Lane), another cousin of the bridegroom, and the Honourable Mrs. Bludyer; the Honourable George Boulter, Lord Levant's son, and his lady, Miss Mango that was; Lord Viscount Castletoddy; Honourable James McMull and Mrs. McMull (formerly Miss Swartz), and a host of fashionables, who have all married into Lombard Street, and done a great deal to ennoble Cornhill.

The young couple had a house near Berkeley Square, and a small villa at Roehampton, among the banking colony there. Fred was considered to have made rather a *mésalliance* by the ladies of his family, whose grandfather had been in a charity school, and who were allied through the husbands with some of the best blood in England. And Maria was bound, by superior pride and great care in the composition of her visiting-book, to make up for the defects of birth; and felt it her duty to see her father and sister as little as possible.

That she should utterly break with the old man, who had still so many scores of thousand pounds to give away, is absurd to suppose. Fred Bullock would never allow her to do that. But she was still young and incapable of hiding her feelings: and by inviting her papa and sister to her third-rate parties, and behaving very coldly to them when they came, and by avoiding Russell Square, and indiscreetly begging her father to quit that odious vulgar place; she did more harm than all Frederick's diplomacy could repair, and perilled her chance of her inheritance like a giddy heedless creature as she was.

'So Russell Square is not good enough for Mrs. Maria, hey?' said the old gentleman, rattling up the carriage-windows, as he and his daughter drove away one night from Mrs. Frederick Bullock's, after dinner. 'So she invites her father and sister to a second day's dinner (if those sides, or ontrys, as she calls 'em, weren't served yesterday, I'm d–d), and to meet City folks and littery men, and keeps the earls and the ladies, and the honourables to herself. Honourables? Damn honourables! I am a plain British merchant, I am: and could buy the beggarly hounds over and over. Lords, indeed! – why, at one of her swarreys I saw one of them speak to a

dam fiddler – a fellar I despise. And they won't come to
Russell Square, won't they? Why, I'll lay my life I've got a
better glass of wine, and pay a better figure for it, and can
show a handsomer service of silver, and can lay a better
dinner on my mahogany, than ever they see on theirs – the
cringing, sneaking, stuck-up fools. Drive on quick, James: I
want to get back to Russell Square – ha, ha!' and he sank
back into the corner with a furious laugh. With such reflections on his own superior merits it was the custom of the
old gentleman not unfrequently to console himself.

Jane Osborne could not but concur in these opinions
respecting her sister's conduct; and when Mrs. Frederick's
firstborn, Frederick Augustus Howard Stanley Devereux Bullock, was born, old Osborne, who was invited to the christening and to be godfather, contented himself with sending
the child a gold cup, with twenty guineas inside it for the
nurse. 'That's more than any of your lords will give, *I'll*
warrant,' he said, and refused to attend at the ceremony.

The splendour of the gift, however, caused great satisfaction to the house of Bullock. Maria thought that her father
was very much pleased with her, and Frederick augured the
best for his little son and heir.

One can fancy the pangs with which Miss Osborne in her
solitude in Russell Square read the *Morning Post*, where her
sister's name occurred every now and then, in the articles
headed 'Fashionable Réunions', and where she had an
opportunity of reading a description of Mrs. F. Bullock's
costume, when presented at the Drawing-room by Lady
Frederica Bullock. Jane's own life, as we have said, admitted
of no such grandeur. It was an awful existence. She had to
get up of black winter's mornings to make breakfast for her
scowling old father, who would have turned the whole house
out of doors if his tea had not been ready at half-past eight.
She remained silent opposite to him, listening to the urn
hissing, and sitting in tremor while the parent read his paper,
and consumed his accustomed portion of muffins and tea.
At half-past nine he rose and went to the City, and she was
almost free till dinner-time, to make visitations in the kitchen
and to scold the servants: to drive abroad and descend upon
the tradesmen, who were prodigiously respectful: to leave
her cards and her papa's at the great glum respectable houses
of their City friends; or to sit alone in the large drawing-

room, expecting visitors; and working at a huge piece of worsted by the fire, on the sofa, hard by the great Iphigenia clock, which ticked and tolled with mournful loudness in the dreary room. The great glass over the mantelpiece, faced by the other great console-glass at the opposite end of the room, increased and multiplied between them the brown holland bag in which the chandelier hung; until you saw these brown holland bags fading away in endless perspectives, and this apartment of Miss Osborne's seemed the centre of a system of drawing-rooms. When she removed the cordovan leather from the grand piano, and ventured to play a few notes on it, it sounded with a mournful sadness, startling the dismal echoes of the house. George's picture was gone, and laid upstairs in a lumber-room in the garret; and though there was a consciousness of him, and father and daughter often instinctively knew that they were thinking of him, no mention was ever made of the brave and once darling son.

At five o'clock Mr. Osborne came back to his dinner, which he and his daughter took in silence (seldom broken, except when he swore and was savage, if the cooking was not to his liking), or which they shared twice in a month with a party of dismal friends of Osborne's rank and age. Old Dr. Gulp and his lady from Bloomsbury Square: old Mr. Frowser, the attorney, from Bedford Row, a very great man, and from his business, hand-in-glove with the 'nobs at the West End'; old Colonel Livermore, of the Bombay Army, and Mrs. Livermore from Upper Bedford Place: old Serjeant Toffy and Mrs. Toffy; and sometimes old Sir Thomas Coffin and Lady Coffin, from Bedford Square. Sir Thomas was celebrated as a hanging judge, and the particular tawny port was produced when he dined with Mr. Osborne.

These people and their like gave the pompous Russell Square merchant pompous dinners back again. They had solemn rubbers of whist, when they went upstairs after drinking, and their carriages were called at half-past ten. Many rich people, whom we poor devils are in the habit of envying, lead contentedly an existence like that above described. Jane Osborne scarcely ever met a man under sixty, and almost the only bachelor who appeared in their society was Mr. Smirk, the celebrated lady's doctor.

I can't say that nothing had occurred to disturb the monotony of this awful existence: the fact is, there had been a secret in poor Jane's life which had made her father more savage and morose than even nature, pride, and overfeeding had made him. This secret was connected with Miss Wirt, who had a cousin an artist, Mr. Smee, very celebrated since as a portrait-painter and R.A., but who once was glad enough to give drawing-lessons to ladies of fashion. Mr. Smee has forgotten where Russell Square is now, but he was glad enough to visit it in the year 1818, when Miss Osborne had instruction from him.

Smee (formerly a pupil of Sharpe of Frith Street, a dissolute, irregular, and unsuccessful man, but a man with great knowledge of his art) being the cousin of Miss Wirt, we say, and introduced by her to Miss Osborne, whose hand and heart were still free after various incomplete love affairs, felt a great attachment for this lady, and it is believed inspired one in her bosom. Miss Wirt was the confidante of this intrigue. I know not whether she used to leave the room where the master and his pupil were painting, in order to give them an opportunity for exchanging those vows and sentiments which cannot be uttered advantageously in the presence of a third party: I know not whether she hoped that should her cousin succeed in carrying off the rich merchant's daughter, he would give Miss Wirt a portion of the wealth which she had enabled him to win – all that is certain is, that Mr. Osborne got some hint of the transaction, came back from the City abruptly, and entered the drawing-room with his bamboo-cane; found the painter, the pupil, and the companion all looking exceedingly pale there; turned the former out of doors with menaces that he would break every bone in his skin, and half an hour afterwards dismissed Miss Wirt likewise, kicking her trunks down the stairs, trampling on her bandboxes, and shaking his fist at her hackney-coach, as it bore her away.

Jane Osborne kept her bedroom for many days. She was not allowed to have a companion afterwards. Her father swore to her that she should not have a shilling of his money if she made any match without his concurrence; and as he wanted a woman to keep his house, he did not choose that she should marry: so that she was obliged to give up all projects with which Cupid had any share. During her papa's life, then, she resigned herself to the manner of existence here described, and was content to be an Old Maid. Her sister, meanwhile, was having children with finer names every year – and the intercourse between the two grew fainter continually. 'Jane and I do not move in the same sphere of life,' Mrs. Bullock said. 'I regard her as a sister, of course' – which means – what does it mean when a lady says that she regards Jane as a sister?

It has been described how the Misses Dobbin lived with their father at a fine villa at Denmark Hill, where there were beautiful graperies and peach-trees which delighted little Georgy Osborne. The Misses Dobbin, who drove often to Brompton to see our dear Amelia, came sometimes to Russell Square, too, to pay a visit to their old acquaintance Miss Osborne. I believe it was in consequence of the commands of their brother the major in India (for whom their papa had a prodigious respect) that they paid attention to Mrs. George; for the major, the godfather and guardian of Amelia's little boy, still hoped that the child's grandfather might be induced to relent towards him, and acknowledge him for the sake of his son. The Miss Dobbins kept Miss Osborne acquainted with the state of Amelia's affairs; how she was living with her father and mother; how poor they were; how they wondered what men, and such men as their brother and dear Captain Osborne, could find in such an insignificant little chit; how she was still, as heretofore, a namby-pamby milk-and-water affected creature – but how the boy was really the noblest little boy ever seen – for the hearts of all women warm towards young children, and the sourest spinster is kind to them.

One day, after great entreaties, on the part of the Misses Dobbin, Amelia allowed little George to go and pass a day with them at Denmark Hill – a part of which day she spent herself in writing to the major in India. She congratulated him on the happy news which his sisters had just conveyed to her. She prayed for his prosperity, and that of the bride he had chosen. She thanked him for a thousand, thousand kind offices and proofs of steadfast friendship to her in her affliction. She told him the last news about little Georgy, and how he was gone to spend that very day with his sisters in the country. She underlined the letter a great deal, and she signed herself affectionately his friend, Amelia Osborne. She forgot to send any message of kindness to Lady O'Dowd, as her wont was – and did not mention Glorvina by name, and only in italics, as the major's *bride*, for whom she begged *blessings*. But the news of the marriage removed the reserve which she had kept up towards him. She was glad to be able to own and feel how warmly and gratefully she regarded him – and as for the idea of being jealous of Glorvina (Glorvina, indeed!), Amelia would have scouted it, if an angel from heaven had hinted it to her.

That night, when Georgy came back in the pony-carriage in which he rejoiced, and in which he was driven by Sir William Dobbin's old coachman, he had round his neck a fine gold chain and watch. He said an old lady, not pretty, had given it him, who cried and kissed him a great deal. But he didn't like her. He liked grapes very much. And he only liked his mamma. Amelia shrunk and started: the timid soul felt a presentiment of terror when she heard that the relations of the child's father had seen him.

Miss Osborne came back to give her father his dinner. He had made a good speculation in the City, and was rather in a good humour that day, and chanced to remark the agitation under which she laboured. 'What's the matter, Miss Osborne?' he deigned to say.

The woman burst into tears. 'Oh, sir,' she said, 'I've seen little George. He is as beautiful as an angel – and so like him!' The old man opposite to her did not say a word, but flushed up, and began to tremble in every limb.

CHAPTER XLIII

IN WHICH THE READER HAS TO DOUBLE THE CAPE

THE astonished reader must be called upon to transport himself ten thousand miles to the military station of Bundlegunge, in the Madras division of our Indian empire, where our gallant old friends of the –th regiment are quartered under the command of the brave colonel, Sir Michael O'Dowd. Time has dealt kindly with that stout officer, as it does ordinarily with men who have good stomachs and good tempers, and are not perplexed over much by fatigue of the brain. The colonel plays a good knife and fork at tiffin, and resumes those weapons with great success at dinner. He smokes his hookah after both meals, and puffs as quietly while his wife scolds him, as he did under the fire of the French at Waterloo. Age and heat have not diminished the activity or the eloquence of the descendant of the Malonys and the Molloys. Her ladyship, our old acquaintance, is as much at home at Madras as at Brussels – in the cantonment as under the tents. On the march you saw her at the head of the regiment seated on a royal elephant, a noble sight. Mounted on that beast, she has been into action with tigers in the jungle: she has been received by native princes, who have welcomed her and Glorvina into the recesses of their zenanas and offered her shawls and jewels which it went to her heart to refuse. The sentries of all arms salute her wherever she makes her appearance: and she touches her hat gravely to their salutation. Lady O'Dowd is one of the greatest ladies in the Presidency of Madras – her quarrel with Lady Smith, wife of Sir Minos Smith the puisne judge, is still remembered by some at Madras, when the colonel's lady snapped her fingers in the judge's lady's face, and said *she'd* never walk behind ever a beggarly civilian. Even now, though it is five-and-twenty years ago, people remember Lady O'Dowd performing a jig at Government House, where she danced down two aides de camp, a major of Madras cavalry and two gentlemen of the Civil Service; and, persuaded by Major Dobbin, C.B., second in command of the –th, to retire to the supper-room, *lassata nondum satiata recessit.*

Peggy O'Dowd is indeed the same as ever: kind in act and thought: impetuous in temper; eager to command: a tyrant over her Michael: a dragon amongst all the ladies of the regiment: a mother to all the young men, whom she tends in their sickness, defends in all their scrapes, and with whom Lady Peggy is immensely popular. But the subalterns' and captains' ladies (the major is unmarried) cabal against her a good deal. They say that Glorvina gives herself airs, and that Peggy herself is intolerably domineering. She interfered with a little congregation which Mrs. Kirk had got up, and laughed the young men away from her sermons, stating that a soldier's wife had no business to be a parson: that Mrs. Kirk would be much better mending her husband's clothes: and, if the regiment wanted sermons, that she had the finest in the world, those of her uncle, the dean. She abruptly put a termination to a flirtation which Lieutenant Stubble of the regiment had commenced with the surgeon's wife, threatening to come down upon Stubble for the money which he had borrowed from her (for the young fellow was still of an extravagant turn) unless he broke off at once and went to the Cape, on sick leave. On the other hand, she housed and sheltered Mrs. Posky, who fled from her bungalow one night, pursued by her infuriate husband, wielding his second brandy bottle, and actually carried Posky through the delirium tremens, and broke him of the habit of drinking, which had grown upon that officer as all evil habits will grow upon men. In a word, in adversity she was the best of comforters, in good fortune the most troublesome of friends; having a perfectly good opinion of herself always, and an indomitable resolution to have her own way.

Among other points, she had made up her mind that Glorvina should marry our old friend Dobbin. Mrs. O'Dowd knew the major's expectations and appreciated his good qualities, and the high character which he enjoyed in his profession. Glorvina, a very handsome, fresh-coloured, black-haired, blue-eyed young lady, who could ride a horse, or play a sonata with any girl out of the County Cork, seemed to be the very person destined to ensure Dobbin's happiness – much more than that poor good little weak-spur'ted Amelia, about whom he used to take on so. – 'Look at Glorvina enter a room,' Mrs. O'Dowd would say, 'and compare her with that poor Mrs. Osborne, who couldn't say boo to a goose. She'd be worthy of you, major – you're a quiet man yourself, and want some one to talk for ye. And though she does not come of such good blood as the Malonys or Molloys, let me tell ye, she's of an ancient family that any nobleman might be proud to marry into.'

But before she had come to such a resolution, and determined to subjugate Major Dobbin by her endearments, it must be owned that Glorvina had practised them a good deal elsewhere. She had had a season in Dublin, and who knows how many in Cork, Killarney, and Mallow? She had flirted with all the marriageable officers whom the dépôts of her country afforded, and all the bachelor squires who seemed eligible. She had been engaged to be married a half score times in Ireland, besides the clergyman at Bath who

used her so ill. She had flirted all the way to Madras with
the captain and chief mate of the *Ramchunder* East Indiaman,
and had a season at the Presidency with her brother and
Mrs. O'Dowd who was staying there, while the major of the
regiment was in command at the station. Everybody admired
her there: everybody danced with her: but no one proposed
who was worth the marrying; one or two exceedingly young
subalterns sighed after her, and a beardless civilian or two;
but she rejected these as beneath her pretensions; and other
and younger virgins than Glorvina were married before her.
There are women, and handsome women too, who have this
fortune in life. They fall in love with the utmost generosity;
they ride and walk with half the Army List, though they draw
near to forty, and yet the Miss O'Gradys are Miss O'Gradys
still: Glorvina persisted that but for Lady O'Dowd's unlucky
quarrel with the judge's lady, she would have made a good
match at Madras, where old Mr. Chutney, who was at the
head of the Civil Service (and who afterwards married Miss
Dolby, a young lady, only thirteen years of age, who had
just arrived from school in Europe), was just at the point
of proposing to her.

Well, although Lady O'Dowd and Glorvina quarrelled a
great number of times every day, and upon almost every
conceivable subject – indeed, if Mick O'Dowd had not
possessed the temper of an angel, two such women constantly
about his ears would have driven him out of his senses –
yet they agreed between themselves on this point, that
Glorvina should marry Major Dobbin, and were determined
that the major should have no rest until the arrangement
was brought about. Undismayed by forty or fifty previous
defeats, Glorvina laid siege to him. She sang Irish Melodies
at him unceasingly. She asked him so frequently and pathetically, will ye come to the bower? that it is a wonder how
any man of feeling could have resisted the invitation. She
was never tired of inquiring, if Sorrow had his young days
faded; and was ready to listen and weep like Desdemona at
the stories of his dangers and his campaigns. It has been
said that our honest and dear old friend used to perform on
the flute in private: Glorvina insisted upon having duets
with him, and Lady O'Dowd would rise and artlessly quit
the room, when the young couple were so engaged. Glorvina
forced the major to ride with her of mornings. The whole

cantonment saw them set out and return. She was constantly
writing notes over to him at his house, borrowing his books,
and scoring with her great pencil-marks such passages of
sentiment or humour as awakened her sympathy. She borrowed his horses, his servants, his spoons, and palankeen; –
no wonder that public rumour assigned her to him, and that
the major's sisters in England should fancy they were about
to have a sister-in-law.

Dobbin, who was thus vigorously besieged, was in the
meanwhile in a state of the most odious tranquillity. He used
to laugh when the young fellows of the regiment joked him
about Glorvina's manifest attentions to him. 'Bah!' said he,
'she is only keeping her hand in – she practises upon me as
she does upon Mrs. Tozer's piano, because it's the most
handy instrument in the station. I am much too battered
and old for such a fine young lady as Glorvina.' And so he
went on riding with her, and copying music and verses into
her albums, and playing at chess with her very submissively;
for it is with these simple amusements that some officers in
India are accustomed to while away their leisure moments;
while others of a less domestic turn hunt hogs, and shoot
snipes, or gamble and smoke cheroots, and betake themselves
to brandy-and-water. As for Sir Michael O'Dowd, though
his lady and her sister both urged him to call upon the major
to explain himself, and not keep on torturing a poor innocent
girl in that shameful way, the old soldier refused point-blank
to have anything to do with the conspiracy. 'Faith, the
major's big enough to choose for himself,' Sir Michael said;
'he'll ask ye when he wants ye;' – or else he would turn the
matter off jocularly, declaring that 'Dobbin was too young
to keep house, and had written home to ask leave of his
mamma'. Nay, he went farther, and in private communications with his major, would caution and rally him – crying,
'Mind your oi, Dob, my boy, them girls is bent on mischief
– me lady has just got a box of gowns from Europe, and
there's a pink satin for Glorvina, which will finish ye, Dob,
if it's in the power of woman or satin to move ye.'

But the truth is, neither beauty nor fashion could conquer
him. Our honest friend had but one idea of a woman in his
head, and that one did not in the least resemble Miss
Glorvina O'Dowd in pink satin. A gentle little woman in
black, with large eyes and brown hair, seldom speaking, save

when spoken to, and then in a voice not the least resembling Miss Glorvina's – a soft young mother tending an infant and beckoning the major up with a smile to look at him – a rosy-cheeked lass coming singing into the room in Russell Square or hanging on George Osborne's arm, happy and loving – there was but this image that filled our honest major's mind by day and by night, and reigned over it always. Very likely Amelia was not like the portrait the major had formed of her: there was a figure in a book of fashions which his sisters had in England, and with which William had made away privately, pasting it into the lid of his desk, and fancying he saw some resemblance to Mrs. Osborne in the print, whereas I have seen it, and can vouch that it is but the picture of a high-waisted gown with an impossible doll's face simpering over it – and, perhaps, Mr. Dobbin's sentimental Amelia was no more like the real one than this absurd little print which he cherished. But what man in love, of us, is better informed? – or is he much happier when he sees and owns his delusion? Dobbin was under this spell. He did not bother his friends and the public much about his feelings, or indeed lose his natural zest or appetite on account of them. His head has grizzled since we saw him last; and a line or two of silver may be seen in the soft brown hair likewise. But his feelings are not in the least changed or oldened; and his love remains as fresh, as a man's recollections of boyhood are.

We have said how the two Miss Dobbins and Amelia, the major's correspondents in Europe, wrote him letters from England; Mrs. Osborne congratulating him with great candour and cordiality upon his approaching nuptials with Miss O'Dowd.

'Your sister has just kindly visited me,' Amelia wrote in her letter, 'and informed me of an *interesting event*, upon which I beg to offer my *most sincere congratulations*. I hope the young lady to whom I hear you are to be *united* will in every respect prove worthy of one who is himself all kindness and goodness. The poor widow has only her prayers to offer, and her cordial, cordial wishes for *your prosperity!* Georgy sends his love to *his dear godpapa*, and hopes that you will not forget him. I tell him that you are about to form *other ties*, with one who I am sure merits *all your affection*, but that although such ties must of course be the strongest and most sacred, and supersede *all others*, yet that I am sure the widow and the child whom you have ever protected and loved will always *have a corner in your heart*.' The letter, which has been before alluded to, went on in this strain, protesting throughout as to the extreme satisfaction of the writer.

This letter, which arrived by the very same ship which brought out Lady O'Dowd's box of millinery from London (and which you may be sure Dobbin opened before any one of the other packets which the mail brought him), put the receiver into such a state of mind that Glorvina, and her pink satin, and everything belonging to her, became perfectly odious to him. The major cursed the talk of women, and the sex in general. Everything annoyed him that day – the parade was insufferably hot and wearisome. Good heavens! was a man of intellect to waste his life, day after day, inspecting cross-belts, and putting fools through their manœuvres? The senseless chatter of the young men at mess was more than ever jarring. What cared he, a man on the high road to forty, to know how many snipes Lieutenant Smith had shot, or what were the performances of Ensign Brown's mare? The jokes about the table filled him with shame. He was too old to listen to the banter of the assistant-surgeon and the slang of the youngsters, at which old O'Dowd, with his bald head and red face, laughed quite easily. The old man had listened to those jokes any time these thirty years – Dobbin himself had been fifteen years hearing them. And after the boisterous dullness of the mess-table, the quarrels and scandal of the ladies of the regiment! It was unbearable, shameful. 'O Amelia, Amelia,' he thought, 'you to whom I have been so faithful – you reproach me! It is because you cannot feel for me, that I drag on this wearisome life. And you reward me after years of devotion by giving me your blessing upon my marriage, forsooth, with this flaunting Irish girl!' Sick and sorry felt poor William: more than ever wretched and lonely. He would like to have done with life and its vanity altogether – so bootless and unsatisfactory the struggle, so cheerless and dreary the prospect seemed to him. He lay all that night sleepless, and yearning to go home. Amelia's letter had fallen as a blank upon him. No fidelity, no constant truth and passion, could move her into warmth. She would not see that he loved her.

Tossing in his bed, he spoke out to her. 'Good God, Amelia!' he said, 'don't you know that I only love you in the world – you, who are a stone to me – you, whom I tended through months and months of illness and grief, and who bade me farewell with a smile on your face, and forgot me before the door shut between us!' The native servants lying outside his verandahs beheld with wonder the major, so cold and quiet ordinarily, at present so passionately moved and cast down. Would she have pitied him had she seen him? He read over and over all the letters which he ever had from her – letters of business relative to the little property which he had made her believe her husband had left to her – brief notes of invitation – every scrap of writing that she had ever sent to him – how cold, how kind, how hopeless, how selfish they were!

Had there been some kind gentle soul near at hand who could read and appreciate this silent generous heart, who knows but that the reign of Amelia might have been over, and that friend William's love might have flowed into a kinder channel? But there was only Glorvina of the jetty ringlets with whom his intercourse was familiar, and this dashing young woman was not bent upon loving the major, but rather on making the major admire *her* – a most vain and hopeless task, too, at least considering the means that the poor girl possessed to carry it out. She curled her hair and showed her shoulders at him, as much as to say, did ye ever see such jet ringlets and such a complexion? She grinned at him so that he might see that every tooth in her head was sound – and he never heeded all these charms. Very soon after the arrival of the box of millinery, and perhaps indeed in honour of it, Lady O'Dowd and the ladies of the King's Regiment gave a ball to the Company's Regiments and the civilians at the station. Glorvina sported the killing pink frock, and the major, who attended the party and walked very ruefully up and down the rooms, never so much as perceived the pink garment. Glorvina danced past him in a fury with all the young subalterns of the station, and the major was not in the least jealous of her performance, or angry because Captain Bangles of the Cavalry handed her to supper. It was not jealousy, or frocks or shoulders, that could move him, and Glorvina had nothing more.

So these two were each exemplifying the Vanity of this

life, and each longing for what he or she could not get. Glorvina cried with rage at the failure. She had set her mind on the major 'more than on any of the others,' she owned, sobbing. 'He'll break my heart, he will, Peggy,' she would whimper to her sister-in-law when they were good friends; 'sure every one of me frocks must be taken in – it's such a skeleton I'm growing.' Fat or thin, laughing or melancholy, on horseback or the music-stool, it was all the same to the major. And the colonel, puffing his pipe and listening to these complaints, would suggest that Glory should have some black frocks out in the next box from London, and told a mysterious story of a lady in Ireland, who died of grief for the loss of her husband before she got e'er a one.

While the major was going on in this tantalizing way, not proposing, and declining to fall in love, there came another ship from Europe bringing letters on board, and amongst them some more for the heartless man. These were home letters bearing an earlier postmark than that of the former packets, and as Major Dobbin recognized among his, the handwriting of his sister, who always crossed and recrossed her letters to her brother – gathered together all the possible bad news which she could collect, abused him and read him lectures with sisterly frankness, and always left him miserable for the day after 'dearest William' had achieved the perusal of one of her epistles – the truth must be told that, dearest William did not hurry himself to break the seal of Miss Dobbin's letter, but waited for a particularly favourable day and mood for doing so. A fortnight before, moreover, he had written to scold her for telling those absurd stories to Mrs. Osborne, and had dispatched a letter in reply to that lady, undeceiving her with respect to the reports concerning him, and assuring her that 'he had no sort of present intention of altering his condition'.

Two or three nights after the arrival of the second package of letters, the major had passed the evening pretty cheerfully at Lady O'Dowd's house, where Glorvina thought that he listened with rather more attention than usual to the 'Meeting of the Wathers', the 'Minsthrel Boy', and one or two other specimens of song with which she favoured him (the truth is, he was no more listening to Glorvina than to the howling of the jackals in the moonlight outside, and the delusion was hers as usual), and having played his game at chess with her (cribbage with the surgeon was Lady O'Dowd's favourite evening pastime), Major Dobbin took leave of the colonel's family at his usual hour, and retired to his own house.

There on his table, his sister's letter lay reproaching him. He took it up, ashamed rather of his negligence regarding it, and prepared himself for a disagreeable hour's communing with that crabbed-handed absent relative. . . . It may have been an hour after the major's departure from the colonel's house – Sir Michael was sleeping the sleep of the just; Glorvina had arranged her black ringlets in the innumerable little bits of paper, in which it was her habit to confine them; Lady O'Dowd, too, had gone to her bed in the nuptial chamber, on the ground-floor, and had tucked her mosquito curtains round her fair form, when the guard at the gates of the commanding-officer's compound beheld Major Dobbin, in the moonlight, rushing towards the house with a swift step and a very agitated countenance, and he passed the sentinel and went up to the windows of the colonel's bedchamber.

'O'Dowd – colonel!' said Dobbin, and kept up a great shouting.

'Heavens, meejor!' said Glorvina of the curl-papers, putting out her head too, from her window.

'What is it, Dob, me boy?' said the colonel, expecting there was a fire in the station, or that the route had come from head quarters.

'I – I must have leave of absence. I must go to England – on the most urgent private affairs,' Dobbin said.

'Good heavens, what has happened!' thought Glorvina, trembling with all the papillotes.

'I want to be off – now – to-night,' Dobbin continued; and the colonel getting up, came out to parley with him.

In the postscript of Miss Dobbin's cross-letter – the major had just come upon a paragraph, to the following effect:– 'I drove yesterday to see your old *acquaintance*, Mrs. Osborne. The wretched place they live at, since they were bankrupts, you know – Mr. S., to judge from a *brass plate* on the door of his hut (it is little better) is a coal-merchant. The little boy, your godson, is certainly a fine child, though forward, and inclined to be saucy and self-willed. But we have taken notice of him as you wish it, and have introduced him to his aunt, Miss O., who was rather pleased with him. Perhaps his grandpapa, not the bankrupt one, who is almost doting, but Mr. Osborne, of Russell Square, may be induced to relent towards the child of your friend, *his erring and self-willed son*. And Amelia will not be ill disposed to give him up. The widow is *consoled*, and is about to marry a reverend gentleman, the Rev. Mr. Binney, one of the curates of Brompton. A poor match. But Mrs. O. is getting old, and I saw a great deal of grey in her hair – she was in very good spirits: and your little godson over-ate himself at our house. Mamma sends her love with that of your affectionate ANN DOBBIN.'

CHAPTER XLIV

A ROUNDABOUT CHAPTER BETWEEN LONDON AND HAMPSHIRE

OUR old friends the Crawleys' family house, in Great Gaunt Street, still bore over its front the hatchment which had been placed there as a token of mourning for Sir Pitt Crawley's demise, yet this heraldic emblem was in itself a very splendid and gaudy piece of furniture, and all the rest of the mansion became more brilliant than it had ever been during the late baronet's reign. The black outer-coating of the bricks was removed, and they appeared with a cheerful, blushing face streaked with white: the old bronze lions of the knocker were gilt handsomely, the railings painted, and the dismallest house in Great Gaunt Street became the smartest in the whole quarter, before the green leaves in Hampshire had replaced those yellowing ones which were on the trees in Queen's Crawley avenue when old Sir Pitt Crawley passed under them for the last time.

A little woman, with a carriage to correspond, was perpetually seen about this mansion; an elderly spinster, accompanied by a little boy, also might be remarked coming thither daily. It was Miss Briggs and little Rawdon, whose business it was to see to the inward renovation of Sir Pitt's house, to superintend the female band engaged in stitching the blinds and hangings, to poke and rummage in the drawers and cupboards crammed with the dirty relics and congregated trumperies of a couple of generations of Lady Crawleys, and to take inventories of the china, the glass, and other properties in the closets and storerooms.

Mrs. Rawdon Crawley was general-in-chief over these arrangements, with full orders from Sir Pitt to sell, barter, confiscate, or purchase furniture: and she enjoyed herself not a little in an occupation which gave full scope to her taste and ingenuity. The renovation of the house was determined upon when Sir Pitt came to town in November to see his lawyers, and when he passed nearly a week in Curzon Street, under the roof of his affectionate brother and sister.

He had put up at an hotel at first; but Becky, as soon as she heard of the baronet's arrival, went off alone to greet him, and returned in an hour to Curzon Street with Sir Pitt in the carriage by her side. It was impossible sometimes to resist this artless little creature's hospitalities, so kindly were they pressed, so frankly and amiably offered. Becky seized Pitt's hand in a transport of gratitude when he agreed to come. 'Thank you,' she said, squeezing it, and looking into the baronet's eyes, who blushed a good deal; 'how happy this will make Rawdon.' She bustled up to Pitt's bedroom, leading on the servants, who were carrying his trunks thither. She came in herself laughing, with a coal-scuttle out of her own room.

A fire was blazing already in Sir Pitt's apartment (it was Miss Briggs's room, by the way, who was sent upstairs to sleep with the maid). 'I knew I should bring you,' she said, with pleasure beaming in her glance. Indeed, she was really and sincerely happy at having him for a guest.

Becky made Rawdon dine out once or twice on business, while Pitt stayed with them, and the baronet passed the happy evening alone with her and Briggs. She went downstairs to the kitchen and actually cooked little dishes for him. 'Isn't it a good salmi?' she said; 'I made it for you. I can make you better dishes than that: and will when you come to see me.'

'Everything you do, you do well,' said the baronet, gallantly. 'The salmi is excellent indeed.'

'A poor man's wife,' Rebecca replied, gaily, 'must make herself useful, you know:' on which her brother-in-law vowed that 'she was fit to be the wife of an emperor, and that to be skilful in domestic duties was surely one of the most charming of woman's qualities'. And Sir Pitt thought, with something like mortification, of Lady Jane at home, and of a certain pie which she had insisted on making, and serving to him at dinner – a most abominable pie.

Besides the salmi, which was made of Lord Steyne's pheasants from his lordship's cottage of Stillbrook, Becky gave her brother-in-law a bottle of white wine, some that Rawdon had brought with him from France, and had picked up for nothing, the little story-teller said; whereas the liquor was, in truth, some White Hermitage from the Marquis of Steyne's famous cellars, which brought fire into the baronet's pallid cheeks and a glow into his feeble frame.

Then when he had drunk up the bottle of *petit vin blanc* she gave him her hand and took him up to the drawing-room, and made him snug on the sofa by the fire, and let him talk as she listened with the tenderest kindly interest, sitting by him, and hemming a shirt for her dear little boy. Whenever Mrs. Rawdon wished to be particularly humble and virtuous, this little shirt used to come out of her work-box. It had got to be too small for Rawdon long before it was finished, though.

Well, Rebecca listened to Pitt, she talked to him, she sang to him, she coaxed him, and cuddled him, so that he found himself more and more glad every day to get back from the lawyer's at Gray's Inn, to the blazing fire in Curzon Street – a gladness in which the men of law likewise participated, for Pitt's harangues were of the longest – and so that when he went away he felt quite a pang at departing. How pretty she looked kissing her hand to him from the carriage and waving her handkerchief when he had taken his place in the mail! She put the handkerchief to her eyes once. He pulled his sealskin cap over his, as the coach drove away, and, sinking back, he thought to himself how she respected him and how he deserved it, and how Rawdon was a foolish dull fellow who didn't half appreciate his wife: and how mum and stupid his own wife was compared to that brilliant little Becky. Becky had hinted every one of these things herself, perhaps, but so delicately and gently, that you hardly knew when or where. And, before they parted, it was agreed that the house in London should be redecorated for the next season, and that the brothers' families should meet again in the country at Christmas.

'I wish you could have got a little money out of him,'

Rawdon said to his wife moodily when the baronet was gone. 'I should like to give something to old Raggles, hanged if I shouldn't. It ain't right, you know, that the old fellow should be kept out of all his money. It may be inconvenient, and he might let to somebody else besides us, you know.'

'Tell him,' said Becky, 'that as soon as Sir Pitt's affairs are settled, everybody will be paid, and give him a little something on account. Here's a cheque that Pitt left for the boy,' and she took from her bag and gave her husband a paper which his brother had handed over to her, on behalf of the little son and heir of the younger branch of the Crawleys.

The truth is, she had tried personally the ground on which her husband expressed a wish that she should venture – tried it ever so delicately, and found it unsafe. Even at a hint about embarrassments, Sir Pitt Crawley was off and alarmed. And he began a long speech, explaining how straitened he himself was in money matters; how the tenants would not pay; how his father's affairs, and the expenses attendant upon the demise of the old gentleman, had involved him; how he wanted to pay off incumbrances; and how the bankers and agents were overdrawn; and Pitt Crawley ended by making a compromise with his sister-in-law, and giving her a very small sum for the benefit of her little boy.

Pitt knew how poor his brother and his brother's family must be. It could not have escaped the notice of such a cool and experienced old diplomatist, that Rawdon's family had nothing to live upon, and that houses and carriages are not to be kept for nothing. He knew very well that he was the proprietor or appropriator of the money, which, according to all proper calculation, ought to have fallen to his younger brother, and he had, we may be sure, some secret pangs of remorse within him, which warned him that he ought to perform some act of justice, or, let us say, compensation, towards these disappointed relations. A just, decent man, not without brains, who said his prayers, and knew his Catechism, and did his duty outwardly through life, he could not be otherwise than aware that something was due to his brother at his hands, and that morally he was Rawdon's debtor.

But, as one reads in the columns of the *Times* newspaper every now and then, queer announcements from the Chan-

cellor of the Exchequer, acknowledging the receipt of 50*l.*
from A.B., or 10*l.* from W.T., as conscience-money, on
account of taxes due by the said A.B. or W.T., which
payments the penitents beg the right honourable gentleman
to acknowledge through the medium of the public press; so
is the Chancellor, no doubt, and the reader likewise, always
perfectly sure that the above-named A.B. and W.T. are only
paying a very small instalment of what they really owe, and
that the man who sends up a twenty pound-note has very
likely hundreds or thousands more for which he ought to
account. Such, at least, are my feelings, when I see A.B. or
W.T.'s insufficient acts of repentance. And I have no doubt
that Pitt Crawley's contrition, or kindness if you will, towards
his younger brother, by whom he had so much profited, was
only a very small dividend upon the capital sum in which
he was indebted to Rawdon. Not everybody is willing to pay
even so much. To part with money is a sacrifice beyond
almost all men endowed with a sense of order. There is
scarcely any man alive who does not think himself meritorious for giving his neighbour five pounds. Thriftless gives,
not from a beneficent pleasure in giving, but from a lazy
delight in spending. He would not deny himself one enjoyment; not his opera-stall, not his horse, not his dinner,
not even the pleasure of giving Lazarus the five pounds.
Thrifty, who is good, wise, just, and owes no man a penny,
turns from a beggar, haggles with a hackney-coachman, or
denies a poor relation, and I doubt which is the most selfish
of the two. Money has only a different value in the eyes
of each.

So, in a word, Pitt Crawley thought he would do something for his brother, and then thought that he would think
about it some other time.

And with regard to Becky, she was not a woman who
expected too much from the generosity of her neighbours,
and so was quite content with all that Pitt Crawley had done
for her. She was acknowledged by the head of the family.
If Pitt would not give her anything, he would get something
for her some day. If she got no money from her brother-in-
law, she got what was as good as money – credit. Raggles
was made rather easy in his mind by the spectacle of the
union between the brothers, by a small payment on the spot,
and by the promise of a much larger sum speedily to be

assigned to him. And Rebecca told Miss Briggs, whose Christmas dividend upon the little sum lent by her, Becky paid with an air of candid joy, and as if her exchequer was brimming over with gold – Rebecca, we say, told Miss Briggs, in strict confidence, that she had conferred with Sir Pitt, who was famous as a financier, on Briggs's special behalf, as to the most profitable investment of Miss B.'s remaining capital; that Sir Pitt, after much consideration, had thought of a most safe and advantageous way in which Briggs could lay out her money; that, being especially interested in her as an attached friend of the late Miss Crawley, and of the whole family, and that long before he left town, he had recommended that she should be ready with the money at a moment's notice, so as to purchase at the most favourable opportunity the shares which Sir Pitt had in his eye. Poor Miss Briggs was very grateful for this mark of Sir Pitt's attention – it came so unsolicited, she said, for she never should have thought of removing the money from the Funds – and the delicacy enhanced the kindness of the office; and she promised to see her man of business immediately, and be ready with her little cash at the proper hour.

And this worthy woman was so grateful for the kindness of Rebecca in the matter, and for that of her generous benefactor, the colonel, that she went out and spent a great part of her half-year's dividend in the purchase of a black velvet coat for little Rawdon, who, by the way, was grown almost too big for black velvet now, and was of a size and age befitting him for the assumption of the virile jacket and pantaloons.

He was a fine open-faced boy, with blue eyes and waving flaxen hair, sturdy in limb, but generous and soft in heart: fondly attaching himself to all who were good to him – to the pony – to Lord Southdown, who gave him the horse (he used to blush and glow all over when he saw that kind young nobleman) – to the groom who had charge of the pony – to Molly, the cook, who crammed him with ghost stories at night, and with good things from the dinner – to Briggs, whom he plagued and laughed at – and to his father especially, whose attachment towards the lad was curious too to witness. Here, as he grew to be about eight years old, his attachments may be said to have ended. The beautiful mother-vision had faded away after a while. During near two years she had scarcely spoken to the child. She disliked him. He had the measles and the whooping-cough. He bored her. One day when he was standing at the landing-place, having crept down from the upper regions, attracted by the sound of his mother's voice, who was singing to Lord Steyne, the drawing-room door opening suddenly, discovered the little spy, who but a moment before had been rapt in delight, and listening to the music.

His mother came out and struck him violently a couple of boxes on the ear. He heard a laugh from the marquis in the inner room (who was amused by this free and artless exhibition of Becky's temper), and fled down below to his friends of the kitchen, bursting in an agony of grief.

'It is not because it hurts me,' little Rawdon gasped out – 'only – only' – sobs and tears wound up the sentence in a storm. It was the little boy's heart that was bleeding. 'Why mayn't I hear her singing? Why don't she ever sing to me – as she does to that bald-headed man with the large teeth?' He gasped out at various intervals these exclamations of rage and grief. The cook looked at the housemaid: the housemaid looked knowingly at the footman – the awful kitchen inquisition which sits in judgement in every house, and knows everything – sat on Rebecca at that moment.

After this incident, the mother's dislike increased to hatred; the consciousness that the child was in the house was a reproach and a pain to her. His very sight annoyed her. Fear, doubt, and resistance sprang up, too, in the boy's own bosom. They were separated from that day of the boxes on the ear.

Lord Steyne also heartily disliked the boy. When they met by mischance, he made sarcastic bows or remarks to the child, or glared at him with savage-looking eyes. Rawdon used to stare him in the face, and double his little fists in return. He knew his enemy; and this gentleman, of all who came to the house, was the one who angered him most. One day the footman found him squaring his fists at Lord Steyne's hat in the hall. The footman told the circumstance as a good joke to Lord Steyne's coachman; that officer imparted it to Lord Steyne's gentleman, and to the servants' hall in general. And very soon afterwards, when Mrs. Rawdon Crawley made her appearance at Gaunt House, the porter who unbarred the gates, the servants of all uniforms in the hall, the functionaries in white waistcoats, who bawled out from landing to landing the names of Colonel and Mrs. Rawdon Crawley, knew about her, or fancied they did. The man who brought her refreshment and stood behind her chair, had talked her character over with the large gentleman in motley-coloured clothes at his side. *Bon Dieu!* it is awful, that servants' inquisition! You see a woman in a great party in a splendid saloon, surrounded by faithful admirers, distributing sparkling glances, dressed to perfection, curled, rouged, smiling and happy:– Discovery walks respectfully up to her, in the shape of a huge powdered man with large calves and a tray of ices – with Calumny (which is as fatal as truth) – behind him, in the shape of the hulking fellow carrying the wafer-biscuits. Madam, your secret will be talked over by those men at their club at the public-house to-night. Jeames will tell Chawls his notions about you over their pipes and pewter beer-pots. Some people ought to have mutes for servants in Vanity Fair – mutes who could not write. If you are guilty, tremble. That fellow behind your chair may be a janissary with a bow-string in his plush breeches pocket. If you are not guilty, have a care of appearances: which are as ruinous as guilt.

'Was Rebecca guilty or not?' The *Vehmgericht* of the servants' hall had pronounced against her.

And, I shame to say, she would not have got credit had they not believed her to be guilty. It was the sight of the Marquis of Steyne's carriage-lamps at her door, contemplated by Raggles, burning in the blackness of midnight, 'that kep' him up,' as he afterwards said; that even more than Rebecca's arts and coaxings.

And so – guiltless very likely – she was writhing and pushing onward towards what they call 'a position in society', and the servants were pointing at her as lost and ruined. So you see Molly, the housemaid, of a morning, watching a spider in the doorpost lay his thread and laboriously crawl up it, until, tired of the sport, she raises her broom and sweeps away the thread and the artificer.

A day or two before Christmas, Becky, her husband and her son made ready and went to pass the holidays at the seat of their ancestors at Queen's Crawley. Becky would have liked to leave the little brat behind, and would have done

so but for Lady Jane's urgent invitations to the youngster;
and the symptoms of revolt and discontent which Rawdon
manifested at her neglect of her son. 'He's the finest boy in
England,' the father said, in a tone of reproach to her, 'and
you don't seem to care for him, Becky, as much as you do
for your spaniel. He shan't bother you much: at home he
will be away from you in the nursery, and he shall go outside
on the coach with me.'

'Where you go yourself because you want to smoke those
filthy cigars,' replied Mrs. Rawdon.

'I remember when you liked 'em though,' answered the
husband.

Becky laughed: she was almost always good-humoured.
'That was when I was on my promotion, Goosey,' she said.
'Take Rawdon outside with you, and give him a cigar too,
if you like.'

Rawdon did not warm his little son for the winter's
journey in this way, but he and Briggs wrapped up the child
in shawls and comforters, and he was hoisted respectfully
on to the roof of the coach in the dark morning, under the
lamps of the 'White Horse Cellar': and with no small delight
he watched the dawn rise, and made his first journey to the
place which his father still called home. It was a journey of
infinite pleasure to the boy, to whom the incidents of the
road afforded endless interest: his father answering to him
all questions connected with it, and telling him who lived
in the great white house to the right, and whom the park
belonged to. His mother, inside the vehicle with her maid
and her furs, her wrappers, and her scent-bottles, made
such a to-do that you would have thought she never had
been in a stage-coach before – much less, that she had been
turned out of this very one to make room for a paying
passenger on a certain journey performed some half-score
years ago.

It was dark again when little Rawdon was wakened up to
enter his uncle's carriage at Mudbury, and he sat and looked
out of it wondering as the great iron gates flew open, and
at the white trunks of the limes as they swept by, until they
stopped, at length, before the light windows of the Hall,
which were blazing and comfortable with Christmas welcome. The hall-door was flung open – a big fire was burning
in the great old fireplace – a carpet was down over the

chequered black flags – 'It's the old Turkey one that used to be in the Ladies' Gallery,' thought Rebecca, and the next instant was kissing Lady Jane.

She and Sir Pitt performed the same salute with great gravity: but Rawdon having been smoking, hung back rather from his sister-in-law, whose two children came up to their cousin: and, while Matilda held out her hand and kissed him, Pitt Binkie Southdown, the son and heir, stood aloof rather, and examined him as a little dog does a big dog.

Then the kind hostess conducted her guests to the snug apartments blazing with cheerful fires. Then the young ladies came and knocked at Mrs. Rawdon's door, under the pretence that they were desirous to be useful, but in reality to have the pleasure of inspecting the contents of her band- and bonnet-boxes, and her dresses which, though black, were of the newest London fashion. And they told her how much the Hall was changed for the better, and how old Lady Southdown was gone, and how Pitt was taking his station in the county, as became a Crawley in fact. Then the great dinner-bell having rung, the family assembled at dinner, at which meal Rawdon Junior was placed by his aunt, the good-natured lady of the house; Sir Pitt being uncommonly attentive to his sister-in-law at his own right hand.

Little Rawdon exhibited a fine appetite, and showed a gentlemanlike behaviour.

'I like to dine here,' he said to his aunt when he had completed his meal, at the conclusion of which, and after a decent grace by Sir Pitt, the young son and heir was introduced, and was perched on a high chair by the baronet's side, while the daughter took possession of the place and the little wine-glass prepared for her near her mother. 'I like to dine here,' said Rawdon Minor, looking up at his relation's kind face.

'Why?' said the good Lady Jane.

'I dine in the kitchen when I am at home,' replied Rawdon Minor, 'or else with Briggs.' But Becky was so engaged with the baronet, her host, pouring out a flood of compliments and delights and raptures, and admiring young Pitt Binkie, whom she declared to be the most beautiful, intelligent, noble-looking little creature, and so like his father, that she did not hear the remarks of her own flesh and blood at the other end of the broad shining table.

As a guest, and it being the first night of his arrival, Rawdon the Second was allowed to sit up until the hour when tea being over, and a great gilt book being laid on the table before Sir Pitt, all the domestics of the family streamed in, and Sir Pitt read prayers. It was the first time the poor little boy had ever witnessed or heard of such a ceremonial.

The house had been much improved even since the baronet's brief reign, and was pronounced by Becky to be perfect, charming, delightful, when she surveyed it in his company. As for little Rawdon, who examined it with the children for his guides, it seemed to him a perfect palace of enchantment and wonder. There were long galleries, and ancient state-bedrooms, there were pictures, and old china, and armour. There were the rooms in which grandpapa died, and by which the children walked with terrified looks. 'Who was grandpapa?' he asked; and they told him how he used to be very old, and used to be wheeled about in a garden-chair, and they showed him the garden-chair one day rotting in the outhouse in which it had lain since the old gentleman had been wheeled away yonder to the church, of which the spire was glittering over the park elms.

The brothers had good occupation for several mornings in examining the improvements which had been effected by Sir Pitt's genius and economy. And as they walked or rode, and looked at them, they could talk without too much boring each other. And Pitt took care to tell Rawdon what a heavy outlay of money these improvements had occasioned; and that a man of landed and funded property was often very hard pressed for twenty pounds. 'There is that new lodge gate,' said Pitt, pointing to it humbly with the bamboo cane, 'I can no more pay for it before the dividends in January than I can fly.'

'I can lend you, Pitt, till then,' Rawdon answered rather ruefully; and they went in and looked at the restored lodge, where the family arms were just new scraped in stone; and where old Mrs. Lock, for the first time these many long years, had tight doors, sound roofs, and whole windows.

CHAPTER XLV

BETWEEN HAMPSHIRE AND LONDON

SIR PITT CRAWLEY had done more than repair fences and restore dilapidated lodges on the Queen's Crawley estate. Like a wise man he had set to work to rebuild the injured popularity of his house, and stop up the gaps and ruins in which his name had been left by his disreputable and thriftless old predecessor. He was elected for the borough speedily after his father's demise; a magistrate, a member of Parliament, a county magnate and representative of an ancient family, he made it his duty to show himself before the Hampshire public, subscribed handsomely to the county charities, called assiduously upon all the county folks, and laid himself out in a word to take that position in Hampshire, and in the Empire afterwards, to which he thought his prodigious talents justly entitled him. Lady Jane was instructed to be friendly with the Fuddlestones, and the Wapshots, and the other famous baronets, their neighbours. Their carriages might frequently be seen in the Queen's Crawley avenue now; they dined pretty frequently at the Hall (where the cookery was so good, that it was clear Lady Jane very seldom had a hand in it), and in return Pitt and his wife most energetically dined out in all sorts of weather, and at all sorts of distances. For though Pitt did not care for joviality, being a frigid man of poor health and appetite, yet he considered that to be hospitable and condescending was quite incumbent on his station, and every time that he got a headache from too long an after-dinner sitting, he felt that he was a martyr to duty. He talked about crops, corn laws, politics, with the best country gentlemen. He (who had been formerly inclined to be a sad freethinker on these points) entered into poaching and game preserving with ardour. He didn't hunt: he wasn't a hunting man: he was a man of books and peaceful habits: but he thought that the breed of horses must be kept up in the country, and that the breed of foxes must therefore be looked to, and for his part, if his friend, Sir Huddlestone Fuddlestone, liked to draw his country, and meet as of old the F. hounds used to do at Queen's Crawley, he should be happy to see him there,

and the gentlemen of the Fuddlestone Hunt. And to Lady
Southdown's dismay too he became more orthodox in his
tendencies every day: gave up preaching in public and
attending meeting-houses; went stoutly to church: called on
the bishop, and all the clergy at Winchester: and made no
objection when the Venerable Archdeacon Trumper asked
for a game of whist. What pangs must have been those of
Lady Southdown, and what an utter castaway she must have
thought her son-in-law for permitting such a godless diversion! and when, on the return of the family from an oratorio
at Winchester, the baronet announced to the young ladies
that he should next year very probably take them to the
'county balls', they worshipped him for his kindness. Lady
Jane was only too obedient, and perhaps glad herself to
go. The dowager wrote off the direst descriptions of her
daughter's worldly behaviour to the authoress of the *Washerwoman of Finchley Common* at the Cape; and her house
in Brighton being about this time unoccupied, returned to
that watering-place, her absence being not very much deplored by her children. We may suppose, too, that Rebecca,
on paying a second visit to Queen's Crawley, did not feel
particularly grieved at the absence of the lady of the medi-
cine-chest; though she wrote a Christmas letter to her
ladyship, in which she respectfully recalled herself to Lady
Southdown's recollection, spoke with gratitude of the delight
which her ladyship's conversation had given her on the
former visit, dilated on the kindness with which her ladyship
had treated her in sickness, and declared that everything at
Queen's Crawley reminded her of her absent friend.

A great part of the altered demeanour and popularity of
Sir Pitt Crawley might have been traced to the counsels of
that astute little lady of Curzon Street. '*You* remain a
baronet – you consent to be a mere country gentleman,' she
said to him, while he had been her guest in London. 'No,
Sir Pitt Crawley, I know you better. I know your talents
and your ambition. You fancy you hide them both: but you
can conceal neither from me. I showed Lord Steyne your
pamphlet on malt. He was familiar with it: and said it was
in the opinion of the whole Cabinet the most masterly thing
that had appeared on the subject. The Ministry has its eye
upon you, and I know what you want. You want to distinguish yourself in Parliament; every one says you are the

finest speaker in England (for your speeches at Oxford are still remembered). You want to be member for the county, where with your own vote and your borough at your back, you can command anything. And you want to be Baron Crawley of Queen's Crawley, and will be before you die. I saw it all. I could read your heart, Sir Pitt. If I had a husband who possessed your intellect as he does your name, I sometimes think I should not be unworthy of him – but – but I am your kinswoman now,' she added with a laugh. 'Poor little penniless I have got a little interest – and who knows, perhaps the mouse may be able to aid the lion.'

Pitt Crawley was amazed and enraptured with her speech. 'How that woman comprehends me!' he said. 'I never could get Jane to read these pages of the malt pamphlet. *She* has no idea that I have commanding talents or secret ambition. So they remember my speaking at Oxford, do they? The rascals! now that I represent my borough and may sit for the county, they begin to recollect me! Why, Lord Steyne cut me at the Levée last year: they are beginning to find out that Pitt Crawley is some one at last. Yes, the man was always the same whom these people neglected: it was only the opportunity that was wanting, and I will show them now that I can speak and act as well as write. Achilles did not declare himself until they gave him the sword. I hold it now, and the world shall yet hear of Pitt Crawley.'

Therefore it was that this roguish diplomatist had grown so hospitable; that he was so civil to oratorios and hospitals; so kind to deans and chapters; so generous in giving and accepting dinners; so uncommonly gracious to farmers on market-days; and so much interested about county business; and that the Christmas at the Hall was the gayest which had been known there for many a long day.

On Christmas Day a great family gathering took place. All the Crawleys from the Rectory came to dine. Rebecca was as frank and fond of Mrs. Bute, as if the other had never been her enemy: she was affectionately interested in the dear girls, and surprised at the progress which they had made in music since her time: and insisted upon encoring one of the duets out of the great song-books which Jim, grumbling, had been forced to bring under his arm from the Rectory. Mrs. Bute, perforce, was obliged to adopt a decent demeanour towards the little adventuress – of course being free to discourse with her daughters afterwards about the absurd respect with which Sir Pitt treated his sister-in-law. But Jim, who had sat next to her at dinner, declared she was a trump: and one and all of the rector's family agreed that the little Rawdon was a fine boy. They respected a possible baronet in the boy, between whom and the title there was only the little sickly pale Pitt Binkie.

The children were very good friends. Pitt Binkie was too little a dog for such a big dog as Rawdon to play with: and Matilda being only a girl, of course not fit companion for a young gentleman who was near eight years old, and going into jackets very soon. He took the command of this small party at once – the little girl and the little boy following him about with great reverence at such times as he condescended to sport with them. His happiness and pleasure in the country were extreme. The kitchen-garden pleased him hugely, the flowers moderately, but the pigeons and the poultry, and the stables when he was allowed to visit them, were delightful objects to him. He resisted being kissed by the Miss Crawleys: but he allowed Lady Jane sometimes to embrace him: and it was by her side that he liked to sit when the signal to retire to the drawing-room being given, the ladies left the gentlemen to their claret – by her side rather than by his mother. For Rebecca seeing that tenderness was the fashion, called Rawdon to her one evening, and stooped down and kissed him in the presence of all the ladies.

He looked her full in the face after the operation, trembling and turning very red, as his wont was when moved. 'You never kiss me at home, mamma,' he said; at which there was a general silence and consternation, and a by no means pleasant look in Becky's eyes.

Rawdon was fond of his sister-in-law, for her regard for his son. Lady Jane and Becky did not get on *quite* so well at this visit as on occasion of the former one, when the colonel's wife was bent upon pleasing. Those two speeches of the child struck rather a chill. Perhaps Sir Pitt was rather too attentive to her.

But Rawdon, as became his age and size, was fonder of the society of the men than of the women; and never wearied of accompanying his sire to the stables, whither the colonel retired to smoke his cigar – Jim, the rector's son, sometimes joining his cousin in that and other amusements. He and the baronet's keeper were very close friends, their mutual taste for 'dawgs' bringing them much together. On one day, Mr. James, the colonel, and Horn, the keeper, went and shot pheasants, taking little Rawdon with them. On another most blissful morning, these four gentlemen partook of the amusement of rat-hunting in a barn, than which sport Rawdon as yet had never seen anything more noble. They stopped up the ends of certain drains in the barn, into the other openings of which ferrets were inserted; and then stood silently aloof with uplifted stakes in their hands, and an anxious little terrier (Mr. James's celebrated 'dawg' Forceps, indeed) scarcely breathing from excitement, listening motionless on three legs, to the faint squeaking of the rats below. Desperately bold at last, the persecuted animals bolted aboveground: the terrier accounted for one, the keeper for another, Rawdon, from flurry and excitement, missed his rat, but on the other hand he half-murdered a ferret.

But the greatest day of all was that on which Sir Huddlestone Fuddlestone's hounds met upon the lawn at Queen's Crawley.

That was a famous sight for little Rawdon. At half-past ten, Tom Moody, Sir Huddlestone Fuddlestone's huntsman, was seen trotting up the avenue, followed by the noble pack of hounds in a compact body – the rear being brought up by the two whips clad in stained scarlet frocks – light hard-featured lads on well-bred lean horses, possessing marvellous dexterity in casting the points of their long heavy whips at the thinnest part of any dog's skin who dares to straggle from the main body, or to take the slightest notice, or even so much as wink at the hares and rabbits starting under their noses.

Next comes boy Jack, Tom Moody's son, who weighs five stone, measures eight-and-forty inches, and will never be any bigger. He is perched on a large rawboned hunter, half covered by a capacious saddle. This animal is Sir Huddlestone Fuddlestone's favourite horse, The Nob. Other horses, ridden by other small boys, arrive from time to time, awaiting their masters, who will come cantering on anon.

Tom Moody rides up to the door of the Hall, where he is welcomed by the butler, who offers him drink, which he declines. He and his pack then draw off into a sheltered corner of the lawn, where the dogs roll on the grass, and play or growl angrily at one another, ever and anon breaking out into furious fight speedily to be quelled by Tom's voice, unmatched at rating, or the snaky thongs of the whips.

Many young gentlemen canter up on thoroughbred hacks, spatterdashed to the knee, and enter the house to drink cherry-brandy and pay their respects to the ladies, or more modest and sportsmanlike, divest themselves of their mud-boots, exchange their hacks for their hunters, and warm their blood by a preliminary gallop round the lawn. Then they collect round the pack in the corner, and talk with Tom Moody of past sport, and the merits of Sniveller and Diamond, and of the state of the country and of the wretched breed of foxes.

Sir Huddlestone presently appears mounted on a clever cob, and rides up to the Hall, where he enters and does the civil thing by the ladies, after which, being a man of few words, he proceeds to business. The hounds are drawn up to the Hall-door, and little Rawdon descends amongst them, excited yet half alarmed by the caresses which they bestow upon him, at the thumps he receives from their waving tails, and at their canine bickerings, scarcely restrained by Tom Moody's tongue and lash.

Meanwhile, Sir Huddlestone has hoisted himself unwield-ily on The Nob: 'Let's try Sowster's Spinney, Tom,' says the baronet: 'Farmer Mangle tells me there are two foxes in it.' Tom blows his horn and trots off, followed by the pack, by the whips, by the young gents from Winchester, by the farmers of the neighbourhood, by the labourers of the parish on foot, with whom the day is a great holiday; Sir Huddlestone bringing up the rear with Colonel Crawley, and the whole *cortège* disappears down the avenue.

The Reverend Bute Crawley (who has been too modest to appear at the public meet before his nephew's windows), and whom Tom Moody remembers forty years back a slender divine riding the wildest horses, jumping the widest brooks, and larking over the newest gates in the country, – his reverence, we say, happens to trot out from the Rectory Lane on his powerful black horse, just as Sir Huddlestone passes; he joins the worthy baronet. Hounds and horsemen disappear, and little Rawdon remains on the door-steps, wondering and happy.

During the progress of this memorable holiday, little Rawdon, if he had got no special liking for his uncle, always awful and cold, and locked up in his study, plunged in justice-business and surrounded by bailiffs and farmers – has gained the good graces of his married and maiden aunts, of the two little folks of the Hall, and of Jim of the Rectory, whom Sir Pitt is encouraging to pay his addresses to one of the young ladies, with an understanding doubtless that he shall be presented to the living when it shall be vacated by his fox-hunting old sire. Jim has given up that sport himself, and confines himself to a little harmless duck or snipe shooting, or a little quiet trifling with the rats during the Christmas holidays, after which he will return to the University and try and not be plucked, once more. He has already eschewed green coats, red neckcloths, and other worldly ornaments, and is preparing himself for a change in his condition. In this cheap and thrifty way Sir Pitt tries to pay off his debt to his family.

Also before this merry Christmas was over, the baronet had screwed up courage enough to give his brother another draft on his bankers, and for no less a sum than a hundred pounds, an act which caused Sir Pitt cruel pangs at first, but which made him glow afterwards to think himself one of the most generous of men. Rawdon and his son went away with the utmost heaviness of heart. Becky and the ladies parted with some alacrity, however: and our friend returned to London to commence those avocations with which we find her occupied when this chapter begins. Under her care the Crawley House in Great Gaunt Street was quite rejuvenescent, and ready for the reception of Sir Pitt and his family, when the baronet came to London to attend his duties in Parliament, and to assume that position in the country for which his vast genius fitted him.

For the first session, this profound dissembler hid his projects and never opened his lips but to present a petition from Mudbury. But he attended assiduously in his place, and learned thoroughly the routine and business of the House. At home he gave himself up to the perusal of Blue Books, to the alarm and wonder of Lady Jane, who thought he was killing himself by late hours and intense application. And he made acquaintance with the ministers, and the chiefs of his party, determining to rank as one of them before many years were over.

Lady Jane's sweetness and kindness had inspired Rebecca with such a contempt for her ladyship as the little woman found no small difficulty in concealing. That sort of goodness and simplicity which Lady Jane possessed annoyed our friend Becky, and it was impossible for her at times not to show, or to let the other divine, her scorn. Her presence, too, rendered Lady Jane uneasy. Her husband talked constantly with Becky. Signs of intelligence seemed to pass between them: and Pitt spoke with her on subjects on which he never thought of discoursing with Lady Jane. The latter did not understand them to be sure, but it was mortifying to remain silent; still more mortifying to know that you had nothing to say, and hear that little audacious Mrs. Rawdon dashing on from subject to subject, with a word for every man, and a joke always pat; and to sit in one's own house alone, by the fireside, and watching all the men round your rival.

In the country, when Lady Jane was telling stories to the children, who clustered about her knees (little Rawdon into the bargain, who was very fond of her) – and Becky came into the room, sneering, with green scornful eyes, poor Lady Jane grew silent under those baleful glances. Her simple little fancies shrank away tremulously, as fairies in the story-books, before a superior bad angel. She could not go on, although Rebecca, with the smallest inflection of sarcasm in her voice, besought her to continue that charming story. And on her side gentle thoughts and simple pleasures were odious to Mrs. Becky, they discorded with her; she hated people for liking them; she spurned children and children-lovers. 'I have no taste for bread-and-butter,' she would say, when caricaturing Lady Jane and her ways to my Lord Steyne.

'No more has a certain person for holy water,' his lordship replied with a bow and a grin, and a great jarring laugh afterwards.

So these two ladies did not see much of each other except upon those occasions, when the younger brother's wife, having an object to gain from the other, frequented her. They my-loved and my-deared each other assiduously, but kept apart generally: whereas Sir Pitt, in the midst of his multiplied avocations, found daily time to see his sister-in-law.

On the occasion of his first Speaker's dinner, Sir Pitt

took the opportunity of appearing before his sister-in-law in his uniform – that old diplomatic suit which he had worn when attaché to the Pumpernickel Legation.

Becky complimented him upon that dress, and admired him almost as much as his own wife and children, to whom he displayed himself before he set out. She said that it was only the thoroughbred gentleman who could wear the court suit with advantage: it was only your men of ancient race whom the *culotte courte* became. Pitt looked down with complacency at his legs, which had not, in truth, much more symmetry or swell than the lean court sword which dangled by his side: looked down at his legs, and thought in his heart that he was killing.

When he was gone, Mrs. Becky made a caricature of his figure, which she showed to Lord Steyne when he arrived. His lordship carried off the sketch, delighted with the accuracy of the resemblance. He had done Sir Pitt Crawley the honour to meet him at Mrs. Becky's house, and had been most gracious to the new baronet and member. Pitt was struck too by the deference with which the great peer treated his sister-in-law, by her ease and sprightliness in the conversation, and by the delight with which the other men of the party listened to her talk. Lord Steyne made no doubt but that the baronet had only commenced his career in public life, and expected rather anxiously to hear him as an orator; as they were neighbours (for Great Gaunt Street leads into Gaunt Square, whereof Gaunt House, as everybody knows, forms one side) my lord hoped that as soon as Lady Steyne arrived in London she would have the honour of making the acquaintance of Lady Crawley. He left a card upon his neighbour in the course of a day or two; having never thought fit to notice his predecessor, though they had lived near each other for near a century past.

In the midst of these intrigues and fine parties and wise and brilliant personages Rawdon felt himself more and more isolated every day. He was allowed to go to the club more: to dine abroad with bachelor friends: to come and go when he liked, without any questions being asked. And he and Rawdon the younger many a time would walk to Gaunt Street, and sit with the lady and the children there while Sir Pitt was closeted with Rebecca, on his way to the House, or on his return from it.

The ex-colonel would sit for hours in his brother's house very silent, and thinking and doing as little as possible. He was glad to be employed of an errand: to go and make inquiries about a horse or a servant: or to carve the roast mutton for the dinner of the children. He was beat and cowed into laziness and submission. Delilah had imprisoned him and cut his hair off, too. The bold and reckless young blood of ten years back was subjugated, and was turned into a torpid, submissive, middle-aged, stout gentleman.

And poor Lady Jane was aware that Rebecca had captivated her husband: although she and Mrs. Rawdon my-deared and my-loved each other every day they met.

CHAPTER XLVI

STRUGGLES AND TRIALS

Our friends at Brompton were meanwhile passing their Christmas after their fashion, and in a manner by no means too cheerful.

Out of the hundred pounds a year, which was about the amount of her income, the widow Osborne had been in the habit of giving up nearly three-fourths to her father and mother, for the expenses of herself and her little boy. With 120*l.* more, supplied by Jos, this family of four people, attended by a single Irish servant who also did for Clapp and his wife, might manage to live in decent comfort through the year, and hold up their heads yet, and be able to give a friend a dish of tea still, after the storms and disappointments of their early life. Sedley still maintained his ascendancy over the family of Mr. Clapp, his ex-clerk. Clapp remembered the time when, sitting on the edge of the chair, he tossed off a bumper to the health of 'Mrs. S—, Miss Emmy, and Mr. Joseph in India', at the merchant's rich table in Russell Square. Time magnified the splendour of those recollections in the honest clerk's bosom. Whenever he came up from the kitchen-parlour to the drawing-room, and partook of tea or gin-and-water with Mr. Sedley, he would say, 'This was not what you was accustomed to once, sir,' and as gravely and reverentially drink the health of the ladies as he had done in the days of their utmost prosperity. He thought Miss 'Melia's playing the divinest music ever performed, and her the finest lady. He never would sit down before Sedley at the club even, nor would he hear that gentleman's character abused by any member of the society. He had seen the first men in London shaking hands with Mr. S——; he said, 'He'd known him in times when Rothschild might be seen on 'Change with him any day, and he owed him personally everythink.'

Clapp, with the best of characters and handwritings, had been able very soon after his master's disaster to find other employment for himself. 'Such a little fish as me can swim in any bucket,' he used to remark, and a member of the house from which old Sedley had seceded was very glad to make use of Mr. Clapp's services, and to reward them with a comfortable salary. In fine, all Sedley's wealthy friends had dropped off one by one, and this poor ex-dependent still remained faithfully attached to him.

Out of the small residue of her income, which Amelia kept back for herself, the widow had need of all the thrift and care possible in order to enable her to keep her darling boy dressed in such a manner as became George Osborne's son, and to defray the expenses of the little school to which, after much misgiving and reluctance, and many secret pangs and fears on her own part, she had been induced to send the lad. She had sat up of nights conning lessons and spelling over crabbed grammars and geography books in order to teach them to Georgy. She had worked even at the Latin accidence, fondly hoping that she might be capable of instructing him in that language. To part with him all day: to send him out to the mercy of a schoolmaster's cane and his schoolfellows' roughness, was almost like weaning him over again, to that weak mother, so tremulous and full of sensibility. He, for his part, rushed off to the school with the utmost happiness. He was longing for the change. That childish gladness wounded his mother, who was herself so grieved to part with him. She would rather have had him more sorry, she thought: and then was deeply repentant within herself, for daring to be so selfish as to wish her own son to be unhappy.

Georgy made great progress in the school, which was kept by a friend of his mother's constant admirer, the Rev. Mr. Binney. He brought home numberless prizes and testimonials of ability. He told his mother countless stories every night about his school companions: and what a fine fellow Lyons was, and what a sneak Sniffin was; and how Steel's father actually supplied the meat for the establishment, whereas Golding's mother came in a carriage to fetch him every Saturday; and how Neat had straps to his trousers – might he have straps? – and how Bull Major was so strong (though only in Eutropius) that it was believed he could lick the usher, Mr. Ward, himself. So Amelia learned to know every one of the boys in that school as well as Georgy himself: and of nights she used to help him in his exercises and puzzle her little head over his lessons as eagerly as if she was herself going in the morning into the presence of the master. Once, after a certain combat with Master Smith, George came home to his mother with a black eye, and bragged prodigiously to his parent and his delighted old grandfather about his valour in the fight, in which, if the truth was known, he did not behave with particular heroism, and in which he decidedly had the worst. But Amelia has never forgiven that Smith to this day, though he is now a peaceful apothecary near Leicester Square.

In these quiet labours and harmless cares the gentle widow's life was passing away, a silver hair or two marking the progress of time on her head, and a line deepening ever so little on her fair forehead. She used to smile at these marks of time. 'What matters it,' she asked, 'for an old woman like me?' All she hoped for was to live to see her son great, famous, and glorious, as he deserved to be. She kept his copy-books, his drawings, and compositions, and showed them about in her little circle, as if they were miracles of genius. She confided some of these specimens to Miss Dobbin; to show them to Miss Osborne, George's aunt, to show them to Mr. Osborne himself – to make that old man repent of his cruelty and ill-feeling towards him who was gone. All her husband's faults and foibles she had buried in the grave with him: she only remembered the lover, who had married her at all sacrifices; the noble husband so brave and beautiful, in whose arms she had hung on the morning when he had gone away to fight, and die gloriously for his King. From heaven the hero must be smiling down upon that paragon of a boy whom he had left to comfort and console her.

We have seen how one of George's grandfathers (Mr. Osborne), in his easy chair in Russell Square, daily grew more violent and moody, and how his daughter, with her fine carriage, and her fine horses, and her name on half the public charity lists of the town, was a lonely, miserable, persecuted old maid. She thought again and again of the beautiful little boy, her brother's son, whom she had seen. She longed to be allowed to drive in the fine carriage to the house in which he lived; and she used to look out day after day as she took her solitary drive in the Park, in hopes that she might see him. Her sister, the banker's lady, occasionally condescended to pay her old home and companion a visit in Russell Square. She brought a couple of sickly children attended by a prim nurse, and in a faint genteel giggling tone cackled to her sister about her fine acquaintance, and how her little Frederick was the image of Lord Claud Lollypop, and her sweet Maria had been noticed by the baroness as they were driving in their donkey-chaise at Roehampton. She urged her to make her papa do something for the darlings. Frederick she had determined should go into the Guards; and if they made an elder son of him (and Mr. Bullock was positively ruining and pinching himself to death to buy land), how was the darling girl to be provided for? 'I expect *you*, dear,' Mrs. Bullock would say, 'for of course my share of our papa's property must go to the head of the house, you know. Dear Rhoda Macmull will disengage the whole of the Castletoddy property as soon as poor dear Lord Castletoddy dies, who is quite epileptic; and little Macduff Macmull will be Viscount Castletoddy. Both the Mr. Bludyers of Mincing Lane have settled their fortunes on Fanny Bludyer's little boy. My darling Frederick must positively be an eldest son; and – and do ask papa to bring us back his account in Lombard Street, will you, dear? It doesn't look well, his going to Stumpy and Rowdy's.' After which kind of speeches, in which fashion and the main chance were blended together, and after a kiss, which was like the contact of an oyster – Mrs. Frederick Bullock would gather her starched nurslings, and simper back into her carriage.

Every visit which this leader of *ton* paid to her family was more unlucky for her. Her father paid more money into Stumpy and Rowdy's. Her patronage became more and more insufferable. The poor widow in the little cottage at Brompton, guarding her treasure there, little knew how eagerly some people coveted it.

On that night when Jane Osborne had told her father that she had seen his grandson, the old man had made her no reply: but he had shown no anger – and had bade her good night on going himself to his room in rather a kindly voice. And he must have meditated on what she said, and have made some inquiries of the Dobbin family regarding her visit; for a fortnight after it took place, he asked her where was her little French watch and chain she used to wear?

'I bought it with my money, sir,' she said in a great fright.

'Go and order another like it, or a better if you can get it,' said the old gentleman, and lapsed again into silence.

Of late, the Miss Dobbins more than once repeated their entreaties to Amelia, to allow George to visit them. His aunt had shown her inclination; perhaps his grandfather himself, they hinted, might be disposed to be reconciled to him. Surely, Amelia could not refuse such advantageous chances for the boy. Nor could she: but she acceded to their overtures with a very heavy and suspicious heart, was always uneasy during the child's absence from her, and welcomed him back as if he was rescued out of some danger. He brought back money and toys, at which the widow looked with alarm and jealousy: she asked him always if he had seen any gentleman – 'Only old Sir William, who drove him about in the four-wheeled chaise, and Mr. Dobbin, who arrived on the beautiful bay horse in the afternoon – in the green coat and pink neckcloth, with the gold-headed whip, who promised to show him the Tower of London, and take him out with the Surrey Hounds.' At last, he said, 'There *was* an old gentleman, with thick eyebrows and a broad hat, and large chain and seals. He came one day as the coachman was lunging Georgy round the lawn on the grey pony. He looked at me very much. He shook very much. I said "My name is Norval" after dinner. My aunt began to cry. She is always crying.' Such was George's report on that night.

Then Amelia knew that the boy had seen his grandfather: and looked out feverishly for a proposal which she was sure would follow, and which came, in fact, in a few days afterwards. Mr. Osborne formally offered to take the boy, and make him heir to the fortune which he had intended that his father should inherit. He would make Mrs. George Osborne an allowance, such as to assure her a decent competency. If Mrs. George Osborne proposed to marry again, as Mr. O. heard was her intention, he would not withdraw that allowance. But it must be understood, that the child would live entirely with his grandfather in Russell Square, or at whatever other place Mr. O. should select; and that he would be occasionally permitted to see Mrs. George Osborne at her own residence. This message was brought or read to her in a letter one day, when her mother was from home, and her father absent as usual, in the City.

She was never seen angry but twice or thrice in her life, and it was in one of these moods that Mr. Osborne's attorney had the fortune to behold her. She rose up trembling and flushing very much as soon as, after reading the letter, Mr. Poe handed it to her, and she tore the paper into a hundred fragments, which she trod on. ' "I marry again! – I take money to part from my child! Who dares insult me by proposing such a thing? Tell Mr. Osborne it is a cowardly letter, sir – a cowardly letter – I will not answer it. I wish you good morning, sir" – and she bowed me out of the room like a tragedy queen,' said the lawyer who told the story.

Her parents never remarked her agitation on that day, and she never told them of the interview. They had their own affairs to interest them, affairs which deeply interested this innocent and unconscious lady. The old gentleman, her father, was always dabbling in speculation. We have seen how the Wine Company and the Coal Company had failed him. But, prowling about the City always eagerly and restlessly still, he lighted upon some other scheme, of which he thought so well that he embarked in it in spite of the remonstrances of Mr. Clapp, to whom indeed he never dared to tell how far he had engaged himself in it. And as it was always Mr. Sedley's maxim not to talk about money matters before women, they had no inkling of the misfortunes that were in store for them until the unhappy old gentleman was forced to make gradual confessions.

The bills of the little household, which had been settled weekly, first fell into arrear. The remittances had not arrived from India, Mr. Sedley told his wife with a disturbed face. As she had paid her bills very regularly hitherto, one or two of the tradesmen to whom the poor lady was obliged to go round asking for time were very angry at a delay, to which they were perfectly used from more irregular customers. Emmy's contribution, paid over cheerfully without any

questions, kept the little company in half rations however.
And the first six months passed away pretty easily: old Sedley
still keeping up with the notion that his shares must rise,
and that all would be well.

No sixty pounds, however, came to help the household
at the end of the half-year; and it fell deeper and deeper
into trouble – Mrs. Sedley, who was growing infirm and
was much shaken, remained silent or wept a great deal with
Mrs. Clapp in the kitchen. The butcher was particularly
surly: the grocer insolent: once or twice little Georgy had
grumbled about the dinners: and Amelia, who still would
have been satisfied with a slice of bread for her own dinner,
could not but perceive that her son was neglected, and
purchased little things out of her private purse to keep the
boy in health.

At last they told her, or told her such a garbled story as
people in difficulties tell. One day, her own money having
been received, and Amelia about to pay it over: she who had
kept an account of the moneys expended by her, proposed
to keep a certain portion back out of her dividend, having
contracted engagements for a new suit for Georgy.

Then it came out that Jos's remittances were not paid;
that the house was in difficulties which Amelia ought to
have seen before, her mother said, but she cared for nothing
or nobody except Georgy. At this she passed all of her money
across the table, without a word, to her mother, and returned
to her room to cry her eyes out. She had a great access of
sensibility too that day, when obliged to go and countermand
the clothes, the darling clothes on which she had set her
heart for Christmas Day, and the cut and fashion of which
she had arranged in many conversations with a small milliner, her friend.

Hardest of all, she had to break the matter to Georgy,
who made a loud outcry. Everybody had new clothes at
Christmas. The others would laugh at him. He *would* have
new clothes. She had promised them to him. The poor
widow had only kisses to give him. She darned the old suit
in tears. She cast about among her little ornaments to see
could she sell anything to procure the desired novelties?
There was her India shawl that Dobbin had sent her. She
remembered in former days going with her mother to a fine
India shop on Ludgate Hill, where the ladies had all sorts

of dealings and bargains in these articles. Her cheeks flushed and her eyes shone with pleasure as she thought of this resource, and she kissed away George to school in the morning, smiling brightly after him. The boy felt that there was good news in her look.

Packing up her shawl in a handkerchief (another of the gifts of the good major), she hid them under her cloak, and walked flushed and eager all the way to Ludgate Hill, tripping along by the Park wall, and running over the crossings, so that many a man turned as she hurried by him, and looked after her rosy pretty face. She calculated how she should spend the proceeds of her shawl: how, besides the clothes, she would buy the books that he longed for, and pay his half-year's schooling; and how she would buy a cloak for her father instead of that old greatcoat which he wore. She was not mistaken as to the value of the major's gift. It was a very fine and beautiful web: and the merchant made a very good bargain when he gave her twenty guineas for her shawl.

She ran on amazed and flurried with her riches to Darton's shop in St. Paul's Churchyard, and there purchased the *Parent's Assistant*, and the *Sandford and Merton* Georgy longed for, and got into the coach there with her parcel, and went home exulting. And she pleased herself by writing in the fly-leaf in her neatest little hand, 'George Osborne, a Christmas gift from his affectionate mother.' The books are extant to this day, with the fair delicate superscription.

She was going from her own room with the books in her hand to place them on George's table, where he might find them on his return from school; when in the passage, she and her mother met. The gilt bindings of the seven handsome little volumes caught the old lady's eye.

'What are those?' she said.

'Some books for Georgy,' Amelia replied; 'I – I promised them to him at Christmas.'

'Books!' cried the elder lady, indignantly, 'books, when the whole house wants bread! Books, when to keep you and your son in luxury, and your dear father out of gaol, I've sold every trinket I had, the India shawl from my back – even down to the very spoons, that our tradesmen mightn't insult us, and that Mr. Clapp, which indeed he is justly entitled, being not a hard landlord, and a civil man, and a father, might have his rent. Oh, Amelia! you break my heart with your books and that boy of yours, whom you are ruining, though part with him you will not. Oh, Amelia, may God send you a more dutiful child than I have had. There's Jos deserts his father in his old age: and there's George, who might be provided for, and who might be rich, going to school like a lord, with a gold watch and chain round his neck – while my dear, dear old man is without a sh–shilling.' Hysteric sobs and cries ended Mrs. Sedley's speech – it echoed through every room in the small house, whereof the other female inmates heard every word of the colloquy.

'Oh, mother, mother!' cried the poor Amelia in reply. 'You told me nothing – I – I promised him the books. I – I only sold my shawl this morning. Take the money – take everything' – and with quivering hands she took out her silver, and her sovereigns – her precious golden sovereigns, which she thrust into the hands of her mother, whence they overflowed and tumbled, rolling down the stairs.

And then she went into her room, and sank down in despair and utter misery. She saw it all now. Her selfishness was sacrificing the boy. But for her he might have wealth, station, education, and his father's place, which the elder George had forfeited for her sake. She had but to speak the words, and her father was restored to competency: and the boy raised to fortune. Oh, what a conviction it was to that tender and stricken heart!

CHAPTER XLVII

GAUNT HOUSE

ALL the world knows that Lord Steyne's town palace stands in Gaunt Square, out of which Great Gaunt Street leads, whither we first conducted Rebecca, in the time of the departed Sir Pitt Crawley. Peering over the railings and through the black trees into the garden of the square, you see a few miserable governesses with wan-faced pupils wandering round and round it, and round the dreary grass-plot in the centre of which rises the statue of Lord Gaunt, who fought at Minden, in a three-tailed wig, and otherwise habited like a Roman Emperor. Gaunt House occupies nearly

a side of the square. The remaining three sides are composed
of mansions that have passed away into Dowagerism; – tall,
dark houses, with window-frames of stone, or picked out of
a lighter red. Little light seems to be behind those lean,
comfortless casements now: and hospitality to have passed
away from those doors as much as the laced lackeys and
link-boys of old times who used to put out their torches in
the blank iron extinguishers that still flank the lamps over
the steps. Brass plates have penetrated into the square –
Doctors, the Diddlesex Bank Western Branch – the English
and European Reunion, &c. – it has a dreary look – nor is
my Lord Steyne's palace less dreary. All I have ever seen
of it is the vast wall in front, with the rustic columns at the
great gate, through which an old porter peers sometimes
with a fat and gloomy red face – and over the wall the garret
and bedroom windows, and the chimneys, out of which there
seldom comes any smoke now. For the present Lord Steyne
lives at Naples, prefering the view of the bay and Capri and
Vesuvius, to the dreary aspect of the wall in Gaunt Square.

A few score yards down New Gaunt Street, and leading
into Gaunt Mews indeed, is a little modest back door, which
you would not remark from that of any of the other stables.
But many a little close carriage has stopped at that door, as
my informant (little Tom Eaves, who knows everything, and
who showed me the place) told me. 'The prince and Perdita
have been in and out of that door, sir,' he has often told
me; 'Marianne Clarke has entered it with the Duke of —. It
conducts to the famous *petits appartements* of Lord Steyne –
one, sir, fitted up all in ivory and white satin, another in
ebony and black velvet; there is a little banqueting-room
taken from Sallust's house at Pompeii, and painted by
Cosway – a little private kitchen, in which every saucepan
was silver, and all the spits were gold. It was there that
Egalité Orleans roasted partridges on the night when he and
the Marquis of Steyne won a hundred thousand from a great
personage at Hombre. Half of the money went to the French
Revolution, half to purchase Lord Gaunt's marquisate and
garter – and the remainder —' but it forms no part of our
scheme to tell what became of the remainder, for every
shilling of which, and a great deal more, little Tom Eaves,
who knows everybody's affairs, is ready to account.

Besides his town palace, the marquis had castles and

palaces in various quarters of the three kingdoms, whereof
the descriptions may be found in the Road-books – Castle
Strongbow, with its woods, on the Shannon shore; Gaunt
Castle, in Carmarthenshire, where Richard II was taken
prisoner – Gauntly Hall in Yorkshire, where I have been
informed there were two hundred silver teapots for the
breakfasts of the guests of the house, with everything to
correspond in splendour; and Stillbrook in Hampshire, which
was my lord's farm, a humble place of residence, of which
we all remember the wonderful furniture which was sold at
my lord's demise by a late celebrated auctioneer.

The Marchioness of Steyne was of the renowned and
ancient family of the Caerlyons, Marquises of Camelot, who
have preserved the old faith ever since the conversion of the
venerable Druid, their first ancestor, and whose pedigree
goes far beyond the date of the arrival of King Brute in
these islands. Pendragon is the title of the eldest son of the
house. The sons have been called Arthurs, Uthers, and
Caradocs, from immemorial time. Their heads have fallen in
many a loyal conspiracy. Elizabeth chopped off the head of
the Arthur of her day, who had been chamberlain to Philip
and Mary, and carried letters between the Queen of Scots
and her uncles the Guises. A cadet of the house was an
officer of the great duke, and distinguished in the famous
St. Bartholomew conspiracy. During the whole of Mary's
confinement, the house of Camelot conspired in her behalf.
It was as much injured by its charges in fitting out an
armament against the Spaniards, during the time of the
Armada, as by the fines and confiscations levied on it by
Elizabeth for harbouring of priests, obstinate recusancy, and
Popish misdoings. A recreant of James's time was momen-
tarily perverted from his religion by the arguments of that
great theologian, and the fortunes of the family somewhat
restored by his timely weakness. But the Earl of Camelot,
of the reign of Charles, returned to the old creed of his
family, and they continued to fight for it, and ruin themselves for it, as long as there was a Stuart left to head or
to instigate a rebellion.

Lady Mary Caerlyon was brought up at a Parisian convent; the Dauphiness Marie Antoinette was her godmother.
In the pride of her beauty she had been married – sold, it
was said – to Lord Gaunt, then at Paris, who won vast sums

from the lady's brother at some of Philip of Orleans's banquets. The Earl of Gaunt's famous duel with the Count de la Marche, of the Grey Musqueteers, was attributed by common report to the pretensions of that officer (who had been a page, and remained a favourite of the Queen) to the hand of the beautiful Lady Mary Caerlyon. She was married to Lord Gaunt while the count lay ill of his wound, and came to dwell at Gaunt House, and to figure for a short time in the splendid Court of the Prince of Wales. Fox had toasted her. Morris and Sheridan had written songs about her. Malmsbury had made her his best bow; Walpole had pronounced her charming; Devonshire had been almost jealous of her; but she was scared by the wild pleasures and gaieties of the society into which she was flung, and after she had borne a couple of sons, shrank away into a life of devout seclusion. No wonder that my Lord Steyne, who liked pleasure and cheerfulness, was not often seen after their marriage, by the side of this trembling, silent, superstitious, unhappy lady.

The before-mentioned Tom Eaves (who has no part in this history, except that he knew all the great folks in London, and the stories and mysteries of each family) had further information regarding my Lady Steyne, which may or may not be true. 'The humiliations,' Tom used to say, 'which that woman has been made to undergo, in her own house, have been frightful; Lord Steyne has made her sit down to table with women with whom I would rather die than allow Mrs. Eaves to associate – with Lady Crackenbury, with Mrs. Chippenham, with Madame de la Cruchecassée, the French secretary's wife' (from every one of which ladies Tom Eaves – who would have sacrificed his wife for knowing them – was too glad to get a bow or a dinner), 'with the *reigning favourite*, in a word. And do you suppose that that woman, of that family, who are as proud as the Bourbons, and to whom the Steynes are but lackeys, mushrooms of yesterday (for after all, they are *not* of the old Gaunts, but of a minor and doubtful branch of the house); do you suppose, I say' (the reader must bear in mind that it is always Tom Eaves who speaks), 'that the Marchioness of Steyne, the haughtiest woman in England, would bend down to her husband so submissively, if there were not some cause? Pooh! I tell you there are *secret reasons*. I tell you, that in the emigration, the Abbé de la Marche who was here and was employed in the Quiberoon business with Puisaye and Tinteniac, was the same colonel of Mousquetaires Gris with whom Steyne fought in the year '86 – that he and the marchioness met again: that it was after the reverend colonel was shot in Brittany, that Lady Steyne took to those extreme practices of devotion which she carries on now: for she is closeted with her director every day – she is at service at Spanish Place, every morning, I've watched her there – that is, I've happened to be passing there – and depend on it there's mystery in her case. People are not so unhappy unless they have something to repent of,' added Tom Eaves with a knowing wag of his head; 'and depend on it, that woman would not be so submissive as she is, if the marquis had not some sword to hold over her.'

So, if Mr. Eaves's information be correct, it is very likely that this lady, in her high station, had to submit to many a private indignity, and to hide many secret griefs under a calm face. And let us, my brethren who have not our names in the Red Book, console ourselves by thinking comfortably how miserable our betters may be, and that Damocles, who sits on satin cushions, and is served on gold plate, has an awful sword hanging over his head in the shape of a bailiff, or an hereditary disease, or a family secret, which peeps out every now and then from the embroidered arras in a ghastly manner, and will be sure to drop one day or the other in the right place.

In comparing, too, the poor man's situation with that of the great, there is (always according to Mr. Eaves) another source of comfort for the former. You who have little or no patrimony to bequeath or to inherit, may be on good terms with your father or your son, whereas the heir of a great prince, such as my Lord Steyne, must naturally be angry at being kept out of his kingdom, and eye the occupant of it with no very agreeable glances. 'Take it as a rule,' this sardonic old Eaves would say, 'the fathers and elder sons of all great families hate each other. The crown prince is always in opposition to the crown or hankering after it. Shakespeare knew the world, my good sir, and when he describes Prince Hal (from whose family the Gaunts pretend to be descended, though they are no more related to John of Gaunt than you are) trying on his father's coronet, he gives you a natural description of all heirs-apparent. If you were heir to a dukedom and a thousand pounds a day, do you mean to say you would not wish for possession? Pooh! And it stands to reason that every great man having experienced this feeling towards his father, must be aware that his son entertains it towards himself; and so they can't but be suspicious and hostile.

'Then again, as to the feeling of elder towards younger sons. My dear sir, you ought to know that every elder brother looks upon the cadets of the house as his natural enemies, who deprive him of so much ready money which ought to be his by right. I have often heard George Mac Turk, Lord Bajazet's eldest son, say that if he had his will when he came to the title, he would do what the sultans do, and clear the estate by chopping off all his younger brothers' heads at once; and so the case is, more or less, with them all. I tell you they are all Turks in their hearts. Pooh! sir, they know the world.' And here, haply a great man coming up, Tom Eaves's hat would drop off his head, and he would rush forward with a bow and a grin, which showed that he knew the world too – in the Tomeavesian way, that is. And having laid out every shilling of his fortune on an annuity, Tom could afford to bear no malice to his nephews and nieces, and to have no other feeling with regard to his betters, but a constant and generous desire to dine with them.

Between the marchioness and the natural and tender regard of mother for children, there was that cruel barrier placed of difference of faith. The very love which she might feel for her sons, only served to render the timid and pious lady more fearful and unhappy. The gulf which separated them was fatal and impassable. She could not stretch her weak arms across it, or draw her children over to that side away from which her belief told her there was no safety. During the youth of his sons, Lord Steyne, who was a good scholar and amateur casuist, had no better sport in the evening after dinner in the country than in setting the boys' tutor, the Reverend Mr. Trail (now my Lord Bishop of Ealing), on her ladyship's director, Father Mole, over their wine, and in putting Oxford against St. Acheul. He cried, 'Bravo, Latimer! Well said, Loyola!' alternately; he promised Mole a bishopric if he would come over; and vowed he would use all his influence to get Trail a cardinal's hat if

he would secede. Neither divine allowed himself to be conquered; and though the fond mother hoped that her youngest
and favourite son would be reconciled to her Church – his
mother Church – a sad and awful disappointment awaited
the devout lady – a disappointment which seemed to be a
judgement upon her for the sin of her marriage.

My Lord Gaunt married, as every person who frequents
the *Peerage* knows, the Lady Blanche Thistlewood, a daughter
of the noble house of Bareacres, before mentioned in this
veracious history. A wing of Gaunt House was assigned to
this couple; for the head of the family chose to govern it,
and while he reigned to reign supreme: his son and heir,
however, living little at home, disagreeing with his wife,
borrowing upon post-obits such moneys as he required
beyond the very moderate sums which his father was disposed to allow him. The marquis knew every shilling of his
son's debts. At his lamented demise, he was found himself
to be possessor of many of his heir's bonds, purchased for
their benefit, and devised by his lordship to the children of
his younger son.

As, to my Lord Gaunt's dismay, and the chuckling delight
of his natural enemy and father, the Lady Gaunt had no
children – the Lord George Gaunt was desired to return from
Vienna, where he was engaged in waltzing and diplomacy,
and to contract a matrimonial alliance with the Honourable
Joan, only daughter of John Johnes, First Baron Helvellyn,
and head of the firm of Jones, Brown, and Robinson, of
Threadneedle Street, Bankers; from which union sprang
several sons and daughters, whose doings do not appertain
to this story.

The marriage at first was a happy and prosperous one.
My Lord George Gaunt could not only read, but write pretty
correctly. He spoke French with considerable fluency; and
was one of the finest waltzers in Europe. With these talents,
and his interests at home, there was little doubt that his
lordship would rise to the highest dignities in his profession.
The lady, his wife, felt that courts were her sphere; and her
wealth enabled her to receive splendidly in those Continental
towns whither her husband's diplomatic duties led him.
There was talk of appointing him minister, and bets were
laid at the Travellers' that he would be ambassador ere long,
when of a sudden, rumours arrived of the secretary's extra-

ordinary behaviour. At a grand diplomatic dinner given by his chief, he had started up, and declared that a *pâté de foie gras* was poisoned. He went to a ball at the hotel of the Bavarian envoy, the Count de Springbock-Hohenlaufen, with his head shaved, and dressed as a Capuchin friar. It was not a masked ball, as some folks wanted to persuade you. It was something queer, people whispered. His grandfather was so. It was in the family.

His wife and family returned to this country, and took up their abode at Gaunt House. Lord George gave up his post on the European Continent, and was gazetted to Brazil. But people knew better; he never returned from that Brazil expedition – never died there – never lived there – never was there at all. He was nowhere: he was gone out altogether. 'Brazil,' said one gossip to another, with a grin – 'Brazil is St. John's Wood. Rio Janeiro is a cottage surrounded by four walls; and George Gaunt is accredited to a keeper, who has invested him with the order of the Strait Waistcoat.' These are the kinds of epitaphs which men pass over one another in Vanity Fair.

Twice or thrice in a week, in the earliest morning, the poor mother went for her sins and saw the poor invalid. Sometimes he laughed at her (and his laughter was more pitiful than to hear him cry); sometimes she found the brilliant dandy diplomatist of the Congress of Vienna dragging about a child's toy, or nursing the keeper's baby's doll. Sometimes he knew her and Father Mole, her director and companion: oftener he forgot her, as he had done wife, children, love, ambition, vanity. But he remembered his dinner-hour, and used to cry if his wine-and-water was not strong enough.

It was the mysterious taint of the blood: the poor mother had brought it from her own ancient race. The evil had broken out once or twice in the father's family, long before Lady Steyne's sins had begun, or her fasts and tears and penances had been offered in their expiation. The pride of the race was struck down as the firstborn of Pharaoh. The dark mark of fate and doom was on the threshold, – the tall old threshold surmounted by coronets and carved heraldry.

The absent lord's children meanwhile prattled and grew on quite unconscious that the doom was over them too. First they talked of their father, and devised plans against his

return. Then the name of the living dead man was less
frequently in their mouths – then not mentioned at all. But
the stricken old grandmother trembled to think that these
too were the inheritors of their father's shame as well as of
his honours: and watched sickening for the day when the
awful ancestral curse should come down on them.

This dark presentiment also haunted Lord Steyne. He
tried to lay the horrid bedside ghost in Red Seas of wine
and jollity, and lost sight of it sometimes in the crowd and
rout of his pleasures. But it always came back to him when
alone, and seemed to grow more threatening with years. 'I
have taken your son,' it said, 'why not you? I may shut you
up in a prison some day like your son George. I may tap
you on the head to-morrow, and away go pleasure and
honours, feasts and beauty, friends, flatterers, French cooks,
fine horses and houses – in exchange for a prison, a keeper,
and a straw mattress like George Gaunt's.' And then my
lord would defy the ghost which threatened him: for he knew
of a remedy by which he could balk his enemy.

So there was splendour and wealth, but no great happiness perchance behind the tall carved portals of Gaunt House
with its smoky coronets and ciphers. The feasts there were
of the grandest in London, but there was not over-much
content therewith, except among the guests who sat at my
lord's table. Had he not been so great a prince very few
possibly would have visited him: but in Vanity Fair the sins
of very great personages are looked at indulgently. '*Nous
regardons à deux fois*' (as the French lady said) before we
condemn a person of my lord's undoubted quality. Some
notorious carpers and squeamish moralists might be sulky
with Lord Steyne, but they were glad enough to come when
he asked them.

'Lord Steyne is really too bad,' Lady Slingstone said, 'but
everybody goes, and of course I shall see that my girls come
to no harm.' 'His lordship is a man to whom I owe much,
everything in life,' said the Right Reverend Doctor Trail,
thinking that the archbishop was rather shaky; and Mrs.
Trail and the young ladies would as soon have missed going
to church as to one of his lordship's parties. 'His morals are
bad,' said little Lord Southdown to his sister, who meekly
expostulated, having heard terrific legends from her mamma
with respect to the doings at Gaunt House; 'but hang it,

he's got the best dry sillery in Europe!' And as for Sir Pitt Crawley, Bart. – Sir Pitt that pattern of decorum, Sir Pitt who had led off at missionary meetings, – he never for one moment thought of not going too. 'Where you see such persons as the Bishop of Ealing and the Countess of Slingstone, you may be pretty sure, Jane,' the baronet would say, 'that *we* cannot be wrong. The great rank and station of Lord Steyne put him in a position to command people in our station in life. The lord lieutenant of a county, my dear, is a respectable man. Besides George Gaunt and I were intimate in early life: he was my junior when we were attachés at Pumpernickel together.'

In a word everybody went to wait upon this great man – everybody who was asked: as you the reader (do not say nay) or I the writer hereof would go if we had an invitation.

CHAPTER XLVIII

IN WHICH THE READER IS INTRODUCED TO THE VERY BEST OF COMPANY

At last Becky's kindness and attention to the chief of her husband's family, were destined to meet with an exceeding great reward; a reward which, though certainly somewhat unsubstantial, the little woman coveted with greater eagerness than more positive benefits. If she did not wish to lead a virtuous life, at least she desired to enjoy a character for virtue, and we know that no lady in the genteel world can possess this desideratum, until she has put on a train and feathers, and has been presented to her sovereign at Court. From that august interview they come out stamped as honest women. The lord chamberlain gives them a certificate of virtue. And as dubious goods or letters are passed through an oven at quarantine, sprinkled with aromatic vinegar, and then pronounced clean – many a lady whose reputation would be doubtful otherwise and liable to give infection, passes through the wholesome ordeal of the royal presence, and issues from it free from all taint.

It might be very well for my Lady Bareacres, my Lady Tufto, Mrs. Bute Crawley in the country, and other ladies who had come into contact with Mrs. Rawdon Crawley, to cry fie at the idea of the odious little adventuress making her curtsy before the sovereign, and to declare, that if dear good Queen Charlotte had been alive, *she* never would have admitted such an extremely ill-regulated personage into Her chaste Drawing-room. But when we consider, that it was the First Gentleman in Europe in whose high presence Mrs. Rawdon passed her examination, and as it were, took her degree in reputation, it surely must be flat disloyalty to doubt any more about her virtue. I, for my part, look back with love and awe to that Great Character in history. Ah, what a high and noble appreciation of Gentlewomanhood there must have been in Vanity Fair, when that revered and august being was invested, by the universal acclaim of the refined and educated portion of this empire, with the title of Premier Gentilhomme of his Kingdom. Do you remember, dear M——, O friend of my youth, how one blissful night five-and-twenty years since, *The Hypocrite* being acted, Elliston being manager, Dowton and Liston performers, two boys had leave from their loyal masters to go out from Slaughter House School where they were educated, and to appear on Drury Lane stage, amongst a crowd which assembled there to greet the King. THE KING? There he was. Beef-eaters were before the august box: the Marquis of Steyne (Lord of the Powder Closet) and other great officers of state were behind the chair on which he sat, *He* sat — florid of face, portly of person, covered with orders, and in a rich curling head of hair — How we sang God save him! How the house rocked and shouted with that magnificent music. How they cheered, and cried, and waved handkerchiefs. Ladies wept: mothers clasped their children: some fainted with emotion. People were suffocated in the pit, shrieks and groans rising up amidst the writhing and shouting mass there of his people who were, and indeed showed themselves almost to be, ready to die for him. Yes, we saw him. Fate cannot deprive us of *that*. Others have seen Napoleon. Some few still exist who have beheld Frederick the Great, Doctor Johnson, Marie Antoinette, &c. — be it our reasonable boast to our children, that we saw George the Good, the Magnificent, the Great.

Well, there came a happy day in Mrs. Rawdon Crawley's existence when this angel was admitted into the paradise of a Court which she coveted; her sister-in-law acting as her godmother. On the appointed day, Sir Pitt and his lady, in their great family carriage (just newly built, and ready for the baronet's assumption of the office of high sheriff of his county), drove up to the little house in Curzon Street, to the edification of Raggles who was watching from his green-grocer's shop, and saw fine plumes within, and enormous bunches of flowers in the breasts of the new livery-coats of the footmen.

Sir Pitt, in a glittering uniform, descended and went into Curzon Street, his sword between his legs. Little Rawdon stood with his face against the parlour window panes, smiling and nodding with all his might to his aunt in the carriage within; and presently Sir Pitt issued forth from the house again, leading forth a lady with grand feathers, covered in a white shawl, and holding up daintily a train of magnificent brocade. She stepped into the vehicle as if she were a princess and accustomed all her life to go to Court, smiling graciously on the footman at the door, and on Sir Pitt, who followed her into the carriage.

Then Rawdon followed in his old Guards' uniform, which had grown wofully shabby, and was much too tight. He was to have followed the procession, and waited upon his sovereign in a cab; but that his good-natured sister-in-law insisted that they should be a family party. The coach was large, the ladies not very big, they would hold their trains in their laps – finally, the four went fraternally together; and their carriage presently joined the line of loyal equipages which was making its way down Piccadilly and St. James's Street, towards the old brick palace where the Star of Brunswick was in waiting to receive his nobles and gentlefolks.

Becky felt as if she could bless the people out of the carriage windows, so elated was she in spirit, and so strong a sense had she of the dignified position which she had at last attained in life. Even our Becky had her weaknesses, and as one often sees how men pride themselves upon excellences which others are slow to perceive: how, for instance, Comus firmly believes that he is the greatest tragic actor in England; how Brown, the famous novelist, longs to be considered, not a man of genius, but a man of fashion; while Robinson, the great lawyer, does not in the least care about his reputation in Westminster Hall, but believes himself incomparable across country, and at a five-barred gate – so to be, and to be thought, a respectable woman, was

Becky's aim in life, and she got up the genteel with amazing assiduity, readiness, and success. We have said, there were times when she believed herself to be a fine lady, and forgot that there was no money in the chest at home – duns round the gate, tradesmen to coax and wheedle – no ground to walk upon, in a word. And as she went to Court in the carriage, the family carriage, she adopted a demeanour so grand, self-satisfied, deliberate, and imposing, that it made even Lady Jane laugh. She walked into the royal apartments with a toss of the head which would have befitted an empress, and I have no doubt had she been one, she would have become the character perfectly.

We are authorized to state that Mrs. Rawdon Crawley's *costume de cour* on the occasion of her presentation to the sovereign was of the most elegant and brilliant description. Some ladies we may have seen – we who wear stars and cordons, and attend the St. James's assemblies, or we who, in muddy boots, dawdle up and down Pall Mall, and peep into the coaches as they drive up with the great folks in their feathers – some ladies of fashion, I say, we may have seen, about two o'clock of the forenoon of a Levée day, as the laced-jacketed band of the Life Guards are blowing triumphal marches seated on those prancing music-stools, their cream-coloured chargers – who are by no means lovely and enticing objects at that early period of noon. A stout countess of sixty, *décolletée*, painted, wrinkled, with rouge up to her drooping eyelids, and diamonds twinkling in her wig, is a wholesome and edifying, but not a pleasant sight. She has the faded look of a St. James's Street illumination, as it may be seen of an early morning, when half the lamps are out, and the others are blinking wanly, as if they were about to vanish like ghosts before the dawn. Such charms as those of which we catch glimpses while her ladyship's carriage passes, should appear abroad at night alone. If even Cynthia looks haggard of an afternoon, as we may see her sometimes in the present winter season, with Phoebus staring her out of countenance from the opposite side of the heavens, how much more can old Lady Castlemouldy keep her head up when the sun is shining full upon it through the chariot windows, and showing all the chinks and crannies with which time has marked her face? No. Drawing-rooms should be announced for November, or the first foggy day: or the elderly sultanas of our Vanity Fair should drive up in closed litters, descend in a covered way, and make their curtsy to the sovereign under the protection of lamplight.

Our beloved Rebecca had no need, however, of any such a friendly halo to set off her beauty. Her complexion could bear any sunshine as yet; and her dress, though if you were to see it now, any present lady of Vanity Fair would pronounce it to be the most foolish and preposterous attire ever worn, was as handsome in her eyes and those of the public, some five-and-twenty years since, as the most brilliant costume of the most famous beauty of the present season. A score of years hence that, too, that milliner's wonder, will have passed into the domain of the absurd, along with all previous vanities. But we are wandering too much. Mrs. Rawdon's dress was pronounced to be *charmante* on the eventful day of her presentation. Even good little Lady Jane was forced to acknowledge this effect, as she looked at her kinswoman; and owned sorrowfully to herself that she was quite inferior in taste to Mrs. Becky.

She did not know how much care, thought, and genius Mrs. Rawdon had bestowed upon that garment. Rebecca had as good taste as any milliner in Europe, and such a clever way of doing things as Lady Jane little understood. The latter quickly spied out the magnificence of the brocade of Becky's train, and the splendour of the lace on her dress.

The brocade was an old remnant, Becky said; and as for the lace, it was a great bargain. She had had it these hundred years.

'My dear Mrs. Crawley, it must have cost a little fortune,' Lady Jane said, looking down at her own lace, which was not nearly so good; and then, examining the quality of the ancient brocade which formed the material of Mrs. Rawdon's court dress, she felt inclined to say that she could not afford such fine clothing, but checked that speech, with an effort, as one uncharitable to her kinswoman.

And yet, if Lady Jane had known all, I think even her kindly temper would have failed her. The fact is, when she was putting Sir Pitt's house in order, Mrs. Rawdon had found the lace and the brocade in old wardrobes, the property of the former ladies of the house, and had quietly carried the goods home, and had suited them to her own little person. Briggs saw her take them, asked no questions, told no stories; but I believe quite sympathized with her on this matter, and so would many another honest woman.

And the diamonds – 'Where the doose did you get the diamonds, Becky?' said her husband, admiring some jewels which he had never seen before, and which sparkled in her ears and on her neck with brilliance and profusion.

Becky blushed a little, and looked at him hard for a moment. Pitt Crawley blushed a little too, and looked out of window. The fact is, he had given her a very small portion of the brilliants; a pretty diamond clasp, which confined a pearl necklace which she wore; and the baronet had omitted to mention the circumstance to his lady.

Becky looked at her husband, and then at Sir Pitt, with an air of saucy triumph, as much as to say, 'Shall I betray you?'

'Guess!' she said to her husband. 'Why, you silly man,' she continued, 'where do you suppose I got them – all except the little clasp, which a dear friend of mine gave me long ago. I hired them, to be sure. I hired them at Mr. Polonius's in Coventry Street. You don't suppose that all the diamonds which go to Court belong to the owners; like those beautiful stones which Lady Jane has, and which are much handsomer than any which I have, I am certain.'

'They are family jewels,' said Sir Pitt, again looking uneasy. And in this family conversation the carriage rolled down the street, until its cargo was finally discharged at the gates of the palace where the sovereign was sitting in state.

The diamonds, which had created Rawdon's admiration, never went back to Mr. Polonius, of Coventry Street, and that gentleman never applied for their restoration; but they retired into a little private repository, in an old desk, which Amelia Sedley had given her years and years ago, and in which Becky kept a number of useful and, perhaps, valuable things, about which her husband knew nothing. To know nothing, or little, is in the nature of some husbands. To hide, in the nature of how many women? O ladies! how many of you have surreptitious milliners' bills? How many of you have gowns and bracelets, which you daren't show, or which you wear trembling? – trembling, and coaxing with smiles the husband by your side, who does not know the new velvet gown from the old one, or the new bracelet from last year's, or has any notion that the ragged-looking yellow lace scarf cost forty guineas, and that Madame Bobinot is writing dunning letters every week for the money!

Thus Rawdon knew nothing about the brilliant diamond ear-rings, or the superb brilliant ornament which decorated the fair bosom of his lady; but Lord Steyne, who was in his place at Court, as Lord of the Powder Closet, and one of the great dignitaries and illustrious defences of the throne of England, and came up with all his stars, garters, collars, and cordons, and paid particular attention to the little woman, knew whence the jewels came, and who paid for them.

As he bowed over her he smiled, and quoted the hackneyed and beautiful lines, from the *Rape of the Lock*, about Belinda's diamonds, 'which Jews might kiss and infidels adore.'

'But I hope your lordship is orthodox,' said the little lady, with a toss of her head. And many ladies round about whispered and talked, and many gentlemen nodded and whispered, as they saw what marked attention the great nobleman was paying to the little adventuress.

What were the circumstances of the interview between Rebecca Crawley, *née* Sharp, and her Imperial Master, it does not become such a feeble and inexperienced pen as mine to attempt to relate. The dazzled eyes close before that Magnificent Idea. Loyal respect and decency tell even the imagination not to look too keenly and audaciously about the sacred audience-chamber, but to back away rapidly, silently, and respectfully, making profound bows out of the August Presence.

This may be said, that in all London there was no more loyal heart than Becky's after this interview. The name of her King was always on her lips, and he was proclaimed by her to be the most charming of men. She went to Colnaghi's and ordered the finest portrait of him that art had produced, and credit could supply. She chose that famous one in which the best of monarchs is represented in a frock-coat with a fur collar, and breeches and silk stockings, simpering on a sofa from under his curly brown wig. She had him painted in a brooch and wore it – indeed she amused and somewhat pestered her acquaintance with her perpetual talk about his urbanity and beauty. Who knows? Perhaps the little woman thought she might play the part of a Maintenon or a Pompadour.

But the finest sport of all after her presentation was to hear her talk virtuously. She had a few female acquaintances, not, it must be owned, of the very highest reputation in Vanity Fair. But being made an honest woman of, so to speak, Becky would not consort any longer with these dubious ones, and cut Lady Crackenbury when the latter nodded to her from her opera-box; and gave Mrs. Washington White the go-by in the ring. 'One must, my dear, show one is somebody,' she said. 'One mustn't be seen with doubtful people. I pity Lady Crackenbury from my heart; and Mrs. Washington White may be a very good-natured person. *You* may go and dine with them, as you like your rubber. But *I* mustn't, and won't; and you will have the goodness to tell Smith to say I am not at home when either of them calls.'

The particulars of Becky's costume were in the newspapers – feathers, lappets, superb diamonds, and all the rest. Lady Crackenbury read the paragraph in bitterness of spirit, and discoursed to her followers about the airs which that woman was giving herself. Mrs. Bute Crawley and her young ladies in the country had a copy of the *Morning Post* from town; and gave a vent to their honest indignation. 'If you had been sandy-haired, green-eyed, and a French rope-dancer's daughter,' Mrs. Bute said to her eldest girl (who, on the contrary, was a very swarthy, short, and snub-nosed young lady), 'you might have had superb diamonds forsooth, and have been presented at Court, by your cousin, the Lady Jane. But you're only a gentlewoman, my poor dear child. You have only some of the best blood in England in your veins, and good principles and piety for your portion. I, myself, the wife of a baronet's younger brother, too, never thought of such a thing as going to Court – nor would other people, if good Queen Charlotte had been alive.' In this way the worthy rectoress consoled herself: and her daughters sighed, and sat over the *Peerage* all night.

A few days after the famous presentation, another great and exceeding honour was vouchsafed to the virtuous Becky. Lady Steyne's carriage drove up to Mr. Rawdon Crawley's door, and the footman, instead of driving down the front of the house, as by his tremendous knocking he appeared to be inclined to do, relented, and only delivered in a couple of cards, on which were engraven the names of the Marchioness of Steyne and the Countess of Gaunt. If these bits of pasteboard had been beautiful pictures, or had had a hundred yards of Malines lace rolled round them, worth twice the number of guineas, Becky could not have regarded them with more pleasure. You may be sure they occupied a conspicuous place in the china bowl on the drawing-room table, where Becky kept the cards of her visitors. Lord! lord! how poor Mrs. Washington White's card and Lady Crackenbury's card, which our little friend had been glad enough to get a few months back, and of which the silly little creature was rather proud once – Lord! lord! I say, how soon at the appearance of these grand court cards, did those poor little neglected deuces sink down to the bottom of the pack. Steyne! Bareacres, Johnes of Helvellyn! and Caerlyon of Camelot! we may be sure that Becky and Briggs looked out those august names in the *Peerage*, and followed the noble races up through all the ramifications of the family tree.

My Lord Steyne coming to call a couple of hours afterwards, and looking about him, and observing everything as was his wont, found his lady's cards already ranged as the trumps of Becky's hand, and grinned, as this old cynic always did at any naïve display of human weakness. Becky came down to him presently: whenever the dear girl expected his lordship, her toilette was prepared, her hair in perfect order, her *mouchoirs*, aprons, scarfs, little morocco slippers, and other female gimcracks arranged, and she seated in some artless and agreeable posture ready to receive him – whenever she was surprised, of course she had to fly to her apartment to take a rapid survey of matters in the glass, and to trip down again to wait upon the great peer.

She found him grinning over the bowl. She was discovered, and she blushed a little. 'Thank you, monseigneur,' she said. 'You see your ladies have been here. How good of you! I couldn't come before – I was in the kitchen making a pudding.'

'I know you were: I saw you through the area-railings as I drove up,' replied the old gentleman.

'You see everything,' she replied.

'A few things, but not that, my pretty lady,' he said, good-naturedly. 'You silly little fibster! I heard you in the room overhead, where I have no doubt you were putting a little rouge on; you must give some of yours to my Lady

Gaunt, whose complexion is quite preposterous; and I heard the bedroom door open, and then you came downstairs.'

'Is it a crime to try and look my best when *you* come here?' answered Mrs. Rawdon, plaintively, and she rubbed her cheek with her handkerchief as if to show there was no rouge at all, only genuine blushes and modesty in her case. About this who can tell? I know there is some rouge that won't come off on a pocket-handkerchief; and some so good that even tears will not disturb it.

'Well,' said the old gentleman, twiddling round his wife's card, 'you are bent upon becoming a fine lady. You pester my poor old life out to get you into the world. You won't be able to hold your own there, you silly little fool. You've got no money.'

'You will get us a place,' interposed Becky, as quick as possible.

'You've got no money, and you want to compete with those who have. You poor little earthenware pipkin, you want to swim down the stream along with the great copper kettles. All women are alike. Everybody is striving for what is not worth the having! Gad! I dined with the King yesterday and we had neck of mutton and turnips. A dinner of herbs is better than a stalled ox very often. You will go to Gaunt House. You give an old fellow no rest until you get there. It's not half so nice as here. You'll be bored there. I am. My wife is as gay as Lady Macbeth, and my daughters as cheerful as Regan and Goneril. I daren't sleep in what they call my bedroom. The bed is like the baldaquin of St. Peter's, and the pictures frighten me. I have a little brass bed in a dressing-room: and a little hair mattress like an anchorite. I am an anchorite. Ho! ho! You'll be asked to dinner next week. And *gare aux femmes*, look out and hold your own! How the women will bully you!' This was a very long speech for a man of few words like my Lord Steyne; nor was it the first which he uttered for Becky's benefit on that day.

Briggs looked up from the work-table at which she was seated in the farther room, and gave a deep sigh as she heard the great marquis speak so lightly of her sex.

'If you don't turn off that abominable sheep-dog,' said Lord Steyne, with a savage look over his shoulder at her, 'I will have her poisoned.'

'I always give my dog dinner from my own plate,' said

Rebecca, laughing mischievously; and having enjoyed for some time the discomfiture of my lord, who hated poor Briggs for interrupting his *tête-à-tête* with the fair colonel's wife, Mrs. Rawdon at length had pity upon her admirer, and calling to Briggs, praised the fineness of the weather to her, and bade her to take out the child for a walk.

'I can't send her away,' Becky said presently, after a pause, and in a very sad voice. Her eyes filled with tears as she spoke, and she turned away her head.

'You owe her her wages? I suppose,' said the peer.

'Worse than that,' said Becky, still casting down her eyes, 'I have ruined her.'

'Ruined her? – then why don't you turn her out?' the gentleman asked.

'Men do that,' Becky answered bitterly. 'Women are not so bad as you. Last year when we were reduced to our last guinea, she gave us everything. She shall never leave me, until we are ruined utterly ourselves, which does not seem far off, or until I can pay her the uttermost farthing.'

'— it, how much is it?' said the peer with an oath. And Becky, reflecting on the largeness of his means, mentioned not only the sum which she had borrowed from Miss Briggs, but one of nearly double the amount.

This caused the Lord Steyne to break out in another brief and energetic expression of anger, at which Rebecca held down her head the more, and cried bitterly. 'I could not help it. It was my only chance. I dare not tell my husband. He would kill me if I told him what I have done. I have kept it a secret from everybody but you – and you forced it from me. Ah, what shall I do, Lord Steyne? for I am very, very unhappy!'

Lord Steyne made no reply except by beating the devil's tattoo, and biting his nails. At last he clapped his hat on his head, and flung out of the room. Rebecca did not rise from her attitude of misery until the door slammed upon him, and his carriage whirled away. Then she rose up with the queerest expression of victorious mischief glittering in her green eyes. She burst out laughing once or twice to herself, as she sat at work; and sitting down to the piano, she rattled away a triumphant voluntary on the keys, which made the people pause under her window to listen to her brilliant music.

That night, there came two notes from Gaunt House for

the little woman, the one containing a card of invitation from Lord and Lady Steyne to a dinner at Gaunt House next Friday: while the other enclosed a slip of grey paper bearing Lord Steyne's signature and the address of Messrs. Jones, Brown, and Robinson, Lombard Street.

Rawdon heard Becky laughing in the night once or twice. It was only her delight at going to Gaunt House and facing the ladies there, she said, which amused her so. But the truth was, that she was occupied with a great number of other thoughts. Should she pay off old Briggs and give her her *congé?* Should she astonish Raggles by settling his account? She turned over all these thoughts on her pillow, and on the next day, when Rawdon went out to pay his morning visit to the club, Mrs. Crawley (in a modest dress with a veil on) whipped off in a hackney-coach to the City: and being landed at Messrs. Jones and Robinson's bank, presented a document there to the authority at the desk, who, in reply, asked her 'How she would take it?'

She gently said 'she would take a hundred and fifty pounds in small notes and the remainder in one note': and passing through St. Paul's Churchyard stopped there and bought the handsomest black silk gown for Briggs which money could buy; and which, with a kiss and the kindest speeches, she presented to the simple old spinster.

Then she walked to Mr. Raggles, inquired about his children affectionately, and gave him fifty pounds on account. Then she went to the livery-man from whom she jobbed her carriages and gratified him with a similar sum. 'And I hope this will be a lesson to you, Spavin,' she said, 'and that on the next Drawing-room day my brother, Sir Pitt, will not be inconvenienced by being obliged to take four of us in his carriage to wait upon His Majesty, because my *own* carriage is not forthcoming.' It appears there had been a difference on the last Drawing-room day. Hence the degradation which the colonel had almost suffered, of being obliged to enter the presence of his sovereign in a hack cab.

These arrangements concluded, Becky paid a visit upstairs to the before-mentioned desk, which Amelia Sedley had given her years and years ago, and which contained a number of useful and valuable little things: in which private museum she placed the one note which Messrs. Jones and Robinson's cashier had given her.

CHAPTER XLIX

IN WHICH WE ENJOY THREE COURSES
AND A DESSERT

W HEN the ladies of Gaunt House were at breakfast that morning Lord Steyne (who took his chocolate in private, and seldom disturbed the females of his household, or saw them except upon public days, or when they crossed each other in the hall, or when from his pit-box at the Opera he surveyed them in their box on the grand tier) – his lordship, we say, appeared among the ladies and the children who were assembled over the tea and toast, and a battle royal ensued à propos of Rebecca.

'My Lady Steyne,' he said, 'I want to see the list for your dinner on Friday; and I want you, if you please, to write a card for Colonel and Mrs. Crawley.'

'Blanche writes them,' Lady Steyne said, in a flutter. 'Lady Gaunt writes them.'

'I will not write to that person,' Lady Gaunt said, a tall and stately lady, who looked up for an instant and then down again after she had spoken. It was not good to meet Lord Steyne's eyes for those who had offended him.

'Send the children out of the room. Go!' said he, pulling at the bell-rope. The urchins, always frightened before him, retired: their mother would have followed too. 'Not you,' he said. 'You stop.'

'My Lady Steyne,' he said, 'once more will you have the goodness to go to the desk, and write that card for your dinner on Friday?'

'My lord, I will not be present at it,' Lady Gaunt said; 'I will go home.'

'I wish you would, and stay there. You will find the bailiffs at Bareacres very pleasant company, and I shall be freed from lending money to your relations, and from your own damned tragedy airs. Who are you to give orders here? You have no money. You've got no brains. You were here to have children, and you have not had any. Gaunt's tired of you; and George's wife is the only person in the family who doesn't wish you were dead. Gaunt would marry again if you were.'

'I wish I were,' her ladyship answered, with tears and rage in her eyes.

'You, forsooth, must give yourself airs of virtue; while my wife, who is an immaculate saint, as everybody knows, and never did wrong in her life, has no objection to meet my young friend, Mrs. Crawley. My Lady Steyne knows that appearances are sometimes against the best of women; that lies are often told about the most innocent of them. Pray, madame, shall I tell you some little anecdotes about my Lady Bareacres, your mamma?'

'You may strike me if you like, sir, or hit any cruel blow,' Lady Gaunt said. To see his wife and daughter suffering always put his lordship into a good humour.

'My sweet Blanche,' he said, 'I am a gentleman, and never lay my hand upon a woman, save in the way of kindness. I only wish to correct little faults in your character. You women are too proud, and sadly lack humility, as Father Mole, I'm sure, would tell my Lady Steyne if he were here. You mustn't give yourselves airs: you must be meek and humble, my blessings. For all Lady Steyne knows, this calumniated, simple, good-humoured Mrs. Crawley is quite innocent – even more innocent than herself. Her husband's character is not good, but it is as good as Bareacres', who has played a little and not paid a great deal, who cheated you out of the only legacy you ever had, and left you a pauper on my hands. And Mrs. Crawley is not very well born; but she is not worse than Fanny's illustrious ancestor, the first de la Jones.'

'The money which I brought into the family, sir,' Lady George cried out —

'You purchased a contingent reversion with it,' the marquis said, darkly. 'If Gaunt dies, your husband may come to his honours; your little boys may inherit them, and who knows what besides? In the meanwhile, ladies, be as proud and virtuous as you like abroad, but don't give *me* any airs. As for Mrs. Crawley's character, I shan't demean myself or that most spotless and perfectly irreproachable lady, by even hinting that it requires a defence. You will be pleased to receive her with the utmost cordiality, as you will receive all persons whom I present in this house. This house?' He broke out with a laugh. 'Who is the master of it? and what is it? This Temple of Virtue belongs to me. And if I invite all Newgate or all Bedlam here, by —, they shall be welcome.'

After this vigorous allocution, to one of which sort Lord Steyne treated his 'Hareem', whenever symptoms of insubordination appeared in his household, the crestfallen women had nothing for it but to obey. Lady Gaunt wrote the invitation which his lordship required, and she and her mother-in-law drove in person, and with bitter and humiliated hearts, to leave the cards on Mrs. Rawdon, the reception of which caused that innocent woman so much pleasure.

There were families in London who would have sacrificed a year's income to receive such an honour at the hands of those great ladies. Mrs. Frederick Bullock, for instance, would have gone on her knees from May Fair to Lombard Street, if Lady Steyne and Lady Gaunt had been waiting in the City to raise her up, and say, 'Come to us next Friday,' – not to one of the great crushes, and grand balls of Gaunt House, whither everybody went, but to the sacred, unapproachable, mysterious, delicious entertainments, to be admitted to one of which was a privilege, and an honour, and a blessing indeed.

Severe, spotless, and beautiful, Lady Gaunt held the very highest rank in Vanity Fair. The distinguished courtesy with which Lord Steyne treated her, charmed everybody who witnessed his behaviour, caused the severest critics to admit how perfect a gentleman he was, and to own that his lordship's heart at least was in the right place.

The ladies of Gaunt House called Lady Bareacres in to their aid, in order to repulse the common enemy. One of Lady Gaunt's carriages went to Hill Street for her ladyship's mother, all whose equipages were in the hands of the bailiffs, whose very jewels and wardrobe, it was said, had been seized by those inexorable Israelites. Bareacres Castle was theirs, too, with all its costly pictures, furniture, and articles of virtu – the magnificent Vandykes; the noble Reynolds pictures; the Lawrence portraits, tawdry and beautiful, and, thirty years ago, deemed as precious as works of real genius; the matchless Dancing Nymph of Canova, for which Lady Bareacres had sat in her youth – Lady Bareacres splendid then, and radiant in wealth, rank, and beauty – a toothless, bald, old woman now – a mere rag of a former robe of state.

Her lord, painted at the same time by Lawrence, as waving his sabre in front of Bareacres Castle, and clothed in his uniform as colonel of the Thistlewood Yeomanry, was a withered, old, lean man in a greatcoat and a Brutus wig: slinking about Gray's Inn of mornings chiefly, and dining alone at clubs. He did not like to dine with Steyne now. They had run races of pleasure together in youth when Bareacres was the winner. But Steyne had more bottom than he, and had lasted him out. The marquis was ten times a greater man now than the young Lord Gaunt of '85; and Bareacres nowhere in the race – old, beaten, bankrupt, and broken down. He had borrowed too much money of Steyne to find it pleasant to meet his old comrade often. The latter, whenever he wished to be merry, used jeeringly to ask Lady Gaunt, why her father had not come to see her? 'He has not been here for four months,' Lord Steyne would say. 'I can always tell by my cheque-book afterwards, when I get a visit from Bareacres. What a comfort it is, my ladies, I bank with one of my sons' fathers-in-law, and the other banks with me!'

Of the other illustrious persons whom Becky had the honour to encounter on this her first presentation to the grand world, it does not become the present historian to say much. There was His Excellency the Prince of Peterwaradin, with his princess; a nobleman tightly girthed, with a large military chest, on which the *plaque* of his order shone magnificently, and wearing the red collar of the Golden Fleece round his neck. He was the owner of countless flocks. 'Look at his face. I think he must be descended from a sheep,' Becky whispered to Lord Steyne. Indeed, his excellency's countenance, long, solemn, and white, with the ornament round his neck, bore some resemblance to that of a venerable bell-wether.

There was Mr. John Paul Jefferson Jones, titularly attached to the American Embassy, and correspondent of the New York *Demagogue*; who, by way of making himself agreeable to the company, asked Lady Steyne, during a pause in the conversation at dinner, how his dear friend, George Gaunt, liked the Brazils? – He and George had been most intimate at Naples, and had gone up Vesuvius together. Mr. Jones wrote a full and particular account of the dinner, which appeared duly in the *Demagogue*. He mentioned the names and titles of all the guests, giving biographical sketches of the principal people. He described the persons of the ladies with great eloquence; the service of the table; the size and costume of the servants; enumerated the dishes and wines served; the ornaments of the sideboard, and the probable value of the plate. Such a dinner he calculated could not be dished up under fifteen or eighteen dollars per head. And he was in the habit, until very lately, of sending over protégés, with letters of recommendation, to the present Marquis of Steyne, encouraged to do so by the intimate terms on which he had lived with his dear friend, the late lord. He was most indignant that a young and insignificant aristocrat, the Earl of Southdown, should have taken the *pas* of him in their procession to the dining-room. 'Just as I was stepping up to offer my hand to a very pleasing and witty fashionable, the brilliant and exclusive Mrs. Rawdon Crawley,' – he wrote – 'the young patrician interposed between me and the lady, and whisked my Helen off without a word of apology. I was fain to bring up the rear with the colonel, the lady's husband, a stout red-faced warrior who distinguished himself at Waterloo, where he had better luck than befell some of his brother red-coats at New Orleans.'

The colonel's countenance on coming into this polite society wore as many blushes as the face of a boy of sixteen assumes when he is confronted with his sister's schoolfellows. It has been told before that honest Rawdon had not been much used at any period of his life to ladies' company. With the men at the club or the mess-room, he was well enough; and could ride, bet, smoke, or play at billiards with the boldest of them. He had had his time for female friendships too: but that was twenty years ago, and the ladies were of the rank of those with whom Young Marlow in the comedy is represented as having been familiar before he became abashed in the presence of Miss Hardcastle. The times are such that one scarcely dares to allude to that kind of company which thousands of our young men in Vanity Fair are frequenting every day, which nightly fills casinos and dancing-rooms, which is known to exist as well as the ring in Hyde Park or the congregation at St. James's – but which the most squeamish if not the most moral of societies is determined to ignore. In a word, although Colonel Crawley was now five-and-forty years of age, it had not been his lot in life to meet with a half-dozen good women, besides his paragon of a wife. All except her and his kind sister Lady Jane, whose gentle nature had tamed and won him, scared the worthy colonel; and on occasion of his first dinner at Gaunt House he was not heard to make a single remark, except to state that the weather was very hot. Indeed Becky would have left him at home, but that virtue ordained that her husband should be by her side to protect the timid and fluttering little creature on her first appearance in polite society.

On her first appearance Lord Steyne stepped forward, taking her hand, and greeting her with great courtesy, and presenting her to Lady Steyne, and their ladyships, her daughters. Their ladyships made three stately curtsies, and the elder lady to be sure gave her hand to the newcomer, but it was as cold and lifeless as marble.

Becky took it, however, with grateful humility; and performing a reverence which would have done credit to the best dancing-master, put herself at Lady Steyne's feet, as it were, by saying that his lordship had been her father's earliest friend and patron, and that she, Becky, had learned to honour and respect the Steyne family from the days of her childhood. The fact is, that Lord Steyne had once purchased a couple of pictures of the late Sharp, and the affectionate orphan could never forget her gratitude for that favour.

The Lady Bareacres then came under Becky's cognizance – to whom the colonel's lady made also a most respectful obeisance: it was returned with severe dignity by the exalted person in question.

'I had the pleasure of making your ladyship's acquaintance at Brussels ten years ago,' Becky said, in the most winning manner. 'I had the good fortune to meet Lady Bareacres, at the Duchess of Richmond's ball, the night before the battle of Waterloo. And I recollect your ladyship, and my Lady Blanche, your daughter, sitting in the carriage in the *porte-cochère* at the inn, waiting for horses. I hope your ladyship's diamonds are safe.'

Everybody's eyes looked into their neighbours'. The famous diamonds had undergone a famous seizure, it appears, about which Becky, of course, knew nothing. Rawdon Crawley retreated with Lord Southdown into a window, where the latter was heard to laugh immoderately, as Rawdon told him the story of Lady Bareacres wanting horses, and 'knuckling down by Jove', to Mrs. Crawley. 'I think I needn't be afraid of *that* woman,' Becky thought. Indeed, Lady Bareacres exchanged terrified and angry looks with her daughter, and retreated to a table, where she began to look at pictures with great energy.

When the potentate from the Danube made his appearance, the conversation was carried on in the French language, and the Lady Bareacres and the younger ladies found, to their farther mortification, that Mrs. Crawley was much better acquainted with that tongue, and spoke it with a much better accent than they. Becky had met other Hungarian magnates with the army in France, in 1816–17. She asked after her friends with great interest. The foreign personages thought that she was a lady of great distinction; and the prince and the princess asked severally of Lord Steyne and the marchioness, whom they conducted to dinner, who was that *petite dame* who spoke so well?

Finally, the procession being formed in the order described by the American diplomatist, they marched into the apartment where the banquet was served: and which, as I have promised the reader he shall enjoy it, he shall have the liberty of ordering himself so as to suit his fancy.

But it was when the ladies were alone that Becky knew the tug of war would come. And then indeed the little woman found herself in such a situation, as made her acknowledge the correctness of Lord Steyne's caution to her to beware of the society of ladies above her own sphere. As they say the persons who hate Irishmen most are Irishmen; so, assuredly, the greatest tyrants over women are women. When poor little Becky, alone with the ladies, went up to the fireplace whither the great ladies had repaired, the great ladies marched away and took possession of a table of drawings. When Becky followed them to the table of drawings, they dropped off one by one to the fire again. She tried to speak to one of the children (of whom she was commonly fond in public places), but Master George Gaunt was called away by his mamma; and the stranger was treated with such cruelty finally, that even Lady Steyne herself pitied her, and went up to speak to the friendless little woman.

'Lord Steyne,' said her ladyship, as her wan cheeks glowed with a blush, 'says you sing and play very beautifully,

Mrs. Crawley – I wish you would do me the kindness to sing to me.'

'I will do anything that may give pleasure to my Lord Steyne or to you,' said Rebecca, sincerely grateful, and seating herself at the piano, began to sing.

She sang religious songs of Mozart, which had been early favourites of Lady Steyne, and with such sweetness and tenderness that the lady lingering round the piano, sat down by its side, and listened until the tears rolled down her eyes. It is true that the opposition ladies at the other end of the room kept up a loud and ceaseless buzzing and talking; but the Lady Steyne did not hear those rumours. She was a child again – and had wandered back through a forty years' wilderness to her convent garden. The chapel organ had pealed the same tones, the organist, the sister whom she loved best of the community, had taught them to her in those early happy days. She was a girl once more, and the brief period of her happiness bloomed out again for an hour – she started when the jarring doors were flung open, and with a loud laugh from Lord Steyne, the men of the party entered full of gaiety.

He saw at a glance what had happened in his absence: and was grateful to his wife for once. He went and spoke to her, and called her by her Christian name, so as again to bring blushes to her pale face – 'My wife says you have been singing like an angel,' he said to Becky. Now there are angels of two kinds, and both sorts, it is said, are charming in their way.

Whatever the previous portion of the evening had been, the rest of that night was a great triumph for Becky. She sang her very best, and it was so good that every one of the men came and crowded round the piano. The women, her enemies, were left quite alone. And Mr. Paul Jefferson Jones thought he had made a conquest of Lady Gaunt by going up to her ladyship, and praising her delightful friend's first-rate singing.

CHAPTER L

CONTAINS A VULGAR INCIDENT

THE Muse, whoever she be, who presides over this Comic History, must now descend from the genteel heights in which she has been soaring, and have the goodness to drop down upon the lowly roof of John Sedley at Brompton, and describe what events are taking place there. Here, too, in this humble tenement, live care, and distrust, and dismay. Mrs. Clapp in the kitchen is grumbling in secret to her husband about the rent, and urging the good fellow to rebel against his old friend and patron and his present lodger. Mrs. Sedley has ceased to visit her landlady in the lower regions now, and indeed is in a position to patronize Mrs. Clapp no longer. How can one be condescending to a lady to whom one owes a matter of forty pound, and who is perpetually throwing out hints for the money? The Irish maidservant has not altered in the least in her kind and respectful behaviour; but Mrs. Sedley fancies that she is growing insolent and ungrateful, and, as the guilty thief who fears each bush an officer, sees threatening innuendoes and hints of capture in all the girl's speeches and answers. Miss Clapp, grown quite a young woman now, is declared by the soured old lady to be an unbearable and impudent little minx. Why Amelia can be so fond of her, or have her in her room so much, or walk out with her so constantly, Mrs. Sedley cannot conceive. The bitterness of poverty has poisoned the life of the once cheerful and kindly woman. She is thankless for Amelia's constant and gentle bearing towards her; carps at her for her efforts at kindness or service; rails at her for her silly pride in her child, and her neglect of her parents. Georgy's house is not a very lively one since uncle Jos's annuity has been withdrawn, and the little family are almost upon famine diet.

Amelia thinks, and thinks, and racks her brain, to find some means of increasing the small pittance upon which the household is starving. Can she give lessons in anything? paint card-racks? do fine work? She finds that women are working hard, and better than she can, for twopence a day. She buys a couple of begilt Bristol boards at the fancy stationer's, and paints her very best upon them – a shepherd with a red waistcoat on one, and a pink face smiling in the midst of a pencil landscape – a shepherdess on the other, crossing a little bridge, with a little dog, nicely shaded. The man of the Fancy Repository and Brompton Emporium of Fine Arts (of whom she bought the screens, vainly hoping that he would re-purchase them when ornamented by her hand) can hardly hide the sneer with which he examines these feeble works of art. He looks askance at the lady who waits in the shop, and ties up the cards again in their envelope of whity-brown paper, and hands them to the poor widow and Miss Clapp, who had never seen such beautiful things in her life, and had been quite confident that the man must give at least two guineas for the screens. They try at other shops in the interior of London, with faint sickening hopes. 'Don't want 'em,' says one. 'Be off,' says another, fiercely. Three and sixpence have been spent in vain – the screens retire to Miss Clapp's bedroom, who persists in thinking them lovely.

She writes out a little card in her neatest hand, and after long thought and labour of composition; in which the public is informed that 'A Lady who has some time at her disposal, wishes to undertake the education of some little girls, whom she would instruct in English, in French, in Geography, in History, and in Music – address A. O., at Mr. Brown's'; and she confides the card to the gentleman of the Fine Art Repository, who consents to allow it to lie upon the counter, where it grows dingy and flyblown. Amelia passes the door wistfully many a time, in hopes that Mr. Brown will have some news to give her; but he never beckons her in. When she goes to make little purchases, there is no news for her. Poor simple lady, tender and weak – how are you to battle with the struggling, violent world?

She grows daily more careworn and sad: fixing upon her child alarmed eyes, whereof the little boy cannot interpret the expression. She starts up of a night and peeps into his room stealthily, to see that he is sleeping and not stolen away. She sleeps but little now. A constant thought and terror is haunting her. How she weeps and prays in the long silent nights – how she tries to hide from herself the thought which will return to her, that she ought to part with the boy, – that she is the only barrier between him and prosperity. She can't, she can't! Not now, at least. Some other day. Oh! it is too hard to think of and to bear.

A thought comes over her which makes her blush and turn from herself, – her parents might keep the annuity – the curate would marry her and give a home to her and the boy. But George's picture and dearest memory are there to rebuke her. Shame and love say no to the sacrifice. She shrinks from it as from something unholy; and such thoughts never found a resting-place in that pure and gentle bosom.

The combat, which we describe in a sentence or two, lasted for many weeks in poor Amelia's heart: during which, she had no confidante: indeed, she could have none: as she would not allow to herself the possibility of yielding: though she was giving way daily before the enemy with whom she had to battle. One truth after another was marshalling itself silently against her, and keeping its ground. Poverty and misery for all, want and degradation for her parents, injustice to the boy – one by one the outworks of the little citadel were taken, in which the poor soul passionately guarded her only love and treasure.

At the beginning of the struggle, she had written off a letter of tender supplication to her brother at Calcutta, imploring him not to withdraw the support which he had granted to their parents, and painting in terms of artless pathos their lonely and hapless condition. She did not know the truth of the matter. The payment of Jos's annuity was still regular: but it was a money-lender in the City who was receiving it: old Sedley had sold it for a sum of money wherewith to prosecute his bootless schemes. Emmy was calculating eagerly the time that would elapse before the letter would arrive and be answered. She had written down the date in her pocket-book of the day when she dispatched it. To her son's guardian, the good major at Madras, she had not communicated any of her griefs and perplexities. She had not written to him since she wrote to congratulate him on his approaching marriage. She thought with sickening despondency, that that friend, – the only one, the one who had felt such a regard for her, – was fallen away.

One day, when things had come to a very bad pass – when the creditors were pressing, the mother in hysteric grief, the father in more than usual gloom, the inmates of the family avoiding each other, each secretly oppressed with his private unhappiness and notion of wrong – the father and daughter happened to be left alone together; and Amelia thought to comfort her father, by telling him what she had done. She had written to Joseph – an answer must come in three or four months. He was always generous, though careless. He could not refuse, when he knew how straitened the circumstances of his parents.

Then the poor old gentleman revealed the whole truth to her – that his son was still paying the annuity, which his own imprudence had flung away. He had not dared to tell it sooner. He thought Amelia's ghastly and terrified look, when, with a trembling, miserable voice he made the confession, conveyed reproaches to him for his concealment.

'Ah!' said he, with quivering lips and turning away, 'you despise your old father now.'

'Oh, papa! it is not that,' Amelia cried out, falling on his neck, and kissing him many times. 'You are always good and kind. You did it for the best. It is not for the money – it is – O my God! my God! have mercy upon me, and give me strength to bear this trial;' and she kissed him again wildly, and went away.

Still the father did not know what that explanation meant, and the burst of anguish with which the poor girl left him. It was that she was conquered. The sentence was passed. The child must go from her – to others – to forget her. Her heart and her treasure – her joy, hope, love, worship – her God, almost! She must give him up; and then – and then she would go to George; and they would watch over the child, and wait for him until he came to them in heaven.

She put on her bonnet, scarcely knowing what she did, and went out to walk in the lanes by which George used to come back from school, and where she was in the habit of going on his return to meet the boy. It was May, a half-holiday. The leaves were all coming out, the weather was brilliant: the boy came running to her, flushed with health, singing, his bundle of school-books hanging by a thong. There he was. Both her arms were round him. No, it was impossible. They could not be going to part. 'What is the matter, mother?' said he; 'you look very pale.'

'Nothing, my child,' she said, and stooped down and kissed him.

That night Amelia made the boy read the story of Samuel to her, and how Hannah, his mother, having weaned him, brought him to Eli the High Priest to minister before the Lord. And he read the song of gratitude which Hannah sang: and which says, Who it is who maketh poor and maketh rich, and bringeth low and exalteth – how the poor shall be raised up out of the dust, and how, in his own might, no man shall be strong. Then he read how Samuel's mother made him a little coat, and brought it to him from year to year when she came up to offer the yearly sacrifice. And then, in her sweet simple way, George's mother made commentaries to the boy upon this affecting story. How Hannah, though she loved her son so much, yet gave him up because of her vow. And how she must always have thought of him as she sat at home, far away, making the little coat: and Samuel, she was sure, never forgot his mother: and how happy she must have been as the time came (and the years pass away very quick) when she should see her boy, and how good and wise he had grown. This little sermon she spoke with a gentle solemn voice, and dry eyes, until she came to the account of their meeting – then the discourse broke off suddenly, the tender heart overflowed, and taking the boy to her breast, she rocked him in her arms, and wept silently over him in a sainted agony of tears.

Her mind being made up, the widow began to take such measures as seemed right to her for advancing the end which she proposed. One day, Miss Osborne, in Russell Square (Amelia had not written the name or number of the house for ten years – her youth, her early story came back to her as she wrote the superscription) – one day Miss Osborne got a letter from Amelia, which made her blush very much and look towards her father, sitting glooming in his place at the other end of the table.

In simple terms, Amelia told her the reasons which had induced her to change her mind respecting her boy. Her father had met with fresh misfortunes which had entirely ruined him. Her own pittance was so small that it would barely enable her to support her parents, and would not suffice to give George the advantages which were his due. Great as her sufferings would be at parting with him, she would, by God's help, endure them for the boy's sake. She knew that those to whom he was going, would do all in their power to make him happy. She described his disposition, such as she fancied it; quick and impatient of control or harshness; easily to be moved by love and kindness. In a postscript, she stipulated that she should have a written agreement, that she should see the child as often as she wished, – she could not part with him under any other terms.

'What? Mrs. Pride has come down, has she?' old Osborne said, when with a tremulous eager voice Miss Osborne read him the letter – 'Reg'lar starved out, hey? ha, ha! I knew she would.' He tried to keep his dignity, and to read his paper as usual, – but he could not follow it. He chuckled and swore to himself behind the sheet.

At last he flung it down: and scowling at his daughter, as his wont was, went out of the room into his study adjoining, from whence he presently returned with a key. He flung it to Miss Osborne.

'Get the room over mine – his room that was – ready,' he said. 'Yes, sir,' his daughter replied in a tremble. It was George's room. It had not been opened for more than ten years. Some of his clothes, papers, handkerchiefs, whips and caps, fishing-rods and sporting gear, were still there. An Army List of 1814, with his name written on the cover; a little dictionary he was wont to use in writing; and the Bible his mother had given him, were on the mantelpiece; with a pair of spurs, and a dried inkstand covered with the dust of ten years. Ah, since that ink was wet, what days and people had passed away! The writing-book still on the table, was blotted with his hand.

Miss Osborne was much affected when she first entered this room with the servants under her. She sank quite pale on the little bed. 'This is blessed news, mam – indeed, mam,' the housekeeper said; 'and the good old times is returning, mam. The dear little feller, to be sure, mam; how happy he will be! But some folks in May Fair, mam, will owe him a grudge, mam;' and she clicked back the bolt which held the window-sash, and let the air into the chamber.

'You had better send that woman some money,' Mr. Osborne said, before he went out. 'She shan't want for nothing. Send her a hundred pound.'

'And I'll go and see her to-morrow?' Miss Osborne asked.

'That's your look out. She don't come in here, mind. No, by —, not for all the money in London. But she mustn't want now. So look out, and get things right.' With which brief speeches Mr. Osborne took leave of his daughter, and went on his accustomed way into the City.

'Here, papa, is some money,' Amelia said that night, kissing the old man, her father, and putting a bill for a hundred pounds into his hands. 'And – and, mamma, don't be harsh with Georgy. He – he is not going to stop with us long.' She could say nothing more, and walked away silently to her room. Let us close it upon her prayers and her sorrow. I think we had best speak little about so much love and grief.

Miss Osborne came the next day, according to the promise contained in her note, and saw Amelia. The meeting between them was friendly. A look and a few words from Miss Osborne showed the poor widow that, with regard to this woman at least, there need be no fear lest she should take the first place in her son's affection. She was cold, sensible, not unkind. The mother had not been so well pleased, perhaps, had the rival been better-looking, younger, more affectionate, warmer-hearted. Miss Osborne, on the other hand, thought of old times and memories, and could not but be touched with the poor mother's pitiful situation. She was conquered, and laying down her arms, as it were, she humbly submitted. That day they arranged together, the preliminaries of the treaty of capitulation.

George was kept from school the next day, and saw his aunt. Amelia left them alone together, and went to her room. She was trying the separation: – as that poor gentle Lady Jane Grey felt the edge of the axe that was to come down and sever her slender life. Days were passed in parleys, visits, preparations. The widow broke the matter to Georgy with great caution; she looked to see him very much affected by the intelligence. He was rather elated than otherwise, and the poor woman turned sadly away. He bragged about the news that day to the boys at school; told them how he was going to live with his grandpapa, his father's father, not the one who comes here sometimes: and that he would be very rich, and have a carriage, and a pony, and go to a much finer school, and when he was rich he would buy Leader's pencil-case, and pay the tart-woman. The boy was the image of his father, as his fond mother thought.

Indeed I have no heart, on account of our dear Amelia's sake, to go through the story of George's last days at home.

At last the day came, the carriage drove up, the little humble packets containing tokens of love and remembrance were ready and disposed in the hall long since – George was in his new suit, for which the tailor had come previously to measure him. He had sprung up with the sun and put on the new clothes; his mother hearing him from the room close by, in which she had been lying, in speechless grief and watching. Days before she had been making preparations for the end; purchasing little stores for the boy's use; marking his books and linen; talking with him and preparing him for the change – fondly fancying that he needed preparation.

So that he had change, what cared he? He was longing for it. By a thousand eager declarations as to what he would do, when he went to live with his grandfather, he had shown the poor widow how little the idea of parting had cast him down. 'He would come and see his mamma often on the pony,' he said: 'he would come and fetch her in the carriage; they would drive in the Park, and she should have everything she wanted.' The poor mother was fain to content herself with these selfish demonstrations of attachment, and tried to convince herself how sincerely her son loved her. He must love her. All children were so: a little anxious for novelty, and – no, not selfish, but self-willed. Her child must have his enjoyments and ambition in the world. She herself, by her own selfishness and imprudent love for him, had denied him his just rights and pleasures hitherto.

I know few things more affecting than that timorous debasement and self-humiliation of a woman. How she owns that it is she and not the man who is guilty: how she takes all the faults on her side: how she courts in a manner punishment for the wrongs which she has not committed, and persists in shielding the real culprit! It is those who injure women who get the most kindness from them – they are born timid and tyrants, and maltreat those who are humblest before them.

So poor Amelia had been getting ready in silent misery for her son's departure, and had passed many and many a long solitary hour in making preparations for the end. George stood by his mother, watching her arrangements without the least concern. Tears had fallen into his boxes; passages had been scored in his favourite books; old toys, relics, treasures had been hoarded away for him, and packed with strange neatness and care, – and of all these things the boy took no note. The child goes away smiling as the mother breaks her heart. By heavens it is pitiful, the bootless love of women for children in Vanity Fair.

A few days are passed: and the great event of Amelia's life is consummated. No angel has intervened. The child is sacrificed and offered up to fate; and the widow is quite alone.

The boy comes to see her often, to be sure. He rides on a pony with the coachman behind him, to the delight of his old grandfather, Sedley, who walks proudly down the lane by his side. She sees him, but he is not her boy any more. Why, he rides to see the boys at the little school, too, and to show off before them his new wealth and splendour. In two days he has adopted a slight imperious air and patronizing manner. He was born to command, his mother thinks, as his father was before him.

It is fine weather now. Of evenings on the days when he does not come, she takes a long walk into London – yes, as far as Russell Square, and rests on the stone by the railing of the garden opposite Mr. Osborne's house. It is so pleasant and cool. She can look up and see the drawing-room windows illuminated, and, at about nine o'clock the chamber in the upper story where Georgy sleeps. She knows – he has told her. She prays there as the light goes out, prays with a humble, humble heart, and walks home shrinking and silent. She is very tired when she comes home. Perhaps she will sleep the better for that long weary walk; and she may dream about Georgy.

One Sunday she happened to be walking in Russell Square, at some distance from Mr. Osborne's house (she could see it from a distance though) when all the bells of Sabbath were ringing, and George and his aunt came out to go to church; a little sweep asked for charity, and the footman, who carried the books, tried to drive him away; but Georgy stopped and gave him money. May God's blessing be on the boy! Emmy ran round the square, and coming up to the sweep, gave him her mite too. All the bells of Sabbath were ringing, and she followed them until she came to the Foundling Church, into which she went. There she sat in a place whence she could see the head of the boy under his father's tombstone. Many hundred fresh children's voices rose up there and sang hymns to the Father Beneficent; and little George's soul thrilled with delight at the burst of glorious psalmody. His mother could not see him for awhile, through the mist that dimmed her eyes.

CHAPTER LI

IN WHICH A CHARADE IS ACTED WHICH MAY
OR MAY NOT PUZZLE THE READER

A FTER Becky's appearance at my Lord Steyne's private and select parties, the claims of that estimable woman as regards fashion, were settled; and some of the very greatest and tallest doors in the metropolis were speedily opened to her – doors so great and tall that the beloved reader and writer hereof may hope in vain to enter at them. Dear brethren, let us tremble before those august portals. I fancy them guarded by grooms of the chamber with flaming silver forks with which they prong all those who have not the right of the entrée. They say the honest newspaper-fellow who sits in the hall and takes down the names of the great ones who are admitted to the feasts, dies after a little time. He can't survive the glare of fashion long. It scorches him up, as the presence of Jupiter in full dress wasted that poor imprudent Semele – a giddy moth of a creature who ruined herself by venturing out of her natural atmosphere. Her myth ought to be taken to heart amongst the Tyburnians, the Belgravians, – her story, and perhaps Becky's too. Ah, ladies! – ask the Reverend Mr. Thurifer if Belgravia is not a sounding brass, and Tyburnia a tinkling cymbal. These are vanities. Even these will pass away. And some day or other (but it will be after our time, thank goodness), Hyde Park Gardens will be no better known than the celebrated horticultural outskirts of Babylon; and Belgrave Square will be as desolate as Baker Street, or Tadmor in the wilderness.

Ladies, are you aware that the Great Pitt lived in Baker Street? What would not your grandmothers have given to be asked to Lady Hester's parties in that now decayed mansion? I have dined in it – *moi qui vous parle*. I peopled the chamber with ghosts of the mighty dead. As we sat soberly drinking claret there with men of to-day, the spirits of the departed came in and took their places round the darksome board. The pilot who weathered the storm tossed off great bumpers of spiritual port: the shade of Dundas did not leave the ghost of a heeltap. – Addington sat bowing and smirking in a ghastly manner, and would not be behindhand when the noiseless bottle went round; Scott, from under bushy eyebrows winked at the apparition of a beeswing; Wilberforce's eyes went up to the ceiling, so that he did not seem to know how his glass went up full to his mouth and came down empty; – up to the ceiling which was above us only yesterday, and which the great of the last days have all looked at. They let the house as a furnished lodging now. Yes, Lady Hester once lived in Baker Street, and lies asleep in the wilderness. Eöthen saw her there – not in Baker Street: but in the other solitude.

It is all vanity to be sure: but who will not own to liking a little of it? I should like to know what well-constituted mind, merely because it is transitory, dislikes roast-beef? That is a vanity; but may every man who reads this, have a wholesome portion of it through life, I beg: aye, though my readers were five hundred thousand. Sit down, gentlemen, and fall to, with a good hearty appetite; the fat, the lean, the gravy, the horse-radish as you like it – don't spare it. Another glass of wine, Jones, my boy – a little bit of the Sunday side. Yes, let us eat our fill of the vain thing, and be thankful therefor. And let us make the best of Becky's aristocratic pleasures likewise – for these too, like all other mortal delights, were but transitory.

The upshot of her visit to Lord Steyne was, that His Highness the Prince of Peterwaradin took occasion to renew his acquaintance with Colonel Crawley, when they met on the next day at the club, and to compliment Mrs. Crawley in the ring of Hyde Park with a profound salute of the hat. She and her husband were invited immediately to one of the prince's small parties at Levant House, then occupied by his highness during the temporary absence from England of its noble proprietor. She sang after dinner to a very little *comité*. The Marquis of Steyne was present, paternally superintending the progress of his pupil.

At Levant House Becky met one of the finest gentlemen and greatest ministers that Europe has produced – the Duc de la Jabotière, then ambassador from the Most Christian King, and subsequently minister to that monarch. I declare I swell with pride as these august names are transcribed by my pen; and I think in what brilliant company my dear Becky is moving. She became a constant guest at the French embassy, where no party was considered to be complete without the presence of the charming Madame Ravdonn Cravley.

Messieurs de Truffigny (of the Périgord family) and Champignac, both attachés of the embassy, were straightway smitten by the charms of the fair colonel's wife: and both declared, according to the wont of their nation (for who ever yet met a Frenchman, come out of England, that has not left half a dozen families miserable, and brought away as many hearts in his pocket-book?) both, I say, declared that they were *au mieux* with the charming Madame Ravdonn.

But I doubt the correctness of the assertion. Champignac was very fond of écarté, and made many *parties* with the colonel of evenings, while Becky was singing to Lord Steyne in the other room; and as for Truffigny, it is a well-known fact that he dared not go to the Travellers', where he owed money to the waiters, and if he had not had the embassy as a dining-place, the worthy young gentleman must have starved. I doubt, I say, that Becky would have selected either of these young men as a person on whom she would bestow her special regard. They ran of her messages, purchased her gloves and flowers, went in debt for opera-boxes for her, and made themselves amiable in a thousand ways. And they talked English with adorable simplicity, and to the constant amusement of Becky and my Lord Steyne. She would mimic one or other to his face, and compliment him on his advance in the English language with a gravity which never failed to tickle the marquis, her sardonic old patron. Truffigny gave Briggs a shawl by way of winning over Becky's confidante, and asked her to take charge of a letter which the simple spinster handed over in public to the person to whom it was addressed; and the composition of which amused everybody who read it greatly. Lord Steyne read it: everybody, but honest Rawdon; to whom it was not necessary to tell everything that passed in the little house in May Fair.

Here, before long, Becky received not only 'the best' foreigners (as the phrase is in our noble and admirable society slang), but some of the best English people too. I don't mean the most virtuous, or indeed the least virtuous, or the cleverest, or the stupidest, or the richest, or the best born, but 'the best' – in a word, people about whom there is no question – such as the great Lady Fitz-Willis, that Patron Saint of Almack's, the great Lady Slowbore, the great

Lady Grizzel Macbeth (she was Lady G. Glowry, daughter of Lord Grey of Glowry), and the like. When the Countess of Fitz-Willis (her ladyship is of the King-street family, see Debrett and Burke) takes up a person, he or she is safe. There is no question about them any more. Not that my Lady Fitz-Willis is any better than anybody else, being, on the contrary, a faded person, fifty-seven years of age, and neither handsome, nor wealthy, nor entertaining; but it is agreed on all sides that she is of the 'best people'. Those who go to her are of the best: and from an old grudge probably to Lady Steyne (for whose coronet her ladyship, then the youthful Georgina Frederica, daughter of the Prince of Wales's favourite, the Earl of Portansherry, had once tried), this great and famous leader of the fashion chose to acknowledge Mrs. Rawdon Crawley: made her a most marked curtsy at the assembly over which she presided: and not only encouraged her son, St. Kitts (his lordship got his place through Lord Steyne's interest), to frequent Mrs. Crawley's house, but asked her to her own mansion, and spoke to her twice in the most public and condescending manner during dinner. The important fact was known all over London that night. People who had been crying fie about Mrs. Crawley, were silent. Wenham, the wit and lawyer, Lord Steyne's righthand man, went about everywhere praising her: some who had hesitated, came forward at once and welcomed her; little Tom Toady, who had warned Southdown about visiting such an abandoned woman, now besought to be introduced to her. In a word, she was admitted to be among the 'best' people. Ah my beloved readers and brethren, do not envy poor Becky prematurely – glory like this is said to be fugitive. It is currently reported that even in the very inmost circles, they are no happier than the poor wanderers outside the zone; and Becky, who penetrated into the very centre of fashion, and saw the great George IV face to face, has owned since that there too was Vanity.

We must be brief in descanting upon this part of her career. As I cannot describe the mysteries of freemasonry, although I have a shrewd idea that it is a humbug: so an uninitiated man cannot take upon himself to portray the great world accurately, and had best keep his opinions to himself whatever they are.

Becky has often spoken in subsequent years of this season

of her life when she moved among the very greatest circles
of the London fashion. Her success excited, elated, and then
bored her. At first no occupation was more pleasant than to
invent and procure (the latter a work of no small trouble
and ingenuity, by the way, in a person of Mrs. Rawdon
Crawley's very narrow means) – to procure, we say, the
prettiest new dresses and ornaments; to drive to fine dinner
parties, where she was welcomed by great people; and from
the fine dinner parties to fine assemblies, whither the same
people came with whom she had been dining, whom she had
met the night before, and would see on the morrow – the
young men faultlessly appointed, handsomely cravatted, with
the neatest glossy boots and white gloves – the elders portly,
brass-buttoned, noble-looking, polite, and prosy – the young
ladies blonde, timid, and in pink – the mothers grand,
beautiful, sumptuous, solemn, and in diamonds. They talked
in English, not in bad French, as they do in the novels.
They talked about each others' houses, and characters, and
families: just as the Joneses do about the Smiths. Becky's
former acquaintances hated and envied her: the poor woman
herself was yawning in spirit. 'I wish I were out of it,' she
said to herself. 'I would rather be a parson's wife, and teach
a Sunday school than this; or a sergeant's lady and ride in
the regimental wagon; or, oh, how much gayer it would be
to wear spangles and trousers, and dance before a booth at
a fair.'

'You would do it very well,' said Lord Steyne, laughing.
She used to tell the great man her ennuis and perplexities
in her artless way – they amused him.

'Rawdon would make a very good Écuyer – Master of the
Ceremonies – what do you call him – the man in the large
boots and the uniform, who goes round the ring cracking
the whip? He is large, heavy, and of a military figure. I
recollect,' Becky continued, pensively, 'my father took me
to see a show at Brookgreen Fair when I was a child; and
when we came home I made myself a pair of stilts, and
danced in the studio to the wonder of all the pupils.'

'I should have liked to see it,' said Lord Steyne.

'I should like to do it now,' Becky continued. 'How Lady
Blinkey would open her eyes, and Lady Grizzel Macbeth
would stare! Hush! silence! there is Pasta beginning to sing.'
Becky always made a point of being conspicuously polite to

the professional ladies and gentlemen who attended at these
aristocratic parties – of following them into the corners
where they sat in silence, and shaking hands with them, and
smiling in the view of all persons. She was an artist herself,
as she said very truly: there was a frankness and humility
in the manner in which she acknowledged her origin, which
provoked, or disarmed, or amused lookers-on, as the case
might be. 'How cool that woman is,' said one; 'what airs of
independence she assumes, where she ought to sit still and
be thankful if anybody speaks to her.' 'What an honest and
good natured soul she is,' said another. 'What an artful little
minx,' said a third. They were all right very likely; but Becky
went her own way, and so fascinated the professional personages, that they would leave off their sore throats in order
to sing at her parties, and give her lessons for nothing.

Yes, she gave parties in the little house in Curzon Street.
Many scores of carriages, with blazing lamps, blocked up
the street, to the disgust of No. 100, who could not rest for
the thunder of the knocking, and of 102, who could not
sleep for envy. The gigantic footmen who accompanied the
vehicles were too big to be contained in Becky's little hall,
and were billeted off in the neighbouring public-houses,
whence, when they were wanted, call-boys summoned them
from their beer. Scores of the great dandies of London
squeezed and trod on each other on the little stairs, laughing
to find themselves there; and many spotless and severe ladies
of *ton* were seated in the little drawing-room, listening to
the professional singers, who were singing according to their
wont, and as if they wished to blow the windows down. And
the day after, there appeared among the fashionable *réunions*
in the *Morning Post*, a paragraph to the following effect:–

'Yesterday, Colonel and Mrs. Crawley entertained a select
party at dinner, at their house in May Fair. Their Excellencies the Prince and Princess of Peterwaradin. H. E. Papoosh
Pasha, the Turkish Ambassador (attended by Kibob Bey,
dragoman of the mission), the Marquess of Steyne, Earl of
Southdown, Mr. Pitt and Lady Jane Crawley, Mr. Wagg,
&c. After dinner, Mrs. Crawley had an assembly, which was
attended by the Duchess (Dowager) of Stilton, Duc de la
Gruyère, Marchioness of Cheshire, Marchese Alessandro
Strachino, Comte de Brie, Baron Schapzuger, Chevalier
Tosti, Countess of Slingstone, and Lady F. Macadam,

Major-General and Lady G. Macbeth, and (2) Miss Mac-
beths, Viscount Paddington, Sir Horace Fogey, Hon. Sands
Bedwin, Bobbachy Bahawder,' and an &c. which the reader
may fill at his pleasure through a dozen close lines of small
type.

And in her commerce with the great our dear friend
showed the same frankness which distinguished her transactions with the lowly in station. On one occasion, when out
at a very fine house, Rebecca was (perhaps rather ostenta-
tiously) holding a conversation in the French language with
a celebrated tenor singer of that nation, while the Lady
Grizzel Macbeth looked over her shoulder scowling at the
pair.

'How very well you speak French,' Lady Grizzel said,
who herself spoke the tongue in an Edinburgh accent most
remarkable to hear.

'I ought to know it,' Becky modestly said, casting down
her eyes. 'I taught it in a school, and my mother was a
Frenchwoman.'

Lady Grizzel was won by her humility, and was mollified
towards the little woman. She deplored the fatal levelling
tendencies of the age, which admitted persons of all classes
into the society of their superiors; but her ladyship owned,
that this one at least was well-behaved, and never forgot her
place in life. She was a very good woman: good to the poor:
stupid, blameless, unsuspicious. – It is not her ladyship's
fault that she fancies herself better than you and me. The
skirts of her ancestors' garments have been kissed for centuries: it is a thousand years, they say, since the tartans of
the head of the family were embraced by the defunct Dun-
can's lords and councillors, when the great ancestor of the
house became King of Scotland.

Lady Steyne, after the music scene, succumbed before
Becky, and perhaps was not disinclined to her. The younger
ladies of the House of Gaunt were also compelled into
submission. Once or twice they set people at her, but they
failed. The brilliant Lady Stunnington tried a passage of
arms with her, but was routed with great slaughter by the
intrepid little Becky. When attacked sometimes, Becky had
a knack of adopting a demure *ingénue* air, under which she
was most dangerous. She said the wickedest things with the
most simple unaffected air when in this mood, and would

take care artlessly to apologize for her blunders, so that all
the world should know that she had made them.

Mr. Wagg, the celebrated wit, and a led captain and
trencherman of my Lord Steyne, was caused by the ladies
to charge her; and the worthy fellow, leering at his patron-
esses, and giving them a wink, as much as to say, 'Now look
out for sport,' one evening began an assault upon Becky,
who was unsuspiciously eating her dinner. The little woman,
attacked on a sudden, but never without arms, lighted up
in an instant, parried and riposted with a home-thrust, which
made Wagg's face tingle with shame; then she returned to
her soup with the most perfect calm and a quiet smile on
her face. Wagg's great patron, who gave him dinners and
lent him a little money sometimes, and whose election,
newspaper, and other jobs Wagg did, gave the luckless fellow
such a savage glance with the eyes as almost made him sink
under the table, and burst into tears. He looked piteously
at my lord, who never spoke to him during dinner, and at
the ladies, who disowned him. At last Becky herself took
compassion upon him, and tried to engage him in talk. He
was not asked to dinner again for six weeks; and Fiche, my
lord's confidential man, to whom Wagg naturally paid a good
deal of court, was instructed to tell him that if he ever dared
to say a rude thing to Mrs. Crawley again, or make her the
butt of his stupid jokes, Milor would put every one of his
notes of hand into his lawyer's hands, and sell him up
without mercy. Wagg wept before Fiche, and implored his
dear friend to intercede for him. He wrote a poem in favour
of Mrs. R. C., which appeared in the very next number of the
Harumscarum Magazine, which he conducted. He implored
her goodwill at parties where he met her. He cringed and
coaxed Rawdon at the club. He was allowed to come back
to Gaunt House after a while. Becky was always good to
him, always amused, never angry.

His lordship's vizier and chief confidential servant (with
a seat in Parliament and at the dinner-table), Mr. Wenham,
was much more prudent in his behaviour and opinions than
Mr. Wagg. However much he might be disposed to hate all
parvenues (Mr. Wenham himself was a stanch old True Blue
Tory, and his father a small coal-merchant in the North of
England), this aide de camp of the marquis never showed
any sort of hostility to the new favourite; but pursued her

with stealthy kindnesses, and a sly and deferential politeness, which somehow made Becky more uneasy than other people's overt hostilities.

How the Crawleys got the money which was spent upon the entertainments with which they treated the polite world, was a mystery which gave rise to some conversation at the time, and probably added zest to these little festivities. Some persons averred that Sir Pitt Crawley gave his brother a handsome allowance: if he did, Becky's power over the baronet must have been extraordinary indeed, and his character greatly changed in his advanced age. Other parties hinted that it was Becky's habit to levy contributions on all her husband's friends: going to this one in tears with an account that there was an execution in the house; falling on her knees to that one, and declaring that the whole family must go to gaol or commit suicide unless such and such a bill could be paid. Lord Southdown, it was said, had been induced to give many hundreds through these pathetic representations. Young Feltham, of the –th Dragoons (and son of the firm of Tiler and Feltham, hatters and army accoutrement-makers), and whom the Crawleys introduced into fashionable life, was also cited as one of Becky's victims in the pecuniary way. People declared that she got money from various simply disposed persons, under pretence of getting them confidential appointments under Government. Who knows what stories were or were not told of our dear and innocent friend? Certain it is, that if she had had all the money which she was said to have begged or borrowed or stolen, she might have capitalized and been honest for life, whereas, – but this is advancing matters.

The truth is that by economy and good management – by a sparing use of ready money and by paying scarcely anybody, – people can manage, for a time at least, to make a great show with very little means: and it is our belief that Becky's much-talked-of parties, which were not, after all was said, very numerous, cost this lady very little more than the wax candles which lighted the walls. Stillbrook and Queen's Crawley supplied her with game and fruit in abundance. Lord Steyne's cellars were at her disposal, and that excellent nobleman's famous cooks presided over her little kitchen, or sent by my lord's order the rarest delicacies from their own. I protest it is quite shameful in the world to abuse a simple creature, as people of her time abused Becky, and I warn the public against believing one-tenth of the stories against her. If every person is to be banished from society who runs into debt and cannot pay − if we are to be peering into everybody's private life, speculating upon their income, and cutting them if we don't approve of their expenditure − why, what a howling wilderness and intolerable dwelling Vanity Fair would be! Every man's hand would be against his neighbour in this case, my dear sir, and the benefits of civilization would be done away with. We should be quarrelling, abusing, avoiding one another. Our houses would become caverns: and we should go in rags because we cared for nobody. Rents would go down. Parties wouldn't be given any more. All the tradesmen of the town would be bankrupt. Wine, wax-lights, comestibles, rouge, crinoline petticoats, diamonds, wigs, Louis Quatorze gimcracks, and old china, park hacks and splendid high-stepping carriage horses − all the delights of life, I say, − would go to the deuce, if people did but act upon their silly principles, and avoid those whom they dislike and abuse. Whereas, by a little charity and mutual forbearance, things are made to go on pleasantly enough: we may abuse a man as much as we like, and call him the greatest rascal unhung − but do we wish to hang him therefore? No. We shake hands when we meet. If his cook is good we forgive him, and go and dine with him; and we expect he will do the same by us. Thus trade flourishes − civilization advances: peace is kept; new dresses are wanted for new assemblies every week; and the last year's vintage of Lafite will remunerate the honest proprietor who reared it.

At the time whereof we are writing, though the Great George was on the throne and ladies wore *gigots* and large combs like tortoise-shell shovels in their hair, instead of the simple sleeves and lovely wreaths which are actually in fashion, the manners of the very polite world were not, I take it, essentially different from those of the present day: and their amusements pretty similar. To us, from outside gazing over the policemen's shoulders at the bewildering beauties as they pass into Court or ball, they may seem beings of unearthly splendour, and in the enjoyment of an exquisite happiness by us unattainable. It is to console some of these dissatisfied beings, that we are narrating our dear

Becky's struggles, and triumphs, and disappointments, of all of which, indeed, as is the case with all persons of merit, she had her share.

At this time the amiable amusement of acting charades had come among us from France: and was considerably in vogue in this country, enabling the many ladies amongst us who had beauty to display their charms, and the fewer number who had cleverness, to exhibit their wit. My Lord Steyne was incited by Becky, who perhaps believed herself endowed with both the above qualifications, to give an entertainment at Gaunt House, which should include some of these little dramas – and we must take leave to introduce the reader to this brilliant *réunion*, and with a melancholy welcome too, for it will be among the very last of the fashionable entertainments to which it will be our fortune to conduct him.

A portion of that splendid room, the picture-gallery of Gaunt House, was arranged as the charade theatre. It had been so used when George III was king; and a picture of the Marquis of Gaunt is still extant, with his hair in powder and a pink ribbon, in a Roman shape, as it was called, enacting the part of Cato in Mr. Addison's tragedy of that name, performed before Their Royal Highnesses the Prince of Wales, the Bishop of Osnaburgh, and Prince William Henry, then children like the actor. One or two of the old properties were drawn out of the garrets, where they had lain ever since, and furbished up anew for the present festivities.

Young Bedwin Sands, then an elegant dandy and Eastern traveller, was manager of the revels. An Eastern traveller was somebody in those days, and the adventurous Bedwin, who had published his quarto, and passed some months under the tents in the desert, was a personage of no small importance. – In his volume there were several pictures of Sands in various Oriental costumes; and he travelled about with a black attendant of most unprepossessing appearance, just like another Brian de Bois Guilbert. Bedwin, his costumes, and black man, were hailed at Gaunt House as very valuable acquisitions.

He led off the first charade. A Turkish officer with an immense plume of feathers (the janissaries were supposed to be still in existence, and the tarboosh had not as yet displaced the ancient and majestic head-dress of the true believers) was seen couched on a divan, and making believe to puff at a *narghile*, in which, however, for the sake of the ladies, only a fragrant pastille was allowed to smoke. The Turkish dignitary yawns and expresses signs of weariness and idleness. He claps his hands and Mesrour the Nubian appears, with bare arms, bangles, and yataghans, every Eastern ornament – gaunt, tall, and hideous. He makes a salaam before my lord the Aga.

A thrill of terror and delight runs through the assembly. The ladies whisper to one another. The black slave was given to Bedwin Sands by an Egyptian pasha in exchange for three dozen of maraschino. He has sewn up ever so many *odalisques* in sacks and tilted them into the Nile.

'Bid the slave-merchant enter,' says the Turkish voluptuary, with a wave of his hand. Mesrour conducts the slave-merchant into my lord's presence: he brings a veiled female with him. He removes her veil. A thrill of applause bursts through the house. It is Mrs. Winkworth (she was a Miss Absolom), with the beautiful eyes and hair. She is in a gorgeous Oriental costume; the black braided locks are twined with innumerable jewels; her dress is covered over with gold piastres. The odious Mahometan expresses himself charmed by her beauty. She falls down on her knees, and entreats him to restore her to the mountains where she was born, and where her Circassian lover is still deploring the absence of his Zuleikah. No entreaties will move the obdurate Hassan. He laughs at the notion of the Circassian bridegroom. Zuleikah covers her face with her hands, and drops down in an attitude of the most beautiful despair. There seems to be no hope for her, when – when the Kislar Aga appears.

The Kislar Aga brings a letter from the Sultan. Hassan receives and places on his head the dread firman. A ghastly terror seizes him, while on the negro's face (it is Mesrour again in another costume) appears a ghastly joy. 'Mercy! mercy!' cries the pasha; while the Kislar Aga, grinning horribly, pulls out – *a bowstring*.

The curtain draws just as he is going to use that awful weapon. Hassan from within bawls out, 'First two syllables' – and Mrs. Rawdon Crawley, who is going to act in the charade, comes forward and compliments Mrs. Winkworth on the admirable taste and beauty of her costume.

The second part of the charade takes place. It is still an Eastern scene. Hassan, in another dress, is in an attitude by Zuleikah, who is perfectly reconciled to him. The Kislar Aga has become a peaceful black slave. It is sunrise on the desert, and the Turks turn their heads eastward and bow to the sand. As there are no dromedaries at hand, the band facetiously plays 'The Camels are coming'. An enormous Egyptian head figures in the scene. It is a musical one, – and, to the surprise of the Oriental travellers, sings a comic song, composed by Mr. Wagg. The Eastern voyagers go off dancing, like Papageno and the Moorish king, in the *Magic Flute*. 'Last two syllables' roars the head.

The last act opens. It is a Grecian tent this time. A tall and stalwart man reposes on a couch there. Above him hang his helmet and shield. There is no need for them now. Ilium is down. Iphigenia is slain. Cassandra is a prisoner in his outer halls. The king of men (it is Colonel Crawley, who, indeed, has no notion about the sack of Ilium or the conquest of Cassandra), the *anax andrôn*, is asleep in his chamber at Argos. A lamp casts the broad shadow of the sleeping warrior flickering on the wall – the sword and shield of Troy glitter in its light. The band plays the awful music of *Don Juan*, before the statue enters.

Aegisthus steals in pale and on tiptoe. What is that ghastly face looking out balefully after him from behind the arras? He raises his dagger to strike the sleeper, who turns in his bed, and opens his broad chest as if for the blow. He cannot strike the noble slumbering chieftain. Clytemnestra glides swiftly into the room like an apparition – her arms are bare and white, – her tawny hair floats down her shoulders, – her face is deadly pale, – and her eyes are lighted up with a smile so ghastly, that people quake as they look at her.

A tremor ran through the room. 'Good God!' somebody said, 'it's Mrs. Rawdon Crawley.'

Scornfully she snatches the dagger out of Aegisthus's hand, and advances to the bed. You see it shining over her head in the glimmer of the lamp, and – and the lamp goes out, with a groan, and all is dark.

The darkness and the scene frightened people. Rebecca performed the part so well, and with such ghastly truth, that the spectators were all dumb, until, with a burst, all the lamps of the hall blazed out again, when everybody began to shout applause. 'Brava! brava!' old Steyne's strident voice was heard roaring over all the rest. 'By —, she'd do it too,' he said between his teeth. The performers were called by the whole house, which sounded with cries of 'Manager! Clytemnestra!' AGAMEMNON could not be got to show in his classical tunic, but stood in the background with Aegisthus and others of the performers of the little play. Mr. Bedwin Sands led on Zuleikah and Clytemnestra. A great personage insisted upon being presented to the charming Clytemnestra. 'Heigh ha? Run him through the body. Marry somebody else, hey?' was the apposite remark made by His Royal Highness.

'Mrs. Rawdon Crawley was quite killing in the part,' said Lord Steyne. Becky laughed; gay, and saucy looking, and swept the prettiest little curtsy ever seen.

Servants brought in salvers covered with numerous cool dainties, and the performers disappeared, to get ready for the second charade-tableau.

The three syllables of this charade were to be depicted in pantomime, and the performance took place in the following wise:—

First syllable. Colonel Rawdon Crawley, C.B., with a slouched hat and a staff, a great coat, and a lantern borrowed from the stables, passed across the stage bawling out, as if warning the inhabitants of the hour. In the lower window are seen two bagmen playing apparently at the game of cribbage, over which they yawn much. To them enters one looking like Boots (the Honourable G. Ringwood), which character the young gentleman performed to perfection, and divests them of their lowering covering; and presently Chambermaid (the Right Honourable Lord Southdown) with two candlesticks, and a warming-pan. She ascends to the upper apartment, and warms the bed. She uses the warming-pan as a weapon wherewith she wards off the attention of the bagmen. She exits. They put on their nightcaps, and pull down the blinds. Boots comes out and closes the shutters of the ground-floor chamber. You hear him bolting and chaining the door within. All the lights go out. The music plays 'Dormez, dormez, chers Amours.' A voice from behind the curtain says, 'First syllable.'

Second syllable. The lamps are lighted up all of a sudden.

The music plays the old air from *John of Paris*, '*Ah, quel plaisir d'être en voyage!*' It is the same scene. Between the first and second floors of the house represented, you behold a sign on which the Steyne arms are painted. All the bells are ringing all over the house. In the lower apartment you see a man with a long slip of paper presenting it to another, who shakes his fist, threatens and vows that it is monstrous. 'Ostler, bring round my gig,' cries another at the door. He chucks Chambermaid (the Right Honourable Lord Southdown) under the chin; she seems to deplore his absence, as Calypso did that of that other eminent traveller, Ulysses. Boots (the Honourable G. Ringwood) passes with a wooden box, containing silver flagons, and cries 'Pots' with such exquisite humour and naturalness, that the whole house rings with applause, and a bouquet is thrown to him. Crack, crack, crack, go the whips. Landlord, chambermaid, waiter rush to the door; but just as some distinguished guest is arriving, the curtains close, and the invisible theatrical manager cries out, 'Second syllable.'

'I think it must be "Hotel",' says Captain Grigg of the Life Guards; there is a general laugh at the captain's cleverness. He is not very far from the mark.

While the third syllable is in preparation, the band begins a nautical medley – 'All in the Downs,' 'Cease, Rude Boreas,' 'Rule, Britannia,' 'In the Bay of Biscay O' – some maritime event is about to take place. A bell is heard ringing as the curtain draws aside. 'Now, gents, for the shore!' a voice exclaims. People take leave of each other. They point anxiously as if towards the clouds, which are represented by a dark curtain, and they nod their heads in fear. Lady Squeams (the Right Honourable Lord Southdown), her lapdog, her bags, reticules, and husband sit down, and cling hold of some ropes. It is evidently a ship.

The captain (Colonel Crawley, C.B.), with a cocked hat and a telescope, comes in, holding his hat on his head, and looks out; his coat-tails fly about as if in the wind. When he leaves go of his hat to use his telescope, his hat flies off, with immense applause. It is blowing fresh. The music rises and whistles louder and louder; the mariners go across the stage staggering, as if the ship was in severe motion. The Steward (the Honourable G. Ringwood) passes reeling by, holding six basins. He puts one rapidly by Lord Squeams –

Lady Squeams giving a pinch to her dog, which begins to howl piteously, puts her pocket-handkerchief to her face, and rushes away as for the cabin. The music rises up to the wildest pitch of stormy excitement, and the third syllable is concluded.

There was a little ballet, *Le Rossignol*, in which Montessu and Noblet used to be famous in those days, and which Mr. Wagg transferred to the English stage as an opera, putting his verse, of which he was a skilful writer, to the pretty airs of the ballet. It was dressed in old French costume, and little Lord Southdown now appeared admirably attired in the disguise of an old woman hobbling about the stage with a faultless crooked stick.

Trills of melody were heard behind the scenes, and gurgling from a sweet pasteboard cottage covered with roses and trellis-work. 'Philomèle, Philomèle,' cries the old woman, and Philomèle comes out.

More applause — it is Mrs. Rawdon Crawley in powder and patches, the most *ravissante* little marquise in the world.

She comes in laughing, humming, and frisks about the stage with all the innocence of theatrical youth — she makes a curtsy. Mamma says, 'Why, child, you are always laughing and singing,' and away she goes with —

THE ROSE UPON MY BALCONY

The rose upon my balcony the morning air perfuming,
Was leafless all the winter-time and pining for the spring;
You ask me why her breath is sweet and why her cheek is blooming,
It is because the sun is out and birds begin to sing.

The nightingale, whose melody is through the greenwood ringing,
Was silent when the boughs were bare and winds were blowing keen;
And if, mamma, you ask of me the reason of his singing;
It is because the sun is out and all the leaves are green.

Thus each performs his part, mamma, the birds have found their
    voices,
The blowing rose a flush, mamma, her bonny cheek to dye;
And there's sunshine in my heart, mamma, which wakens and rejoices,
And so I sing and blush, mamma, and that's the reason why.

During the intervals of the stanzas of this ditty, the good-natured personage addressed as mamma by the singer, and

whose large whiskers appeared under her cap, seemed very
anxious to exhibit her maternal affection by embracing the
innocent creature who performed the daughter's part. Every
caress was received with loud acclamations of laughter by
the sympathizing audience. At its conclusion (while the
music was performing a symphony as if ever so many birds
were warbling) the whole house was unanimous for an
encore: and applause and bouquets without end were showered
upon the NIGHTINGALE of the evening. Lord Steyne's voice
of applause was loudest of all. Becky, the nightingale, took
the flowers which he threw to her, and pressed them to her
heart with the air of a consummate comedian. Lord Steyne
was frantic with delight. His guests' enthusiasm harmonized
with his own. Where was the beautiful black-eyed houri
whose appearance in the first charade had caused such
delight? She was twice as handsome as Becky, but the
brilliancy of the latter had quite eclipsed her. All voices were
for her. Stephens, Caradori, Ronzi de Begnis, people compared her to one or the other; and agreed with good reason,
very likely, that had she been an actress none on the stage
would have surpassed her. She had reached her culmination:
her voice rose trilling and bright over the storm of applause:
and soared as high and joyful as her triumph. There was a
ball after the dramatic entertainments, and everybody pressed
round Becky as the great point of attraction of the evening.
The royal personage declared with an oath, that she was
perfection, and engaged her again and again in conversation.
Little Becky's soul swelled with pride and delight at these
honours; she saw fortune, fame, fashion before her. Lord
Steyne was her slave; followed her everywhere, and scarcely
spoke to any one in the room beside; and paid her the
most marked compliments and attention. She still appeared
in her marquise costume, and danced a minuet with Monsieur de Truffigny, Monsieur le Duc de la Jabotière's attaché;
and the duke, who had all the traditions of the ancient court,
pronounced that Madame Crawley was worthy to have been
a pupil of Vestris, or to have figured at Versailles. Only a
feeling of dignity, the gout, and the strongest sense of duty
and personal sacrifice, prevented his excellency from dancing
with her himself; and he declared in public, that a lady who
could talk and dance like Mrs. Rawdon, was fit to be
ambassadress at any court in Europe. He was only consoled

when he heard that she was half a Frenchwoman by birth. 'None but a compatriot,' his excellency declared, 'could have performed that majestic dance in such a way.'

Then she figured in a waltz with Monsieur de Klingenspohr, the Prince of Peterwaradin's cousin and attaché. The delighted prince, having less *retenue* than his French diplomatic colleague, insisted upon taking a turn with the charming creature, and twirled round the ball-room with her, scattering the diamonds out of his boot-tassels and hussar jacket until his highness was fairly out of breath. Papoosh Pasha himself would have liked to dance with her if that amusement had been the custom of his country. The company made a circle round her, and applauded as wildly as if she had been a Noblet or a Taglioni. Everybody was in ecstasy; and Becky too, you may be sure. She passed by Lady Stunnington with a look of scorn. She patronized Lady Gaunt and her astonished and mortified sister-in-law – she *écrasé*'d all rival charmers. As for poor Mrs. Winkworth, and her long hair and great eyes, which had made such an effect at the commencement of the evening; where was she now? Nowhere in the race. She might tear her long hair and cry her great eyes out; but there was not a person to heed or to deplore the discomfiture.

The greatest triumph of all was at supper-time. She was placed at the grand exclusive table with his royal highness the exalted personage before mentioned, and the rest of the great guests. She was served on gold plate. She might have had pearls melted into her champagne if she liked – another Cleopatra; and the potentate of Peterwaradin would have given half the brilliants off his jacket for a kind glance from those dazzling eyes. Jabotière wrote home about her to his Government. The ladies at the other tables, who supped off mere silver, and marked Lord Steyne's constant attention to her, vowed it was a monstrous infatuation, a gross insult to ladies of rank. If sarcasm could have killed, Lady Stunnington would have slain her on the spot.

Rawdon Crawley was scared at these triumphs. They seemed to separate his wife farther than ever from him somehow. He thought with a feeling very like pain how immeasurably she was his superior.

When the hour of departure came, a crowd of young men followed her to her carriage, for which the people without bawled, the cry being caught up by the link-men who were stationed outside the tall gates of Gaunt House, congratulating each person who issued from the gate and hoping his lordship had enjoyed this noble party.

Mrs. Rawdon Crawley's carriage, coming up to the gate after due shouting, rattled into the illuminated courtyard, and drove up to the covered way. Rawdon put his wife into the carriage, which drove off. Mr. Wenham had proposed to him to walk home, and offered the colonel the refreshment of a cigar.

They lighted their cigars by the lamp of one of the many link-boys outside, and Rawdon walked on with his friend Wenham. Two persons separated from the crowd and followed the two gentlemen; and when they had walked down Gaunt Square a few score of paces, one of the men came up, and touching Rawdon on the shoulder, said, 'Beg your pardon, colonel, I vish to speak to you most particular.' The gentleman's acquaintance gave a loud whistle as the latter spoke, at which signal a cab came clattering up from those stationed at the gate of Gaunt House – and the aide de camp ran round and placed himself in front of Colonel Crawley.

That gallant officer at once knew what had befallen him. He was in the hands of the bailiffs. He started back, falling against the man who had first touched him.

'We're three on us – it's no use bolting,' the man behind said.

'It's you, Moss, is it?' said the colonel, who appeared to know his interlocutor. 'How much is it?'

'Only a small thing,' whispered Mr. Moss, of Cursitor Street, Chancery Lane, and assistant officer to the Sheriff of Middlesex – 'one hundred and sixty-six, six and eight-pence, at the suit of Mr. Nathan.'

'Lend me a hundred, Wenham, for God's sake,' poor Rawdon said – 'I've got seventy at home.'

'I've not got ten pounds in the world,' said poor Mr. Wenham – 'Good night, my dear fellow.'

'Good night,' said Rawdon ruefully. And Wenham walked away – and Rawdon Crawley finished his cigar as the cab drove under Temple Bar.

CHAPTER LII

IN WHICH LORD STEYNE SHOWS HIMSELF IN A
MOST AMIABLE LIGHT

W HEN Lord Steyne was benevolently disposed, he did nothing by halves, and his kindness towards the Crawley family did the greatest honour to his benevolent discrimination. His lordship extended his goodwill to little Rawdon: he pointed out to the boy's parents the necessity of sending him to a public school; that he was of an age now when emulation, the first principles of the Latin language, pugilistic exercises, and the society of his fellow boys would be of the greatest benefit to the boy. His father objected that he was not rich enough to send the child to a good public school; his mother, that Briggs was a capital mistress for him, and had brought him on (as indeed was the fact) famously in English, the Latin rudiments, and in general learning: but all these objections disappeared before the generous perseverance of the Marquis of Steyne. His lordship was one of the governors of that famous old collegiate institution called the Whitefriars. It had been a Cistercian convent in old days, when the Smithfield, which is contiguous to it, was a tournament ground. Obstinate heretics used to be brought thither convenient for burning hard by. Harry VIII, the Defender of the Faith, seized upon the monastery and its possessions, and hanged and tortured some of the monks who could not accommodate themselves to the pace of his reform. Finally, a great merchant bought the house and land adjoining, in which, and with the help of other wealthy endowments of land and money, he established a famous foundation hospital for old men and children. An extern school grew round the old almost monastic foundation, which subsists still with its middle-age costume and usages: and all Cistercians pray that it may long flourish.

Of this famous house, some of the greatest noblemen, prelates, and dignitaries in England are governors: and as the boys are very comfortably lodged, fed, and educated, and subsequently inducted to good scholarships at the University and livings in the Church, many little gentlemen are devoted to the ecclesiastical profession from their tenderest years,

and there is considerable emulation to procure nominations
for the foundations. It was originally intended for the sons
of poor and deserving clerics and laics; but many of the
noble governors of the Institution, with an enlarged and
rather capricious benevolence, selected all sorts of objects
for their bounty. To get an education for nothing, and a
future livelihood and profession assured, was so excellent a
scheme, that some of the richest people did not disdain it;
and not only great men's relations, but great men themselves,
sent their sons to profit by the chance – right reverend
prelates sent their own kinsmen or the sons of their clergy,
while, on the other hand, some great noblemen did not
disdain to patronize the children of their confidential servants, – so that a lad entering this establishment had every
variety of youthful society wherewith to mingle.

Rawdon Crawley, though the only book which he studied
was the *Racing Calendar*, and though his chief recollections
of polite learning were connected with the floggings which
he received at Eton in his early youth, had that decent and
honest reverence for classical learning which all English
gentlemen feel, and was glad to think that his son was to
have a provision for life, perhaps, and a certain opportunity
of becoming a scholar. And although his boy was his chief
solace and companion, and endeared to him by a thousand
small ties, about which he did not care to speak to his wife,
who had all along shown the utmost indifference to their
son, yet Rawdon agreed at once to part with him, and to
give up his own greatest comfort and benefit for the sake of
the welfare of the little lad. He did not know how fond he
was of the child until it became necessary to let him go
away, When he was gone, he felt more sad and downcast
than he cared to own – far sadder than the boy himself, who
was happy enough to enter a new career, and find companions of his own age. Becky burst out laughing once or twice,
when the colonel, in his clumsy, incoherent way, tried to
express his sentimental sorrows at the boy's departure. The
poor fellow felt that his dearest pleasure and closest friend
was taken from him. He looked often and wistfully at the
little vacant bed in his dressing-room, where the child used
to sleep. He missed him sadly of mornings, and tried in vain
to walk in the Park without him. He did not know how
solitary he was until little Rawdon was gone. He liked the

people who were fond of him; and would go and sit for long hours with his good-natured sister, Lady Jane, and talk to her about the virtues, and good looks, and hundred good qualities of the child.

Young Rawdon's aunt, we have said, was very fond of him, as was her little girl, who wept copiously when the time for her cousin's departure came. The elder Rawdon was thankful for the fondness of mother and daughter. The very best and honestest feelings of the man came out in these artless outpourings of paternal feeling in which he indulged in their presence, and encouraged by their sympathy. He secured not only Lady Jane's kindness, but her sincere regard, by the feelings which he manifested, and which he could not show to his own wife. The two kinswomen met as seldom as possible. Becky laughed bitterly at Jane's feelings and softness; the other's kindly and gentle nature could not but revolt at her sister's callous behaviour.

It estranged Rawdon from his wife more than he knew or acknowledged to himself. She did not care for the estrangement. Indeed, she did not miss him or anybody. She looked upon him as her errand-man and humble slave. He might be ever so depressed or sulky, and she did not mark his demeanour, or only treated it with a sneer. She was busy thinking about her position or her pleasures or her advancement in society; she ought to have held a great place in it, that is certain.

It was honest Briggs who made up the little kit for the boy which he was to take to school. Molly, the housemaid, blubbered in the passage when he went away – Molly kind and faithful in spite of a long arrear of unpaid wages. Mrs. Becky could not let her husband have the carriage to take the boy to school. Take the horses into the City! – such a thing was never heard of. Let a cab be brought. She did not offer to kiss him when he went: nor did the child propose to embrace her: but gave a kiss to old Briggs (whom, in general, he was very shy of caressing), and consoled her by pointing out that he was to come home on Saturdays, when she would have the benefit of seeing him. As the cab rolled towards the City, Becky's carriage rattled off to the Park. She was chattering and laughing with a score of young dandies by the Serpentine, as the father and son entered at the old gates of the school – where Rawdon left the child, and came away with a sadder, purer feeling in his heart than perhaps that poor battered fellow had ever known since he himself came out of the nursery.

He walked all the way home very dismally, and dined alone with Briggs. He was very kind to her, and grateful for her love and watchfulness over the boy. His conscience smote him that he had borrowed Briggs's money and aided in deceiving her. They talked about little Rawdon a long time, for Becky only came home to dress and go out to dinner – and then he went off uneasily to drink tea with Lady Jane, and tell her of what had happened, and how little Rawdon went off like a trump, and how he was to wear a gown and little knee-breeches, and how young Blackball, Jack Blackball's son, of the old regiment, had taken him in charge and promised to be kind to him.

In the course of a week, young Blackball had constituted little Rawdon his fag, shoeblack, and breakfast toaster; initiated him into the mysteries of the Latin grammar, and thrashed him three or four times; but not severely. The little chap's good-natured honest face won his way for him. He only got that degree of beating which was, no doubt, good for him; and as for blacking shoes, toasting bread, and fagging in general, were these offices not deemed to be necessary parts of every young English gentleman's education?

Our business does not lie with the second generation and Master Rawdon's life at school, otherwise the present tale might be carried to any indefinite length. The colonel went to see his son a short time afterwards, and found the lad sufficiently well and happy, grinning and laughing in his little black gown and little breeches.

His father sagaciously tipped Blackball, his master, a sovereign, and secured that young gentleman's goodwill towards his fag. As a protégé of the great Lord Steyne, the nephew of a county member, and son of a colonel and C.B., whose name appeared in some of the most fashionable parties in the *Morning Post*, perhaps the school authorities were disposed not to look unkindly on the child. He had plenty of pocket-money, which he spent in treating his comrades royally to raspberry tarts, and he was often allowed to come home on Saturdays to his father, who always made a jubilee of that day. When free, Rawdon would take him to the play, or send him thither with the footman; and on Sundays he went to church with Briggs and Lady Jane and his cousins. Rawdon marvelled over his stories about school, and fights, and fagging. Before long, he knew the names of all the masters and the principal boys as well as little Rawdon himself. He invited little Rawdon's crony from school, and made both the children sick with pastry, and oysters, and porter after the play. He tried to look knowing over the Latin grammar when little Rawdon showed him what part of that work he was 'in'. 'Stick to it, my boy,' he said to him with much gravity, 'there's nothing like a good classical education! nothing!'

Becky's contempt for her husband grew greater every day. 'Do what you like – dine where you please – go and have ginger-beer and sawdust at Astley's, or psalm-singing with Lady Jane – only don't expect *me* to busy myself with the boy. I have your interests to attend to, as you can't attend to them yourself. I should like to know where you would have been now, and in what sort of a position in society, if I had not looked after you?' Indeed, nobody wanted poor old Rawdon at the parties whither Becky used to go. She was often asked without him now. She talked about great people as if she had the fee-simple of May Fair; and when the Court went into mourning, she always wore black.

Little Rawdon being disposed of, Lord Steyne, who took such a parental interest in the affairs of this amiable poor family, thought that their expenses might be very advantageously curtailed by the departure of Miss Briggs; and that Becky was quite clever enough to take the management of her own house. It has been narrated in a former chapter, how the benevolent nobleman had given his protégée money to pay off her little debt to Miss Briggs, who however still remained behind with her friends; whence my lord came to the painful conclusion that Mrs. Crawley had made some other use of the money confided to her than that for which her generous patron had given the loan. However, Lord Steyne was not so rude as to impart his suspicions upon this head to Mrs. Becky, whose feelings might be hurt by any controversy on the money question, and who might have a thousand painful reasons for disposing otherwise of his lordship's generous loan. But he determined to satisfy himself of the real state of the case, and instituted the necessary inquiries in a most cautious and delicate manner.

In the first place he took an early opportunity of pumping Miss Briggs. That was not a difficult operation. A very little encouragement would set that worthy woman to talk volubly, and pour out all within her. And one day when Mrs. Rawdon had gone out to drive (as Mr. Fiche, his lordship's confidential servant, easily learned at the livery stables where the Crawleys kept their carriage and horses, or rather, where the livery-man kept a carriage and horses for Mr. and Mrs. Crawley) – my lord dropped in upon the Curzon Street house – asked Briggs for a cup of coffee – told her that he had good accounts of the little boy at school – and in five minutes found out from her that Mrs. Rawdon had given her nothing except a black silk gown, for which Miss Briggs was immensely grateful.

He laughed within himself at this artless story. For the truth is our dear friend Rebecca had given him a most circumstantial narration of Briggs's delight at receiving her money – eleven hundred and twenty-five pounds – and in what securities she had invested it; and what a pang Becky herself felt in being obliged to pay away such a delightful sum of money. 'Who knows,' the dear woman may have thought within herself, 'perhaps he may give me a little more?' My lord, however, made no such proposal to the little schemer – very likely thinking that he had been sufficiently generous already.

He had the curiosity, then, to ask Miss Briggs about the state of her private affairs – and she told his lordship candidly what her position was – how Miss Crawley had left her a legacy – how her relatives had had part of it – how Colonel Crawley had put out another portion, for which she had the best security and interest – and how Mr. and Mrs. Rawdon had kindly busied themselves with Sir Pitt, who was to dispose of the remainder most advantageously for her, when he had time. My lord asked how much the colonel had already invested for her, and Miss Briggs at once and truly told him that the sum was six hundred and odd pounds.

But as soon as she had told her story, the voluble Briggs repented of her frankness, and besought my lord not to tell Mr. Crawley of the confessions which she had made. 'The colonel was so kind – Mr. Crawley might be offended and pay back the money, for which she could get no such good interest anywhere else.' Lord Steyne, laughing, promised he never would divulge their conversation, and when he and Miss Briggs parted he laughed still more.

'What an accomplished little devil it is!' thought he. 'What a splendid actress and manager! She had almost got a second supply out of me the other day, with her coaxing ways. She beats all the women I have ever seen in the course of all my well-spent life. They are babies compared to her. I am a greenhorn myself, and a fool in her hands – an old fool. She is unsurpassable in lies.' His lordship's admiration for Becky rose immeasurably at this proof of her cleverness. Getting the money was nothing – but getting double the sum she wanted, and paying nobody – it was a magnificent stroke. And Crawley, my lord thought – Crawley is not such a fool as he looks and seems. He has managed the matter cleverly enough on his side. Nobody would ever have supposed from his face and demeanour that he knew anything about this money business; and yet he put her up to it, and has spent the money, no doubt. In this opinion my lord, we know, was mistaken; but it influenced a good deal his behaviour towards Colonel Crawley, whom he began to treat with even less than that semblance of respect which he had formerly shown towards that gentleman. It never entered into the head of Mrs. Crawley's patron that the little lady might be making a purse for herself; and, perhaps, if the truth must be told, he judged of Colonel Crawley by his experience of other husbands, whom he had known in the course of the long and well-spent life, which had made him acquainted with a great deal of the weakness of mankind. My lord had bought so many men during his life that he was surely to be pardoned for supposing that he had found the price of this one.

He taxed Becky upon the point on the very first occasion when he met her alone, and he complimented her, good-humouredly, on her cleverness in getting more than the money which she required. Becky was only a little taken aback. It was not the habit of this dear creature to tell falsehoods, except when necessity compelled, but in these great emergencies it was her practice to lie very freely; and in an instant she was ready with another neat, plausible, circumstantial

story which she administered to her patron. The previous
statement which she had made to him was a falsehood – a
wicked falsehood: she owned it; but who had made her tell
it? 'Ah, my lord,' she said, 'you don't know all I have to
suffer and bear in silence: you see me gay and happy before
you – you little know what I have to endure when there is
no protector near me. It was my husband, by threats and
the most savage treatment, forced me to ask for that sum
about which I deceived you. It was he, who, foreseeing that
questions might be asked regarding the disposal of the
money, forced me to account for it as I did. He took the
money. He told me he had paid Miss Briggs; I did not want,
I did not dare to doubt him. Pardon the wrong which a
desperate man is forced to commit, and pity a miserable
woman.' She burst into tears as she spoke. Persecuted virtue
never looked more bewitchingly wretched.

They had a long conversation, driving round and round
the Regent's Park in Mrs. Crawley's carriage together, a
conversation of which it is not necessary to repeat the details;
but the upshot of it was, that, when Becky came home, she
flew to her dear Briggs with a smiling face, and announced
that she had some very good news for her. Lord Steyne had
acted in the noblest and most generous manner. He was
always thinking how and when he could do good. Now that
little Rawdon was gone to school, a dear companion and
friend was no longer necessary to her. She was grieved
beyond measure to part with Briggs; but her means required
that she should practise every retrenchment, and her sorrow
was mitigated by the idea that her dear Briggs would be far
better provided for by her generous patron than in her
humble home. Mrs. Pilkington, the housekeeper at Gauntly
Hall, was growing exceedingly old, feeble, and rheumatic:
she was not equal to the work of superintending that vast
mansion, and must be on the look out for a successor. It
was a splendid position. The family did not go to Gauntly
once in two years. At other times the housekeeper was the
mistress of the magnificent mansion – had four covers daily
for her table; was visited by the clergy and the most respectable people of the country – was the lady of Gauntly, in
fact; and the two last housekeepers before Mrs. Pilkington
had married rectors of Gauntly; but Mrs. P. could not, being
the aunt of the present rector. The place was not to be hers

yet; but she might go down on a visit to Mrs. Pilkington and see whether she would like to succeed her.

What words can paint the ecstatic gratitude of Briggs! All she stipulated for was that little Rawdon should be allowed to come down and see her at the Hall. Becky promised this – anything. She ran up to her husband when he came home, and told him the joyful news. Rawdon was glad, deuced glad; the weight was off his conscience about poor Briggs's money. She was provided for, at any rate, but – but his mind was disquiet. He did not seem to be all right somehow. He told little Southdown what Lord Steyne had done, and the young man eyed Crawley with an air which surprised the latter.

He told Lady Jane of this second proof of Steyne's bounty, and she, too, looked odd and alarmed; so did Sir Pitt. 'She is too clever and – and gay to be allowed to go from party to party without a companion,' both said. 'You must go with her, Rawdon, wherever she goes, and you *must* have somebody with her – one of the girls from Queen's Crawley, perhaps, though they were rather giddy guardians for her.'

Somebody Becky should have. But in the meanwhile it was clear that honest Briggs must not lose her chance of settlement for life; and so she and her bags were packed, and she set off on her journey. And so two of Rawdon's out-sentinels were in the hands of the enemy.

Sir Pitt went and expostulated with his sister-in-law upon the subject of the dismissal of Briggs, and other matters of delicate family interest. In vain she pointed out to him how necessary was the protection of Lord Steyne for her poor husband; how cruel it would be on their part to deprive Briggs of the position offered to her. Cajolements, coaxings, smiles, tears could not satisfy Sir Pitt, and he had something very like a quarrel with his once admired Becky. He spoke of the honour of the family: the unsullied reputation of the Crawleys; expressed himself in indignant tones about her receiving those young Frenchmen – those wild young men of fashion, my Lord Steyne himself whose carriage was always at her door, who passed hours daily in her company, and whose constant presence made the world talk about her. As the head of the house he implored her to be more prudent. Society was already speaking lightly of her. Lord

Steyne, though a nobleman of the greatest station and talents, was a man whose attentions would compromise any woman; he besought, he implored, he commanded his sister-in-law to be watchful in her intercourse with that nobleman.

Becky promised anything and everything Pitt wanted; but Lord Steyne came to her house as often as ever, and Sir Pitt's anger increased. I wonder was Lady Jane angry or pleased that her husband at last found fault with his favourite Rebecca? Lord Steyne's visits continuing, his own ceased; and his wife was for refusing all further intercourse with that nobleman, and declining the invitation to the Charade-night which the marchioness sent to her; but Sir Pitt thought it was necessary to accept it, as his royal highness would be there.

Although he went to the party in question, Sir Pitt quitted it very early, and his wife, too, was very glad to come away. Becky hardly so much as spoke to him or noticed her sister-in-law. Pitt Crawley declared her behaviour was monstrously indecorous, reprobated in strong terms the habit of play-acting and fancy-dressing, as highly unbecoming a British female; and after the charades were over, took his brother Rawdon severely to task for appearing himself, and allowing his wife to join in such improper exhibitions.

Rawdon said she should not join in any more such amusements, but indeed, and perhaps from hints from his elder brother and sister, he had already become a very watchful and exemplary domestic character. He left off his clubs and billiards. He never left home. He took Becky out to drive: he went laboriously with her to all her parties. Whenever my Lord Steyne called, he was sure to find the colonel. And when Becky proposed to go out without her husband, or received invitations for herself, he peremptorily ordered her to refuse them; and there was that in the gentleman's manner which enforced obedience. Little Becky, to do her justice, was charmed with Rawdon's gallantry. If he was surly, she never was. Whether friends were present or absent she had always a kind smile for him, and was attentive to his pleasure and comfort. It was the early days of their marriage over again: the same good humour, *prévenances*, merriment, and artless confidence and regard. 'How much pleasanter it is,' she would say, 'to have you by my side in the carriage than that foolish old Briggs! Let us always go on so, dear Rawdon. How nice it would be, and how happy we should always be, if we had but the money!' He fell asleep after dinner in his chair; he did not see the face opposite to him, haggard, weary, and terrible; it lighted up with fresh candid smiles when he woke. It kissed him gaily. He wondered that he had ever had suspicions. No, he never had suspicion; all those dumb doubts and surly misgivings which had been gathering on his mind were mere idle jealousies. She was fond of him; she always had been. As for her shining in society it was no fault of hers; she was formed to shine there. Was there any woman who could talk, or sing, or do anything like her? If she would but like the boy! Rawdon thought. But the mother and son never could be brought together.

And it was while Rawdon's mind was agitated with these doubts and perplexities that the incident occurred which was mentioned in the last chapter; and the unfortunate colonel found himself a prisoner away from home.

CHAPTER LIII

A RESCUE AND A CATASTROPHE

FRIEND Rawdon drove on then to Mr. Moss's mansion in Cursitor Street, and was duly inducted into that dismal place of hospitality. Morning was breaking over the cheerful house-tops of Chancery Lane as the rattling cab woke up the echoes there. A little pink-eyed Jew-boy, with a head as ruddy as the rising morn, let the party into the house, and Rawdon was welcomed to the ground-floor apartments by Mr. Moss, his travelling companion and host, who cheerfully asked him if he would like a glass of something warm after his drive.

The colonel was not so depressed as some mortals would be, who, quitting a palace and a *placens uxor*, find themselves barred into a spunging-house, for, if the truth must be told, he had been a lodger at Mr. Moss's establishment once or twice before. We have not thought it necessary in the previous course of this narrative to mention these trivial little domestic incidents: but the reader may be assured that they can't unfrequently occur in the life of a man who lives on nothing a year.

Upon his first visit to Mr. Moss, the colonel, then a
bachelor, had been liberated by the generosity of his aunt;
on the second mishap, little Becky, with the greatest spirit
and kindness, had borrowed a sum of money from Lord
Southdown, and had coaxed her husband's creditor (who
was her shawl, velvet gown, lace pocket-handkerchief, trinket, and gimcrack purveyor, indeed) to take a portion of the
sum claimed, and Rawdon's promissory note for the remainder: so on both these occasions the capture and release had
been conducted with the utmost gallantry on all sides, and
Moss and the colonel were therefore on the very best of
terms.

'You'll find your old bed, colonel, and everything comfortable,' that gentleman said, 'as I may honestly say. You
may be pretty sure its kep aired, and by the best of company,
too. It was slep in the night afore last by the Honourable
Capting Famish, of the Fiftieth Dragoons, whose mar took
him out, after a fortnight, jest to punish him, she said. But,
Law bless you, I promise you, he punished my champagne,
and had a party ere every night – reglar tip-top swells, down
from the clubs and the West End – Capting Ragg, the
Honourable Deuceace, who lives in the Temple, and some
fellers as knows a good glass of wine, I warrant you. I've
got a Doctor of Diwinity upstairs, five gents in the coffee-
room, and Mrs. Moss has a tably-dy-hoty at half-past five,
and a little cards or music afterwards, when we shall be most
happy to see you.'

'I'll ring, when I want anything,' said Rawdon, and went
quietly to his bedroom. He was an old soldier, we have said,
and not to be disturbed by any little shocks of fate. A weaker
man would have sent off a letter to his wife on the instant
of his capture. 'But what is the use of disturbing her night's
rest?' thought Rawdon. 'She won't know whether I am in
my room or not. It will be time enough to write to her when
she has had her sleep out, and I have had mine. It's only a
hundred-and-seventy, and the deuce is in it if we can't raise
that.' And so, thinking about little Rawdon (whom he would
not have know that he was in such a queer place), the colonel
turned into the bed lately occupied by Captain Famish, and
fell asleep. It was ten o'clock when he woke up, and the
ruddy-headed youth brought him, with conscious pride, a
fine silver dressing-case, wherewith he might perform the

operation of shaving. Indeed Mr. Moss's house, though somewhat dirty, was splendid throughout. There were dirty-trays, and wine-coolers *en permanence* on the side board, huge dirty gilt cornices, with dingy yellow satin hangings to the barred windows which looked into Cursitor Street – vast and dirty gilt picture-frames surrounding pieces sporting and sacred, all of which works were by the greatest masters; and fetched the greatest prices, too, in the bill transactions, in the course of which they were sold and bought over and over again. The colonel's breakfast was served to him in the same dingy and gorgeous plated ware. Miss Moss, a dark-eyed maid in curl-papers appeared with the teapot, and, smiling, asked the colonel how he had slept? and she brought him in the *Morning Post*, with the names of all the great people who had figured at Lord Steyne's entertainment the night before. It contained a brilliant account of the festivities, and of the beautiful and accomplished Mrs. Rawdon Craw-ley's admirable personifications.

After a lively chat with this lady (who sat on the edge of the breakfast-table in an easy attitude displaying the drapery of her stocking and an ex-white satin shoe, which was down at heel), Colonel Crawley called for pens and ink, and paper; and being asked how many sheets, chose one which was brought to him between Miss Moss's own finger and thumb. Many a sheet had that dark-eyed damsel brought in; many a poor fellow had scrawled and blotted hurried lines of entreaty, and paced up and down that awful room until his messenger brought back the reply. Poor men always use messengers instead of the post. Who has not had their letters with the wafers wet, and the announcement that a person is waiting in the hall?

Now on the score of his application, Rawdon had not many misgivings.

DEAR BECKY (Rawdon wrote), *I hope you slept well*. Don't be *frightened* if I don't bring you in your *coffy*. Last night as I was coming home smoking, I met with an *accadent*. I was *nabbed* by Moss of Cursitor Street – from whose *gilt and splendid parler* I write this – the same that had me this time two years. Miss Moss brought in my tea – she is grown very *fat*, and as usual, had *her stockens down at heal*.

It's Nathan's business – a hundred-and-fifty – with costs, hundred-and-seventy. Please send me my desk and some *cloths* – I'm in pumps and a white tye (something like Miss M.'s stockings) – I've seventy in it. And as soon as you get this, Drive to Nathan's – offer him seventy-five down, and ask *him to renew* – say I'll take wine – we may as well have some dinner sherry; but not *picturs*, they're too dear.

If he won't stand it. Take my ticker and such of your things as you can *spare*, and send them to Balls – we must, of coarse, have the sum to-night. It won't do to let it stand over, as to-morrow's Sunday; the beds here are not very *clean*, and there may be other things out against me – I'm glad it an't Rawdon's Saturday for coming home. God bless you.

Yours in haste, R. C.

PS. – Make haste and come.

This letter, sealed with a wafer, was dispatched by one of the messengers who are always hanging about Mr. Moss's establishment; and Rawdon, having seen him depart, went out in the courtyard, and smoked his cigar with a tolerably easy mind – in spite of the bars overhead; for Mr. Moss's courtyard is railed in like a cage, lest the gentlemen who are boarding with him should take a fancy to escape from his hospitality.

Three hours, he calculated, would be the utmost time required, before Becky should arrive and open his prison doors: and he passed these pretty cheerfully in smoking, in reading the paper, and in the coffee-room with an acquaintance, Captain Walker, who happened to be there, and with whom he cut for sixpences for some hours, with pretty equal luck on either side.

But the day passed away and no messenger returned, – no Becky. Mr. Moss's tably-de-hoty was served at the appointed hour of half-past five, when such of the gentlemen lodging in the house as could afford to pay for the banquet, came and partook of it in the splendid front parlour before described, and with which Mr. Crawley's temporary lodging communicated, when Miss M. (Miss Hem, as her papa called her) appeared without the curl-papers of the morning, and Mrs. Hem did the honours of a prime boiled leg of mutton and turnips, of which the colonel ate with a very faint appetite. Asked whether he would 'stand' a bottle of champagne for the company, he consented, and the ladies drank to his 'ealth, and Mr. Moss, in the most polite manner 'looked towards him'.

In the midst of this repast, however, the door-bell was heard, – young Moss of the ruddy hair, rose up with the keys and answered the summons, and coming back, told the colonel that the messenger had returned with a bag, a desk and a letter, which he gave him. 'No ceremony, colonel, I beg,' said Mrs. Moss, with a wave of her hand, and he opened the letter rather tremulously. – It was a beautiful letter, highly scented, on a pink paper, and with a light green seal.

MON PAUVRE CHER PETIT (Mrs. Crawley wrote), I could not sleep *one wink* for thinking of what had become of *my odious old monstre:* and only got to rest in the morning after sending for Mr. Blench (for I was in a fever), who gave me a composing draught and left orders with Finette that I should be disturbed *on no account.* So that my poor old man's messenger, who had *bien mauvaise mine*, Finette says, and *sentait le genièvre*, remained in the hall for some hours waiting my bell. You may fancy my state when I read your poor dear old ill-spelt letter.

Ill as I was, I instantly called for the carriage, and as soon as I was dressed (though I couldn't drink a drop of chocolate – I assure you I couldn't without my *monstre* to bring it to me), I drove *ventre à terre* to Nathan's. I saw him – I wept – I cried – I fell at his odious knees. Nothing would mollify the horrid man. He would have all the money, he said, or keep my poor *monstre* in prison. I drove home with the intention of paying that *triste visite chez mon oncle* (when every trinket I have should be at your disposal though they would not fetch a hundred pounds, for some, you know, are with *ce cher oncle* already), and found Milor there with the Bulgarian old sheep-faced monster, who had come to compliment me upon last night's performances. Paddington came in, too, drawling and lisping and twiddling his hair; so did Champignac, and his chef – everybody with *foison* of compliments and pretty speeches – plaguing poor me, who longed to be rid of them, and was thinking *every moment of the time of mon pauvre prisonnier.*

When they were gone, I went down on my knees to Milor; told him we were going to pawn everything, and begged and prayed him to give me two hundred pounds. He pish'd and psha'd in a fury – told me not to be such a fool as to pawn – and said he would see whether he could lend me the money. At last he went away, promising that he would send it me in the morning: when I will bring it to my poor old monster with a kiss from his affectionate

BECKY.

I am writing in bed. Oh, I have such a headache and such a heartache!

When Rawdon read over this letter, he turned so red and looked so savage that the company at the table d'hôte easily perceived that bad news had reached him. All his suspicions,

which he had been trying to banish, returned upon him. She
could not even go out and sell her trinkets to free him. She
could laugh and talk about compliments paid to her, whilst
he was in prison. Who had put him there? Wenham had
walked with him. Was there. . . . He could hardly bear to
think of what he suspected. Leaving the room hurriedly, he
ran into his own – opened his desk, wrote two hurried lines,
which he directed to Sir Pitt or Lady Crawley, and bade
the messenger carry them at once to Gaunt Street, bidding
him to take a cab, and promising him a guinea if he was
back in an hour.

In the note he besought his dear brother and sister, for
the sake of God; for the sake of his dear child and his
honour; to come to him and relieve him from his difficulty.
He was in prison: he wanted a hundred pounds to set him
free – he entreated them to come to him.

He went back to the dining-room after dispatching his
messenger, and called for more wine. He laughed and talked
with a strange boisterousness, as the people thought. Sometimes he laughed madly at his own fears, and went on
drinking for an hour; listening all the while for the carriage
which was to bring his fate back.

At the expiration of that time, wheels were heard whirling
up to the gate – the young janitor went out with his gatekeys.
It was a lady whom he let in at the bailiff's door.

'Colonel Crawley,' she said, trembling very much. He
with a knowing look, locked the outer door upon her – then
unlocked and opened the inner one, and calling out, 'Colonel, you're wanted,' led her into the back parlour, which
he occupied.

Rawdon came in from the dining-parlour where all those
people were carousing, into his back-room; a flare of coarse
light following him into the apartment where the lady stood,
still very nervous.

'It is I, Rawdon,' she said, in a timid voice, which she
strove to render cheerful. 'It is Jane.' Rawdon was quite
overcome by that kind voice and presence. He ran up to her
– caught her in his arms – gasped out some inarticulate
words of thanks, and fairly sobbed on her shoulder. She did
not know the cause of his emotion.

The bills of Mr. Moss were quickly settled, perhaps to
the disappointment of that gentleman, who had counted on

having the colonel as his guest over Sunday at least; and Jane, with beaming smiles and happiness in her eyes, carried away Rawdon from the bailiff's house, and they went homewards in the cab in which she had hastened to his release. 'Pitt was gone to a Parliamentary dinner,' she said, 'when Rawdon's note came, and so, dear Rawdon, I – I came myself;' and she put her kind hand in his. Perhaps it was well for Rawdon Crawley that Pitt was away at that dinner. Rawdon thanked his sister a hundred times, and with an ardour of gratitude which touched and almost alarmed that soft-hearted woman. 'Oh,' said he, in his rude, artless way, 'you – you don't know how I'm changed since I've known you, and – and little Rawdy. I – I'd like to change somehow. You see I want – I want – to be —.' – He did not finish the sentence, but she could interpret it. And that night after he left her, and as she sat by her own little boy's bed, she prayed humbly for that poor wayworn sinner.

Rawdon left her and walked home rapidly. It was nine o'clock at night. He ran across the streets, and the great squares of Vanity Fair, and at length came up breathless opposite his own house. He started back and fell against the railings, trembling as he looked up. The drawing-room windows were blazing with light. She had said that she was in bed and ill. He stood there for some time, the light from the rooms on his pale face.

He took out his door-key and let himself into the house. He could hear laughter in the upper rooms. He was in the ball-dress in which he had been captured the night before. He went silently up the stairs; leaning against the banisters at the stair-head. – Nobody was stirring in the house besides – all the servants had been sent away. Rawdon heard laughter within – laughter and singing. Becky was singing a snatch of the song of the night before; a hoarse voice shouted, 'Brava! Brava!' – it was Lord Steyne's.

Rawdon opened the door and went in. A little table with a dinner was laid out – and wine and plate. Steyne was hanging over the sofa on which Becky sat. The wretched woman was in a brilliant full toilette, her arms and all her fingers sparkling with bracelets and rings; and the brilliants on her breast which Steyne had given her. He had her hand in his, and was bowing over it to kiss it, when Becky started up with a faint scream as she caught sight of Rawdon's white face. At the next instant she tried a smile, a horrid smile, as if to welcome her husband: and Steyne rose up, grinding his teeth, pale, and with fury in his looks.

He, too, attempted a laugh – and came forward holding out his hand. 'What, come back! How d'ye do, Crawley?' he said, the nerves of his mouth twitching as he tried to grin at the intruder.

There was that in Rawdon's face which caused Becky to fling herself before him. 'I am innocent, Rawdon,' she said; 'before God, I am innocent.' She clung hold of his coat, of his hands; her own were all covered with serpents, and rings, and baubles. 'I am innocent. – Say I am innocent,' she said to Lord Steyne.

He thought a trap had been laid for him, and was as furious with the wife as with the husband. 'You innocent! Damn you,' he screamed out. 'You innocent! Why, every trinket you have on your body is paid for by me. I have given you thousands of pounds which this fellow has spent, and for which he has sold you. Innocent, by —! You're as innocent as your mother, the ballet-girl, and your husband the bully. Don't think to frighten me as you have done others. Make way, sir, and let me pass;' and Lord Steyne seized up his hat, and, with flame in his eyes, and looking his enemy fiercely in the face, marched upon him, never for a moment doubting that the other would give way.

But Rawdon Crawley springing out, seized him by the neckcloth, until Steyne, almost strangled, writhed, and bent under his arm. 'You lie, you dog!' said Rawdon. 'You lie, you coward and villain!' And he struck the peer twice over the face with his open hand, and flung him bleeding to the ground. It was all done before Rebecca could interpose. She stood there trembling before him. She admired her husband, strong, brave, and victorious.

'Come here,' he said. – She came up at once.

'Take off those things.' – She began, trembling, pulling the jewels from her arms, and the rings from her shaking fingers, and held them all in a heap, quivering and looking up at him. 'Throw them down,' he said, and she dropped them. He tore the diamond ornament out of her breast, and flung it at Lord Steyne. It cut him on his bald forehead. Steyne wore the scar to his dying day.

'Come upstairs,' Rawdon said to his wife. 'Don't kill me, Rawdon,' she said. He laughed savagely. – 'I want to see if that man lies about the money as he has about me. Has he given you any?'

'No,' said Rebecca, 'that is —'

'Give me your keys,' Rawdon answered, and they went out together.

Rebecca gave him all the keys but one: and she was in hopes that he would not have remarked the absence of that. It belonged to the little desk which Amelia had given her in early days, and which she kept in a secret place. But Rawdon flung open boxes and wardrobes, throwing the multifarious trumpery of their contents here and there, and at last he found the desk. The woman was forced to open it. It contained papers, love-letters many years old – all sorts of small trinkets and woman's memoranda. And it contained a pocket-book with bank-notes. Some of these were dated ten years back, too, and one was quite a fresh one – a note for a thousand pounds which Lord Steyne had given her.

'Did he give you this?' Rawdon said.

'Yes,' Rebecca answered.

'I'll send it to him to-day,' Rawdon said (for day had dawned again, and many hours had passed in this search), 'and I will pay Briggs, who was kind to the boy, and some of the debts. You will let me know where I shall send the rest to you. You might have spared me a hundred pounds, Becky, out of all this – I have always shared with you.'

'I am innocent,' said Becky. And he left her without another word.

What were her thoughts when he left her? She remained for hours after he was gone, the sunshine pouring into the room, and Rebecca sitting alone on the bed's edge. The drawers were all opened and their contents scattered about, – dresses and feathers, scarfs and trinkets, a heap of tumbled vanities lying in a wreck. Her hair was falling over her shoulders; her gown was torn where Rawdon had wrenched the brilliants out of it. She heard him go downstairs a few minutes after he left her, and the door slamming and closing on him. She knew he would never come back. He was gone for ever. Would he kill himself? – she thought – not until after he had met Lord Steyne. She thought of her long past life, and all the dismal incidents of it. Ah, how dreary it seemed, how miserable, lonely and profitless! Should she take laudanum, and end it, too – have done with all hopes, schemes, debts, and triumphs? The French maid found her in this position – sitting in the midst of her miserable ruins with clasped hands and dry eyes. The woman was her accomplice and in Steyne's pay. '*Mon Dieu*, madame, what has happened?' she asked.

What *had* happened? Was she guilty or not? She said not; but who could tell what was truth which came from those lips; or if that corrupt heart was in this case pure? All her lies and her schemes, all her selfishness and her wiles, all her wit and genius had come to this bankruptcy. The woman closed the curtains, and with some entreaty and show of kindness, persuaded her mistress to lie down on the bed. Then she went below and gathered up the trinkets which had been lying on the floor, since Rebecca dropped them there at her husband's orders, and Lord Steyne went away.

CHAPTER LIV

SUNDAY AFTER THE BATTLE

T HE mansion of Sir Pitt Crawley in Great Gaunt Street was just beginning to dress itself for the day, as Rawdon, in his evening costume, which he had now worn two days, passed by the scared female who was scouring the steps, and entered into his brother's study. Lady Jane, in her morning-gown, was up and above stairs in the nursery, superintending the toilettes of her children, and listening to the morning prayers which the little creatures performed at her knee. Every morning she and they performed this duty privately, and before the public ceremonial at which Sir Pitt presided, and at which all the people of the household were expected to assemble. Rawdon sat down in the study before the baronet's table, set out with the orderly Blue Books and the letters, the neatly docketed bills and symmetrical pamphlets; the locked account-books, desks, and dispatch boxes, the Bible, the *Quarterly Review*, and the *Court Guide*, which all stood as if on parade awaiting the inspection of their chief.

A book of family sermons, one of which Sir Pitt was in the habit of administering to his family on Sunday mornings, lay ready on the study table, and awaiting his judicious selection. And by the sermon-book was the *Observer* newspaper, damp and neatly folded, and for Sir Pitt's own private use. His gentleman alone took the opportunity of perusing the newspaper before he laid it by his master's desk. Before he had brought it into the study that morning, he had read in the journal a flaming account of 'Festivities at Gaunt House', with the names of all the distinguished personages invited by the Marquis of Steyne to meet his royal highness. Having made comments upon this entertainment to the housekeeper and her niece as they were taking early tea and hot buttered toast in the former lady's apartment, and wondered how the Rawding Crawleys could git on, the valet had damped and folded the paper once more, so that it looked quite fresh and innocent against the arrival of the master of the house.

Poor Rawdon took up the paper and began to try and read it until his brother should arrive. But the print fell blank upon his eyes; and he did not know in the least what he was reading. The Government news and appointments (which Sir Pitt as a public man was bound to peruse, otherwise he would by no means permit the introduction of Sunday papers into his household), the theatrical criticisms, the fight for a hundred pounds a side between the Barking Butcher and the Tutbury Pet, the Gaunt House chronicle itself, which contained a most complimentary though guarded account of the famous charades of which Mrs. Becky had been the heroine – all these passed as in a haze before Rawdon, as he sat waiting the arrival of the chief of the family.

Punctually, as the shrill-toned bell of the black marble study clock began to chime nine, Sir Pitt made his appearance, fresh, neat, smugly shaved, with a waxy clean face, and stiff shirt collar, his scanty hair combed and oiled, trimming his nails as he descended the stairs majestically, in a starched cravat and a grey flannel dressing-gown – a real old English gentleman, in a word – a model of neatness and every propriety. He started when he saw poor Rawdon in his study in tumbled clothes, with bloodshot eyes, and his hair over his face. He thought his brother was not sober, and had been out all night on some orgy. 'Good gracious, Rawdon,' he said, with a blank face, 'what brings you here at this time of the morning? Why ain't you at home?'

'Home,' said Rawdon, with a wild laugh. 'Don't be frightened, Pitt. I'm not drunk. Shut the door; I want to speak to you.'

Pitt closed the door and came up to the table, where he sat down in the other arm-chair – that one placed for the reception of the steward, agent, or confidential visitor who came to transact business with the baronet – and trimmed his nails more vehemently than ever.

'Pitt, it's all over with me,' the colonel said, after a pause. 'I'm done.'

'I always said it would come to this,' the baronet cried peevishly, and beating a tune with his clean-trimmed nails. 'I warned you a thousand times. I can't help you any more. Every shilling of my money is tied up. Even the hundred pounds that Jane took you last night were promised to my lawyer to-morrow morning; and the want of it will put me to great inconvenience. I don't mean to say that I won't assist you ultimately. But as for paying your creditors in full, I might as well hope to pay the National Debt. It is madness, sheer madness, to think of such a thing. You must come to a compromise. It's a painful thing for the family; but everybody does it. There was George Kitely, Lord Ragland's son, went through the court last week, and was what they call whitewashed, I believe. Lord Ragland would not pay a shilling for him, and —'

'It's not money I want,' Rawdon broke in. 'I'm not come to you about myself. Never mind what happens to me —'

'What is the matter, then?' said Pitt, somewhat relieved.

'It's the boy,' said Rawdon, in a husky voice. 'I want you to promise me that you will take charge of him when I'm gone. That dear good wife of yours has always been good to him; and he's fonder of her than he is of his. . . . – Damn it. Look here, Pitt – you know that I was to have had Miss Crawley's money. I wasn't brought up like a younger brother: but was always encouraged to be extravagant and kep idle. But for this I might have been quite a different man. I didn't do my duty with the regiment so bad. You know how I was thrown over about the money, and who got it.'

'After the sacrifices I have made, and the manner in which I have stood by you, I think this sort of reproach is useless,' Sir Pitt said. 'Your marriage was your own doing, not mine.'

'That's over now,' said Rawdon. – 'That's over now.' And

the words were wrenched from him with a groan, which made his brother start.

'Good God! is she dead?' Sir Pitt said, with a voice of genuine alarm and commiseration.

'I wish *I* was,' Rawdon replied. 'If it wasn't for little Rawdon I'd have cut my throat this morning – and that damned villain's too.'

Sir Pitt instantly guessed the truth, and surmised that Lord Steyne was the person whose life Rawdon wished to take. The colonel told his senior briefly, and in broken accents, the circumstances of the case. 'It was a regular plan between that scoundrel and her,' he said. 'The bailiffs were put upon me: I was taken as I was going out of his house: when I wrote to her for money, she said she was ill in bed, and put me off to another day. And when I got home I found her in diamonds and sitting with that villain alone.' He then went on to describe hurriedly the personal conflict with Lord Steyne. To an affair of that nature, of course, he said, there was but one issue: and after his conference with his brother, he was going away to make the necessary arrangements for the meeting which must ensue. 'And as it may end fatally for me,' Rawdon said with a broken voice, 'and as the boy has no mother, I must leave him to you and Jane, Pitt – only it will be a comfort to me if you will promise me to be his friend.'

The elder brother was much affected, and shook Rawdon's hand with a cordiality seldom exhibited by him. Rawdon passed his hand over his shaggy eyebrows. 'Thank you, brother,' said he. 'I know I can trust your word.'

'I will, upon my honour,' the baronet said. And thus, and almost mutely, this bargain was struck between them.

Then Rawdon took out of his pocket the little pocket-book which he had discovered in Becky's desk; and from which he drew a bundle of the notes which it contained. 'Here's six hundred,' he said – 'you didn't know I was so rich. I want you to give the money to Briggs, who lent it to us – and who was so kind to the boy – and I've always felt ashamed of having taken the poor old woman's money. And here's some more – I've only kept back a few pounds – which Becky may as well have, to get on with.' As he spoke he took hold of the other notes to give to his brother: but his hands shook, and he was so agitated that the pocket-book fell from him, and out of it the thousand-pound note which had been the last of the unlucky Becky's winnings.

Pitt stooped and picked them up, amazed at so much wealth. 'Not that,' Rawdon said; 'I hope to put a bullet into the man whom that belongs to.' He had thought to himself, it would be a fine revenge to wrap a ball in the note, and kill Steyne with it.

After this colloquy the brothers once more shook hands and parted. Lady Jane had heard of the colonel's arrival, and was waiting for her husband in the adjoining dining-room, with female instinct, auguring evil. The door of the dining-room happened to be left open, and the lady of course was issuing from it as the two brothers passed out of the study. She held out her hand to Rawdon, and said she was glad he was come to breakfast; though she could perceive, by his haggard unshorn face, and the dark looks of her husband, that there was very little question of breakfast between them. Rawdon muttered some excuses about an engagement, squeezing hard the timid little hand which his sister-in-law reached out to him. Her imploring eyes could read nothing but calamity in his face; but he went away without another word. Nor did Sir Pitt vouchsafe her any explanation. The children came up to salute him, and he kissed them in his usual frigid manner. The mother took both of them close to herself, and held a hand of each of them as they knelt down to prayers, which Sir Pitt read to them, and to the servants in their Sunday suits or liveries, ranged upon chairs on the other side of the hissing tea-urn. Breakfast was so late that day, in consequence of the delays which had occurred, that the church bells began to ring whilst they were sitting over their meal: and Lady Jane was too ill, she said, to go to church, though her thoughts had been entirely astray during the period of family devotion.

Rawdon Crawley meanwhile hurried on from Great Gaunt Street, and knocking at the great bronze Medusa's head which stands on the portal of Gaunt House, brought out the purple Silenus in a red and silver waistcoat, who acts as porter of that palace. The man was scared also by the colonel's dishevelled appearance, and barred the way as if afraid that the other was going to force it. But Colonel Crawley only took out a card and enjoined him particularly to send it in to Lord Steyne, and to mark the address written on it, and say that Colonel Crawley would be all day after one o'clock at the Regent Club in St. James's Street – not at home. The fat red-faced man looked after him with astonishment as he strode away; so did the people in their Sunday clothes who were out so early; the charity boys with shining faces, the greengrocer lolling at his door, and the publican shutting his shutters in the sunshine, against service commenced. The people joked at the cabstand about his appearance, as he took a carriage there, and told the driver to drive him to Knightsbridge Barracks.

All the bells were jangling and tolling as he reached that place. He might have seen his old acquaintance Amelia on her way from Brompton to Russell Square had he been looking out. Troops of schools were on their march to church, the shiny pavement and outsides of coaches in the suburbs were thronged with people out upon their Sunday pleasure; but the colonel was much too busy to take any heed of these phenomena, and, arriving at Knightsbridge, speedily made his way up to the room of his old friend and comrade Captain Macmurdo, who Crawley found, to his satisfaction, was in barracks.

Captain Macmurdo, a veteran officer and Waterloo man, greatly liked by his regiment, in which want of money alone prevented him from attaining the highest ranks, was enjoying the forenoon calmly in bed. He had been at a fast supper-party, given the night before by Captain the Honourable George Cinqbars, at his house in Brompton Square, to several young men of the regiment, and a number of ladies of the *corps de ballet*, and old Mac, who was at home with people of all ages and ranks, and consorted with generals, dog-fanciers, opera-dancers, bruisers, and every kind of person, in a word, was resting himself after the night's labours, and, not being on duty, was in bed.

His room was hung round with boxing, sporting, and dancing pictures, presented to him by comrades as they retired from the regiment, and married and settled into quiet life. And as he was now nearly fifty years of age, twenty-four of which he had passed in the corps, he had a singular museum. He was one of the best shots in England, and, for a heavy man, one of the best riders; indeed, he and Crawley had been rivals when the latter was in the army. To be brief, Mr. Macmurdo was lying in bed, reading in *Bell's Life* an account of that very fight between the Tutbury Pet and the Barking Butcher, which has been before mentioned – a venerable bristly warrior, with a little close-shaved grey head, with a silk nightcap, a red face and nose, and a great dyed moustache.

When Rawdon told the captain he wanted a friend, the latter knew perfectly well on what duty of friendship he was called to act, and indeed had conducted scores of affairs for his acquaintances with the greatest prudence and skill. His Royal Highness the late lamented Commander-in-chief had had the greatest regard for Macmurdo on this account; and he was the common refuge of gentlemen in trouble.

'What's the row about, Crawley, my boy?' said the old warrior. 'No more gambling business, hey, like that when we shot Captain Marker?'

'It's about – about my wife,' Crawley answered, casting down his eyes and turning very red.

The other gave a whistle. 'I always said she'd throw you over,' he began:– indeed there were bets in the regiment and at the clubs regarding the probable fate of Colonel Crawley, so lightly was his wife's character esteemed by his comrades and the world; but seeing the savage look with which Rawdon answered the expression of this opinion, Macmurdo did not think fit to enlarge upon it further.

'Is there no way out of it, old boy?' the captain continued in a grave tone. 'Is it only suspicion, you know, or – or what is it? Any letters? Can't you keep it quiet? Best not make any noise about a thing of that sort if you can help it.' 'Think of his only finding her out now,' the captain thought to himself, and remembered a hundred particular conversations at the mess-table, in which Mrs. Crawley's reputation had been torn to shreds.

'There's no way but one out of it,' Rawdon replied – 'and there's only a way out of it for one of us, Mac – do you understand? I was put out of the way: arrested: I found 'em alone together. I told him he was a liar and a coward, and knocked him down and thrashed him.'

'Serve him right,' Macmurdo said. 'Who is it?'

Rawdon answered it was Lord Steyne.

'The deuce! a marquis! they said he – that is, they said you —'

'What the devil do you mean?' roared out Rawdon; 'do

you mean that you ever heard a fellow doubt about my wife, and didn't tell me, Mac?'

'The world's very censorious, old boy,' the other replied. 'What the deuce was the good of my telling you what any tom-fools talked about?'

'It was damned unfriendly, Mac,' said Rawdon, quite overcome; and, covering his face with his hands, he gave way to an emotion, the sight of which caused the tough old campaigner opposite him to wince with sympathy. 'Hold up, old boy,' he said; 'great man or not, we'll put a bullet in him, damn him. As for women, they're all so.'

'You don't know how fond I was of that one,' Rawdon said, half inarticulately. 'Damme, I followed her like a footman. I gave up everything I had to her. I'm a beggar because I would marry her. By Jove, sir, I've pawned my own watch in order to get her anything she fancied: and she – she's been making a purse for herself all the time, and grudged me a hundred pound to get me out of quod.' He then, fiercely and incoherently, and with an agitation under which his counsellor had never before seen him labour, told Macmurdo the circumstances of the story. His adviser caught at some stray hints in it.

'She may be innocent, after all,' he said. 'She says so. Steyne has been a hundred times alone with her in the house before.'

'It may be so,' Rawdon answered, sadly; 'but this don't look very innocent:' and he showed the captain the thousand-pound note which he had found in Becky's pocket-book. 'This is what he gave her, Mac: and she kep it unknown to me: and with this money in the house, she refused to stand by me when I was locked up.' The captain could not but own that the secreting of the money had a very ugly look.

Whilst they were engaged in their conference, Rawdon dispatched Captain Macmurdo's servant to Curzon Street, with an order to the domestic there to give up a bag of clothes of which the colonel had great need. And during the man's absence, and with great labour and a Johnson's Dictionary, which stood them in much stead, Rawdon and his second composed a letter, which the latter was to send to Lord Steyne. Captain Macmurdo had the honour of waiting upon the Marquis of Steyne, on the part of Colonel Rawdon

Crawley, and begged to intimate that he was empowered by the colonel to make any arrangements for the meeting which, he had no doubt, it was his lordship's intention to demand, and which the circumstances of the morning had rendered inevitable. Captain Macmurdo begged Lord Steyne, in the most polite manner, to appoint a friend, with whom he (Captain M'M.) might communicate, and desired that the meeting might take place with as little delay as possible.

In a postscript the captain stated that he had in his possession a bank-note for a large amount, which Colonel Crawley had reason to suppose was the property of the Marquis of Steyne. And he was anxious, on the colonel's behalf, to give up the note to its owner.

By the time this note was composed, the captain's servant returned from his mission to Colonel Crawley's house in Curzon Street, but without the carpet-bag and portmanteau, for which he had been sent; and with a very puzzled and odd face.

'They won't give 'em up,' said the man; 'there's a regular shinty in the house; and everything at sixes and sevens. The landlord's come in and took possession. The servants was a-drinkin' up in the drawing-room. They said – they said you had gone off with the plate, colonel,' – the man added after a pause:– 'One of the servants is off already. And Simpson, the man as was very noisy and drunk indeed, says nothing shall go out of the house until his wages is paid up.'

The account of this little revolution in May Fair astonished and gave a little gaiety to an otherwise very *triste* conversation. The two officers laughed at Rawdon's discomfiture.

'I'm glad the little 'un isn't at home,' Rawdon said, biting his nails. 'You remember him, Mac, don't you, in the Riding School? How he sat the kicker to be sure! didn't he?'

'That he did, old boy,' said the good-natured captain.

Little Rawdon was then sitting, one of fifty gown-boys, in the chapel of Whitefriars School: thinking, not about the sermon, but about going home next Saturday, when his father would certainly tip him, and perhaps would take him to the play.

'He's a regular trump, that boy,' the father went on, still musing about his son. 'I say, Mac, if anything goes wrong – if I drop – I should like you to – to go and see him, you know: and say that I was very fond of him, and that. And

– dash it – old chap, give him these gold sleeve-buttons: it's all I've got.' He covered his face with his black hands; over which the tears rolled and made furrows of white. Mr. Macmurdo had also occasion to take off his silk night-cap and rub it across his eyes.

'Go down and order some breakfast,' he said to his man in a loud cheerful voice. – 'What'll you have, Crawley? Some devilled kidneys and a herring – let's say – And, Clay, lay out some dressing things for the colonel: we were always pretty much of a size, Rawdon, my boy, and neither of us ride so light as we did when we first entered the corps.' With which, and leaving the colonel to dress himself, Macmurdo turned round towards the wall, and resumed the perusal of *Bell's Life*, until such time as his friend's toilette was complete, and he was at liberty to commence his own.

This, as he was about to meet a lord, Captain Macmurdo performed with particular care. He waxed his moustachios into a state of brilliant polish, and put on a tight cravat and a trim buff waistcoat: so that all the young officers in the mess-room, whither Crawley had preceded his friend, complimented Mac on his appearance at breakfast, and asked if he was going to be married that Sunday?

CHAPTER LV

IN WHICH THE SAME SUBJECT IS PURSUED

B ECKY did not rally from the state of stupor and confusion in which the events of the previous night had plunged her intrepid spirit, until the bells of the Curzon Street chapels were ringing for afternoon service, and rising from her bed she began to ply her own bell, in order to summon the French maid who had left her some hours before.

Mrs. Rawdon Crawley rang many times in vain; and though, on the last occasion, she rang with such vehemence as to pull down the bell-rope, Mademoiselle Fifine did not make her appearance, – no, not though her mistress, in a great pet, and with the bell-rope in her hand, came out to the landing-place with her hair over her shoulders, and screamed out repeatedly for her attendant.

The truth is, she had quitted the premises for many

hours, and upon that permission which is called French leave among us. After picking up the trinkets in the drawing-room, Mademoiselle had ascended to her own apartments, packed and corded her own boxes there, tripped out and called a cab for herself, brought down her trunks with her own hand, and without ever so much as asking the aid of any of the other servants, who would probably have refused it, as they hated her cordially, and without wishing any one of them good-bye, had made her exit from Curzon Street.

The game, in her opinion, was over in that little domestic establishment. Fifine went off in a cab, as we have known more exalted persons of her nation to do under similar circumstances: but, more provident or lucky than these, she secured not only her own property, but some of her mistress's (if indeed that lady could be said to have any property at all) – and not only carried off the trinkets before alluded to, and some favourite dresses on which she had long kept her eye, but four richly gilt Louis Quatorze candlesticks, six gilt Albums, *Keepsakes*, and *Books of Beauty*, a gold enamelled snuff-box which had once belonged to Madame du Barri, and the sweetest little inkstand and mother-of-pearl blotting-book, which Becky used when she composed her charming little pink notes, had vanished from the premises in Curzon Street together with Mademoiselle Fifine, and all the silver laid on the table for the little *festin* which Rawdon interrupted. The plated ware Mademoiselle left behind her was too cumbrous probably, for which reason, no doubt, she also left the fire-irons, the chimney-glasses, and the rosewood cottage piano.

A lady very like her subsequently kept a milliner's shop in the Rue du Helder at Paris, where she lived with great credit and enjoyed the patronage of my Lord Steyne. This person always spoke of England as of the most treacherous country in the world, and stated to her young pupils that she had been *affreusement volé* by natives of that island. It was no doubt compassion for her misfortunes which induced the Marquis of Steyne to be so very kind to Madame de Saint-Amaranthe. May she flourish as she deserves, – she appears no more in our quarter of Vanity Fair.

Hearing a buzz and a stir below, and indignant at the impudence of those servants who would not answer her summons, Mrs. Crawley flung her morning robe round her, and descended majestically to the drawing-room, whence the noise proceeded.

The cook was there with blackened face, seated on the beautiful chintz sofa by the side of Mrs. Raggles, to whom she was administering maraschino. The page with the sugar-loaf buttons, who carried about Becky's pink notes, and jumped about her little carriage with such alacrity, was now engaged putting his fingers into a cream dish; the footman was talking to Raggles, who had a face full of perplexity and woe – and yet, though the door was open, and Becky had been screaming a half-dozen of times a few feet off, not one of her attendants had obeyed her call. 'Have a little drop, do'ee now, Mrs. Raggles,' the cook was saying as Becky entered, the white cashmere dressing-gown flouncing around her.

'Simpson! Trotter!' the mistress of the house cried in great wrath. 'How dare you stay here when you heard me call? How dare you sit down in my presence? Where's my maid?' The page withdrew his fingers from his mouth with a momentary terror: but the cook took off a glass of mara-schino, of which Mrs. Raggles had had enough, staring at Becky over the little gilt glass as she drained its contents. The liquor appeared to give the odious rebel courage.

'*Your* sofy, indeed!' Mrs. Cook said. 'I'm a-settin' on Mrs. Raggles's sofy. Don't you stir, Mrs. Raggles, mum. I'm a-settin' on Mr. and Mrs. Raggles's sofy, which they bought with honest money, and very dear it cost 'em, too. And I'm thinkin' if I set here until I'm paid my wages, I shall set a precious long time, Mrs. Raggles; and set I will, too – ha! ha!' and with this she filled herself another glass of the liquor, and drank it with a more hideously satirical air.

'Trotter! Simpson! turn that drunken wretch out,' screamed Mrs. Crawley.

'I shawn't,' said Trotter the footman; 'turn out yourself. Pay our selleries, and turn me out too. *We'll* go fast enough.'

'Are you all here to insult me?' cried Becky, in a fury; 'when Colonel Crawley comes home I'll —'

At this the servants burst into a hoarse haw-haw, in which, however, Raggles, who still kept a most melancholy countenance, did not join. 'He ain't a-coming back,' Mr. Trotter resumed. 'He sent for his things, and I wouldn't let 'em go, although Mr. Raggles would: and I don't b'lieve he's no more a colonel than I am. He's hoff: and I suppose you're a-goin' after him. You're no better than swindlers, both on you. Don't be a-bullyin' *me*. I won't stand it. Pay us our selleries, I say. Pay us our selleries.' It was evident, from Mr. Trotter's flushed countenance and defective intonation, that he, too, had had recourse to vinous stimulus.

'Mr. Raggles,' said Becky, in a passion of vexation, 'you will not surely let me be insulted by that drunken man?' 'Hold your noise. Trotter; do now,' said Simpson the page. He was affected by his mistress's deplorable situation, and succeeded in preventing an outrageous denial of the epithet 'drunken' on the footman's part.

'Oh, mam,' said Raggles, 'I never thought to live to see this year day. I've known the Crawley family ever since I was born. I lived butler with Miss Crawley for thirty years; and I little thought one of that family was a-goin' to ruing me – yes, ruing me' – said the poor fellow with tears in his eyes. 'Har you a-goin' to pay me? You've lived in this 'ouse four year. You've 'ad my substance: my plate and linning. You ho me a milk and butter bill of two 'undred pound, you must 'ave noo laid heggs for your homlets, and cream for your spanil dog.'

'She didn't care what her own flesh and blood had,' interposed the cook. 'Many's the time, he'd have starved but for me.'

'He's a charaty boy now, cooky,' said Mr. Trotter, with a drunken 'ha! ha!' – and honest Raggles continued, in a lamentable tone, an enumeration of his griefs. All he said was true. Becky and her husband had ruined him. He had bills coming due next week and no means to meet them. He would be sold up and turned out of his shop and his house, because he had trusted to the Crawley family. His tears and lamentations made Becky more peevish than ever.

'You all seem to be against me,' she said, bitterly. 'What do you want? I can't pay you on Sunday. Come back to-morrow and I'll pay you everything. I thought Colonel Crawley had settled with you. He will to-morrow. I declare to you upon my honour that he left home this morning with fifteen hundred pounds in his pocket-book. He has left me nothing. Apply to him. Give me a bonnet and shawl and let me go out and find him. There was a difference between us this morning. You all seem to know it. I promise you upon my word that you shall all be paid. He has got a good appointment. Let me go out and find him.'

This audacious statement caused Raggles and the other personages present to look at one another with a wild surprise, and with it Rebecca left them. She went upstairs and dressed herself this time without the aid of her French maid. She went into Rawdon's room, and there saw that a trunk and bag were packed ready for removal, with a pencil direction that they should be given when called for; then she went into the Frenchwoman's garret; everything was clean, and all the drawers emptied there. She bethought herself of the trinkets which had been left on the ground, and felt certain that the woman had fled. 'Good Heavens! was ever such ill luck as mine?' she said; 'to be so near, and to lose all. Is it all too late? No; there was one chance more.'

She dressed herself, and went away unmolested this time, but alone. It was four o'clock. She went swiftly down the streets (she had no money to pay for a carriage), and never stopped until she came to Sir Pitt Crawley's door, in Great Gaunt Street. Where was Lady Jane Crawley? She was at church. Becky was not sorry. Sir Pitt was in his study, and had given orders not to be disturbed – she must see him – she slipped by the sentinel in livery at once, and was in Sir Pitt's room before the astonished baronet had even laid down the paper.

He turned red and started back from her with a look of great alarm and horror.

'Do not look so,' she said. 'I am not guilty, Pitt, dear Pitt; you were my friend once. Before God, I am not guilty. I seem so. Everything is against me. And oh! at such a moment! just when all my hopes were about to be realized: just when happiness was in store for us.'

'Is this true, what I see in the paper, then?' Sir Pitt said – a paragraph in which had greatly surprised him.

'It is true. Lord Steyne told me on Friday night, the night of that fatal ball. He has been promised an appointment any time these six months. Mr. Martyr, the Colonial Secretary, told him yesterday that it was made out. That unlucky arrest ensued; that horrible meeting. I was only guilty of too much devotedness to Rawdon's service. I have received Lord Steyne alone a hundred times before. I confess I had money of which Rawdon knew nothing. Don't you know how

careless he is of it, and could I dare to confide it to him?'
And so she went on with a perfectly connected story, which
she poured into the ears of her perplexed kinsman.

It was to the following effect. Becky owned, and with
perfect frankness, but deep contrition, that having remarked
Lord Steyne's partiality for her (at the mention of which
Pitt blushed), and being secure of her own virtue, she had
determined to turn the great peer's attachment to the
advantage of herself and her family. 'I looked for a peerage
for you, Pitt,' she said (the brother-in-law again turned red).
'We have talked about it. Your genius and Lord Steyne's
interest made it more than probable, had not this dreadful
calamity come to put an end to all our hopes. But, first, I
own that it was my object to rescue my dear husband, –
him whom I love in spite of all his ill usage and suspicions
of me, – to remove him from the poverty and ruin which
was impending over us. I saw Lord Steyne's partiality for
me,' she said, casting down her eyes. 'I own that I did
everything in my power to make myself pleasing to him, and
as far as an honest woman may, to secure his – his esteem.
It was only on Friday morning that the news arrived of the
death of the governor of Coventry Island, and my lord
instantly secured the appointment for my dear husband. It
was intended as a surprise for him, – he was to see it in the
papers to-day. Even after that horrid arrest took place (the
expenses of which Lord Steyne generously said he would
settle, so that I was in a manner prevented from coming to
my husband's assistance), my lord was laughing with me,
and saying that my dearest Rawdon would be consoled when
he read of his appointment in the paper, in that shocking
spun – bailiff's house. And then – then he came home. His
suspicions were excited, – the dreadful scene took place
between my lord and my cruel, cruel Rawdon, – and, oh,
my God, what will happen next? Pitt, dear Pitt! pity me,
and reconcile us!' And as she spoke she flung herself down
on her knees, and bursting into tears, seized hold of Pitt's
hand, which she kissed passionately.

It was in this very attitude that Lady Jane, who, returning
from church, ran to her husband's room directly she heard
Mrs. Rawdon Crawley was closeted there, found the baronet
and his sister-in-law.

'I am surprised that woman has the audacity to enter this

house,' Lady Jane said, trembling in every limb, and turning quite pale. (Her ladyship had sent out her maid directly after breakfast, who had communicated with Raggles and Rawdon Crawley's household, who had told her all, and a great deal more than they knew, of that story, and many others besides). 'How dare Mrs. Crawley to enter the house of – of an honest family?'

Sir Pitt started back, amazed at his wife's display of vigour. Becky still kept her kneeling posture, and clung to Sir Pitt's hand.

'Tell her that she does not know all. Tell her that I am innocent, dear Pitt,' she whimpered out.

'Upon my word, my love, I think you do Mrs. Crawley injustice,' Sir Pitt said; at which speech Rebecca was vastly relieved. 'Indeed I believe her to be —'

'To be what?' cried out Lady Jane, her clear voice thrilling, and her heart beating violently as she spoke. 'To be a wicked woman – a heartless mother, a false wife? She never loved her dear little boy, who used to fly here and tell me of her cruelty to him. She never came into a family but she strove to bring misery with her, and to weaken the most sacred affections with her wicked flattery and false-hoods. She has deceived her husband, as she has deceived everybody; her soul is black with vanity, worldliness, and all sorts of crime. I tremble when I touch her. I keep my children out of her sight. I —'

'Lady Jane!' cried Sir Pitt, starting up, 'this is really language —'

'I have been a true and faithful wife to you, Sir Pitt,' Lady Jane continued, intrepidly; 'I have kept my marriage vow as I made it to God, and have been obedient and gentle as a wife should. But righteous obedience has its limits, and I declare that I will not bear that – that woman again under my roof: if she enters it, I and my children will leave it. She is not worthy to sit down with Christian people. You – you must choose, sir, between her and me;' and with this my lady swept out of the room, fluttering with her own audacity, and leaving Rebecca and Sir Pitt not a little astonished at it.

As for Becky, she was not hurt; nay, she was pleased. 'It was the diamond clasp you gave me,' she said to Sir Pitt, reaching him out her hand; and before she left him (for which event you may be sure my Lady Jane was looking out from her dressing-room window in the upper story) the baronet had promised to go and seek out his brother, and endeavour to bring about a reconciliation.

Rawdon found some of the young fellows of the regiment seated in the mess-room at breakfast, and was induced without much difficulty to partake of that meal, and of the devilled legs of fowls and soda-water with which these young gentlemen fortified themselves. Then they had a conversation befitting the day and their time of life: about the next pigeon-match at Battersea, with relative bets upon Ross and Osbaldiston; about Mademoiselle Ariane of the French Opera, and who had left her, and how she was consoled by Panther Carr; and about the fight between the Butcher and the Pet, and the probabilities that it was a cross. Young Tandyman, a hero of seventeen, laboriously endeavouring to get up a pair of moustachios, had seen the fight, and spoke in the most scientific manner about the battle, and the condition of the men. It was he who had driven the Butcher on to the ground in his drag, and passed the whole of the previous night with him. Had there not been foul play he must have won it. All the old files of the Ring were in it: and Tandyman wouldn't pay; no, dammy, he wouldn't pay. It was but a year since the young cornet, now so knowing a hand in Cribb's parlour, had a still lingering liking for toffy, and used to be birched at Eton.

So they went on talking about dancers, fights, drinking, demireps, until Macmurdo came down and joined the boys and the conversation. He did not appear to think that any especial reverence was due to their boyhood; the old fellow cut in with stories, to the full as choice as any the youngest rake present had to tell; – nor did his own grey hairs, nor their smooth faces detain him. Old Mac was famous for his good stories. He was not exactly a lady's man; that is, men asked him to dine rather at the houses of their mistresses than of their mothers. There can scarcely be a life lower, perhaps, than his; but he was quite contented with it, such as it was, and led it in perfect good nature, simplicity, and modesty of demeanour.

By the time Mac had finished a copious breakfast, most of the others had concluded their meal. Young Lord Varinas

was smoking an immense meerschaum pipe, while Captain
Hugues was employed with a cigar: that violent little devil
Tandyman, with his little bull-terrier between his legs, was
tossing for shillings with all his might (that fellow was always
at some game or other) against Captain Deuceace; and Mac
and Rawdon walked off to the club, neither, of course,
having given any hint of the business which was occupying
their minds. Both, on the other hand, had joined pretty gaily
in the conversation; as, why should they interrupt it? Feasting, drinking, ribaldry, laughter, go on alongside of all sorts
of other occupations in Vanity Fair, – the crowds were
pouring out of church as Rawdon and his friend passed down
St. James's Street and entered into their club.

The old bucks and *habitués*, who ordinarily stand gaping
and grinning out of the great front window of the club, had
not arrived at their posts as yet, – the newspaper-room was
almost empty. One man was present whom Rawdon did not
know; another to whom he owed a little score for whist, and
whom, in consequence, he did not care to meet; a third was
reading the *Royalist* (a periodical famous for its scandal and
its attachment to Church and King) Sunday paper at the
table, and, looking up at Crawley with some interest, said,
'Crawley, I congratulate you.'

'What do you mean?' said the colonel.

'It's in the *Observer* and the *Royalist* too,' said Mr. Smith.

'What?' Rawdon cried, turning very red. He thought that
the affair with Lord Steyne was already in the public prints.
Smith looked up wondering and smiling at the agitation
which the colonel exhibited as he took up the paper, and,
trembling, began to read.

Mr. Smith and Mr. Brown (the gentleman with whom
Rawdon had the outstanding whist account) had been talking
about the colonel just before he came in.

'It is come just in the nick of time,' said Smith. 'I suppose
Crawley had not a shilling in the world.'

'It's a wind that blows everybody good,' Mr. Brown said.
'He can't go away without paying me a pony he owes me.'

'What's the salary?' asked Smith.

'Two or three thousand,' answered the other. 'But the
climate's so infernal, they don't enjoy it long. Liverseege
died after eighteen months of it: and the man before went
off in six weeks, I hear.'

'Some people say his brother is a very clever man. I always found him a d— bore,' Smith ejaculated. 'He must have good interest, though. He must have got the colonel the place.'

'*He!*' said Brown, with a sneer. – 'Pooh. – It was Lord Steyne got it.'

'How do you mean?'

'A virtuous woman is a crown to her husband,' answered the other, enigmatically, and went to read his papers.

Rawdon, for his part, read in the *Royalist* the following astonishing paragraph:–

GOVERNORSHIP OF COVENTRY ISLAND. – H.M.S. *Yellowjack*, Commander Jaunders, has brought letters and papers from Coventry Island. H.E. Sir Thomas Liverseege had fallen a victim to the prevailing fever at Swamptown. His loss is deeply felt in the flourishing colony. We hear that the Governorship has been offered to Colonel Rawdon Crawley, C.B., a distinguished Waterloo officer. We need not only men of acknowledged bravery, but men of administrative talents to superintend the affairs of our colonies; and we have no doubt that the gentleman selected by the Colonial Office to fill the lamented vacancy which has occurred at Coventry Island is admirably calculated for the post which he is about to occupy.

'Coventry Island! where was it? who had appointed him to the government? You must take me out as your secretary, old boy,' Captain Macmurdo said, laughing; and as Crawley and his friend sat wondering and perplexed over the announcement, the club waiter brought in to the colonel a card, on which the name of Mr. Wenham was engraved, who begged to see Colonel Crawley.

The colonel and his aide de camp went out to meet the gentleman, rightly conjecturing that he was an emissary of Lord Steyne. 'How d'ye do, Crawley? I am glad to see you,' said Mr. Wenham, with a bland smile, and grasping Crawley's hand with great cordiality.

'You come, I suppose, from —'

'Exactly,' said Mr. Wenham.

'Then this is my friend Captain Macmurdo of the Life Guards Green.'

'Delighted to know Captain Macmurdo, I'm sure,' Mr. Wenham said, and tendered another smile and shake of the hand to the second, as he had done to the principal. Mac

put out one finger, armed with a buckskin glove, and made
a very frigid bow to Mr. Wenham over his tight cravat. He
was, perhaps, discontented at being put in communication
with a *pékin*, and thought that Lord Steyne should have sent
him a colonel at the very least.

'As Macmurdo acts for me, and knows what I mean,'
Crawley said, 'I had better retire and leave you together.'

'Of course,' said Macmurdo.

'By no means, my dear colonel,' Mr. Wenham said; 'the
interview which I had the honour of requesting was with
you personally, though the company of Captain Macmurdo
cannot fail to be also most pleasing. In fact, captain, I hope
that our conversation will lead to none but the most agreeable
results, very different from those which my friend Colonel
Crawley appears to anticipate.'

'Humph!' said Captain Macmurdo. Be hanged to these
civilians, he thought to himself, they are always for arranging
and speechifying. Mr. Wenham took a chair which was
not offered to him – took a paper from his pocket, and
resumed:–

'You have seen this gratifying announcement in the papers
this morning, colonel? Government has secured a most
valuable servant, and you, if you accept office, as I presume
you will, an excellent appointment. Three thousand a year,
delightful climate, excellent government-house, all your own
way in the colony, and a certain promotion. I congratulate
you with all my heart. I presume you know, gentlemen, to
whom my friend is indebted for this piece of patronage?'

'Hanged if I know,' the captain said: his principal turned
very red.

'To one of the most generous and kindest men in the
world, as he is one of the greatest – to my excellent friend,
the Marquis of Steyne.'

'I'll see him d— before I take his place,' growled out
Rawdon.

'You are irritated against my noble friend,' Mr. Wenham
calmly resumed: 'and now, in the name of common sense
and justice, tell me why?'

'*Why?*' cried Rawdon, in surprise.

'Why? Dammy!' said the captain, ringing his stick on the
ground.

'Dammy, indeed,' said Mr. Wenham, with the most

agreeable smile; 'still, look at the matter as a man of the world – as an honest man, and see if you have not been in the wrong. You come home from a journey, and find – what? – my Lord Steyne supping at your house in Curzon Street with Mrs. Crawley. Is the circumstance strange or novel? Has he not been a hundred times before in the same position? Upon my honour and word as a gentleman' (Mr. Wenham here put his hand on his waistcoat, with a parliamentary air), 'I declare I think that your suspicions are monstrous and utterly unfounded, and that they injure an honourable gentleman who has proved his goodwill towards you by a thousand benefactions – and a most spotless and innocent lady.'

'You don't mean to say that – that Crawley's mistaken?' said Mr. Macmurdo.

'I believe that Mrs. Crawley is as innocent as my wife, Mrs. Wenham,' Mr. Wenham said, with great energy. 'I believe that, misled by an infernal jealousy, my friend here strikes a blow against not only an infirm and old man of high station, his constant friend and benefactor, but against his wife, his own dearest honour, his son's future reputation, and his own prospects in life.

'I will tell you what happened,' Mr. Wenham continued, with great solemnity; 'I was sent for this morning by my Lord Steyne, and found him in a pitiable state, as, I need hardly inform Colonel Crawley, any man of age and infirmity would be after a personal conflict with a man of your strength. I say to your face; it was a cruel advantage you took of that strength, Colonel Crawley. It was not only the body of my noble and excellent friend which was wounded – his heart, sir, was bleeding. A man whom he had loaded with benefits and regarded with affection, had subjected him to the foulest indignity. What was this very appointment, which appears in the journals of to-day, but a proof of his kindness to you? When I saw his lordship this morning I found him in a state pitiable indeed to see: and as anxious as you are to revenge the outrage committed upon him, by blood. You know he has given his proofs, I presume, Colonel Crawley?'

'He has plenty of pluck,' said the colonel. 'Nobody ever said he hadn't.'

'His first order to me was to write a letter of challenge,

and to carry it to Colonel Crawley. One or other of you, he said, must not survive the outrage of last night.'

Crawley nodded. 'You're coming to the point, Wenham,' he said.

'I tried my utmost to calm Lord Steyne. "Good God! sir," I said, "how I regret that Mrs. Wenham and myself had not accepted Mrs. Crawley's invitation to sup with her!"'

'She asked you to sup with her?' Captain Macmurdo said.

'After the Opera. Here's the note of invitation – stop – no, this is another paper – I thought I had it, but it's of no consequence, and I pledge you my word to the fact. If we had come, and it was only one of Mrs. Wenham's headaches which prevented us – she suffers under them a good deal, especially in the spring – if we had come, and you had returned home, there would have been no quarrel, no insult, no suspicion – and so it is positively because my poor wife has a headache that you are to bring death down upon two men of honour, and plunge two of the most excellent and ancient families in the kingdom into disgrace and sorrow.'

Mr. Macmurdo looked at his principal with the air of a man profoundly puzzled; and Rawdon felt with a kind of rage that his prey was escaping him. He did not believe a word of the story, and yet, how discredit or disprove it?

Mr. Wenham continued with the same fluent oratory, which in his place in Parliament he had so often practised – 'I sat for an hour or more by Lord Steyne's beside, beseeching, imploring Lord Steyne to forgo his intention of demanding a meeting. I pointed out to him that the circumstances were after all suspicious – they were suspicious. I acknowledge it, any man in your position might have been taken in – I said that a man furious with jealousy is to all intents and purposes a madman, and should be as such regarded – that a duel between you must lead to the disgrace of all parties concerned – that a man of his lordship's exalted station had no right in these days, when the most atrocious revolutionary principles, and the most dangerous levelling doctrines are preached among the vulgar, to create a public scandal; and that, however innocent, the common people would insist that he was guilty. In fine, I implored him not to send the challenge.'

'I don't believe one word of the whole story,' said Rawdon, grinding his teeth. 'I believe it a d— lie, and that you're in it, Mr. Wenham. If the challenge don't come from him, by Jove it shall come from me.'

Mr. Wenham turned deadly pale at this savage interruption of the colonel, and looked towards the door.

But he found a champion in Captain Macmurdo. That gentleman rose up with an oath, and rebuked Rawdon for his language. 'You put the affair into my hands, and you shall act as I think fit, by Jove, and not as you do. You have no right to insult Mr. Wenham with this sort of language; and dammy, Mr. Wenham, you deserve an apology. And as for a challenge to Lord Steyne, you may get somebody else to carry it, I won't. If my lord, after being thrashed, chooses to sit still, dammy let him. And as for the affair with – with Mrs. Crawley, my belief is, there's nothing proved at all: that your wife's innocent, as innocent as Mr. Wenham says she is: and at any rate, that you would be a d—fool not to take the place and hold your tongue.'

'Captain Macmurdo, you speak like a man of sense,' Mr. Wenham cried out, immensely relieved – 'I forget any words that Colonel Crawley has used in the irritation of the moment.'

'I thought you would,' Rawdon said, with a sneer.

'Shut your mouth, you old stoopid,' the captain said, good-naturedly. 'Mr. Wenham ain't a fighting man; and quite right, too.'

'This matter, in my belief,' the Steyne emissary cried, 'ought to be buried in the most profound oblivion. A word concerning it should never pass these doors. I speak in the interest of my friend, as well as of Colonel Crawley, who persists in considering me his enemy.'

'I suppose Lord Steyne won't talk about it very much,' said Captain Macmurdo; 'and I don't see why our side should. The affair ain't a very pretty one, any way you take it; and the less said about it the better. It's you are thrashed, and not us; and if you are satisfied, why, I think, we should be.'

Mr. Wenham took his hat, upon this, and Captain Macmurdo following him to the door, shut it upon himself and Lord Steyne's agent, leaving Rawdon chafing within. When the two were on the other side, Macmurdo looked hard at the other ambassador, and with an expression of anything but respect on his round jolly face.

'You don't stick at a trifle, Mr. Wenham,' he said.

'You flatter me, Captain Macmurdo,' answered the other, with a smile. 'Upon my honour and conscience, now, Mrs. Crawley did ask us to sup after the Opera.'

'Of course; and Mrs. Wenham had one of her headaches. I say, I've got a thousand-pound note here, which I will give you if you will give me a receipt, please; and I will put the note up in an envelope for Lord Steyne. My man shan't fight him. But we had rather not take his money.'

'It was all a mistake, – all a mistake, my dear sir,' the other said, with the utmost innocence of manner; and was bowed down the club steps by Captain Macmurdo, just as Sir Pitt Crawley ascended them. There was a slight acquaintance between these two gentlemen; and the captain, going back with the baronet to the room where the latter's brother was, told Sir Pitt, in confidence, that he had made the affair all right between Lord Steyne and the colonel.

Sir Pitt was well pleased, of course, at this intelligence; and congratulated his brother warmly upon the peaceful issue of the affair, making appropriate moral remarks upon the evils of duelling, and the unsatisfactory nature of that sort of settlement of disputes.

And after this preface, he tried with all his eloquence to effect a reconciliation between Rawdon and his wife. He recapitulated the statements which Becky had made, pointed out the probabilities of their truth, and asserted his own firm belief in her innocence.

But Rawdon would not hear of it. 'She has kep money concealed from me these ten years,' he said. 'She swore, last night only, she had none from Steyne. She knew it was all up, directly I found it. If she's not guilty, Pitt, she's as bad as guilty; and I'll never see her again, – never.' His head sank down on his chest as he spoke the words; and he looked quite broken and sad.

'Poor old boy,' Macmurdo said, shaking his head.

Rawdon Crawley resisted for some time the idea of taking the place which had been procured for him by so odious a patron: and was also for removing the boy from the school where Lord Steyne's interest had placed him. He was induced, however, to acquiesce in these benefits by the entreaties of his brother and Macmurdo: but mainly by the latter pointing out to him what a fury Steyne would be in, to think that his enemy's fortune was made through his means.

When the Marquis of Steyne came abroad after his accident, the Colonial Secretary bowed up to him and congratulated himself and the Service upon having made so excellent an appointment. These congratulations were received with a degree of gratitude which may be imagined on the part of Lord Steyne.

The secret of the rencontre between him and Colonel Crawley was buried in the profoundest oblivion, as Wenham said; that is by the seconds and the principals. But before that evening was over it was talked of at fifty dinner-tables in Vanity Fair. Little Cackleby himself went to seven evening parties, and told the story with comments and emendations at each place. How Mrs. Washington White revelled in it! The Bishopess of Ealing was shocked beyond expression: the bishop went and wrote his name down in the visiting-book at Gaunt House that very day. Little Southdown was sorry: so you may be sure was his sister Lady Jane, very sorry. Lady Southdown wrote it off to her other daughter at the Cape of Good Hope. It was town-talk for at least three days, and was only kept out of the newspapers by the exertions of Mr. Wagg, acting upon a hint from Mr. Wenham.

The bailiffs and brokers seized upon poor Raggles in Curzon Street, and the late fair tenant of that poor little mansion was in the meanwhile – where? Who cared? Who asked after a day or two? Was she guilty or not? We all know how charitable the world is, and how the verdict of Vanity Fair goes when there is a doubt. Some people said she had gone to Naples in pursuit of Lord Steyne; whilst others averred that his lordship quitted that city, and fled to Palermo on hearing of Becky's arrival; some said she was living in Bierstadt, and had become a *dame d'honneur* to the Queen of Bulgaria; some that she was at Boulogne; and others, at a boarding-house at Cheltenham.

Rawdon made her a tolerable annuity; and we may be sure that she was a woman who could make a little money go a great way, as the saying is. He would have paid his debts on leaving England, could he have got any Insurance Office to take his life; but the climate of Coventry Island was so bad that he could borrow no money on the strength of his salary. He remitted, however, to his brother punctually, and wrote to his little boy regularly every mail. He kept Macmurdo in cigars; and sent over quantities of shells, cayenne pepper, hot pickles, guava jelly, and colonial produce to Lady Jane. He sent his brother home the *Swamp Town Gazette*, in which the new governor was praised with immense enthusiasm; whereas the *Swamp Town Sentinel*, whose wife was not asked to Government House, declared that his excellency was a tyrant, compared to whom Nero was an enlightened philanthropist. Little Rawdon used to like to get the papers and read about his excellency.

His mother never made any movement to see the child. He went home to his aunt for Sundays and holidays; he soon knew every bird's-nest about Queen's Crawley, and rode out with Sir Huddlestone's hounds, which he admired so on his first well-remembered visit to Hampshire.

CHAPTER LVI

GEORGY IS MADE A GENTLEMAN

GEORGY OSBORNE was now fairly established in his grandfather's mansion in Russell Square: occupant of his father's room in the house, and heir-apparent of all the splendours there. The good looks, gallant bearing, and gentlemanlike appearance of the boy won the grandsire's heart for him. Mr. Osborne was as proud of him as ever he had been of the elder George.

The child had many more luxuries and indulgences than had been awarded to his father. Osborne's commerce had prospered greatly of late years. His wealth and importance in the City had very much increased. He had been glad enough in former days to put the elder George to a good private school; and a commission in the army for his son had been a source of no small pride to him: for little George and his future prospects the old man looked much higher. He would make a gentleman of the little chap, was Mr. Osborne's constant saying regarding little Georgy. He saw him in his mind's eye, a collegian, a Parliament-man, – a baronet, perhaps. The old man thought he would die contented if he could see his grandson in a fair way to such honours. He would have none but a tip-top college man to

educate him, – none of your quacks and pretenders, – no,
no. A few years before, he used to be savage, and inveigh
against all parsons, scholars, and the like, – declaring that
they were a pack of humbugs, and quacks, that weren't fit
to get their living but by grinding Latin and Greek, and a
set of supercilious dogs, that pretended to look down upon
British merchants and gentlemen, who could buy up half a
hundred of 'em. He would mourn now, in a very solemn
manner, that his own education had been neglected, and
repeatedly point out, in pompous orations to Georgy, the
necessity and excellence of classical acquirements.

When they met at dinner the grandsire used to ask the
lad what he had been reading during the day, and was greatly
interested at the report the boy gave of his own studies:
pretending to understand little George when he spoke
regarding them. He made a hundred blunders, and showed
his ignorance many a time. It did not increase the respect
which the child had for his senior. A quick brain and a better
education elsewhere showed the boy very soon that his
grandsire was a dullard: and he began accordingly to command him and to look down upon him; for his previous
education, humble and contracted as it had been, had made
a much better gentleman of Georgy than any plans of his
grandfather could make him. He had been brought up by a
kind, weak, and tender woman, who had no pride about
anything, but about him, and whose heart was so pure and
whose bearing was so meek and humble, that she could not
but needs be a true lady. She busied herself in gentle offices
and quiet duties; if she never said brilliant things, she never
spoke or thought unkind ones: guileless and artless, loving
and pure, indeed how could our poor little Amelia be other
than a real gentlewoman?

Young Georgy lorded over this soft and yielding nature:
and the contrast of its simplicity and delicacy with the coarse
pomposity of the dull old man with whom he next came in
contact, made him lord over the latter too. If he had been
a prince royal he could not have been better brought up to
think well of himself.

Whilst his mother was yearning after him at home, and
I do believe every hour of the day, and during most hours
of the sad lonely nights, thinking of him, this young gentleman had a number of pleasures and consolations adminis-

tered to him, which made him for his part bear the separation from Amelia very easily. Little boys who cry when they
are going to school – cry because they are going to a very
uncomfortable place. It is only a very few who weep from
sheer affection. When you think that the eyes of your
childhood dried at the sight of a piece of ginger-bread, and
that a plum-cake was a compensation for the agony of parting
with your mamma and sisters; oh, my friend and brother,
you need not be too confident of your own fine feelings.

Well, then, Master George Osborne had every comfort
and luxury that a wealthy and lavish old grandfather thought
fit to provide. The coachman was instructed to purchase for
him the handsomest pony which could be bought for money;
and on this George was taught to ride, first at a riding-
school, whence, after he had performed satisfactorily without
stirrups, and over the leaping-bar, he was conducted through
the New Road to Regent's Park, and then to Hyde Park,
where he rode in state with Martin the coachman behind
him. Old Osborne, who took matters more easily in the City
now, where he left his affairs to his junior partners, would
often ride out with Miss O. in the same fashionable direction.
As little Georgy came cantering up with his dandified air,
and his heels down, his grandfather would nudge the lad's
aunt, and say, 'Look, Miss O.' And he would laugh, and
his face would grow red with pleasure, as he nodded out of
the window to the boy, as the groom saluted the carriage,
and the footman saluted Master George. Here too his aunt,
Mrs. Frederick Bullock (whose chariot might daily be seen
in the Ring, with bullocks *or* emblazoned on the panels and
harness, and three pasty-faced little Bullocks, covered with
cockades and feathers, staring from the windows), – Mrs.
Frederick Bullock, I say, flung glances of the bitterest hatred
at the little upstart as he rode by with his hand on his side
and his hat on one ear, as proud as a lord.

Though he was scarcely eleven years of age, Master
George wore straps and the most beautiful little boots like
a man. He had gilt spurs and a gold-headed whip, and a
fine pin in his handkerchief; and the neatest little kid gloves
which Lamb's Conduit Street could furnish. His mother had
given him a couple of neck-cloths, and carefully hemmed
and made some little shirts for him; but when her Samuel
came to see the widow, they were replaced by much finer

linen. He had little jewelled buttons in the lawn shirt-fronts. Her humble presents had been put aside – I believe Miss Osborne had given them to the coachman's boy. Amelia tried to think she was pleased at the change. Indeed, she was happy and charmed to see the boy looking so beautiful.

She had had a little black profile of him done for a shilling; and this was hung up by the side of another portrait over her bed. One day the boy came on his accustomed visit, galloping down the little street at Brompton, and bringing, as usual, all the inhabitants to the windows to admire his splendour, and with great eagerness, and a look of triumph in his face, he pulled a case out of his great-coat – (it was a natty white great-coat, with a cape and a velvet collar) – pulled out a red morocco case, which he gave her.

'I bought it with my own money, mamma,' he said. 'I thought you'd like it.'

Amelia opened the case, and giving a little cry of delighted affection, seized the boy and embraced him a hundred times. It was a miniature of himself, very prettily done (though not half handsome enough, we may be sure, the widow thought). His grandfather had wished to have a picture of him by an artist whose works, exhibited in a shop-window, in Southampton Row, had caught the old gentleman's eyes; and George, who had plenty of money, bethought him of asking the painter how much a copy of the little portrait would cost, saying that he would pay for it out of his own money, and that he wanted to give it to his mother. The pleased painter executed the copy for a small price; and old Osborne himself, when he heard of the incident, growled out his satisfaction, and gave the boy twice as many sovereigns as he paid for the miniature.

But what was the grandfather's pleasure compared to Amelia's ecstasy? That proof of the boy's affection charmed her so, that she thought no child in the world was like hers for goodness. For long weeks after, the thought of his love made her happy. She slept better with the picture under her pillow; and how many, many times did she kiss it, and weep and pray over it! A small kindness from those she loved made that timid heart grateful. Since her parting with George she had had no such joy and consolation.

At his new home Master George ruled like a lord: at dinner he invited the ladies to drink wine with the utmost coolness, and took off his champagne in a way which charmed his old grandfather. 'Look at him,' the old man would say, nudging his neighbour with a delighted purple face, 'did you ever see such a chap? Lord, Lord! he'll be ordering a dressing-case next, and razors to shave with; I'm blest if he won't.'

The antics of the lad did not, however, delight Mr. Osborne's friends so much as they pleased the old gentleman. It gave Mr. Justice Coffin no pleasure to hear Georgy cut into the conversation and spoil his stories. Colonel Fogey was not interested in seeing the little boy half tipsy. Mr. Serjeant Toffy's lady felt no particular gratitude when, with a twist of his elbow, he tilted a glass of port wine over her yellow satin, and laughed at the disaster: nor was she better pleased, although old Osborne was highly delighted, when Georgy 'whopped' her third boy (a young gentleman a year older than Georgy, and by chance home for the holidays from Dr. Tickleus's at Ealing School) in Russell Square. George's grandfather gave the boy a couple of sovereigns for that feat, and promised to reward him further for every boy above his own size and age whom he whopped in a similar manner. It is difficult to say what good the old man saw in these combats; he had a vague notion that quarrelling made boys hardy, and that tyranny was a useful accomplishment for them to learn. English youth have been so educated time out of mind, and we have hundreds of thousands of apologists and admirers of injustice, misery, and brutality, as perpetrated among children.

Flushed with praise and victory over Master Toffy, George wished naturally to pursue his conquests further, and one day as he was strutting about in prodigiously dandified new clothes, near St. Pancras, and a young baker's boy made sarcastic comments upon his appearance, the youthful patrician pulled off his dandy jacket with great spirit, and giving it in charge to the friend who accompanied him (Master Todd, of Great Coram Street, Russell Square, son of the junior partner of the house of Osborne and Co.) – George tried to whop the little baker. But the chances of war were unfavourable this time, and the little baker whopped Georgy; who came home with a rueful black eye and all his fine shirt frill dabbled with the claret drawn from his own little nose. He told his grandfather that he had been in combat with a giant; and frightened his poor mother at Brompton with long, and by no means authentic, accounts of the battle.

This young Todd, of Coram Street, Russell Square, was Master George's great friend and admirer. They both had a taste for painting theatrical characters; for hard-bake and raspberry tarts; for sliding and skating in the Regent's Park and the Serpentine, when the weather permitted; for going to the play, whither they were often conducted, by Mr. Osborne's orders, by Rowson, Master George's appointed body-servant; with whom they sat in great comfort in the pit.

In the company of this gentleman they visited all the principal theatres of the metropolis – knew the names of all the actors from Drury Lane to Sadler's Wells: and performed, indeed, many of the plays to the Todd family and their youthful friends, with West's famous characters, on their pasteboard theatre. Rowson, the footman, who was of a generous disposition, would not unfrequently, when in cash, treat his young master to oysters after the play, and to a glass of rum-shrub for a nightcap. We may be pretty certain that Mr. Rowson profited in his turn, by his young master's liberality and gratitude for the pleasures to which the footman inducted him.

A famous tailor from the West End of the town, – Mr. Osborne would have none of your City or Holborn bunglers he said, for the boy (though a City tailor was good enough for *him*) – was summoned to ornament little George's person, and was told to spare no expense in so doing. So, Mr. Woolsey of Conduit Street, gave a loose to his imagination, and sent the child home fancy trousers, fancy waistcoats, and fancy jackets enough to furnish a school of little dandies. Georgy had little white waistcoats for evening parties, and little cut velvet waistcoats for dinners, and a dear little darling shawl dressing-gown, for all the world like a little man. He dressed for dinner every day, 'like a regular West End swell,' as his grandfather remarked; one of the domestics was affected to his especial service, attended him at his toilette, answered his bell, and brought him his letters always on a silver tray.

Georgy, after breakfast, would sit in the arm-chair in the dining-room, and read the *Morning Post*, just like a grown-up man. 'How he *du* dam and swear,' the servants would

cry, delighted at his precocity. Those who remembered the
captain, his father, declared Master George was his pa every
inch of him. He made the house lively by his activity, his
imperiousness, his scolding, and his good nature.

George's education was confided to a neighbouring scholar
and private pedagogue who 'prepared young noblemen and
gentlemen for the Universities, the senate, and the learned
professions: whose system did not embrace the degrading
corporal severities, still practised at the ancient places of
education, and in whose family the pupils would find the
elegances of refined society and the confidence and affection
of a home'. It was in this way that the Reverend Lawrence
Veal of Hart Street, Bloomsbury, and domestic chaplain to
the Earl of Bareacres, strove, with Mrs. Veal, his wife, to
entice pupils.

By thus advertising and pushing sedulously, the domestic
chaplain and his lady generally succeeded in having one or
two scholars by them: who paid a high figure: and were
thought to be in uncommonly comfortable quarters. There
was a large West Indian, whom nobody came to see, with a
mahogany complexion, a woolly head, and an exceedingly
dandified appearance; there was another hulking boy, of
three-and-twenty, whose education had been neglected, and
whom Mr. and Mrs. Veal were to introduce into the polite
world; there were two sons of Colonel Bangles of the East
India Company's Service. These four sat down to dinner at
Mrs. Veal's genteel board, when Georgy was introduced to
her establishment.

Georgy was, like some dozen other pupils, only a day boy;
he arrived in the morning under the guardianship of his
friend Mr. Rowson, and if it was fine, would ride away in
the afternoon on his pony, followed by the groom. The wealth
of his grandfather was reported in the school to be prodigious.
The Rev. Mr. Veal used to compliment Georgy upon it
personally, warning him that he was destined for a high
station; that it became him to prepare, by sedulity and docility
in youth, for the lofty duties to which he would be called in
mature age; that obedience in the child was the best preparation for command in the man; and that he therefore begged
George would not bring toffy into the school, and ruin the
health of the Masters Bangles, who had everything they
wanted at the elegant and abundant table of Mrs. Veal.

With respect to learning, 'the Curriculum,' as Mr. Veal loved to call it, was of prodigious extent: and the young gentlemen in Hart Street might learn a something of every known science. The Rev. Mr. Veal had an orrery, an electrifying machine, a turning lathe, a theatre (in the washhouse), a chemical apparatus, and what he called a select library of all the works of the best authors of ancient and modern times and languages. He took the boys to the British Museum, and descanted upon the antiquities and the specimens of natural history there, so that audiences would gather round him as he spoke, and all Bloomsbury highly admired him as a prodigiously well-informed man. And whenever he spoke (which he did almost always), he took care to produce the very finest and longest words of which the vocabulary gave him the use; rightly judging, that it was as cheap to employ a handsome, large, and sonorous epithet, as to use a little stingy one.

Thus he would say to George in school, 'I observed on my return home from taking the indulgence of an evening's scientific conversation with my excellent friend Dr. Bulders – a true archaeologian, gentlemen, a true archaeologian – that the windows of your venerated grandfather's almost princely mansion in Russell Square were illuminated as if for the purposes of festivity. Am I right in my conjecture, that Mr. Osborne entertained a society of chosen spirits round his sumptuous board last night?'

Little Georgy, who had considerable humour, and used to mimic Mr. Veal to his face with great spirit and dexterity, would reply, that Mr. V. was quite correct in his surmise.

'Then those friends who had the honour of partaking of Mr. Osborne's hospitality, gentlemen, had no reason, I will lay any wager, to complain of their repast. I myself have been more than once so favoured. (By the way, Master Osborne, you came a little late this morning, and have been a defaulter in this respect more than once.) I myself, I say, gentlemen, humble as I am, have been found not unworthy to share Mr. Osborne's elegant hospitality. And though I have feasted with the great and noble of the world – for I presume that I may call my excellent friend and patron, the Right Honourable George, Earl of Bareacres, as one of the number – yet I assure you that the board of the British merchant was to the full as richly served, and his reception

as gratifying and noble. Mr. Bluck, sir, we will resume, if
you please, that passage of Eutropius, which was interrupted
by the late arrival of Master Osborne.'

To this great man George's education was for some time
entrusted. Amelia was bewildered by his phrases, but thought
him a prodigy of learning. That poor widow made friends
of Mrs. Veal, for reasons of her own. She liked to be in the
house, and see Georgy coming to school there. She liked to
be asked to Mrs. Veal's *conversazioni*, which took place
once a month (as you were informed on pink cards, with
AΘHNH engraved on them), and where the professor welcomed his pupils and their friends to weak tea and scientific
conversation. Poor little Amelia never missed one of these
entertainments, and thought them delicious so long as she
might have Georgy sitting by her. And she would walk from
Brompton in any weather, and embrace Mrs. Veal with
tearful gratitude for the delightful evening she had passed,
when, the company having retired, and Georgy gone off with
Mr. Rowson, his attendant, poor Mrs. Osborne put on her
cloaks and her shawls preparatory to walking home.

As for the learning which Georgy imbibed under this
voluble master of a hundred sciences, to judge from the
weekly reports which the lad took home to his grandfather,
his progress was remarkable. The names of a score or more
of desirable branches of knowledge were printed on a table,
and the pupil's progress in each was marked by the professor.
In Greek Georgy was pronounced *aristos*, in Latin *optimus*,
in French *très bien*, and so forth: and everybody had prizes
for everything at the end of the year. Even Mr. Swartz, the
woolly-headed young gentleman, and half-brother to the
Honourable Mrs. McMull, and Mr. Bluck, the neglected
young pupil of three-and-twenty from the agricultural dis-
tricts, and that idle young scapegrace of a Master Todd
before mentioned, received little eighteenpenny books, with
'Athene' engraved in them, and a pompous Latin inscription
from the professor to his young friends.

The family of this Master Todd were hangers-on of the
house of Osborne. The old gentleman had advanced Todd
from being a clerk to be a junior partner in his establishment.

Mr. Osborne was the godfather of young Master Todd
(who in subsequent life wrote Mr. Osborne Todd on his
cards, and became a man of decided fashion), while Miss

Osborne had accompanied Miss Maria Todd to the font, and gave her protégée a Prayer-book, a collection of tracts, a volume of very Low Church poetry, or some such memento of her goodness every year. Miss O. drove the Todds out in her carriage now and then: when they were ill, her footman, in large plush smalls and waistcoat, brought jellies and delicacies from Russell Square to Coram Street. Coram Street trembled and looked up to Russell Square indeed: and Mrs. Todd, who had a pretty hand at cutting out paper trimmings for haunches of mutton, and could make flowers, ducks, &c., out of turnips and carrots in a very creditable manner, would go to 'the Square', as it was called, and assist in the preparations incident to a great dinner, without even so much as thinking of sitting down to the banquet. If any guest failed at the eleventh hour, Todd was asked to dine. Mrs. Todd and Maria came across in the evening, slipped in with a muffled knock, and were in the drawing-room by the time Miss Osborne and the ladies under her convoy reached that apartment; and ready to fire off duets and sing until the gentlemen came up. Poor Maria Todd; poor young lady! How she had to work and thrum at these duets and sonatas in the Street, before they appeared in public in the Square!

Thus it seemed to be decreed by fate, that Georgy was to domineer over everybody with whom he came in contact, and that friends, relatives, and domestics were all to bow the knee before the little fellow. It must be owned that he accommodated himself very willingly to this arrangement. Most people do so. And Georgy liked to play the part of master, and perhaps had a natural aptitude for it.

In Russell Square everybody was afraid of Mr. Osborne, and Mr. Osborne was afraid of Georgy. The boy's dashing manners, and off-hand rattle about books and learning, his likeness to his father (dead unreconciled in Brussels yonder), awed the old gentleman, and gave the young boy the mastery. The old man would start at some hereditary feature or tone unconsciously used by the little lad, and fancy that George's father was again before him. He tried by indulgence to the grandson to make up for harshness to the elder George. People were surprised at his gentleness to the boy. He growled and swore at Miss Osborne as usual: and would smile when George came down late for breakfast.

Miss Osborne, George's aunt, was a faded old spinster, broken down by more than forty years of dullness and coarse usage. It was easy for a lad of spirit to master *her*. And whenever George wanted anything from her, from the jampots in her cupboards, to the cracked and dry old colours in her paint-box (the old paint-box which she had had when she was a pupil of Mr. Smee, and was still almost young and blooming), Georgy took possession of the object of his desire, which obtained, he took no further notice of his aunt.

For his friends and cronies, he had a pompous old schoolmaster, who flattered him, and a toady, his senior, whom he could thrash. It was dear Mrs. Todd's delight to leave him with her youngest daughter, Rosa Jemima, a darling child of eight years old. The little pair looked so well together, she would say (but not to the folks in 'the Square', we may be sure), – 'Who knows what might happen? Don't they make a pretty little couple?' the fond mother thought.

The broken-spirited, old, maternal grandfather was likewise subject to the little tyrant. He could not help respecting a lad who had such fine clothes, and rode with a groom behind him. Georgy, on his side, was in the constant habit of hearing coarse abuse and vulgar satire levied at John Sedley, by his pitiless old enemy, Mr. Osborne. Osborne used to call the other the old pauper, the old coalman, the old bankrupt, and by many other such names of brutal contumely. How was little George to respect a man so prostrate? A few months after he was with his paternal grandfather, Mrs. Sedley died. There had been little love between her and the child. He did not care to show much grief. He came down to visit his mother in a fine new suit of mourning, and was very angry that he could not go to a play upon which he had set his heart.

The illness of that old lady had been the occupation and perhaps the safeguard of Amelia. What do men know about women's martyrdoms? We should go mad had we to endure the hundredth part of those daily pains which are meekly borne by many women. Ceaseless slavery meeting with no reward; constant gentleness and kindness met by cruelty as constant; love, labour, patience, watchfulness, without even so much as the acknowledgement of a good word; all this, how many of them have to bear in quiet, and appear abroad with cheerful faces, as if they felt nothing. Tender slaves that they are, they must needs be hypocrites and weak.

From her chair Amelia's mother had taken to her bed, which she had never left; and from which Mrs. Osborne herself was never absent except when she ran to see George. The old lady grudged her even those rare visits; she, who had been a kind, smiling, good-natured mother once, in the days of her prosperity, but whom poverty and infirmities had broken down. Her illness or estrangement did not affect Amelia. They rather enabled her to support the other calamity under which she was suffering, and from the thoughts of which she was kept by the ceaseless calls of the invalid. Amelia bore her harshness quite gently; smoothed the uneasy pillow; was always ready with a soft answer to the watchful, querulous voice; soothed the sufferer with words of hope, such as her pious simple heart could best feel and utter, and closed the eyes that had once looked so tenderly upon her.

Then all her time and tenderness were devoted to the consolation and comfort of the bereaved old father, who was stunned by the blow which had befallen him, and stood utterly alone in the world. His wife, his honour, his fortune, everything he loved best had fallen away from him. There was only Amelia to stand by and support with her gentle arms the tottering, heart-broken, old man. We are not going to write the history; it would be too dreary and stupid. I can see Vanity Fair yawning over it *d'avance*.

One day as the young gentlemen were assembled in the study at the Rev. Mr. Veal's, and the domestic chaplain to the Right Honourable the Earl of Bareacres was spouting away as usual – a smart carriage drove up to the door decorated with the statue of Athene, and two gentlemen stepped out. The young Masters Bangles rushed to the window, with a vague notion that their father might have arrived from Bombay. The great hulking scholar of three-and-twenty, who was crying secretly over a passage of Eutropius, flattened his neglected nose against the panes, and looked at the drag, as the *laquais de place* sprang from the box and let out the persons in the carriage.

'It's a fat one and a thin one,' Mr. Bluck said, as a thundering knock came to the door.

Everybody was interested, from the domestic chaplain himself, who hoped he saw the fathers of some future pupils, down to Master Georgy, glad of any pretext for laying his book down.

The boy in the shabby livery, with the faded copper buttons, who always thrust himself into the tight coat to open the door, came into the study and said, 'Two gentlemen want to see Master Osborne.' The professor had had a trifling altercation in the morning with that young gentleman, owing to a difference about the introduction of crackers in school-time; but his face resumed its habitual expression of bland courtesy, as he said, 'Master Osborne, I give you full permission to go and see your carriage friends – to whom I beg you to convey the respectful compliments of myself and Mrs. Veal.'

Georgy went into the reception-room, and saw two strangers, whom he looked at with his head up, in his usual haughty manner. One was fat, with moustachios, and the other was lean and long, in a blue frock-coat, with a brown face, and a grizzled head.

'My God, how like he is!' said the long gentleman, with a start. 'Can you guess who we are, George?'

The boy's face flushed up, as it did usually when he was moved, and his eyes brightened. 'I don't know the other,' he said, 'but I should think you must be Major Dobbin.'

Indeed it was our old friend. His voice trembled with pleasure as he greeted the boy, and taking both the other's hands in his own, drew the lad to him.

'Your mother has talked to you about me – has she?' he said.

'That she has,' Georgy answered, 'hundreds and hundreds of times.'

CHAPTER LVII

EOTHEN

I T was one of the many causes for personal pride with which old Osborne chose to recreate himself, that Sedley, his ancient rival, enemy, and benefactor, was in his last days so utterly defeated and humiliated, as to be forced to accept pecuniary obligations at the hands of the man who had most

injured and insulted him. The successful man of the world
cursed the old pauper, and relieved him from time to time.
As he furnished George with money for his mother, he gave
the boy to understand by hints, delivered in his brutal, coarse
way, that George's maternal grandfather was but a wretched
old bankrupt and dependant, and that John Sedley might
thank the man to whom he already owed ever so much
money, for the aid which his generosity now chose to
administer. George carried the pompous supplies to his
mother and the shattered old widower whom it was now the
main business of her life to tend and comfort. The little
fellow patronized the feeble and disappointed old man.

It may have shown a want of 'proper pride' in Amelia
that she chose to accept these money benefits at the hands
of her father's enemy. But proper pride and this poor lady
had never had much acquaintance together. A disposition
naturally simple and demanding protection; a long course of
poverty and humility, of daily privations, and hard words,
of kind offices and no returns, had been her lot ever since
womanhood almost, or since her luckless marriage with
George Osborne. You who see your betters, bearing up
under this shame every day, meekly suffering under the
slights of fortune, gentle and unpitied, poor, and rather
despised for their poverty, do you ever step down from your
prosperity and wash the feet of these poor wearied beggars?
The very thought of them is odious and low. 'There must
be classes – there must be rich and poor,' Dives says,
smacking his claret – (it is well if he even sends the broken
meat out to Lazarus sitting under the window). Very true;
but think how mysterious and often unaccountable it is –
that lottery of life which gives to this man the purple and
fine linen, and sends to the other rags for garments and dogs
for comforters.

So I must own, that without much repining, on the
contrary with something akin to gratitude, Amelia took the
crumbs that her father-in-law let drop now and then and
with them fed her own parent. Directly she understood it
to be her duty, it was this young woman's nature (ladies,
she is but thirty still, and we choose to call her a young
woman even at that age) – it was, I say, her nature to
sacrifice herself and to fling all that she had at the feet of
the beloved object. During what long thankless nights had

she worked out her fingers for little Georgy whilst at home with her; what buffets, scorns, privations, poverties had she endured for father and mother! And in the midst of all these solitary resignations and unseen sacrifices, she did not respect herself any more than the world respected her; but I believe thought in her heart that she was a poor-spirited, despicable little creature, whose luck in life was only too good for her merits. O you poor women! O you poor secret martyrs and victims, whose life is a torture, who are stretched on racks in your bedrooms, and who lay your heads down on the block daily at the drawing-room table; every man who watches your pains, or peers into those dark places where the torture is administered to you, must pity you – and – and thank God that he has a beard. I recollect seeing, years ago, at the prison for idiots and madmen at Bicêtre, near Paris, a poor wretch bent down under the bondage of his imprisonment and his personal infirmity, to whom one of our party gave a half penny worth of snuff in a *cornet* or 'screw' of paper. The kindness was too much for the poor epileptic creature. He cried in an anguish of delight and gratitude: if anybody gave you and me a thousand a year, or saved our lives, we could not be so affected. And so, if you properly tyrannize over a woman, you will find a halfp'orth of kindness act upon her, and bring tears into her eyes, as though you were an angel benefiting her.

Some such boons as these were the best which Fortune allotted to poor little Amelia. Her life, begun not unprosperously, had come down to this – to a mean prison and a long, ignoble bondage. Little George visited her captivity sometimes, and consoled it with feeble gleams of encouragement. Russell Square was the boundary of her prison: she might walk thither occasionally, but was always back to sleep in her cell at night; to perform cheerless duties; to watch by thankless sick-beds; to suffer the harassment and tyranny of querulous disappointed old age. How many thousands of people are there, women for the most part, who are doomed to endure this long slavery? – who are hospital nurses without wages, – sisters of Charity, if you like, without the romance and the sentiment of sacrifice, – who strive, fast, watch, and suffer, unpitied; and fade away ignobly and unknown. The hidden and awful Wisdom which apportions the destinies of mankind is pleased so to humiliate and cast down the tender, good, and wise; and to set up the selfish, the foolish, or the wicked. Oh, be humble, my brother, in your prosperity! Be gentle with those who are less lucky, if not more deserving. Think, what right have you to be scornful, whose virtue is a deficiency of temptation, whose success may be a chance, whose rank may be an ancestor's accident, whose prosperity is very likely a satire.

They buried Amelia's mother in the churchyard at Brompton; upon just such a rainy, dark day, as Amelia recollected when first she had been there to marry George. Her little boy sat by her side in pompous new sables. She remembered the old pew-woman and clerk. Her thoughts were away in other times as the parson read. But that she held George's hand in her own, perhaps she would have liked to change places with . . . Then, as usual, she felt ashamed of her selfish thoughts, and prayed inwardly to be strengthened to do her duty.

So she determined with all her might and strength to try and make her old father happy. She slaved, toiled, patched and mended, sang and played backgammon, read out the newspaper, cooked dishes for old Sedley, walked him out sedulously into Kensington Gardens or the Brompton lanes, listened to his stories with untiring smiles and affectionate hypocrisy, or sat musing by his side and communing with her own thoughts and reminiscences, as the old man, feeble and querulous, sunned himself on the garden benches and prattled about his wrongs or his sorrows. What sad, unsatisfactory thoughts those of the widow were! The children running up and down the slopes and broad paths in the gardens, reminded her of George who was taken from her: her selfish, guilty love, in both instances, had been rebuked and bitterly chastised. She strove to think it was right that she should be so punished. She was such a miserable wicked sinner. She was quite alone in the world.

I know that the account of this kind of solitary imprisonment is insufferably tedious, unless there is some cheerful or humorous incident to enliven it, – a tender gaoler, for instance, or a waggish commandant of the fortress, or a mouse to come out and play about Latude's beard and whiskers, or a subterranean passage under the castle, dug by Trenck with his nails and a toothpick: the historian has no such enlivening incident to relate in the narrative of Amelia's captivity. Fancy her, if you please, during this period, very sad, but always ready to smile when spoken to; in a very mean, poor, not to say vulgar position of life; singing songs, making puddings, playing cards, mending stockings, for her old father's benefit. So, never mind, whether she be a heroine or no; or you and I, however old, scolding, and bankrupt; – may we have in our last days a kind soft shoulder on which to lean, and a gentle hand to soothe our gouty old pillows.

Old Sedley grew very fond of his daughter after his wife's death; and Amelia had her consolation in doing her duty by the old man.

But we are not going to leave these two people long in such a low and ungenteel station of life. Better days, as far as worldly prosperity went, were in store for both. Perhaps the ingenious reader has guessed who was the stout gentleman who called upon Georgy at his school in company with our old friend Major Dobbin. It was another old acquaintance returned to England, and at a time when his presence was likely to be of great comfort to his relatives there.

Major Dobbin having easily succeeded in getting leave from his good-natured commandant to proceed to Madras, and thence probably to Europe, on urgent private affairs, never ceased travelling night and day until he reached his journey's end, and had directed his march with such celerity, that he arrived at Madras in a high fever. His servants who accompanied him, brought him to the house of the friend, with whom he had resolved to stay until his departure for Europe, in a state of delirium; and it was thought for many, many days that he would never travel farther than the burying-ground of the church of St. George's, where the troops should fire a salvo over his grave, and where many a gallant officer lies far away from his home.

Here as the poor fellow lay tossing in his fever, the people who watched him might have heard him raving about Amelia. The idea that he should never see her again depressed him in his lucid hours. He thought his last day was come; and he made his solemn preparations for departure: setting his affairs in this world in order, and leaving the little property of which he was possessed to those whom he most desired to benefit. The friend in whose house he was located witnessed his testament. He desired to be buried with a little brown hair-chain which he wore round his neck, and which, if the truth must be known, he had got from Amelia's maid at Brussels, when the young widow's hair was cut off, during the fever which prostrated her after the death of George Osborne on the plateau of Mount St. John.

He recovered, rallied, relapsed again, having undergone such a process of blood-letting and calomel as showed the strength of his original constitution. He was almost a skeleton when they put him on board the *Ramchunder* East Indiaman, Captain Bragg, from Calcutta touching at Madras; and so weak and prostrate, that his friend who had tended him through his illness, prophesied that the honest major would never survive the voyage, and that he would pass some morning, shrouded in flag and hammock, over the ship's side, and carrying down to the sea with him, the relic that he wore at his heart. But whether it was the sea air, or the hope which sprang up in him afresh, from the day that the ship spread her canvas and stood out of the roads towards *home*, our friend began to amend, and he was quite well (though as gaunt as a greyhound) before they reached the Cape. 'Kirk will be disappointed of his majority this time,' he said with a smile: 'he will expect to find himself gazetted by the time the regiment reaches home.' For it must be premised that while the major was lying ill at Madras, having made such a prodigious haste to go thither, the gallant –th which had passed many years abroad, which after its return from the West Indies had been balked of its stay at home by the Waterloo campaign, and had been ordered from Flanders to India, had received orders home; and the major might have accompanied his comrades, had he chosen to wait for their arrival at Madras.

Perhaps he was not inclined to put himself in his exhausted state again under the guardianship of Glorvina. 'I think Miss O'Dowd would have done for me,' he said, laughingly, to a fellow-passenger, 'if we had had her on board, and when she had sunk me, she would have fallen upon you, depend upon it, and carried you in as a prize to Southampton, Jos, my boy.'

For indeed it was no other than our stout friend who was also a passenger on board the *Ramchunder*. He had passed ten years in Bengal. – Constant dinners, tiffins, pale ale, and

claret, the prodigious labours of cutcherry, and the refreshment of brandy-pawnee which he was forced to take there,
had their effect upon Waterloo Sedley. A voyage to Europe
was pronounced necessary for him – and having served his
full time in India, and had fine appointments which had
enabled him to lay by a considerable sum of money, he was
free to come home and stay with a good pension, or to return
and resume that rank in his service to which his seniority
and his vast talents entitled him.

He was rather thinner than when we last saw him, but
had gained in majesty and solemnity of demeanour. He had
resumed the moustachios to which his services at Waterloo
entitled him, and swaggered about on deck in a magnificent
velvet cap with a gold band, and a profuse ornamentation
of pins and jewellery about his person. He took breakfast in
his cabin, and dressed as solemnly to appear on the quarter-
deck, as if he was going to turn out for Bond Street, or the
Course at Calcutta. He brought a native servant with him,
who was his valet and pipe-bearer; and who wore the Sedley
crest in silver on his turban. That oriental menial had a
wretched life under the tyranny of Jos Sedley. Jos was as
vain of his person as a woman, and took as long a time at
his toilette as any fading beauty. The youngsters among the
passengers, young Chaffers of the 150th, and poor little
Ricketts, coming home after his third fever, used to draw
out Sedley at the cuddy-table, and make him tell prodigious
stories about himself and his exploits against tigers and
Napoleon. He was great when he visited the Emperor's tomb
at Longwood, when to these gentlemen and the young
officers of the ship, Major Dobbin not being by, he described
the whole battle of Waterloo, and all but announced that
Napoleon never would have gone to St. Helena at all but
for him, Jos Sedley.

After leaving St. Helena he became very generous, disposing of a great quantity of ship's stores, claret, preserved
meats, and great casks packed with soda-water, brought out
for his private delectation. There were no ladies on board:
the major gave the *pas* of precedency to the civilian, so that
he was the first dignitary at table; and treated by Captain
Bragg, and the officers of the *Ramchunder*, with the respect
which his rank warranted. He disappeared rather in a panic
during a two-days' gale, in which he had the port-holes of

his cabin battened down; and remained in his cot reading the *Washerwoman of Finchley Common*, left on board the *Ramchunder* by the Right Honourable the Lady Emily Hornblower, wife of the Rev. Silas Hornblower, then on their passage out to the Cape, where the reverend gentleman was a missionary: but, for common reading, he had brought a stock of novels and plays which he lent to the rest of the ship, and rendered himself agreeable to all by his kindness and condescension.

Many and many a night as the ship was cutting through the roaring dark sea, the moon and stars shining overhead, and the bell singing out the watch, Mr. Sedley and the major would sit on the quarter-deck of the vessel talking about home, as the major smoked his cheroot, and the civilian puffed at the hookah which his servant prepared for him.

In these conversations it was wonderful with what perseverance and ingenuity Major Dobbin would manage to bring the talk round to the subject of Amelia and her little boy. Jos, a little testy about his father's misfortunes and unceremonious applications to him, was soothed down by the major, who pointed out the elder's ill fortunes and old age. He would not perhaps like to live with the old couple: whose ways and hours might not agree with those of a younger man, accustomed to different society (Jos bowed at this compliment): but, the major pointed out, how advantageous it would be for Jos Sedley to have a house of his own in London, and not a mere bachelor's establishment as before: how his sister Amelia would be the very person to preside over it; how elegant, how gentle she was, and of what refined good manners. He recounted stories of the success which Mrs. George Osborne had had in former days at Brussels, and in London, where she was much admired by people of very great fashion: and he then hinted how becoming it would be for Jos to send Georgy to a good school and make a man of him; for his mother and her parents would be sure to spoil him. In a word this artful major made the civilian promise to take charge of Amelia and her unprotected child. He did not know as yet what events had happened in the little Sedley family: and how death had removed the mother, and riches had carried off George from Amelia. But the fact is, that every day and always, this love-smitten and middle-aged gentleman was thinking about Mrs. Osborne, and his whole heart was bent upon doing her good. He coaxed, wheedled, cajoled, and complimented Jos Sedley with a perseverance and cordiality of which he was not aware himself, very likely: but some men who have unmarried sisters or daughters even, may remember how uncommonly agreeable gentlemen are to the male relations when they are courting the females; and perhaps this rogue of a Dobbin was urged by a similar hypocrisy.

The truth is, when Major Dobbin came on board the *Ramchunder*, very sick, and for the three days she lay in the Madras roads, he did not begin to rally, nor did even the appearance and recognition of his old acquaintance, Mr. Sedley, on board much cheer him, until after a conversation which they had one day, as the major was laid languidly on the deck. He said then he thought he was doomed; he had left a little something to his godson in his will; and he trusted Mrs. Osborne would remember him kindly, and be happy in the marriage she was about to make. 'Married? not the least,' Jos answered; 'he had heard from her: she made no mention of the marriage, and by the way, it was curious, she wrote to say that Major Dobbin was going to be married, and hoped that *he* would be happy.' What were the dates of Sedley's letters from Europe? The civilian fetched them. They were two months later than the major's; and the ship's surgeon congratulated himself upon the treatment adopted by him towards his new patient, who had been consigned to shipboard by the Madras practitioner with very small hopes indeed; for, from that day, the very day that he changed the draught, Major Dobbin began to mend. And thus it was that deserving officer, Captain Kirk, was disappointed of his majority.

After they passed St. Helena, Major Dobbin's gaiety and strength was such as to astonish all his fellow-passengers. He larked with the midshipmen, played singlestick with the mates, ran up the shrouds like a boy, sang a comic song one night to the amusement of the whole party assembled over their grog after supper, and rendered himself so gay, lively, and amiable, that even Captain Bragg, who thought there was nothing in his passenger, and considered he was a poor-spirited feller at first, was constrained to own that the major was a reserved but well-informed and meritorious officer. 'He ain't got distangy manners, dammy,' Bragg observed to his first mate; 'he wouldn't do at Government House, Roper, where his lordship and Lady William was as kind to me, and shook hands with me before the whole company and asking me at dinner to take beer with him before the commander-in-chief himself; he ain't got manners, but there's something about him —.' And thus Captain Bragg showed that he possessed discrimination as a man, as well as ability as a commander.

But a calm taking place when the *Ramchunder* was within ten days' sail of England, Dobbin became so impatient and ill-humoured as to surprise those comrades who had before admired his vivacity and good temper. He did not recover until the breeze sprang up again, and was in a highly excited state when the pilot came on board. Good God, how his heart beat as the two friendly spires of Southampton came in sight!

CHAPTER LVIII

OUR FRIEND THE MAJOR

OUR major had rendered himself so popular on board the *Ramchunder*, that when he and Mr. Sedley descended into the welcome shore-boat which was to take them from the ship, the whole crew, men and officers, the great Captain Bragg himself leading off, gave three cheers for Major Dobbin, who blushed very much, and ducked his head in token of thanks. Jos, who very likely thought the cheers were for himself, took off his gold-laced cap and waved it majestically to his friends, and they were pulled to shore and landed with great dignity at the pier, whence they proceeded to the 'Royal George' Hotel.

Although the sight of that magnificent round of beef, and the silver tankard suggestive of real British home-brewed ale and porter, which perennially greet the eyes of the traveller returning from foreign parts, who enters the coffee-room of the 'George', are so invigorating and delightful, that a man entering such a comfortable snug homely English inn, might well like to stop some days there, yet Dobbin began to talk about a post-chaise instantly, and was no sooner at Southampton than he wished to be on the road to London. Jos, however, would not hear of moving that evening. Why was he to pass the night in a post-chaise, instead of a great large undulating downy feather bed which was there ready to replace the horrid little narrow crib in which the portly Bengal gentleman had been confined during the voyage? He could not think of moving till his baggage was cleared, or of travelling until he could do so with his chillum. So the major was forced to wait over that night, and dispatched a letter to his family announcing his arrival; entreating from Jos a promise to write to his own friends. Jos promised, but didn't keep his promise. The captain, the surgeon, and one or two passengers came and dined with our two gentlemen at the inn; Jos exerting himself in a sumptuous way in ordering the dinner: and promising to go to town the next day with the major. The landlord said it did his eyes good to see Mr. Sedley take off his first pint of porter. If I had time and dared to enter into digressions, I would write a chapter about that first pint of porter drunk upon English ground. Ah, how good it is! It is worth while to leave home for a year, just to enjoy that one draught.

Major Dobbin made his appearance the next morning very neatly shaved and dressed, according to his wont. Indeed it was so early in the morning, that nobody was up in the house except that wonderful boots of an inn who never seems to want sleep; and the major could hear the snores of the various inmates of the house roaring through the corridors as he creaked about in those dim passages. Then the sleepless boots went shirking round from door to door, gathering up at each the Bluchers, Wellingtons, Oxonians, which stood outside. Then Jos's native servant arose and began to get ready his master's ponderous dressing apparatus, and prepare his hookah: then the maidservants got up, and meeting the dark man in the passages, shrieked, and mistook him for the devil. He and Dobbin stumbled over their pails in the passages as they were scouring the decks of the 'Royal George'. When the first unshorn waiter appeared and unbarred the door of the inn, the major thought that the time for departure was arrived, and ordered a post-chaise to be fetched instantly, that they might set off.

He then directed his steps to Mr. Sedley's room, and opened the curtains of the great large family bed wherein Mr. Jos was snoring. 'Come, up, Sedley,' the major said, 'it's time to be off; the chaise will be at the door in half an hour.'

Jos growled from under the counterpane to know what the time was; but when he at last extorted from the blushing major (who never told fibs, however much they might be to his advantage) what was the real hour of the morning, he broke out into a volley of bad language, which we will not repeat here, but by which he gave Dobbin to understand that he would jeopardy his soul if he got up at that moment, that the major might go and be hanged, that he would not travel with Dobbin, and that it was most unkind and ungentlemanlike to disturb a man out of his sleep in that way; on which the discomfited major was obliged to retreat, leaving Jos to resume his interrupted slumbers.

The chaise came up presently, and the major would wait no longer.

If he had been an English nobleman travelling on a pleasure tour, or a newspaper courier bearing dispatches (Government messages are generally carried much more quietly), he could not have travelled more quickly. The postboys wondered at the fees he flung amongst them. How happy and green the country looked as the chaise whirled rapidly from milestone to milestone, through neat country towns where landlords came out to welcome him with smiles and bows; by pretty roadside inns, where the signs hung on the elms, and horses and wagoners were drinking under the chequered shadow of the trees; by old halls and parks; rustic hamlets clustered round ancient grey churches – and through the charming friendly English landscape. Is there any in the world like it? To a traveller returning home it looks so kind – it seems to shake hands with you as you pass through it. Well, Major Dobbin passed over all this through from Southampton to London, and without noting much beyond the milestones along the road. You see he was so eager to see his parents at Camberwell.

He grudged the time lost between Piccadilly and his old haunt at the Slaughters', whither he drove faithfully. Long years had passed since he saw it last, since he and George, as young men, had enjoyed many a feast, and held many a revel there. He had now passed into the stage of old-fellow-hood. His hair was grizzled, and many a passion and feeling of his youth had grown grey in that interval. There, however, stood the old waiter at the door in the same greasy black suit, with the same double chin and flaccid face, with the same huge bunch of seals at his fob, rattling his money in his pockets as before, and receiving the major as if he had gone away only a week ago. 'Put the major's things in twenty-three, that's his room,' John said, exhibiting not the least surprise. 'Roast fowl for your dinner, I suppose. You ain't got married? They said you was married – the Scotch surgeon of yours was here. No, it was Captain Humby of the Thirty-third, as was quartered with the –th in Injee. Like any warm water? What do you come in a chay for – ain't the coach good enough?' And with this, the faithful waiter, who knew and remembered every officer who used the house, and with whom ten years were but as yesterday, led the way up to Dobbin's old room, where stood the great moreen bed, and the shabby carpet, a thought more dingy, and all the old black furniture covered with faded chintz, just as the major recollected them in his youth.

He remembered George pacing up and down the room, and biting his nails, and swearing that the governor must come round, and that if he didn't, he didn't care a straw, on the day before he was married. He could fancy him walking in, banging the door of Dobbin's room, and his own hard by –

'You ain't got young,' John said, calmly surveying his friend of former days.

Dobbin laughed. 'Ten years and a fever don't make a man young, John,' he said. 'It is you that are always young: – No, you are always old.'

'What became of Captain Osborne's widow?' John said. 'Fine young fellow that. Lord, how he used to spend his money. He never came back after that day he was married from here. He owes me three pound at this minute. Look here, I have it in my book. "April 10, 1815, Captain Osborne: 3l." I wonder whether his father would pay me,' and so saying, John of the Slaughters' pulled out the very morocco pocketbook in which he had noted his loan to the captain, upon a greasy faded page still extant, with many other scrawled memoranda regarding the bygone frequenters of the house.

Having inducted his customer into the room, John retired with perfect calmness; and Major Dobbin, not without a

blush and a grin at his own absurdity, chose out of his kit
the very smartest and most becoming civil costume he
possessed, and laughed at his own tanned face and grey hair,
as he surveyed them in the dreary little toilet-glass on the
dressing-table.

'I'm glad old John didn't forget me,' he thought. 'She'll
know me, too, I hope.' And he sallied out of the inn, bending
his steps once more in the direction of Brompton.

Every minute incident of his last meeting with Amelia
was present to the constant man's mind as he walked towards
her house. The arch and the Achilles statue were up since
he had last been in Piccadilly; a hundred changes had
occurred which his eye and mind vaguely noted. He began
to tremble as he walked up the lane from Brompton, that
well-remembered lane leading to the street where she lived.
Was she going to be married or not? If he were to meet her
with the little boy – Good God, what should he do? He saw
a woman coming to him with a child of five years old – was
that she? He began to shake at the mere possibility. When
he came up to the row of houses, at last, where she lived,
and to the gate, he caught hold of it and paused. He might
have heard the thumping of his own heart. 'May God
Almighty bless her, whatever has happened,' he thought to
himself. 'Psha! she may be gone from here,' he said, and
went in through the gate.

The window of the parlour which she used to occupy was
open, and there were no inmates in the room. The major
thought he recognized the piano, though, with the picture
over it, as it used to be in former days, and his perturbations
were renewed. Mr. Clapp's brass plate was still on the door,
at the knocker of which Dobbin performed a summons.

A buxom-looking lass of sixteen, with bright eyes and
purple cheeks, came to answer the knock, and looked hard
at the major as he leant back against the little porch.

He was as pale as a ghost, and could hardly falter out
the words – 'Does Mrs. Osborne live here?'

She looked him hard in the face for a moment – and then
turning, white too – said, 'Lord bless me – it's Major
Dobbin.' She held out both her hands shaking – 'Don't you
remember me?' she said, 'I used to call you Major Sugarplums.' On which, and I believe it was for the first time
that he ever so conducted himself in his life, the major took

the girl in his arms and kissed her. She began to laugh and cry hysterically, and calling out 'Ma, Pa!' with all her voice, brought up those worthy people, who had already been surveying the major from the casement of the ornamental kitchen, and were astonished to find their daughter in the little passage in the embrace of a great tall man in a blue frock-coat and white duck trousers.

'I'm an old friend,' he said – not without blushing though. 'Don't you remember me, Mrs. Clapp, and those good cakes you used to make for tea? – Don't you recollect me, Clapp? I'm George's godfather, and just come back from India!' A great shaking of hands ensued – Mrs. Clapp was greatly affected and delighted; she called upon Heaven to interpose a vast many times in that passage.

The landlord and landlady of the house led the worthy major into the Sedleys' room (whereof he remembered every single article of furniture, from the old brass ornamented piano, once a natty little instrument, Stothard maker, to the screens and the alabaster miniature tombstone, in the midst of which ticked Mr. Sedley's gold watch), and there as he sat down in the lodger's vacant arm-chair, the father, the mother, and the daughter, with a thousand ejaculatory breaks in the narrative, informed Major Dobbin of what we know already, but of particulars in Amelia's history of which he was not aware – namely, of Mrs. Sedley's death, of George's reconcilement with his grandfather Osborne, of the way in which the widow took on at leaving him, and of other particulars of her life. Twice or thrice he was going to ask about the marriage question, but his heart failed him. He did not care to lay it bare to these people. Finally, he was informed that Mrs. O. was gone to walk with her pa in Kensington Gardens, whither she always went with the old gentleman (who was very weak and peevish now, and led her a sad life, though she behaved to him like an angel, to be sure), of a fine afternoon after dinner.

'I'm very much pressed for time,' the major said, 'and have business to-night of importance. I should like to see Mrs. Osborne though. Suppose Miss Polly would come with me and show me the way.'

Miss Polly was charmed and astonished at this proposal. 'She knew the way. She would show Major Dobbin. She had often been with Mr. Sedley when Mrs. O. was gone –

was gone Russell Square way: and knew the bench where
he liked to sit.' She bounced away to her apartment, and
appeared presently in her best bonnet and her mamma's
yellow shawl and large pebble brooch, of which she assumed
the loan in order to make herself a worthy companion for
the major.

That officer, then, in his blue frock-coat and buckskin
gloves, gave the young lady his arm, and they walked away
very gaily. He was glad to have a friend at hand for the
scene which he dreaded somehow. He asked a thousand more
questions from his companion about Amelia: his kind heart
grieved to think that she should have had to part with her
son. How did she bear it? Did she see him often? Was Mr.
Sedley pretty comfortable now in a worldly point of view?
Polly answered all these questions of Major Sugarplums to
the very best of her power.

And in the midst of their walk an incident occurred
which, though very simple in its nature, was productive of
the greatest delight to Major Dobbin. A pale young man
with feeble whiskers and a stiff white neckcloth came walking
down the lane, *en sandwich*: - having a lady, that is, on each
arm. One was a tall and commanding middle-aged female,
with features and a complexion similar to those of the
clergyman of the Church of England by whose side she
marched, and the other a stunted little woman with a dark
face, ornamented by a fine new bonnet and white ribbons,
and in a smart pelisse with a rich gold watch in the midst
of her person. The gentleman, pinioned as he was by these
two ladies, carried further a parasol, shawl, and basket, so
that his arms were entirely engaged, and of course he was
unable to touch his hat in acknowledgement of the curtsy
with which Miss Mary Clapp greeted him.

He meekly bowed his head in reply to her salutation,
which the two ladies returned in a patronizing air, and at
the same time looking severely at the individual in the blue
coat and bamboo cane, who accompanied Miss Polly.

'Who's that,' asked the major, amused by the group, and
after he had made way for the three to pass up the lane.
Mary looked at him rather roguishly.

'That is our curate, the Reverend Mr. Binney' (a twitch
from Major Dobbin), 'and his sister Miss B. Lord bless us,
how she did use to worret us at Sunday-school; and the

other lady, the little one with a cast in her eye, and the handsome watch, is Mrs. Binney – Miss Grits that was; her pa was a grocer, and kept the Little Original Gold Tea Pot in Kensington Gravel Pits. They were married last month, and are just come back from Margate. She's five thousand pound to her fortune; but her and Miss B., who made the match, have quarrelled already.'

If the major had twitched before, he started now, and slapped the bamboo on the ground with an emphasis which made Miss Clapp cry, 'Law,' and laugh too. He stood for a moment silent with open mouth looking after the retreating young couple, while Miss Mary told their history; but he did not hear beyond the announcement of the reverend gentleman's marriage; his head was swimming with felicity. After this rencontre he began to walk double quick towards the place of his destination; and yet they were too soon (for he was in a great tremor at the idea of a meeting for which he had been longing any time these ten years) – through the Brompton lanes, and entering at the little old portal in Kensington Garden wall.

'There they are,' said Miss Polly, and she felt him again start back on her arm. She was a confidante at once of the whole business. She knew the story as well as if she had read it in one of her favourite novel-books – *Fatherless Fanny*, or the *Scottish Chiefs*.

'Suppose you were to run on and tell her,' the major said. Polly ran forward, her yellow shawl streaming in the breeze.

Old Sedley was seated on a bench, his handkerchief placed over his knees, prattling away according to his wont, with some old story about old times, to which Amelia had listened, and awarded a patient smile many a time before. She could of late think of her own affairs, and smile or make other marks of recognition of her father's stories, scarcely hearing a word of the old man's tales. As Mary came bouncing along, and Amelia caught sight of her, she started up from her bench. Her first thought was, that something had happened to Georgy; but the sight of the messenger's eager and happy face dissipated that fear in the timorous mother's bosom.

'News! News!' cried the emissary of Major Dobbin. 'He's come! He's come!'

'Who is come?' said Emmy, still thinking of her son.

'Look there,' answered Miss Clapp, turning round and pointing; in which direction Amelia looking, saw Dobbin's lean figure and long shadow stalking across the grass. Amelia started in her turn, blushed up, and, of course, began to cry. At all this simple little creature's fêtes, the *grandes eaux* were accustomed to play.

He looked at her – oh, how fondly – as she came running towards him, her hands before her, ready to give them to him. She wasn't changed. She was a little pale: a little stouter in figure. Her eyes were the same, the kind trustful eyes. There were scarce three lines of silver in her soft brown hair. She gave him both her hands as she looked up flushing and smiling through her tears into his honest homely face. He took the two little hands between his two, and held them there. He was speechless for a moment. Why did he not take her in his arms, and swear that he would never leave her? She must have yielded: she could not but have obeyed him.

'I – I've another arrival to announce,' he said, after a pause.

'Mrs. Dobbin?' Amelia said, making a movement back – Why didn't he speak?

'No,' he said, letting her hands go: 'who has told you those lies? – I mean, your brother Jos came in the same ship with me, and is come home to make you all happy.'

'Papa, papa!' Emmy cried out, 'here are news! My brother is in England. He is come to take care of you. – Here is Major Dobbin.'

Mr. Sedley started up, shaking a great deal, and gathering up his thoughts. Then he stepped forward and made an old-fashioned bow to the major, whom he called Mr. Dobbin, and hoped his worthy father, Sir William, was quite well. He proposed to call upon Sir William, who had done him the honour of a visit a short time ago. Sir William had not called upon the old gentleman for eight years – it was that visit he was thinking of returning.

'He is very much shaken,' Emmy whispered, as Dobbin went up and cordially shook hands with the old man.

Although he had such particular business in London that evening, the major consented to forgo it upon Mr. Sedley's invitation to him to come home and partake of tea. Amelia put her arm under that of her young friend with the yellow shawl, and headed the party on their return homewards, so that Mr. Sedley fell to Dobbin's share. The old man walked very slowly, and told a number of ancient histories about himself and his poor Bessy, his former prosperity, and his bankruptcy. His thoughts, as is usual with failing old men, were quite in former times. The present, with the exception of the one catastrophe which he felt, he knew little about. The major was glad to let him talk on. His eyes were fixed upon the figure in front of him — the dear little figure always present to his imagination and in his prayers, and visiting his dreams wakeful or slumbering.

Amelia was very happy, smiling, and active all that evening; performing her duties as hostess of the little entertainment with the utmost grace and propriety, as Dobbin thought. His eyes followed her about as they sat in the twilight. How many a time had he longed for that moment, and thought of her far away under hot winds and in weary marches, gentle and happy, kindly ministering to the wants of old age, and decorating poverty with sweet submission — as he saw her now. I do not say that his taste was the highest or that it is the duty of great intellects to be content with a bread-and-butter paradise, such as sufficed our simple old friend; but his desires were of this sort whether for good or bad; and, with Amelia to help him, he was as ready to drink as many cups of tea as Doctor Johnson.

Amelia seeing this propensity, laughingly encouraged it; and looked exceedingly roguish as she administered to him cup after cup. It is true she did not know that the major had had no dinner, and that the cloth was laid for him at the Slaughters', and a plate laid thereon to mark that the table was retained, in that very box in which the major and George had sat many a time carousing, when she was a child just come home from Miss Pinkerton's school.

The first thing Mrs. Osborne showed the major was Georgy's miniature, for which she ran upstairs on her arrival at home. It was not half handsome enough of course for the boy, but wasn't it noble of him to think of bringing it to his mother? Whilst her papa was awake she did not talk much about Georgy. To hear about Mr. Osborne and Russell Square was not agreeable to the old man, who very likely was unconscious that he had been living for some months past mainly on the bounty of his richer rival; and lost his temper if allusion was made to the other.

Dobbin told him all, and a little more perhaps than all, that had happened on board the *Ramchunder*; and exaggerated Jos's benevolent dispositions towards his father, and resolution to make him comfortable in his old days. The truth is, that during the voyage the major had impressed this duty most strongly upon his fellow-passenger and extorted promises from him that he would take charge of his sister and her child. He soothed Jos's irritation with regard to the bills which the old gentleman had drawn upon him, gave a laughing account of his own sufferings on the same score, and of the famous consignment of wine with which the old man had favoured him: and brought Mr. Jos, who was by no means an ill-natured person when well pleased and moderately flattered, to a very good state of feeling regarding his relatives in Europe.

And in fine I am ashamed to say that the major stretched the truth so far as to tell old Mr. Sedley that it was mainly a desire to see his parent which brought Jos once more to Europe.

At his accustomed hour Mr. Sedley began to doze in his chair, and then it was Amelia's opportunity to commence her conversation, which she did with great eagerness; – it related exclusively to Georgy. She did not talk at all about her own sufferings at breaking from him, for indeed this worthy woman, though she was half-killed by the separation from the child, yet thought it was very wicked in her to repine at losing him; but everything concerning him, his virtues, talents, and prospects, she poured out. She described his angelic beauty; narrated a hundred instances of his generosity and greatness of mind whilst living with her: how a royal duchess had stopped and admired him in Kensington Gardens; how splendidly he was cared for now, and how he had a groom and a pony; what quickness and cleverness he had, and what a prodigiously well-read and delightful person the Reverend Lawrence Veal was, George's master. 'He knows *everything*,' Amelia said. 'He has the most delightful parties. You who are so learned yourself, and have read so much, and are so clever and accomplished – don't shake your head and say No – *he* always used to say you were – you will be charmed with Mr. Veal's parties. The last Tuesday in every month. He says there is no place in the bar or the senate that Georgy may not aspire to. Look here,' and she went to the piano-drawer and drew out a theme of Georgy's composition. This great effort of genius, which is still in the possession of George's mother, is as follows: –

On Selfishness. – Of all the vices which degrade the human character, Selfishness is the most odious and contemptible. An undue love of Self leads to the most monstrous crimes; and occasions the greatest misfortunes both in *States and Families*. As a selfish man will impoverish his family and often bring them to ruin: so a selfish king brings ruin on his people and often plunges them into war.

Example: The selfishness of Achilles, as remarked by the poet Homer, occasioned a thousand woes to the Greeks – μυρί Ἀχαιοιζ ἄλγε ἔθηκε – (Hom. *Il.* A. 2). The selfishness of the late Napoleon Bonaparte occasioned innumerable wars in Europe, and caused him to perish, himself, in a miserable island – that of St. Helena in the Atlantic Ocean.

We see by these examples that we are not to consult our own interest and ambition, but that we are to consider the interest of others as well as our own.

GEORGE S. OSBORNE.

ATHENÈ HOUSE, April 24, 1827.

'Think of him writing such a hand, and quoting Greek too, at his age,' the delighted mother said. 'Oh, William,' she added, holding out her hand to the major – 'what a treasure Heaven has given me in that boy! He is the comfort of my life – and he is the image of – of him that's gone!'

'Ought I to be angry with her for being faithful to him?' William thought. 'Ought I to be jealous of my friend in the grave, or hurt that such a heart as Amelia's can love only once and for ever? O George, George, how little you knew the prize you had, though.' This sentiment passed rapidly through William's mind, as he was holding Amelia's hand, whilst the handkerchief was veiling her eyes.

'Dear friend,' she said, pressing the hand which held hers, 'how good, how kind you always have been to me! See! papa is stirring. You will go and see Georgy to-morrow, won't you?'

'Not to-morrow,' said poor old Dobbin. 'I have business.' He did not like to own that he had not as yet been to his parents' and his dear sister Anne – a remissness for which I am sure every well-regulated person will blame the major. And presently he took his leave, leaving his address behind

him for Jos, against the latter's arrival. And so the first day
was over, and he had seen her.

When he got back to the Slaughters', the roast fowl was
of course cold, in which condition he ate it for supper. And
knowing what early hours his family kept, and that it would
be needless to disturb their slumbers at so late an hour, it
is on record, that Major Dobbin treated himself to half-price
at the Haymarket Theatre that evening, where let us hope
he enjoyed himself.

CHAPTER LIX

THE OLD PIANO

T HE major's visit left old John Sedley in a great state of
agitation and excitement. His daughter could not induce
him to settle down to his customary occupations or amusements that night. He passed the evening fumbling amongst
his boxes and desks, untying his papers with trembling
hands, and sorting and arranging them against Jos's arrival.
He had them in the greatest order – his tapes and his files,
his receipts, and his letters with lawyers and correspondents;
the documents relative to the Wine Project (which failed
from a most unaccountable accident, after commencing with
the most splendid prospects), the Coal Project (which only
a want of capital prevented from becoming the most successful scheme ever put before the public), the Patent Saw-
mills and Sawdust Consolidation Project, &c. &c. – All night,
until a very late hour, he passed in the preparation of these
documents, trembling about from one room to another, with
a quivering candle and shaky hands. – Here's the wine
papers, here's the sawdust, here's the coals; here's my letters
to Calcutta and Madras, and replies from Major Dobbin,
C.B., and Mr. Joseph Sedley to the same. 'He shall find no
irregularity about *me*, Emmy,' the old gentleman said.

Emmy smiled. 'I don't think Jos will care about seeing
those papers, papa,' she said.

'You don't know anything about business, my dear,'
answered the sire, shaking his head with an important air.
And it must be confessed that on this point Emmy was very
ignorant, and that it is a pity, some people are so knowing.
All these twopenny documents arranged on a side table, old

Sedley covered them carefully over with a clean bandanna handkerchief (one out of Major Dobbin's lot), and enjoined the maid and landlady of the house, in the most solemn way, not to disturb those papers, which were arranged for the arrival of Mr. Joseph Sedley the next morning, 'Mr. Joseph Sedley of the Honourable East India Company's Bengal Civil Service.'

Amelia found him up very early the next morning, more eager, more hectic, and more shaky than ever. 'I didn't sleep much, Emmy, my dear,' he said. 'I was thinking of my poor Bessy. I wish she was alive, to ride in Jos's carriage once again. She kept her own, and became it very well.' And his eyes filled with tears, which trickled down his furrowed old face. Amelia wiped them away, and smilingly kissed him, and tied the old man's neckcloth in a smart bow, and put his brooch into his best shirt frill, in which, in his Sunday suit of mourning, he sat from six o'clock in the morning awaiting the arrival of his son.

There are some splendid tailors' shops in the High Street of Southampton, in the fine plate-glass windows of which hang gorgeous waistcoats of all sorts, of silk and velvet, and gold and crimson, and pictures of the last new fashions in which those wonderful gentlemen with quizzing glasses, and holding on to little boys with the exceeding large eyes and curly hair, ogle ladies in riding habits prancing by the Statue of Achilles at Apsley House. Jos, although provided with some of the most splendid vests that Calcutta could furnish, thought he could not go to town until he was supplied with one or two of these garments, and selected a crimson satin, embroidered with gold butterflies, and a black and red velvet tartan with white stripes and a rolling collar, with which, and a rich blue satin stock and a gold pin, consisting of a five-barred gate with a horseman in pink enamel jumping over it, he thought he might make his entry into London with some dignity. For Jos's former shyness and blundering blushing timidity had given way to a more candid and courageous self-assertion of his worth. 'I don't care about owning it,' Waterloo Sedley would say to his friends, 'I am a dressy man:' and though rather uneasy if the ladies looked at him at the Government House balls, and though he blushed and turned away alarmed under their glances, it was chiefly from a dread lest they should make love to him, that he avoided them, being averse to marriage altogether. But there was no such swell in Calcutta as Waterloo Sedley, I have heard say: and he had the handsomest turn-out, gave the best bachelor dinners, and had the finest plate in the whole place.

To make these waistcoats for a man of his size and dignity took at least a day, part of which he employed in hiring a servant to wait upon him and his native; and in instructing the agent who cleared his baggage, his boxes, his books, which he never read; his chests of mangoes, chutney, and curry-powders; his shawls for presents to people whom he didn't know as yet; and the rest of his *Persicos apparatus*.

At length, he drove leisurely to London on the third day, and in the new waistcoat; the native, with chattering teeth, shuddering in a shawl on the box by the side of the new European servant, Jos puffing his pipe at intervals within, and looking so majestic, that the little boys cried 'Hooray,' and many people thought he must be a governor-general. *He*, I promise, did not decline the obsequious invitation of the landlords to alight and refresh himself in the neat country towns. Having partaken of a copious breakfast, with fish, and rice, and hard eggs, at Southampton, he had so far rallied at Winchester as to think a glass of sherry necessary. At Alton he stepped out of the carriage, at his servant's request, and imbibed some of the ale for which the place is famous. At Farnham he stopped to view the Bishop's Castle, and to partake of a light dinner of stewed eels, veal cutlets, and French beans, with a bottle of claret. He was cold over Bagshot Heath, where the native chattered more and more, and Jos Sahib took some brandy-and-water; in fact, when he drove into town, he was as full of wine, beer, meat, pickles, cherry-brandy, and tobacco, as the steward's cabin of a steam-packet. It was evening when his carriage thundered up to the little door in Brompton, whither the affectionate fellow drove first, and before hying to the apartments secured for him by Mr. Dobbin at the Slaughters'.

All the faces in the street were in the windows; the little maidservant flew to the wicket-gate, the Mesdames Clapp looked out from the casement of the ornamented kitchen; Emmy, in a great flutter, was in the passage among the hats and coats, and old Sedley in the parlour inside, shaking all over. Jos descended from the post-chaise and down the creaking swaying steps in awful state, supported by the new valet from Southampton and the shuddering native, whose brown face was now livid with cold, and of the colour of a turkey's gizzard. He created an immense sensation in the passage presently, where Mrs. and Miss Clapp, coming perhaps to listen at the parlour door, found Loll Jewab shaking upon the hall bench under the coats, moaning in a strange piteous way, and showing his yellow eyeballs and white teeth.

For, you see, we have adroitly shut the door upon the meeting between Jos and the old father, and the poor little gentle sister inside. The old man was very much affected: so, of course, was his daughter: nor was Jos without feeling. In that long absence of ten years, the most selfish will think about home and early ties. Distance sanctifies both. Long brooding over those lost pleasures exaggerates their charm and sweetness. Jos was unaffectedly glad to see and shake the hand of his father, between whom and himself there had been a coolness — glad to see his little sister, whom he remembered so pretty and smiling, and pained at the alteration which time, grief, and misfortune had made in the shattered old man. Emmy had come out to the door in her black clothes and whispered to him of her mother's death, and not to speak of it to their father. There was no need of this caution, for the elder Sedley himself began immediately to speak of the event, and prattled about it, and wept over it plenteously. It shocked the Indian not a little, and made him think of himself less than the poor fellow was accustomed to do.

The result of the interview must have been very satisfactory, for when Jos had reascended his post-chaise, and had driven away to his hotel, Emmy embraced her father tenderly, appealing to him with an air of triumph, and asking the old man whether she did not always say that her brother had a good heart?

Indeed, Joseph Sedley, affected by the humble position in which he found his relations, and in the expansiveness and overflowing of heart occasioned by the first meeting, declared that they should never suffer want or discomfort any more, that he was at home for some time at any rate, during which his house and everything he had should be

theirs: and that Amelia would look very pretty at the head
of his table – until she would accept one of her own.

She shook her head sadly, and had, as usual, recourse to
the waterworks. She knew what he meant. She and her
young confidante, Miss Mary, had talked over the matter
most fully, the very night of the major's visit: beyond which
time the impetuous Polly could not refrain from talking of
the discovery which she had made, and describing the start
and tremor of joy by which Major Dobbin betrayed himself
when Mr. Binney passed with his bride, and the major
learned that he had no longer a rival to fear. 'Didn't you
see how he shook all over when you asked if he was married,
and he said, "Who told you those lies?" Oh, ma'am,' Polly
said, 'he never kept his eyes off you; and I'm sure he's grown
grey a-thinking of you.'

But Amelia, looking up at her bed, over which hung the
portraits of her husband and son, told her young protégée,
never, never, to speak on that subject again; that Major
Dobbin had been her husband's dearest friend, and her own
and George's most kind and affectionate guardian; that she
loved him as a brother – but that a woman who had been
married to such an angel as that, and she pointed to the
wall, could never think of any other union. Poor Polly sighed:
she thought what she should do if young Mr. Tomkins, at
the surgery, who always looked at her so at church, and
who, by those mere aggressive glances had put her timorous
little heart into such a flutter that she was ready to surrender
at once, – what she should do if he were to die? She knew
he was consumptive, his cheeks were so red, and he was so
uncommon thin in the waist.

Not that Emmy, being made aware of the honest major's
passion, rebuffed him in any way, or felt displeased with
him. Such an attachment from so true and loyal a gentleman
could make no woman angry. Desdemona was not angry with
Cassio, though there is very little doubt she saw the lieutenant's partiality for her (and I for my part believe that many
more things took place in that sad affair than the worthy
Moorish officer ever knew of); why, Miranda was even very
kind to Caliban, and we may be pretty sure for the same
reason. Not that she would encourage him in the least, –
the poor uncouth monster – of course not. No more would
Emmy by any means encourage her admirer, the major. She

would give him that friendly regard, which so much excellence and fidelity merited; she would treat him with perfect cordiality and frankness until he made his proposals: and *then* it would be time enough for her to speak, and to put an end to hopes which never could be realized.

She slept, therefore, very soundly that evening, after the conversation with Miss Polly, and was more than ordinarily happy, in spite of Jos's delaying. 'I am glad he is not going to marry that Miss O'Dowd,' she thought. 'Colonel O'Dowd never could have a sister fit for such an accomplished man as Major William.' Who was there amongst her little circle, who would make him a good wife? Not Miss Binney, she was too old and ill-tempered; Miss Osborne? – too old, too. Little Polly was too young. Mrs. Osborne could not find anybody to suit the major before she went to sleep.

However, when the postman made his appearance, the little party were put out of suspense, by the receipt of a letter from Jos to his sister, who announced, that he felt a little fatigued after his voyage, and should not be able to move on that day, but that he would leave Southampton early the next morning, and be with his father and mother at evening. Amelia, as she read out the letter to her father, paused over the latter word; her brother, it was clear, did not know what had happened in the family. Nor could he: for the fact is, that though the major rightly suspected that his travelling companion never would be got into motion in so short a space as twenty-four hours, and would find some excuse for delaying, yet Dobbin had not written to Jos to inform him of the calamity which had befallen the Sedley family; being occupied in talking with Amelia until long after post-hour.

The same morning brought Major Dobbin a letter to the Slaughters' Coffee-house from his friend at Southampton; begging dear Dob to excuse Jos for being in a rage when awakened the day before (he had a confounded headache, and was just in his first sleep), and entreating Dob to engage comfortable rooms at the Slaughters' for Mr. Sedley and his servants. The major had become necessary to Jos during the voyage. He was attached to him, and hung upon him. The other passengers were away to London. Young Ricketts and little Chaffers went away on the coach that day – Ricketts on the box, and taking the reins from Botley; the doctor was off to his family at Portsea; Bragg gone to town to his co-partners; and the first mate busy in the unloading of the *Ramchunder*. Mr. Jos was very lonely at Southampton, and got the landlord of the 'George' to take a glass of wine with him that day; at the very hour at which Major Dobbin was seated at the table of his father, Sir William, where his sister found out (for it was impossible for the major to tell fibs) that he had been to see Mrs. George Osborne.

Jos was so comfortably situated in St. Martin's Lane, he could enjoy his hookah there with such perfect ease, and could swagger down to the theatres, when minded, so agreeably, that, perhaps, he would have remained altogether at the Slaughters' had not his friend, the major, been at his elbow. That gentleman would not let the Bengalee rest until he had executed his promise of having a home for Amelia and his father. Jos was a soft fellow in anybody's hands; Dobbin most active in anybody's concerns but his own; the civilian was, therefore, an easy victim to the guileless arts of this good-natured diplomatist, and was ready to do, to purchase, hire, or relinquish whatever his friend thought fit. Loll Jewab, of whom the boys about St. Martin's Lane used to make cruel fun whenever he showed his dusky counten- ance in the street, was sent back to Calcutta in the *Lady Kicklebury* East Indiaman, in which Sir William Dobbin had a share; having previously taught Jos's European the art of preparing curries, pilaws, and pipes. It was a matter of great delight and occupation to Jos to superintend the building of a smart chariot, which he and the major ordered in the neighbouring Long Acre: and a pair of handsome horses were jobbed, with which Jos drove about in state in the Park, or to call upon his Indian friends. Amelia was not seldom by his side on these excursions, when also Major Dobbin would be seen in the back seat of the carriage. At other times old Sedley and his daughter took advantage of it: and Miss Clapp, who frequently accompanied her friend, had great pleasure in being recognized as she sat in the carriage, dressed in the famous yellow shawl, by the young gentleman at the surgery, whose face might commonly be seen over the window-blinds as she passed.

Shortly after Jos's first appearance at Brompton, a dismal scene, indeed, took place at that humble cottage, at which the Sedleys had passed the last ten years of their life. Jos's carriage (the temporary one, not the chariot under construction) arrived one day and carried off old Sedley and his daughter – to return no more. The tears that were shed by the landlady and the landlady's daughter at that event were as genuine tears of sorrow as any that have been outpoured in the course of this history. In their long acquaintanceship and intimacy they could not recall a harsh word that had been uttered by Amelia. She had been all sweetness and kindness, always thankful, always gentle, even when Mrs. Clapp lost her own temper, and pressed for the rent. When the kind creature was going away for good and all, the landlady reproached herself bitterly for ever having used a rough expression to her – how she wept, as they stuck up with wafers on the window, a paper notifying that the little rooms so long occupied were to let! They never would have such lodgers again, that was quite clear. After-life proved the truth of this melancholy prophecy: and Mrs. Clapp revenged herself for the deterioration of mankind by levying the most savage contributions upon the tea-caddies and legs of mutton of her *locataires*. Most of them scolded and grumbled; some of them did not pay: none of them stayed. The landlady might well regreat those old, old friends, who had left her.

As for Miss Mary, her sorrow at Amelia's departure was such as I shall not attempt to depict. From childhood upwards she had been with her daily, and had attached herself so passionately to that dear good lady, that when the grand barouche came to carry her off into splendour, she fainted in the arms of her friend, who was indeed scarcely less affected than the good-natured girl. Amelia loved her like a daughter. During eleven years the girl had been her constant friend and associate. The separation was a very painful one indeed to her. But it was of course arranged that Mary was to come and stay often at the grand new house whither Mrs. Osborne was going; and where Mary was sure she would never be so happy as she had been in their humble cot, as Miss Clapp called it in the language of the novels which she loved.

Let us hope she was wrong in her judgement. Poor Emmy's days of happiness had been very few in that humble cot. A gloomy Fate had oppressed her there. She never liked

to come back to the house after she had left it, or to face
the landlady who had tyrannized over her when ill-humoured
and unpaid, or when pleased, had treated her with a coarse
familiarity scarcely less odious. Her servility and fulsome
compliments when Emmy was in prosperity were not more
to that lady's liking. She cast about notes of admiration all
over the new house, extolling every article of furniture or
ornament; she fingered Mrs. Osborne's dresses, and calculated their price. Nothing could be too good for that sweet
lady, she vowed and protested. But in the vulgar sycophant
who now paid court to her, Emmy always remembered the
coarse tyrant who had made her miserable many a time, to
whom she had been forced to put up petitions for time,
when the rent was overdue; who cried out at her extravagance if she bought delicacies for her ailing mother or father;
who had seen her humble and trampled upon her.

Nobody ever heard of these griefs, which had been part
of our poor little woman's lot in life. She kept them secret
from her father, whose improvidence was the cause of much
of her misery. She had to bear all the blame of his misdoings,
and indeed was so utterly gentle and humble as to be made
by nature for a victim.

I hope she is not to suffer much more of that hard usage.
And, as in all griefs, there is said to be some consolation, I
may mention that poor Mary, when left at her friend's
departure in a hysterical condition, was placed under the
medical treatment of the young fellow from the surgery,
under whose care she rallied after a short period. Emmy,
when she went away from Brompton, endowed Mary with
every article of furniture that the house contained: only
taking away her pictures (the two pictures over the bed) and
her piano – that little old piano which had now passed into
a plaintive jingling old age, but which she loved for reasons
of her own. She was a child when first she played on it:
and her parents gave it her. It had been given to her again
since, as the reader may remember, when her father's house
was gone to ruin, and the instrument was recovered out of
the wreck.

Major Dobbin was exceedingly pleased when, as he was
superintending the arrangements of Jos's new house, which
the major insisted should be very handsome and comfortable;
the cart arrived from Brompton, bringing the trunks and

bandboxes of the emigrants from that village, and with them the old piano. Amelia would have it up in her sitting-room, a neat little apartment on the second floor, adjoining her father's chamber: and where the old gentleman sat commonly of evenings.

When the men appeared then bearing this old music-box, and Amelia gave orders that it should be placed in the chamber aforesaid, Dobbin was quite elated. 'I'm glad you've kept it,' he said in a very sentimental manner. 'I was afraid you didn't care about it.'

'I value it more than anything I have in the world,' said Amelia.

'*Do* you, Amelia?' cried the major. The fact was, as he had bought it himself, though he never said anything about it, it never entered into his head to suppose that Emmy should think anybody else was the purchaser, and as a matter of course, he fancied that she knew the gift came from him. 'Do you, Amelia?' he said; and the question, the great question of all, was trembling on his lips, when Emmy replied –

'Can I do otherwise? – did not *he* give it me?'

'I did not know,' said poor old Dob, and his countenance fell.

Emmy did not note the circumstance at the time, nor take immediate heed of the very dismal expression which honest Dobbin's countenance assumed; but she thought of it afterwards. And then it struck her, with inexpressible pain and mortification too, that it was William who was the giver of the piano; and not George as she had fancied. It was not George's gift; the only one which she had received from her lover, as she thought – the thing she had cherished beyond all others – her dearest relic and prize. She had spoken to it about George; played his favourite airs upon it; sat for long evening hours, touching, to the best of her simple art, melancholy harmonies on the keys, and weeping over them in silence. It was not George's relic. It was valueless now. The next time that old Sedley asked her to play, she said it was shockingly out of tune, that she had a headache, that she couldn't play.

Then, according to her custom, she rebuked herself for her pettishness and ingratitude, and determined to make a reparation to honest William for the slight she had not expressed to him, but had felt for his piano. A few days afterwards, as they were seated in the drawing-room, where Jos had fallen asleep with great comfort after dinner, Amelia said with rather a faltering voice to Major Dobbin, –

'I have to beg your pardon for something.'

'About what?' said he.

'About – about that little square piano. I never thanked you for it when you gave it me, many, many years ago, before I was married. I thought somebody else had given it. Thank you, William.' She held out her hand; but the poor little woman's heart was bleeding; and as for her eyes, of course they were at their work.

But William could hold no more. 'Amelia, Amelia,' he said, 'I did buy it for you. I loved you then as I do now. I must tell you. I think I loved you from the first minute that I saw you, when George brought me to your house, to show me the Amelia whom he was engaged to. You were but a girl in white, with large ringlets; you came down singing – do you remember? – and we went to Vauxhall. Since then I have thought of but one woman in the world, and that was you. I think there is no hour of the day has passed for twelve years that I haven't thought of you. I came to tell you this before I went to India, but you did not care, and I hadn't the heart to speak. You did not care whether I stayed or went.'

'I was very ungrateful,' Amelia said.

'No; only indifferent,' Dobbin continued desperately. 'I have nothing to make a woman to be otherwise. I know what you are feeling now. You are hurt in your heart at that discovery about the piano; and that it came from me and not from George. I forgot, or I should never have spoken of it so. It is for me to ask your pardon for being a fool for a moment, and thinking that years of constancy and devotion might have pleaded with you.'

'It is you who are cruel now,' Amelia said, with some spirit. 'George is my husband, here and in heaven. How could I love any other but him? I am his now as when you first saw me, dear William. It was he who told me how good and generous you were, and who taught me to love you as a brother. Have you not been everything to me and my boy? Our dearest, truest, kindest friend and protector? Had you come a few months sooner perhaps you might have spared me that – that dreadful parting. Oh, it nearly killed me, William – but you didn't come, though I wished and prayed for you to come, and they took him too away from me. Isn't he a noble boy, William? Be his friend still and mine' – and here her voice broke, and she hid her face on his shoulder.

The major folded his arms round her, holding her to him as if she was a child, and kissed her head. 'I will not change, dear Amelia,' he said. 'I ask for no more than your love. I think I would not have it otherwise. Only let me stay near you, and see you often.'

'Yes, often,' Amelia said. And so William was at liberty to look and long: as the poor boy at school who has no money may sigh after the contents of the tart-woman's tray.

CHAPTER LX

RETURNS TO THE GENTEEL WORLD

G OOD fortune now begins to smile upon Amelia. We are glad to get her out of that low sphere in which she has been creeping hitherto, and introduce her into a polite circle, not so grand and refined as that in which our other female friend, Mrs. Becky, has appeared, but still having no small pretensions to gentility and fashion. Jos's friends were all from the three presidencies, and his new house was in the comfortable Anglo-Indian district of which Moira Place is the centre. Minto Square, Great Clive Street, Warren Street, Hastings Street, Ochterlony Place, Plassey Square, Assaye Terrace ('Gardens' was a felicitous word not applied to stucco houses with asphalte terraces in front, so early as 1827) – who does not know these respectable abodes of the retired Indian aristocracy, and the quarter which Mr. Wenham calls the Black Hole, in a word? Jos's position in life was not grand enough to entitle him to a house in Moira Place, where none can live but retired Members of Council, and partners of Indian firms (who break after having settled a hundred thousand pounds on their wives, and retire into comparative penury, to a country place and four thousand a year): he engaged a comfortable house of a second- or third-rate order in Gillespie Street, purchasing the carpets, costly mirrors and handsome and appropriate planned furniture by Seddons, from the assignees of Mr. Scape, lately admitted partner into the great Calcutta house of Fogle, Fake, and Cracksman, in which poor Scape had embarked seventy thousand pounds, the earnings of a long and honourable life, taking Fake's place, who retired to a princely park in Sussex (the Fogles have been long out of the firm, and Sir Horace Fogle is about to be raised to the peerage as Baron Bandanna) – admitted, I say, partner into the great agency house of Fogle and Fake two years before it failed for a million, and plunged half the Indian public into misery and ruin.

Scape, ruined, honest, and broken-hearted at sixty-five years of age, went out to Calcutta to wind up the affairs of the house. Walter Scape was withdrawn from Eton, and put into a merchant's house. Florence Scape, Fanny Scape, and their mother, faded away to Boulogne, and will be heard of no more. To be brief, Jos stepped in and bought their carpets and sideboards, and admired himself in the mirrors which had reflected their kind handsome faces. The Scape tradesmen, all honourably paid, left their cards, and were eager to supply the new household. The large men in white waistcoats, who waited at Scape's dinners, greengrocers, bank-porters, and milkmen in their private capacity, left their addresses, and ingratiated themselves with the butler. Mr. Chummy, the chimney-purifier, who had swep the last three families, tried to coax the butler and the boy under him, whose duty it was to go out covered with buttons and with stripes down his trousers, for the protection of Mrs. Amelia whenever she chose to walk abroad.

It was a modest establishment. The butler was Jos's valet also, and never was more drunk than a butler in a small family should be who has a proper regard for his master's wine. Emmy was supplied with a maid, grown on Sir William Dobbin's suburban estate; a good girl, whose kindness and humility disarmed Mrs. Osborne, who was at first terrified at the idea of having a servant to wait upon herself, who did not in the least know how to use one, and who always spoke to domestics with the most reverential politeness. But this maid was very useful in the family, in dexterously tending old Mr. Sedley, who kept almost entirely to his own quarter of the house, and never mixed in any of the gay doings which took place there.

Numbers of people came to see Mrs. Osborne. Lady

Dobbin and daughters were delighted at her change of fortune, and waited upon her. Miss Osborne from Russell Square came in her grand chariot with the flaming hammer-cloth emblazoned with the Leeds arms. Jos was reported to be immensely rich. Old Osborne had no objection that Georgy should inherit his uncle's property as well as his own. 'Damn it, we will make a man of the feller,' he said; 'and I'll see him in Parliament before I die. *You* may go and see his mother, Miss O., though I'll never set eyes on her:' and Miss Osborne came. Emmy, you may be sure, was very glad to see her, and so be brought nearer to George. That young fellow was allowed to come much more frequently than before to visit his mother. He dined once or twice a week in Gillespie Street, and bullied the servants and his relations there, just as he did in Russell Square.

He was always respectful to Major Dobbin, however, and more modest in his demeanour when that gentleman was present. He was a clever lad, and afraid of the major. George could not help admiring his friend's simplicity, his good humour, his various learning quietly imparted, his general love of truth and justice. He had met no such man as yet in the course of his experience, and he had an instinctive liking for a gentleman. He hung fondly by his godfather's side; and it was his delight to walk in the Parks and hear Dobbin talk. William told George about his father, about India and Waterloo, about everything but himself. When George was more than usually pert and conceited, the major made jokes at him, which Mrs. Osborne thought very cruel. One day, taking him to the play, and the boy declining to go into the pit because it was vulgar, the major took him to the boxes, left him there, and went down himself to the pit. He had not been seated there very long, before he felt an arm thrust under his, and a dandy little hand in a kid-glove squeezing his arm. George had seen the absurdity of his ways, and come down from the upper region. A tender laugh of benevolence lighted up old Dobbin's face and eyes as he looked at the repentant little prodigal. He loved the boy, as he did everything that belonged to Amelia. How charmed she was when she heard of this instance of George's goodness! Her eyes looked more kindly on Dobbin than they ever had done. She blushed, he thought, after looking at him so.

Georgy never tired of his praises of the major to his mother. 'I like him, mamma, because he knows such lots of things; and he ain't like old Veal, who is always bragging and using such long words, don't you know? The chaps call him "Longtail" at school. I gave him the name; ain't it capital? But Dob reads Latin like English, and French and that; and when we go out together he tells me stories about my papa, and never about himself; though I heard Colonel Buckler, at grandpapa's, say that he was one of the bravest officers in the army, and had distinguished himself ever so much. Grandpapa was quite surprised, and said "*That* feller! why, I didn't think he could say Bo to a goose" – but *I* know he could, couldn't he, mamma?'

Emmy laughed: she thought it was very likely the major could do thus much.

If there was a sincere liking between George and the major, it must be confessed that between the boy and his uncle no great love existed. George had got a way of blowing out his cheeks, and putting his hands in his waistcoat pockets, and saying, 'God bless my soul, you don't say so,' so exactly after the fashion of old Jos, that it was impossible to restrain from laughter. The servants would explode at dinner if the lad, asking for something which wasn't at table, put on that countenance and used that favourite phrase. Even Dobbin would shoot out a sudden peal at the boy's mimicry. If George did not mimic his uncle to his face, it was only by Dobbin's rebukes and Amelia's terrified entreaties that the little scapegrace was induced to desist. And the worthy civilian being haunted by a dim consciousness that the lad thought him an ass, and was inclined to turn him into ridicule, used to be extremely timorous, and, of course, doubly pompous and dignified in the presence of Master Georgy. When it was announced that the young gentleman was expected in Gillespie Street to dine with his mother, Mr. Jos commonly found that he had an engagement at the club. Perhaps nobody was much grieved at his absence. On those days Mr. Sedley would commonly be induced to come out from his place of refuge in the upper stories; and there would be a small family party, whereof Major Dobbin pretty generally formed one. He was the *ami de la maison*; old Sedley's friend, Emmy's friend, Georgy's friend, Jos's counsel and adviser. 'He might almost as well be at Madras for anything *we* see of him,' Miss Ann Dobbin remarked, at Camberwell. Ah! Miss Ann, did it not strike you that it was not *you* whom the major wanted to marry?

Joseph Sedley then led a life of dignified otiosity such as became a person of his eminence. His very first point, of course, was to become a member of the Oriental Club: where he spent his mornings in the company of his brother Indians, where he dined, or whence he brought home men to dine.

Amelia had to receive and entertain these gentlemen and their ladies. From these she heard how soon Smith would be in Council; how many lacs Jones had brought home with him; how Thomson's House in London had refused the bills drawn by Thomson, Kibobjee and Co., the Bombay House, and how it was thought the Calcutta House must go too; how very imprudent, to say the least of it, Mrs. Brown's conduct (wife of Brown of the Ahmednuggar Irregulars) had been with young Swankey of the Body Guard, sitting up with him on deck until all hours, and losing themselves as they were riding out at the Cape; how Mrs. Hardyman had had out her thirteen sisters, daughters of a country curate, the Rev. Felix Rabbits, and married eleven of them, seven high up in the service; how Hornby was wild because his wife would stay in Europe, and Trotter was appointed collector at Ummerapoora. This and similar talk took place, at the grand dinners all round. They had the same conversation; the same silver dishes; the same saddles of mutton, boiled turkeys, and entrées. Politics set in a short time after dessert, when the ladies retired upstairs and talked about their complaints and their children.

Mutato nomine, it is all the same. Don't the barristers' wives talk about Circuit? – don't the soldiers' ladies gossip about the Regiment? – don't the clergymen's ladies discourse about Sunday-schools, and who takes whose duty? – don't the very greatest ladies of all talk about that small clique of persons to whom they belong, and why shall our Indian friends not have their own conversation? – only I admit it is slow for the laymen whose fate it sometimes is to sit by and listen.

Before long Emmy had a visiting-book, and was driving about regularly in a carriage, calling upon Lady Bludyer (wife of Major-General Sir Roger Bludyer, K.C.B., Bengal Army); Lady Huff, wife of Sir G. Huff, Bombay ditto; Mrs.

Pice, the lady of Pice the director, &c. We are not long in using ourselves to changes in life. That carriage came round to Gillespie Street every day; that buttony boy sprang up and down from the box with Emmy's and Jos's visiting cards; at stated hours Emmy and the carriage went for Jos to the club, and took him an airing; or, putting old Sedley into the vehicle, she drove the old man round the Regent's Park. The lady's maid and the chariot, the visiting-book and the buttony page, became soon as familiar to Amelia as the humble routine of Brompton. She accommodated herself to one as to the other. If Fate had ordained that she should be a duchess, she would even have done that duty too. She was voted, in Jos's female society, rather a pleasing young person – not much in her, but pleasing, and that sort of thing.

The men, as usual, liked her artless kindness and simple refined demeanour. The gallant young Indian dandies at home on furlough – immense dandies these – chained and moustached – driving in tearing cabs, the pillars of the theatres, living at West End hotels, – nevertheless admired Mrs. Osborne, liked to bow to her carriage in the Park, and to be admitted to have the honour of paying her a morning visit. Swankey of the Body Guard himself, that dangerous youth, and the greatest buck of all the Indian army now on leave, was one day discovered by Major Dobbin *tête à tête* with Amelia, and describing the sport of pig-sticking to her with great humour and eloquence; and he spoke afterwards of a d–d king's officer that's always hanging about the house – a long, thin, queer-looking oldish fellow – a dry fellow though, that took the shine out of a man in the talking line.

Had the major possessed a little more personal vanity he would have been jealous of so dangerous a young buck, as that fascinating Bengal captain. But Dobbin was of too simple and generous a nature to have any doubts about Amelia. He was glad that the young men should pay her respect; and that others should admire her. Ever since her womanhood almost, had she not been persecuted and undervalued? It pleased him to see how kindness brought out her good qualities, and how her spirits gently rose with her prosperity. Any person who appreciated her paid a compliment to the major's good judgement – that is, if a man may be said to have good judgement who is under the influence of Love's delusion.

After Jos went to Court, which we may be sure he did as a loyal subject of his sovereign (showing himself in his full Court suit at the club, whither Dobbin came to fetch him in a very shabby old uniform), he who had always been a stanch Loyalist and admirer of George IV, became such a tremendous Tory and pillar of the State, that he was for having Amelia to go to a Drawing-room too. He somehow had worked himself up to believe that he was implicated in the maintenance of the public welfare, and that the sovereign would not be happy unless Jos Sedley and his family appeared to rally round him at St. James's.

Emmy laughed. 'Shall I wear the family diamonds, Jos?' she said.

'I wish you would let me buy you some,' thought the major. 'I should like to see any that were too good for you.'

CHAPTER LXI

IN WHICH TWO LIGHTS ARE PUT OUT

HERE came a day when the round of decorous pleasures and solemn gaieties in which Mr. Jos Sedley's family indulged, was interrupted by an event which happens in most houses. As you ascend the staircase of your house from the drawing-towards the bedroom floors, you may have remarked a little arch in the wall right before you, which at once gives light to the stair which leads from the second story to the third (where the nursery and servants' chambers commonly are), and serves for another purpose of utility, of which the undertaker's men can give you a notion. They rest the coffins upon that arch, or pass them through it so as not to disturb in any unseemly manner the cold tenant slumbering within the black ark.

That second-floor arch in a London house, looking up and down the well of the staircase, and commanding the main thoroughfare by which the inhabitants are passing; by which cook lurks down before daylight to scour her pots and pans in the kitchen; by which young master stealthily ascends, having left his boots in the hall, and let himself in after dawn from a jolly night at the club; down which miss comes rustling in fresh ribbons and spreading muslins, brilliant and beautiful, and prepared for conquest and the ball;

or Master Tommy slides, preferring the banisters for a mode
of conveyance, and disdaining danger and the stair; down which
the mother is fondly carried smiling in her strong husband's
arms, as he steps steadily step by step, and followed by the
monthly nurse, on the day when the medical man has
pronounced that the charming patient may go downstairs;
up which John lurks to bed, yawning with a sputtering tallow
candle, and to gather up before sunrise the boots which are
awaiting him in the passages: – that stair, up or down which
babies are carried, old people are helped, guests are marshalled to the ball, the parson walks to the christening, the
doctor to the sick-room, and the undertaker's men to the
upper floor – what a memento of Life, Death, and Vanity
it is – that arch and stair – if you choose to consider it, and
sit on the landing, looking up and down the well! The doctor
will come up to us too for the last time there, my friend in
motley. The nurse will look in at the curtains, and you take
no notice – and then she will fling open the windows for a
little, and let in the air. Then they will pull down all the
front blinds of the house and live in the back rooms – then
they will send for the lawyer and other men in black, &c.
– Your comedy and mine will have been played then, and
we shall be removed, oh how far, from the trumpets, and
the shouting, and the posture-making. If we are gentlefolks
they will put hatchments over our late domicile, with gilt
cherubim, and mottoes stating that there is 'Quiet in Heaven'.
Your son will new furnish the house, or perhaps let it, and
go into a more modern quarter; your name will be among
the 'Members Deceased', in the lists of your clubs next year.
However much you may be mourned, your widow will like
to have her weeds neatly made – the cook will send or come
up to ask about dinner – the survivors will soon bear to look
at your picture over the mantelpiece, which will presently
be deposed from the place of honour, to make way for the
portrait of the son who reigns.

Which of the dead are most tenderly and passionately
deplored? Those who love the survivors the least, I believe.
The death of a child occasions a passion of grief and frantic
tears, such as your end, brother reader, will never inspire.
The death of an infant which scarce knew you, which a
week's absence from you would have caused to forget you,
will strike you down more than the loss of your closest

friend, or your first-born son – a man grown like yourself, with children of his own. We may be harsh and stern with Judah and Simeon – our love and pity gushes out for Benjamin, the little one. And if you are old, as some reader of this may be or shall be – old and rich, or old and poor – you may one day be thinking for yourself – 'These people are very good round about me; but they won't grieve too much when I am gone. I am very rich, and they want my inheritance – or very poor, and they are tired of supporting me.'

The period of mourning for Mrs. Sedley's death was only just concluded, and Jos scarcely had had time to cast off his black and appear in the splendid waistcoats which he loved, when it became evident to those about Mr. Sedley, that another event was at hand, and that the old man was about to go seek for his wife in the dark land whither she had preceded him. 'The state of my father's health,' Jos Sedley solemnly remarked at the club, 'prevents me from giving my *large* parties this season: but if you will come in quietly at half-past six, Chutney, my boy, and take a homely dinner with one or two of the old set – I shall be always glad to see you.' So Jos and his acquaintances dined and drank their claret among themselves in silence; whilst the sands of life were running out in the old man's glass upstairs. The velvet-footed butler brought them their wine; and they composed themselves to a rubber after dinner; at which Major Dobbin would sometimes come and take a hand: and Mrs. Osborne would occasionally descend, when her patient above was settled for the night, and had commenced one of those lightly troubled slumbers which visit the pillow of old age.

The old man clung to his daughter during this sickness. He would take his broths and medicines from scarcely any other hand. To tend him became almost the sole business of her life. Her bed was placed close by the door which opened into his chamber, and she was alive at the slightest noise or disturbance from the couch of the querulous invalid. Though, to do him justice, he lay awake many an hour, silent and without stirring, unwilling to awaken his kind and vigilant nurse.

He loved his daughter with more fondness now, perhaps, than ever he had done since the days of her childhood. In the discharge of gentle offices and kind filial duties, this simple creature shone most especially. 'She walks into the room as silently as a sunbeam,' Mr. Dobbin thought, as he saw her passing in and out from her father's room: a cheerful sweetness lighting up her face as she moved to and fro, graceful and noiseless. When women are brooding over their children, or busied in a sick-room, who has not seen in their faces those sweet angelic beams of love and pity?

A secret feud of some years standing was thus healed: and with a tacit reconciliation. In these last hours and touched by her love and goodness, the old man forgot all his grief against her, and wrongs which he and his wife had many a long night debated: how she had given up everything for her boy: how she was careless of her parents in their old age and misfortune, and only thought of the child: how absurdly and foolishly, impiously indeed she took on, when George was removed from her. Old Sedley forgot these charges as he was making up his last account, and did justice to the gentle and uncomplaining little martyr. One night when she stole into his room, she found him awake, when the broken old man made his confession. 'Oh, Emmy, I've been thinking we were very unkind and unjust to you,' he said, and put out his cold and feeble hand to her. She knelt down and prayed by his bedside, as he did too, having still hold of her hand. When our turn comes, friend, may we have such company in our prayers.

Perhaps as he was lying awake then, his life may have passed before him – his early hopeful struggles, his manly successes and prosperity, his downfall in his declining years, and his present helpless condition – no chance of revenge against Fortune, which had had the better of him – neither name nor money to bequeath – a spent-out, bootless life of defeat and disappointment, and the end here! Which, I wonder, brother reader, is the better lot, to die prosperous and famous, or poor and disappointed? To have, and to be forced to yield; or to sink out of life, having played and lost the game? That must be a strange feeling, when a day of our life comes and we say, '*To-morrow*, success or failure won't matter much: and the sun will rise, and all the myriads of mankind go to their work or their pleasure as usual, but I shall be out of the turmoil.'

So there came one morning and sunrise, when all the

world got up and set about its various works and pleasures, with the exception of old John Sedley, who was not to fight with fortune, or to hope or scheme any more: but to go and take up a quiet and utterly unknown residence in a church-yard at Brompton by the side of his old wife.

Major Dobbin, Jos, and Georgy followed his remains to the grave, in a black cloth coach. Jos came on purpose from the 'Star and Garter' at Richmond, whither he retreated after the deplorable event. He did not care to remain in the house, with the – under the circumstances, you understand. But Emmy stayed and did her duty as usual. She was bowed down by no especial grief, and rather solemn than sorrowful. She prayed that her own end might be as calm and painless, and thought with trust and reverence of the words which she had heard from her father during his illness, indicative of his faith, his resignation, and his future hope.

Yes, I think that will be the better ending of the two, after all. Suppose you are particularly rich and well-to-do, and say on that last day, 'I am very rich; I am tolerably well known; I have lived all my life in the best society, and, thank Heaven, come of a most respectable family. I have served my King and country with honour. I was in Parliament for several years, where, I may say, my speeches were listened to, and pretty well received. I don't owe any man a shilling: on the contrary, I lent my old college friend, Jack Lazarus, fifty pounds, for which my executors will not press him. I leave my daughters with ten thousand pounds a piece – very good portions for girls: I bequeath my plate and furniture, my house in Baker Street, with a handsome jointure, to my widow for her life; and my landed property, besides money in the Funds, and my cellar of well-selected wine in Baker Street, to my son. I leave twenty pound a year to my valet; and I defy any man after I am gone to find anything against my character.' Or suppose, on the other hand, your swan sings quite a different sort of dirge, and you say, 'I am a poor, blighted, disappointed old fellow, and have made an utter failure through life. I was not endowed either with brains or with good fortune: and confess that I have com-mitted a hundred mistakes and blunders. I own to having forgotten my duty many a time. I can't pay what I owe. On my last bed I lie utterly helpless and humble: and I pray forgiveness for my weakness, and throw myself with a contrite heart at the feet of the Divine Mercy.' Which of these two speeches, think you, would be the best oration for your own funeral? Old Sedley made the last; and in that humble frame of mind, and holding by the hand of his daughter, life and disappointment and vanity sank away from under him.

'You see,' said old Osborne to George, 'what comes of merit and industry, and judicious speculations, and that. Look at me and my banker's account. Look at your poor grandfather Sedley, and his failure. And yet he was a better man than I was, this day twenty years – a better man I should say by ten thousand pound.'

Beyond these people and Mr. Clapp's family, who came over from Brompton to pay a visit of condolence, not a single soul alive ever cared a penny piece about old John Sedley, or remembered the existence of such a person.

When old Osborne first heard from his friend Colonel Buckler (as little Georgy has already informed us) how distinguished an officer Major Dobbin was, he exhibited a great deal of scornful incredulity, and expressed his surprise how ever such a feller as that should possess either brains or reputation. But he heard of the major's fame from various members of his society. Sir William Dobbin had a great opinion of his son, and narrated many stories illustrative of the major's learning, valour, and estimation in the world's opinion. Finally, his name appeared in the lists of one or two great parties of the nobility; and this circumstance had a prodigious effect upon the old aristocrat of Russell Square.

The major's position, as guardian to Georgy, whose possession had been ceded to his grandfather, rendered some meetings between the two gentlemen inevitable; and it was in one of these that old Osborne, a keen man of business, looking into the major's accounts with his ward and the boy's mother, got a hint which staggered him very much, and at once pained and pleased him, that it was out of William Dobbin's own pocket that a part of the fund had been supplied upon which the poor widow and the child had subsisted.

When pressed upon the point, Dobbin, who could not tell lies, blushed and stammered a good deal, and finally confessed. 'The marriage,' he said (at which his interlocu-

tor's face grew dark), 'was very much my doing. I thought
my poor friend had gone so far, that retreat from his
engagement would have been dishonour to him and death
to Mrs. Osborne; and I could do no less, when she was left
without resources, than give what money I could spare to
maintain her.'

'Major D.,' Mr. Osborne said, looking hard at him, and
turning very red too – 'You did me a great injury; but give
me leave to tell you, sir, you are an honest feller. There's
my hand, sir, though I little thought that my flesh and blood
was living on you –' and the pair shook hands, with great
confusion on Major Dobbin's part, thus found out in his act
of charitable hypocrisy.

He strove to soften the old man, and reconcile him
towards his son's memory. 'He was such a noble fellow,' he
said, 'that all of us loved him, and would have done anything
for him. I, as a young man in those days, was flattered
beyond measure by his preference for me; and was more
pleased to be seen in his company than in that of the
commander-in-chief. I never saw his equal for pluck and
daring, and all the qualities of a soldier;' and Dobbin told
the old father as many stories as he could remember regarding the gallantry and achievements of his son. 'And Georgy
is so like him,' the major added.

'He's so like him that he makes me tremble sometimes,'
the grandfather said.

On one or two evenings the major came to dine with Mr.
Osborne (it was during the time of the sickness of Mr.
Sedley), and as the two sat together in the evening after
dinner all their talk was about the departed hero. The father
boasted about him according to his wont, glorifying himself
in recounting his son's feats and gallantry, but his mood was
at any rate better and more charitable than that in which he
had been disposed until now to regard the poor fellow; and
the Christian heart of the kind major was pleased at these
symptoms of returning peace and goodwill. On the second
evening old Osborne called Dobbin, William, just as he used
to do at the time when Dobbin and George were boys
together; and the honest gentleman was pleased by that mark
of reconciliation.

On the next day at breakfast when Miss Osborne, with
the asperity of her age and character, ventured to make some

remark reflecting slightingly upon the major's appearance
or behaviour – the master of the house interrupted her.
'You'd have been glad enough to git him for yourself, Miss
O. But them grapes are sour. Ha! ha! Major William is a
fine feller.'

'That he is, grandpapa,' said Georgy, approvingly; and
going up close to the old gentleman, he took a hold of his
large grey whiskers, and laughed in his face good-humouredly
and kissed him. And he told the story at night to his mother:
who fully agreed with the boy. 'Indeed he is,' she said. 'Your
dear father always said so. He is one of the best and most
upright of men.' Dobbin happened to drop in very soon
after this conversation, which made Amelia blush perhaps;
and the young scapegrace increased the confusion by telling
Dobbin the other part of the story. 'I say, Dob,' he said,
'there's such an uncommon nice girl wants to marry you.
She's plenty of tin: she wears a front: and she scolds the
servants from morning till night.'

'Who is it?' asked Dobbin.

'It's Aunt O.,' the boy answered, 'grandpapa said so. And
I say, Dob, how prime it would be to have you for my
uncle.' Old Sedley's quavering voice from the next room at
this moment weakly called for Amelia, and the laughing
ended.

That old Osborne's mind was changing was pretty clear.
He asked George about his uncle sometimes, and laughed at
the boy's imitation of the way in which Jos said 'God-bless-
my-soul', and gobbled his soup. Then he said, 'It's not
respectful, sir, of you younkers to be imitating of your
relations. Miss O., when you go out a-driving to-day, leave
my card upon Mr. Sedley, do you hear? There's no quarrel
betwigst me and him, anyhow.'

The card was returned, and Jos and the major were asked
to dinner, – to a dinner the most splendid and stupid that
perhaps ever Mr. Osborne gave; every inch of the family
plate was exhibited, and the best company was asked. Mr.
Sedley took down Miss O. to dinner, and she was very
gracious to him; whereas she hardly spoke to the major, who
sat apart from her, and by the side of Mr. Osborne, very
timid. Jos said, with great solemnity, it was the best clear
turtle soup he had ever tasted in his life; and asked Mr.
Osborne where he got his madeira?

'It is some of Sedley's wine,' whispered the butler to his master. 'I've had it a long time, and paid a good figure for it, too,' Mr. Osborne said aloud to his guest; and then whispered to his right-hand neighbour how he had got it 'at the old chap's sale'.

More than once he asked the major about – about Mrs. George Osborne – a theme on which the major could be very eloquent when he chose. He told Mr. Osborne of her sufferings – of her passionate attachment to her husband, whose memory she worshipped still – of the tender and dutiful manner in which she had supported her parents and given up her boy, when it seemed to her her duty to do so. 'You don't know what she endured, sir,' said honest Dobbin, with a tremor in his voice; 'and I hope and trust you will be reconciled to her. If she took your son away from you, she gave hers to you; and however much you loved your George, depend on it, she loved hers ten times more.'

'By God, you are a good feller, sir,' was all Mr. Osborne said. It had never struck him that the widow would feel any pain at parting with the boy, or that his having a fine fortune could grieve her. A reconciliation was announced as speedy and inevitable; and Amelia's heart already began to beat at the notion of the awful meeting with George's father.

It was never, however, destined to take place. Old Sedley's lingering illness and death supervened, after which a meeting was for some time impossible. That catastrophe and other events may have worked upon Mr. Osborne. He was much shaken of late, and aged, and his mind was working inwardly. He had sent for his lawyers, and probably changed something in his will. The medical man who looked in, pronounced him shaky, agitated, and talked of a little blood, and the sea-side; but he took neither of these remedies.

One day when he should have come down to breakfast, his servant, missing him, went into his dressing-room, and found him lying at the foot of the dressing-table, in a fit. Miss Osborne was apprised; the doctors were sent for; Georgy stopped away from school; the bleeders and cuppers came. Osborne partially regained cognizance; but never could speak again, though he tried dreadfully once or twice, and in four days he died. The doctors went down; the under-taker's men went up the stairs; and all the shutters were shut towards the garden in Russell Square. Bullock rushed

from the City in a hurry. 'How much money had he left to
that boy? – not half, surely? Surely share and share alike
between the three?' It was an agitating moment.

What was it that poor old man had tried once or twice
in vain to say? I hope it was that he wanted to see Amelia,
and be reconciled before he left the world to the dear and
faithful wife of his son: it was most likely that; for his will
showed that the hatred which he had so long cherished had
gone out of his heart.

They found in the pocket of his dressing-gown the letter
with the great red seal, which George had written him from
Waterloo. He had looked at the other papers, too, relative
to his son, for the key of the box in which he kept them
was also in his pocket, and it was found the seals and
envelopes had been broken – very likely on the night before
the seizure, when the butler had taken him tea into his study,
and found him reading in the great red family Bible.

When the will was opened, it was found that half the
property was left to George, and the remainder between the
two sisters. Mr. Bullock to continue, for their joint benefit,
the affairs of the commercial house, or to go out, as he
thought fit. An annuity of five hundred pounds, chargeable
on George's property, was left to his mother, 'the widow of
my beloved son George Osborne,' who was to resume the
guardianship of the boy.

'Major William Dobbin, my beloved son's friend,' was
appointed executor; 'and as out of his kindness and bounty,
and with his own private funds, he maintained my grandson,
and my son's widow, when they were otherwise without
means of support' (the testator went on to say), 'I hereby
thank him heartily for his love and regard for them; and
beseech him to accept such a sum as may be sufficient to
purchase his commission as a lieutenant-colonel, or to be
disposed of in any way he may think fit.'

When Amelia heard that her father-in-law was reconciled
to her, her heart melted, and she was grateful for the fortune
left to her. But when she heard how Georgy was restored
to her, and knew how and by whom, and how it was
William's bounty that supported her in poverty, how it was
William who gave her her husband and her son – oh, then
she sank on her knees, and prayed for blessings on that
constant and kind heart: she bowed down and humbled

herself, and kissed the feet, as it were, of that beautiful and generous affection.

And gratitude was all that she had to pay back for such admirable devotion and benefits – only gratitude! If she thought of any other return, the image of George stood up out of the grave, and said, 'You are mine, and mine only, now and for ever.'

William knew her feelings: had he not passed his whole life in divining them?

When the nature of Mr. Osborne's will became known to the world, it was edifying to remark how Mrs. George Osborne rose in the estimation of the people forming her circle of acquaintance. The servants of Jos's establishment, who used to question her humble orders, and say they would 'ask master', whether or not they could obey, never thought now of that sort of appeal. The cook forgot to sneer at her shabby old gowns (which, indeed, were quite eclipsed by that lady's finery when she was dressed to go to church of a Sunday evening); the others no longer grumbled at the sound of her bell, or delayed to answer that summons. The coachman, who grumbled that his osses should be brought out, and his carriage made into an ospital for that old feller and Mrs. O., drove her with the utmost alacrity now, and trembling lest he should be superseded by Mr. Osborne's coachman, asked 'what them there Russell Square coachmen knew about town, and whether *they* was fit to sit on a box before a lady?' Jos's friends, male and female, suddenly became interested about Emmy, and cards of condolence multiplied on her hall-table. Jos himself, who had looked on her as a good-natured harmless pauper, to whom it was his duty to give victuals and shelter, paid her and the rich little boy, his nephew, the greatest respect – was anxious that she should have change and amusement after her troubles and trials, 'poor dear girl' – and began to appear at the break-fast-table, and most particularly to ask how she would like to dispose of the day.

In her capacity of guardian to Georgy, she, with the consent of the major, her fellow-trustee, begged Miss Osborne to live in the Russell Square house as long as ever she chose to dwell there; but that lady, with thanks, declared that she never could think of remaining alone in that melancholy mansion, and departed in deep mourning, to Cheltenham, with a couple of her old domestics. The rest were liberally paid and dismissed; the faithful old butler, whom Mrs. Osborne proposed to retain, resigning and preferring to invest his savings in a public-house, where, let us hope, he was not unprosperous. Miss Osborne not choosing to live in Russell Square, Mrs. Osborne also, after consultation, declined to occupy the gloomy old mansion there. The house was dismantled; the rich furniture and effects, the awful chandeliers and dreary blank mirrors packed away and hidden, the rich rosewood drawing-room suite was muffled in straw, the carpets were rolled up and corded, the small select library of well-bound books were stowed into two wine chests, and the whole paraphernalia rolled away in several enormous vans to the Pantechnicon, where they were to lie until Georgy's majority. And the great heavy dark plate-chests went off to Messrs. Stumpy and Rowdy, to lie in the cellars of those eminent bankers until the same period should arrive.

One day Emmy with George in her hand and clad in deep sables went to visit the deserted mansion which she had not entered since she was a girl. The place in front was littered with straw where the vans had been laden and rolled off. They went into the great blank rooms, the walls of which bore the marks where the pictures and mirrors had hung. Then they went up the great blank stone staircases into the upper rooms, into that where grandpapa died, as George said in a whisper, and then higher still into George's own room. The boy was still clinging by her side, but she thought of another besides him. She knew that it had been his father's room as well as his own.

She went up to one of the open windows (one of those at which she used to gaze with a sick heart when the child was first taken from her) and thence as she looked out she could see over the trees of Russell Square, the old house in which she herself was born, and where she had passed so many happy days of sacred youth. They all came back to her, the pleasant holidays, the kind faces, the careless, joyful past times; and the long pains and trials that had since cast her down. She thought of these and of the man who had been her constant protector, her good genius, her sole benefactor, her tender and generous friend.

'Look here, mother,' said Georgy, 'here's a G. O. scratched on the glass with a diamond; I never saw it before, *I* never did it.'

'It was your father's room long, long before you were born, George,' she said, and she blushed as she kissed the boy.

She was very silent as they drove back to Richmond where they had taken a temporary house: where the smiling lawyers used to come bustling over to see her (and we may be sure noted the visit in the bill): and where of course there was a room for Major Dobbin too, who rode over frequently, having much business to transact in behalf of his little ward.

Georgy at this time was removed from Mr. Veal's on an unlimited holiday, and that gentleman was engaged to prepare an inscription for a fine marble slab, to be placed up in the Foundling under the monument of Captain George Osborne.

The female Bullock, aunt of Georgy, although despoiled by that little monster of one-half of the sum which she expected from her father, nevertheless showed her charitableness of spirit by being reconciled to the mother and the boy. Roehampton is not far from Richmond, and one day the chariot, with the golden Bullocks emblazoned on the panels, and the flaccid children within, drove to Amelia's house at Richmond; and the Bullock family made an irruption into the garden, where Amelia was reading a book, Jos was in an arbour placidly dipping strawberries into wine, and the major in one of his Indian jackets was giving a back to Georgy, who chose to jump over him. He went over his head, and bounded into the little advance of Bullocks, with immense black bows in their hats, and huge black sashes, accompanying their mourning mamma.

'He is just of the age for Rosa,' the fond parent thought, and glanced towards that dear child, an unwholesome little miss of seven years of age.

'Rosa, go and kiss your dear cousin,' Mrs. Frederick said. 'Don't you know me, George? – I am your aunt.'

'*I* know you well enough,' George said; 'but I don't like kissing, please;' and he retreated from the obedient caresses of his cousin.

'Take me to your dear mamma, you droll child,' Mrs.

Frederick said; and those ladies accordingly met, after an absence of more than fifteen years. During Emmy's cares and poverty the other had never once thought about coming to see her; but now that she was decently prosperous in the world, her sister-in-law came to her as a matter of course.

So did numbers more. Our old friend, Miss Swartz, and her husband came thundering over from Hampton Court, with flaming yellow liveries, and was as impetuously fond of Amelia as ever. Swartz would have liked her always if she could have seen her. One must do her that justice. But, *que voulez-vous?* – in this vast town one has not the time to go and seek one's friends; if they drop out of the rank they disappear, and we march on without them. Who is ever missed in Vanity Fair?

But so, in a word, and before the period of grief for Mr. Osborne's death had subsided, Emmy found herself in the centre of a very genteel circle indeed; the members of which could not conceive that anybody belonging to it was not very lucky. There was scarce one of the ladies that hadn't a relation a peer, though the husband might be a drysalter in the City. Some of the ladies were very blue and well informed; reading Mrs. Somerville, and frequenting the Royal Institution; others were severe and Evangelical, and held by Exeter Hall. Emmy, it must be owned, found herself entirely at a loss in the midst of their clavers, and suffered wofully on the one or two occasions in which she was compelled to accept Mrs. Frederick Bullock's hospitalities. That lady persisted in patronizing her, and determined most graciously to form her. She found Amelia's milliners for her, and regulated her household and her manners. She drove over constantly from Roehampton, and entertained her friend with faint fashionable fiddlefaddle and feeble Court slipslop. Jos liked to hear it, but the major used to go off growling at the appearance of this woman, with her twopenny gentility. He went to sleep under Frederick Bullock's bald head, after dinner, at one of the banker's best parties (Fred was still anxious that the balance of the Osborne property should be transferred from Stumpy and Rowdy's to them), and whilst Amelia, who did not know Latin, or who wrote the last crack article in the *Edinburgh*, and did not in the least deplore, or otherwise, Mr. Peel's late extraordinary tergiversation in the fatal Catholic Relief Bill, sat dumb amongst the ladies in the grand drawing-room, looking out upon velvet lawns, trim gravel walks, and glistening hothouses.

'She seems good-natured but insipid,' said Mrs. Rowdy; 'that major seems to be particularly *épris*.'

'She wants *ton* sadly,' said Mrs. Hollyock. 'My dear creature, you never will be able to form her.'

'She is dreadfully ignorant or indifferent,' said Mrs. Glowry, with a voice as if from the grave, and a sad shake of the head and turban – 'I asked her if she thought that it was in 1836, according to Mr. Jowls, or in 1839, according to Mr. Wapshot, that the Pope was to fall: and she said – "Poor Pope! I hope not – What has he done?" '

'She is my brother's widow, my dear friends,' Mrs. Frederick replied, 'and as such I think we're all bound to give her every attention and instruction on entering into the world. You may fancy there can be no *mercenary* motive in those whose *disappointments* are well known.'

'That poor dear Mrs. Bullock,' said Rowdy to Hollyock, as they drove away together – 'she is always scheming and managing. She wants Mrs. Osborne's account to be taken from our house to hers – and the way in which she coaxes that boy, and makes him sit by that blear-eyed little Rosa, is perfectly ridiculous.'

'I wish Glowry was choked with her Man of Sin and her Battle of Armageddon,' cried the other; and the carriage rolled away over Putney Bridge.

But this sort of society was too cruelly genteel for Emmy: and all jumped for joy when a foreign tour was proposed.

CHAPTER LXII

AM RHEIN

THE above every-day events had occurred, and a few weeks had passed, when, on one fine morning, Parliament being over, the summer advanced, and all the good company in London about to quit that city for their annual tour in search of pleasure or health, the *Batavier* steamboat left the Tower stairs laden with a goodly company of English fugitives. The quarterdeck awnings were up, and the benches and gangways crowded with scores of rosy children, bustling nursemaids, ladies in the prettiest pink bonnets and summer dresses, gentlemen in travelling caps and linen jackets, whose moustachios had just begun to sprout for the ensuing tour; and stout trim old veterans with starched neckcloths and neat-brushed hats, such as have invaded Europe any time since the conclusion of the war, and carry the national Goddem into every city of the Continent. The congregation of hat-boxes, and Bramah desks, and dressing-cases, was prodigious. There were jaunty young Cambridge men travelling with their tutor, and going for a reading excursion to Nonnenwerth or Königswinter: there were Irish gentlemen, with the most dashing whiskers and jewellery, talking about horses incessantly, and prodigiously polite to the young ladies on board, whom, on the contrary, the Cambridge lads and their palefaced tutor avoided with maiden coyness: there were old Pall Mall loungers bound for Ems and Wiesbaden, and a course of waters to clear off the dinners of the season, and a little roulette and *trente-et-quarante* to keep the excitement going: there was old Methuselah, who had married his young wife, with Captain Papillon of the Guards holding her parasol and guide-books: there was young May who was carrying off his bride on a pleasure tour (Mrs. Winter that was, and who had been at school with May's grandmother); there was Sir John and my lady with a dozen children, and corresponding nursemaids; and the great grandee Bareacres family that sat by themselves near the wheel, stared at everybody, and spoke to no one. Their carriages, emblazoned with coronets, and heaped with shining imperials, were on the fore-deck; locked in with a dozen more such vehicles: it was difficult to pass in and out amongst them: and the poor inmates of the fore-cabin had scarcely any space for locomotion. These consisted of a few magnificently attired gentlemen from Houndsditch, who brought their own provisions, and could have bought half the gay people in the grand saloon; a few honest fellows with moustachios and portfolios, who set to sketching before they had been half an hour on board; one or two French *femmes de chambre* who began to be dreadfully ill by the time the boat had passed Greenwich; a groom or two who lounged in the neighbourhood of the horse-boxes under their charge, or leaned over the side by the paddle-wheels, and talked about who was good for the Leger, and what they stood to win or lose for the Goodwood Cup.

All the couriers, when they had done plunging about the ship, and had settled their various masters in the cabins or on the deck, congregated together and began to chatter and smoke; the Hebrew gentlemen joining them and looking at the carriages. There was Sir John's great carriage that would hold thirteen people; my Lord Methuselah's carriage, my Lord Bareacres's chariot, britzka, and fourgon, that anybody might pay for who liked. It was a wonder how my lord got the ready money to pay for the expenses of the journey. The Hebrew gentlemen knew how he got it. They knew what money his lordship had in his pocket at that instant, and what interest he paid for it, and who gave it him. Finally, there was a very neat, handsome travelling carriage, about which the gentlemen speculated.

'*A qui cette voiture-là?*' said one gentleman-courier with a large morocco money-bag and ear-rings, to another with ear-rings and a large morocco money-bag.

'*C'est à Kirsch, je bense – je l'ai vu toute à l'heure – qui brenait des sangviches dans la voiture,*' said the courier, in a fine German French.

Kirsch emerging presently from the neighbourhood of the hold where he had been bellowing instructions intermingled with polyglot oaths to the ship's men engaged in secreting the passengers' luggage, came to give an account of himself to his brother interpreters. He informed them that the carriage belonged to a nabob from Calcutta and Jamaica, enormously rich, and with whom he was engaged to travel; and at this moment a young gentleman who had been warned off the bridge between the paddle-boxes, and who had dropped thence on to the roof of Lord Methuselah's carriage, from which he had made his way over other carriages and imperials until he had clambered on to his own, descended thence and through the window into the body of the carriage to the applause of the couriers looking on.

'*Nous allons avoir une belle traversée*, Monsieur George,' said the courier, with a grin, as he lifted his gold-laced cap.

'D– your French,' said the young gentleman, 'where's the biscuits, eh?' Whereupon Kirsch answered him in the English language or in such an imitation of it as he could command, – for though he was familiar with all languages, Mr. Kirsch was not acquainted with a single one and spoke all with indifferent volubility and incorrectness.

The imperious young gentleman who gobbled the biscuits (and indeed it was time to refresh himself, for he had breakfasted at Richmond full three hours before) was our young friend George Osborne. Uncle Jos and his mamma were on the quarter-deck with a gentleman of whom they used to see a good deal, and the four were about to make a summer tour.

Jos was seated at that moment on deck under the awning, and pretty nearly opposite to the Earl of Bareacres and his family, whose proceedings absorbed the Bengalee almost entirely. Both the noble couple looked rather younger than in the eventful year '15, when Jos remembered to have seen them at Brussels (indeed he always gave out in India that he was intimately acquainted with them). Lady Bareacres's hair which was then dark was now a beautiful golden auburn, whereas Lord Bareacres's whiskers, formerly red, were at present of a rich black with purple and green reflections in the light. But changed as they were, the movements of the noble pair occupied Jos's mind entirely. The presence of a lord fascinated him, and he could look at nothing else.

'Those people seem to interest you a good deal,' said Dobbin, laughing and watching him. Amelia too laughed. She was in a straw bonnet with black ribbons, and otherwise dressed in mourning: but the little bustle and holiday of the journey pleased and excited her, and she looked particularly happy.

'What a heavenly day!' Emmy said, and added, with great originality, 'I hope we shall have a calm passage.'

Jos waved his hand scornfully, glancing at the same time under his eyelids at the great folks opposite. 'If you had made the voyages *we* have,' he said, 'you wouldn't much care about the weather.' But nevertheless, traveller as he was, he passed the night direfully sick in his carriage, where his courier tended him with brandy-and-water and every luxury.

In due time this happy party landed at the quays of Rotterdam, whence they were transported by another steamer to the city of Cologne. Here the carriage and the family took to the shore, and Jos was not a little gratified to see his arrival announced in the Cologne newspapers as '*Herr Graf Lord von Sedley, nebst Begleitung, aus London.*' He had his Court dress with him: he had insisted that Dobbin should bring his regimental paraphernalia: he announced that it was his intention to be presented at some foreign Courts, and pay his respects to the sovereigns of the countries which he honoured with a visit.

Wherever the party stopped, and an opportunity was offered, Mr. Jos left his own card and the major's upon 'Our Minister'. It was with great difficulty that he could be restrained from putting on his cocked hat and tights to wait upon the English consul at the Free City of Judenstadt, when that hospitable functionary asked our travellers to dinner. He kept a journal of his voyage, and noted elaborately the defects or excellences of the various inns at which he put up, and of the wines and dishes of which he partook.

As for Emmy, she was very happy and pleased. Dobbin used to carry about for her her stool and sketch-book, and admired the drawings of the good-natured little artist, as they never had been admired before. She sat upon steamers' decks and drew crags and castles, or she mounted upon donkeys and ascended to ancient robber-towers, attended by her two aides de camp, Georgy and Dobbin. She laughed and the major did too, at his droll figure on donkey-back, with his long legs touching the ground. He was the interpreter for the party, having a good military knowledge of the German language; and he and the delighted George fought the campaigns of the Rhine and the Palatinate. In the course of a few weeks, and by assiduously conversing with Herr Kirsch on the box of the carriage, Georgy made prodigious advance in the knowledge of High Dutch, and could talk to hotel waiters and postilions in a way that charmed his mother, and amused his guardian.

Mr. Jos did not much engage in the afternoon excursions of his fellow travellers. He slept a good deal after dinner, or basked in the arbours of the pleasant inn-gardens. Pleasant Rhine gardens! Fair scenes of peace and sunshine – noble purple mountains, whose crests are reflected in the magnificent stream – who has ever seen you, that has not a grateful memory of those scenes of friendly repose and beauty? To lay down the pen, and even to think of that beautiful Rhineland makes one happy. At this time of summer evening, the cows are trooping down from the hills, lowing and with their bells tinkling, to the old town, with its old moats, and gates, and spires, and chestnut-trees, with long blue shadows stretching over the grass; the sky and the river below flame in crimson and gold; and the moon is already out, looking pale towards the sunset. The sun sinks behind the great castle-crested mountains, the night falls suddenly, the river grows darker and darker, lights quiver in it from the windows in the old ramparts, and twinkle peacefully in the villages under the hills on the opposite shore.

So Jos used to go to sleep a good deal with his bandanna over his face and be very comfortable, and read all the English news, and every word of Galignani's admirable newspaper (may the blessings of all Englishmen who have ever been abroad rest on the founders and proprietors of that piratical print!) and whether he woke or slept his friends did not very much miss him. Yes, they were very happy. They went to the Opera often of evenings – to those snug, unassuming, dear old operas in the German towns, where the noblesse sits and cries, and knits stockings on the one side, over against the bourgeoisie on the other; and his transparency the duke and his transparent family, all very fat and good-natured, come and occupy the great box in the middle; and the pit is full of the most elegant slim-waisted officers with straw-coloured moustaches, and twopence a day on full pay. Here it was that Emmy found her delight, and was introduced for the first time to the wonders of Mozart and Cimarosa. The major's musical taste has been before alluded to, and his performances on the flute commended. But perhaps the chief pleasure he had in these operas was in watching Emmy's rapture while listening to them. A new world of love and beauty broke upon her when she was introduced to those divine compositions: this lady had the keenest and finest sensibility, and how could she be indifferent when she heard Mozart? The tender parts of *Don Juan* awakened in her raptures so exquisite that she would ask herself when she went to say her prayers of a night, whether it was not wicked to feel so much delight as that with which *Vedrai Carino* and *Batti, Batti* filled her gentle little bosom? But the major, whom she consulted upon this head, as her theological adviser (and who himself had a pious and reverent soul), said that for his part, every beauty of art or nature made him thankful as well as happy; and that the pleasure to be had in listening to fine music, as in looking at the stars in the sky, or at a beautiful landscape or picture, was a benefit for which we might thank Heaven as sincerely as for any other worldly blessing. And in reply to some faint objections of Mrs. Amelia's (taken from certain theological works like the *Washerwoman of Finchley Common* and others of that school, with which Mrs. Osborne had been furnished during her life at Brompton) he told her an Eastern fable of the Owl who thought that the sunshine was unbearable for the eyes, and that the Nightingale was a most over-rated bird. 'It is one's nature to sing and the other's to hoot,' he said, laughing, 'and with such a sweet voice as you have yourself, you must belong to the Bulbul faction.'

I like to dwell upon this period of her life, and to think that she was cheerful and happy. You see she has not had too much of that sort of existence as yet, and has not fallen in the way of means to educate her tastes or her intelligence. She has been domineered over hitherto by vulgar intellects. It is the lot of many a woman. And as every one of the dear sex is the rival of the rest of her kind, timidity passes for folly in their charitable judgements; and gentleness for dullness; and silence – which is but timid denial of the unwelcome assertion of ruling folks, and tacit protestantism – above all, finds no mercy at the hands of the female Inquisition. Thus, my dear and civilized reader, if you and I were to find ourselves this evening in a society of greengrocers, let us say; it is probable that our conversation would not be brilliant; if, on the other hand, a greengrocer should find himself at your refined and polite tea-table, where everybody was saying witty things, and everybody of fashion and repute tearing her friends to pieces in the most delightful manner, it is possible that the stranger would not be very talkative, and by no means interesting or interested.

And it must be remembered, that this poor lady had never met a gentleman in her life until this present moment. Perhaps these are rarer personages than some of us think for. Which of us can point out many such in his circle – men whose aims are generous, whose truth is constant, and not only constant in its kind, but elevated in its degree; whose want of meanness makes them simple: who can look the world honestly in the face with an equal manly sympathy for the great and the small? We all know a hundred whose coats are very well made, and a score who have excellent manners, and one or two happy beings who are what they call, in the inner circles, and have shot into the very centre

and bull's-eye of the fashion; but of gentlemen how many?
Let us take a little scrap of paper and each make out his
list.

My friend the major I write, without any doubt, in mine.
He had very long legs, a yellow face, and a slight lisp, which
at first was rather ridiculous. But his thoughts were just, his
brains were fairly good, his life was honest and pure, and
his heart warm and humble. He certainly had very large
hands and feet, which the two George Osbornes used to
caricature and laugh at; and their jeers and laughter perhaps
led poor little Emmy astray as to his worth. But have we
not all been misled about our heroes, and changed our
opinions a hundred times? Emmy, in this happy time, found
that hers underwent a very great change in respect of the
merits of the major.

Perhaps it was the happiest time of both their lives
indeed, if they did but know it – and who does? Which of
us can point out and say that 'was the culmination – that
was the summit of human joy? But at all events, this couple
were very decently contented and enjoyed as pleasant a
summer tour as any pair that left England that year. Georgy
was always present at the play, but it was the major who
put Emmy's shawl on after the entertainment; and in the
walks and excursions the young lad would be on ahead, and
up a tower-stair or a tree, whilst the soberer couple were
below, the major smoking his cigar with great placidity and
constancy, whilst Emmy sketched the site or the ruin. It was
on this very tour that I, the present writer of a history of
which every word is true, had the pleasure to see them first,
and to make their acquaintance.

It was at the little comfortable ducal town of Pumpernickel
(that very place where Sir Pitt Crawley had been so distinguished as an attaché; but that was in early, early days, and
before the news of the battle of Austerlitz sent all the English
diplomatists in Germany to the right-about) that I first saw
Colonel Dobbin and his party. They had arrived with the
carriage and courier at the 'Erbprinz' Hotel, the best of the
town, and the whole party dined at the table d'hôte. Everybody remarked the majesty of Jos, and the knowing way in
which he sipped, or rather sucked, the Johannisberger, which
he ordered for dinner. The little boy, too, we observed, had

a famous appetite, and consumed *Schinken* and *Braten*, and *Kartoffeln*, and cranberry jam, and salad, and pudding, and roast fowls, and sweetmeats, with a gallantry that did honour to his nation. After about fifteen dishes, he concluded the repast with dessert, some of which he even carried out of doors; for some young gentlemen at table, amused with his coolness and gallant free and easy manner, induced him to pocket a handful of macaroons, which he discussed on his way to the theatre, whither everybody went in the cheery social little German place. The lady in black, the boy's mamma, laughed and blushed, and looked exceedingly pleased and shy as the dinner went on, and at the various feats and instances of *espièglerie* on the part of her son. The colonel – for so he became very soon afterwards – I remember joked the boy with a great deal of grave fun, pointing out dishes which he *hadn't* tried, and entreating him not to balk his appetite, but to have a second supply of this or that.

It was what they call a *Gast-rolle* night at the Royal Grand Ducal Pumpernickelisch Hof – or Court – Theatre: and Madame Schroeder Devrient, then in the bloom of her beauty and genius, performed the part of the heroine in the wonderful opera of *Fidelio*. From our places in the stalls we could see our four friends of the table d'hôte, in the loge which Schwendler of the 'Erbprinz' kept for his best guests: and I could not help remarking the effect which the magnificent actress and music produced upon Mrs. Osborne, for so we had heard the stout gentleman in the moustachios call her. During the astonishing Chorus of the Prisoners over which the delightful voice of the actress rose and soared in the most ravishing harmony, the English lady's face wore such an expression of wonder and delight that it struck even little Fipps, the *blasé* attaché, who drawled out, as he fixed his glass upon her, 'Gayd, it really does one good to see a woman caypable of that stayt of excaytement.' And in the Prison Scene where Fidelio, rushing to her husband, cries '*Nichts, nichts, mein Florestan*', she fairly lost herself and covered her face with her handkerchief. Every woman in the house was snivelling at the time: but I suppose it was because it was predestined that I was to write this particular lady's memoirs, that I remarked her.

The next day they gave another piece of Beethoven: *Die Schlacht bei Vittoria*. Malbrook is introduced at the beginning of the performance, as indicative of the brisk advance of the French Army. Then come drums, trumpets, thunder of artillery, and groans of the dying, and at last in a grand triumphal swell, 'God save the King' is performed.

There may have been a score of Englishmen in the house, but at the burst of that beloved and well-known music, every one of them, we young fellows in the stalls, Sir John and Lady Bullminster (who had taken a house at Pumpernickel for the education of their nine children), the fat gentleman with the moustachios, the long major in white duck trousers, and the lady with the little boy upon whom he was so sweet: even Kirsch, the courier in the gallery, stood bolt upright in their places, and proclaimed themselves to be members of the dear old British nation. As for Tapeworm, the chargé d'affaires, he rose up in his box and bowed and simpered, as if he would represent the whole empire. Tapeworm was nephew and heir of old Marshal Tiptoff, who has been introduced in this story as General Tiptoff, just before Waterloo, who was colonel of the – th regiment, in which Major Dobbin served, and who died in this year full of honours, and of an aspic of plovers' eggs; when the regiment was graciously given by his majesty to Colonel Sir Michael O'Dowd, K.C.B., who had commanded it in many glorious fields.

Tapeworm must have met with Colonel Dobbin at the house of the colonel's colonel, the marshal, for he recognized him on this night at the theatre; and with the utmost condescension, his majesty's minister came over from his own box, and publicly shook hands with his new-found friend.

'Look at that infernal sly-boots of a Tapeworm,' Fipps whispered, examining his chief from the stalls. 'Wherever there's a pretty woman he always twists himself in.' And I wonder what were diplomatists made for but for that?

'Have I the honour of addressing myself to Mrs. Dobbin?' asked the secretary, with a most insinuating grin.

Georgy burst out laughing, and said, 'By Jove, that *is* a good un.' – Emmy and the major blushed: we saw them from the stalls.

'This lady is Mrs. George Osborne,' said the major, 'and this is her brother, Mr. Sedley, a distinguished officer of the Bengal Civil Service: permit me to introduce him to your lordship.'

My lord nearly sent Jos off his legs, with the most fascinating smile. 'Are you going to stop in Pumpernickel?' he said. 'It is a dull place: but we want some nice people, and we would try and make it *so* agreeable to you. Mr. – Ahum – Mrs. – Oho. I shall do myself the honour of calling upon you to-morrow at your inn.' – And he went away with a Parthian grin and glance, which he thought must finish Mrs. Osborne completely.

The performance over, the young fellows lounged about the lobbies, and we saw the society take its departure. The duchess dowager went off in her jingling old coach, attended by two faithful and withered old maids of honour, and a little snuffy spindle-shanked gentleman in waiting, in a brown jasey and a green coat covered with orders – of which the star and the grand yellow cordon of the order of St. Michael of Pumpernickel was most conspicuous. The drums rolled, the guards saluted, and the old carriage drove away.

Then came his transparency the duke and transparent family, with his great officers of state and household. He bowed serenely to everybody. And amid the saluting of the guards and the flaring of the torches of the running footman, clad in scarlet, the transparent carriages drove away to the old Ducal Schloss, with its towers and pinnacles standing on the Schlossberg. Everybody in Pumpernickel knew everybody. No sooner was a foreigner seen there than the Minister of Foreign Affairs, or some other great or small officer of state, went round to the 'Erbprinz,' and found out the name of the new arrival.

We watched them too, out of the theatre. Tapeworm had just walked off, enveloped in his cloak, with which his gigantic chasseur was always in attendance, and looking as much as possible like Don Juan. The Prime Minister's lady had just squeezed herself into her sedan, and her daughter, the charming Ida, had put on her calash and clogs; when the English party came out, the boy yawning drearily, the major taking great pains in keeping the shawl over Mrs. Osborne's head, and Mr. Sedley looking grand, with a crush opera-hat on one side of his head, and his hand in the stomach of a voluminous white waistcoat. We took off our hats to our acquaintances of the table d'hôte, and the lady, in return, presented us with a little smile and a curtsy, for which everybody might be thankful.

The carriage from the inn, under the superintendence of the bustling Mr. Kirsch, was in waiting to convey the party; but the fat man said he would walk, and smoke his cigar on his way homewards; so the other three, with nods and smiles to us, went without Mr. Sedley, Kirsch, with the cigar-case, following in his master's wake.

We all walked together, and talked to the stout gentleman about the *agréments* of the place. It was very agreeable for the English. There were shooting parties and battues; there was a plenty of balls and entertainments at the hospitable Court; the society was generally good, the theatre excellent, and the living cheap.

'And our minister seems a most delightful and affable person,' our new friend said. 'With such a representative, and – and a good medical man, I can fancy the place to be most eligible. Good night, gentlemen.' And Jos creaked up the stairs to bedward, followed by Kirsch, with a flambeau. We rather hoped that nice-looking woman would be induced to stay some time in the town.

CHAPTER LXIII

IN WHICH WE MEET AN OLD ACQUAINTANCE

SUCH polite behaviour as that of Lord Tapeworm did not fail to have the most favourable effect upon Mr. Sedley's mind, and the very next morning, at breakfast, he pronounced his opinion that Pumpernickel was the pleasantest little place of any which he had visited on their tour. Jos's motives and artifices were not very difficult of comprehension: and Dobbin laughed in his sleeve, like a hypocrite as he was, when he found by the knowing air of the civilian and the off-hand manner in which the latter talked about Tapeworm Castle, and the other members of the family, that Jos had been up already in the morning, consulting his travelling *Peerage*. Yes, he had seen the Right Honourable the Earl of Bagwig, his lordship's father; he was sure he had, he had met him at – at the Levée – didn't Dob remember? and when the diplomatist called on the party, faithful to his promise, Jos received him with such a salute and honours as were seldom accorded to the little envoy. He winked at Kirsch on his excellency's arrival, and that emissary, instructed beforehand, went out and superintended an entertainment of cold meats, jellies, and other delicacies, brought in upon trays, and of which Mr. Jos absolutely insisted that his noble guest should partake.

Tapeworm, so long as he could have an opportunity of admiring the bright eyes of Mrs. Osborne (whose freshness of complexion bore daylight remarkably well) was not ill pleased to accept any invitation to stay in Mr. Sedley's lodgings; he put one or two dexterous questions to him about India and the dancing-girls there; asked Amelia about that beautiful boy who had been with her, and complimented the astonished little woman upon the prodigious sensation which she had made in the house; and tried to fascinate Dobbin by talking of the late war, and the exploits of the Pumpernickel contingent under the command of the hereditary prince, now Duke of Pimpernickel.

Lord Tapeworm inherited no little portion of the family gallantry, and it was his happy belief, that almost every woman upon whom he himself cast friendly eyes, was in love with him. He left Emmy under the persuasion that she was slain by his wit and attractions, and went home to his lodgings to write a pretty little note to her. She was not fascinated; only puzzled by his grinning, his simpering, his scented cambric handkerchief, and his high-heeled lacquered boots. She did not understand one-half the compliments which he paid; she had never, in her small experience of mankind, met a professional lady's man as yet, and looked upon my lord as something curious rather than pleasant; and if she did not admire, certainly wondered at him. Jos, on the contrary, was delighted. 'How very affable his lordship is,' he said; 'how very kind of his lordship to say he would send his medical man! Kirsch, you will carry our cards to the Count de Schlüsselback directly: the major and I will have the greatest pleasure in paying our respects at Court as soon as possible. Put out my uniform, Kirsch, – both our uniforms. It is a mark of politeness which every English gentleman ought to show to the countries which he visits to pay his respects to the sovereigns of those countries, as to the representatives of his own.'

When Tapeworm's doctor came, Doctor von Glauber, body physician to H.S.H. the Duke, he speedily convinced Jos that the Pumpernickel mineral springs and the doctor's particular treatment would infallibly restore the Bengalee to youth and slimness. 'Dere came here last year,' he said, 'Sheneral Bulkeley, an English sheneral, tvice so pic as you, sir. I sent him back qvite tin after tree months, and he danced vid Baroness Glauber at the end of two.'

Jos's mind was made up: the springs, the doctor, the Court, and the chargé d'affaires convinced him, and he proposed to spend the autumn in these delightful quarters. – And punctual to his word, on the next day the chargé d'affaires presented Jos and the major to Victor Aurelius XVII, being conducted to their audience with that sovereign by the Count de Schlüsselback, marshal of the Court.

They were straightway invited to dinner at Court, and their intention of staying in the town being announced, the politest ladies of the whole town instantly called upon Mrs. Osborne; and as not one of these, however poor they might be, was under the rank of a baroness, Jos's delight was beyond expression. He wrote off to Chutney at the club to say that the Service was highly appreciated in Germany, that he was going to show his friend, the Count de Schlüsselback, how to stick a pig in the Indian fashion, and that his august friends, the duke and duchess, were everything that was kind and civil.

Emmy, too, was presented to the august family, and as mourning is not admitted in Court on certain days, she appeared in a pink crape dress, with a diamond ornament in the corsage, presented to her by her brother, and she looked so pretty in this costume that the duke and Court (putting out of the question the major, who had scarcely ever seen her before in an evening dress, and vowed that she did not look five-and-twenty) all admired her excessively.

In this dress she walked a polonaise with Major Dobbin at a Court ball, in which easy dance Mr. Jos had the honour of leading out the Countess of Schlüsselback, an old lady with a humpback, but with sixteen good quarters of nobility, and related to half the royal houses of Germany.

Pumpernickel stands in the midst of a happy valley, through which sparkles – to mingle with the Rhine some- where, but I have not the map at hand to say exactly at what point – the fertilizing stream of the Pump. In some places the river is big enough to support a ferry-boat, in others to turn a mill; in Pumpernickel itself, the last transparency but three, the great and renowned Victor Aurelius XIV, built a magnificent bridge, on which his own statue rises, surrounded by water-nymphs and emblems of victory, peace, and plenty; he has his foot on the neck of a prostrate Turk (history says he engaged and ran a janissary through the body at the relief of Vienna by Sobieski); but, quite undisturbed by the agonies of that prostrate Mahometan, who writhes at his feet in the most ghastly manner – the prince smiles blandly, and points with his truncheon in the direction of the Aurelius-platz, where he began to erect a new place that would have been the wonder of his age, had the great-souled prince but funds to complete it. But the completion of Monplaisir (*Monblaisir* the honest German folks call it) was stopped for lack of ready money, and it and its park and garden are now in rather a faded condition, and not more than ten times big enough to accommodate the Court of the reigning sovereign.

The gardens were arranged to emulate those of Versailles, and amidst the terraces and groves there are some huge allegorical waterworks still, which spout and froth stupendously upon fête-days, and frighten one with their enormous aquatic insurrections. There is the Trophonius' cave in which, by some artifice, the leaden Tritons are made not only to spout water, but to play the most dreadful groans out of their lead conchs – there is the Nymph-bath and the Niagara cataract which the people of the neighbourhood admire beyond expression, when they come to the yearly fair at the opening of the Chamber, or to the fêtes with which the happy little nation still celebrates the birthdays and marriage-days of its princely governors.

Then from all the towns of the duchy which stretches for nearly ten miles, – from Bolkum, which lies on its western frontier bidding defiance to Prussia, from Grogwitz, where the prince has a hunting-lodge, and where his dominions are separated by the Pump river from those of the neighbouring Prince of Potzenthal: from all the little villages, which besides these three great cities, dot over the happy principality – from the farms and the mills along the Pump, come troops of people in red petticoats and velvet head-dresses, or with three-cornered hats and pipes in their mouths, who flock to the Residenz and share in the pleasures of the fair and the festivities there. Then the theatre is open for nothing, then the waters of Monblaisir begin to play (it is lucky that there is company to behold them, for one would be afraid to see them alone) – then there come mountebanks and riding troupes (the way in which his transparency was fascinated by one of the horse-riders, is well known, and it is believed that *La Petite Vivandière*, as she was called, was a spy in the French interest), and the delighted people are permitted to march through room after room of the grand ducal palace, and admire the slippery floor, the rich hangings, and the spittoons at the doors of all the innumerable chambers. There is one pavilion at Monblaisir which Aurelius Victor XV had arranged – a great prince but too fond of pleasure – and which I am told is a perfect wonder of licentious elegance. It is painted with the story of Bacchus and Ariadne, and the table works in and out of the room by means of a windlass, so that the company was served without any intervention of domestics. But the place was shut up by Barbara, Aurelius XV's widow, a severe and devout princess of the house of Bolkum and regent of the duchy during her son's glorious minority, and after the death of her husband, cut off in the pride of his pleasures.

The theatre of Pumpernickel is known and famous in that quarter of Germany. It languished a little when the present duke in his youth insisted upon having his own operas played there, and it is said one day, in a fury from his place in the orchestra, when he attended a rehearsal, broke a bassoon on the head of the chapel master, who was conducting, and led too slow; and during which time the Duchess Sophia wrote domestic comedies which must have been very dreary to witness. But the prince executes his music in private now, and the duchess only gives away her plays to the foreigners of distinction who visit her kind little Court.

It is conducted with no small comfort and splendour. When there are balls, though there may be four hundred people at supper, there is a servant in scarlet and lace to attend upon every four, and every one is served on silver. There are festivals and entertainments going continually on; and the duke has his chamberlains and equerries, and the duchess her mistress of the wardrobe and ladies of honour just like any other and more potent potentates.

The Constitution is or was a moderate despotism, tempered by a Chamber that might or might not be elected. I never certainly could hear of its sitting in my time at Pumpernickel. The Prime Minister had lodgings in a second floor; and the Foreign Secretary occupied the comfortable lodgings over Zwieback's Conditorei. The army consisted of a magnificent band that also did duty on the stage, where it was quite pleasant to see the worthy fellows marching in Turkish dresses with rouge on and wooden scimitars, or as Roman warriors with ophicleides and trombones, – to see them again, I say, at night, after one had listened to them all the morning in the Aurelius-platz, where they performed opposite the café where we breakfasted. Besides the band, there was a rich and numerous staff of officers, and I believe a few men. Besides the regular sentries, three or four men, habited as hussars, used to do duty at the palace, but I never saw them on horseback, and *au fait*, what was the use of cavalry in a time of profound peace? – and whither the deuce should the hussars ride?

Everybody – everybody that was noble, of course, for as for the bourgeois, we could not quite be expected to take notice of *them* – visited his neighbour. H.E. Madame de Burst received once a week, H.E. Madame de Schnurrbart had her night – the theatre was open twice a week, the Court graciously received once, so that a man's life might in fact be a perfect round of pleasure, in the unpretending Pumpernickel way.

That there were feuds in the place, no one can deny. Politics ran very high at Pumpernickel, and parties were very bitter. There was the Strumpff faction and the Lederlung party, the one supported by our envoy and the other by the French chargé d'affaires, M. de Macabau. Indeed it sufficed for our minister to stand up for Madame Strumpff, who was clearly the greatest singer of the two, and had three more notes in her voice than Madame Lederlung her rival – it sufficed, I say, for our minister to advance *any* opinion, to have it instantly contradicted by the French diplomatist.

Everybody in the town was ranged in one or other of these factions. The Lederlung was a prettyish little creature certainly, and her voice (what there was of it) was very sweet, and there is no doubt that the Strumpff was not in her first youth and beauty, and certainly too stout; when she came on in the last scene of the *Sonnambula* for instance, in her night-chemise with a lamp in her hand, and had to go out of the window and pass over the plank of the mill, it was all she could do to squeeze out of the window, and the plank used to bend and creak again under her weight – but how she poured out the finale of the opera! and with what a burst of feeling she rushed into Elvino's arms – almost fit to smother him! Whereas the little Lederlung – but a truce to this gossip – the fact is, that these two women were the two flags of the French and the English party at Pumpernickel, and the society was divided in its allegiance to those two great nations.

We had on our side the Home Minister, the Master of the Horse, the duke's private secretary, and the prince's tutor: whereas of the French party were the Foreign Minister, the commander-in-chief's lady, who had served under Napoleon, and the Hofmarschall and his wife, who was glad enough to get the fashions from Paris, and always had them and her caps by M. de Macabau's courier. The secretary of his chancery was little Grignac, a young fellow as malicious as Satan, and who made caricatures of Tapeworm in all the albums of the place.

Their head-quarters and table d'hôte were established at the Pariser Hof, the other inn of the town; and though, of course, these gentlemen were obliged to be civil in public, yet they cut at each other with epigrams that were as sharp as razors, as I have seen a couple of wrestlers in Devonshire, lashing at each other's shins, and never showing their agony upon a muscle of their faces. Neither Tapeworm nor Macabau ever sent home a dispatch to his Government, without a most savage series of attacks upon his rival. For instance, on our side we would write: 'The interests of Great Britain in this place, and throughout the whole of Germany, are perilled by the continuance in office of the present French envoy: this man is of a character so infamous that he will stick at no falsehood, or hesitate at no crime, to attain his ends. He poisons the mind of the Court against the English minister, represents the conduct of Great Britain in the most odious and atrocious light, and is unhappily backed by a minister whose ignorance and necessities are as notorious as his influence is fatal.' On their side they would say: 'M. de Tapeworm continues his system of stupid insular arrogance and vulgar falsehood against the greatest nation in the world. Yesterday he was heard to speak lightly of Her Royal

Highness Madame the Duchess of Berri; on a former occasion he insulted the heroic Duke of Angoulême, and dared to insinuate that H.R.H. the Duke of Orleans was conspiring against the august throne of the lilies. His gold is prodigated in every direction which his stupid menaces fail to frighten. By one and the other, he has won over creatures of the Court here – and, in fine, Pumpernickel will not be quiet, Germany tranquil, France respected, or Europe content, until this poisonous viper be crushed under heel;' and so on. When one side or the other had written any particularly spicy dispatch, news of it was sure to slip out.

Before the winter was far advanced it is actually on record that Emmy took a night and received company with great propriety and modesty. She had a French master who complimented her upon the purity of her accent and her facility of learning; the fact is she had learned long ago, and grounded herself subsequently in the grammar, so as to be able to teach it to George; and Madame Strumpff came to give her lessons in singing, which she performed so well and with such a true voice that the major's windows, who had lodgings opposite under the Prime Minister, were always open to hear the lesson. Some of the German ladies, who are very sentimental and simple in their tastes, fell in love with her and began to call her *Du* at once. These are trivial details, but they relate to happy times. The major made himself George's tutor, and read Caesar and mathematics with him, and they had a German master and rode out of evenings by the side of Emmy's carriage – she was always too timid, and made a dreadful outcry at the slightest disturbance on horseback. So she drove about with one of her dear German friends, and Jos asleep on the back seat of the barouche.

He was becoming very sweet upon the Gräfin Fanny de Butterbrod, a very gentle tender-hearted and unassuming young creature, a canoness and countess in her own right, but with scarcely ten pounds per year to her fortune, and Fanny for her part declared that to be Amelia's sister was the greatest delight that Heaven could bestow on her, and Jos might have put a countess's shield and coronet by the side of his own arms on his carriage and forks; when – when events occurred, and those grand fêtes given upon the marriage of the Hereditary Prince of Pumpernickel with the lovely Princess Amelia of Humbourg-Schlippenschloppen took place.

At this festival the magnificence displayed was such as had not been known in the little German place since the days of the prodigal Victor XIV. All the neighbouring princes, princesses, and grandees were invited to the feast. Beds rose to half a crown per night in Pumpernickel, and the army was exhausted in providing guards of honour for the highnesses, serenities, and excellencies, who arrived from all quarters. The princess was married by proxy, at her father's residence, by the Count de Schlüsselback. Snuff-boxes were given away in profusion (as we learned from the Court jeweller, who sold and afterwards bought them again), and bushels of the Order of St. Michael of Pumpernickel were sent to the nobles of the Court, while hampers of the cordons and decorations of the Wheel of St. Catherine of Schlippenschloppen were brought to ours. The French envoy got both. 'He is covered with ribbons like a prize cart-horse,' Tapeworm said, who was not allowed by the rules of his service to take any decorations: 'Let him have the cordons; but with whom is the victory?' The fact is, it was a triumph of British diplomacy: the French party having proposed and tried their utmost to carry a marriage with a princess of the house of Potztausend-Donnerwetter, whom, as a matter of course, we opposed.

Everybody was asked to the fêtes of the marriage. Garlands and triumphal arches were hung across the road to welcome the young bride. The great St. Michael's Fountain ran with uncommonly sour wine, while that in the Artillery Place frothed with beer. The great waters played; and poles were put up in the park and gardens for the happy peasantry, which they might climb at their leisure, carrying off watches, silver forks, prize sausages hung with pink ribbon, &c., at the top. Georgy got one, wrenching it off, having swarmed up the pole to the delight of the spectators, and sliding down with the rapidity of a fall of water. But it was for the glory's sake merely. The boy gave the sausage to a peasant, who had very nearly seized it, and stood at the foot of the mast, blubbering, because he was unsuccessful.

At the French chancellerie they had six more lampions in their illumination than ours had; but our transparency, which represented the young couple advancing, and Discord flying away, with the most ludicrous likeness to the French ambassador, beat the French picture hollow; and I have no doubt got Tapeworm the advancement and the Cross of the Bath, which he subsequently attained.

Crowds of foreigners arrived for the fêtes: and of English of course. Besides the Court balls, public balls were given at the Town Hall and the Redoute, and in the former place there was a room for *trente-et-quarante* and roulette established, for the week of the festivities only, and by one of the great German companies from Ems or Aix-la-Chapelle. The officers or inhabitants of the town were not allowed to play at these games, but strangers, peasants, ladies were admitted, and any one who chose to lose or win money.

That little scapegrace Georgy Osborne amongst others, whose pockets were always full of dollars, and whose relations were away at the grand festival of the Court, came to the Stadthaus ball in company of his uncle's courier, Mr. Kirsch, and having only peeped into a play-room at Baden-Baden when he hung on Dobbin's arm, and where, of course, he was not permitted to gamble, came eagerly to this part of the entertainment, and hankered round the tables where the croupiers and the punters were at work. Women were playing; they were masked, some of them; this licence was allowed in these wild times of carnival.

A woman with light hair, in a low dress, by no means so fresh as it had been, and with a black mask on, through the eyelets of which her eyes twinkled strangely, was seated at one of the roulette-tables with a card and a pin, and a couple of florins before her. As the croupier called out the colour and number, she pricked on the card with great care and regularity, and only ventured her money on the colours after the red or black had come up a certain number of times. It was strange to look at her.

But in spite of her care and assiduity she guessed wrong, and the last two florins followed each other under the croupier's rake, as he cried out, with his inexorable voice, the winning colour and number. She gave a sigh, a shrug with her shoulders, which were already too much out of her gown, and dashing the pin through the card on to the table, sat thrumming it for a while. Then she looked round her, and saw Georgy's honest face staring at the scene. The little scamp! what business had he to be there?

When she saw the boy, at whose face she looked hard
through her shining eyes and mask, she said, '*Monsieur n'est
pas joueur.*'

'*Non, madame,*' said the boy: but she must have known,
from his accent, of what country he was, for she answered
him, with a slight foreign tone, 'You have nevare played –
will you do me a littl' favour?'

'What is it?' said Georgy, blushing again. Mr. Kirsch was
at work for his part at the *rouge et noir,* and did not see his
young master.

'Play this for me, if you please, put it on any number,
any number.' And she took from her bosom a purse, and
out of it a gold piece, the only coin there, and she put it
into George's hand. The boy laughed, and did as he was
bid. The number came up sure enough. There is a power
that arranges that, they say, for beginners.

'Thank you,' said she, pulling the money towards her;
'thank you. What is your name?'

'My name's Osborne,' said Georgy, and was fingering in
his own pockets for dollars, and just about to make a trial,
when the major, in his uniform, and Jos, *en marquis,* from
the Court ball, made their appearance. Other people finding
the entertainment stupid, and preferring the fun at the
Stadthaus, had quitted the palace ball earlier; but it is
probable the major and Jos had gone home and found the
boy's absence, for the former instantly went up to him, and
taking him by the shoulder, pulled him briskly back from
the place of temptation. Then, looking round the room,
he saw Kirsch employed as we have said, and going up to
him, asked how he dared to bring Mr. George to such a
place.

'*Laissez-moi tranquille,*' said Mr. Kirsch, very much excited
by play and wine. '*Il faut s'amuser, parbleu. Je ne suis pas au
service de monsieur.*'

Seeing his condition, the major did not choose to argue
with the man; but contented himself with drawing away
George, and asking Jos if he would come away. He was
standing close by the lady in the mask, who was playing
with pretty good luck now; and looking on much interested
at the game.

'Hadn't you better come, Jos,' the major said, 'with
George and me?'

'I'll stop and go home with that rascal, Kirsch,' Jos said; and for the same reason of modesty, which he thought ought to be preserved before the boy, Dobbin did not care to remonstrate with Jos, but left him and walked home with Georgy.

'Did you play?' asked the major, when they were out, and on their way home.

The boy said, 'No.'

'Give me your word of honour as a gentleman, that you never will.'

'Why?' said the boy: 'it seems very good fun.' And, in a very eloquent and impressive manner, the major showed him why he shouldn't, and would have enforced his precepts by the example of Georgy's own father, had he liked to say anything that should reflect on the other's memory. When he had housed him he went to bed, and saw his light, in the little room outside of Amelia's, presently disappear. Amelia's followed half an hour afterwards. I don't know what made the major note it so accurately.

Jos, however, remained behind over the play-table; he was no gambler, but not averse to the little excitement of the sport now and then; and he had some napoleons chinking in the embroidered pockets of his Court waistcoat. He put down one over the fair shoulder of the little gambler before him, and they won. She made a little movement to make room for him by her side, and just took the skirt of her gown from a vacant chair there.

'Come and give me good luck,' she said, still in a foreign accent, quite different from that frank and perfectly English 'Thank you,' with which she had saluted Georgy's *coup* in her favour. The portly gentleman, looking round to see that nobody of rank observed him, sat down; he muttered, 'Ah, really, well now, God bless my soul. I'm very fortunate; I'm sure to give you good fortune,' – and other words of compliment and confusion.

'Do you play much?' the foreign mask said.

'I put a nap or two down,' said Jos, with a superb air, flinging down a gold piece.

'Yes; ay nap after dinner,' said the mask, archly. But Jos looking frightened, she continued, in her pretty French accent, 'You do not play to win. No more do I. I play to forget, but I cannot. I cannot forget old times, monsieur.

Your little nephew is the image of his father; and you – you
are not changed – but yes, you are. Everybody changes,
everybody forgets; nobody has any heart.'

'Good God, who is it?' asked Jos, in a flutter.

'Can't you guess, Joseph Sedley?' said the little woman,
in a sad voice, and undoing her mask, she looked at him.
'You have forgotten me.'

'Good Heavens! Mrs. Crawley!' gasped out Jos.

'Rebecca,' said the other, putting her hand on his; but
she followed the game still, all the time she was looking at
him.

'I am stopping at the "Elephant",' she continued. 'Ask
for Madame de Raudon. I saw my dear Amelia to-day; how
pretty she looked, and how happy! So do you! Everybody
but me, who am wretched, Joseph Sedley.' And she put her
money over from the red to the black, as if by a chance
movement of her hand, and while she was wiping her eyes
with a pocket-handkerchief fringed with torn lace.

The red came up again, and she lost the whole of that
stake. 'Come away,' she said. 'Come with me a little – we
are old friends, are we not, dear Mr. Sedley?'

And Mr. Kirsch having lost all his money by this time,
followed his master out into the moonlight, where the
illuminations were winking out, and the transparency over
our mission was scarcely visible.

CHAPTER LXIV

A VAGABOND CHAPTER

WE must pass over a part of Mrs. Rebecca Crawley's
biography with that lightness and delicacy which the
world demands – the moral world, that has, perhaps, no
particular objection to vice, but an insuperable repugnance
to hearing vice called by its proper name. There are things
we do and know perfectly well in Vanity Fair, though we
never speak them: as the Ahrimanians worship the devil, but
don't mention him: and a polite public will no more bear
to read an authentic description of vice than a truly-refined
English or American female will permit the word 'breeches'
to be pronounced in her chaste hearing. And yet, madam,
both are walking the world before our faces every day,

without much shocking us. If you were to blush every time they went by, what complexions you would have! It is only when their naughty names are called out that your modesty has any occasion to show alarm or sense of outrage, and it has been the wish of the present writer, all through this story, deferentially to submit to the fashion at present prevailing, and only to hint at the existence of wickedness in a light, easy, and agreeable manner, so that nobody's fine feelings may be offended. I defy any one to say that our Becky, who has certainly some vices, has not been presented to the public in a perfectly genteel and inoffensive manner. In describing this siren, singing and smiling, coaxing and cajoling, the author, with modest pride, asks his readers all round, has he once forgotten the laws of politeness, and showed the monster's hideous tail above water? No! Those who like may peep down under waves that are pretty transparent, and see it writhing and twirling, diabolically hideous and slimy, flapping amongst bones, or curling round corpses; but above the water line, I ask, has not everything been proper, agreeable, and decorous, and has any the most squeamish immoralist in Vanity Fair a right to cry fie? When, however, the siren disappears and dives below, down among the dead men, the water of course grows turbid over her, and it is labour lost to look into it ever so curiously. They look pretty enough when they sit upon a rock, twanging their harps and combing their hair, and sing, and beckon to you to come and hold the looking-glass; but when they sink into their native element, depend on it those mermaids are about no good, and we had best not examine the fiendish marine cannibals, revelling and feasting on their wretched pickled victims. And so, when Becky is out of the way, be sure that she is not particularly well employed, and that the less that is said about her doings is in fact the better.

If we were to give a full account of her proceedings during a couple of years that followed after the Curzon Street catastrophe, there might be some reason for people to say this book was improper. The actions of very vain, heartless, pleasure-seeking people are very often improper (as are many of yours, my friend with the grave face and spotless reputation; – but that is merely by the way); and what are those of a woman without faith – or love – or character? And I am inclined to think that there was a period in Mrs.

Becky's life, when she was seized, not by remorse, but by a
kind of despair, and absolutely neglected her person, and
did not even care for her reputation.

This *abattement* and degradation did not take place all at
once: it was brought about by degrees, after her calamity,
and after many struggles to keep up – as a man who goes
overboard hangs on to a spar whilst any hope is left, and
then flings it away and goes down, when he finds that
struggling is in vain.

She lingered about London whilst her husband was making preparations for his departure to his seat of government;
and it is believed made more than one attempt to see her
brother-in-law, Sir Pitt Crawley, and to work upon his
feelings which she had almost enlisted in her favour. As Sir
Pitt and Mr. Wenham were walking down to the House of
Commons, the latter spied Mrs. Rawdon in a black veil, and
lurking near the palace of the legislature. She sneaked away
when her eyes met those of Wenham, and indeed never
succeeded in her designs upon the baronet.

Probably Lady Jane interposed. I have heard that she quite
astonished her husband by the spirit which she exhibited in
this quarrel, and her determination to disown Mrs. Becky.
Of her own movement, she invited Rawdon to come and
stop in Gaunt Street until his departure for Coventry Island,
knowing that with him for a guard Mrs. Becky would not
try to force her door: and she looked curiously at the
superscriptions of all the letters which arrived for Sir Pitt,
lest he and his sister-in-law should be corresponding. Not
but that Rebecca could have written had she a mind: but
she did not try to see or to write to Pitt at his own house,
and after one or two attempts consented to his demand that
the correspondence regarding her conjugal differences should
be carried on by lawyers only.

The fact was, that Pitt's mind had been poisoned against
her. A short time after Lord Steyne's accident Wenham had
been with the baronet; and given him such a biography of
Mrs. Becky as had astonished the member for Queen's
Crawley. He knew everything regarding her; who her father
was; in what year her mother danced at the Opera; what
had been her previous history, and what her conduct during
her married life:– as I have no doubt that the greater part
of the story was false and dictated by interested malevolence,

it shall not be repeated here. But Becky was left with a sad, sad reputation in the esteem of a country gentleman and relative who had been once rather partial to her.

The revenues of the governor of Coventry Island are not large. A part of them were set aside by his excellency for the payment of certain outstanding debts and liabilities, the charges incident on his high situation required considerable expense; finally, it was found that he could not spare to his wife more than three hundred pounds a year, which he proposed to pay to her on an undertaking that she would never trouble him. Otherwise: scandal, separation, Doctors' Commons would ensue. But it was Mr. Wenham's business, Lord Steyne's business, Rawdon's, everybody's – to get her out of the country, and hush up a most disagreeable affair.

She was probably so much occupied in arranging these affairs of business with her husband's lawyers, that she forgot to take any step whatever about her son, the little Rawdon, and did not even once propose to go and see him. That young gentleman was consigned to the entire guardianship of his aunt and uncle, the former of whom had always possessed a great share of the child's affection. His mamma wrote him a neat letter from Boulogne when she quitted England, in which she requested him to mind his book, and said she was going to take a Continental tour, during which she would have the pleasure of writing to him again. But she never did for a year afterwards, and not indeed, until Sir Pitt's only boy, always sickly, died of whooping-cough and measles: – then Rawdon's mamma wrote the most affectionate composition to her darling son, who was made heir of Queen's Crawley by this accident, and drawn more closely than ever to the kind lady, whose tender heart had already adopted him. Rawdon Crawley, then grown a tall, fine lad, blushed when he got the letter. 'Oh, Aunt Jane, you are my mother!' he said; 'and not – and not that one.' But he wrote back a kind and respectful letter to Mrs. Rebecca, then living at a boarding-house at Florence. – But we are advancing matters.

Our darling Becky's first flight was not very far. She perched upon the French coast at Boulogne, that refuge of so much exiled English innocence; and there lived in rather a genteel, widowed manner, with a *femme de chambre* and a couple of rooms, at an hotel. She dined at the table d'hôte, where people thought her very pleasant, and where she entertained her neighbours by stories of her brother, Sir Pitt, and her great London acquaintance: talking that easy, fashionable slipslop, which has so much effect upon certain folks of small breeding. She passed with many of them for a person of importance; she gave little tea-parties in her private room, and shared in the innocent amusements of the place, – in sea-bathing, and in jaunts in open carriages, in strolls on the sands, and in visits to the play. Mrs. Burjoice, the printer's lady, who was boarding with her family at the hotel for the summer, and to whom her Burjoice came of a Saturday and Sunday, voted her charming; until that little rogue of a Burjoice began to pay her too much attention. But there was nothing in the story, only that Becky was always affable, easy, and good-natured – and with men especially.

Numbers of people were going abroad as usual at the end of the season, and Becky had plenty of opportunities of finding out by the behaviour of her acquaintances of the great London world the opinion of 'society' as regarded her conduct. One day it was Lady Partlet and her daughters whom Becky confronted as she was walking modestly on Boulogne pier, the cliffs of Albion shining in the distance across the deep blue sea. Lady Partlet marshalled all her daughters round her with a sweep of her parasol, and retreated from the pier darting savage glances at poor little Becky who stood alone there.

On another day the packet came in. It had been blowing fresh, and it always suited Becky's humour to see the droll woebegone faces of the people as they emerged from the boat. Lady Slingstone happened to be on board this day. Her ladyship had been exceedingly ill in her carriage, and was greatly exhausted and scarcely fit to walk up the plank from the ship to the pier. But all her energies rallied the instant she saw Becky smiling roguishly under a pink bonnet: and giving her a glance of scorn, such as would have shrivelled up most women, she walked into the Custom House quite unsupported. Becky only laughed: but I don't think she liked it. She felt she was alone, quite alone: and the far-off shining cliffs of England were impassable to her.

The behaviour of the men had undergone too I don't know what change. Grinstone showed his teeth and laughed in her face with a familiarity that was not pleasant. Little Bob Suckling, who was cap in hand to her three months before, and would walk a mile in the rain to see for her carriage in the line at Gaunt House, was talking to Fitzoof of the Guards (Lord Heehaw's son) one day upon the jetty, as Becky took her walk there. Little Bobby nodded to her over his shoulder without moving his hat, and continued his conversation with the heir of Heehaw. Tom Raikes tried to walk into her sitting-room at the inn with a cigar in his mouth: but she closed the door upon him and would have locked it only that his fingers were inside. She began to feel that she was very lonely indeed. 'If *he'd* been here,' she said, 'those cowards would never have dared to insult me.' She thought about 'him' with great sadness, and perhaps longing – about his honest, stupid, constant kindness and fidelity: his never-ceasing obedience; his good humour; his bravery and courage. Very likely she cried, for she was particularly lively, and had put on a little extra rouge when she came down to dinner.

She rouged regularly now: and – and her maid got cognac for her besides that which was charged in the hotel bill.

Perhaps the insults of the men were not, however, so intolerable to her as the sympathy of certain women. Mrs. Crackenbury and Mrs. Washington White passed through Boulogne on their way to Switzerland. (The party were protected by Colonel Horner, young Beaumoris, and of course old Crackenbury, and Mrs. White's little girl.) *They* did not avoid her. They giggled, cackled, tattled, condoled, consoled, and patronized her until they drove her almost wild with rage. To be patronized by *them!* she thought, as they went away simpering after kissing her. And she heard Beaumoris's laugh ringing on the stair, and knew quite well how to interpret his hilarity.

It was after this visit that Becky, who had paid her weekly bills, Becky who had made herself agreeable to everybody in the house, who smiled at the landlady, called the waiters 'monsieur', and paid the chambermaids in politeness and apologies, what far more than compensated for a little niggardliness in point of money (of which Becky never was free), that Becky, we say, received a notice to quit from the landlord, who had been told by some one that she was quite an unfit person to have at his hotel, where English ladies would not sit down with her. And she was forced to fly into lodgings, of which the dullness and solitude were most wearisome to her.

Still she held up, in spite of these rebuffs, and tried to make a character for herself, and conquer scandal. She went to church very regularly, and sang louder than anybody there. She took up the cause of the widows of the ship-wrecked fishermen, and gave work and drawings for the Quashyboo Mission; she subscribed to the Assembly, and *wouldn't* waltz. In a word, she did everything that was respectable, and that is why we dwell upon this part of her career with more fondness than upon subsequent parts of her history, which are not so pleasant. She saw people avoiding her, and still laboriously smiled upon them; you never could suppose from her countenance what pangs of humiliation she might be enduring inwardly.

Her history was after all a mystery. Parties were divided about her. Some people, who took the trouble to busy themselves in the matter, said that she was the criminal; whilst others vowed that she was as innocent as a lamb, and that her odious husband was in fault. She won over a good many by bursting into tears about her boy, and exhibiting the most frantic grief when his name was mentioned, or she saw anybody like him. She gained good Mrs. Alderney's heart in that way, who was rather the queen of British Boulogne, and gave the most dinners and balls of all the residents there, by weeping when Master Alderney came from Doctor Swishtail's academy to pass his holidays with his mother. 'He and her Rawdon were of the same age, and *so* like,' Becky said, in a voice choking with agony; whereas there was five years' difference between the boys' ages, and no more likeness between them than between my respected reader and his humble servant. Wenham, when he was going abroad, on his way to Kissingen to join Lord Steyne, enlightened Mrs. Alderney on this point, and told her how he was much more able to describe little Rawdon than his mamma, who notoriously hated him, and never saw him; how he was thirteen years old, while little Alderney was but nine; fair, while the other darling was dark, – in a word, caused the lady in question to repent of her good humour.

Whenever Becky made a little circle for herself with incredible toils and labour, somebody came and swept it down rudely, and she had all her work to begin over again. It was very hard: very hard; lonely, and disheartening.

There was Mrs. Newbright, who took her up for some time, attracted by the sweetness of her singing at church, and by her proper views upon serious subjects, concerning which in former days, at Queen's Crawley, Mrs. Becky had had a good deal of instruction. – Well, she not only took tracts, but she read them. She worked flannel petticoats for the Quashyboos – cotton nightcaps for the Cocoanut Indians – painted hand-screens for the conversion of the Pope and the Jews – sat under Mr. Rowls on Wednesdays, Mr. Huggleton on Thursdays, attended two Sunday services at church, besides Mr. Bawler, the Darbyite, in the evening, and all in vain. Mrs. Newbright had occasion to correspond with the Countess of Southdown about the Warming-pan Fund for the Feejee Islanders (for the management of which admirable charity both these ladies formed part of a female committee), and having mentioned her 'sweet friend', Mrs. Rawdon Crawley, the dowager countess wrote back such a letter regarding Becky, with such particulars, hints, facts, falsehoods, and general comminations, that intimacy between Mrs. Newbright and Mrs. Crawley ceased forthwith: and all the serious world of Tours, where this misfortune took place, immediately parted company with the reprobate. Those who know the English colonies abroad know that we carry with us our pride, pills, prejudices, Harvey-sauces, cayenne-peppers, and other Lares, making a little Britain wherever we settle down.

From one colony to another Becky fled uneasily. From Boulogne to Dieppe, from Dieppe to Caen, from Caen to Tours – trying with all her might to be respectable, and alas! always found out some day or other, and pecked out of the cage by the real daws.

Mrs. Hook Eagles took her up at one of these places:– a woman without a blemish in her character, and a house in Portman Square. She was staying at the hotel at Dieppe, whither Becky fled, and they made each other's acquaintance first at sea, where they were swimming together, and subsequently at the table d'hôte of the hotel. Mrs. Eagles had heard, – who indeed had not? – some of the scandal of the Steyne affair; but after a conversation with Becky, she pronounced that Mrs. Crawley was an angel, her husband a ruffian, Lord Steyne an unprincipled wretch, as everybody knew, and the whole case against Mrs. Crawley, an infamous and wicked conspiracy of that rascal Wenham. 'If you were a man of any spirit, Mr. Eagles, you would box the wretch's ears the next time you see him at the club,' she said to her husband. But Eagles was only a quiet old gentleman, husband to Mrs. Eagles, with a taste for geology, and not tall enough to reach anybody's ears.

The Eagles then patronized Mrs. Rawdon, took her to live with her at her own house at Paris, quarrelled with the ambassador's wife because she would not receive her protégée, and did all that lay in woman's power to keep Becky straight in the paths of virtue and good repute.

Becky was very respectable and orderly at first, but the life of humdrum virtue grew utterly tedious to her before long. It was the same routine every day, the same dullness and comfort, the same drive over the same stupid Bois de Boulogne, the same company of an evening, the same Blair's Sermon of a Sunday night – the same opera always being acted over and over again: Becky was dying of weariness, when, luckily for her, young Mr. Eagles came from Cambridge, and his mother, seeing the impression which her little friend made upon him, straightway gave Becky warning.

Then she tried keeping house with a female friend; then the double *ménage* began to quarrel and get into debt. Then she determined upon a boarding-house existence, and lived for some time at that famous mansion kept by Madame de St. Amour, in the Rue Royale at Paris, where she began exercising her graces and fascinations upon the shabby dandies and fly-blown beauties who frequented her landlady's salons. Becky loved society, and, indeed, could no more exist without it than an opium-eater without his dram, and she was happy enough at the period of her boarding-house life. 'The women here are as amusing as those in May Fair,' she told an old London friend who met her – 'only, their dresses are not quite so fresh. The men wear cleaned gloves, and are sad rogues, certainly, but they are not worse than Jack This, and Tom That. The mistress of the house is a little vulgar, but I don't think she is so vulgar as Lady —' and here she named the name of a great leader of fashion that I would die rather than reveal. In fact, when you saw Madame de St. Amour's rooms lighted up of a night, men with *plaques* and *cordons* at the écarté tables, and the women at a little distance, you might fancy yourself for a while in good society, and that madame was a real countess. Many people did so fancy: and Becky was for a while one of the most dashing ladies of the countess's salons.

But it is probable that her old creditors of 1815 found her out and caused her to leave Paris, for the poor little woman was forced to fly from the city rather suddenly; and went thence to Brussels.

How well she remembered the place! She grinned as she looked up at the little *entresol* which she had occupied, and thought of the Bareacres family, bawling for horses and flight, as their carriage stood in the *porte-cochère* of the hotel. She went to Waterloo and to Laeken, where George Osborne's monument much struck her. She made a little sketch of it. 'That poor Cupid!' she said; 'how dreadfully he was in love with me, and what a fool he was! I wonder whether little Emmy is alive. It was a good little creature: and that fat brother of hers. I have his funny fat picture still among my papers. They were kind simple people.'

At Brussels Becky arrived, recommended by Madame de St. Amour to her friend, Madame la Comtesse de Borodino, widow of Napoleon's general, the famous Count de Borodino, who was left with no resource by the deceased hero but that of a table d'hôte and an écarté table. Second-rate dandies and *roués*, widow ladies who always have a lawsuit, and very simple English folks, who fancy they see 'Continental society' at these houses, put down their money, or ate their meals, at Madame de Borodino's tables. The gallant young fellows treated the company round to champagne at the table d'hôte, rode out with the women, or hired horses on country excursions, clubbed money to take boxes at the play or the Opera, betted over the fair shoulders of the ladies at the écarté tables, and wrote home to their parents in Devonshire about their felicitous introduction to foreign society.

Here, as at Paris, Becky was a boarding-house queen: and ruled in select *pensions*. She never refused the champagne, or the bouquets, or the drives into the country, or the private boxes; but what she preferred was the écarté at night, – and she played audaciously. First she played only for a little, then for five-franc pieces, then for napoleons, then for notes: then she would not be able to pay her month's *pension*: then she borrowed from the young gentlemen: then she got into cash again, and bullied Madame de Borodino, whom she had coaxed and wheedled before: then she was playing for ten sous at a time, and in a dire state of poverty: then her quarter's allowance would come in, and she would pay off Madame de Borodino's score: and would once more take the cards against Monsieur de Rossignol, or the Chevalier de Raff.

When Becky left Brussels, the sad truth is, that she owed three months' *pension* to Madame de Borodino, of which fact, and of the gambling, and of the drinking, and of the going down on her knees to the Reverend Mr. Muff, Ministre Anglican, and borrowing money of him, and of her coaxing and flirting with Milor Noodle, son of Sir Noodle, pupil of the Rev. Mr. Muff, whom she used to take into her private room, and of whom she won large sums at écarté – of which fact, I say, and of a hundred of her other knaveries, the Countess de Borodino informs every English person who stops at her establishment, and announces that Madame Rawdon was no better than a *vipère*.

So our little wanderer went about setting up her tent in various cities of Europe, as restless as Ulysses or Bampfylde Moore Carew. Her taste for disrespectability grew more and more remarkable. She became a perfect Bohemian ere long, herding with people whom it would make your hair stand on end to meet.

There is no town of any mark in Europe but it has its little colony of English raffs – men whose names Mr. Hemp, the officer, reads out periodically at the Sheriffs' Court – young gentlemen of very good family often, only that the latter disowns them; frequenters of billiard-rooms and estaminets, patrons of foreign races and gaming-tables. They people the debtors' prisons – they drink and swagger – they fight and brawl – they run away without paying – they have duels with French and German officers – they cheat Mr. Spoony at écarté – they get the money, and drive off to Baden in magnificent britzkas – they try their infallible martingale, and lurk about the tables with empty pockets, shabby bullies, penniless bucks, until they can swindle a Jew banker with a sham bill of exchange, or find another Mr. Spoony to rob. The alternations of splendour and misery which these people undergo are very queer to view. Their life must be one of great excitement. Becky – must it be owned? – took to this life, and took to it not unkindly. She went about from town to town among these Bohemians. The lucky Mrs. Rawdon was known at every play-table in Germany. She and Madame de Cruchecassée kept house at Florence together. It is said she was ordered out of Munich; and my friend Mr. Frederic Pigeon avers that it was at her house at Lausanne that he was hocussed at supper and lost eight hundred pounds to Major Loder and the Honourable Mr. Deuceace. We are bound, you see, to give some account of Becky's biography: but of this part, the less, perhaps, that is said the better.

They say, that when Mrs. Crawley was particularly down on her luck, she gave concerts and lessons in music here and there. There was a Madame de Raudon who certainly had a *matinée musicale* at Wildbad, accompanied by Herr Spoff, premier pianist to the Hospodar of Wallachia, and my little friend Mr. Eaves, who knew everybody, and had travelled everywhere, always used to declare that he was at Strasburg in the year 1830, when a certain Madame Rebecque made her appearance in the opera of the *Dame Blanche*, giving occasion to a furious row in the theatre there. She was hissed off the stage by the audience, partly from her own incompetency, but chiefly from the ill-advised sympathy of some persons in the *parquet* (where the officers of the garrison had their admissions); and Eaves was certain that the unfortunate *débutante* in question was no other than Mrs. Rawdon Crawley.

She was, in fact, no better than a vagabond upon this earth. When she got her money she gambled; when she had gambled it she was put to shifts to live; who knows how or by what means she succeeded? It is said that she once was seen at St. Petersburg, but was summarily dismissed from that capital by the police: so that there cannot be any possibility of truth in the report that she was a Russian spy at Teplitz and Vienna afterwards. I have even been informed, that at Paris she discovered a relation of her own, no less a person than her maternal grandmother, who was not by any means a Montmorenci, but a hideous old box-opener at a theatre on the Boulevards. The meeting between them, of which other persons, as it is hinted elsewhere, seem to have been acquainted, must have been a very affecting interview.

The present historian can give no certain details regarding the event.

It happened at Rome once, that Mrs. de Rawdon's half-year's salary had just been paid into the principal banker's there, and, as everybody who had a balance of above five hundred scudi was invited to the balls which this prince of merchants gave during the winter, Becky had the honour of a card, and appeared at one of the Prince and Princess Polonia's splendid evening entertainments. The princess was of the family of Pompili, lineally descended from the second King of Rome, and Egeria of the house of Olympus, while the prince's grandfather, Alessandro Polonia, sold wash-balls, essences, tobacco, and pocket-handkerchiefs, ran errands for gentlemen, and lent money in a small way. All the great company in Rome thronged to his saloons – princes, dukes, ambassadors, artists, fiddlers, monsignori, young bears with their leaders – every rank and condition of man. His halls blazed with light and magnificence; were resplendent with gilt frames (containing pictures) and dubious antiques: and the enormous gilt crown and arms of the princely owner, a gold mushroom on a crimson field (the colour of the pocket-handkerchiefs which he sold), and the silver fountain of the Pompili family shone all over the roof, doors, and panels of the house, and over the grand velvet baldaquins prepared to receive popes and emperors.

So Becky, who had arrived in the diligence from Florence, and was lodged at an inn in a very modest way, got a card for Prince Polonia's entertainment, and her maid dressed her with unusual care, and she went to this fine ball leaning on the arm of Major Loder, with whom she happened to be travelling at the time (the same man who shot Prince Ravioli at Naples the next year, and was caned by Sir John Buckskin for carrying four kings in his hat besides those which he used in playing at écarté) – and this pair went into the rooms together, and Becky saw a number of old faces, which she remembered in happier days, when she was not innocent, but not found out. Major Loder knew a great number of foreigners, keen-looking whiskered men with dirty striped ribbons in their button-holes, and a very small display of linen; but his own countrymen, it might be remarked, eschewed the major. Becky, too, knew some ladies here and there – French widows, dubious Italian countesses, whose husbands had treated them ill – faugh – what shall we say, we who have moved among some of the finest company of Vanity Fair, of this refuse and sediment of rascals? If we play, let it be with clean cards, and not with this dirty pack. But every man who has formed one of the innumerable army of travellers has seen these marauding irregulars hanging on, like Nym and Pistol, to the main force; wearing the king's colours, and boasting of his commission, but pillaging for themselves, and occasionally gibbeted by the roadside.

Well, she was hanging on the arm of Major Loder, and they went through the rooms together, and drank a great quantity of champagne at the buffet, where the people, and especially the major's irregular corps, struggled furiously for refreshments, of which when the pair had had enough, they pushed on until they reached the duchess's own pink velvet saloon, at the end of the suite of apartments (where the statue of the Venus is, and the great Venice looking-glasses, framed in silver), and where the princely family were entertaining their most distinguished guests at a round table at supper. It was just such a little select banquet as that of which Becky recollected that she had partaken at Lord Steyne's – and there he sat at Polonia's table, and she saw him.

The scar cut by the diamond on his white, bald, shining forehead, made a burning red mark; his red whiskers were dyed of a purple hue, which made his pale face look still paler. He wore his collar and orders, his blue ribbon and garter. He was a greater prince than any there, though there was a reigning duke and a royal highness, with their princesses, and near his lordship was seated the beautiful Countess of Belladonna, *née* de Glandier, whose husband (the Count Paolo della Belladonna) so well known for his brilliant entomological collections, had been long absent on a mission to the Emperor of Morocco.

When Becky beheld that familiar and illustrious face, how vulgar all of a sudden did Major Loder appear to her, and how that odious Captain Rook did smell of tobacco! In one instant she resumed her fine-ladyship, and tried to look and feel as if she was in May Fair once more. 'That woman looks stupid and ill-humoured,' she thought; 'I am sure she can't amuse him. No, he must be bored by her – he never was by me.' A hundred such touching hopes, fears, and memories palpitated in her little heart, as she looked with her brightest eyes (the rouge which she wore up to her eyelids made them twinkle) towards the great nobleman. Of a Star and Garter night Lord Steyne used also to put on his grandest manner, and to look and speak like a great prince, as he was. Becky admired him, smiling sumptuously, easy, lofty, and stately. Ah, *bon Dieu*, what a pleasant companion he was, what a brilliant wit, what a rich fund of talk, what a grand manner! – and she had exchanged this for Major Loder, reeking of cigars and brandy-and-water, and Captain Rook with his horse-jockey jokes and prize-ring slang, and their like. 'I wonder whether he will know me,' she thought. Lord Steyne was talking and laughing with a great and illustrious lady at his side, when he looked up and saw Becky.

She was all over in a flutter as their eyes met, and she put on the very best smile she could muster, and dropped him a little, timid, imploring curtsy. He stared aghast at her for a minute, as Macbeth might on beholding Banquo's sudden appearance at his ball-supper; and remained looking at her with open mouth, when that horrid Major Loder pulled her away.

'Come away into the supper-room, Mrs. R.,' was that gentleman's remark; 'seeing those nobs grubbing away has made me peckish too. Let's go and try the old governor's champagne.' Becky thought the major had had a great deal too much already.

The day after she went to walk on the Pincian Hill – the Hyde Park of the Roman idlers – possibly in hopes to have another sight of Lord Steyne. But she met another acquaintance there: it was Mr. Fiche, his lordship's confidential man, who came up nodding to her rather familiarly and putting a finger to his hat. 'I knew that madame was here,' he said; 'I followed her from her hotel. I have some advice to give madame.'

'From the Marquis of Steyne?' Becky asked resuming as much of her dignity as she could muster, and not a little agitated by hope and expectation.

'No,' said the valet; 'it is from me. Rome is very unwholesome.'

'Not at this season, Monsieur Fiche – not till after Easter.'

'I tell madame it is unwholesome now. There is always

malaria for some people. That cursed marsh wind kills many at all seasons. Look, Madame Crawley, you were always *bon enfant*, and I have an interest in you, *parole d'honneur*. Be warned. Go away from Rome, I tell you – or you will be ill and die.'

Becky laughed, though in rage and fury. 'What! assassinate poor little me?' she said. 'How romantic! Does my lord carry bravos for couriers, and stilettos in the fourgons? Bah! I will stay, if but to plague him. I have those who will defend me whilst I am here.'

It was Monsieur Fiche's turn to laugh now. 'Defend you,' he said, 'and who? The major, the captain, any one of those gambling men whom madame sees, would take her life for a hundred louis. We know things about Major Loder (he is no more a major than I am my lord the marquis) which would send him to the galleys or worse. We know everything, and have friends everywhere. We know whom you saw at Paris, and what relations you found there. Yes, madame may stare, but we do. And how was it that no minister on the Continent would receive madame? She has offended somebody: who never forgives – whose rage redoubled when he saw you. He was like a madman last night when he came home. Madame de Belladonna made him a scene about you, and fired off in one of her furies.'

'Oh, it was Madame de Belladonna, was it?' Becky said, relieved a little, for the information she had just got had scared her.

'No – she does not matter – she is always jealous. I tell you it was monseigneur. You did wrong to show yourself to him. And if you stay here you will repent it. Mark my words. Go. Here is my lord's carriage' – and seizing Becky's arm, he rushed down an alley of the garden as Lord Steyne's barouche, blazing with heraldic devices, came whirling along the avenue, borne by the almost priceless horses, and bearing Madame de Belladonna lolling on the cushions, dark, sulky, and blooming, a King Charles in her lap, a white parasol swaying over her head, and old Steyne stretched at her side with a livid face and ghastly eyes. Hate, or anger, or desire, caused them to brighten now and then still; but ordinarily, they gave no light, and seemed tired of looking out on a world of which almost all the pleasure and all the best beauty had palled upon the wornout wicked old man.

'Monseigneur has never recovered the shock of that night,
never,' Monsieur Fiche whispered to Mrs. Crawley as the
carriage flashed by, and she peeped out at it from behind
the shrubs that hid her. 'That was a consolation at any rate,'
Becky thought.

Whether my lord really had murderous intentions towards
Mrs. Becky, as Monsieur Fiche said – (since monseigneur's
death he has returned to his native country, where he lives
much respected, and has purchased from his prince the title
of Baron Ficci), – and the factotum objected to have to do
with assassination; or whether he simply had a commission
to frighten Mrs. Crawley out of a city where his lordship
proposed to pass the winter, and the sight of her would be
eminently disagreeable to the great nobleman, is a point
which has never been ascertained: but the threat had its
effect upon the little woman, and she sought no more to
intrude herself upon the presence of her old patron.

Everybody knows the melancholy end of that nobleman,
which befell at Naples two months after the French Revolution of 1830: when the Most Honourable George Gustavus,
Marquis of Steyne, Earl of Gaunt and of Gaunt Castle, in
the Peerage of Ireland, Viscount Hellborough, Baron Pitch-
ley and Grillsby, a Knight of the Most Noble Order of the
Garter, of the Golden Fleece of Spain, of the Russian Order
of St. Nicholas of the First Class, of the Turkish Order of
the Crescent, First Lord of the Powder Closet and Groom
of the Back Stairs, Colonel of the Gaunt or Regent's Own
Regiment of Militia, a Trustee of the British Museum, an
Elder Brother of the Trinity House, a Governor of the White
Friars, and D.C.L., – died, after a series of fits, brought on,
as the papers said, by the shock occasioned to his lordship's
sensibilities by the downfall of the ancient French monarchy.

An eloquent catalogue appeared in a weekly print,
describing his virtues, his magnificence, his talents, and his
good actions. His sensibility, his attachment to the illustrious
House of Bourbon, with which he claimed an alliance, were
such that he could not survive the misfortunes of his august
kinsmen. His body was buried at Naples, and his heart –
that heart which always beat with every generous and noble
emotion – was brought back to Castle Gaunt in a silver urn.
'In him,' Mr. Wagg said, 'the poor and the Fine Arts have
lost a beneficent patron, society one of its most brilliant

ornaments, and England one of her loftiest patriots and statesmen,' &c., &c.

His will was a good deal disputed, and an attempt was made to force from Madame de Belladonna the celebrated jewel called the 'Jew's-eye' diamond, which his lordship always wore on his forefinger, and which it was said that she removed from it after his lamented demise. But his confidential friend and attendant, Monsieur Fiche, proved that the ring had been presented to the said Madame de Belladonna two days before the marquis's death; as were the bank-notes, jewels, Neapolitan and French bonds, &c., found in his lordship's secretaire, and claimed by his heirs, from that injured woman.

CHAPTER LXV

FULL OF BUSINESS AND PLEASURE

THE day after the meeting at the play-table, Jos had himself arrayed with unusual care and splendour, and without thinking it necessary to say a word to any member of his family regarding the occurrences of the previous night, or asking for their company in his walk, he sallied forth at an early hour, and was presently seen making inquiries at the door of the 'Elephant' Hotel. In consequence of the fêtes the house was full of company, the tables in the street were already surrounded by persons smoking and drinking the national small beer, the public rooms were in a cloud of smoke, and Mr. Jos having, in his pompous way, and with his clumsy German, made inquiries for the person of whom he was in search, was directed to the very top of the house, above the first-floor rooms where some travelling pedlars had lived, and were exhibiting their jewellery and brocades; above the second-floor apartments occupied by the *état-major* of the gambling firm; above the third-floor rooms, tenanted by the band of renowned Bohemian vaulters and tumblers; and so on to the little cabins of the roof, where, among students, bagmen, small tradesmen, and country-folks, come in for the festival, Becky had found a little nest; – as dirty a little refuge as ever beauty lay hid in.

Becky liked the life. She was at home with everybody in the place, pedlars, punters, tumblers, students and all. She was of a wild, roving nature, inherited from father and mother, who were both Bohemians, by taste and circumstance: if a lord was not by, she would talk to his courier with the greatest pleasure; the din, the stir, the drink, the smoke, the tattle of the Hebrew pedlars, the solemn, braggart ways of the poor tumblers, the *sournois* talk of the gambling-table officials, the songs and swagger of the students, and the general buzz and hum of the place had pleased and tickled the little woman, even when her luck was down, and she had not wherewithal to pay her bill. How pleasant was all the bustle to her now that her purse was full of the money which little Georgy had won for her the night before!

As Jos came creaking and puffing up the final stairs, and was speechless when he got to the landing, and began to wipe his face and then to look for No. 92, the room where he was directed to seek for the person he wanted, the door of the opposite chamber, No. 90, was open, and a student, in jack-boots and a dirty *Schlafrock*, was lying on the bed smoking a long pipe; whilst another student in long yellow hair and a braided coat, exceeding smart and dirty too, was actually on his knees at No. 92, bawling through the keyhole supplications to the person within.

'Go away,' said a well-known voice, which made Jos thrill; 'I expect somebody; I expect my grandpapa. He mustn't see you there.'

'Angel Engländerin!' bellowed the kneeling student with the whity-brown ringlets and the large finger-ring, 'do take compassion upon us. Make an appointment. Dine with me and Fritz at the inn in the park. We will have roast pheasants and porter, plum-pudding and French wine. We shall die if you don't.'

'That we will,' said the young nobleman on the bed; and this colloquy Jos overheard, though he did not comprehend it, for the reason that he had never studied the language in which it was carried on.

'*Newmero kattervang dooze, si vous plaît*,' Jos said in his grandest manner, when he was able to speak.

'*Quater fang tooce!*' said the student, starting up, and he bounced into his own room, where he locked the door, and where Jos heard him laughing with his comrade on the bed.

The gentleman from Bengal was standing disconcerted by this incident, when the door of the 92 opened of itself, and

Becky's little head peeped out, full of archness and mischief. She lighted on Jos. 'It's you,' she said, coming out. 'How I have been waiting for you! Stop! not yet – in one minute you shall come in.' In that instant she put a rouge-pot, a brandy-bottle, and a plate of broken meat into the bed, gave one smooth to her hair, and finally let in her visitor.

She had, by way of morning robe, a pink domino, a trifle faded and soiled, and marked here and there with pomatum; but her arms shone out from the loose sleeves of the dress, very white and fair, and it was tied round her little waist, so as not ill to set off the trim little figure of the wearer. She led Jos by the hand into her garret. 'Come in,' she said. 'Come and talk to me. Sit yonder on the chair;' and she gave the civilian's hand a little squeeze, and laughingly placed him upon it. As for herself, she placed herself on the bed – not on the bottle and plate, you may be sure – on which Jos might have reposed, had be chosen that seat; and so there she sat, and talked with her old admirer.

'How little years have changed you,' she said, with a look of tender interest. 'I should have known you anywhere. What a comfort it is amongst strangers to see once more the frank honest face of an old friend!'

The frank honest face, to tell the truth, at this moment bore any expression but one of openness and honesty: it was, on the contrary, much perturbed and puzzled in look. Jos was surveying the queer little apartment in which he found his old flame. One of her gowns hung over the bed, another depending from a hook of the door: her bonnet obscured half the looking-glass, on which, too, lay the prettiest little pair of bronze boots; a French novel was on the table by the bedside, with a candle, not of wax. Becky thought of popping that into the bed too, but she only put in the little paper nightcap, with which she had put the candle out on going to sleep.

'I should have known you anywhere,' she continued; 'a woman never forgets some things. And you were the first man I ever – I ever saw.'

'Was I, really?' said Jos. 'God bless my soul, you – you don't say so.'

'When I came with your sister from Chiswick, I was scarcely more than a child,' Becky said. 'How is that dear love? Oh, her husband was a sad wicked man, and of course it was of me that the poor dear was jealous. As if I cared about him, heigho! when there was somebody – but no – don't let us talk of old times;' and she passed her handkerchief with the tattered lace across her eyelids.

'Is not this a strange place,' she continued, 'for a woman, who has lived in a very different world too, to be found in? I have had so many griefs and wrongs, Joseph Sedley, I have been made to suffer so cruelly, that I am almost made mad sometimes. I can't stay still in any place, but wander about always restless and unhappy. All my friends have been false to me – all. There is no such thing as an honest man in the world. I was the truest wife that ever lived, though I married my husband out of pique, because somebody else – but never mind that. I was true, and he trampled upon me, and deserted me. I was the fondest mother. I had but one child, one darling, one hope, one joy, which I held to my heart with a mother's affection, which was my life, my prayer, my – my blessing; and they – they tore it from me – tore it from me;' and she put her hand to her heart with a passionate gesture of despair, burying her face for a moment on the bed.

The brandy-bottle inside clinked up against the plate which held the cold sausage. Both were moved, no doubt, by the exhibition of so much grief. Max and Fritz were at the door listening with wonder to Mrs. Becky's sobs and cries. Jos, too, was a good deal frightened and affected at seeing his old flame in this condition. And she began forthwith to tell her story – a tale so neat, simple, and artless, that it was quite evident, from hearing her, that if ever there was a white-robed angel escaped from heaven to be subject to the infernal machinations and villany of fiends here below, that spotless being – that miserable, unsullied martyr – was present on the bed before Jos – on the bed, sitting on the brandy-bottle.

They had a very long, amicable, and confidential talk there; in the course of which, Jos Sedley was somehow made aware (but in a manner that did not in the least scare or offend him) that Becky's heart had first learned to beat at his enchanting presence: that George Osborne had certainly paid an unjustifiable court to *her*, which might account for Amelia's jealousy, and their little rupture; but that Becky never gave the least encouragement to the unfortunate

officer, and that she had never ceased to think about Jos
from the very first day she had seen him, though, of course,
her duties as a married woman were paramount – duties
which she had always preserved, and would, to her dying
day, or until the proverbially bad climate in which Colonel
Crawley was living, should release her from a yoke which
his cruelty had rendered odious to her.

Jos went away, convinced that she was the most virtuous,
as she was one of the most fascinating of women, and
revolving in his mind all sorts of benevolent schemes for her
welfare. Her persecutions ought to be ended: she ought to
return to the society of which she was an ornament. He
would see what ought to be done. She must quit that place
and take a quiet lodging. Amelia must come and see her,
and befriend her. He would go and settle about it, and
consult with the major. She wept tears of heartfelt gratitude
as she parted from him, and pressed his hand as the gallant
stout gentleman stooped down to kiss hers.

So Becky bowed Jos out of her little garret with as much
grace as if it was a palace of which she did the honours;
and that heavy gentleman having disappeared down the
stairs, Hans and Fritz came out of their hole, pipe in mouth,
and she amused herself by mimicking Jos to them as she
munched her cold bread and sausage and took draughts of
her favourite brandy-and-water.

Jos walked over to Dobbin's lodgings with great solemnity,
and there imparted to him the affecting history with which
he had just been made acquainted, without, however, mentioning the play business of the night before. And the two
gentlemen were laying their heads together, and consulting
as to the best means of being useful to Mrs. Becky, while
she was finishing her interrupted *déjeuner à la fourchette*.

How was it that she had come to that little town? How
was it that she had no friends and was wandering about
alone? Little boys at school are taught in their earliest Latin
book, that the path of Avernus is very easy of descent. Let
us skip over the interval in the history of her downward
progress. She was not worse now than she had been in the
days of her prosperity:– only a little down on her luck.

As for Mrs. Amelia, she was a woman of such a soft and
foolish disposition, that when she heard of anybody unhappy,
her heart straightway melted towards the sufferer; and as

she had never thought or done anything mortally guilty herself, she had not that abhorrence for wickedness which distinguishes moralists much more knowing. If she spoiled everybody who came near her with kindness and compliments, – if she begged pardon of all her servants for troubling them to answer the bell, – if she apologized to a shop-boy who showed her a piece of silk, or made a curtsy to a street-sweeper, with a complimentary remark upon the elegant state of his crossing – and she was almost capable of every one of these follies – the notion that an old acquaintance was miserable was sure to soften her heart; nor would she hear of anybody's being deservedly unhappy. A world under such legislation as hers, would not be a very orderly place of abode; but there are not many women, at least not of the rulers, who are of her sort. This lady, I believe, would have abolished all gaols, punishments, handcuffs, whippings, poverty, sickness, hunger, in the world; and was such a mean-spirited creature, that – we are obliged to confess it – she could even forget a mortal injury.

When the major heard from Jos of the sentimental adventure which had just befallen the latter, he was not, it must be owned, nearly as much interested as the gentleman from Bengal. On the contrary, his excitement was quite the reverse from a pleasurable one; he made use of a brief but improper expression regarding a poor woman in distress, saying, in fact, – 'The little minx, has she come to light again?' He never had had the slightest liking for her; but had heartily mistrusted her from the very first moment when her green eyes had looked at, and turned away from, his own.

'That little devil brings mischief wherever she goes,' the major said, disrespectfully. 'Who knows what sort of life she has been leading; and what business has she here abroad and alone? Don't tell me about persecutors and enemies; an honest woman always has friends, and never is separated from her family. Why has she left her husband? He may have been disreputable and wicked, as you say. He always was. I remember the confounded blackleg, and the way in which he used to cheat and hoodwink poor George. Wasn't there a scandal about their separation? I think I heard something,' cried out Major Dobbin, who did not care much about gossip; and whom Jos tried in vain to convince that

Mrs. Becky was in all respects a most injured and virtuous female.

'Well, well; let's ask Mrs. George,' said that arch-diplomatist of a major. 'Only let us go and consult *her*. I suppose you will allow that *she* is a good judge at any rate, and knows what is right in such matters.'

'H'm! Emmy is very well,' said Jos, who did not happen to be in love with his sister.

'Very well? by Gad, sir, she's the finest lady I ever met in my life,' bounced out the major. 'I say at once, let us go and ask her if this woman ought to be visited or not – I will be content with her verdict.' Now this odious, artful rogue of a major was thinking in his own mind that he was sure of his case. Emmy, he remembered, was at one time cruelly and deservedly jealous of Rebecca, never mentioned her name but with a shrinking and terror – a jealous woman never forgives, thought Dobbin: and so the pair went across the street to Mrs. George's house, where she was contentedly warbling at a music-lession with Madame Strumpff.

When that lady took her leave, Jos opened the business with his usual pomp of words. 'Amelia, my dear,' said he, 'I have just had the most extraordinary – yes – God bless my soul! the most extraordinary adventure – an old friend – yes, a most interesting old friend of yours, and I may say in old times, has just arrived here, and I should like you to see her.'

'Her!' said Amelia, 'who is it? Major Dobbin, if you please not to break my scissors.' The major was twirling them round by the little chain from which they sometimes hung to their lady's waist, and was thereby endangering his own eye.

'It is a woman whom I dislike very much,' said the major doggedly; 'and whom you have no cause to love.'

'It is Rebecca, I'm sure it is Rebecca,' Amelia said, blushing, and being very much agitated.

'You are right; you always are,' Dobbin answered. Brussels, Waterloo, old, old times, griefs, pangs, remembrances, rushed back into Amelia's gentle heart, and caused a cruel agitation there.

'Don't let me see her,' Emmy continued. 'I couldn't see her.'

'I told you so,' Dobbin said to Jos.

'She is very unhappy, and – and that sort of thing,' Jos urged. 'She is very poor and unprotected: and has been ill – exceedingly ill – and that scoundrel of a husband has deserted her.'

'Ah!' said Amelia.

'She hasn't a friend in the world,' Jos went on, not undexterously; 'and she said she thought she might trust in you. She's so miserable, Emmy. She has been almost mad with grief. Her story quite affected me:– 'upon my word and honour, it did – never was such a cruel persecution borne so angelically, I may say. Her family has been most cruel to her.'

'Poor creature!' Amelia said.

'And if she can get no friend, she says she thinks she'll die,' Jos proceeded, in a low tremulous voice. – 'God bless my soul! do you know that she tried to kill herself? She carries laudanum with her – I saw the bottle in her room – such a miserable little room – at a third-rate house, the "Elephant," up in the roof at the top of all. I went there.'

This did not seem to affect Emmy. She even smiled a little. Perhaps she figured Jos to herself panting up the stair.

'She's beside herself with grief,' he resumed. 'The agonies that woman has endured are quite frightful to hear of. She had a little boy of the same age as Georgy.'

'Yes, yes, I think I remember,' Emmy remarked. 'Well?'

'The most beautiful child ever seen,' Jos said, who was very fat, and easily moved, and had been touched by the story Becky told; 'a perfect angel, who adored his mother. The ruffians tore him shrieking out of her arms, and have never allowed him to see her.'

'Dear Joseph,' Emmy cried out, starting up at once, 'let us go and see her this minute.' And she ran into her adjoining bedchamber, tied on her bonnet in a flutter, came out with her shawl on her arm, and ordered Dobbin to follow.

He went and put her shawl – it was a white Cashmere, consigned to her by the major himself from India – over her shoulders. He saw there was nothing for it but to obey; and she put her hand into his arm, and they went away.

'It is number 92, up four pair of stairs,' Jos said, perhaps not very willing to ascend the steps again; but he placed himself in the window of his drawing-room, which commands the place on which the 'Elephant' stands, and saw the pair marching through the market.

It was as well that Becky saw them too from her garret;
for she and the two students were chattering and laughing
there; they had been joking about the appearance of Becky's
grandpapa – whose arrival and departure they had witnessed
– but she had time to dismiss them, and have her little room
clear before the landlord of the 'Elephant', who knew that
Mrs. Osborne was a great favourite at the Serene Court, and
respected her accordingly, led the way up the stairs to the
roof-story, encouraging miladi and Herr Major as they
achieved the ascent.

'Gracious lady, gracious lady!' said the landlord, knocking
at Becky's door; he had called her madame the day before,
and was by no means courteous to her.

'Who is it?' Becky said, putting out her head, and she
gave a little scream. There stood Emmy in a tremble, and
Dobbin, the tall major with his cane.

He stood still watching, and very much interested at the
scene; but Emmy sprang forward with open arms towards
Rebecca, and forgave her at that moment and embraced her
and kissed her with all her heart. Ah, poor wretch, when
was your lip pressed before by such pure kisses?

CHAPTER LXVI

AMANTIUM IRAE

FRANKNESS and kindness like Amelia's were likely to
touch even such a hardened little reprobate as Becky.
She returned Emmy's caresses and kind speeches with something very like gratitude, and an emotion which, if it was
not lasting, for a moment was almost genuine. That was a
lucky stroke of hers about the child 'torn from her arms
shrieking'. It was by that harrowing misfortune that Becky
had won her friend back, and it was one of the very first
points, we may be certain, upon which our poor simple little
Emmy began to talk to her new-found acquaintance.

'And so they took your darling child from you,' our
simpleton cried out. 'Oh, Rebecca, my poor dear suffering
friend, I know what it is to lose a boy, and to feel for those
who have lost one. But please Heaven yours will be restored
to you, as a merciful, merciful Providence has brought me
back mine.'

'The child, my child? Oh, yes, my agonies were frightful,'
Becky owned, not perhaps without a twinge of conscience.
It jarred upon her, to be obliged to commence instantly to
tell lies in reply to so much confidence and simplicity. But
that is the misfortune of beginning with this kind of forgery.
When one fib becomes due as it were, you must forge
another to take up the old acceptance; and so the stock of
your lies in circulation inevitably multiplies, and the danger
of detection increases every day.

'My agonies,' Becky continued, 'were terrible (I hope she
won't sit down on the bottle) when they took him away from
me; I thought I should die; but I fortunately had a brain
fever, during which my doctor gave me up, and – and I
recovered, and – and here I am, poor and friendless.'

'How old is he?' Emmy asked.

'Eleven,' said Becky.

'Eleven!' cried the other. 'Why, he was born the same
year with Georgy, who is —'

'I know, I know,' Becky cried out, who had in fact quite
forgotten all about little Rawdon's age. 'Grief has made me
forget so many things, dearest Amelia. I am very much
changed: half wild sometimes. He was eleven when they took
him away from me. Bless his sweet face; I have never seen
it again.'

'Was he fair or dark?' went on that absurd little Emmy.
'Show me his hair.'

Becky almost laughed at her simplicity. 'Not to-day, love,
– some other time, when my trunks arrive from Leipsic,
whence I came to this place, – and a little drawing of him,
which I made in happy days.'

'Poor Becky, poor Becky!' said Emmy. 'How thankful,
how thankful I ought to be!' (though I doubt whether that
practice of piety inculcated upon us by our womankind in
early youth, namely, to be thankful because we are better
off than somebody else, be a very rational religious exercise;)
and then she began to think as usual, how her son was the
handsomest, the best, and the cleverest boy in the whole
world.

'You will see my Georgy,' was the best thing Emmy could
think of to console Becky. If anything could make her
comfortable that would.

And so the two women continued talking for an hour or

more, during which Becky had the opportunity of giving her
new friend a full and complete version of her private history.
She showed how her marriage with Rawdon Crawley had
always been viewed by the family with feelings of the utmost
hostility; how her sister-in-law (an artful woman) had poisoned her husband's mind against her; how he had formed
odious connexions, which had estranged his affections from
her; how she had borne everything – poverty, neglect,
coldness from the being whom she most loved – and all for
the sake of her child; how, finally, and by the most flagrant
outrage, she had been driven into demanding a separation
from her husband, when the wretch did not scruple to ask
that she should sacrifice her own fair fame so that he might
procure advancement through the means of a very great and
powerful but unprincipled man – the Marquis of Steyne,
indeed. The atrocious monster!

This part of her eventful history Becky gave with the
utmost feminine delicacy, and the most indignant virtue.
Forced to fly her husband's roof by this insult, the coward
had pursued his revenge, by taking her child from her. And
thus Becky said she was a wanderer, poor, unprotected,
friendless, and wretched.

Emmy received this story, which was told at some length,
as those persons who are acquainted with her character may
imagine that she would. She quivered with indignation at
the account of the conduct of the miserable Rawdon and the
unprincipled Steyne. Her eyes made notes of admiration for
every one of the sentences in which Becky described the
persecutions of her aristocratic relatives, and the falling away
of her husband. (Becky did not abuse him. She spoke rather
in sorrow than in anger. She had loved him only too fondly:
and was he not the father of her boy?) And as for the
separation scene from the child, while Becky was reciting it,
Emmy retired altogether behind her pocket-handkerchief, so
that the consummate little tragedian must have been charmed
to see the effect which her performance produced on her
audience.

Whilst the ladies were carrying on their conversation,
Amelia's constant escort, the major (who, of course, did not
wish to interrupt their conference, and found himself rather
tired of creaking about the narrow stair passage of which
the roof brushed the nap from his hat), descended to the

ground-floor of the house and into the great room common
to all the frequenters of the 'Elephant', out of which the
stair led. This apartment is always in a fume of smoke, and
liberally sprinkled with beer. On a dirty table stand scores
of corresponding brass candlesticks with tallow candles for
the lodgers, whose keys hang up in rows over the candles.
Emmy had passed blushing through the room anon, where
all sorts of people were collected; Tyrolese glove-sellers and
Danubian linen-merchants, with their packs; students recruit-
ing themselves with *Butterbrods* and meat; idlers, playing
cards or dominoes, on the sloppy, beery tables; tumblers
refreshing during the cessation of their performances; – in
a word, all the *fumum* and *strepitus* of a German inn in
fair-time. The waiter brought the major a mug of beer, as
a matter of course; and he took out a cigar, and amused
himself with that pernicious vegetable and a newspaper until
his charge should come down to claim him.

Max and Fritz came presently downstairs, their caps on
one side, their spurs jingling, their pipes splendid with coats-
of-arms and full-blown tassels, and they hung up the key of
No. 90 on the board, and called for the ration of *Butterbrod*
and beer. The pair sat down by the major, and fell into a
conversation of which he could not help hearing somewhat.
It was mainly about *Fuchs* and *Philister*, and duels and
drinking-bouts at the neighbouring University of Schoppen-
hausen, from which renowned seat of learning they had just
come in the *Eilwagen*, with Becky, as it appeared, by their
side, and in order to be present at the bridal fêtes at
Pumpernickel.

'The little *Engländerin* seems to be *en bays de gonnaiss-
ance*,' said Max, who knew the French language, to Fritz,
his comrade. 'After the fat grandfather went away, there
came a pretty little compatriot. I heard them chattering and
whimpering together in the little woman's chamber.'

'We must take the tickets for her concert,' Fritz said.
'Hast thou any money, Max?'

'Bah,' said the other, 'the concert is a concert *in nubibus*.
Hans said that she advertised one at Leipzig: and the
Burschen took many tickets. But she went off without singing. She said in the coach yesterday that her pianist had
fallen ill at Dresden. She cannot sing, it is my belief: her
voice is as cracked as thine, O thou beer-soaking Renowner!'

'It is cracked; *I* hear her trying out of her window a *schrecklich* English ballad, called "De Rose upon de Balgony".'

'*Saufen* and *Singen* go not together,' observed Fritz with the red nose, who evidently preferred the former amusement. 'No, thou shalt take none of her tickets. She won money at the *trente-et-quarante* last night. I saw her: she made a little English boy play for her. We will spend thy money there or at the theatre, or we will treat her to French wine or cognac in the Aurelius-garden, but the tickets we will not buy. What sayest thou? Yet another mug of beer?' and one and another successively having buried their blond whiskers in the mawkish draught, curled them and swaggered off into the fair.

The major, who had seen the key of number 90 put up on its hook, and had heard the conversation of the two young university bloods, was not at a loss to understand that their talk related to Becky. 'The little devil is at her old tricks,' he thought, and he smiled as he recalled old days, when he had witnessed the desperate flirtation with Jos, and the ludicrous end of that adventure. He and George had often laughed over it subsequently, and until a few weeks after George's marriage, when he also was caught in the little Circe's toils, and had an understanding with her which his comrade certainly suspected, but preferred to ignore. William was too much hurt or ashamed to ask to fathom that disgraceful mystery, although once, and evidently with remorse on his mind, George had alluded to it. It was on the morning of Waterloo as the young men stood together in front of their line, surveying the black masses of Frenchmen who crowned the opposite heights, and as the rain was coming down, 'I have been mixing in a foolish intrigue with a woman,' George said. 'I am glad we were marched away. If I drop, I hope Emmy will never know of that business. I wish to God it had never been begun!' And William was pleased to think, and had more than once soothed poor George's widow with the narrative, that Osborne, after quitting his wife, and after the action of Quatre Bras, on the first day, spoke gravely and affectionately to his comrade of his father and his wife. On these facts, too, William had insisted very strongly in his conversations with the elder Osborne: and had thus been the means of reconciling the old gentleman to his son's memory, just at the close of the elder man's life.

'And so this devil is still going on with her intrigues,' thought William. 'I wish she were a hundred miles from here. She brings mischief wherever she goes.' And he was pursuing these forebodings and this uncomfortable train of thought, with his head between his hands, and the *Pumpernickel Gazette* of last week unread under his nose, when somebody tapped his shoulder with a parasol, and he looked up and saw Mrs. Amelia.

This woman had a way of tyrannizing over Major Dobbin (for the weakest of all people will domineer over somebody), and she ordered him about, and patted him, and made him fetch and carry just as if he was a great Newfoundland dog. He liked, so to speak, to jump into the water if she said 'High, Dobbin!' and to trot behind her with her reticule in his mouth. This history has been written to very little purpose if the reader has not perceived that the major was a spoony.

'Why did you not wait for me, sir, to escort me downstairs?' she said, giving a little toss of her head, and a most sarcastic curtsy.

'I couldn't stand up in the passage,' he answered, with a comical deprecatory look; and, delighted to give her his arm, and to take her out of the horrid smoky place, he would have walked off without even so much as remembering the waiter, had not the young fellow run after him and stopped him on the threshold of the 'Elephant', to make him pay for the beer which he had not consumed. Emmy laughed: she called him a naughty man, who wanted to run away in debt; and, in fact, made some jokes suitable to the occasion and the small-beer. She was in high spirits and good humour, and tripped across the market-place very briskly. She wanted to see Jos that instant. The major laughed at the impetuous affection Mrs. Amelia exhibited; for, in truth, it was not very often that she wanted her brother 'that instant'.

They found the civilian in his saloon on the first floor; he had been pacing the room, and biting his nails, and looking over the market-place towards the 'Elephant' a hundred times at least during the past hour, whilst Emmy was closeted with her friend in the garret, and the major was beating the tattoo on the sloppy tables of the public room below, and he was, on his side too, very anxious to see Mrs. Osborne.

'Well?' said he.

'The poor dear creature, how she has suffered!' Emmy said.

'God bless my soul, yes,' Jos said, wagging his head, so that his cheeks quivered like jellies.

'She may have Payne's room; who can go upstairs,' Emmy continued. Payne was a staid English maid and personal attendant upon Mrs. Osborne, to whom the courier, as in duty bound, paid court, and whom Georgy used to 'lark' dreadfully with accounts of German robbers and ghosts. She passed her time chiefly in grumbling, in ordering about her mistress, and in stating her intention to return the next morning to her native village of Clapham. 'She may have Payne's room,' Emmy said.

'Why, you don't mean to say you are going to have that woman into the *house*?' bounced out the major, jumping up.

'Of course we are,' said Amelia, in the most innocent way in the world. 'Don't be angry, and break the furniture, Major Dobbin. Of course we are going to have her here.'

'Of course, my dear,' Jos said.

'The poor creature, after all her sufferings,' Emmy continued: 'her horrid banker broken and run away: her husband – wicked wretch – having deserted her and taken her child away from her' (here she doubled her two little fists and held them in a most menacing attitude before her, so that the major was charmed to see such a dauntless virago) – 'the poor dear thing! quite alone and absolutely forced to give lessons in singing to get her bread – and not have her here!'

'Take lessons, my dear Mrs. George,' cried the major, 'but don't have her in the house. I implore you, don't.'

'Pooh,' said Jos.

'You who are always good and kind: always used to be, at any rate: I'm astonished at you, Major William,' Amelia cried. 'Why, what is the moment to help her but when she is so miserable? Now is the time to be of service to her. The oldest friend I ever had, and not —'

'She was not always your friend, Amelia,' the major said, for he was quite angry. This allusion was too much for Emmy, who looking the major almost fiercely in the face, said, 'For shame, Major Dobbin!' and, after having fired this shot, she walked out of the room with a most majestic air, and shut her own door briskly on herself and her outraged dignity.

'To allude to *that!*' she said, when the door was closed. 'Oh, it was cruel of him to remind me of it,' and she looked up at George's picture, which hung there as usual, with the portrait of the boy underneath. 'It was cruel of him. If I had forgiven it, ought he to have spoken? No. And it is from his own lips that I know how wicked and groundless my jealousy was; and that you were pure – Oh yes, you were pure, my saint in heaven!'

She paced the room trembling and indignant. She went and leaned on the chest of drawers over which the picture hung, and gazed and gazed at it. Its eyes seemed to look down on her with a reproach that deepened as she looked. The early dear, dear memories of that brief prime of love rushed back upon her. The wound which years had scarcely cicatrized bled afresh, and oh, how bitterly! She could not bear the reproaches of the husband there before her. It couldn't be. Never, never!

Poor Dobbin; poor old William! That unlucky word had undone the work of many a year – the long laborious edifice of a life of love and constancy – raised, too, upon what secret and hidden foundations, wherein lay buried passions, uncounted struggles, unknown sacrifices – a little word was spoken, and down fell the fair palace of hope – one word, and away flew the bird which he had been trying all his life to lure!

William, though he saw by Amelia's looks that a great crisis had come, nevertheless continued to implore Sedley, in the most energetic terms, to beware of Rebecca: and he eagerly, almost frantically, adjured Jos not to receive her. He besought Mr. Sedley to inquire at least regarding her: told him how he had heard that she was in the company of gamblers and people of ill repute: pointed out what evil she had done in former days: how she and Crawley had misled poor George into ruin: how she was now parted from her husband, by her own confession, and, perhaps, for good reason. What a dangerous companion she would be for his sister, who knew nothing of the affairs of the world! William implored Jos, with all the eloquence which he could bring to bear, and a great deal more energy than this quiet gentleman was ordinarily in the habit of showing, to keep Rebecca out of his household.

Had he been less violent, or more dexterous, he might

have succeeded in his supplications to Jos; but the civilian
was not a little jealous of the airs of superiority which
the major constantly exhibited towards him, as he fancied
(indeed, he had imparted his opinions to Mr. Kirsch, the
courier, whose bills Major Dobbin checked on this journey,
and who sided with his master), and he began a blustering
speech about his competency to defend his own honour, his
desire not to have his affairs meddled with, his intention, in
fine, to rebel against the major, when the colloquy – rather
a long and stormy one – was put an end to in the simplest
way possible, namely, by the arrival of Mrs. Becky, with a
porter from the 'Elephant' Hotel, in charge of her very
meagre baggage.

She greeted her host with affectionate respect, and made
a shrinking, but amicable, salutation to Major Dobbin, who,
as her instinct assured her at once, was her enemy, and had
been speaking against her; and the bustle and clatter consequent upon her arrival brought Amelia out of her room.
Emmy went up and embraced her guest with the greatest
warmth, and took no notice of the major, except to fling
him an angry look – the most unjust and scornful glance
that had perhaps ever appeared in that poor little woman's
face since she was born. But she had private reasons of her
own, and was bent upon being angry with him. And Dobbin,
indignant at the injustice, not at the defeat, went off, making
her a bow quite as haughty as the killing curtsy with which
the little woman chose to bid him farewell.

He being gone, Emmy was particularly lively and affectionate to Rebecca, and bustled about the apartments and
installed her guest in her room with an eagerness and activity
seldom exhibited by our placid little friend. But when an
act of injustice is to be done, especially by weak people, it
is best that it should be done quickly; and Emmy thought
she was displaying a great deal of firmness and proper feeling
and veneration for the late Captain Osborne in her present
behaviour.

Georgy came in from the fêtes for dinner-time, and found
four covers laid as usual; but one of the places was occupied
by a lady, instead of by Major Dobbin. 'Hullo! where's Dob?'
the young gentleman asked, with his usual simplicity of
language. 'Major Dobbin is dining out, I suppose,' his
mother said; and, drawing the boy to her, kissed him a great

deal, and put his hair off his forehead, and introduced him
to Mrs. Crawley. 'This is my boy, Rebecca,' Mrs. Osborne
said – as much as to say – can the world produce anything
like that? Becky looked at him with rapture, and pressed his
hand fondly. 'Dear boy!' she said – 'he is just like my —'
Emotion choked her further utterance; but Amelia understood, as well as if she had spoken, that Becky was thinking
of her own blessed child. However, the company of her friend
consoled Mrs. Crawley, and she ate a very good dinner.

During the repast, she had occasion to speak several
times, when Georgy eyed her and listened to her. At the
dessert Emmy was gone out to superintend further domestic
arrangements: Jos was in his great chair dozing over *Galignani*: Georgy and the new arrival sat close to each other: he
had continued to look at her knowingly more than once, and
at last, he laid down the nutcrackers.

'I say,' said Georgy.

'What do you say?' Becky said, laughing.

'You're the lady I saw in the mask at the *rouge et noir*.'

'Hush! you little sly creature,' Becky said, taking up his
hand and kissing it. 'Your uncle was there too, and mamma
mustn't know.'

'Oh, no – not by no means,' answered the little fellow.

'You see we are quite good friends already,' Becky said
to Emmy, who now re-entered; and it must be owned that
Mrs. Osborne had introduced a most judicious and amiable
companion into her house.

William, in a state of great indignation, though still
unaware of all the treason that was in store for him, walked
about the town wildly until he fell upon the Secretary of
Legation, Tapeworm, who invited him to dinner. As they
were discussing that meal, he took occasion to ask the
secretary whether he knew anything about a certain Mrs.
Rawdon Crawley, who had, he believed, made some noise
in London; and then Tapeworm, who of course knew all the
London gossip, and was besides a relative of Lady Gaunt,
poured out into the astonished major's ears such a history
about Becky and her husband as astonished the querist, and
supplied all the points of this narrative, for it was at that
very table years ago that the present writer had the pleasure
of hearing the tale. Tufto, Steyne, the Crawleys, and their

history – everything connected with Becky and her previous life passed under the record of the bitter diplomatist. He knew everything and a great deal besides, about all the world:– in a word, he made the most astounding revelations to the simple-hearted major. When Dobbin said that Mrs. Osborne and Mr. Sedley had taken her into their house, Tapeworm burst into a peal of laughter which shocked the major, and asked if they had not better send into the prison, and take in one or two of the gentlemen in shaved heads and yellow jackets, who swept the streets of Pumpernickel, chained in pairs, to board and lodge, and act as tutor to that little scapegrace Georgy.

This information astonished and horrified the major not a little. It had been agreed in the morning (before meeting with Rebecca) that Amelia should go to the Court ball that night. That would be the place where he should tell her. The major went home and dressed himself in his uniform, and repaired to Court in hopes to see Mrs. Osborne. She never came. When he returned to his lodgings all the lights in the Sedley tenement were put out. He could not see her till the morning. I don't know what sort of a night's rest he had with this frightful secret in bed with him.

At the earliest convenient hour in the morning he sent his servant across the way with a note, saying, that he wished very particularly to speak with her. A message came back to say, that Mrs. Osborne was exceedingly unwell, and was keeping her room.

She, too, had been awake all that night. She had been thinking of a thing which had agitated her mind a hundred times before. A hundred times on the point of yielding, she had shrunk back from a sacrifice which she felt was too much for her. She couldn't, in spite of his love and constancy, and her own acknowledged regard, respect, and gratitude. What are benefits, what is constancy, or merit? One curl of a girl's ringlet, one hair of a whisker, will turn the scale against them all in a minute. They did not weigh with Emmy more than with other women. She had tried them; wanted to make them pass; could not; and the pitiless little woman had found a pretext, and determined to be free.

When at length, in the afternoon, the major gained admission to Amelia, instead of the cordial and affectionate greeting to which he had been accustomed now for many a long day, he received the salutation of a curtsy, and of a little gloved hand, retracted the moment after it was accorded to him.

Rebecca, too, was in the room, and advanced to meet him with a smile and an extended hand. Dobbin drew back rather confusedly. 'I – I beg your pardon, ma'am,' he said; 'but I am bound to tell you that it is not as your friend that I am come here now.'

'Pooh! damn! don't let us have this sort of thing!' Jos cried out, alarmed, and anxious to get rid of a scene.

'I wonder what Major Dobbin has to say against Rebecca?' Amelia said in a low, clear voice with a slight quiver in it, and a very determined look about the eyes.

'I will *not* have this sort of thing in my house,' Jos again interposed. 'I say I will not have it: and Dobbin, I beg, sir, you'll stop it.' And he looked round trembling and turning very red, and gave a great puff, and made for his door.

'Dear friend!' Rebecca said with angelic sweetness, 'do hear what Major Dobbin has to say against me.'

'I will *not* hear it, I say,' squeaked out Jos at the top of his voice, and, gathering up his dressing-gown, he was gone.

'We are only two women,' Amelia said. 'You can speak now, sir.'

'This manner towards me is one which scarcely becomes you, Amelia,' the major answered haughtily; 'nor I believe am I guilty of habitual harshness to women. It is not a pleasure to me to do the duty which I am come to do.'

'Pray, proceed with it quickly, if you please, Major Dobbin,' said Amelia, who was more and more in a pet. The expression of Dobbin's face, as she spoke in this imperious manner, was not pleasant.

'I came to say – and as you stay, Mrs. Crawley, I must say it in your presence – that I think you – you ought not to form a member of the family of my friends. A lady who is separated from her husband, who travels not under her own name, who frequents public gaming-tables —'

'It was to the ball I went,' cried out Becky.

'– is not a fit companion for Mrs. Osborne and her son,' Dobbin went on: 'and I may add that there are people here who know you, and who profess to know that regarding your conduct, about which I don't even wish to speak before – before Mrs. Osborne.'

'Yours is a very modest and convenient sort of calumny, Major Dobbin,' Rebecca said. 'You leave me under the weight of an accusation which, after all, is unsaid. What is it? Is it unfaithfulness to my husband? I scorn it, and defy anybody to prove it – I defy you, I say. My honour is as untouched as that of the bitterest enemy who ever maligned me. Is it of being poor, forsaken, wretched, that you accuse me? Yes, I am guilty of those faults, and punished for them every day. Let me go, Emmy. It is only to suppose that I have not met you, and I am no worse to-day than I was yesterday. It is only to suppose that the night is over and the poor wanderer is on her way. Don't you remember the song we used to sing in old, dear old days? I have been wandering ever since then – a poor castaway, scorned for being miserable, and insulted because I am alone. Let me go: my stay here interferes with the plans of this gentleman.'

'Indeed it does, madam,' said the major. 'If I have any authority in this house —'

'Authority, none!' broke out Amelia. 'Rebecca, you stay with me. *I* won't desert you, because you have been persecuted, or insult you, because – because Major Dobbin chooses to do so. Come away, dear.' And the two women made towards their door.

William opened it. As they were going out, however, he took Amelia's hand, and said – 'Will you stay a moment and speak to me?'

'He wishes to speak to you away from me,' said Becky, looking like a martyr. Amelia gripped her hand in reply.

'Upon my honour it is not about you that I am going to speak,' Dobbin said. 'Come back, Amelia,' and she came. Dobbin bowed to Mrs. Crawley, as he shut the door upon her. Amelia looked at him, leaning against the glass: her face and her lips were quite white.

'I was confused when I spoke just now,' the major said, after a pause; 'and I misused the word "authority".'

'You did,' said Amelia, with her teeth chattering.

'At least I have claims to be heard,' Dobbin continued.

'It is generous to remind me of our obligations to you,' the woman answered.

'The claims I mean, are those left me by George's father,' William said.

'Yes, and you insulted his memory. You did yesterday. You know you did. And I will never forgive you. Never!' said Amelia. She shot out each little sentence in a tremor of anger and emotion.

'You don't mean that, Amelia?' William said, sadly. 'You don't mean that these words, uttered in a hurried moment, are to weigh against a whole life's devotion. I think that George's memory has not been injured by the way in which I have dealt with it, and if we are come to bandying reproaches, I at least merit none from his widow and the mother of his son. Reflect, afterwards when – when you are at leisure, and your conscience will withdraw this accusation. It does even now.' Amelia held down her head.

'It is not that speech of yesterday,' he continued, 'which moves you. That is but the pretext, Amelia, or I have loved you and watched you for fifteen years in vain. Have I not learned in that time to read all your feelings, and look into your thoughts? I know what your heart is capable of: it can cling faithfully to a recollection, and cherish a fancy; but it can't feel such an attachment as mine deserves to mate with, and such as I would have won from a woman more generous than you. No, you are not worthy of the love which I have devoted to you. I knew all along that the prize I had set my life on was not worth the winning; that I was a fool, with fond fancies, too, bartering away my all of truth and ardour against your little feeble remnant of love. I will bargain no more: I withdraw. I find no fault with you. You are very good-natured, and have done your best; but you couldn't – you couldn't reach up to the height of the attachment which I bore you, and which a loftier soul than yours might have been proud to share. Good-bye, Amelia! I have watched your struggle. Let it end. We are both weary of it.'

Amelia stood scared and silent as William thus suddenly broke the chain by which she held him, and declared his independence and superiority. He had placed himself at her feet so long that the poor little woman had been accustomed to trample upon him. She didn't wish to marry him, but she wished to keep him. She wished to give him nothing, but that he should give her all. It is a bargain not unfrequently levied in love.

William's sally had quite broken and cast her down. *Her* assault was long since over and beaten back.

'Am I to understand then, – that you are going – away, – William?' she said.

He gave a sad laugh. 'I went once before,' he said, 'and came back after twelve years. We were young then, Amelia. Good-bye. I have spent enough of my life at this play.'

Whilst they had been talking, the door into Mrs. Osborne's room had opened ever so little; indeed, Becky had kept a hold of the handle, and had turned it on the instant when Dobbin quitted it; and she heard every word of the conversation that had passed between these two. 'What a noble heart that man has,' she thought, 'and how shamefully that woman plays with it.' She admired Dobbin; she bore him no rancour for the part he had taken against her. It was an open move in the game, and played fairly. 'Ah!' she thought, 'if I could have had such a husband as that – a man with a heart and brains too! I would not have minded his large feet;' and running into her room, she absolutely bethought herself of something, and wrote him a note, beseeching him to stop for a few days – not to think of going – and that she could serve him with A.

The parting was over. Once more poor William walked to the door and was gone; and the little widow, the author of all this work, had her will, and had won her victory, and was left to enjoy it as she best might. Let the ladies envy her triumph.

At the romantic hour of dinner Mr. Georgy made his appearance, and again remarked the absence of 'Old Dob'. The meal was eaten in silence by the party; Jos's appetite not being diminished, but Emmy taking nothing at all.

After the meal, Georgy was lolling in the cushions of the old window, a large window, with three sides of glass abutting from the gable, and commanding on one side the market place, where the 'Elephant' is, his mother being busy hard by, when he remarked symptoms of movement at the major's house on the other side of the street.

'Hullo!' said he, 'there's Dob's trap – they are bringing it out of the courtyard.' The 'trap' in question was a carriage which the major had bought for six pounds sterling, and about which they used to rally him a good deal.

Emmy gave a little start, but said nothing.

'Hullo!' Georgy continued, 'there's Francis coming out with the portmanteaus, and Kunz, the one-eyed postilion,

coming down the market with three *Schimmels*. Look at his
boots and yellow jacket, – ain't he a rum one? Why – they're
putting the horses to Dobs's carriage. Is he going anywhere?'

'Yes,' said Emmy, 'he is going on a journey.'

'Going a journey; and when is he coming back?'

'He is – not coming back,' answered Emmy.

'Not coming back!' cried out Georgy, jumping up. 'Stay
here, sir,' roared out Jos. 'Stay, Georgy,' said his mother,
with a very sad face. The boy stopped; kicked about the
room, jumped up and down from the window-seat with
his knees, and showed every symptom of uneasiness and
curiosity.

The horses were put to. The baggage was strapped on.
Francis came out with his master's sword, cane, and umbrella
tied up together, and laid them in the well, and his desk
and old tin cocked-hat case, which he placed under the seat.
Francis brought out the stained old blue cloak lined with
red camlet, which had wrapped the owner up any time these
fifteen years, and had '*manchen Sturm erlebt*', as a favourite
song of those days said. It had been new for the campaign
of Waterloo, and had covered George and William after the
night of Quatre Bras.

Old Burcke, the landlord of the lodgings, came out, then
Francis, with more packages – final packages – then Major
William, – Burcke wanted to kiss him. The major was adored
by all people with whom he had to do. It was with difficulty
he could escape from this demonstration of attachment.

'By Jove, I *will* go!' screamed out George. 'Give him this,'
said Becky, quite interested, and put a paper into the boy's
hand. He had rushed down the stairs and flung across the
street in a minute – the yellow postilion was cracking his
whip gently.

William had got into the carriage, released from the
embraces of his landlord. George bounded in afterwards and
flung his arms round the major's neck (as they saw from
the window), and began asking him multiplied questions.
Then he felt in his waistcoat-pocket and gave him a note.
William seized at it rather eagerly, he opened it trembling,
but instantly his countenance changed, and he tore the paper
in two, and dropped it out of the carriage. He kissed Georgy
on the head, and the boy got out, doubling his fists into his
eyes, and with the aid of Francis. He lingered with his hand

on the panel. *Fort, Schwager!* The yellow postilion cracked his whip prodigiously, up sprang Francis to the box, away went the *Schimmels*, and Dobbin with his head on his breast. He never looked up as they passed under Amelia's window: and Georgy, left alone in the street, burst out crying in the face of all the crowd.

Emmy's maid heard him howling again during the night, and brought him some preserved apricots to console him. She mingled her lamentations with his. All the poor, all the humble, all honest folks, all good men who knew him, loved that kind-hearted and simple gentleman.

As for Emmy, had she not done her duty? She had her picture of George for a consolation.

CHAPTER LXVII

WHICH CONTAINS BIRTHS, MARRIAGES, AND DEATHS

WHATEVER Becky's private plan might be by which Dobbin's true love was to be crowned with success, the little woman thought that the secret might keep, and indeed, being by no means so much interested about anybody's welfare as about her own, she had a great number of things pertaining to herself to consider, and which concerned her a great deal more than Major Dobbin's happiness in this life.

She found herself suddenly and unexpectedly in snug comfortable quarters: surrounded by friends, kindness, and good-natured simple people, such as she had not met with for many a long day; and, wanderer as she was by force and inclination, there were moments when rest was pleasant to her. As the most hardened Arab that ever careered across the Desert over the hump of a dromedary, likes to repose sometimes under the date-trees by the water; or to come into the cities, walk in the bazaars, refresh himself in the baths, and say his prayers in the Mosques, before he goes out again marauding; Jos's tents and pilau were pleasant to his little Ishmaelite. She picketed her steed, hung up her weapons, and warmed herself comfortably by his fire. The halt in that roving, restless life, was inexpressibly soothing and pleasant to her.

So, pleased herself, she tried with all her might to please everybody; and we know that she was eminent and successful

as a practitioner in the art of giving pleasure. As for Jos,
even in that little interview in the garret at the 'Elephant'
Inn, she had found means to win back a great deal of his
goodwill. In the course of a week, the civilian was her sworn
slave and frantic admirer. He didn't go to sleep after dinner,
as his custom was, in the much less lively society of Amelia.
He drove out with Becky in his open carriage. He asked
little parties and invented festivities to do her honour.
Tapeworm, the chargé d'affaires, who had abused her so
cruelly, came to dine with Jos, and then came every day to
pay his respects to Becky. Poor Emmy, who was never very
talkative, and more glum and silent than ever after Dobbin's
departure, was quite forgotten when this superior genius
made her appearance. The French minister was as much
charmed with her as his English rival. The German ladies,
never particularly squeamish as regards morals, especially in
English people, were delighted with the cleverness and wit
of Mrs. Osborne's charming friend; and though she did not
ask to go to Court, yet the most august and transparent
personages there heard of her fascinations, and were quite
curious to know her. When it became known that she was
noble, of an ancient English family, that her husband was a
colonel of the Guard, excellenz and governor of an island,
only separated from his lady by one of those trifling differences which are of little account in a country where
Werther is still read, and the *Wahlverwandschaften* of Goethe
is considered an edifying moral book; nobody thought of
refusing to receive her in the very highest society of the
little duchy; and the ladies were even more ready to call her
Du, and to swear eternal friendship for her, than they had
been to bestow the same inestimable benefits upon Amelia.
Love and Liberty are interpreted by those simple Germans
in a way which honest folks in Yorkshire and Somersetshire
little understand; and a lady might, in some philosophic and
civilized towns, be divorced ever so many times from her
respective husbands, and keep her character in society. Jos's
house never was so pleasant since he had a house of his
own, as Rebecca caused it to be. She sang, she played, she
laughed, she talked in two or three languages; she brought
everybody to the house: and she made Jos believe that it
was his own great social talents and wit which gathered the
society of the place round about him.

As for Emmy, who found herself not in the least mistress of her own house, except when the bills were to be paid, Becky soon discovered the way to soothe and please her. She talked to her perpetually about Major Dobbin sent about his business, and made no scruple of declaring her admiration for that excellent, high-minded gentleman, and of telling Emmy that she had behaved most cruelly regarding him. Emmy defended her conduct, and showed that it was dictated only by the purest religious principles; that a woman once, &c., and to such an angel as him whom she had had the good fortune to marry, was married for ever; but she had no objection to hear the major praised as much as every Becky chose to praise him; and indeed brought the conversation round to the Dobbin subject a score of times every day.

Means were easily found to win the favour of Georgy and the servants. Amelia's maid, it has been said, was heart and soul in favour of the generous major. Having at first disliked Becky for being the means of dismissing him from the presence of her mistress, she was reconciled to Mrs. Crawley subsequently, because the latter became William's most ardent admirer and champion. And in these mighty conclaves in which the two ladies indulged after their parties, and while Miss Payne was 'brushing their 'airs', as she called the yellow locks of the one, and the soft brown tresses of the other, this girl, always put in her word for that dear good gentleman Major Dobbin. Her advocacy did not make Amelia angry any more than Rebecca's admiration of him. She made George write to him constantly, and persisted in sending mamma's kind love in a postcript. And as she looked at her husband's portrait of nights, it no longer reproached her – perhaps she reproached it, now William was gone.

Emmy was not very happy after her heroic sacrifice. She was very *distraite*, nervous, silent, and ill to please. The family had never known her so peevish. She grew pale and ill. She used to try and sing certain songs (*Einsam bin ich, nicht alleine*, was one of them; that tender love-song of Weber's, which, in old-fashioned days, young ladies, and when you were scarcely born, showed that those who lived before you knew too how to love and to sing); – certain songs, I say, to which the major was partial; and as she warbled them in the twilight in the drawing-room, she would break off in the midst of the song, and walk into her neighbouring apartment, and there, no doubt, take refuge in the miniature of her husband.

Some books still subsisted, after Dobbin's departure, with his name written in them; a German Dictionary, for instance, with 'William Dobbin, –th Reg.', in the fly-leaf; a guide-book with his initials, and one or two other volumes which belonged to the major. Emmy cleared these away, and put them on the drawers, where she placed her workbox, her desk, her Bible, and Prayer-book, under the pictures of the two Georges. And the major, on going away, having left his gloves behind him, it is a fact that Georgy, rummaging his mother's desk some time afterwards, found the gloves neatly folded up, and put away in what they call the secret drawers of the desk.

Not caring for society, and moping there a great deal, Emmy's chief pleasure in the summer evenings was to take long walks with Georgy (during which Rebecca was left to the society of Mr. Joseph), and then the mother and son used to talk about the major in a way which even made the boy smile. She told him that she thought Major William was the best man in all the world; the gentlest and the kindest, the bravest, and the humblest. Over and over again, she told him how they owed everything which they possessed in the world to that kind friend's benevolent care of them; how he had befriended them all through their poverty and misfor-tunes; watched over them when nobody cared for them; how all his comrades admired him, though he never spoke of his own gallant actions; how Georgy's father trusted him beyond all other men, and had been constantly befriended by the good William. 'Why, when your papa was a little boy,' she said, 'he often told me that it was William who defended him against a tyrant at the school where they were; and their friendship never ceased from that day until the last, when your dear father fell.'

'Did Dobbin kill the man who killed papa?' Georgy said. 'I'm sure he did, or he would if he could have caught him; wouldn't he, mother? When I'm in the army, won't I hate the French? – that's all.'

In such colloquies the mother and the child passed a great deal of their time together. The artless woman had made a confidant of the boy. He was as much William's friend as was everybody else who knew him well.

By the way, Mrs. Becky, not to be behindhand in sentiment, had got a miniature too hanging up in her room, to
the surprise and amusement of most people, and the delight
of the original, who was no other than our friend Jos. On
her first coming to favour the Sedleys with a visit, the little
woman, who had arrived with a remarkably small shabby
kit, was perhaps ashamed of the meanness of her trunks and
bandboxes, and often spoke with great respect about her
baggage left behind at Leipzig, which she must have from
that city. When a traveller talks to you perpetually about
the splendour of his luggage, which he does not happen to
have with him; my son, beware of that traveller! He is ten
to one, an impostor.

Neither Jos nor Emmy knew this important maxim. It
seemed to them of no consequence whether Becky had a
quantity of very fine clothes in invisible trunks; but as her
present supply was exceedingly shabby, Emmy supplied her
out of her own stores, or took her to the best milliner in
the town, and there fitted her out. It was no more torn
collars now, I promise you, and faded silks trailing off at
the shoulder. Becky changed her habits with her situation
in life – the rouge-pot was suspended – another excitement
to which she had accustomed herself was also put aside, or
at least only indulged in in privacy; as when she was
prevailed on by Jos of a summer evening, Emmy and the
boy being absent on their walks, to take a little spirit-and-
water. But if she did not indulge – the courier did: that
rascal Kirsch could not be kept from the bottle; nor could
he tell how much he took when he applied to it. He was
sometimes surprised himself at the way in which Mr. Sedley's cognac diminished. Well, well; this is a painful subject.
Becky did not very likely indulge so much as she used before
she entered a decorous family.

At last the much-bragged-about boxes arrived from Leipzig; – three of them, not by any means large or splendid; –
nor did Becky appear to take out any sort of dresses or
ornaments from the boxes when they did arrive. But out of
one, which contained a mass of her papers (it was that very
box which Rawdon Crawley had ransacked in his furious
hunt for Becky's concealed money), she took a picture with
great glee, which she pinned up in her room, and to which
she introduced Jos. It was the portrait of a gentleman in

pencil, his face having the advantage of being painted up in pink. He was riding on an elephant, away from some coconut trees, and a pagoda: it was an Eastern scene.

'God bless my soul, it is my portrait,' Jos cried out. It was he indeed, blooming in youth and beauty, in a nankeen jacket of the cut of 1804. It was the old picture that used to hang up in Russell Square.

'I bought it,' said Becky, in a voice trembling with emotion; 'I went to see if I could be of any use to my kind friends. I have never parted with that picture – I never will.'

'Won't you?' Jos cried, with a look of unutterable rapture and satisfaction. 'Did you really now value it for my sake?'

'You know I did, well enough,' said Becky; 'but why speak, – why think, – why look back? It is too late now!'

That evening's conversation was delicious for Jos. Emmy only came in to go to bed very tired and unwell. Jos and his fair guest had a charming *tête-à-tête*, and his sister could hear, as she lay awake in her adjoining chamber, Rebecca singing over to Jos the old songs of 1815. He did not sleep for a wonder, that night, any more than Amelia.

It was June, and, by consequence, high season in London; Jos, who read the incomparable *Galignani* (the exile's best friend) through every day, used to favour the ladies with extracts from his paper during their breakfast. Every week in this paper there is a full account of military movements, in which Jos, as a man who had seen service, was especially interested. On one occasion he read out:–

'ARRIVAL OF THE – th REGIMENT. – GRAVESEND, June 20. – The *Ramachunder*, East Indiaman, came into the river this morning, having on board 14 officers, and 132 rank and file of this gallant corps. They have been absent from England fourteen years, having been embarked the year after Waterloo, in which glorious conflict they took an active part, and having subsequently distinguished themselves in the Burmese war. The veteran colonel, Sir Michael O'Dowd, K.C.B., with his lady and sister, landed here yesterday with Captains Posky, Stubble, Macraw, Malony; Lieutenants Smith, Jones, Thompson, F. Thomson; Ensigns Hicks and Grady; the band on the pier playing the national anthem, and the crowd loudly cheering the gallant veterans as they went into Wayte's Hotel, where a sumptuous banquet was provided for the defenders of Old England. During the repast, which we need not say was served up in Wayte's best style, the cheering continued so enthusiastically, that Lady O'Dowd and the colonel came forward to the balcony, and drank the healths of their fellow-countrymen in a bumper of Wayte's best claret.'

On a second occasion Jos read a brief announcement:— Major Dobbin had joined the –th regiment at Chatham; and subsequently he promulgated accounts of the presentations at the Drawing-room, of Colonel Sir Michael O'Dowd, K.C.B., Lady O'Dowd (by Mrs. Molloy Malony of Ballymalony), and Miss Glorvina O'Dowd (by Lady O'Dowd). Almost directly after this, Dobbin's name appeared among the lieutenant-colonels: for old Marshal Tiptoff had died during the passage of the –th from Madras, and the Sovereign was pleased to advance Colonel Sir Michael O'Dowd to the rank of major-general on his return to England, with an intimation that he should be colonel of the distinguished regiment which he had so long commanded.

Amelia had been made aware of some of these movements. The correspondence between George and his guardian had not ceased by any means: William had even written once or twice to her since his departure, but in a manner so unconstrainedly cold, that the poor woman felt now in her turn that she had lost her power over him, and that, as he had said, he was free. He had left her, and she was wretched. The memory of his almost countless services, and lofty and affectionate regard, now presented itself to her, and rebuked her day and night. She brooded over those recollections according to her wont: saw the purity and beauty of the affection with which she had trifled, and reproached herself for having flung away such a treasure.

It was gone indeed. William had spent it all out. He loved her no more, he thought, as he had loved her. He never could again. That sort of regard, which he had proffered to her for so many faithful years, can't be flung down and shattered, and mended so as to show no scars. The little heedless tyrant had so destroyed it. No, William thought again and again, 'It was myself I deluded, and persisted in cajoling; had she been worthy of the love I gave her, she would have returned it long ago. It was a fond mistake. Isn't the whole course of life made up of such? and suppose I had won her, should I not have been disenchanted the day after my victory? Why pine, or be ashamed of my defeat?' The more he thought of this long passage of his life, the more clearly he saw his deception. 'I'll go into harness again,' he said, 'and do my duty in that state of life in which it has pleased Heaven to place me. I will see that the buttons of the recruits are properly bright, and that the sergeants make no mistakes in their accounts. I will dine at mess, and listen to the Scotch surgeon telling his stories. When I am old and broke, I will go on half-pay, and my old sisters shall scold me. I have *geliebt und gelebet* as the girl in *Wallenstein* says. I am done. – Pay the bills and get me a cigar: find out what there is at the play to-night, Francis; to-morrow we cross by the *Batavier*.' He made the above speech, whereof Francis only heard the last two lines, pacing up and down the Boompjes at Rotterdam. The *Batavier* was lying in the basin. He could see the place on the quarter-deck, where he and Emmy had sat on the happy voyage out. What had that little Mrs. Crawley to say to him? Psha! to-morrow we will put to sea, and return to England, home, and duty!

After June all the little Court society of Pumpernickel used to separate, according to the German plan, and make for a hundred watering-places, where they drank at the wells; rode upon donkeys; gambled at the *redoutes*, if they had money and a mind; rushed with hundreds of their kind, to gor-mandize at the tables d'hôte; and idled away the summer. The English diplomatists went off to Toeplitz and Kissingen, their French rivals shut up their chancellerie and whisked away to their darling Boulevard de Gand. The transparent reigning family took, too, to the waters, or retired to their hunting-lodges. Everybody went away having any preten-sions to politeness, and, of course, with them, Doctor von Glauber, the Court doctor, and his baroness. The seasons for the baths were the most productive periods of the doctor's practice – he united business with pleasure, and his chief place of resort was Ostend, which is much frequented by Germans, and where the doctor treated himself and his spouse to what he called a 'dib' in the sea.

His interesting patient, Jos, was a regular milch cow to the doctor, and he easily persuaded the civilian, both for his own health's sake and that of his charming sister, which was really very much shattered, to pass the summer at that hideous seaport town. Emmy did not care where she went much. Georgy jumped at the idea of a move. As for Becky, she came as a matter of course in the fourth place inside of the fine barouche Mr. Jos had bought: the two domestics being on the box in front. She might have some misgivings about the friends whom she should meet at Ostend, and who might be likely to tell ugly stories – but, bah! she was strong enough to hold her own. She had cast such an anchor in Jos now as would require a strong storm to shake. That incident of the picture had finished him. Becky took down her elephant, and put it into the little box which she had had from Amelia ever so many years ago. Emmy also came off with her Lares, – her two pictures, – and the party, finally, were lodged in an exceedingly dear and uncomfortable house at Ostend.

There Amelia began to take baths, and get what good she could from them, and though scores of people of Becky's acquaintance passed her and cut her, yet Mrs. Osborne, who walked about with her, and who knew nobody, was not aware of the treatment experienced by the friend whom she had chosen so judiciously as a companion; indeed, Becky never thought fit to tell her what was passing under her innocent eyes.

Some of Mrs. Rawdon Crawley's acquaintances, however, acknowledged her readily enough, – perhaps more readily than she would have desired. Among those were Major Loder (unattached), and Captain Rook (late of the Rifles), who might be seen any day on the Dyke, smoking and staring at the women, and who speedily got an introduction to the hospitable board and select circle of Mr. Joseph Sedley. In fact, they would take no denial; they burst into the house whether Becky was at home or not, walked into Mrs. Osborne's drawing-room, which they perfumed with their coats and moustachios, called Jos 'old buck', and invaded his dinner-table, and laughed and drank for long hours there.

'What can they mean?' asked Georgy, who did not like these gentlemen. 'I heard the major say to Mrs. Crawley yesterday, 'No, no, Becky, you shan't keep the old buck to

yourself. We must have the bones in, or dammy, I'll split.'
What could the major mean, mamma?'

'Major! don't call *him* major!' Emmy said. 'I'm sure I
can't tell what he meant.' His presence and that of his friends
inspired the little lady with intolerable terror and aversion.
They paid her tipsy compliments; they leered at her over
the dinner-table. And the captain made her advances that
filled her with sickening dismay, nor would she ever see him
unless she had George by her side.

Rebecca, to do her justice, never would let either of these
men remain alone with Amelia; the major was disengaged
too, and swore he would be the winner of her. A couple of
ruffians were fighting for this innocent creature, gambling
for her at her own table; and though she was not aware of
the rascals' designs upon her, yet she felt a horror and
uneasiness in their presence, and longed to fly.

She besought, she entreated Jos to go. Not he. He was
slow of movement, tied to his doctor, and perhaps to some
other leading-strings. At least Becky was not anxious to go
to England.

At last she took a great resolution – made the great
plunge. She wrote off a letter to a friend whom she had on
the other side of the water; a letter about which she did not
speak a word to anybody, which she carried herself to the
post under her shawl, nor was any remark made about it;
only that she looked very much flushed and agitated when
Georgy met her: and she kissed him and hung over him a
great deal that night. She did not come out of her room
after her return from her walk. Becky thought it was Major
Loder and the captain who frightened her.

'She mustn't stop here,' Becky reasoned with herself. 'She
must go away, the silly little fool. She is still whimpering
after that gaby of a husband – dead (and served right!) these
fifteen years. She shan't marry either of these men. It's too
bad of Loder. No; she shall marry the bamboo-cane, I'll
settle it this very night.'

So Becky took a cup of tea to Amelia in her private
apartment, and found that lady in the company of her
miniatures, and in a most melancholy and nervous condition.
She laid down the cup of tea.

'Thank you,' said Amelia.

'Listen to me, Amelia,' said Becky, marching up and

down the room before the other, and surveying her with a
sort of contemptuous kindness. 'I want to talk to you. You
must go away from here and from the impertinences of these
men. I won't have you harassed by them; and they will insult
you if you stay. I tell you they are rascals; men fit to send
to the hulks. Never mind how I know them. I know everybody. Jos can't protect you, he is too weak, and wants a
protector himself. You are no more fit to live in the world
than a baby in arms. You must marry, or you and your
precious boy will go to ruin. You must have a husband, you
fool; and one of the best gentlemen I ever saw has offered
you a hundred times, and you have rejected him, you silly,
heartless, ungrateful little creature!'

'I tried – I tried my best, indeed I did, Rebecca,' said
Amelia, deprecatingly, 'but I couldn't forget —;' and she
finished the sentence by looking up at the portrait.

'Couldn't forget *him!*' cried out Becky, 'that selfish humbug, that low-bred Cockney dandy, that padded booby, who
had neither wit, nor manners, nor heart, and was no more
to be compared to your friend with the bamboo-cane than
you are to Queen Elizabeth! Why, the man was weary of
you, and would have jilted you, but that Dobbin forced him
to keep his word. He owned it to me. He never cared for
you. He used to sneer about you to me, time after time; and
made love to me the week after he married you.'

'It's false! It's false! Rebecca,' cried out Amelia, starting
up.

'Look there, you fool,' Becky said, still with provoking
good humour, and taking a little paper out of her belt, she
opened it and flung it into Emmy's lap. 'You know his
handwriting. He wrote that to me – wanted me to run away
with him – gave it me under your nose, the day before he
was shot – and served him right!' Becky repeated.

Emmy did not hear her; she was looking at the letter. It
was that which George had put into the bouquet and given
to Becky on the night of the Duke of Richmond's ball. It
was as she said: the foolish young man had asked her to fly.

Emmy's head sank down, and for almost the last time in
which she shall be called upon to weep in this history, she
commenced that work. Her head fell to her bosom, and her
hands went up to her eyes; and there for awhile, she gave
way to her emotions, as Becky stood on and regarded her.

Who shall analyse those tears, and say whether they were sweet or bitter? Was she most grieved, because the idol of her life was tumbled down and shivered at her feet; or indignant that her love had been so despised; or glad because the barrier was removed which modesty had placed between her and a new, a real affection? 'There is nothing to forbid me now,' she thought. 'I may love him with all my heart now. Oh, I will, I will, if he will but let me, and forgive me.' I believe it was this feeling rushed over all the others which agitated that gentle little bosom.

Indeed, she did not cry so much as Becky expected – the other soothed and kissed her – a rare mark of sympathy with Mrs. Becky. She treated Emmy like a child, and patted her head. 'And now let us get pen and ink, and write to him to come this minute,' she said.

'I – I wrote to him this morning,' Emmy said, blushing exceedingly.

Becky screamed with laughter – '*Un biglietto,*' she sang out with Rosina, '*eccolo quà!* ' – the whole house echoed with her shrill singing.

Two mornings after this little scene, although the day was rainy and gusty, and Amelia had had an exceedingly wakeful night, listening to the wind roaring, and pitying all travellers by land and by water, yet she got up early, and insisted upon taking a walk on the Dyke with Georgy; and there she paced as the rain beat into her face, and she looked out westward across the dark sea line, and over the swollen billows which came tumbling and frothing to the shore. Neither spoke much, except now and then, when the boy said a few words to his timid companion, indicative of sympathy and protection.

'I hope he won't cross in such weather,' Emmy said.

'I bet ten to one he does,' the boy answered. 'Look, mother, there's the smoke of the steamer.' It was that signal, sure enough.

But though the steamer was under weigh, he might not be on board; he might not have got the letter; he might not choose to come. – A hundred fears poured one over the other into the little heart, as fast as the waves on to the Dyke.

The boat followed the smoke into sight. Georgy had a dandy telescope, and got the vessel under view in the most skilful manner. And he made appropriate nautical comments upon the manner of the approach of the steamer as she came nearer and nearer, dipping and rising in the water. The signal of an English steamer in sight went fluttering up to the mast on the pier. I dare say Mrs. Amelia's heart was in a similar flutter.

Emmy tried to look through the telescope over George's shoulder, but she could make nothing of it. She only saw a black eclipse bobbing up and down before her eyes.

George took the glass again and raked the vessel. 'How she does pitch!' he said. 'There goes a wave slap over her bows. There's only two people on deck besides the steersman. There's a man lying down, and a – chap in a – cloak with a – Hooray! – It's Dob by Jingo!' He clapped-to the telescope and flung his arms round his mother. As for that lady: let us say what she did in the words of a favourite poet – Δακρυόεν γελασάσα. She was sure it was William. It could be no other. What she had said about hoping that he would not come was all hypocrisy. Of course he would come: what could he do else but come? She knew he would come.

The ship came swiftly nearer and nearer. As they went in to meet her at the landing-place at the Quay, Emmy's knees trembled so that she scarcely could run. She would have liked to kneel down and say her prayers of thanks there. Oh, she thought, she would be all her life saying them!

It was such a bad day that as the vessel came alongside of the Quay there were no idlers abroad; scarcely even a commissioner on the look-out for the few passengers in the steamer. That young scapegrace George had fled too: and as the gentleman in the old cloak lined with red stuff stepped on to the shore, there was scarcely any one present to see what took place, which was briefly this:–

A lady in a dripping white bonnet and shawl, with her two little hands out before her, went up to him, and in the next minute she had altogether disappeared under the folds of the old cloak, and was kissing one of his hands with all her might; whilst the other, I suppose, was engaged in holding her to his heart (which her head just about reached) and in preventing her from tumbling down. She was murmuring something about – forgive – dear William – dear, dear, dearest friend – kiss, kiss, kiss, and so forth – and in fact went on under the cloak in an absurd manner.

When Emmy emerged from it, she still kept tight hold of one of William's hands, and looked up in his face. It was full of sadness and tender love and pity. She understood its reproach, and hung down her head.

'It was time you sent for me, dear Amelia,' he said.

'You will never go again, William.'

'No, never,' he answered: and pressed the dear little soul once more to his heart.

As they issued out of the Custom-house precincts, Georgy broke out on them, with his telescope up to his eye, and a loud laugh of welcome; he danced round the couple, and performed many facetious antics as he led them up to the house. Jos wasn't up yet; Becky not visible (though she looked at them through the blinds). Georgy ran off to see about breakfast. Emmy, whose shawl and bonnet were off in the passage in the hands of Mrs. Payne, now went to undo the clasp of William's cloak, and – we will, if you please, go with George and look after breakfast for the colonel. The vessel is in port. He has got the prize he has been trying for all his life. The bird has come in at last. There it is with its head on his shoulder, billing and cooing close up to his heart, with soft outstretched fluttering wings. This is what he has asked for every day and hour for eighteen years. This is what he pined after. Here it is – the summit, the end – the last page of the third volume. Good-bye, colonel – God bless you, honest William! – Farewell, dear Amelia – Grow green again, tender little parasite, round the rugged old oak to which you cling!

Perhaps it was compunction towards the kind and simple creature who had been the first in life to defend her, perhaps it was a dislike to all such sentimental scenes, – but Rebecca, satisfied with her part in the transaction, never presented herself before Colonel Dobbin and the lady whom he married. 'Particular business,' she said, took her to Bruges, whither she went; and only Georgy and his uncle were present at the marriage ceremony. When it was over, and Georgy had rejoined his parents, Mrs. Becky returned (just for a few days) to comfort the solitary bachelor Joseph Sedley. He preferred a Continental life, he said, and declined to join in housekeeping with his sister and her husband.

Emmy was very glad in her heart to think that she had

written to her husband before she read or knew of that letter of George's. 'I knew it all along,' William said; 'but could I use that weapon against the poor fellow's memory? It was that which made me suffer so when you —'

'Never speak of that day again,' Emmy cried out, so contrite and humble, that William turned off the conversation, by his account of Glorvina and dear old Peggy O'Dowd, with whom he was sitting when the letter of recall reached him. 'If you hadn't sent for me,' he added with a laugh, 'who knows what Glorvina's name might be now?'

At present it is Glorvina Posky (now Mrs. Major Posky), she took him on the death of his first wife; having resolved never to marry out of the regiment. Lady O'Dowd is also so attached to it that, she says, if anything were to happen to Mick, bedad she'd come back and marry some of 'em. But the major-general is quite well, and lives in great splendour at O'Dowdstown, with a pack of beagles, and (with the exception of perhaps their neighbour, Hoggarty of Castle Hoggarty) he is the first man of his county. Her ladyship still dances jigs, and insisted on standing up to the master of the horse at the Lord Lieutenant's last ball. Both she and Glorvina declared that Dobbin had used the latter *sheamfully*, but Posky falling in, Glorvina was consoled, and a beautiful turban from Paris appeased the wrath of Lady O'Dowd.

When Colonel Dobbin quitted the service, which he did immediately after his marriage, he rented a pretty little country place in Hampshire, not far from Queen's Crawley, where, after the passing of the Reform Bill, Sir Pitt and his family constantly resided now. All idea of a peerage was out of the question, the baronet's two seats in Parliament being lost. He was both out of pocket and out of spirits by that catastrophe, failed in his health, and prophesied the speedy ruin of the Empire.

Lady Jane and Mrs. Dobbin became great friends – there was a perpetual crossing of pony-chaises between the Hall and the Evergreens, the colonel's place (rented of his friend Major Ponto, who was abroad with his family). Her ladyship was godmother to Mrs. Dobbin's child, which bore her name, and was christened by the Rev. James Crawley, who succeeded his father in the living; and a pretty close friendship subsisted between the two lads, George and Rawdon, who hunted and shot together in the vacations, were both

entered of the same college at Cambridge, and quarrelled
with each other about Lady Jane's daughter, with whom they
were both, of course, in love. A match between George and
that young lady was long a favourite scheme of both the
matrons, though I have heard that Miss Crawley herself
inclined towards her cousin.

Mrs. Rawdon Crawley's name was never mentioned by
either family. There were reasons why all should be silent
regarding her. For wherever Mr. Joseph Sedley went, she
travelled likewise; and that infatuated man seemed to be
entirely her slave. The colonel's lawyers informed him that
his brother-in-law had effected a heavy insurance upon his
life, whence it was probable that he had been raising money
to discharge debts. He procured prolonged leave of absence
from the East India House, and indeed his infirmities were
daily increasing.

On hearing the news about the insurance, Amelia, in a
good deal of alarm, entreated her husband to go to Brussels,
where Jos then was, and inquire into the state of his affairs.
The colonel quitted home with reluctance (for he was deeply
immersed in his *History of the Punjaub*, which still occupies
him, and much alarmed about his little daughter, whom he
idolizes, and who was just recovering from the chicken-pox),
and went to Brussels and found Jos living at one of the
enormous hotels in that city. Mrs. Crawley, who had her
carriage, gave entertainments, and lived in a very genteel
manner, occupied another suite of apartments in the same
hotel.

The colonel, of course, did not desire to see that lady,
or even think proper to notify his arrival at Brussels, except
privately to Jos by a message through his valet. Jos begged
the colonel to come and see him that night, when Mrs.
Crawley would be at a *soirée*, and when they could meet
alone. He found his brother-in-law in a condition of pitiable
infirmity; and dreadfully afraid of Rebecca, though eager in
his praises of her. She tended him through a series of
unheard-of illnesses, with a fidelity most admirable. She had
been a daughter to him. 'But – but – oh for God's sake, do
come and live near me, and – and – see me sometimes,'
whimpered out the unfortunate man.

The colonel's brow darkened at this. 'We can't, Jos,' he
said. 'Considering the circumstances, Amelia can't visit you.'

'I swear to you – I swear to you on the Bible,' gasped out Joseph, wanting to kiss the book, 'that she is as innocent as a child, as spotless as your own wife.'

'It may be so,' said the colonel, gloomily; 'but Emmy can't come to you. Be a man, Jos: break off this disreputable connexion. Come home to your family. We hear your affairs are involved.'

'Involved!' cried Jos. 'Who has told such calumnies? All my money is placed out most advantageously. Mrs. Crawley – that is – I mean, – it is laid out to the best interest.'

'You are not in debt, then? Why did you insure your life?'

'I thought – a little present to her – in case anything happened; and you know my health is so delicate – common gratitude you know – and I intend to leave all my money to you – and I can spare it out of my income, indeed I can,' cried out William's weak brother-in-law.

The colonel besought Jos to fly at once – to go back to India, whither Mrs. Crawley could not follow him; to do anything to break off a connexion which might have the most fatal consequences to him.

Jos clasped his hands, and cried, – 'He would go back to India. He would do anything; only he must have time: they mustn't say anything to Mrs. Crawley:– she'd – she'd kill me if she knew it. You don't know what a terrible woman she is,' the poor wretch said.

'Then, why not come away with me?' said Dobbin in reply; but Jos had not the courage. 'He would see Dobbin again in the morning: he must on no account say that he had been there. He must go now. Becky might come in.' And Dobbin quitted him full of forebodings.

He never saw Jos more. Three months afterwards Joseph Sedley died at Aix-la-Chapelle. It was found that all his property had been muddled away in speculations, and was represented by valueless shares in different bubble companies. All his available assets were the two thousand pounds for which his life was insured, and which were left equally between his beloved 'sister Amelia, wife of, &c., and his friend and invaluable attendant during sickness, Rebecca, wife of Lieutenant-Colonel Rawdon Crawley, C.B.,' who was appointed administratrix.

The solicitor of the Insurance Company swore it was the

blackest case that ever had come before him; talked of sending a commission to Aix to examine into the death, and the company refused payment of the policy. But Mrs., or Lady Crawley, as she styled herself, came to town at once (attended with her solicitors, Messrs. Burke, Thurtell & Hayes, of Thavies Inn), and dared the company to refuse the payment. They invited examination, they declared that she was the object of an infamous conspiracy, which had been pursuing her all through life, and triumphed finally. The money was paid, and her character established, but Colonel Dobbin sent back his share of the legacy to the Insurance Office, and rigidly declined to hold any communication with Rebecca.

She never was Lady Crawley, though she continued so to call herself. His Excellency Colonel Rawdon Crawley died of yellow fever at Coventry Island, most deeply beloved and deplored, and six weeks before the demise of his brother Sir Pitt. The estate consequently devolved upon the present Sir Rawdon Crawley, Bart.

He, too, has declined to see his mother, to whom he makes a liberal allowance; and who, besides, appears to be very wealthy. The baronet lives entirely at Queen's Crawley, with Lady Jane and her daughter; whilst Rebecca, Lady Crawley, chiefly hangs about Bath and Cheltenham, where a very strong party of excellent people consider her to be a most injured woman. She has her enemies. Who has not? Her life is her answer to them. She busies herself in works of piety. She goes to church, and never without a footman. Her name is in all the Charity Lists. The Destitute Orange-girl, the Neglected Washerwoman, the Distressed Muffin-man, find in her a fast and generous friend. She is always having stalls at Fancy Fairs for the benefit of these hapless beings. Emmy, her children, and the colonel, coming to London some time back, found themselves suddenly before her at one of these fairs. She cast down her eyes demurely and smiled as they started away from her: Emmy scurrying off on the arm of George (now grown a dashing young gentleman), and the colonel seizing up his little Janey, of whom he is fonder than of anything in the world – fonder even than of his *History of the Punjaub*.

'Fonder than he is of me,' Emmy thinks, with a sigh. But he never said a word to Amelia, that was not kind and gentle; or thought of a want of hers that he did not try to gratify.

Ah! *Vanitas Vanitatum!* Which of us is happy in this world? Which of us has his desire? or, having it, is satisfied? — Come, children, let us shut up the box and the puppets, for our play is played out.